WHITE HAVEN
WINTER
WHITE HAVEN WITCHES BOOKS FOUR - SIX
TJ GREEN

White Haven Winter: Witches Books 4-6
Mountolive Publishing

ISBN 978-0-9951386-5-0

Editing by Missed Period Editing
Cover Design by Fiona Jayde Media

To My Readers - you're amazing xx

Other Titles by TJ Green

Rise of the King Series
Call of the King
The Silver Tower
The Cursed Sword
Tom's Arthurian Legacy Box Set

White Haven Witches
Buried Magic
Magic Unbound
Magic Unleashed
All Hallows' Magic
Undying Magic
Crossroads Magic

Invite from the author -

You can get two free short stories, Excalibur Rises and Jack's Encounter, by subscribing to my newsletter. You will also receive free character sheets of all the main White Haven Witches.

By staying on my mailing list you'll receive free excerpts of my new books, as well as short stories, news of giveaways, and a chance to join my launch team. I'll also be sharing information about other books in this genre you might enjoy.

Details can be found at the end of *White Haven Winter*.

Cast of Characters

Avery Hamilton - owns Happenstance Books
Alex Bonneville - owns The Wayward Son pub
Reuben Jackson - owns Greenlane Nursery
Elspeth Robinson - owns The Silver Bough
Briar Ashworth - owns Charming Balms Apothecary
Mathias Newton - DI with Cornwall Police
Caspian Faversham - CEO Kernow Shipping
Shadow Walker of the Dark Ways

ALL HALLOWS' MAGIC

WHITE HAVEN WITCHES (BOOK 4)

TJ GREEN

1

Avery looked out of the window of Happenstance Books and sighed. Winter was on its way.

Rain lashed down and water poured along the gutters, carrying crumpled leaves and debris. The street was populated by only a few hardened individuals who scurried from shop to shop, looking windblown and miserable.

She watched a young man struggle down the road, his arms wrapped around him in an effort to keep his leather jacket sealed. He really wasn't dressed for the weather. He had a beanie pulled low over his head, and she suspected it was soaked.

He paused in front of her shop and looked up at the sign, hesitated for the briefest of seconds, and then pushed the door open, making the door chimes ring. A swirl of damp air whooshed in before he shut it behind him and shook himself like a dog. He was of average height with a slim build, and his jeans hung off his hips. He pulled his woollen hat off and wiped the rain from his face, revealing light brown hair shorn close to his scalp. He looked up and caught Avery's eye.

Avery smiled. "Welcome. You've picked a great day for shopping."

He smiled weakly in response, but it was clear that his mind wasn't on the weather. "I had no choice. I'm looking for someone."

Avery frowned, sensing she already knew what was coming. She'd been feeling unsettled for days, and tried to put it down to the change in the seasons and the coming of Samhain in a couple of weeks. Unfortunately, that didn't explain the unusual tarot readings she'd had recently. "Who are you looking for?"

He looked around nervously, noting a few customers tucked into the armchairs she had placed around the displays and in corners. The blues album playing in the background contributed to the mellow feel, and the shop smelt of old paper and incense. Nevertheless, his eyes were filled with fear.

Avery smiled again, gently. "Come and talk to me at the counter. No one will hear you." She moved around behind the till, sat on a stool, and hoped the young man would feel less threatened with something between them.

He followed her, leaning on the counter and dropping his voice. "I'm new to White Haven. I arrived here recently with my family, drawn by the magic here. We've been trying to work out where it comes from—or rather, who," he said, rushing on, "and you're one of the people I've narrowed it down to."

Up close, Avery could see his pallor under his stubble, and his fear was more obvious. Despite that, he looked her straight in the eye, as if daring her to disagree. She kept her voice low and even. "May I ask how you can detect magic?"

"I may have some ability," he said, vaguely.

Avery hesitated, casting her awareness out. She could sense something unusual about him, but he didn't feel like a witch. He was risking a lot, she could tell, and suddenly it seemed mean to be so circumspect. "Your abilities have served you well. How can I help?"

"My brother is ill. He needs a healer."

"Why don't you take him to a doctor?"

"They would ask too many questions."

"I'm not a healer. Not a good one, anyway." His face fell. "But I do know someone who is. Can you tell me more?"

"Not here. Later. Can you come to this address?" He reached into his pocket, pulled a piece of paper out, and slid it across the counter.

She glanced at it, recognising the street. It ran along the coast on the hillside. There was no way that just she and Briar were going there. She didn't sense danger, but she didn't know him or his family. "Okay. But there'll be more than two of us, is that okay? We're all trustworthy."

He swallowed. "That's fine. So are we." With that he turned and left, a blast of cold air swirling behind him.

Avery went to the window and watched him run up the street, wondering where he was from, what magic he possessed, and where this visit would lead. It seemed the relative peace of the last few months wouldn't last.

Since Lughnasadh, the night they had successfully fought off the Mermaids with the aid of the Nephilim, life in White Haven had calmed down. She and the other four witches—El, Briar, Alex, and Reuben—had been able to get on with their lives without fear of being attacked. Their magic, released from the binding spell, still hung above the town, but it had reduced in size. The unusual level of spirit activity had continued, which meant they were still casting banishing spells regularly, but the three paranormal investigators—Dylan, Ben, and Cassie—monitored most of that.

Avery was disturbed from her thoughts by movement in her peripheral vision, and she turned to see Sally, her friend and shop manager, coming back from lunch.

Sally frowned. "You look deep in thought."

"I've just had a visitor."

"Oh?" Sally raised her eyebrows.

"He's scared and needs our help."

Sally knew all about Avery and other witches' powers. "You don't know him, I presume?"

"No. He's just arrived in White Haven. I need to phone Briar and Alex."

"All good. Have your lunch and take your time. It's not like we're run off our feet."

Avery nodded and headed to the room at the back of the shop where there was a small kitchen and stock room. From here there was a door that led to her flat above the shop, and she headed through it and up the stairs.

Her flat was in its usual, chaotic state. Books were scattered everywhere, the warm woollen blanket on the sofa was rumpled and half on the floor, and the room needed a good tidying. That would have to wait. It was cool, the central heating turned low, and she adjusted it slightly so it would be warmer for the evening. She pulled her phone from the back pocket of her jeans and called Briar while she put the kettle on and heated some soup.

Out of all of the witches, Briar was the most skilled at Earth magic and healing. She ran Charming Balms Apothecary and lived alone in a cottage off one of the many lanes in White Haven. Fortunately, Briar was free that evening, and after Avery arranged to collect her at six, she called Alex, hoping he wouldn't be too busy at work.

Alex owned The Wayward Son, a pub close to the harbour, and he was Avery's boyfriend, although she always felt really weird calling him that. It sounded like they were fourteen. But what else could she call him. Her lover? That sounded too French, and somehow seedy. Her partner? Sort of, but they didn't live together. Anyway, whatever she called him, he was all hers and completely hot, and she was smitten. They'd got together in the summer, and things were still going strong.

"Hey kitten," he said when he answered her call. "How are you?"

"Kitten! I like that. I'm good, what about you?"

"Busy. The pub is pretty full for the lunch rush. I'm not exactly sure where they're coming from in this weather, but I can't complain."

"It's quiet here," she explained, leaning against the counter and stirring her soup. "But that's okay. Look, I'll get to the point. I've had a visitor, no one we know, but he knows we're witches and needs our help. Are you free tonight?"

She could hear the concern in his voice and the background noise fade away as he moved rooms. "What do you mean? He knows about US?"

"Yes, but he wouldn't explain. I sensed some kind of magic, but he's not a witch. He said he needs a healer, so I'm picking up Briar at six. Can you come with us?"

"Yes, absolutely. And I'll stay at yours tonight, if that's okay?"

She grinned. "Of course. See you later."

***

It was dark by the time the group pulled up outside the whitewashed house on Beachside Road. It was a double-fronted Victorian villa, used for holiday rentals. A portion of the front lawn had been turned into a drive, and an old Volvo hatchback took up most of the space.

"First impressions?" Briar asked from where she sat next to Avery on the front bench of her Bedford van. She was petite and pretty, and her long dark hair was pulled back into a loose ponytail.

"I can't feel anything magical," Avery said, feeling puzzled but also relieved.

"Me, neither," Alex agreed. He sat on the end, next to the passenger window, looking at the house. Like Briar he was dark haired, but far from petite. He was tall and lean, with abs to die for, and his arms were covered in tattoos. He often wore his shoulder length hair down, but tonight it was pulled back into a top knot and his jaw was covered in stubble. "It worries me. Didn't you even get a name?"

"Nope. He didn't stick around long enough," Avery answered. "But I didn't get anything dodgy from him. He was just scared."

"Come on," Briar said, pushing Alex to move. "If someone's hurt, we need to get on with it."

The rain still lashed down, and they raced up the path and sheltered beneath the porch as Avery knocked on the door.

A young woman with long, purple hair opened the door and scowled. "Who are you?"

"Charming," Alex said, amused. "We were invited."

A voice yelled, "Piper! You bloody well know who it is. Let them in."

Piper glared at them and then turned and stomped off, leaving the witches to let themselves in.

Briar smirked and shut the door behind them. "She seems fun."

They stood in a large hallway with doors on both sides, and directly ahead stairs led to the upper level. Piper had already disappeared, but the man Avery met earlier bounded down the staircase, looking both relieved and harassed. "Thanks for coming. I wasn't sure you would. Follow me." He immediately turned to head back up the stairs.

Alex called him back. "Hold on, mate. Before we go any further, who are you, and what's going on?"

He stood for a second, speechless, and then seemed to gather his wits. "Sorry. I'm not thinking straight. I'm Josh." He shook their hands. "My brother is really ill, and I'm worried he might not survive. That's what's upsetting Piper, too. She has a weird way of showing it. Look, I get that you're worried, but I'm not a threat. It's easier if I just show you."

It seemed that was all they would get from Josh, and he ran up the stairs. Alex glanced at Briar and Avery, and followed him. Avery could already feel their combined magic gathering, but she still didn't sense any magic from elsewhere. She gave a last sweep of the hall and then followed the others up the stairs.

On the first floor, Avery detected a strange smell. She wrinkled her nose. It was odd, unpleasant, and cloying.

Josh led them into a room at the back of the house, and as soon as they stepped inside, the smell magnified and Avery tried not to heave.

They were in a large bedroom, and in the double bed in the centre of the room a man lay writhing in a disturbed sleep. A young woman sat next to him, watching with concern, and trying to hold his hand. She looked up when they entered, and a mixture of fear and relief washed over her.

WHAT IS GOING ON HERE?

The man was covered in a sheen of sweat, and his hair stuck to his head. He was bare-chested, but most of his trunk and one of his arms was wrapped in soiled bandages, and it was from these wounds that the smell emanated.

Briar ran forward. "By the Great Goddess! What the hell's happened to him? His wounds are infected!"

The young woman stood, moving out of the way. "Can you help him?"

Briar barely glanced at her. "I'll try. You should have come to me sooner. What's his name?" She placed her box of herbs, balms, and potions on the floor, and started to peel the man's bandages away. He immediately cried out, his arms flailing, and Alex leapt forward to help restrain him.

Josh explained, "He's Hunter, my older brother. This is my twin sister, Holly."

Holly nodded briefly at them, and then went back to watching her brother helplessly. Avery could see the similarity between her and Josh. They both had light brown hair and hazel eyes, although Holly was shorter than her brother, and her hair fell in a wavy bob to her shoulders. The man writhing on the bed had dark, almost black hair, a light tan, and a muscular build.

Avery asked, "What happened to him?"

Josh met her eyes briefly and then watched Hunter again. "He was attacked several days ago. We've been on the road, and only got here recently. It has taken me a while to track you down."

Avery watched Briar resort to using a sharp pair of scissors to cut the bandages away. Avery recoiled as the smell hit her, and then gasped at the size of the wounds. He had long, deep claw marks across his chest, back, and left arm, and they were inflamed and oozing pus. As Briar pulled the sheet away, they saw more bandages around his legs.

Alex looked up. "What the hell did this? And why didn't you go to a doctor?"

"Because they would have involved the police," Josh explained. "We can't afford that to happen."

As they watched Hunter twist and turn, Avery scented magic, and she looked around, alarmed. Briar and Alex must have too, because they paused momentarily.

"What's causing that?" Avery asked sharply, raising her hands, ready to defend herself.

"What?" Josh asked, his eyes wide.

"Magic. We can sense it now."

"Oh no," he answered. "He's changing again."

"He's what?"

But Avery could barely finish the question when Hunter shimmered in a strange way, as if his body was melting, and then his shape changed into a huge wolf, snarling and twisting on the bed.

"Holy crap!" Alex exclaimed, leaping backwards out of the way of his snapping jaws. "He's a *Shifter*! Why the hell didn't you warn us?"

"Because we hoped you wouldn't have to know," Holly said tearfully, running forward with Josh to try and calm her brother down. In a split second, she changed into a wolf too, leaving her clothes behind as she leapt onto the bed. She yelped, and her presence seemed to calm Hunter down. Within seconds, he lay back on the bed, panting heavily. His wounds looked even worse in this form if that was possible; his fur was matted and bloodstained.

Avery dropped her hands and sighed heavily. "You're all Shifters?"

"'Fraid so," Josh said with a weak smile.

"So, I guess he was attacked by another Shifter?"

"You could say that."

Briar leaned back on her heels. "This will probably make things a bit trickier."

"But can you still help?"

"Yes! I'm a good healer, but I have limited experience with Shifters."

Like none, Avery thought, just like the rest of them.

Briar continued, "Does he change a lot at the moment?"

Josh nodded. "He doesn't seem to be able to control it. His change won't last long, but we think it's getting in the way of his healing. His wounds keep opening, and we can't get them clean."

She nodded and thought for a second. "I need to give him a sedative. It will calm him down, which will hopefully prevent him from shifting."

"You have a spell for that?" Josh asked.

Briar shrugged. "In theory. I'll have to make it stronger than usual. I need your kitchen to make a slight change to one of the potions I have with me."

"I presume you're all witches, then?" Josh asked. "I mean, I thought that's what I sensed, but I wasn't sure."

"Yes, we are," Avery said. "But we'll talk later. For now, let Briar work her magic."

2

Josh escorted Briar to the kitchen, leaving Avery with Alex and the two Shifters.

Alex looked across the bed at Avery. "Well, this is new."

She grinned. "Isn't it?"

"I just wish I didn't have the feeling they've brought trouble with them."

"They seem harmless—for wolves. At least they're not Mermaids," she said, referring to the summer when they'd been attacked by the Daughters of Llyr. She looked at Holly. "Can you understand me, wolfy?"

Holly thumped her tail on the bed and Avery laughed. "This is so weird." She sobered up when she looked at Hunter. "He's in a bad way."

"Briar will fix him," Alex said, confidently. "If she can cure demon burns, she can stop infected wounds."

"They sound like they're from up north somewhere," Avery observed. "Cumbria or Lancashire, maybe."

"In that case, they've travelled a long way to get here. I wonder what they're running from?"

"It's not what, it's who," a young, petulant voice said from behind them.

Piper. She stood in the doorway, pouting in her low-slung jeans and t-shirt, her pale brown eyes made up with dark purple makeup that matched her hair.

"Was it some sort of turf war?" Alex asked from where he leaned against the wall, keeping a watchful eye on Hunter.

"Yes. And we lost. Or rather, he did. And now we're stuck here, miles from home." Her voice dripped with resentment and Holly growled at her, and before they could ask Piper anything else, she turned with a flounce and disappeared.

"She's such a delight," Alex said dryly. "I like her more every time I see her."

Avery glanced at Holly, who was now watching Hunter whimper in his sleep, twitching as if he was dreaming.

"I would imagine this has been a nightmarish few days for all of them," Avery observed.

Within minutes Briar returned with Josh, carrying a gently steaming potion. Josh was carrying a bowl of hot water. Briar had barely settled herself by the bed when Hunter shimmered again and changed back to human form. "Oh good. This will make life easier," she said. "Alex, help lift his head, please."

Between them they manoeuvred Hunter into a sitting position and Briar trickled the potion between his lips, whispering a spell as she did so. Within seconds he relaxed and his breathing deepened, and Alex lowered him back on the bed.

"Right, time to clean up this mess," Briar said resolutely. She chose a selection of herbs and dropped them into the water, and then started to clean the wounds with a soft cloth.

"So, what happened?" Avery asked Josh. "Piper said he lost a fight."

"We live in a small hamlet in Cumbria called Chapel Stile. It's right in the centre of the Lake District, and perfect for Shifters. It's remote and there's plenty of space for us. Quite a few Shifter families live in the area, and we generally get along well. Until recently." He fell silent for a moment, and Avery wondered if that's all he would tell them, but then he rubbed his face and sighed. "The head of one of the other families died recently and his son took over. He's now the pack's Alpha. He's imposing some new rules and we didn't like them. Hunter was pretty vocal about it, and he was attacked."

"If you don't mind me saying, that sounds quite medieval," Avery said, wondering how bad the new rules could be that made someone want to fight.

"It is. Nothing has happened like that for years." He looked Avery in the eye, finally. "We were taken by surprise. Hunter's a good man. He looks after us, and he's been in his fair share of fights—Shifters are always territorial—but this fight was really vicious."

Avery looked at Hunter's wounds. "It looks like he was trying to kill him."

Josh nodded grimly. "I think he was."

"You should have settled the score, Josh." Piper spoke from behind them again. She leaned on the doorframe, her tone accusatory.

"Shut up, Piper," he shot back. "You're talking rubbish, as usual. If I'd fought, then we'd both be in this mess, and you and Holly would be in big trouble. You know what Cooper is like. He's a misogynist bully."

She glared at him, but dropped her eyes to the floor, seemingly in agreement. "I want to go home."

Josh's tone softened. "So do I, but I'm not sure that's possible anymore."

"Have you lost your house?" Avery asked, incredulous.

"No. I just meant it would be dangerous to return. We might have to sell. Can we have your permission to live here, at least for now?"

Avery was speechless, but Alex snorted from across the bed where he was helping Briar. "Mate, you don't need our permission. Stay here as long as you like."

"He's right, we don't own White Haven," Avery agreed, perplexed by his question. "You can live here if that's what you decide."

"Are there other Shifters in the area?"

"Not as far as I know," she answered. "But then again, this place keeps surprising us lately."

"We like the wild places—the moors, the peaks, and the lakes. But you are on the edge of moorland here."

"Yes, and there are weirder things than Shifters around, I can assure you," she said, thinking of the Nephilim. "Are there witches in Cumbria?"

"Oh yes. And they align with Cooper."

"We align with no one except each other," Alex explained. "Is anyone likely to follow you here?"

"I hope not," Josh said, not meeting their eyes.

Avery had a horrible feeling he wasn't sure about that.

***

The following evening, Avery met the other witches at Alex's flat above the pub, and Newton, their friend the Detective Inspector, joined them.

They had ordered in Thai food, and delicious aromas wafted around the room. Reuben, as usual, had filled his plate, and sat on the sofa with it perched on his knee. He and El were a couple, and El spent a lot of her weekends at Greenlane Manor, Reuben's huge estate. They were both tall and blonde, laid back and well suited. Briar was single, and although she and Newton seemed to have something going for a while, since their battle with the Mermaids, it had fizzled. Newton still struggled to reconcile their magic with his job. He also struggled with the Nephilim sticking around, and he wasn't too happy about Shifters arriving in White Haven, either.

"Shifters? Do you mean Shapeshifters?"

"I don't know any other kind of Shifter," Briar said, annoyed.

"How long are they planning to stay?"

She frowned at him. "As long as they need! And Hunter is badly injured, so he'll have to stay until he's better. That could be weeks."

"How was he tonight?" Alex asked her.

"Slightly better. His wounds don't smell anymore. He'll have scars, though."

"Was he still changing without control?" Avery asked.

"No. My sedative sorted that out. He woke this morning and had some food, and then I dosed him up for the day again."

"He was awake? That's good, right?" El asked from where she sat in her favourite corner of the sofa. "I'd like to meet them."

"And you will, but they're keeping a low profile for now, until Hunter's better," Briar explained.

"Well, I think I should meet him," Newton said, decisively. "We don't want trouble here."

Briar glared at him again. She had very little patience with Newton lately. "They won't bring trouble! Stop being so patriarchal."

"I'm a detective. It's my job."

"It's your job to solve murders. They haven't murdered anyone!"

An awkward silence fell, and Reuben leapt in. "Well, I heard from Gabreel the other day, or Gabe, as he prefers to be called."

"The Nephilim?" Alex asked.

"Well, I don't know another Gabreel," Reuben said with a smirk.

"What did he want?"

"A job for Asher, one of his winged buddies." Reuben owned Greenlane Nurseries, and although it was the winter months, they still had a couple of large greenhouses that they kept stocked, ready for the spring and summer months. They also sold lots of shrubs that kept the place ticking over all year.

"A Nephilim who likes gardening. Nice," Avery said. "Did you offer him a job?"

"I did. A couple of the teens we employed left for University a few weeks ago, so he can fill in for them. He'll start next week. Fully legit, too. They have paperwork and everything."

Newton looked suspicious. "How have they got that?"

"I don't know and I don't care," Reuben said, forking up another mouthful of noodles.

"Strange you should say that," Alex said. "Gabreel came looking for a job with me, too. Well, for Amaziah, actually. Zee for short. So, he starts behind the bar next week."

"Which one is he?" El asked, frowning. "I'm trying to put faces to names."

"Hawk-nose, black hair, dark-skinned—if that helps?"

"Vaguely. The last time I saw them was in a storm, and to be honest, I can't remember them clearly."

"Well, it sounds like we'll be seeing a lot more of some of them," Alex said, helping himself to more food.

Briar looked thoughtful. "I could offer one of them some part-time work. Cassie can only help out a couple of days now that term has started again."

Cassie was one of the ghost-hunters they'd met in the summer; she'd started working with Briar to learn about magic, and to learn a few simple spells to help with their paranormal investigations. She studied Parapsychology at Penryn University with Ben. Dylan, the third member, studied English Folklore.

Newton frowned and looked as if he might complain again, but Briar gave him a challenging stare and he wisely chose not to comment. Avery tried not to smirk. However, Alex simply nodded. "Great, I'll let Gabreel know. I think he's trying to set up a security business as a long-term plan, which sort of makes sense. I think some of the others have managed to get bartending jobs across town."

El placed her empty plate on the coffee table. "So, what are we doing about Samhain this year? I presume we're going to celebrate together?"

Samhain, or All Hallows' Eve, was one of the important dates in the calendar for witches, one of the eight Sabbats, and they'd taken to celebrating them together. The celebrations consisted of feasting, celebrating the turn of the seasons, and cementing their relationships with each other. It was also a time to remember the dead and their ancestors. The energy of such gatherings would be significant, but generally no magic was performed.

Avery groaned. "Genevieve wants us to celebrate with the other covens. It came up at the last meeting. I've been meaning to tell you."

Genevieve Byrne was the leader of the Witches Council, which governed the thirteen covens of Cornwall, and Avery was White Haven's representative. The meetings took place every couple of months, and the latest had been only a few days ago. Avery had refused the invitation to join the celebrations for Lughnasadh after Genevieve declined to help defend White Haven against the Mermaids. She still felt a guilty pleasure over telling Genevieve where to stick the invite.

"Really?" Briar asked, excited. "I'd love to meet everyone!"

"Me, too!" El agreed. "Don't you?"

"I guess so," Avery said, shrugging. "I like it when we do our own thing, but it will be a good chance to meet all the other covens."

"I'm game," Reuben said, having finally finished eating. "One giant party. Sounds great!"

Alex smiled and winked at Avery. "Sounds like that's a yes from us. Where will we all meet?"

"Rasmus's house. He has large grounds on the edge of Newquay, surrounded by a wood. It's very private, apparently. It's where the covens celebrate all the Sabbats. I'll get in touch with Genevieve and give her the good news."

3

The next day was Saturday, the rain had eased, and cheered on by the bright autumnal sunshine, Sally had started to decorate the shop for Halloween.

"Don't you think there are a few too many decorations?" Avery observed from the counter. Sally was stringing up toy skeletons, witches, and ghouls in the windows and around the shelves. On the counter were strings of fairy lights, and in the room at the back of the shop was a mountain of fake pumpkins, ready to fill any gaps.

"No. The more the merrier. It's Halloween, Avery, in under two weeks! The most important date in White Haven!" She grinned, her face flushed, hair tied up on her head, and her sleeves rolled up. "I've got plans for the corner in the next room. You're going to set it up as a reading corner, and we're going to do evening readings of scary stories for kids. I've arranged it with the local school."

"You have?" Avery's heart sank. Lots of kids in her shop. They'd cause havoc! She looked around at her neat displays and tried to dispel the vision from her head.

Sally sighed. "Avery, trust me. It will bring in lots of customers, and parents will be here to supervise them."

"Who's going to read to them?" she asked. Please don't let it be me.

"Me, of course." Dan said, joining them from across the room where he'd been chatting to some customers. Dan was Avery's assistant who was also doing post-grad English studies. He'd also almost met his doom at the hands of Nixie, one of the Mermaids. "It'll be fun."

"Great," Avery said, slightly relieved. "I presume I'll still have to do something?"

"Yes. You, like us, will be dressed up and helping customers stock up on books and their occult needs."

Avery narrowed her eyes. "What do you mean, dressed up?"

Both Sally and Dan looked very pleased with themselves, and Avery had a sinking feeling.

"Well," Dan said, "I'm going to be Dracula. I have a very long, sweeping cloak that I can wrap myself in. I can't wait."

Avery raised an eyebrow. "Really? I didn't take you for a fancy dress type of guy."

"There's a lot you don't know about me, Avery," he said with a certain aloofness. "Sally will be dressed as a zombie. And guess what you'll be?"

"Please don't say a witch."

"Of course you'll be a witch."

She lowered her voice. "Isn't that a bit obvious, all things considered?"

"No. It's perfect. Very meta."

Sally agreed. "I've already bought you a big witch's hat."

"You're kidding me! We haven't done this any other year!"

"Change is good," Sally insisted. "Besides, the Town Council want to make this a really good festival, seeing as Lughnasadh ended earlier than planned."

That was their fault, Avery reflected, since they'd had to get Eve, a weather witch from St Ives, to make a huge storm to cover up their fight with the Mermaids on the beach. It had worked, but consequently the crowds had fled the beach earlier than usual.

Sally continued, "And Stan, our Councillor slash Druid is coming to inspect all the shops."

"I give up," Avery declared. "All right. I suppose it will be fine."

"It will be great, trust us," Dan said, smirking. "I can't wait to see you in costume."

"Be careful," Avery said, "Or I might just hex you."

They were interrupted by the arrival of Ben, one of the ghost-hunters. Avery turned to him with relief. "Hey, Ben. Keeping busy?"

Ben was average height with a stocky build and short, dark hair. He was wearing jeans, a university hoodie, and a jacket shrugged over the top. He greeted the others and then said, "Too busy. Spirit sightings are going up, particularly around Old Haven Church."

"Really? I thought things were slowing down."

"So did I, but not anymore."

"Halloween magic?" Dan asked, wide-eyed.

"Oh please," Avery said. "You missing all the action from the summer?"

"Not really. I'll leave you to it," he said sheepishly, and he and Sally went back to decorating the shop.

Ben fished in his pocket and pulled out his phone. "I'm wondering if these might have anything to do with it. I took pictures of a couple of things we found hanging on the trees around the cemetery."

He showed Avery a photo of a bundle of twigs in the shape of a pentagram strung up high on the branch of a tree.

Avery frowned. "That's weird. I wonder how long it's been there."

"Not long at all. We normally scope out the area every time we go up there, which is reasonably frequently. We have a few night vision cameras set up, courtesy of the vicar."

"The vicar? James?"

"Yep, the same one who looks after the Church of All Souls. He kept in touch after the events there," he said meaningfully, referring to the appearance of the Nephilim and the death of Harry, the verger. Avery was astonished. She had no idea he'd kept in touch with Ben and the others.

"Why didn't you say so?"

"I didn't think of it. Anyway, this is a proven hot spot, so we like to keep tabs on it. This," he said, indicating the photo, "appeared in the last week."

Avery was perplexed. Who could be placing those around the church grounds? Was there another witch in the area they didn't know about? And what were they hoping to achieve? She made a decision. "Show me."

***

Old Haven Church looked beautiful in the weak sunshine. The large, grey blocks of local stone it was made from looked golden in the light, and long shadows were already streaking across the old, lichen-covered gravestones.

Avery looked across to the Jacksons' Mausoleum where Gil, Reuben's brother, had been laid to rest only months before, at the beginning of the summer. Beneath it was a hidden room where previous generations of the witches had gathered to celebrate magical rites. She shivered. It was a creepy place, and she hoped she never had to go back there. Ben had no idea about the hidden room, but he knew all about Reuben's brother and how he died.

The church was locked and the grounds were deserted, and Ben led the way down winding paths between the graves to an older part of the cemetery at the rear. Old Haven Church was out of town, high on the hill above the coast, and very few services or burials were held there anymore. Gil's had been an exception because of the family mausoleum.

At the edge of the oldest graves at the rear of the cemetery was a small wood. The trees were a mixture of mainly oak and beech with some shrubby undergrowth, and at this time of year their branches were bare except for a few hardy leaves clinging on. The rest were thick underfoot.

"This is where we've set up the cameras," Ben explained, as he pointed to a couple of devices situated in a sheltered spot on the edge of the wood, protected from the elements by a wooden box. "We've found that this place is the most likely to have spirit manifestations—probably because it's the oldest part of the grounds. We train the cameras on the graves. But the weird twig-things are further in."

The wood was left to grow wild and unkempt, and he led Avery through the tangle of branches and over fallen, mossy tree limbs and rotting trunks to a small clearing. He pointed to where one item swung from the branch of a huge, gnarled tree in the centre, twigs and feathers bound together in an odd shape. "Does it have a name?"

Avery frowned, puzzled as to who had put them there. "Witch runes, witch twigs, spell-casters. They have lots of names. Their intent is more to offer the warning that a witch is around, to scare others, too. They look spooky to the uninitiated. But why are they here?"

Ben looked as puzzled as she did. "Would Reuben have put them here? Because of his brother?"

"No. This is not Reuben's style. It's pretty old school, to be honest." Avery moved closer and squinted up at it. "I'm not sure I recognise this sign." She pulled her phone out of her bag and snapped a picture of it so she could look it up later.

"Why don't you take it with you?" Ben asked.

"I don't know who's put it there, and I'd rather they don't know that we know it's here. And I can feel the magic around them. I don't suppose you have any footage of whoever put it there?"

"No. They obviously spotted the cameras." He shrugged, "I mean, we haven't tried to hide them. And whoever put these here could have approached from any direction. This wood backs onto fields with only the low church wall between them."

Avery looked around, astonished. "I honestly did not know that the wood was this big, and I certainly didn't know there was a clearing in the middle of it." She turned and explored the surrounding trees, looking carefully to see if there were any more hidden in the tangle of branches, but apart from the couple Ben had told her about, she couldn't see any. And then realisation dawned, and she groaned. "This is a yew tree. That changes everything."

Ben looked confused. "Why?"

"Because yews have huge significance. They're present in churchyards across the whole country. Some have several, many at the gates of the church. They protect against evil, but they are also guardians to the Underworld, death, and the afterlife. Churches were built next to them deliberately," she mused, "not the other way around. Many yews are hundreds, if not thousands, of years old."

"Another case of Christians jumping on pagan traditions?"

"Absolutely. They are a potent force for protection against evil. " Avery pointed. "Look at it. The trunk isn't like a normal tree. It has several trunks forming one tree, and the older it gets, the more the trunks are hollowed out, forming a space within the tree. It keeps its needles all year round, and every bit of it is poisonous."

Ben stepped into the space. "You can walk right into and through this one. It's huge."

Avery frowned. "I'm going to do a bit more research on yews. As for the witch-signs, there's too few to create a big spell, but maybe whoever's put them there is starting slowly. When are you next due to come here?"

"Another couple of days, why?"

"Keep me informed if any more appear. I think we have another witch in White Haven, and I don't know what he or she wants. I'm worried it's nothing good."

Ben led the way back to the edge of the grove and started to exchange the camera memory cards while they were talking. "I'll check these later. If there's anything interesting, I'll let you know. If there's spirit activity, do you want to come up one night?"

She sighed. "I suppose so. And I'd better tell the others."

4

The next night, Avery was with Briar at the Shifters' house. Hunter was sitting up in bed, wincing as Briar inspected his wounds, and Avery stood to the side watching, Josh and Holly next to her.

"They look better," Briar said, looking pleased. "They're already closing up. How do you feel?"

He watched her deft hands admiringly. *Interesting. It seems Briar has another fan.* "I feel a lot better. What did you do?" His voice was deep and resonant with a Cumbrian accent, yet surprisingly gentle.

Briar smiled briefly. "I used some healing Earth magic. Combined with your own natural magic, it worked well. They were nasty wounds. You're lucky I got to you before the infection killed you."

"I know. Thank you," he said, his eyes appraising her.

Hunter, when he wasn't as white as a sheet and covered in sweat, was handsome in a reliable, easy on the eyes kind of way. His dark hair was tousled, and his muscled physique was fit and athletic, although covered in scars. A lot of him was on show, despite the sheet draped around him.

"Before you put my dressings back on," he continued, "can I have a shower? I smell like crap."

"Of course," Briar said, stepping away from the bed. "It'll help clean your bites."

He smiled and stood, pulling the sheet around him. Avery turned to Josh and Holly. "How are you two feeling?"

"Happier now that he's well," Holly said, watching her brother leave the room. She met Avery's eyes. "I still don't know what we're going to do, but at least we have some thinking time."

"We have to go back at some point," Josh pointed out. "I don't think we can stay here forever."

"I know, but part of me doesn't want to fight Cooper." Holly sat on the bed and looked at her feet. "If we go back, it means more fighting, and Hunter might not survive."

"He might win," Josh pointed out.

"Perhaps, but how long would it last?" Holly said, glaring at her brother. "Cooper wants us to influence his businesses at the expense of our own. It's a nightmare, but I don't think it's worth losing a life over. And even though Hunter is a good fighter, he's not a killer. We can sell our house and move here!"

Once again, Piper appeared in the doorway like a ghost. "I don't want to move here. This isn't home!"

"You want to fight Cooper? Go ahead!" Holly said, her voice dripping with disdain. "I'd like to see how far you get. Hunter fights better than any of us, and look what happened to him."

"We ran away. You're cowards," Piper spat.

"Take that back!" Holly leapt to her feet, her voice dropping to a snarl.

"Never." Piper squared up to her. "We ran, and I'm ashamed."

"Shut up, Piper," Josh warned, pushing her away. "Holly has a very short temper right now. You want to get a few bites, too?"

Holly's eyes had turned a molten yellow, and her face started to lose its human appearance. Avery stepped back, alarmed, and she noticed Briar did the same. Avery instinctively called the wind to her, and a gust blew around the room and energy sparkled in her hands.

That was enough to snap Holly out it; her shoulders dropped and her eyes returned to their normal pale brown, watching Avery warily.

"Sorry. Instinct," Avery murmured. "How much control do you have over shapeshifting? I mean, I've never met a Shifter before."

"Very good control," Josh said before Holly could respond. "Except when you're as injured as Hunter, or provoked. But Holly knew what she was doing, didn't you?" He was clearly expecting Holly to apologise.

"I'm tired," she explained. "And annoyed at someone's constant whingeing."

Piper just glared.

"Are you all wolves?"

"Yep, runs in the family—like witchcraft, I guess," Josh said, sitting on the edge of the bed.

"And you turn from a young age?"

"Not really until our teens. Some earlier, some later, but that's the average."

Briar had been listening as she prepared more bandages and salve for Hunter's wounds. "I guess you learn to control it as you grow, like we do. I can sense it—it's a different sort of magic."

Avery agreed. "Me, too. I could sense it when you first walked in my shop. It's stronger when you're worried."

Holly laughed. "The Wolf creeps closer to the surface, then. It's a defence thing."

Briar looked up, frowning. "So, where are your parents? Can't they help with this Cooper guy?"

"'Fraid, not," Josh said, his voice tight. "They both died a few years ago. Car accident." He didn't elaborate further.

"Sorry," Briar murmured, and Avery added her condolences.

Piper narrowed her eyes. "You're asking a lot of questions."

"We're curious, that's all. Ask us about being a witch if you want," Avery shot back.

"Don't care," she said simply and flounced out of the room.

"Sorry," Josh said, sighing. "She's not normally so nightmarish. She's just missing home. And she adores Hunter, so she's been more scared than she wants to admit. She'll come round."

"She'd better," Holly said, following her out of the room.

As she left, Hunter strode back in with a towel wrapped around his lower half, his sheet in his hands. "That's better. I'm all yours," he said, smiling at Briar.

His injuries haven't affected his libido, Avery thought.

"Your injuries are horrendous," Avery said, noting them fully now that he was standing. Huge claw marks were raked down his back and side, and also across his chest. One streaked across his neck, almost hitting his cheek. And he was covered in bruises. "They must hurt."

He winced as he sat down close to Briar. "They do, but the potions helped. Thanks for allowing us to stay here, and helping us."

"I'm sure Josh must have explained that's not how it works in White Haven. You don't need our permission to be here."

"But you've given it, right? Allowed us Sanctuary?" He was strangely insistent.

"Yes. If you want permission, you've got it," she said, bewildered.

"And you are witches?" he asked, wincing again as Briar dressed his wounds with a salve.

"Yes. There are five of us in White Haven, and more across Cornwall. But you have witches in the Lakes, I understand," she said, remembering what Josh had told her.

"Yes, and they control what goes on. They wouldn't appreciate unknown paranormal creatures showing up unannounced."

Strange. She had so much to learn about other witches. "Maybe it's because there are a lot of Shifters where you come from. What about this Cooper character? How much control does he have?"

"Not as much as he wants." Hunter scowled, and Avery wasn't sure if it was in pain or from the thought of Cooper. "He caught me by surprise, the bastard. That's why I'm so badly injured. But I'll go back when I'm healed."

Josh almost jumped in surprise. "We will? I wasn't sure you'd want to."

"Of course I want to," Hunter said, glaring at Josh. "Our home is there. You didn't think I was just going to roll over and let him think he'd won, did you?"

"I wasn't sure what you'd want to do, if I'm honest. He almost killed you, and I had to protect our sisters and get out of there."

Hunter's eyes softened momentarily. "And you did the right thing. But I will go back. It's not over."

Briar spoke softly as she unrolled a long bandage. "Well, you'd better prepare yourself for a long wait. These will take weeks to heal. If you fight too soon, they'll open up again. Lift your arm."

He smiled at her and did as instructed, watching her as she leaned in and wrapped the bandage around his chest, turning slightly to help her.

"At least I know if I get injured again you could help," he said, pleased with himself.

"Not if you're in Cumbria I won't. It's a bit far."

"You wouldn't visit?" he teased.

"Nope. I have a business to run." She kept her head down and concentrated on his dressings.

He fell silent and Avery tried not to smirk. "What do you guys do for a living?"

Josh answered, Hunter clearly distracted by Briar. "We have a family business, taking groups of tourists around the Lakes—day trips, walks, kayaking, hiking, camping. We know the place like the back of our hands."

"Does everyone know what you are?"

"No way. It's a Shifter community, but nobody outside the pack knows. That's the beauty of the Lakes. It's wild and areas of it are remote, so we can shift with complete privacy."

"We keep a low profile, too, as much as possible," Avery said. "Will anyone come looking for you here?"

"Let's hope not," Josh said, tiredly running his hands across his face. Avery noticed, however, he refused to meet her eyes. "We don't aim to bring any trouble to you."

"Don't worry. We handle trouble pretty well."

***

"I think you have an admirer," Avery said to Briar as they walked down the hill into White Haven. It was a calm night, cold and clear, and stars sparkled in the sky above them. It would frost later, the chill was already gathering. Avery pulled her jacket together and huddled into her scarf.

"He's a flirt," Briar said, embarrassed. "It means nothing."

Avery adopted a teasing, singsong voice. "Hunter and Briar sitting in a tree, K-I-S-S-I-N-G."

"You have to be kidding me! How old are you?" Briar exclaimed.

"Sorry," Avery said, laughing. "It's nice. He's nice. I can sort of see you together."

"Really? Mr Hunter Shapeshifter, I'm going back to fight the big bad wolf. I don't think so."

"Do you and Newton catch-up anymore?" Avery asked, hoping she wasn't prying too much.

"No. I'm a witch, he's a detective. It doesn't work. And besides, I have work to keep me busy right now."

"Never too busy for love."

"That's because you're all loved up with Alex. It's not a complaint," she added quickly. "I'm pleased for you. Anyway, moving on from my love life, why are we meeting tonight?"

"I think there's a rogue witch in White Haven. Come on, get a move on. Last one in the pub gets the round."

They arrived at The Wayward Son breathless and with flushed cheeks. Briar was surprisingly quick, and Avery followed her through the door wishing she hadn't made the bet. She headed to the bar and ordered two glasses of wine, white for Briar and red for her, but Simon, one of the regular bar staff, gestured up towards the ceiling. "I wouldn't bother. He's got wine upstairs. He said to send you up."

"Fair enough," Avery said, and they wound their way through the crowded tables to the small room at the back of the pub, and the stairs that led to Alex's flat.

He answered the door with a flourish. "Welcome, ladies." He leaned in and gave Avery a breath-taking kiss, and Briar sidled past them. "Missed you," he murmured.

"Get a room," Reuben yelled from the sofa in Alex's living room.

Avery laughed and headed into the flat as Alex closed the door behind her. "Thanks, Reuben. As usual, you completely spoil the mood."

El was leaning against the counter that separated the kitchen from the living area, giggling. "That's what he's here for. How're our Shifter friends?"

Briar shrugged her jacket off and put it on the back of a chair. "Hunter's better. But he'll be scarred for life. There's some stuff I can't heal."

"Will they go back?"

Avery nodded. "Oh, yes. He intends to fight this Cooper guy."

"I'd do the same," Reuben said. "Let's face it, we did it here. You protect your own space."

"Well, he's not well enough yet," Briar answered. She took the glass of wine that El passed to her. "By the way, Gabe, the Nephilim, came into my shop today, and he brought Eli with him. I think they're shortening all their names so they blend in a bit more. Eliphaz sounds so Old Testament."

"And?" Avery asked, curious.

"Eli is starting with me on Monday—tomorrow, in fact!" She looked baffled. "I must admit, I didn't think one of them would want to work in my shop. It's not exactly exciting. He's going to be bored stupid."

Alex laughed. "It's money. I'm sure he'll be fine. Which one is he?"

"He's tall—"

"Aren't they all?" Avery interrupted.

"Olive-skinned, green-eyed, brown hair, clean-shaven. And silent. Didn't say a word. This could be really weird. Cassie never stops talking."

Reuben grunted. "Just one more thing for the locals to comment on. Ash started a few days ago, too. He's pretty quiet, but can he carry stuff! He works twice as hard as anybody else."

"I wonder where else we'll see them around town?" Avery asked. "In fact, I've been trying to work out which one was at the Church in Harecombe."

"Maybe it's better we don't know," El said.

Alex started to get food ready in the kitchen. "We're bound to work it out one day. Zee starts his first shift tomorrow, so let's hope he can communicate. It's better in a pub to have chatty bar staff."

As he was talking, Avery's phone rang, and she reached into her bag and saw it was Ben. She inwardly sighed. I know what this is about. "Hey, Ben. Let me guess. More witch-marks."

"Plenty more," he answered. "And things are starting to look really weird at Old Haven."

"They are?" she asked, alarmed. The others all turned at her tone. "How weird?"

"There's some sort of design burnt into the ground. Do you want to see?"

She groaned. "Couldn't you have called in the daytime?"

"I've only just found it! Trust me. You'll want to see this."

"You skulk about at night? In the freezing cold?"

"It's the job! Get your ass over here."

He rang off and she looked up at the others. "I had meant to tell you all over dinner, but guess what? Dinner will have to wait. We're heading to Old Haven Church."

***

Old Haven was dark. Very dark. There were no street lights, and no lights along the paths that snaked around the graves. The air was crisp, a low ground mist had started to rise, and an owl hooted in the distance.

"This had better be good," Reuben complained. "I'm freezing my ass off and I'm not in the mood for spirit banishing. If this is Caspian's doing, I'll fry him."

Avery had told them about the witch-signs on the way over, and they had speculated about who could be putting them there.

"This is not Caspian," Avery said firmly. "He's far more direct. And I think he's too busy to be sticking up witch-signs at Old Haven. "

"I agree," Alex said, striding quickly along the path, his torch illuminating the way ahead. "He'd be more sophisticated than this."

It wasn't long before they heard voices and saw lights ahead of them, illuminating the trees' bare branches. The ghost-hunters. They stood huddled together, and turned when they heard the others approach.

"Hey, guys," Dylan greeted them. He was wearing a large puffer jacket that swelled his slim frame. "Glad you could make it."

"I had nothing better to do than drink beer and eat," Reuben said sarcastically.

Dylan grinned. "You'll be glad you came!"

"Will I? I'm not sure about that. So what are we all so excited about?"

"Follow me!"

Dylan led them into the clearing in the centre of the grove and pointed his torch at the ground.

A rune was scorched into the earth.

"What the hell is that?" El exclaimed, dropping to a crouch and reaching out tentatively to touch the scorch marks.

"Well, it's why you're here," Ben said, testily. "We've never seen anything like it before. And there are more of these." He pointed to the yew tree. From its branches hung dozens of witch-signs—twigs of all shapes and sizes, making strange runic shapes.

Avery shivered. The glow from the torch lit the witch-marks up and cast strange shadows on the trees. Coupled with the very large rune burnt into the ground, it was undeniably weird. "Why did you come here at this hour?"

"We came to check the cameras and do some readings with the gear, and I thought I'd check the yew while we were here."

"I can feel the hum of magic here, can you?" she asked the other witches.

"It's faint, but yes, I feel it," Briar said, pointing her torch up into the twisted tree branches.

El lifted her fingers from where she'd touched the scorched mark and sniffed. "Nothing but earth and witch fire. I don't recognise the sign, either." She stood and played her torch over the ground.

"You looking for more marks?" Alex asked.

El nodded. "I can't help but think this is incomplete."

"I agree," he said. "I think this is the start of something bigger. If we compare it to the portal openings, it would have to have more symbols to be effective."

Avery looked across at Alex, startled. She'd been examining the witch-twigs, trying to make out some of the shapes and symbols. "You think it's a portal door?"

"I think it will be, once it's complete."

"Here," El shouted from the edge of the undergrowth. "There's another mark scorched into the ground." She pulled out her phone and started to snap photos as the others joined her.

"What is it?" Briar asked, frowning.

"Looks like a runic letter."

"Could this be the start of a portal to summon demons again?" Reuben asked, alarmed. The last person who'd summoned demons had been Alicia, Gil's widow, who was now also dead, killed by one of her own demons in Reuben's house.

Alex shrugged. He was their own expert in banishing demons, and knew the most about portal signs. "These portals come in all sorts of shapes and sizes, so maybe?" He looked at them apologetically. "Sorry. It's hard to know at this stage."

"Can't you just get rid of the symbol?" Cassie asked.

"I'll try," Briar volunteered. She crouched, and Avery felt her magic rise as she touched the earth. Briar was the most skilled at Earth magic, and it looked as if she was trying to erase the sign by using the earth to swallow it. However, after a few moments of intense concentration, during which the grass surrounding it started to grow, nothing happened to the scorched ground. She shook her head. "No. The earth resists it. Alex, do you want to try?"

He nodded. "Sure." He stood silently for a few moments, and then started to recite a spell, directing his energy to the mark on the floor. Nothing happened, and he sighed. "Damn it."

However, his magic triggered something else. The witch-signs in the trees above their heads started to vibrate, and the magic they felt emanating from them started to grow, pulsing in the air around the group. And then there was a flash of bright white light and a shock wave of magic rolled out, catching all of them unaware. It lifted them off the ground and threw them back several feet. Avery crashed into a tree trunk and crumpled in a heap, where she lay dazed for a few seconds.

Aware they could be attacked again, she struggled to sit up and blinked, trying to clear her vision. She instantly summoned air, meaning to send a whirlwind into the branches above when she hear Alex shout, "No! No one do anything."

She heard the groans of the others around her, and as the flash cleared from her vision, she saw the dark outlines of the others around her, sprawled on the ground, or lying awkwardly against trees. The sizzle of scorched earth filled the air, and she watched the signs on the ground glow with a fiery light before it faded to embers. Otherwise, the feel of magic was diminishing.

"Bollocks!" Reuben exclaimed. "I've hit my bloody head."

"I think I broke my camera," Dylan groaned.

"But is everyone okay?" Alex asked. From the sound of his voice, he was a few feet to Avery's left. Every single light had gone out, shorted by the magic.

There was a grumble of responses, but everyone seemed generally unharmed.

Ben swore. "What the hell was that?"

"Trigger protection response," Alex said. "This is more sophisticated magic than I thought."

Avery sent a couple of witch lights up, hoping that wouldn't trigger anything else. Thankfully it didn't, showing only her friends struggling to rise to their feet.

"Why didn't my magic trigger it?" Briar asked. She stood, brushing leaves and dirt off her skirt and boots.

"I presume my spell was a more direct assault than your Earth magic," Alex guessed. "Sorry guys."

"Not your fault," El said. "We sort of asked you to."

Once they were all standing, and a few more witch lights had been sent up, they inspected the witch-signs and the sigils on the ground. The sigils still glowed from where they had been burnt into the earth again, but the witch-twigs hung from the trees, as seemingly harmless as they had been when they arrived, although a faint glow marked where they had been attached to the branches.

"I don't think we could cut them free even if we wanted to," El noted thoughtfully. "I might be able to fashion a suitable spell into one of my silver daggers that would enable us to sever the magic attaching them to the tree. When we're ready."

Alex nodded. "Sounds good. But we do nothing until we know more about what we're dealing with here."

"What do you think's going on?" Cassie asked, slightly shaken.

"Well, Samhain is coming," Reuben said, "when the veils between worlds are at their thinnest. I think someone is trying to capitalise on that by creating a breach."

"When you say worlds, which ones are you talking about?" Dylan asked, perplexed.

Reuben's grin was devilish in the dim light. "All worlds—spirits, demons, other realities, and who knows what else. This is an old church with an old cemetery, quiet and secluded, and lots of power is manifesting here. It's going to be a fun Halloween, guys!"

5

The next morning, Happenstance Books glowed with golden light in the weak autumnal sunshine, enhanced by the enormous amount of fairy lights and fake candles glittering in corners and lighting up carved pumpkins.

"Excellent job, Sally!" Stan the Councillor and town Druid said, as he looked around the shop with delight. "I can always trust you to get on board with the town's celebrations."

Avery carefully said nothing, except smiled and raised an ironic eyebrow. She too was amazed by the amount of stuff Sally had managed to pack into the shop. She'd thought it had looked full the other day, but that was nothing compared to how it looked now.

"Thanks, Stan," Sally said, grinning. "I love this time of year, and I love Halloween! We're starting our storytelling evening at the beginning of Halloween week." She pointed to the printed posters that were placed around the shop and in the window.

"Fantastic!" Stan nodded happily as he strolled around the shop, Sally at his side, with Avery trailing after them. "I might be able to bring my grandchildren one night."

He wasn't dressed at all like a Druid today. His long cloak that he'd worn on the beach at Lughnasadh had gone, and instead he was in a regular dark grey suit and white shirt, his one concession to Halloween, an artful skeleton on his tie.

He continued, "I think Halloween is everyone's favourite celebration. Most shops are looking fantastic. And of course, the plans for the bonfire at the White Haven Castle are well underway."

"Will you be officiating again, Stan?" Avery asked.

He turned to her and grinned. "Of course! I wouldn't miss it. Let's hope rain doesn't ruin everything again. What a dreadful storm last time!" His face fell. "Such a shame, and the evening weather prediction had been so good…"

A rush of guilt swept over Avery again. "Oh well, you know what the weather forecasts are like. They're never accurate. I'm sure this time it will be fine."

"And you'll come?" he asked. "It's a week from Saturday, so obviously not Halloween proper, but close enough. We'll combine it with Guy Fawkes too, of course."

The town celebrations for the pagan and Christian festivals always fell on the closest Saturday, and of course five days after Halloween it was Guy Fawkes night, so the celebrations were on the Saturday in between.

Avery grinned. "Of course. I love a good bonfire and firework display. And, of course, your libations to the Gods."

Stan laughed. "Well, you'd know all about that wouldn't you, with all your books on the occult here."

For one horrible second, Avery had wondered if he was about to say something else, but she recovered swiftly. "Of course. I'm fascinated by it."

"We all are! It's the lifeblood of White Haven. The place is steeped in it. My niece is staying with me at the moment, and she loves all of this stuff! Doesn't live here, you understand," he dropped his voice conspiratorially. "Just visiting while her mother goes through a nasty divorce. I must tell her to come and visit here. She'd love it."

"Of course," Sally said, smiling. "It would be lovely to meet her."

"Yes, I'll mention it to her. Anyway," he said abruptly, "I must get on. I have more shops to visit. Keep up the good work, and I'll see you both soon!" And with that, he swept from the shop with a regal wave, and Avery let out a huge sigh. "Bloody Hell, I wondered what he was going to say then."

"You worry too much," Sally said, straightening a display. "So you're going to the bonfire?"

"Yeah, it won't clash with anything we're doing, and it's always fun. Well, hopefully more fun than last time."

"I take it you'll be doing your own celebrations?"

"We have the honour of sharing our celebrations as part of the thirteen covens of Cornwall—on the actual night of Samhain, of course!"

Sally widened her eyes with surprise. "Wow! So you're going? I thought the initial thrill of being part of the Council had worn off?"

Avery groaned. "It has, sort of. But seeing as Genevieve asked again, and I told her to stick it last time, I thought I should show some good will." She shrugged. "Besides, the others should meet the other covens, and it will be good to see Nate, Eve, Oswald, and Ulysses again." She referred to the other witches who lived in Mevagissey and St Ives, and who had helped them defeat the Mermaids.

"Have you told them about your problem up at Old Haven?"

Avery had told Sally about the witch-signs and sigils earlier that day. "No, not yet. Hopefully it's something we won't need help with." She headed to the back room, leaving Sally to return to the counter. "I'm going to make some coffee, do you want one?"

"Yes, please. And bring biscuits!"

As Avery made coffee, she pondered the witch-signs they had found at Old Haven. Someone was clearly trying to manifest something, but what? She and Alex had talked late into the night, trying to figure out what the sigil was. It looked nothing like the ones they had seen for demon summoning, but then again, it may not be complete yet. Reuben had talked about other worlds, but she presumed he was just spit-balling as usual. But he was right in one sense. Samhain was known for the fact that the veils between worlds became thin and beings could pass between them, especially the world of the dead, when spirits walked abroad. She had a horrible feeling Helena, her ghostly relative, would be more active during Samhain. But old tales also talked about Faeries—the worlds of the Other—when the Fey and other strange beings could cross into their world, or of course the other way around.

There were lots of tales about mythical creatures and Cornwall had many of their own. Cornish Piskies, or Pixies as they were called elsewhere, were small sprites who were mischievous, but mostly harmless, and known to lead travellers astray. There were also Spriggans, little creatures their local beach was named after, who were supposed to be spiteful and vengeful to those who had wronged them. They left Changelings—Faery children—in place of mortal ones. And Cornwall was well known for its tin mines. The remnants of many were strewn across the land and believed to be inhabited by Knockers, who had large heads and wizened faces and who knocked on the walls of a mine just before a cave collapse. Those tales, like those of Mermaids and giants, were children's stories, but Mermaids had proved to be only too real, and Piskies and Spriggans were supposed to be present in the real world, lurking where they couldn't be seen. Faeries, creatures of the Other—they lived *somewhere else.*

Of course, there were the tales of magic about King Arthur and Tintagel Castle on the North Coast of Cornwall. Morgan Le Fay was allegedly King Arthur's half-sister, depending on which stories you read, and she was half-Fey, as her name suggested. She was a witch who moved between the worlds of the Fey and mortals. According to tales from all over Britain and Europe, the Other also contained dragons, dryads, nymphs, and other mythical creatures. It was a place where time passed differently. A day in the Other, could be hundreds of years on Earth. Avery shivered. There were many tales about travellers who had crossed to the Other and returned years later, only to find their loved ones dead. She wasn't sure which was the more unnerving—demons or Faeries with their clever wiles and manipulations.

And of course there was the yew tree. She still needed to read up on that.

Just as she'd poured coffee and made up her mind to distract herself in the shop, someone knocked at the door and pushed it slowly open. James the vicar peered around the edge. He smiled tentatively. "May I come in and talk?"

A sinking feeling flooded through Avery. *He's going to ask about Old Haven.*

She pasted a smile on her face. "Of course. I haven't seen you for while. How are you?"

He threaded through the boxes, looking around curiously as he always did. "I've been better." He looked her straight in the eye. "You know why I'm here, of course."

"I presume you have questions about Old Haven Church."

He nodded. "Why is my church being targeted again, Avery?"

"I didn't know Old Haven was your church."

"Old Haven belongs to the Church of England. It's part of my area, especially because it's used only occasionally. It doesn't need a full-time vicar."

Avery frowned, recalling Gil's funeral. "My friend died in the summer and was buried there, in the Jackson's mausoleum. You weren't there then."

"I had some leave. Someone stood in for me. You haven't answered my question," he said softly.

"I honestly don't know why Old Haven is being targeted." He looked so anxious she knew she couldn't brush him off. "Take a seat. I'll take Sally her drink, and then we'll chat."

She rushed out the door, plonked Sally's drink and a pack of biscuits in front of her, and said, "Give me fifteen minutes. If I'm not out, come and get me."

Sally smirked and nodded, and Avery took a deep breath and headed to the back room.

James was idly flicking through a book on local history, but he put it down as soon as she walked in.

"Do you want a coffee?" she asked, remembering her manners.

"Just a biscuit will do."

She pushed a pack of chocolate digestives over and watched as he took a bite of one. "I'm not sure what's happening at Old Haven, but it's definitely different from what happened at All Souls."

"In what way?"

"Well, someone is trying to manipulate events at Old Haven. Someone is placing witch-signs in the trees, and there's a sign burnt into the earth now. That didn't happen at All Souls. The spirit there arrived all on its own." Avery inwardly winced. *Not exactly true, but she couldn't tell James about the portal under the Church.*

James's lips tightened. "Witchcraft! Someone is performing witchcraft at Old Haven? That's sacred ground. Hallowed. Consecrated to God!" His voice rose with anger.

"Witches are not demons," Avery said, her voice also rising with indignation. "Witches are good. They are not repelled by hallowed earth. Many worship the Goddess, not the Christian God. It doesn't make them evil."

"You speak from experience," James said knowingly, his eyebrows raised.

"Yes," she said, sick of his accusations and stupid ignorance. "I know about witchcraft. There's good and bad to the craft, as there is to anything. But I'm pretty sure this is not about inviting demons into Old Haven." As she said it, a certainty rushed through her, and she was convinced she was right. Her being resonated with it.

He leaned forward. "Then what are the witch-signs for? They are creepy and unholy and I want them gone."

"We cannot move them. Yet."

He narrowed his eyes at her and then sat back. "That's exactly what Ben said. Why? They're just twigs."

"Look, you asked Ben to keep an eye on the place, so he is. There have been increased spirit sightings there. It's an old church, with old graves. Halloween is coming. Maybe somebody wants to stir up ghosts and scare people. Or maybe it's something else. He came to me for advice, and I suggested that we don't move the signs yet. You have to trust me, James. We'll move them when we can."

"Well, that's the trouble Avery, I'm not sure I can trust you."

Avery's heart thudded painfully in her chest. "So, why are you here?"

"I'm assessing my options."

"What's that supposed to mean?" she shot back, annoyed. "We helped you at All Souls, and I'll help you now, but we need time and space to do it."

James rose to his feet, the chair scraping along the floor. "I've wrestled with my conscience ever since the events in the summer. I'm not sure what happened then, but I have to accept I wilfully looked the other way. I will not again. I've decided I'm going to call the police."

Avery stood, too. "And what will they do?"

"I want them to catalogue it and issue a trespass notice. I don't want whoever it is doing this to think they can keep doing this."

"And what about Ben and the filming?"

"I will allow that, but not the witch-signs. I'm going to get them down as soon as possible. And I want the press there."

"The press! Are you nuts? Old Haven will be invaded! I thought you would hate that. In fact, that's exactly what you wanted to avoid at All Souls!"

"I've changed my mind. I will make it clear that this will not be tolerated." And with that, he turned and marched out the door.

***

"I'm worried James is going to get hurt," Avery said to Alex.

"I'm sure he'll be fine. Especially if the press and the police will be there," he answered, trying to reassure her. "What could go wrong?"

"Everything!" she huffed. "I wonder if I should go."

"Don't talk bollocks," he said, incredulous. "You can't use magic, and you being there will look suspicious. Let James go ahead and do what he has to. I guarantee if he can tear those signs down, they'll be back overnight. In fact, he probably *can't* tear them down. They're reinforced with magic."

"That's what worries me. He could get hurt. And what would be on film?"

"Nothing! Magic will fry the footage."

"Well, from what Ben told me, it's happening tomorrow at midday."

It was a few hours after James had announced his intention to remove the signs, and Avery and Alex sat at the corner table in Penny Lane Bistro, exactly where they had sat months earlier when they were planning to break in and hunt for Helena's grimoire. In fact, Penny Lane Bistro had been Helena's house with her husband, and it was from there that she had been dragged to her trial for being a witch.

"When did he phone?" Alex asked, referring to Ben.

"At about six. I'd been trying to warn him about what James was planning, but he was testing psychic subjects at the university."

Alex smirked. "Were they psychic?"

"It doesn't look like it," she said, laughing. "Anyway, James had already told him. The press couldn't scramble in time for today, so that's why it's happening tomorrow. They were very interested, apparently."

"Of course they were. It's the perfect Halloween story. Especially after the deaths in the churches over the summer."

"I guess there isn't much we can do. I've told Ben to stand as far back as possible." Avery sighed. "I thought we'd ended things with James quite well, and now I find he's been fuming for months. It sucks."

Alex leaned forward and held her hand, stroking her palm. "I know. But we're witches and he's a vicar. And we did act very suspiciously. Anyway, I'm starving. Let's order food first and then we can talk."

"Does your stomach always come first?" Avery asked petulantly.

"Not always." He turned to the menu. "I'm having steak. What about you?"

"You always have steak."

"I'm a red-blooded male and I've been on my feet all day. You?"

"Venison," Avery said decisively. She sipped her red wine and decided he was right. There was nothing she could do about James. Ben and the others would be there—they were going to be interviewed about ghosts. They could keep an eye on James. "So, how's Zee working out?" she asked after they placed their order.

"Brilliant."

"Really?"

"Yep. He's tall and striking, he works hard, and the ladies love him. Including half the bar staff," he added with a frown.

Avery laughed. "Oh! A ladies' man?"

"I'm not sure I'd say that. He's just charming—and huge. And mysterious. I think that helps."

"Mysterious how?"

Alex sipped his pint as he thought. "He doesn't talk about himself much—understandably. No one knows where he comes from or what he does outside of work. And let's face it—we don't know much more, either. I just know they live in that big house on the edge of the moor that's available for long-term rentals. I have no idea how they arranged it, or who sorted their paperwork, and I don't want to know."

"How's Newton with him?" Newton often drank in The Wayward Son, but he was very suspicious of the Nephilim.

Alex raised his eyebrows and exhaled heavily. "Polite but brusque. He'll come around. I don't think it helps that the very handsome Eli is working with Briar."

"Really! Jealous? Well, he should have made a move when he had the chance." She took a satisfying sip of wine. "I'm a bit disappointed. They would have made such a nice couple. But, it's his own fault. "

"You're a hard woman, Avery Hamilton," Alex said, holding her hand and gazing at her in the way that was guaranteed to send her stomach somersaulting. "Remind me to never get on your bad side."

She met his dark chocolate eyes and felt her heart skip a beat. "Keep treating me like this and I don't think you ever will."

"Ever? I like that," he said, rubbing her palm again, and Avery allowed herself a twinge of excitement at the thought that this may last longer than any relationship she'd ever had before.

She wasn't sure if she was pleased or bitterly resentful when the waiter brought their food and their conversation turned more mundane, but just after nine they were interrupted by Alex's phone.

"Hey Reuben," Alex started, but then he fell silent and looked alarmed. Really alarmed. Avery's stomach tightened with worry. "Reuben, I need you to stay calm until we get there. Give us five." He looked at Avery. "Something's wrong with El. We need to go."

6

El was lying on the floor in the middle of her lounge, unconscious.

Her long, blonde hair was spread around her, looking bright against the dark red of the rug beneath her. Her face was pale, and her limbs were spread wide. She was wearing skinny jeans and a t-shirt, and her feet were bare.

The door to her flat had been open and they found Reuben at her side, kneeling as he shook her gently. "She won't rouse at all!" He looked at them, panic filling his eyes.

Avery felt for her pulse. "How long has she been like this?"

"About fifteen minutes. It happened just before I called you." Reuben was almost breathless with worry.

"What were you doing?" Alex asked calmly.

"We'd just had dinner. I'd cooked and was tidying the kitchen, and she walked from the table to join me and just fell!"

"No headaches, dizziness, anything weird? Any sign of fainting?" Alex asked.

"No! It was a normal night and she just collapsed. Should I call an ambulance? I wasn't sure if it was magic."

Interesting suggestion.

"Have you called Briar?" Avery asked.

"I couldn't get through," he explained.

"I'll try." Alex rose to his feet and started to pace as he pulled his phone out of his pocket.

El's pulse was fluttering wildly under Avery's fingers and her eyes seemed to be moving rapidly beneath her closed lids.

Avery looked around the room, perplexed, and asked a question, not really expecting Reuben to answer. "I wonder if she's possessed or something?"

He frowned. "Why do you ask that?"

"Well, you wondered if it was magic. She's young and healthy. Why would she collapse?"

The more she thought about it, the more likely this seemed and she stood, too, looking around the room, eyes narrowed.

"Let's think. We know there's another witch in White Haven. There are witch-signs at Old Haven, and strange sigils on the ground. Someone is trying to conjure something. They must know we're witches—or at least that there are witches in White Haven. Josh could recognise magic and he's a Shifter, so another witch would know us. Maybe that's even why they're here," she said, thinking out loud.

"Are you suggesting that whoever it is, is targeting us?" Reuben asked, wide-eyed. "Some bastard has hexed El?"

"Maybe." Avery shrugged. "That's the only logical solution—improbable though that seems."

Alex joined them. "I got hold of Briar. She was at the Shifters' house with Hunter. They're coming now."

"Both of them?" Avery asked, confused.

"He wants to help," Alex explained. "Not sure whether it's us though or Briar. But, all help is welcome."

"We need to look for witch-signs, symbols, runes, hex marks—anything," Avery said. "I'm wondering if she's been cursed by our mysterious newcomer."

Alex nodded. "Reuben, you monitor El. Yell loudly if anything changes. We'll search the flat."

"And the foyer," Reuben suggested, reaching for El's hand.

"Good idea. I'll look there now," Avery said, heading for the lift.

El's flat was situated on the top floor of an old converted warehouse, next to White Haven harbour. The foyer was locked, and visitors had to ring to be let in, but that wouldn't bother a witch. It was easy to open locks—electronic or otherwise.

The trouble was, Avery thought as she examined the lobby, which contained a large plant, a small table, the entrance doors to the two ground floor flats and not much else, *a hex bag or something in the lobby would surely affect the whole building.*

Outside the locked area of the foyer was the entrance with a row of locked post boxes. There were only five other flats here—two on each floor, including the ground floor. Avery looked in El's post box, but it was empty other than a couple of advertising flyers.

She headed out of the building and around the perimeter, not knowing what she was looking for, but hoping to see something unusual.

Once outside she inhaled deeply, enjoying the fresh sea air and sharp bite of brine and seaweed. The tide was in, and the fishing boats and small sailing ships bobbed on the gently moving water. The harsh glare from the street lamps showed that the road next to the harbour was mostly deserted, other than a few people wandering past on their way to and from pubs and restaurants. The fish and chip shop had steamy windows, and the faint smell of chips and vinegar drifted towards her. Avery shivered. It was cold and she could feel rain in the air.

Avery set off around the side of the building. There was only a short distance separating it from the sea, and as she progressed further around the back of the warehouse, the sounds of the town fell away and she heard the glug and lap of the water.

She felt a prickle run down her spine.

Someone was watching her.

Avery froze, slowed her breathing, and sent out her magic, gently. She didn't want to alarm whoever was watching her.

She turned slowly, scanning the area. To the right all she could see was the road snaking around the edges of the town, past the arcade with Viking Ink above it, heading towards Spriggan Beach.

No. Nothing from that direction.

Avery examined the walls and ground, looking for witch-marks or sigils, all the while feeling the prickle between her shoulder blades, but the building looked and felt normal. This attack was definitely directed at El, and whoever was watching wanted to see their reaction.

She looked towards the deeply shadowed path under the wall on the far side of the harbour. *Someone was there. Should she engage them now?* She had no idea of how strong they were or what they could do. It could be a trap for all she knew.

Quickly, before she changed her mind, she sent a spell to chill the blood—unpleasant, but not fatal. Within seconds there was a cry, and Avery saw a bright blue light flash across the water towards her. She rolled, threw up her defences, and deflected the energy bolt. A figure sprinted towards the road. Avery saw a coil of rope lying on the quayside and she flicked another spell towards it, seeing it rise with satisfaction and trip up the unknown enemy. Her assailant rolled quickly and sent a well-aimed curse at her. Avery flew backwards, hitting the wall of the building with a crushing *thump.*

She dragged herself off the cold floor and stood ready to fight, but it was too late. Her attacker had gone.

Avery ran back down the quay, hoping to see someone running along the street, but instead met Briar and Hunter as they sprinted from the road. Briar was breathless. "Sorry! I got here as quick as I could. Is she okay?"

"She was, but I've been out here for the last fifteen minutes. Someone, another witch, was lurking over there." Avery pointed to where her attacker had been hiding.

Hunter narrowed his eyes. "Show me. I have a better sense of smell than any of you. I may be able to detect something."

If Hunter was still suffering from his injuries, Avery couldn't tell. He looked fighting fit, and he reeked of confidence and aggression.

Briar agreed. "You carry on. I'll head up to El." Without waiting for their response, she headed inside, and Hunter followed Avery.

"You feeling better, then?" Avery asked as they walked.

"Much," he said, grinning. "Briar's a good healer."

"She is. She's a good witch."

"Single?" Hunter cocked a quizzical eye at her.

Avery smiled, despite her worry about El. "Yes. Single. Don't you live a long way from here?"

"Not at the moment I don't."

Avery appraised him. His hands were thrust into his leather jacket pockets, and his jeans hugged his hips. Leather boots completed the picture, along with his charming, confident grin. He was a darker, cockier version of his younger brother, Josh, and he was very different from Newton. "She's not the love 'em and leave 'em type," she advised him, quickening her step. "You hurt her, I'll boil your balls."

"Yes ma'am," he said with a smirk.

"I mean it." They had reached the far side of the harbour, and the opening between the two walls yawned wide and dark, the waves choppy where the calm water met the open sea. "This is where my attacker was watching me and the building. I can feel a residual tingle of magic."

Hunter dropped to his hands and knees and sniffed the ground. Old lobster pots and rope were coiled on the side; the scent of fish and the sea was strong. Avery was certain he wouldn't be able to smell much, but she was wrong.

"Female, old." He sniffed again, looking puzzled. "*Very* old."

Avery frowned. "But my attacker was agile. They ran and rolled. An old person couldn't do that. You must be detecting something else."

He looked up at her and shook his head. "No. I can smell other stuff, of course—fishermen, fish, seaweed, dogs, cats. But I sense magic, too. Old magic from an old person." He seemed very certain.

"How old is *very* old? And how can you tell from a smell?"

He rose to his feet and sighed. "It's hard to explain, but energy has signatures—you can probably detect that, too?"

"Yes, but this isn't energy, it's age."

"Oh, age has energy, too. For example, you smell of youth and vitality, and—" he inhaled deeply. "Roses and honeysuckle. And red wine. And a musky male." He grinned. "Dinner date? And very strong magic. Your magic," he pressed on before she could respond, "is a mixture of old and new. I sense another presence around you. Something smoky and complex, and a trace of violets." He frowned, perplexed. "Someone even older than your mysterious attacker."

Avery was astonished. "You must be able to scent Helena, my resident ghostly ancestor."

"You keep very interesting company, Avery."

"If Helena feels very old, and our attacker not so old, how old are we talking?"

He shrugged and set off down the wall, following the scent. "Hard to say with any great accuracy. How old is Helena?"

"Nearly five hundred years."

He raised his eyebrows. "So, I would guess maybe two hundred. Or thereabouts."

Avery felt goose bumps caress her skin that had nothing to do with the chill October air. "But how could someone that old still be alive?"

He smirked. "Magic?"

***

Twenty minutes later, Avery and Hunter arrived back in El's flat after unsuccessfully trying to follow the scent into town. Unfortunately, the overwhelming smells of others made it too hard, and they lost all trace in the narrow lanes that ran into the centre.

Alex looked up when they entered, frowning slightly. "I was getting worried. What happened?"

"Something really weird," Avery answered, trying to get her head around Hunter's news. El still lay prone on the floor, her breathing shallow, the others crouched next to her. "How's El?"

"No change. But we have found this." Alex gestured towards a silver necklace on the floor that was hard to see because it was almost under a side table. "It's cursed. Clever."

"How do you know?" Avery asked, puzzled.

"I've been trying to retrace her steps," Reuben explained, "and I remembered that as she came over to join me, she paused by this side table and said something like, 'Oh, there you are!' I thought she was talking to me, but then she picked the necklace up and dropped like a stone. I didn't think the two were related. I feel like such an idiot!"

"Don't," Avery reassured him. "Why would you think of a curse? And are we sure it is?"

"Yes, it's definitely cursed," Briar said emphatically. She held her hands a couple of inches above El and ran them over her in a sweeping motion. "I can feel the energy field around the necklace. Whatever you do, don't touch it. But it's muted, disguised somehow. And I can't feel anything from El. Normally, when I'm healing, I can feel how the body's energies feel wrong, but not now. There's just a void." She glanced up. "It's really weird. I just can't decide how it works."

Avery headed over to the necklace and crouched next to it, careful not to touch. She held her hand above it, feeling with her magic; Briar was right.

Alex asked, "How did this witch get hold of her necklace in the first place?"

"I have no idea!" Reuben said. "Like you said, she wears a lot of jewellery. And she didn't mention a missing necklace."

"Well, whoever is causing this," Avery mused, "was outside the warehouse, on the harbour wall, watching. Maybe they activated it from outside."

Briar shook her head. "No. It was already cursed. I think they were enjoying the repercussions, don't you?"

"Maybe." Avery shrugged, perplexed.

"Any clue as to who it is?" Alex asked.

"Someone very old," Hunter said, joining the conversation. Until then he'd been pacing around the room like a sniffer dog. "I can smell them here, too."

"They've been in this flat?" Avery spun around to look at him. "I can't feel other magic!"

"I can. It's faint, but I'm good. I'd be even better in wolf form. If I could have changed in the street, I would have been able to follow them with ease."

"Wolves in White Haven? I don't think so," Avery said.

He grinned. "Tell people I'm a husky. That would work."

"Can we just cure her now and ponder how it was cursed later?" Reuben asked, a dangerous edge to his voice.

Briar sighed. "It's not that simple, Reuben. We have to work out what type of curse it is to lift it." She pulled her Athame and a small, velvet bag out of her medicines box, and then joined Avery. She placed her Athame under the necklace, lifted it gingerly and examined it again. El's cursed necklace was a long silver chain with an ornate amulet attached, and it looked perfectly normal. Briar dropped it in the bag, tying it securely.

Reuben almost growled in frustration. "How long can this last? I know bugger all about curses!"

"If we can't break it, it could last forever," Briar said, securing the necklace in the box. "And that would kill her." Her words fell into deafening silence. "However, there's some healing magic I need to perform that will buy us some time. Can you carry her to her bed?"

While Briar and Reuben ministered to El, Alex joined Hunter and Avery. "You said this attacker was old? What do you mean?"

"I mean, you have a two hundred-year old—and then some—witch, or something, running around White Haven cursing its resident witches," Hunter answered, a slight preen of arrogance to his tone.

"Well, you can put your famous nose to the test and check out Old Haven Church tomorrow. I want to know if our two problems are caused by the same person."

7

El remained unconscious, but Briar promised to stay with her, as did Hunter and Reuben. Alex and Avery left after making sure the others would call with updates.

"Hunter's pretty cocky," Alex said, as they headed to his flat above The Wayward Son.

"But pretty useful." Avery slipped her small hand into Alex's, savouring his warmth. "That nose of his sensed things I couldn't. Yes, I sensed magic, but not age."

Alex shook his head. "A really old witch must mean some sort of alchemy is involved, and maybe a quest."

"Alchemy? Quest?" Avery looked up at him, confused. "What do you mean?"

"Would you want to live for hundreds of years unless you had something to achieve? Our ancestors were powerful, so were some of the others in the Witches Council. They're all dead. Magic does not normally enhance your lifespan, unless…" He looked at her speculatively.

"Unless you do a deal of some sort, or some really dark magic," Avery finished.

"Because you want to *do something.*"

"How can you expand your lifespan for over two hundred years? Have you ever seen a spell for that?"

Alex shook his head. "No. But I know alchemy promised such things."

"The gift of immortality is a myth, Alex."

"But it might not be immortality. It might be a way of eking out life, bit by bit, until you achieve what you set out to do."

"And that would be to open some kind of portal—if the two are linked?" Avery suggested.

"Maybe."

"So, why target El?"

"Because she said she could make a knife or sword that could cut through the magic securing the witch-signs. Eliminating El means the witch-signs remain. This witch has ears and eyes we don't know about."

"A traitor?"

Alex frowned. "I don't think so. A seer maybe? Scrying? Someone who can do it better than me." He threw back his head and shouted. "Can you see us now? We'll find you, old one." He turned to Avery and grinned.

"Silly bugger."

"But sexy as hell, right?" He pulled her close for a long, lingering kiss.

"Now who's cocky?" Avery said as she got her breath back.

"I'll show you cocky." They had reached his flat, and he opened the back gate of the pub with a wicked glint in his eye.

***

Old Haven Church was draped in mist and drizzle when the group arrived there at nine the next morning.

Briar had phoned Avery at six saying that El was still unconscious and that she was staying with her all day. Neither she nor Reuben had slept much, and Briar had asked Eli to cover her shop. As worried as Alex and Avery were, there was nothing they could do, and they decided to go ahead with their meeting.

Hunter was leaning against the main door of the church, sheltering under the broad porch, Piper next to him. She scowled when she saw them, but he gave a wolfish grin. "Ready for some hunting?"

"Always," Alex said as he led the way to the grove of trees.

Hunter matched Alex's stride. "How's your friend?"

"Not good."

"Sorry. Briar was sure she'd figure out something this morning."

"She was trying to be positive, but I think we all know it's not going to be that simple. The more we can find out now, the more we'll help El."

Hunter nodded, quickening his pace.

"Are you helping, too?" Avery asked Piper, hoping to draw her out of her sulk.

She shrugged. "There's not much else to do."

Avery resisted the urge to roll her eyes and said dryly, "Good for you."

Once they reached the wood, Alex said, "We need to work quickly. The press and the police will be here at twelve, with the vicar."

"It'll take minutes only," Hunter reassured them.

As soon as they reached the clearing, Avery shivered. "The magic has grown stronger. Can you feel it, Alex?"

Alex placed his hand on the yew's knotty trunk. "Yeah, and not just around us. The tree has a…" He paused, thinking for a moment. "A pulse, or a breath—it's like the tree's breathing."

There were now dozens of witch-signs hanging not only from the branches of the yew, but also in the surrounding trees, and Avery watched their strange forms and patterns turning in the damp, autumnal air. "I can feel *them,* too, shimmering with magic. It's so unusual."

"In what way?" Hunter asked, as he lifted his head and sniffed the air.

"It feels deeper, older almost—"

"Wilder," Alex said, before she could continue. "Like wild magic just coming to life."

Avery smiled softly at Alex. "That's *exactly* what it feels like!"

Hunter looked thoughtfully between the two of them, nodding, and then stripped his clothes off without a second thought and shifted into a beautiful black wolf with a grey muzzle.

Although Avery was expecting it, it was still a shock. For a few moments his body shimmered and then dissolved, and a wolf was standing there instead. However, Hunter was bigger than a normal, non-shifting wolf—or so Avery thought. *Like I spend a lot of time with wolves.* He stood at least level with her waist, and his paws were enormous. Even in wolf form, she could still see the scars from his fight, where his thick coat was ragged and patchy.

Hunter immediately started sniffing the ground, and they watched him search among the tree roots and narrow animal tracks.

Avery watched him start searching and turned back to Alex. "What does this mean? Wild magic?"

"Isn't all magic wild?" Piper asked, looking mildly bored.

"Yes and no," Avery said, struggling to explain. "The magic we use is disciplined, taught and practiced for generations, guided and shaped by spells and the elements. This feels like it has no borders, no restraints. Plenty for us to think about."

Piper shrugged and fell silent again.

While Hunter searched, Avery thought about the cameras at the edge of the wood. "I wonder if Dylan had any luck with the footage."

"He hasn't called you?" Alex asked.

"No. I bet that jolt of magic fried everything the other night."

Alex stepped into the yew's hollow trunk and rubbed his hand across the gnarled surface. "I wonder how old this is. It must pre-date the church."

"I agree," Avery said. "I managed to catch up on some lore about them. I know they were sacred to Druids. They believed they linked to one's ancestors and guarded a person's path into the Otherworld. It's also sacred to Hecate and the Crone."

"Hecate and the Crone?" Piper asked, curiosity overcoming her sullenness. She leaned against a beech tree, half watching them, half watching her brother.

"Hecate is the Greek Goddess of magic and witchcraft, the moon and ghosts, and one of the many Gods and Goddesses who are sacred to the night and the Underworld," Avery explained. "She is closely linked to the Celtic Goddess, of which there are three aspects—the Maiden, the Mother, and the Crone. The Crone is the old lady we will all become. She relates to death and as such also guards the Underworld." She smiled. "You, as I am still, are in our maiden phase."

"It sounds stupid." Piper eyes flashed a challenge.

"So does the idea of people turning into wolves, and yet you do," Avery pointed out.

"There's a lot of talk about Underworld and Otherworlds in all of this," Alex said, ignoring Piper.

Avery nodded. "In all the reading I've done, the thing that's mentioned most frequently is the yew's links to the Otherworld. And that sigil burnt into the ground in front of the trunk must have something to do with that—I think so, anyway."

Alex sighed. "And we still haven't identified what that sigil is yet."

Hunter paced around their feet. In seconds he shifted back to human form, completely naked, and Avery tried to avert her eyes. *Shifter's aren't shy.* Alex caught her glance, his eyes filled with laughter.

"Well, it's the same smell I found before," Hunter said, a trace of humour in his eyes as if he knew Avery was uncomfortable.

Smug git.

He continued, "An old woman, and old magic. Very different from you guys." He shivered, and headed for his clothes, pulling his jeans on. "And powerful."

"No other scents that suggest she's working with someone?" Alex asked.

"No. Plenty of other human scents, but nothing remotely witchy. In fact," he lifted his head and inhaled. "Some of them are coming now."

As he spoke, Avery heard voices and turned to see Dylan and Ben arrive. "Hey guys," Ben said cheerily. "Didn't think you were coming today."

"We're leaving soon," Avery reassured him, and introduced them to Piper and Hunter. "You're early."

"I was about to check the footage," Dylan said, "but we heard your voices and thought we'd say hi." He looked around, noticing the newly arrived witch-signs. "Wow. Someone's been busy!"

"Yeah, too busy," Alex said, despondently. "You think you'll have any film at all?"

He grimaced. "Unfortunately, I think there's too much magic around for anything to record now. The footage just buzzes." He caught Piper looking at him and grinned, his teeth glinting white against his dark skin.

Piper's interest shot up and for the first time, Avery saw her actually smile. "Cool. Can you show me?"

"Sure. Follow me."

Hunter watched her follow Dylan back through the trees and sighed. "She's bloody hard work sometimes."

"Maybe she just needs a distraction," Avery said. "Looks like she's found one."

Ben had been gazing around the clearing. "This place is seriously creepy. You guys need to get out of here. The police are coming soon, and the press will set up early. James is on his way, too."

"All right," Avery said. "Please try to stop James from touching the witch-signs. I don't think they're safe, and I think he could get a nasty shock."

"I'll try, but I think we'll fail," Ben said. "He's getting angrier about this by the minute."

"Well, so is the witch doing this. She cursed El last night, using one of her own necklaces." She told him what they'd discovered the night before.

Ben looked worried. "This is getting dangerous."

"Doesn't it always?"

"If there's anything we can do to help El, let me know."

"Will do. And if there's anything you can find out about this site, let us know. I'm going to do some research." Avery looked around at the grove. "This has to have relevance to what the witch wants to do."

"Come on, we better go," Alex said, and followed Hunter as he walked back to the cemetery.

Avery nodded. "Call me later, Ben?"

"If we're all still alive," Ben answered.

Avery was pretty sure he wasn't joking.

***

Before Alex and Avery returned home, they headed to El's flat, hoping to see her awake and well, but they were disappointed. She lay under her quilt, unnaturally still.

Briar leaned against the doorframe. "This curse is strong. I can't shift it."

"Even though she isn't touching the necklace?" Avery asked.

"Yep." Briar headed back to the lounge and pointed to where it lay on a side table under a glass cover that looked like one of El's shop displays. "The necklace is still cursed, too. I haven't dared touch it. I have attempted a few spells to try to discover the type of curse, but it's well-disguised."

Reuben was in the kitchen, trying to keep busy. He looked terrible. His eyes were dark with lack of sleep, and thick stubble was already covering his chin and cheeks. "And while the curse remains, El remains under its enchantment."

Briar explained, "Many of my spells are for healing Earth magic. Not many talk about breaking curses. Have you got any suitable spells?"

"I can't think of any off the top of my head, but I can certainly look," Avery said. "I'm heading back to the flat now, so all being well, I'll get straight on it."

"Me, too," Alex agreed. "In fact, I'm not working until later today, so I can stay if you need to head to your shop, Briar? I can grab my grimoires, bring them back here, and keep an eye on El."

She smiled at him gratefully. "Yes, please. There are a few things I need to check on and some herbs I want to collect. I'll come back this afternoon."

"Same goes, Reuben. You should go home and get some sleep."

"Absolutely not. The business is fine, and El is more important."

"Well okay, but you have to try to sleep here. Briar can give you something. You look like shit."

"Cheers, mate." Reuben's normal buoyant humour had deserted him. "That's because I feel like it. I can't believe someone would do this to El!"

"It could have been anyone of us. In fact," Alex said, looking at all of them, "it still could be. Be suspicious of anyone. We need to try and find how she got to El's necklace—whether it was from the shop or here—and we need to increase our protection spells. One of us could be next."

8

Avery walked up the winding streets of White Haven, having declined a lift back. She needed the fresh air to clear her brain, and her shop was only ten minutes from the harbour.

Despite the grim circumstances and her preoccupation with the curse and the strange events at Old Haven Church, her surroundings made her smile. The murk of the day was lifted by the decorations in the shops and cafes. The windows were filled with pumpkins, witches riding on brooms, skeletons, vampires, ghosts and ghouls, and strings of lights. In another week or so, all of these items would be replaced by Christmas decorations, and they would all gear up for another round of celebrations. The Town Council had already decorated the streets with festive lights, but for now, the focus was clearly on All Hallows' Eve.

The numbers of shoppers were lower, now that the summer holidays were over, and on the way Avery nodded to, or stopped and spoke to the locals as they went about their business. This weekend, however, the streets would once again fill with visitors as people came for the fun of Halloween.

Realising she was close to El's shop, Avery ducked down a side street to speak to Zoey, a practicing Wicca Witch.

As usual, Zoey stood behind the counter looking immaculate. Her hair was cut into a blunt bob, but this time the tips were died neon blue, and her makeup was perfect. She didn't often smile, but as soon as Avery entered, her eyes lightened. "How's El? Better?"

"Sorry, no," Avery said, heading over and leaning on the counter. "I've come to see if you remember anything weird happening here over the last day or two?"

Zoey's face fell in disappointment. "I've been thinking of nothing else, ever since Reuben told me. Nothing unusual has happened. We've had some regular customers and some new ones, but no one has struck me as odd."

"No sign of a break-in, I presume?"

"No, why?"

"Someone has been in El's flat. We think it's a woman, an old woman who potentially appears as someone much younger. I just wondered if you'd seen anything."

"Everything has been completely normal," she explained, perplexed. "I've been trying to think of anything that could help, but I just can't!"

"It's okay," Avery said, smiling softly. "We'll get her back, somehow. In the meantime, do you need help with her shop?"

"No. I can manage. I pretty much run the place anyway."

"Okay. If anything occurs to you, no matter how small, let us know."

Frustrated that there was nothing more to learn, Avery continued on to her favourite coffee shop, bought three coffees and a selection of pastries, and headed back to Happenstance Books.

"Anything going on here?" she asked, placing everything on the counter.

"Nope," Dan said, reaching immediately for a pastry, and nodding to the stacks behind her. "Other than that you've got a visitor."

"I have? Who?"

A familiar drawl made her skin prickle. "Me. I have a few questions." She turned to see Caspian emerge from one of the deep armchairs placed around the shop. He was dressed in a dark grey suit, with a pale grey, linen shirt open at the neck. The scent of expensive aftershave drifted over to her, and she noted his well-groomed hair and expensive leather shoes, all topped with a heavy, knee-length wool coat.

"Oh, goodie. I've so missed you," Avery said dryly.

He allowed the faintest of smiles to crease his face, and then it was gone. "Of course you have. I'm a delight. After you," he said, gesturing to the back of the shop.

She grimaced, considered refusing, and then decided she may as well get it over with—as soon as he asked nicely. She folded her arms across her chest. "Say please!"

"Do we have to do this?"

"Yes. They're called manners. It's about time you learned some."

She could hear Dan sniggering into his pastry and tried to ignore it.

Caspian narrowed his eyes, sighed, and then said with exaggerated politeness, "May I please speak to you privately, Ms Hamilton?"

"Why, certainly, Mr Faversham," she replied as she grabbed a coffee and pastry and carried them to the back room.

"Not one for me?" he asked, leaning forward to open the door for her.

"Had I been expecting you, of course I would have bought one." *Liar!* "Instead," she said, resolutely refusing to share her own and reaching for a pack of biscuits, "Would you like a Hob Nob?"

"Splendid, my favourite," he said, sinking into a chair at the table. He crunched into one with great satisfaction, and Avery's lips twitched with amusement. *Who'd have thought Caspian would like a Hob Nob?*

She sat opposite him and reflected on the strange conversations she often had at this table. As she took a bite of her custard-filled croissant, she hoped the sugar would be enough to sustain her. "I gather this is not a social call?"

"No. I'm wondering what on Earth possessed you to let the vicar summon the press up to Old Haven to film him removing witch-signs."

"Well, short of me glamouring the vicar, there was actually no way of stopping him. And besides, how do you know?" Once again, she felt annoyed. His ability to piss her off in seconds was uncanny.

He smirked as he reached for another biscuit. "I have my methods."

"A sneak in the press, you mean?"

"We all have ways of staying in touch with the local news. So, what *is* going on at Old Haven?"

Avery debated how much to tell him, and they watched each other silently across the table for a few seconds. Despite the very rocky start to their relationship, and the fact that Caspian had been responsible for Gil's death, they seemed to have reached an unspoken truce. She chewed on her croissant, savouring it for a moment before coming to a decision.

"There's an unknown witch in White Haven. She has cursed El, and seems to be powering up a spell in Old Haven Church, centred on the old yew tree in the grove behind the churchyard. I presume she thought the place was so quiet that no one would notice what she was up to. Fortunately, Ben and the others head up there quite regularly, and they spotted them. Initially there were just a couple of witch-signs hanging from the branches, but now there are more of them, and two sigils burnt into the ground. The power there is palpable and growing."

Caspian leaned forward. "El is cursed?"

Avery was shocked. That wasn't what she thought he'd lead with. "Yes. Her necklace. We found it on the floor of her flat. Reuben remembered that she picked it up and then collapsed. But we can't work out what sort of curse it is. And she's unconscious. A very weird, unnatural stillness." Avery hesitated for a second, worry bubbling up inside her. "We can't break it, yet. Briar has tried—she's better at that sort of thing—but I'm about to start searching for spells, too."

"Curse spells are notoriously difficult to break," Caspian said. "They have a tendency to rebound on those attempting to break them. Unless you're the one that cast it, of course."

"I know. That's why we're being careful." She tried unsuccessfully to temper her sarcasm.

"A necklace, you say? Silver?"

"Yes."

"Silver holds magic very well, it will be tricky." He broke off and looked into the distance. "I'll give it some thought."

Really? "Thanks, Caspian. We'd appreciate it."

The surprise must have showed on her face, because he grimaced. "I am not without sympathy, and my family grimoires contain many curses."

No surprise there.

He continued, "In the meantime, what will you do to counteract the press at Old Haven?"

Avery snorted. "It's Halloween. Hopefully people will put it down to some prank or hoax. And it's very likely their cameras won't work. Dylan's don't anymore."

"What was he filming?"

"Ghost activity. That place can be volatile."

He leaned back thoughtfully. "Interesting. But that's good—the cameras, I mean. And any leads on this witch?"

"None. But she's old. Very old, according to—" Avery caught herself in time. She wasn't sure she wanted Caspian to know about the Shifters. "From what we can tell, anyway."

"A time-walker?"

Avery almost choked on her coffee. "A *what*?"

He smiled. "Some witches have learnt to defy time. If she's the one who cast your spell, you'll struggle. They're very powerful."

"I've never heard of a time-walker!"

"So, there are some things I can teach you, after all!" he smirked.

"Go on," she said, wanting to throw the remains of her pastry at him.

He shrugged. "They have learnt the secret of defying aging. Immortal creatures, maybe, but essentially time stretches for them. But it takes energy. A lot of it. She'll be staying somewhere close to natural resources she can draw on to replenish her energy. Somewhere isolated."

"Surely the sea is a great natural resource?"

"Yes, but huge and unwieldy. Running water, such as a spring or river, is better. Of course, your abundance of magic over the town will help."

"No one's drawing on that as far as I can tell."

"*Yet,*" he said, reaching for another biscuit. "And now for my next item of business. There are Shifters in White Haven."

"Wow. You really run a spy network, don't you?" Avery said, annoyed.

"I have been approached by the Device witches from Cumbria."

The name sounded vaguely familiar to Avery, but she couldn't quite place it. "Who?"

"You really are an ingénue, aren't you?"

"Don't push me, Caspian."

"Have you heard of the Pendle witches?"

"Of course I have. I'm not an idiot."

He spread his hands wide, smirking.

She groaned. *Of course!*

The Device witches were an old family that went back at least to the sixteenth century, and probably further. They had gained notoriety when they feuded with another family of witches, headed by Anne Whittle, and then both were brought to the attention of the authorities and tried for witchcraft. The families were commonly referred to as the Demdike family, after "Old Demdike," head of the Devices, and the Chattoxes after "Mother Chattox," head of the Whittles. Together they were called the Pendle witches after the area in Lancashire they lived in. The story was notorious because they were accused of ten murders by the use of witchcraft. Of the twelve alleged witches who were brought to trial, ten were found guilty and hanged, one was found not guilty, and the other died in prison.

Caspian continued, "Their descendants, like ours, survived, and they remain two of the most powerful witch families in the north of England. The Devices are now in Cumbria and have been for many years, after moving on from Pendle. They rule with an iron fist. You know there are many Shifters there?"

Avery felt a deep, sinking sensation in the pit of her stomach. "Yes. Some fled after one of them was attacked. He was near death when they came to me."

"That's not the story I heard," he said softly. "They attacked first, and the family they attacked wants revenge—a rematch. Demdike, also known as Alice Device, will see it happens."

Avery fell silent for a moment, her thoughts whirring. "But they fled here after saying they were attacked by some guy called Cooper. They sought Sanctuary here. They claim victim."

Caspian frowned. "Well, I imagine somewhere between the two tales lies the truth. Either way, Alice—the leader of their family—will ensure that the Shifters return. They will arrive here tomorrow. Expect a visit."

Avery frowned, still confused. "Why did they call you and not me?"

"Over the years our families have done business together, but not for a long time. However, in cases such as these, it was natural they should speak to me, as I know you."

"But why are they coming to see *me*?"

Caspian shook his head slowly. "Avery, you have much to learn. It is because you allowed them Sanctuary."

That word again.

She looked at him, astonished. "What year is this, Caspian? We don't grant Sanctuary like some feudal system. People come and go, and are free to live here!"

"That may be so for normal people, but for those like us, who live on the peripheries of the normal world, some old school polices still apply. Especially as viewed by the Devices. Some old families quite like their feudal systems."

"Like yours, you mean? Your unwillingness to let us gain our grimoires."

He shuffled uncomfortably in his chair. "My father's wishes could not be ignored. Do you want my advice or not?"

"Well, you don't offer it often, so go on."

He met her gaze steadily across the table. "Shifters like that system, too. They are wolves—pack animals, despite their human form. Cumbria is wild country, that's why they live there. It is remote, wolves can disappear there. You do not want a Shifter war here. Did the Shifters *ask* for Sanctuary?"

"Yes. And I laughed, but said of course they could stay here."

"Well, there you are then. I suggest you get your boy repaired and send him on his way." He smiled. "He helped you detect the old witch, didn't he?"

"Yes."

"Don't owe him too many favours. It might come back to bite you."

"We saved his life. He better be bloody grateful, or it will come back to bite *him*."

Caspian smiled, and it almost made him look charming. "That's why I like you, Avery. You have fire, and undeniable magic. If you ever get tired of Alex, give me a call."

And with that, he left, leaving Avery staring after him.

9

Avery was seething. Did Caspian just make a pass at her? *Cheeky bastard.* As if she would ever think about having an affair with him!

Sally laughed when she told her about their conversation. "He's just trying to get a rise out of you, Avery. Ignore him. He will say anything to inflame you."

Dan agreed, although he qualified it with, "But he is single. Why? He's rich, good looking. A wanker, yes, but still… He might mean it."

"I don't care if he means it. How dare he!"

"He's a guy. You can't blame him for trying, Avery," Dan said, frowning. "You have no idea what it's like to be a man and expected to make the first move. It doesn't matter how confident you are, it's still awkward. Give him a break."

"I have a boyfriend. Aren't there mates' rules or something?"

"Yeah, but he and Alex are not mates," he pointed out.

Avery huffed. "Traitor. That's the last time I save you from a Mermaid."

"Ouch. It's a good thing I've sworn off women, then." He grinned and reached for another pastry. "At least I have food to console me."

"So, what else did Caspian want? You were talking a while," Sally said.

They were all standing around the counter. The shop was empty, and outside the rain had returned in such a downpour that the other side of the street was a blur. Happenstance Books seemed isolated from the outside world. Incense smoke drifted around the room, B.B. King was playing, and a tingle of magic hung on the air. Avery loved afternoons like this.

"He came to warn me about the Shifters and the imminent arrival of the ex-Pendle witches," Avery said, and went on to explain their conversation.

Sally looked worried. "Do you think the Shifters are playing you?"

"Lying, you mean? About what really happened?"

"Maybe. You don't know anything about them. They turn up here, one of them nearly dead, and ask for help. They've told you their side of the story. You have no idea what else went on."

Avery fell silent for a moment. Sally was right. She needed to ask some more questions.

Damn it.

***

The old Volvo that was normally parked in front of the house was missing.

Avery paused for a moment on the doorstep before she knocked, and cast her witchy senses wide. She sensed their Shifter magic, but nothing else. Summoning her courage, she knocked resolutely, and for a while, nothing happened.

She was about to knock again when Holly answered the door, looking surprised. "Oh, it's you. I thought Briar had arrived early."

"No. Briar is a little tied up with our friend, El. Can I come in?"

Holly looked wary, but then said, "Sure, but Hunter's out."

"That's fine. I have a few questions, and I hope you can help." *Softly, softly.* She didn't want the door slammed in her face. Blasting the door back open with her witch powers wasn't on her to-do list for the day.

Holly shrugged. "I can try." She turned and led the way to the kitchen at the back of the house. The rain had slowed to a drizzle, and mist swirled around the back garden. Holly turned the kettle on. "Want a drink?"

"Tea sounds lovely." Thank the Goddess for tea. It seemed to pave the way for any conversation.

Avery had debated with herself on how best to start this conversation, and she realised there was no easy way. She could hedge around the fight and what really happened, but ultimately decided honesty was the best way.

"Alice Device is coming to see me tomorrow."

Holly dropped the cup she was holding and looked at Avery in shock. The noise of the shattering cup was ignored as each met the other's eyes. Holly was frozen in place.

Avery spoke softly. "Would you like to sit down?"

Holly nodded and fumbled for a chair, sinking into it absently. She was still mute, and she looked at the table.

"Why is Old Demdike coming to see me?"

"I didn't think they would follow us here." Holly's hands started to shake, and she placed them on her lap, out of Avery's sight.

"What happened in Cumbria?"

Holly swallowed nervously. "I'm not sure Hunter would want me sharing this."

"I don't give a crap what Hunter wants. What happened?"

Holly looked at her, her eyes silently pleading.

"I can't face the Devices without knowing what really happened. Weakness is not an option."

Holly exhaled heavily. "Cooper is the pack leader and Hunter challenged him. He lost, and we fled."

"Oh! So Hunter wasn't attacked in some stealth manoeuvre, he actually challenged Cooper. He started the fight."

"Yes."

"Why lie? And what's the big deal? Cooper is still the pack leader. Why are they coming here?"

"He needs to swear loyalty and renounce his claim to the leadership. He fled—*we* fled—before he could do this. Hunter wants to challenge again. He's buying himself time."

"Time to heal."

Holly nodded. "Yes. If he loses after a challenge, we lose everything. We move to the bottom of the pack. Loss of privileges. And I'm still expected to marry Cooper."

Avery felt the air start to rise and her hair lifted as a gust of wind rattled around the kitchen. Holly looked around, alarmed and confused. "You are to do what?"

"Marry Cooper. We are the oldest families. It's expected. I don't like him. I never have. Hunter was trying to protect me."

Avery was incensed. "You're not a piece of meat! What the hell system do you live in? It's the twenty-first century, Holly!"

"Are you causing that wind?"

"Yes! I can make a frigging hurricane if I want! Are you serious?"

"Yes. Shifters are pack animals. It's patriarchal. And the pack leader is strongly allied to the Devices—Old Demdike. They carry their history with them."

"I have history! We all have." Avery shot up from the table and started pacing the room, energy balling in her hands. She was pretty sure Holly was being honest with her. Avery could usually sense lies—witches were good at that—but their Shifter magic was clouding her judgement. "Are you telling me the truth? Because if I defend you tomorrow, I want to make sure I know absolutely everything. I can make your life just as miserable as them." *Not entirely true, but they didn't have to know that.*

"Yes! Hunter would hate you to know this—he hates to fail. He thought he could take Cooper on. It's knocked his confidence and almost killed him—because of me. I begged him to do it!" Holly started to cry. "I should just suck it up. Marriage to the pack leader is something many other Shifters would want."

"Only if they're stupid," Piper said. Once again she'd sidled to the door, and she stood watching them.

"But you want to go home," Holly said, annoyed. "At my expense."

"Not true." Piper joined them at the table, her shoulders bowed. "I want to go home, yes, but not with those consequences."

"And what does Josh think?" Avery asked.

"Like us, he thinks it's time for change. It would be good for the whole pack," Holly said.

"And what about the other members?"

"Some agree, others don't. There are a lot of us."

"The younger ones definitely want change," Piper said, "I know they do. I think they'll be gutted that Hunter lost."

"They would know?" Avery was struggling to understand the pack rules and what exactly a challenge consisted of.

"Oh, yes. The pack was there, watching the outcome."

"How exactly did you get Hunter away, if it was an arranged fight and everyone was watching?"

"Josh picked another fight, and we sneaked him out in the chaos. We have broken every rule there is," Piper explained, slightly triumphant, and it brought a brief smile to Avery's face.

"I like your style!" Avery fell silent for a second, thinking. "Do the witches interfere with fights?"

"I'm pretty sure not," Holly said, but doubt lurked behind her eyes.

"So, just to be clear, Hunter wasn't ambushed. He picked the fight and lost?"

Holly nodded. "Yes. And we have to return to finish it. We either submit, Hunter dies, or we are exiled."

Avery felt her annoyance settle into cold, hard steel and she sat down. "Why are you in White Haven? Why not somewhere else?"

"We wanted to put a lot of distance between us and them, and this is a long way south. And then we sensed the magic here. It's strong. You're strong. We needed your help, and we needed someone who could stand up to the Devices, if they came looking. We honestly didn't think they would—at least, not so soon. They're mean, Avery. They'll drag us back before we're ready to go.""No, they won't. I'll make sure of that."

***

Avery marched into The Wayward Son with fire burning in her soul. Alex was behind the bar serving a customer, and for a second, he didn't see her. The sight of him calmed her down, fractionally.

His lean, muscled frame looked good in his jeans and black t-shirt. As usual, stubble covered his cheeks and chin, and his hair fell loosely to his shoulders. Her stomach somersaulted. *He was so hot.* And the absolute opposite of Caspian in every way. He looked up and grinned when he saw her, and her stomach flipped once more. Even now, months after they had got together, he still gave her goose bumps.

"Hi, gorgeous," he said, leaning over the bar to kiss her. "I didn't think I'd be seeing you 'til later."

She cupped his face between her hands and kissed him back, enjoying his heat and scent, before she broke away. "Hi, handsome. I've missed you."

"Good," he said, a gentle smile playing across his lips. "But why do I sense there's another reason for your early visit?"

"There have been a few developments with our new friends. Can you get away from the bar for a while? I'm going to call the others, too."

"Sure, give me half an hour. But there's no El, remember, or Reuben. He'll be with her."

"Shit." She rubbed her face. "Have you heard how she is?"

"No change. I called Reuben earlier." He gestured to a stool at the end of the bar, well away from prying ears. "Grab a seat and I'll get you a drink. Want some food?"

At the mention of food, her stomach grumbled and she checked her watch. It was nearly three. No wonder she was hungry. "Yeah, a bowl of fries, please." And then another thought struck her. "What happened at the church?"

"I haven't heard." He placed a glass of red wine in front of her.

Avery reached for her phone. "Crap, let's hope no news is good news. I'll call Ben."

Before she could make the call, a blast of cold, damp air gusted into the bar, and Avery looked up to see a grim-faced Newton approaching. "Newton! Didn't expect to see you here at this time."

Newton did not waste time on niceties. "What the bloody hell is going on at Old Haven Church?"

"Were you there today?"

"Yes, I was there, and it would have been nice if you'd have given me some warning!" His face was thunderous.

"But you deal with murders, why were you there?"

"Because with all the weird shit I've been dealing with lately, my boss has decided that I'm now the new go-to guy for paranormal crap."

"And that's bad?" Avery asked tentatively, before taking a large gulp of wine. It was going to be one of those days.

"Yes! I don't want to be the poster boy for paranormal Cornwall!"

Alex slid a pint of the local Doom beer in front of him. "On the house, mate. You look like you need it."

Newton looked like he was about to protest, and then slid on to a stool next to Avery and drank some anyway. "Cheers."

"So, what happened with the vicar?"

"He ended up being blasted off his ladder. The camera exploded, the cameraman received third-degree burns, and the interviewer, some perky blonde called Sarah, passed out with fright."

Avery put her glass down in shock, glanced at an equally shocked Alex, and asked, "Is James okay?"

"No. He's in hospital, unconscious, with a broken arm."

Avery's hand flew to her mouth. "Oh, no. And Ben and the others?"

"Fine, if not shocked. They were watching from the edge of the clearing."

"And you're okay?" she asked, faltering as he fixed his glare on her.

"No! I'm bloody furious! You said nothing about this! Neither of you!" He turned his glare on Alex.

"Clearly a mistake," Alex said, glancing nervously at Avery, "and could you lower your voice?"

Avery glanced around to see a few heads looking their way.

Newton grimaced, and continued in a low menacing tone. "Why didn't you tell me?"

"I honestly forgot, and didn't really think anything would come of it," Avery said. "I'm so sorry, Newton. We've got a lot on with the Shifters, and with El being cursed."

"Cursed?" His eyes widened with surprise.

"Sorry, didn't we tell you about that, either?"

"Why don't you two head up to my flat?" Alex suggested, seeing that Newton was about to go apoplectic, "and you can get Newton up to date. I'll join you as soon as I can."

With that, Avery headed upstairs, wishing she had some moral support.

Newton paced Alex's flat as Avery gave him all the latest news, everything except about the Cumbrian witches, which could wait until Alex arrived.

"Will they still run the news story?" Avery asked.

"Of course they will. It may even make national coverage."

"But there's no footage of the actual incident?"

"No. But they sent another crew and they have interviewed Ben and me, well away from the grove. The magic there is interfering with their equipment—not that they know it's magic, of course. I suggested that this is a hoax for Halloween—a very good one. One that went wrong," he said, glaring again.

Avery sat on the floor cushion in front of the fire and warmed her hands, finding comfort in the bright flames. The day was already darkening outside, and Alex's flat was gloomy, lit only by the fire and one lamp in the corner. She liked it like this, it matched her mood, and the quiet, broken only by the crackle of the flames, allowed her to think.

She looked up at Newton. "Please come and sit down."

He frowned but acquiesced, sitting in the large, leather armchair." It's starting again, isn't it?"

"Yes, and we have no idea what this witch is seeking to do at Old Haven, other than maybe open some kind of gateway. It's well protected, and the magic there is growing stronger every day."

The door swung open just then and Alex came in, carrying two bowls of fries, and he sat on the sofa, placing both on the coffee table next to Avery. "Here you go. For you, too if you want some, Newton."

Newton nodded and took a chip absently.

"You filled him in?" Alex asked.

"Yes, and now I have more news for both of you," she said as she pulled a bowl of fries closer.

Between munching on chips, she let them know about Caspian's visit and her chat with the Shifters.

Alex groaned and leaned back, rubbing his face. "Great, just great. Have you heard from them yet?"

"No, but it's just a matter of time."

"Okay," Alex said, coming to a decision. "Let's head to El's flat, meet Briar and Reuben there, and work out what we do next. Want to join us, Newton?"

"Of course I bloody do."

10

By the time they reached El's flat, the rain was pouring again, streaming down El's windows and blurring the view. Her flat, however, was a warm cocoon of light and colour, and Avery, Alex, and Newton shook off their jackets and joined Reuben and Briar in the lounge.

"Any improvement with El?" Avery asked, sure she'd be disappointed with the answer.

"A very tiny amount." Briar looked hopeful, which dispelled some of the shadows beneath her eyes. Reuben looked even worse than he had before.

"Really? How?" Alex asked, placing a bag full of books on the table.

"I've found a couple of spells that talk about lifting curses, so I've been experimenting with them. She's not conscious, but her eyes are flickering a little. I hope that means something's happening. Sorry—that's vague, but I feel like I'm swimming in the dark here."

Briar led the way to El's bedroom, where she lay covered only in a sheet. The room was warm and the blinds were half-closed, keeping the space dim and shadowy. Candles had been placed around the bed, and the air was rich with the scent of incense. A symbol had been drawn on El's forehead, and a line of runes scrawled on her hands and feet. An amethyst was placed over the symbol on her head.

Briar watched her with troubled eyes. "I've been trying to draw the curse out, but without knowing what it is, it's hard. I've examined the necklace as much as possible, but haven't had much success. I'm scared to touch it without protection."

Avery sighed with annoyance at her forgetfulness. "That reminds me. Caspian has offered to help break El's curse."

Reuben had followed them into the room, and he leaned against the doorframe, frowning. "I don't want him anywhere near her! How does that wanker even know about this?"

"Because I was blessed by a visit from him," Avery said, feeling anything but lucky. "He came to give me some information about the Shifters, but as soon as he knew El was cursed, he offered his help. It's unlikely, I know, but it seemed genuine. He says his grimoires have lots of spells on curses and breaking them."

Newton snorted. "Of course they have."

"That's what I said, but I think we should seriously consider his offer." She looked at Alex. "What do you think?"

He shrugged. "Part of me agrees with Reuben, but if you can't make any headway, Briar…"

Briar nodded thoughtfully. "Let me think on it while you bring us up to speed with our Shifter friends." She led them back to the living area.

"You're not seriously thinking of accepting Caspian's help?" Reuben asked, looking aghast.

"I am. The longer she's cursed, the worse she'll get. She'll be dehydrated and starving, and who knows what else."

Reuben sighed with resignation and went to get drinks while Avery told them all about the Devices and their relationship with the Shifters, and about the possibility of their mysterious witch being a time-walker.

"Wow. A lot's been happening while I've been here," Briar said thoughtfully. "Hunter didn't mention this when I checked his wounds early this morning." Then she frowned. "Did he shift again?"

"Er, yes. Is that bad?"

Briar looked exasperated. "Yes! He's a terrible patient. Every time he shifts it disturbs his wounds."

"They did look pretty red," Avery confessed.

"So, you're saying he picked this fight? He confessed!"

"Yes and no," Avery said. "I only know what happened because I went to their house after Caspian visited me and found Holly and Piper at home alone. They told me all about the real circumstances of the fight, and it rings true."

"Well, we always suspected they were holding something back," Alex said. "This puts things in a whole different light."

"They lied to us," Reuben argued. "And brought trouble to White Haven."

"It's something we can deal with," Avery said, trying to reassure him. "And you don't need to get involved. You have El to worry about."

"I'm feeling pretty useless at the moment," he said, running his fingers through his hair. "I've read the grimoires back to front for solutions to curses, and the stuff I've found hasn't been much help with El. I could do with something else to try."

Avery sighed. "We're not looking for a fight. We are buying time for the Shifters. I don't know much about how they live, but it sounds a patriarchal nightmare." She shrugged. "And until I meet with the Devices, we don't even know what they want."

Newton looked impatient. "I'm more concerned about the events right on our doorstep—Old Haven Church, to be precise. What are we doing about that?"

Briar glared at him. "El is my concern right now, Newton."

He looked momentarily chastened. "Well, yes, of course, but the vicar has just been blasted by magic in front of a news crew. We need to stop this from escalating."

"Bloody hell," Alex said, leaning against the back of the sofa and rubbing his eyes. "Once this gets out, paranormal obsessives are going to flock to Old Haven. What a bloody nightmare."

"Yes they will, which puts them in danger," Newton said, thinking through the implications. He rounded on them angrily. "I can't believe you didn't tell me about this!"

"Oh, get over it," Briar said abruptly. "We've had other things to worry about."

Avery inwardly flinched. Briar could be so scathing to Newton now. However, he didn't care. "It's my job, Briar. *You* get over it."

They glared at each other for a few seconds before Reuben hurriedly intervened with a few bottles of beer from the fridge. "So, what's the plan?"

Alex leaned forward decisively. "Old Haven Church is old, but the site it's on is even older. The yew tree has been there for hundreds of years, probably pre-dating the church, which was built somewhere in the thirteenth century. Yews have huge significance. They symbolise death and rebirth, which is partly why churches were built next to them. At Old Haven, it's in the centre of a grove of trees. We need to know more about that site. Why has the witch picked there?"

"You're looking at me with that fevered gleam in your eye," Reuben noted. "What do want me to do?'

"We've brought lots of books with us," Alex started.

"Yes, books on local history, tree lore, old rites… And we thought while you're looking over El…" Avery continued.

"Sure, I could do research." Reuben nodded. "It will help keep me busy. I'm starting to go a bit screwy here."

Avery smiled, "Thanks."

"And what are you going to do?" he asked.

"As I mentioned, Caspian suggested that the witch is a time-walker. She has managed to manipulate time to live longer. He says that takes a lot of energy, and we should look at sources of elemental energy to help her renew, particularly water—fresh water."

"A time-walker? It's a term I've heard of, but I don't know much else," Briar confessed.

"Neither do we," Alex said. "But I have an idea for where to find her. We're going to spirit walk."

Reuben frowned. "That could be dangerous if she can do that, too."

"But I can cover a lot of area that way, and I might be able to pick up her energy signature."

Avery added, "He won't be alone. We'll go together."

"Where will you look?"

"Natural springs, waterfalls—I need to start checking uncle Google," Alex said.

"And what about protecting Old Haven Church from paranormal obsessives?" Newton asked, still bristling with annoyance. "The police can't do this."

Alex smiled. "Our friend, Gabe, is looking for some security work."

Newton looked stunned. "The Nephilim guy?"

"It's a great fit, surely! Nephilim protecting the Church. Perfect," Alex said, grinning. "In fact, I'll call him now."

"No, wait," Avery said, stilling his hand. "Let me check with James first. Is he at home, Newton?"

"Maybe. It depends if he's conscious, or has concussion."

Avery sat silently thinking for a moment. She really didn't want to talk to James after their conversation, but she knew she had to. He was injured because she hadn't intervened more forcefully, and the church grounds would be swamped with paranormal enthusiasts unless they acted quickly. And she liked him, despite their differences. He was a good man, and she wanted to help him. "I'll call him now. And Briar, what do you want to do about Caspian's offer of help?"

"Call him. We need all the help we can get."

Avery promptly called Caspian before James. He answered with a slow drawl. "Avery. What a pleasure."

She cut to the chase. "Did you mean what you offered earlier? About El?"

"Of course."

"Then could you come to El's flat? Briar has made virtually no progress, and we need help now."

Avery could sense him bristling with smugness at being asked, and she fought to subdue her annoyance. "It will be my pleasure. I'll be there within the hour."

"Do you need the address?"

"Of course not. I know where she lives." And with that he hung up, leaving her infuriated.

She then called James, but it went straight to voicemail. She looked up at Alex. "I'm going to his house. Want to come?"

"Sure. Newton, we'll call you with news about the Nephilim and the church. Until then, see if you can post a couple of police up there for a short time. We don't need anyone else to get injured."

"And what about these other Device witches?" Newton asked, concerned.

"We'll deal with those when they arrive."

***

"I'm not sure how pleased he will be to see us," Avery said to Alex as they stood poised on James's doorstep, ready to knock.

Alex smiled that slow, sexy smile that always turned her knees to water. "You're adorable, you know that?"

She flushed with pleasure. "Well, thanks, but that doesn't help me right now."

"I'm telling you that you're adorable, and that doesn't help?"

She laughed. "It's awesome, and you're adorable, too. But I don't think James thinks I am."

"Clearly he's an idiot," he said softly as he leaned in for a kiss that left her breathless, and she pushed him away playfully.

"We're snogging on the vicar's doorstep. Behave!"

He laughed as she knocked on the door, and they heard footsteps approach from the other side. The woman who answered looked to be in her late thirties, with shoulder-length brown hair and tired eyes. She was petite in build, shorter than Avery, and she looked up, frowning uncertainly. "Can I help you?"

"Hi, I'm Avery, and this is Alex. Any chance we can chat to James for a moment?"

As soon as Avery mentioned their names her face fell, a trace of fear flashed through her eyes, and she stepped back. Avery's stomach turned. *Was this woman afraid of her?*

"What do you want?"

"Just to talk. I heard he was hurt earlier today."

"Yes, thanks to *you*. His arm's broken and he banged his head."

"And that's why we're here. I did ask him not to go there today," Avery said gently. "Are you his wife? You must be worried. We want to help."

For one horrible moment, Avery thought she was going to slam the door in her face and wondered if they would have to glamour her, which she didn't really want to do. But then his wife stepped back again, opening the door wider. "Come in. I'll take you to him."

They stepped inside and Avery held her hand out, "And your name is?"

She hesitated for a second, and then shook her offered hand. "Elise."

Alex did the same, and gave her his most gleaming smile. "Thanks, Elise. We appreciate this."

She turned her back and led them down a wide entrance hall, and Avery and Alex exchanged a furtive glance. *This was going to be hard.*

The house was warm from the central heating, the entrance hall and corridor were panelled with wood, and the floor covered with rugs. Stray toys were strewn along the way, and as they walked, Elise picked them up wearily. They entered a living room, filled with the chaos of family life, and passing through it, she led them to a door at the back of the house. She knocked tentatively and then pushed the door open. "James, you have visitors."

It was a study, lit with a single lamp, and furnished with a desk overflowing with papers, and several bookcases full of books. James was reclining in a large armchair, the material of the arms and headrest worn thin over the years. A fire was burning low in the hearth, and he sat looking into the flames, vacant. He didn't turn his head.

Elise glanced at them, and then marched over to the fire and threw another log on, prodding it back into life.

Avery moved around the front of the chair very slowly, as if she was approaching a scared child, and dropped to her knees so she was at his eye level. "Hi James, how are you?"

For a second he didn't move, and then he raised his eyes slowly to meet hers, cradling his left arm, which was now encased in plaster. "Not great."

"I'm really sorry you were hurt today, we both are." She nodded to Alex, who now moved into James's line of sight, and he sat cross-legged on the floor, nodding at James in sympathy. Avery continued, "How are you feeling?"

"Pretty confused actually, Avery." He looked across her towards Elise, and Elise straightened and left the room. He waited until her steps retreated. "I'm not exactly sure what happened today, but I'm pretty sure it wasn't a hoax."

"What do you think it was, then?" Avery felt her throat constrict with worry, but she kept her expression calm and relaxed.

James looked away, back into the fire. "I felt a jolt of something flash up my arm and through my body. It felt like every nerve ending was on fire, and it just threw me, right off the ladder and back against a tree. But I saw something..."

Avery looked at Alex, who appeared calm, but she knew he was as worried as she was. She prompted James, "What did you see?"

"A face, a woman's face. Old eyes, so very old. Haunted."

"How did you see her face?"

"In my mind." He turned to her, his eyes equally haunted, and lifted his uninjured hand, pointing to his head. "Right in here. Just for a second. And a voice was shouting something like, 'No, run away, preacher man.' Then I blacked out, but her face is stuck here. Every time I close my eyes, I see her."

Alex frowned and leaned forward. "Did you feel anything? Any emotion?"

"Yes." His eyes moved to Alex. "A raging anger. Who is she?"

"We don't know," Alex confessed. "But we're trying to find out."

"Would you recognise her again?" Avery asked, eagerly.

"Oh, yes. Definitely."

"That may help us, I guess," Avery mused.

James added, "There's power around there. I sensed it. It was eerie. It felt very different from when that spirit was in the church. Those *things* on the tree, you called them witch-signs. Is she a witch? Are *you*?"

Avery felt her breath catch in her throat and she faltered for a second. Before she could respond, James leapt in. "Yes, I see it in your face." He looked at Alex. "Are *you*?"

Alex kept his gaze firmly locked with James's. "There are many definitions of a witch."

James allowed himself a brief smile. "Semantics. What's your definition?"

"What's yours?" Alex countered.

For a few seconds the room was silent, and all Avery could hear were the shifting embers, crackling logs in the fire, and the quiet *tick-tock* of the clock on the wall, which seemed to get louder with every passing moment.

A new hardness entered James's voice. "I've heard of Wicca, of course—witches who celebrate the seasons, who worship the Goddess, who forgo the one true God. But there are also those who sign pacts with the Devil, who wear the Devil's mark, who have familiars who do their bidding, who cast spells and engage with the occult. Which are you?"

Avery sighed and hardened her tone too as she came to a decision. This was not the time for lies, and if this went badly, they could still glamour him. "There are no witches who sign pacts with the Devil, James. That's medieval nonsense. Innocent men and women were burned for it, including my ancestor, Helena Marchmont. But yes, I am a witch. I perform magic, natural magic." She watched James's face change and his eyes widen with surprise. "*Actual* magic. It has been passed down to me through the centuries, and to Alex, from his family. We have no pacts with anyone, and we are good, our magic used to protect. We protect White Haven, and that includes you."

His eyes narrowed with suspicion and doubt. "What do you mean, 'actual magic?'"

Avery glanced at Alex, and he nodded. Turning to James, she summoned air, and a small breeze drifted around her, lifting her hair. She sent it around the room, ruffling the papers on his desk and lifting them until they floated freely for a few seconds, and then moving on to brush across Alex and James's hair, too. James started, the shock clear on his face. Alex then turned to the fire and made the flames grow higher and higher, creating twisting shapes within them, and then he held his palm out and summoned a flame onto his hands.

James edged back in his chair, a mixture of fear and wonder in his eyes. "Actual magic," he said, exhaling softly.

"Elemental magic," Avery corrected, watching his reaction.

"I think I'm concussed."

Avery smiled. "You might be, but it is real. And it has nothing to do with the Devil."

Alex was watching James carefully, and he leaned forward. "We're trusting you with this information, James. It's a secret—between us."

James nodded in acceptance. "You could have lied."

"Yes, we could have—and still can."

"Are there more than just you two?"

Alex hesitated a second. "Yes, but we won't tell you who they are. It's not important."

James accepted this silently. "And this woman in my head?"

"Another witch, but we have no idea who she is or what she wants," Avery answered. "It's important we keep people away from Old Haven right now."

"And that includes you," Alex added.

"Do those paranormal investigators know about you?"

Avery nodded. "Please believe me when I say that we are safe, James. You have nothing to fear from us, but you also have no idea of the nature of magic and how dangerous it can be. It is powerful and mysterious, and can be used for ill by those who choose to do so."

"Like that witch. She threatened me," he said, starting to get angry.

"Which is why you need to stay out of it," Alex said, insistent.

James stared at him, and it was clear that his moment of wonder was ebbing back towards fear and suspicion. *Had they just made a terrible mistake?* "How do we stop what's happening at Old Haven?"

"We're working on it," Alex said. "But we need time and space."

"As I told you yesterday," Avery said, unable to keep the impatience from her voice.

"You can't just remove those things with your—" he swallowed, "magic?"

"No. But we can protect the area. We have friends who can help; they work in security. Shall I ask them?" Alex asked.

"Who are they?" James looked warily between them. "Other witches?"

"No. But they're strong, and no one can do this better. Their manager," Avery said, inwardly wincing at the lie, "is called Gabe, and you're welcome to meet him."

"All right," he said, resignation and desperation all over his face. "Now, please go and let me try to get my head around this. What do we tell the press?"

Alex smiled. "You don't want them to know now? Because they saw a lot there today."

"No. Not now." He held his hand to his head again, looking appalled. "Can you imagine what they'd say?"

Avery rose to her feet. "They ended up interviewing Newton, the DI, and Ben and the others, so it's already done. Not sure if that will calm anything down, though. We'll be in touch."

11

Once again, Avery and Alex sat within a protective circle on the rug in front of Alex's fire, just as they had done the first time that Avery spirit walked with him.

The room was dimly lit with only candles and firelight, and Avery sat cross-legged and knee-to-knee with Alex. He held the small, silver goblet filled with the potion to help them enter the necessary mind state, and he took a sip before passing it to Avery. She grimaced as she sipped and then passed it back. She had forgotten how bitter it was. "Where are we going first?"

"Up to Old Haven. I thought it would be interesting to see how it appears in our spirit state," he said, reaching forward and squeezing her hands. "And then on from there over the moors. Maybe follow the river up the valley."

Avery nodded. "Do you remember the last time we did this?"

"Of course. It was the first time I kissed you."

Avery reached forward and stroked his cheek, feeling a wave of longing rush over her. "Lucky me. I misjudged you then."

"I know, but I forgive you," he said cheekily, and then pulled her in for a kiss again. "Stop being so distracting. We have work to do."

"All right, I'll distract you later." She lay down and held his hand as they had done before, and listened to him say the spell that helped their spirits leave their body.

She felt herself slip from consciousness into some strange dreamstate, and as before, Alex lifted from his body first and floated above her, his body shimmering silver, a cord linking him back to his corporeal self.

He smiled down at her and pulled gently, and she felt the jolt as she floated to join him. His voice resonated in her head. *Do you need to go around the room again first?*

No, I'm fine, she replied. *Let's get on with it.*

He turned and pulled her through the walls of his flat and out above the streets of White Haven. Although it was cold out she felt perfectly warm and comfortable, impervious to the autumn weather, but the elemental energies looked very different tonight. Rain and wind swirled about them, and the sky overhead was heavy with brooding clouds, appearing purple and grey on this plane. Street lights still sparked brightly below them, and Avery could see the auras of the people who were braving the weather. Above the town was the faint pulse of their magic, released on the night when they broke the binding spell, much smaller than it had been. However, Alex didn't hesitate, pulling her quickly over the town and towards Old Haven on the hill.

There were no people up there. The landscape was quiet and dark, and the bulk of the church was solid below them. But behind it, a dark red glow seemed to vibrate in the night. *Can you see it?* Alex asked, his voice in her head as he guided them closer.

Yes. That's a pretty threatening energy signature. A red aura around a person could mean passion, energy, and strength, but when it was cloudy and tinged with black as this was, it meant anger and negativity. *Does that reflect the witch's aura?* Avery asked. Alex understood this better than she did.

Probably. She built this spell, and as we thought, it's very strong.

As they moved closer, staying clear of the energy field, Avery saw silvery sigils glowing around the area. Wards.

She means business, Alex said. *I wonder if these were added today, after James's attempt to remove the witch-signs.*

Maybe the area doesn't need protecting by Gabe. These wards would discourage anyone from getting closer.

The runes were protective, but also defensive, and Avery could feel their power from here. She wondered what sort of a spell it was.

Maybe James's attempt to remove a witch-sign triggered them, and that's why he heard her in his head? Alex suggested.

Avery agreed, but was distracted by something beneath the cloudy red area that seemed to emanate from the yew itself. *Can you see that?* She pointed towards the heart of the tree.

The yew's trunk and branches were flush with a green aura, indicating life and vitality, and all the other trees and bushes vibrated with the same colour.

The yew's, however, was darker and richer, Avery thought probably as a sign of its great age. But within its hollow trunk, she saw a faintly iridescent, white glow.

Alex twisted as he tried to get a better view. *That's a different energy signature.*

I agree. But what does it mean?

I think that whatever she's doing is working, and a portal is starting to form.

But to where? The last one we saw was full of fire and darkness.

Hopefully not to demon realms, then. The witch-signs are resonating, too.

He was right. There were lots of them hanging in the yew and the surrounding trees, and they also glowed with rainbow colours, shaking slightly with power.

Come on, he said, sighing. There's nothing more we can do here. Let's try to find her.

They ranged onwards, looking for something that might link Old Haven to where the witch was hiding, but there was nothing.

They passed over swollen streams and rushing rivers, heavy with rainfall. Small waterfalls churned their energy and threw up clouds of moisture, but nothing suggested a witch might be close. They even looked for absences of light that might indicate something was blocking them, but saw nothing.

Alex drew her attention to the moors, well away from White Haven and other small communities. He pointed down to racing shapes, streaking across the ground. Four of them in all, and they seemed to be hunting a small, fleeing creature. *The Shifters.*

Avery gasped. *You're right!* As they dropped lower, she saw how huge and fast they were. They were intent on their quarry, which Avery thought was a fox, and she looked away as they moved around it in a pincer movement. *I love foxes! They can't kill it.*

It's what they do...they're wolves. But Avery detected a trace of regret in his tone, too—if you could call it a tone in your head.

Not tonight they don't, she said, annoyed. She hadn't tried to use her powers on this plane since the last time she spirit walked, but she quickly spelled a charm of protection over the fox, blanketing its scent and draping it in shadow. Then she sent its scent down a false path, causing the wolves to veer in the wrong direction. She smiled gleefully at Alex as the fox ran across the moors to freedom, the wolves now far away.

Avery Hamilton, that was very sneaky, Alex said approvingly.

I know, but I don't care. It's not like they'll starve.

Come on. We're not getting anywhere here. Let's go home.

They headed back to White Haven, passing over the roads that branched below them. Alex's eyes narrowed and he pointed towards dark shapes moving on the road that led directly to the town, a dark mass of grey and black around a swiftly moving car, easy to see against the glow of street lights. *I think the Devices are here.*

If their auras are anything to go by, they are not happy, Avery said.

They dropped down until they were much closer to the car and tried to see inside. There were three figures; a driver and two others in the back seat, from whom a wave of power and determination emanated.

Avery realised one of the witches in the back seat was turning to look out of the window, as if they detected their presence, and she pulled Alex away. *The fun's about to begin.*

***

Avery spent the night at Alex's. They initially talked about how to deal with the Devices, but then, the world tuned out by the wind and rain, Avery decided that getting naked with Alex was much more fun. The Devices could wait.

She woke in the middle of the night, wondering what the weird noise she heard was. For a few seconds, she lay dazed, trying to analyse the sound, and then turned to Alex, but the bed was empty.

Alarmed, she woke completely, leapt out of bed, and pulled on a t-shirt before heading into the main room where she found Alex slumped on the floor of the kitchen, talking to himself—or someone in his mind. *Crap.* Avery dropped next to him, debating whether to try and wake him, but that could be dangerous.

The room was dark, other than the leak of light from the street lamps through the blinds. She spelled the lamps on, but the room looked as normal, and she couldn't detect another presence among them.

She rolled him onto his back and lifted his eyelids. His eyes were white, rolled back into his head, and he continued to whisper words she couldn't make out. He felt icy cold, his skin was pale, and his fists were clenched. She ran to the sofa and pulled a cushion and a blanket free, and then placed the cushion under his head and draped the rug over him.

Months ago, Nate, one of the witches from St Ives, had warned Alex that his visions may get stronger, and for a while, they had. Their troubles with the Mermaids and the Nephilim seemed to have opened floodgates of receptiveness that had led to headaches and sudden collapses. They had been tied to the witches' activities in White Haven, and once he'd had a vision of Gabe, the Nephilim, and had been propelled into his head unexpectedly. It had happened a couple of times at work, alarming his staff, and he had passed it off as exhaustion. With Nate's help he had been able to get them under control, and now they happened only intermittently.

Tonight's efforts must have triggered them again. Avery hated it when this happened; she was powerless to stop them, or bring him out of them. She sat, frustrated, hoping it would end quickly, when she felt the tingle of magic as Alex's protective wards around his pub started to vibrate. Someone was trying to break them.

She jumped to her feet, hands raised, and added her own magic to Alex's spells. For a short time it seemed to be working, and then with a hollow *boom*, the charms fell and she saw an inky black mass start to twist in the middle of the living area. Someone was using witch-flight, which Avery had tried but struggled to master. She quickly threw up a protective barrier of shimmering white energy, blocking whatever it was from coming closer; they might be in the flat, but it wasn't over yet. She was tempted to send a blast of fire at it, but she also wanted to know who it was.

The swirl of darkness coalesced into the figure of a tall woman, standing with arms raised, her dark eyes boring into Avery. She was wearing contemporary dress—dark trousers tucked into knee-length leather boots, a shirt, and a long jacket, and she had long, silky auburn hair, framing a pale face. In the instant before she attacked, Avery registered the shock on her face. *She hadn't expected me to be here.* Before Avery could do anything, the witch sent a blast of pure energy at her, which would have swept her off her feet if it hadn't been for her shield that effectively blocked it.

Avery used her shield as a weapon, propelling it forward with a wave of icy air, and sweeping the unknown witch off her feet and sending her crashing against the far wall. Before she could respond, Avery pinned her there, lifting her off the floor so that her legs dangled inches from the ground.

"How dare you enter uninvited!" Avery yelled, both furious and afraid.

"How dare you look for me!" the woman retorted in a husky voice. She managed to lift her hands and sent a wave of power towards Avery with a swiftness that caught Avery unawares, and she flew backwards, hitting the kitchen cabinets painfully. She fell, winded, and only just managed to find her feet and repel another attack, this one a jet of witch-fire that spewed from the woman's hands across the room. Avery could feel the heat from here, and she managed to deflect it onto a houseplant, which burst into flames.

Alex was still immobile on the ground, and Avery's heart was banging painfully in her chest. She had to stop this woman, *now.*

Avery used elemental air to lift the burning plant off the ground and send it spinning across the room back towards the witch, who in turn hurled it against the wall and advanced across the space. Avery advanced too, but rather than strike with magic, she ran full tilt across the room and rugby-tackled the witch. They crashed into the sofa and rolled over it and onto the coffee table, before falling onto the rug on the far side, barely missing the wide stone hearth of the fireplace.

The witch was winded from her unexpected attack, and taking advantage, Avery punched her in the face. The woman's head flew back in shock, striking the floor, and anger filled her dark eyes. In a sudden display of power, she propelled Avery up until she had her pinned to the ceiling in a vice grip of magic. She held her left arm upwards and tightened her hands as if she was squeezing, and Avery felt her ribs contract. She couldn't breathe and she felt her vision start to blacken at the edges.

With her right hand, the witch wiped the blood trickling from her lip. She stared up at Avery. "You'll regret that, bitch."

Avery couldn't move or speak; her grip was immense. *Shit. She's going to kill me.*

And then out of her peripheral vision, Avery saw Alex rise to his feet, and a huge fireball hurtled across the room.

It hit the witch before she even knew what was happening, and she was immediately enveloped in flames. In a split second she disappeared, taking the flames with her, and Avery plummeted onto the floor, half hitting the coffee table before she dropped to the ground.

For a few seconds, she couldn't breathe and she lay winded, trying to see beyond the encroaching blackness. She felt rather than saw Alex come to a skidding halt next to her. "Avery. Thank the Gods, you're alive."

"Barely," she croaked. The blackness started to recede and she saw his anxious face above hers. "I think I've broken some ribs. That really bloody hurts." She gingerly lifted her left hand and felt her side. Even inhaling hurt.

Alex tenderly felt around her head, and then her left side. "How's your breathing?"

"Painful. Help me sit up."

He eased a hand around her back and virtually lifted her into a sitting position.

"Ouch, ouch, ouch," she said with every incremental movement. Once she got her breath back, she squinted at Alex. He looked equally terrible, with dark shadows beneath his eyes. "How are you? I thought you were unconscious."

"I was. I could feel her mind wrapped around mine like a thick cloud. It was impenetrable, until you did *something*. You must have caused her to lose concentration. I lay still for a few seconds before I acted, and just tried to summon my power."

Avery smiled at him and cupped his cheek. "Lucky me. I think she was about to kill me."

"I would have killed her first. No question." He leaned forward and kissed her gently. "Should I call Briar?"

"No. Let her rest. I'll survive 'til morning. What about you?"

"I'll be fine eventually. I'm just pissed off she caught me unawares. And I need to get my protection spells up again." He flopped back on the ground, staring up at the ceiling, clutching his stomach. "I feel sick."

"I'll make you something," Avery said, trying to struggle to her feet before giving up. "In a minute." She looked over at Alex. "She thought you were alone. She was pretty shocked to see me. If I hadn't been here, I'm not sure what she would have done."

Alex was silent for a second. "Do you think she'd have killed me?"

"I'm not sure. Maybe. She certainly wants us out of action. First El, and now you." A horrible thought struck her. "Maybe she's already attacked Briar and Reuben. I need to call them, it can't wait."

Avery stood slowly, wincing with every movement, pulled her phone from her bag where it sat on the kitchen bench, and called Reuben. It rang for a while before he answered. "Avery. It's four in the morning. This better be good."

"We were attacked in Alex's flat. I wanted to make sure you were okay."

"What!" His tone changed as his brain flipped into gear. "Are you both okay?"

"Yes, just. Are you? Is Briar with you?"

"Yeah, she's sleeping on the couch. Well, she was." She could hear him moving about, and he lowered his voice as he said something to Briar. "Yep, nothing happened here."

Relief swept though Avery. "Good. Is Caspian still there?"

"No, he went home hours ago, but he'll be back later."

"Will he?" Avery thought her confusion would never end. "Why?"

"Well, shockingly, he's been pretty useful." Reuben sounded annoyed but also pleased, not surprisingly. He'd pretty much vowed to hate Caspian forever after he killed Gil.

Avery came to a decision. "I'll let you get back to sleep, but we'll head over in a few hours. This witch means business, and we need to decide what to do."

"Sure, laters," Reuben said, yawning before he hung up.

"So, they're okay?" Alex asked from where he still lay stretched out on the rug.

"Yep. Come on. Let's get your wards up again."

He groaned, sat up, looked around at his flat, and frowned. "And maybe clean. You two made quite a mess."

He was right. The sofa cushions were strewn across the floor, soil was scattered *everywhere*, and the remains of the burnt plant were smeared across the wall and now lay smoking on the floor. Candles and other objects were either on the floor or in random places, and pictures were hanging askew on the wall. On top of that, the smell of smoke hung on the air.

"Your lovely flat! Sorry," Avery said, feeling terrible.

He grinned, rose to his feet, and joined her in the kitchen. "All fixable. Well, maybe not the plant. The important thing is that you're okay." He frowned. "Why is there a bruise on your chin?"

"Is there?" Avery touched it gently. "I think I smacked it off her elbow when I rugby-tackled her."

Alex started to laugh. "And there's blood on your knuckles."

"I punched her, too."

"That's my girl," he said. And then he frowned. "Is that your blood? Because if she's got it…"

He didn't need to explain. Hair and blood were great assets to a witch, and you didn't want an enemy getting hold of them. They could be used to make a poppet—a small figure of someone that you could spell and manipulate.

"No. I'm pretty sure it's hers. I spilt her lip."

"Good. Let's use it." He threw her a tissue. "Wipe it up and keep it safe."

12

The next morning, Avery creaked out of bed; every muscle ached, and her ribs felt like they were on fire. After she'd phoned Sally and explained she wouldn't be going in to work until later—and asked her to feed her cats—everyone headed to El's flat. By the time Avery and Alex arrived, Caspian was already there.

The mood in El's flat was all business. Spell books, history books, and reference books were spread everywhere. Incense hung in the air, and the central heating was turned up high, dispelling the cold gloom that lurked outside the windows. Caspian and Briar were seated at El's small dining table, deep in discussion, and Reuben was cross-legged on the floor, an open book on his lap, and a cup of coffee steaming at his elbow. Intriguingly, a selection of different shaped Alembic jars stood in a row on the kitchen workbench, each filled with unrecognisable substances. It looked like a chemistry lab.

It was odd seeing Caspian there, dressed in jeans and a t-shirt rather than a suit, and he looked up as they entered, his eyes brushing across Alex before coming to rest on Avery. She met his eyes briefly before she looked at the others, calling, "Hi, guys."

"Hey Ave, Alex," Reuben said, twisting to look at them. "You two recovered?"

"Just about." Alex headed to El's open kitchen and placed fresh pastries down, closely followed by Avery with a tray of coffees. "Well, maybe not Avery. She's a bit sore." He pulled her close and kissed her forehead.

"But I did manage to buy coffees despite feeling battered and bruised," she explained with a grimace.

Briar groaned in appreciation and joined them at the counter. "You stars. Just what I needed. Can I do anything to help you heal, Avery?"

Avery shook her head. "No, El's more important. As is coffee. Two lattes, two flat whites, and a moccachino in case someone wanted a chocolate hit, too," Avery said, pointing them out.

"Mine!" Reuben shouted. He held up his hand expectantly.

Briar turned to him. "You've got a coffee!"

"I can have two!" he protested.

"It's all yours, don't panic." She picked it up and took it over to him.

Caspian walked over to join them, smiling smugly. "One for me, too? I am lucky."

"Well, you're helping, so why not?" Avery said, trying to avoid his stare.

"And you even get a pastry," Alex said, archly. "Must be your lucky day."

Caspian gave him the coolest of smiles. "To be here with all of you fills my heart with joy."

Briar sighed, exasperated. "Stop it, both of you. We're actually making good progress, thanks to Caspian."

Alex adopted a lofty expression. "Good. So is El out of her curse-coma yet?"

"No, but we now know what type of curse it is," Caspian said. He pointed to the table where the cursed necklace lay on folds of velvet, well out of reach of an accidental touch. "I found some spells which work to reveal the nature of the curse, and through a process of elimination—"

"Endless elimination," Reuben added with a groan.

Caspian ignored him. "By testing various potions and herbs in the alembic jars, we have found it is an earth-based curse."

"What does that mean?" Avery asked between sips of coffee.

"Earth elemental magic, bound into the silver, has suffocated El's mind and bound her magic into Earth and darkness."

Avery paused, horrified. "That sounds awful. So, her mind is trapped—as if she's buried alive?"

"Sort of," Briar said. "If there's an excess of Earth magic, then we'll need Air, Fire, and Water to balance it."

"The witch attacked me last night," Alex said, thoughtfully. "And I experienced a similar sensation. She suffocated me, and I thought it was with her mind, but after thinking about it, the weight of it suggested an earthiness. I was almost crushed under it."

"So, our new arrival is an Earth witch," Caspian said thoughtfully.

Avery frowned. "But she travelled using witch-flight. I thought that was something only an Air witch could do?"

He shrugged. "If she's been around as long as we think, she's probably mastered many skills most of us would never achieve in one lifetime."

"But I'm an Earth witch," Briar said, offended. "I don't do things like that!"

Caspian sighed. "We can do as many positive or negative things with our powers as we choose, you know that, Briar. Earth can nurture and create life, or suffocate and bury it. Fire can warm or burn, air can caress or batter like a hurricane, and water can give life or drown it." He took a sip of coffee and reached for a croissant. "Using Earth magic to curse is also quite inspired at this time of year."

"Of course," Briar said. "Its season is winter, its nature is grounding, and the cave, its natural manifestation of protection, can be a prison."

Alex nodded thoughtfully. "El's predominant strength is Fire. The complete opposite to Earth on the natural cycle."

"But how do we break it?" Reuben asked impatiently. He still sat on the rug, watching them through narrowed eyes.

Caspian suggested, "We free El from its binding using all the elements. It will take all of us, but now that we know what we're fighting, we can target it more effectively."

"And we've almost finalised the spell," Briar added.

Avery felt a flush of relief race through her. "Fantastic. When?"

"Noon." Caspian moved back to his spell book. "Earth magic is strongest at midnight, therefore weakest at midday. Fire is strongest at midday. We need to place her in the centre of a pentagram. We'll draw it on the floor." He pointed to where Reuben sat in the middle of the rug, and then looked back at Avery and Alex. "You injured the witch last night?"

Alex nodded. "A combination of a fireball, a rugby tackle, and a punch to her face."

"You punched her?" Briar asked, wide-eyed.

"Avery did," Alex explained with pride as he pulled her close and kissed her cheek.

"Nice one!"

Avery laughed, but was uncomfortably aware of Caspian's appreciative glance in her direction, and she studiously ignored it.

"Good," Caspian said. "She'll be recovering, and that will make our life easier. A spell, as you know, is always connected to the witch who cast it, and it's no different with curses."

"And is El at all improved today?" Avery asked.

Briar shook her head. "No. She has sunk deeper into the coma again."

Their conversation was interrupted by Avery's phone ringing, and she saw it was Sally. She retreated to the far corner of the room as she answered it. "Hi Sally, everything okay?"

"I'm afraid not, Avery." Sally's voice sounded clipped with annoyance. "You have two visitors here who are refusing to go until they have spoken to you. They are interfering with the smooth running of this shop."

Avery imagined Sally was staring right at them as she spoke. *It must be the Devices.*

"Did they give a name?"

"No, other than that they have travelled a long way to see you."

"Well, tell them I have business to attend to, and will see them when I'm free," she answered. And then she dropped her voice, just in case they could hear her. "And don't offer them coffee."

She looked across to Alex as she hung up. "The Devices are here."

"Great. Right on cue," Alex said.

"Need my help?" Caspian drawled.

"No," Avery said abruptly, and then she softened her tone, remembering he was helping them. "You concentrate on El. Me and Alex will meet them and will be back here before midday. Need us to bring anything?"

"Alex, do whatever you need to do to prepare yourself to connect with El's spirit. Avery, just bring yourself."

***

"What's going on with Caspian?" Alex asked Avery as they walked up the hill towards Happenstance Books. "He seemed *odd* around you. Creepier than normal."

Avery paused for a second, and then decided honesty was the best option. "He told me if I got bored with you to give him a call."

"He did *what?*" Alex asked, stopping in the middle of the street. "The cheeky bastard!"

She turned to him and laughed. "Very. Clearly I won't, because he's an arse and you're awesome, so you have nothing to worry about, other than maybe me punching him, too."

"I'd pay to see that," he said, and then he frowned. "When did he say that? You didn't tell me."

She rubbed her face, moving out of the way of a local who nodded as he passed. "Yesterday? When he came to ask about Old Haven and the press. So much has happened, I just haven't had a chance to say."

He looked mildly offended. "As long as that's the only reason."

"Of course it is," Avery said, rushing to reassure him. She pulled him into a shop doorway, out of the drizzle, and wrapped her arms around him, inhaling his gorgeous Alex scent. "You know I have zero interest in Caspian."

"Just checking," he murmured, his dark eyes appraising her.

She rose on her tiptoes and kissed him. "Never doubt my feelings for you, or my loathing of Caspian."

He grinned. "Come on then, or the Devices will be steaming."

***

As soon as Avery entered Happenstance Books, she could feel a chill in the atmosphere, and it didn't have anything to do with the heating.

Sally silently glowered at a couple of witches who sat on the sofa under the window, watching everyone with steely eyes. Other customers had retreated to the far reaches of the shop, leaving the main area deserted. Avery met Sally's furious glance with raised eyebrows, and immediately turned to the newcomers, who rose as one to greet her.

There was a man and a woman waiting. Avery estimated the woman was in her sixties, with long, white hair and a fine-boned, aristocratic face, accentuated with high cheekbones and pale brown eyes that were almost amber. She wore a long, sweeping black coat that covered clothes made of velvet and silk. The man was younger, maybe late forties, with salt and pepper hair brushed into a neat side-part. His clothes were also clearly expensive; a sharp, three-piece suit and a fine wool overcoat. Power emanated from them. In fact, Avery was pretty sure they were projecting it to instil fear. Unfortunately, all it did was annoy her.

Avery spoke first. "I believe you're waiting for me? I'm Avery Hamilton, and this is Alex Bonneville."

The woman answered, a trace of Lancashire to her accent. "We did not expect to wait so long, Ms Hamilton."

"I don't know why not. It's not like you made an appointment to see me."

Her expression froze, and she almost hissed. "Mr Faversham advised you I would be coming."

"But he is not my secretary. And your name is?"

Avery could tell the woman was itching to use magic, and she felt Alex bristling beside her. "Alice Device, and my son, Jeremy Device."

"Excellent. Please follow me." She led the way once more to her back room, Alex following at the rear.

Once inside with the door firmly closed, Alex leaned against it watchfully, and Alice rounded on her. "Your impertinence is outrageous."

"So is yours!" Avery said. "This is *my* shop, you arrive here unannounced and uninvited, and then have the nerve to criticise me. What century are you from?"

"Our apologies," Jeremy said, intervening smoothly. "We have travelled a long way. I think you know. I detected your unique—" he paused, "*energy* from last night. It was you, wasn't it? Hovering over our car?"

Avery turned to him speculatively. "Yes. We thought you'd noticed us. Impressive."

"One of my gifts." He bowed his head, but didn't drop his eyes.

Avery took a deep breath and gestured to the table and chairs in the centre of the small room. "We're tired, too. Please take a seat."

Alice looked dismissively around the room, which was as usual, filled with boxes of stock. "May we not sit somewhere more comfortable?"

Avery had no intention of taking them up to her flat. "Unfortunately not."

"We'll get to the point," Alice said, still standing. "The Shifters, Hunter Chadwick and his family, have hidden here. They are to return to Cumbria immediately."

"Have you asked them?" Avery knew that they had not, because their old-fashioned views meant they had to ask the witches of the town first.

"Of course not," Alice confirmed. "They are under your protection."

"Yes, they are," Avery said, deciding that although she hadn't understood exactly what she had agreed to initially, they absolutely were now. "Returning to Cumbria at the present time is out of the question."

Alice stared down her nose at Avery. "You clearly have no understanding of what they have done."

"I believe Hunter challenged some guy called Cooper to save his sister, and unfortunately lost the fight. His brother affected a rescue due to the severity of Hunter's injuries. He is still healing."

"That *guy* is Cooper Dacre, the leader of the pack, and he demands Hunter makes peace or die in a re-challenge. The fight was not completed. It leaves the whole pack in a state of flux. It is unacceptable."

Interesting that a pack suffered from political instability.

"Hunter suspects interference, and fears for his family."

"How dare you suggest we interfered with the fight," Alice said, bright red spots of fury springing up on her pale cheeks.

"*I* didn't, he did, and actually didn't mention you at all." Avery paused, letting her inference hang on the air. "You may return to Cumbria now and we will tell you when he is fit enough to travel."

"He returns with us today."

"No. They sought Sanctuary, and we granted it. We decide when he is ready to leave."

Alice fell silent, glaring at Avery with seething resentment, and Avery knew there was nothing she could do. Emboldened by her progress, and feeling Alex's solidarity from behind, she asked, "Did you oversee the fight?"

"We witness all challenges."

Avery decided guile might be best. "I don't understand the rules of Shifters and their society. It's complex to those who don't participate in it. You work hand in hand with the ruling pack? The Dacres?"

"Yes. It has been our way for hundreds of years."

"So, should a challenger win, your allegiance is to them?"

Alice blinked. "Yes, of course."

"Sounds fascinating. I would love to witness a challenge, wouldn't you, Alex?"

"Absolutely," she heard him reply.

Avery continued. "I believe Hunter is planning to challenge again, once he recovers and seeks to leave White Haven. I would like to watch, if that's possible. I have never been to Cumbria, and of course it's an area famous for its rich history of witches, your family included."

"Challenges can be bloody affairs, Miss Hamilton, and are absolutely forbidden to outsiders," Alice said, and a wave of magic reached a snaky tendril out between them, as if probing Avery's defences.

Avery stopped it dead. "Such a shame."

Alice's features suddenly transformed, and her facade of grace disappeared into a snarl as a flare of magic reared up between them. "You mess with things that are beyond your reach, young witch."

At that, Avery had enough, and a swirl of wind rose around her, whipping her hair up and off her face and pushing Alice back a step. "They asked for our help, and they will get it. Don't you dare threaten me! You have no authority in White Haven!"

Alice lifted her chin defiantly. "And you will have none in Cumbria. Step carefully, Ms Hamilton. Jeremy. A card, please."

Jeremy reached into his pocket and extracted a business card that he handed wordlessly to Avery. She received it without breaking eye contact with Alice. "Thank you. I will inform you when he is fit to travel."

Alex opened the door and without another word, Alice swept from the room, Jeremy following, and within seconds they heard the shrill jingle of the door bells as they left the shop.

Avery looked up at Alex. "Holy cow."

"I think we've just made another enemy," he said, kissing her forehead gently.

13

El's flat had been transformed in Avery and Alex's absence. The blinds were shut and there were candles everywhere, brightening the space with a golden glow. The sofa had been pushed back, the rug rolled up, and a pentacle had been drawn on the floor—a circle that encompassed a pentagram.

The scent of natural oils filled the rooms from several oil burners, and Avery detected mint and rosemary, among others. As she breathed deeply, she felt her head clear and new resolve fill her. "An energising spell," she said to no one in particular.

Briar was still putting the finishing touches on the pentagram, but she glanced up at her. "To help with lifting the curse."

"Good thinking." She slipped her shoes off, and placed her coat in the corner, out of the way, as Alex did the same.

"How did the meeting go?" Caspian asked. He too was ready for the spell. He already sat at the pentagram point of Fire, his grimoire in front of him, and he had also removed his shirt, revealing a pale, lightly muscled chest on which a strange rune had been drawn. The design was echoed in many smaller runes that trailed down his arms and hands in one long chain.

"Depends on which way you look at it," Avery explained. "They left without the Shifters, but they weren't happy."

"But guess who's going to Cumbria when the Shifters return?" Alex said, settling himself at the point of the Spirit at the top of the pentagram. He looked at Caspian. "I presume this is where you want me to sit."

Caspian nodded distractedly. "You're going to Cumbria? Is that wise?"

"We have no choice." Avery sat at the point of Air, between Alex and Caspian. "I suspect they will interfere with the fight. Holly pretty much accused them of it."

"Haven't we got enough going on?" Reuben asked, exiting the bathroom wrapped in only a towel and rubbing his hair dry with another.

"Well, we're not going now!" Avery chided him, trying to look only at his face. Reuben's remarkable physique was very disconcerting. "And why are you showering *now*?"

"I went for a surf," he explained. "I needed to clear my head and connect with my magic. I've found it's the best way for me to do it. Back in a tic, and I'll bring El," he said as he bounded out of the room.

When he returned in board shorts and a t-shirt, he carried El in his arms, and he carefully placed her in the centre of the pentagram, her head at the point of Spirit within inches of Alex, and her arms and legs spread to the other elements. She was clothed in loose white cotton trousers and shirt, her skin was pale, almost grey, and her lips were colourless. Avery's heart sank. She looked on the verge of death, and all other concerns fled from her mind. The only important thing now was El.

Reuben sat at the point of Water, completing the pentagram, as Briar sat at Earth. A candle burned in front of each of them, the colours corresponding to the elements.

"What now?" Alex asked, looking to Briar, but Caspian answered.

"El's mind is cursed by the Earth element, and she suffocates beneath the weight of it. She's hanging on by a thread. We need to draw it out, and destroy it. Alex, you must reach for her mind, help her surface, lead her to light and warmth. She will be confused. The rest of us will balance the elements. Briar, as an Earth witch, will be the best placed to bring Earth out of her, and I will nurture with Fire, El's own element."

"Is that your natural element?" Avery asked, realising she hadn't got a clue what Caspian's strengths were.

"No. Like you, my strength is Air, which is why I have witch-flight. No other elemental strength can master that." He looked puzzled for a moment. "Have you mastered it yet?"

"No, it evades me," she confessed.

"I can give you some pointers," he said, his dark eyes holding hers for a second before he turned back to his grimoire. "Anyway, I will fill the place of Fire. I can add my strength to El's emerging power. And then comes the hard part. The curse is like a live thing—it will try to attach itself to something else. I suggested we put it into another animal, like a rabbit. That would be the cleanest option."

"But I said no," Briar interrupted, glaring at Caspian. "I will not allow the death of another creature. And the curse *would* kill a creature that small."

"So, we must trap the curse in something else." He gestured to where a large jar of water sat at his side. "You may be wondering why I am covered in runes. They will help to draw the curse up and out into this where we can trap it. It is decidedly more difficult and not without great risk, but if we don't, El will die."

The risks they were taking suddenly sank in, and Avery turned to him, shocked. "The curse will pass *through* you? But what if you can't control it, or restrain it?"

"As soon as the curse lifts from her body, you must join your strength to mine and help me. All except Alex. Never let go of your connection to her mind. *Never*!"

Alex nodded, and then closed his eyes to compose himself.

"You didn't answer my question," Avery said, staring at Caspian.

"I will be cursed if I fail, so I do not intend to fail." He looked to his left at Briar, and then Reuben next to her. "Repeat the words of the spell after me. This will not be quick—or pretty—so be prepared."

It was now a few minutes to midday and the rain had returned, filling the flat with a muted, steady drumming that drowned out the sounds of the town. Avery stared at her candle, took deep, calming breaths, and then closed her eyes as she waited for Caspian to begin.

He started to intone the spell, line by line, which they repeated after him. He called upon each of the elements, and Avery opened her eyes to watch him. His voice was sure and steady, and as he called upon each element, their respective candles flared brighter. Avery felt Air surge to her, and she channelled it, holding it close. Caspian reached forward to hold El's left foot, and they each reached forward too, grasping the closest limb, which for Avery was El's left hand.

El's skin gave off an unearthly chill, which reinforced Caspian's belief that she was close to death. Avery's resolve strengthened. She could not lose El. *Reuben could not lose El.* Avery looked up at Alex, but his eyes were closed as he held El's head gently between his hands. An empty potion bottle sat next to him on the floor, and she realised he'd taken something to help his spirit reach El.

At Caspian's nod, she released Air through her fingers and into El's, feeling it course through them both, invigorating El's senses. She felt Fire from Caspian and Water from Reuben, and lastly the lightest touch of Earth from Briar, carefully so as not to overwhelm.

And then the battle began. Slowly, as if from the darkest depths of the ocean, a heavy swell of icy cold started to lift, wrapping its weight around all of them. For a second, Avery felt herself panic as its dense fingers started to envelop her, and dread filled her thoughts. *Nothing would work. They would all die. It was pointless, why even try?*

But Air cleansed her thoughts, and the scent of the energising spell reinforced her will. The curse was trying to undermine them, seeking their weaknesses.

Caspian was calling it to him, opening his body to it, but it struggled, resisting his call, clinging on to El like a fungus. All the elements were mingling now, and although Avery's eyes were open, watching El's immovable form, her mind battled beneath the surface of her skin.

Their battle to banish the curse lasted for a long time. They gained and then lost as the curse ebbed and flowed, its strength waxing and waning, until finally the weirdest thing happened. The Earth curse reared up like a cobra, straight out of her body, a dark surging mass of brown and toxic green, streaming out of El's pores as the other elements gained strength. Caspian called it once more and it headed into the rune on his chest. Caspian cried out like a wild animal as the rune blazed with a fiery light.

Caspian still held El's foot tightly, and Avery felt his connection. She raced through El's body, joining her power with his, and felt Reuben and Briar do the same. All of his runes blazed, and she saw the curse swirl around the blazing marks as Caspian herded it down his arm to the water at his side. He plunged his left hand into the jar, his features screwed up with tension and concentration—and pain. He roared again and drew on all of them.

He was right. The curse was like a wild animal, and it kicked and surged and battled beneath Caspian's skin, the runes barely containing it.

Part of Avery's awareness was still with El, and she felt her stir, life creeping back into her limbs. Alex was there, a faint presence, but he was concentrating only on El's mind.

Caspian's hand was fully immersed in the water and he pushed the now thrashing curse out. It clung on desperately, wriggling like a giant eel beneath Caspian's skin. With one final act of will, he cast it out of his body. The water churned like it contained a maelstrom, and Avery lifted its lid with a jet of air, and slapped it on the jar with a resounding *smack*.

Silence fell and Caspian sprawled backwards on the floor, his chest heaving, the runes glowing with a dirty red light.

Reuben and Briar deflated like balloons, falling forward over their knees. Avery could barely breathe. Her ribs ached again, her head thudded, and stars swam before her eyes. The cloying feel of the curse seemed to hang around, but El stirred like a cat after a long nap.

Alex opened his eyes and called softly, "El, can you hear me?"

For a second she said nothing, and his voice became more urgent. "I feel you, El, you're here. Open your eyes."

And then she groaned. "What the hell just happened? And why am I starving?"

Alex laughed with relief. "Welcome back."

Reuben let out a weak cry of delight and shuffled forward to hold her, pulling her into his lap, and Avery reached for Alex's hand. "Well done. Are you all right?"

"Exhausted, but okay. You?"

"Same." She looked over at Caspian and Briar. "Are you both okay?"

"I guess so," Briar said, shuddering. "That was horrible, just horrible. I feel tainted. For a long while there, I felt we were doomed to fail."

"I think that's the effect of the curse," Alex said. "It was designed to crush you, mentally and physically."

Caspian was still silent, and Avery shuffled over to him. "Caspian, speak to me. Are you okay?" The runes had smeared off his skin, but they had scarred his body; she could see red welts starting to blister. She looked at Alex and Briar anxiously. "Guys, I think something's wrong."

But then he opened his eyes and croaked, "I'm okay. Barely. Someone seal that jar before the damn thing gets out again." And then he closed his eyes tightly again.

Briar had already prepared a spell to seal the jar, and she rose wearily to her feet and cast it. The water within was murky, and reminded Avery of the binding spell Helena and the other witches had cast that sealed Caspian's ancestor, Octavia, within it. She presumed he would remember this, too. She looked at him lying on the floor, his chest rising and falling in shallow breaths. He had risked much to help them, more than she had initially realised. More than she had herself, she felt ashamed to admit. She hadn't realised the effects of the curse would be so serious until it was almost too late. *What did this do to their relationship with him?*

As if he sensed her staring, he opened his eyes. "Something on your mind, Avery?"

"Many things. You could have died then. And your runes seem to be baked in."

He held his arms up and laughed dryly. "So it seems. They will fade in time."

"I have a balm that will help," Briar said, her expression serious. "That was incredibly brave, Caspian. I'll be honest, we couldn't have done it without you. I had no idea how to break that curse."

Alex spoke from behind them, his tone suspicious. "Most unlike you, Caspian. What's going on?"

Caspian sat up slowly and looked at them one by one, considering his words. "Time has proven to me that you are not my enemy."

"You're still responsible for my brother's death, and you tried to kill me once," Reuben said, still holding El in his lap, and Caspian's head fell. "But, you've saved El, and while Gil's death can never be forgotten, this is a start. Thank you."

Caspian considered him for a moment in silence, and then nodded. "Good. Then I guess I should go."

"Not yet, you won't," Briar said. "You have injuries I need to heal."

El croaked, "Can you all stop talking and get me some food!"

Briar leapt to her feet and headed to her box of healing balms and potions. "No food for you yet, El. It's too soon. You haven't had food in your stomach for almost 48 hours. I have a healing potion for you to drink first, and then plenty of water."

"Then food?" El lifted her pale face and squinted at them.

"Soup only," Briar chided.

Avery laughed. "Good to have you back, El! Nice to see nothing much has changed." She looked at her watch. "That took ages!"

"I told you it would take time," Caspian explained. "It was a deep curse, well thought out, well executed. Our mysterious witch has impressive powers. We need to decide what to do now."

Avery smiled. He seemed to have involved himself in their fight, which was unexpected.

But let's face it. We need all the help we can get.

Alex must have shared the same thought. "She's attacked three of us, admittedly one by default. Are you sure you want to involve yourself in this?"

"With luck, she won't know about me yet. That gives us an advantage."

Alex stretched and rose to his feet. "We'd better plan our next steps."

***

El still looked pale, but Briar's potions and soup had restored some of her colour. She sat curled up next to Reuben on the sofa, her head on his lap, covered by a blanket.

The blinds were open, but the day was still dark with thick clouds and pouring rain. They had cleared the pentagram and circle, and cleansed the air of negative energies, and now they sat around drinking tea and eating biscuits.

"So," Reuben summarised, "El has been cursed, you were attacked, Alex, in your sleep, your protection spells were shattered, and Avery was battered like a ragdoll. Have I missed anything?"

Avery was affronted. "We did get the better of her, eventually."

"Only because you were there," Caspian pointed out. "Who knows what may have happened to Alex if you weren't."

"Maybe we need safety in numbers," Briar suggested. She was sitting on the floor, leaning back against the armchair, her feet curled under her. "She's seems to be singling us out for attack."

Caspian agreed. "As it gets closer to Samhain, it might get worse. Whatever she's planning must coincide with that night. She does not want you interfering."

"You should all move in with me," Reuben said decisively. "I have plenty of room."

"But what about my shop?" Avery asked.

"I'm not suggesting we don't go out. Everyone still goes to work, but at night we're vulnerable. There are too many people around in the day to attack."

Alex nodded. "You're right. It would be safest, and then we could ward your house with our combined magic."

"Can I bring my cats? I'm not leaving them behind," Avery pleaded.

Reuben smiled at her. "Of course you can."

"All right then. From when? Tonight?"

"Yes. We've saved El. If the witch knows, she could try again." He looked at the others. "Agreed?"

"Agreed," they all murmured.

"Before I go," Caspian said, "may I ask what you've found about Old Haven's site? The grove?"

Reuben shrugged. "Sure. Not much as yet, unfortunately. But, I've been doing a bit of reading around the Druids of ancient Britain. They revered trees and developed a whole system of belief and the Ogham alphabet around them. The oak was the tree they revered the most, but the yew is considered the link to the spiritual world through our ancestors, and are the guardians to the Otherworld. It has particular significance at Samhain, when the gateways between worlds are at their thinnest. And Samhain is also the night of the Crone. That grove behind Old Haven is probably a remnant of one of many old groves revered by the Druids. And we all know that because of the pagan beliefs about the yew, churches were built next to them. Old Haven is no different. The groves are power centres if used in the right way, and this witch is clearly manipulating it."

"To open a gateway to the dead?" Briar asked.

"Or Faerie," Reuben said, looking amused. "It sounds ridiculous, but…"

"When me and Alex were there yesterday morning," Avery said, "I could feel the wild magic there. It felt different, ancient, as if anything could happen."

Alex added, "We spirit walked last night. There was a strange light within the yew tree's hollow trunk, as if a portal or a doorway was already starting to build."

Caspian nodded. "Any sign of the witch?"

"None. She has disguised herself well."

Caspian rose to his feet. "If you find anything else, let me know, and I'll do the same. The repercussions of opening this portal could be big. I mean, is she planning on closing it again, or is it to remain open forever, allowing passage back and forth? That could be disastrous. Such a portal between the worlds of Fey and man hasn't existed for years—if that's what it is." He frowned. "Are you all planning to attend the Samhain celebrations for the Witches Council?"

"I said we would," Avery said. "But this could change everything."

"Genevieve would not be happy if you failed to attend again."

"She'd also be furious if we allowed a doorway to open to another world. Maybe we could come for a short time and try to do both," Avery suggested.

Caspian laughed as he headed out the door. "Good luck with that!"

14

Avery was exhausted. She needed a good sleep, but she still had a few hours' worth of work to finish first. And then she'd have to let Hunter and the other Shifters know about the Devices' visit.

She sighed as she entered Happenstance Books. It was a hive of activity; Sally and Dan were both busy at the till, serving a line of customers.

Avery busied herself helping out the many kids with their parents who were looking for spooky reads. The children's section, like the rest of the shop, was fully decorated for Halloween, and Dan had prepared the reading area for the storytelling that would start the next night, which marked one week until Halloween. Late night Thursday shopping would continue until Christmas, a request disguised as an order by the Town Council.

Avery inwardly sighed, as part of her wished it were already over. This time of the year was so busy, but she couldn't complain. Business meant money. If only she didn't have a rogue witch, the Devices, and Shifters to deal with. As soon as Sally and Dan were free from customers, she updated them on El and everything else.

They looked horrified. "I didn't know about El!" Dan said, perched on the stool behind the counter. "Why didn't you say something?"

"Sorry, the last couple of days have been so busy, I guess I didn't want to worry you. But look, you both need to be vigilant. Anything strange happens, let me know. I'm increasing my protection on the shop, and I'll be sleeping at Reuben's until this is over—all of us will be there. And I'll take the cats."

Sally frowned, and pointed at her chin. "Is that bruise from last night?"

Avery nodded, feeling gently to see if it had swollen. "Unfortunately. This woman frightens me. She has no boundaries."

"And the Devices? That pair were insufferable," Sally complained.

"They've hopefully gone by now, but it's not over. Far from it. But that battle is for another time." She mulled on the fact that once they got through

Samhain, there was a whole other problem to deal with in Cumbria, and she had no idea how that would go. "I just wish we weren't staying open so late on Thursday. I don't like the idea of you leaving here at that time of night."

"It's not me I'm worried about," Sally said. "And between all you witches, there are lots of staff to target. She can't be everywhere at once. Besides, it sounds like she's too busy at Old Haven."

Avery nodded, slightly comforted by Sally's logic. "True. Come on. Let's lock up. Tomorrow's going to be a long day, so I think we need a good night's rest."

"Pub for me," Dan said with a grin. "I'll try not to overdo it. Coming for a quick one?"

Sally shook her head. "I better get back for the kids. And I'll bake a cake for us to keep us going tomorrow," she added with a smile.

"Yes!" Dan said, punching the air. "I love your baking, Sally."

She looked at him with a warning in her eye. "And I'll be bringing in cupcakes for the kids. They are not for you! *Not one*!"

"Spoilsport," Dan grumbled as he shrugged his jacket on.

"And I'm going to pack and reinforce my protection spells on the shop," Avery said.

"Okay," Dan called with a spring in his step as he headed towards the door. "Don't forget, it's dress-up day tomorrow. Halloween week is here! Your costume is in the back."

"Bollocks!" Avery said with feeling.

***

Avery locked up the shop, picked up the box containing her costume from the back room, turned the lights off, and wandered up to her flat.

The cats greeted her by rubbing her legs and yowling for food. She tickled their ears and fed them, locked the cat flap that led to the garden so they couldn't make a bolt for freedom, and then pulled their carry cages out of the cupboard. Then she headed up to her bedroom to pack. In the end she decided to take only a few clothing items for the night and evening, since she could change for work when she arrived back in the morning. She grimaced at the box. *Damn it. She had to dress up.*

She held up the costume to the light. It was a long dress with a bodice, the skirt made of panels of black and green, and there was a thick belt with a silver buckle to wrap around her waist. A full-length, dark green cloak and black witch's hat finished it off, along with lace-up calf-height boots that languished in the box. She had to giggle. It was her own fault; she shouldn't have let Sally go and choose it for her.

Leaving the costume on her bed, she checked her shelves for useful books to pack with her grimoires, and also gathered her own spell casting equipment—her Athame, chalice, and silver bowl. She felt naked without them close by. A prickle at her neck alerted her to Helena's arrival, her ghostly ancestor, and she turned slowly, always unnerved at her appearance.

Helena stood stock-still in the middle of the room, watching Avery. As always, she wore a long black dress, over which was draped a long cloak, and her dark hair fell across her shoulders and down her back. A faint whiff of violets wafted across the room, and her pretty face creased into a frown.

Avery nodded to her, noticing that she was more corporeal than she had appeared for months. *Was this the effect of Samhain?* "You look worried, Helena. Don't be. I'll be back. A rogue witch is making life difficult."

In the blink of an eye, Helena reappeared inches from Avery, and Avery stepped back, startled. "Bloody Hell, Helena, what are you doing?"

Helena leaned forward and lifted her hand, as if to brush Avery's face. Avery's heart was thudding in her chest. Helena hadn't been this close to her in a long time, and it reminded her of when she'd possessed her body and her mind. *What if she wanted to do that now? What if she was stronger now, and could do it without being invited?* She'd wanted to kill her then, and it was for that reason that Avery had warded her bedroom against her. But, she reminded herself, Helena had helped her find the spell to unveil the Mermaids during the summer. *I have nothing to fear.*

Helena opened her mouth and started to speak, but Avery couldn't hear anything. "I can't hear you, I'm sorry."

Helena gestured again towards Avery's bruise and frowned. Avery never ceased to be astonished by Helena's awareness, and it was definitely stronger than usual. "I don't know who she is! She's trying to open a portal at Old Haven Church. We don't know why or for what purpose. But she's strong. I'm not safe here at night."

Helena stepped back and moved towards the town map that Avery still had pinned to her wall, the map that marked the old pentagram over the town based on the houses where all of the witches' ancestors lived. She pointed to Old Haven Church on the map.

"Yes, that's the place," Avery said.

Helena's expression changed to one of alarm, and then she pointed to Avery's bags with a questioning glance.

"I'm going to Greenlane Manor," she said, pointing it out on the map. "The Jacksons' place."

Helena nodded and then disappeared.

Avery looked around the room, perplexed. "Helena?"

Weird. Maybe she'd gone to Old Haven? Avery shook her head. There was no point waiting. Sometimes she didn't see Helena for weeks; she always wondered where she went. To the spirit realm, or other places in White Haven?

Regardless, it was time to go to Reuben's.

***

Alex had decided to take his own car to Greenlane Manor as he was working until last orders, so Avery went on her own, finding only Briar's car waiting in the driveway.

The house was dark, other than lights by the front door and a couple of lights on the first floor. She knocked at the door, and within seconds Reuben flung it open, and the sound of drum and bass thudded after him. He grinned at her. "Come in. I'm cooking, so I hope you're hungry." He reached forward, took her bag, and led the way to the kitchen, and she followed with her cats. "I'll show you your room in a minute. I just need to check the food."

"Honestly, you didn't need to cook, Reuben," she said, quickening her pace to keep up with him. "I presumed we'd order in." She followed him down the long hall, lined with antiques, into the kitchen at the back of the house, which was a vision of high tech modernity. There seemed to be an acre of work surfaces and gleaming stainless steel appliances, and the smell of something spicy tickled her nose. And it was a mess. Bowls, spices, and chopping boards were strewn with the remnants of food. "Wow! You've really taken up the whole kitchen, Reu!"

"I know." He didn't sound the least bit regretful. "I'm a creative cook. But trust me, it will taste great!"

"I believe you," she said, watching him as he turned down the sound system, artfully built into the wall, and then stirred a large pot, turning the heat down. He dipped a spoon in and tasted it. "Perfect. You like curry spicy, right?"

"Of course. What is it?"

"Lamb *Maas*. My specialty. El loves it. This is her treat," he said with a wink. Underneath his forced cheer, Avery could see the worry on his face, and she squeezed his arm.

"Is she okay? Any after-effects of the curse?"

He frowned and ruffled his dark blond hair. "She's sleeping at the moment, but she seemed a bit flat actually, once the relief of being awake had worn off. I think the curse has left her feeling depressed."

"It doesn't surprise me. It was pretty toxic. You must have felt it."

"Yeah, true. I did. I guess I just wanted her to bounce back to normal."

"I'm sure she will, she's resilient, but she was out for almost two days. Any longer and we'd have had to take her to hospital for a drip. How the hell would we have explained that?" Avery rubbed her face. "It was way more serious than I thought. I'm sorry I didn't help you find a solution. I just thought it was something easy that Briar could break."

Reuben shrugged. "You were side-tracked with other things."

"Not an excuse. El's my friend. Nothing's more important than her."

"Avery, you did what you could, and helped when you were needed most. And you're right—she'll be fine. It will just take time." Her cats meowed pitifully, and Reuben looked down at them and laughed. "I think your cats are going stir crazy. Let me show you your room."

He lifted her bag once more and took her up a small set of stairs, almost hidden in the corner of the kitchen, which led onto the first floor landing. He guided her down a series of passageways until he reached a door. He flung it open and announced, "Your room, madam. With Alex, of course—unless you'd rather have your own?"

"No, you twit, of course not." She gasped as she looked at the room properly. "Holy cow, Reuben. This is amazing!"

"I know. This is all Alicia's doing," he said, referring to his brother, Gil's dead wife. "She may have been a devious, two-faced, demon-summoning bitch, but she did have great design skills."

Avery's eyes were wide as she entered the room and admired the highly polished wooden floor covered in expensive Persian rugs, rich colours, gorgeous antique furniture, and fine linen. "Who normally sleeps here?"

"No one. I just make sure Deb, the housekeeper, keeps it ready."

Avery marvelled at the awesome things that money could buy, and pulled the curtains back to peek at the view. The room overlooked the back garden that was partially illuminated with accent lights pointing up into the trees, but it was otherwise dark, a light grey colour marking the sea at the end of the garden.

She turned to him. "Thanks, Reuben. This is fantastic. You know I may never move out now."

"And that would be fine. You have an en suite, too," he said, pointing to a door on the right. "I'll go back to the kitchen, come down when you're ready. I thought we'd eat somewhere between seven and eight," he said vaguely.

"What about the protection spell for the house?"

"We'll do that later." Halfway out of the door, he hesitated. "By the way, Briar's about three doors down the hall, that way," he said pointing to the left. "Laters."

Once she was alone, Avery freed the cats, who scampered off to explore, stretching out as if they had been imprisoned for hours. Then she looked around the room again, unpacked her few belongings, gasped at the beauty of the bathroom, poked around in drawers and cupboards, and then threw herself on the bed and grinned. She loved her flat, but this was amazing. And she'd be sharing it with Alex. As she lay there, propped up on the full pillows, she realised how busy her head was with worries about Shifters, the Devices, strange portals, and Druids' trees. Maybe she'd rest her eyes, just for a short while.

The next thing she knew, there was a light tapping at her door, and Briar called out, "Avery, are you all right?"

Avery peeled an eye open and groaned. "Yes, come in!"

Briar popped her head around the door. "Were you asleep?"

"I didn't mean to be. It sort of snuck up on me." She sat up, blinking the sleep away. "I didn't know I was so tired."

"Not surprising, considering you were attacked last night." Briar headed over carrying two glasses of wine, one white and one red. She handed the glass of red to Avery. "Reuben sent me up with this."

"Wow. He's a great host." She took an appreciative sip. "Perfect. And how are you?"

Briar sat on the end of the bed, legs crossed, sipping her wine. "Okay, but like you, I need a good sleep. Breaking that curse took it out of me. It was slippery." She shuddered. "Yuck. How are your bruises?"

"It's my ribs, really," Avery said, feeling her left side. "I crashed onto Alex's coffee table, and it completely winded me. Now it just aches."

Briar considered her silently. "You were lucky. Things could have been much worse. Come on, let's go and eat, and then we can protect this place—properly. I want a good night's sleep without fear of attack."

Reuben was waiting in the snug next to the kitchen, sitting next to El. It was a small, cosy living area, much less formal than the large lounge at the front of the house. It was filled with an overstuffed corner sofa, squashy armchairs, and a huge TV screen was fixed on the wall. An ornate wood burner was placed in the corner, and a crackling blaze heated the room.

"Hey, El! You're up," Briar said, sitting next to her. "How are you?"

El still looked pale. "I've been better, but I'll survive."

"Good to see you up and about," Avery echoed. "At least you have Reuben to look after you."

El laughed weakly. "He's doing a great job. I can't wait to eat some proper food."

Reuben interrupted, pointing at the screen. "Guess who's on the TV?"

Newton's face was there in close up, talking to the interviewer, and a view of Old Haven Church was in the background.

"Oh no," Avery said, "has something else happened?"

"As predicted, quite a few ghost-hunters have turned up, trying to get access to the grounds, and the police have had to intervene. And look who's there now."

The interview was from earlier in the day. Dark grey skies loomed over the churchyard, and Newton was wearing a heavy coat with the collar turned up. Reuben turned the volume up, and they heard Newton explain how the Church had hired a private firm to protect the grounds. The camera panned back to show the alarmingly tall Gabreel staring intently at the interviewer as she asked, "Do you think this is overkill on the part of the Church to cordon off the grounds of a place of worship?"

Gabreel frowned. "My job is to protect the public from harm, and as there seems to be a hoaxer at this site who has no qualms about injuring innocent people, I think it's the best thing the Church could do right now."

"And how do you plan to protect this area?"

"I have half a dozen staff who will take turns monitoring the grounds, day and night."

"Is that all? This is quite a large site."

"I have a very effective team," he said, with a look that almost dared her to disagree.

"But what will you do?" she pressed, clearly spoiling for an argument.

"Patrol the grounds."

At his tone of finality, she turned back to Newton. "And do the police approve of this plan of action?"

"Absolutely," he said. "The police are not a private security force. Obviously, we support this decision, and are currently working to identify the hoaxer. Several people were injured yesterday as a result of this hoax, and they will be prosecuted when found. The security firm allows us the time to follow up leads."

The camera panned around now to frame the interviewer, who must be the perky blonde that Newton had referred to the day before. "So, for now, the Church grounds are closed, and we advise all ghost-hunters to stay away from the area for their own safety. Sarah Rutherford, Cornwall News."

Reuben muted the TV again. "Do you think we should check the place out again?"

"Now?" Avery asked, horrified.

"No, tomorrow," he said, looking at her like she'd gone mad. "Gabe's up there doing his thing. I'm sure everything will be okay. And besides, the food is ready."

They spent the rest of the evening eating, drinking, and relaxing, and by the time Alex arrived, Avery was already half dozing on the sofa, lulled by the warmth and good company. He joined them on the sofa after grabbing a beer.

"Everybody's talking about Old Haven Church," Alex informed the group.

"Everyone?" Avery asked, doubtful.

"*Everyone*! 'Who's responsible?' 'Is it serious?' 'How badly was the vicar hurt?' 'Is there a demon gateway in the Church grounds?' 'Is Halloween magic making spirits rise from the dead?' 'How bad will it get by the time Halloween arrives?'" He listed everything off and rolled his eyes. "Everyone has an opinion, and everyone wants this to be the worst thing possible. Most people are really excited, and quite a few are planning a midnight visit."

Reuben laughed. "I'm tempted to go myself, just to see how Gabe handles it. Is Zee going?"

"Yep," Alex answered in between sips of beer. "Not that he told the punters that. It will be a nice surprise for them to see him at his other job."

El yawned and asked, "So, what now?"

Reuben smiled. "Now we ward the house with a kick-ass protection spell, and then we sleep."

15

Avery was woken by the insistent ringing of her phone as it vibrated its way across the bedside table.

She grabbed it and answered before she even registered who was calling. "Yes?" she groaned.

A hysterical female voice answered. "Avery! Alice has taken Hunter and Holly! We need help!"

Avery's brain kicked in and she shot up, aware of Alex waking next to her. *Piper*. She put the phone on speaker and flicked a lamp on. "*What*? Are you kidding?"

"No! They barged their way into the house, attacked Josh and me so we couldn't fight, and have taken Hunter and Holly! I thought you said we were protected!" Anger entered Piper's voice as she accused Avery of lying.

"You were! No, you *are*. I told them that." She was halfway out of bed now. "Where have they taken them?"

"Cumbria, of course! To fight Cooper."

"We'll follow them," Avery said decisively.

"You'll come now?"

Alex intervened, a restraining hand on Avery's arm. "*No*. There's no point. We are not going to engage them on the road. It's too dangerous for everyone. When will the challenge take place?"

"As soon as they can arrange it, probably midnight tomorrow. Maybe the day after. We have to go now!"

Avery's mind was whirring with possibilities as she looked at Alex's resigned face. "No, Piper, Alex is right. We can achieve nothing right now. But we WILL go with you, tomorrow morning. We'll all travel together. Now, promise me that you'll wait."

Piper was silent for a moment. "What if they hurt them?"

"Be logical," Alex said, his eyes heavy with sleep. "Hunter needs to fight, and Holly is collateral. We follow tomorrow. Agreed?"

Her voice was quiet. "Yes, okay. You won't change your mind?"

"Absolutely not," Avery said firmly. "I have a score to settle with them. They have violated your Sanctuary. See you tomorrow morning. We'll be at yours at eight."

She rang off and looked at Alex. "That bitch!"

"Caspian warned you about them."

"These are their rules, not mine!"

"Maybe they didn't think you meant it."

"Did I sound like I meant it?"

"Yes. But they're old school and used to getting their own way. Are you sure you want to follow them up there? This will get ugly."

"Yes!" Avery said, incensed. "Don't you?"

He held his hands up in surrender. "Of course! Now come here." He spelled the lights out and lay down, pulling her close. "Try to sleep. We've got a long day tomorrow."

***

The morning had started badly. Alex and Avery had met as agreed at the Shifters' house, only to find that their Volvo had been sabotaged and wouldn't start, and neither Alex nor Avery could spell it to start again. They ended up going back to Reuben's in Avery's van and borrowing Gil's BMW that was still in the garage. Driving the seven-hour journey to Cumbria wasn't possible with either Piper or Josh unsecured in the back of Avery's van. By the time they left it was closer to nine, and the rush hour traffic was still in full swing. Alex was taking the first stint at the wheel, as he was far more used to the Cornish roads than Josh or Piper.

The one good thing about having to head up to Cumbria, Avery mused as Alex navigated onto the A roads that led to the motorway and the north, was that she could put off having to dress up as a witch in her own shop. When she phoned Sally to tell her she had to take a couple of days off, she accused her of doing it deliberately.

"I did not! This is an emergency," she stressed. "I'm sorry, I really am. And I'll get the others to keep an eye on you. Call either Briar or Reuben if you're worried about anything. Or Newton." She knew he'd help if he could. "Anything suspicious, don't hesitate."

"All right," Sally sighed. "But I was looking forward to today."

"I was looking forward to your cake, and to seeing you two dressed up. But I'll be back, and I'll wear that stupid costume then."

"Stay safe, Avery. I don't like the Devices, and I don't trust them. Be careful."

"I will," she promised.

The other witches hadn't been happy when she saw them at breakfast, either. "We should all go," Reuben said recklessly. Now that El was better, his usual bounce had returned, and Avery could tell he was itching for action.

Alex just looked at him with a measured stare. "El is still recovering from her curse, and we still have a rogue witch down here. You three have to stay and look after White Haven. We'll be okay."

"Take my short sword," El had insisted, referring to the sword she had fashioned that enhanced elemental magic. "You can collect it from my shop. You both wield it well, and it may help you."

That sword was now in the boot of the car, and Avery could feel its magic from where she sat in the back next to Piper, who chewed her lip and fidgeted as she gazed out of the window.

"Tell me about the pack," Avery said, as much to distract her as to learn more about what they were facing. "How many are in it?"

"About ten families, all spread across the small towns and villages in the Lake District. That makes about 30 or 40 Shifters," she estimated.

"Including children?" Alex asked, listening as he drove.

Josh shook his head. "No. They are not full pack members until they hit 16."

"And do regular people have relationships with Shifters?" Avery asked.

"Sure," Piper said, "or else there would be a lot of incest! Consequently, not all children are Shifters. You can usually tell by the early teens. When hormones kick in, that's when shifting starts. Some kids miss a lot of school until they start to control their changes. You really don't want to shift in class!"

"So, I guess, you live under the radar, like we do?"

Josh looked over his shoulder. "Yep. Just as we told you. We have a regular business, but the pack always comes first. You swear fealty to it at 16."

"Does the community know, or even suspect, that Shifters live among them?"

"Maybe, but no one says anything. We're spread across the countryside. It's big, remote, and we take care not to draw attention to ourselves."

Alex twisted in his seat slightly, still watching the road. "So, this challenge. What is it, where does it happen?"

"Castlerigg Stone Circle. Anyone can challenge the leader—the Alpha—but most don't unless something really bad is happening. The Alpha is strong, and brings stability."

Avery frowned. "So how long has Cooper been the Alpha?"

"Just under a year. He succeeded his father."

"Is that normal?"

Josh glanced at Piper nervously. "Not really. Normally, the strongest succeeds. When an old leader grows too weak, others challenge him. But there hasn't been a real challenge for hundreds of years. It was a line of succession."

"Why?" Avery asked, sensing something suspicious.

Piper answered, her tone dry. "The Dacres are a very rich family. They have power and influence and like to maintain leadership. They fight dirty and have the Devices on their side, and to be honest, many other members, too. They take care of us if we take care of them. Unfortunately, laying claim to Holly was one step too far. To take them on is huge. Hunter didn't care about that."

Avery was struggling to understand. "So, Holly marrying Cooper is politically motivated. But why her? If they're so rich, what makes her special?"

"Because we are one of the oldest families, and have a strong line of Shifters. Alphas have come from our family in the past. It's believed that we will create other strong Shifters. Plus, when two Shifters mate, their children are *always* Shifters, too. Cooper wants Shifter kids. He has no brothers or sisters. He needs an heir if his family is to continue to be the Alpha."

"You said other women would like that chance, so why not choose them?"

"Because there aren't many Shifter women, that's why," Josh said. "Shifters are more likely to be male."

Piper smiled softly. "We're rare, and therefore precious."

Avery exhaled heavily, "Wow. That's mad. What a weird life."

"Any weirder than yours?" Piper asked, narrowing her eyes.

"Yes! I don't get married off to some witch just because I'm a female with a strong lineage, for breeding purposes!"

"And," Alex added, "witches are pretty much an even split of male and female, despite the popular image being that witches are women."

Avery thought for a moment. "Are there other Shifter communities across the country?"

"Sure," Josh answered. "Many farther north than us, especially in Scotland. There is some movement between packs, but it's not common. Newcomers bring challenges."

"And new packs?"

"Happen rarely," he said. "Unless you can persuade some members to leave together. They have to be really unhappy to do that. It means moving to a completely new area."

"So Hunter has to win, or what would happen?"

"Everything we said," Piper explained. "Holly will marry Cooper, and essentially Hunter has to swear fealty to him."

"But I don't think he will," Josh added, worried. "He'd rather die first."

"And Cooper would be only too pleased to see that happen," Piper said, and then turned and looked out of the window.

"And Holly?" Avery asked. "She wouldn't refuse Cooper?"

"Like we said. He's powerful. He influences businesses and the locals. One word from him and our business could fold. We'd become virtual outsiders in our own community, and our income would be gone. We'd have to leave and start again. Our whole lives are there—friends, work, our home. Holly knows what the consequences would be."

"So she'd essentially sacrifice herself for all of you," Avery said, not sure whether to admire Holly's decision or not.

"Yep," Josh said, looking uncomfortable.

Alex sounded incredulous as he put in, "You know that life elsewhere would be fine. You'd start again. So what?"

Josh looked at him sharply. "Would you?"

"If it meant saving Avery, or anyone else I loved from that, of course I would."

Avery blinked in shock. *Loved? Was that meant for her? Did he love her?* They'd never had that conversation. *Did she love him?* She looked at him for a moment, meeting his eyes in the rear-view mirror. *Yes, of course she did.*

She dragged her gaze away and turned back to Josh. "Would you challenge?"

"I'm tempted, but I know my limits. I'm not as strong as Hunter or Cooper."

Alex glanced at him. "You must have good friends—other Shifters who would support you."

Josh nodded. "Yes, we do. I phoned them early this morning. We have a couple of families who are really sympathetic to us, and are willing to help us discretely, but no one who would put their life on the line. I've asked them to tell us if they hear anything about a meet. They agree with me. It will happen tonight, but there's no word yet."

"We need to meet them, before the challenge. There must be a way of trying to get them to help you," Alex said, insistent.

Josh rounded on him, annoyed. "*How?* We can't guarantee we'll win. I keep telling you, and you're not listening. We don't have that kind of support or leverage! *We are completely screwed!*" Josh's eyes had taken on a frightening yellow ring that looked like fire around his pupils, and they could hear a small snarl in the back of his throat. Piper shot upright, out of her relaxed slump on the backseat, and Avery felt a tingle in her palms as she summoned her magic.

"Calm the fuck down, Josh. It's just a question—*I'm trying to help!*" Alex yelled back.

Piper reached forward a hand and laid it on Josh's arm. "Josh, please."

He took a deep breath and looked away, out of the window, and Avery felt the tension subside.

"Tell me about the Devices," Avery said, hoping to find other avenues to help. "Everything. What are their motivations, weaknesses, roles in the community?"

Piper spoke up first. "Like the Dacres, they're rich. Big house, good community standing, own many local businesses."

Alex snorted. "No wonder they reached out to Caspian. Their families sound similar."

"Why do they care if Cooper loses?" Avery asked.

"They know that other pack members would rather keep our lives more independent, away from the influence of the Devices. They would lose their power over us."

"Does that matter?" Avery asked, incredulous.

"It does to them."

"And does anyone know of their links to the Pendle witches of the sixteenth century?"

"Maybe a few locals make the connection, but no one would believe they're witches," Josh said, turning around. Avery was relieved to see that his eyes had returned to their normal colour. "Same as you and your ancestor, Helena."

Avery looked at him, astonished. "How do you know about that?"

"Briar told us. We were asking about all of you and your history. She explained the mysterious cloud of power above White Haven. That's what drew us to you."

Avery thought for a moment, watching the countryside streak by. They were on the A30, passing through the rugged beauty of Bodmin Moor, looking more brooding than usual under the grey overcast conditions.

She exchanged a worried glance with Alex in the rear-view mirror, and she knew exactly what he was thinking. *How would the Devices interfere, and what could they do to stop them?*

"How many Devices are there?" she asked abruptly.

"Alice, her daughter, Rose, and Rose's two children, who are both younger than me, and Jeremy and his children. I don't think Alice's grandchildren will interfere, just Jeremy and Rose."

Avery realised she had no idea how they'd captured the others the night before, so she asked now, feeling it would help her understand how they fought.

"They knocked on the door like civilised people," Piper said. "It was nine at night. Hunter answered, and they said they wanted to talk, that they understood we were under your Sanctuary, but they needed to discuss terms. He was suspicious, but let them in."

Josh continued. "We were in the lounge, and we came to the door to see what was happening. As they entered, Jeremy did something—released *something* from his hands."

"Yeah, it was like this little cloud of blackness," Piper said, struggling to articulate what it was. "But it rushed across to us like a mini whirlwind, and that's all I remember."

Avery frowned. "You passed out?"

"Yep," Josh said. "When we woke up, it was three in the morning, and we were freezing our asses off on the floor. Hunter and Holly had gone."

"You're sure they'd have headed back home?" Alex asked.

"Yes. They'll have either gone to Cooper's house or their own place."

"So, if they've travelled all night, they'll be there by now," Avery said. It was about seven hours to Cumbria, give or take some time for stops and traffic.

"They won't want to waste any more time," Alex said. "They know you'll follow. Can this fight happen in the day?"

"No." Josh shook his head. "All challenges take place at midnight, in the open, at Castlerigg Stone Circle."

"Are you sure?" Avery asked.

"Always," Piper agreed. "It's sacred ground, our spiritual home."

Piper was looking tired, and the shadows under eyes were darkening. Her normal retreat into snark had gone, and instead she looked defeated as she leaned back against the seat and closed her eyes.

Avery fell silent, trying to come up with a plan, which she decided was virtually impossible without knowing how the night would unfold. She thought of El's sword in the back of the car, and was glad they'd brought it with them. Tonight could get very ugly.

16

Avery took over the driving from Alex just before Birmingham, negotiating the horrible M5/M6 interchange on the way to the north, and the traffic was horrendous, slowing their progress to a crawl in places. They'd finally had a call from Josh's friend mid-morning, who confirmed the challenge was to take place that night, but there was no other news. While Avery drove, Josh and Piper slept in the back of the car; they would all need their strength for the night ahead.

Josh drove the last two hours of the journey, and they finally exited the M6 and followed the A590 and then the A591 to Ambleside. Josh was navigating them to the Devices house, where they hoped to see Hunter and Holly.

"I doubt they'll be there," Alex said. "They'll have hidden them somewhere. They must know we'd look for them. Or at least you would." He grinned suddenly. "They must have hoped that damaging your Volvo would have stopped you. Idiots."

"Agreed," Josh said. "They will hide them before taking them to Castlerigg. They won't risk the challenge being stopped now. Once there, the pack will ensure it happens."

"Will they?" Avery asked. "Why?"

"A challenge leaves uncertainty. No one wants that."

Avery shook her head, perplexed. If some of them wanted change, surely they should support Hunter. Many were obviously scared of Cooper and his supporters. Avery already hated him. He sounded like a bully.

The Devices lived on the outskirts of Ambleside, a popular tourist town in the centre of the Lake District at the head of Lake Windermere, surrounded by rugged hills and tumbling streams. As they passed the lake, it was dusk and they again hit traffic. Avery checked her watch, worried. It was nearly six. Traffic, road works, and a couple of stops had delayed them all along the way, and who knows what might delay them further here.

They wound down narrow lanes, but because of the encroaching night, Avery caught only a glimpse of the wild beauty of the landscape, though she couldn't help but get lost in the view. It was wilder than Cornwall and the perfect place for wolves to roam free, unseen and unheard. By the time they got to Ambleside, their surroundings were lost in darkness, but the town looked quaint with its winding streets of grey stone buildings, and the bright yellow of street lights illuminating shops and pubs. Any other time Avery would have loved to wonder the streets and explore, but there was no time for that now.

The Devices' house was a large stone building, set at the bottom of a hill. It had a long drive, which offered only a peek at the house, and for added privacy, it was surrounded by a large, walled garden offering glimpses of mature trees and shrubs.

Josh parked at the side of the road and turned to the others. "At least the darkness will offer us some cover. Once we slip into the grounds, me and Piper will change and head to the house as wolves. Maybe you should wait here until we give you the all clear?"

Alex looked incredulous. "No way. They're witches and are obviously quite happy to use their power against you. We're coming."

"Agreed," Avery said, reaching for the door handle. "We should check for magical traps and protection spells."

They exited the car and Avery shivered as she pulled her jacket on, thankful she'd borrowed El's heavy parka. It was cold, almost icy, with the wind bringing a chill from the mountains. She reached into the boot for El's sword. "Do you want it, Alex?"

He shook his head. "No, you use it better than me. But stay close."

The lane they were on was deserted, and Alex and Avery stood at the bottom of the drive, feeling for magic. "Nothing yet," Alex declared.

"Same." Avery looked at Josh and Piper, who were clearly itching to go. "Be careful!"

They nodded and slipped into the shrubs at the edge of the drive, shedding their clothes quickly and then shifting effortlessly into two beautiful wolves, Piper slightly smaller than Josh. In seconds, they had gone.

Alex followed their path into the shrubs, and Avery followed him. They edged their way up to the house, warily feeling their way, and slapping small branches aside. The wolves had disappeared.

"I don't like this," Alex whispered. "It's too quiet."

"The grounds are big. They'll have more protection closer to the house," Avery reasoned.

Her breath escaped in white clouds, and she wished she'd brought her gloves with her. Avery whispered a small warming spell, and felt her coat start to heat. She'd learnt that one from Eve, the witch from St Ives. *Thank the gods for weather witches.*

The attack was unexpected—the Devices had hidden it well.

As they came in sight of the house, a wall of darkness shot up from the ground, enveloping them completely. It felt sticky and cloying, and Avery quickly became disorientated. She dropped to her knees, pleased to feel the damp ground beneath her. She flared a light into her hands, but the blackness swallowed it. She couldn't feel Alex at all.

Shit!

She cried out, *"Alex!"*

Silence.

She tried again, this time grounding herself completely with the earth. She pulled its power into her hands and cast a lightning bolt ahead of her, hoping Alex was still to her left. The smell of magic and ozone was overpowering, but the oily darkness receded slightly.

She inwardly smacked herself. The air was still and heavy; what she needed was wind. She created a mini tornado, drawing the oily darkness into its centre. Within a few seconds it lifted and she sent the tornado away to the far side of the garden.

She turned to where Alex had stood only moments earlier, but he was gone.

For a second Avery panicked, and then she took a deep breath. *Smoke and mirrors. He was here somewhere.*

A wolf's howl broke the silence over to her right. After one final look for Alex, she turned, heading towards the sound.

A second howl followed the first, and her skin prickled. It was tempting to run, but that would be too dangerous. She broke free of the shrubs and the house appeared in front of her, on the other side of a lawn and large flowerbeds.

No one was in sight. She headed to the right, towards the sounds of the howl. There was another, much closer, and the large shape of a wolf came into view, its lips drawn back to reveal large teeth, a snarl building in the back of its throat.

It was Josh, she was sure. He had dark brown fur with a white stripe down his nose, she'd noticed when he'd changed, and he was bigger than Piper.

But something was wrong.

He advanced towards her as if he didn't know her, and Avery fell back into the shadows, watching him. She raised her hands just as he sprang at her, covering meters of ground in mere seconds. She sent a blast of energy at him and it struck him in the chest.

He rolled away, stunned, but quickly regained his footing. He howled again and Avery's blood curdled. She'd always wondered where that expression came from, and now she knew. A wolf's howl was terrifying.

He launched across the small space between them again and she struck, too, desperately not wanting to hurt him, but aware that one wrong move on her part would see her throat ripped out.

She was too slow. His paws landed on her chest, throwing her to the floor, and she was winded, crying out in pain as her injured ribs screamed in protest. Shocked, she struck out, sending out a wave of power so strong that it lifted him into the air and threw him back against a tree.

She staggered to her feet, ready to fight again. But then he looked at her, shaking his big, shaggy head with confusion, and she saw recognition flash into his eyes.

He bowed his head, whimpered, and then shifted. The very human Josh shivered and curled into a foetal position, and Avery ran over.

"I'm so sorry. Are you okay?"

He nodded. "I just need a minute. I don't know what came over me. I didn't recognise you at all. You were just someone—an enemy."

"Some weird spell. I plunged into one, too and have lost Alex."

Just then, another howl sounded behind the house.

"Time to go," Josh said. "Stay close."

He changed again, rose to his feet, and loped off around the house, Avery jogging to keep up.

The house was in complete darkness. There was no way anyone was here. These traps were to confuse and delay them, and they were working.

A sudden pain in her head made her stumble and fall, and Josh returned to her side, nuzzling her hand. A voice filled her head. *Avery, it's Alex. Can you hear me?*

Relief flooded though her, and she answered in her mind. *Yes! Where are you?*

Somewhere in the garden. It's dark. I can't get out, but I feel the earth beneath me, and can hear the trees. It's like I've been blinded.

Have you seen Piper?

I can hear howling, but that's all.

I'm coming. Stay with me.

She rose to her feet and sent out a witch light, illuminating the trees and a path that ran behind the house. She was sure now that no one was here. They had planned this to delay them, keep them here all night if necessary, all in order to miss the challenge.

Bollocks to them. They would not win.

She sent out light after light, floating around the garden, and then decided to cast a finding spell. Alex's scent was all over her, and she was wearing his scarf. She quickly cast the spell and a small, blue light appeared out of the air; she followed it across the garden.

She hadn't gone too far when Piper appeared, snarling on the path ahead of her. *Oh no. Not again.*

But this time, Josh intervened. As Piper leapt at Avery, Josh leapt at her, and the wolves collided mid-leap. They hit the ground, a snarling, tumbling mass of teeth and fur.

As soon as she had a clear shot, Avery sent of couple of blasts of pure energy at Piper, and like Josh, it seemed to shock her out of whatever spell had confused her. She whined as recognition flooded through her and both of them turned and headed off across the garden.

Alex. Can you hear us? Avery again communicated to him in her head. She could feel his presence, and his worry.

You're muffled, he replied. As if you're overhead.

You must be underground, she reasoned. They probably have a cellar or a basement. Can you see anything yet?

Something is binding my magic. I can't spell anything, other than to speak to you.

A howl disturbed Avery's attention, and she ran towards the sound. Josh and Piper were pawing at the ground, raking back dirt, and Avery joined them. They were at the back of the garden, next to an old shed, and Avery could see metal gleaming beneath the dirt.

"I hear you!" Alex shouted audibly from beneath her feet.

Relief flooded though Avery and she called to the wolves, "Stand back. I'm going to try something."

Avery used elemental air to move the earth, wielding it like a shovel to push it out of the way. As she dumped it to the side, she saw a hatch in the ground, like an old air raid shelter. Magic sang from it, crackling around the edges. "Alex, I've found a hatch. It's spelled shut. Bear with me."

She could feel a combination of Earth and Fire magic. The Earth must be giving Alex that suffocating blanket feeling that was blinding him, much like El's curse had. She tried a few different spells, attempting to break through whatever was holding Alex inside, but nothing worked. She sat back, thinking for a moment. El's sword wielded Ice Fire—maybe that would do it.

"Josh, Piper. I need the sword in the back of the car. Can you get it?" Josh nodded and loped off across the garden, returning within a couple of minutes, the blade between his teeth. Avery shouted, "Alex, if you can feel anything, make for the edges and crouch down."

She held the sword, activating its magic by sending a shiver of fire along its blade, and then pressed the point to the tin panel and felt the crack of magic. She cast a banishing spell at the same time as she plunged the sword through the tin as if it were butter. As soon as it punctured the metal, a *pop* sounded and Avery was thrown backwards several feet, leaving the sword in the metal. Josh changed form and took over, dragging the sword through the metal as sparks were thrown around them. An oily black cloud seeped out of the jagged tear, and he stepped back, coughing. Avery whisked it into the shed and sealed it in. Again she used her magic to peel the metal back and she peered in and saw Alex crouched on the floor about eight feet down, arms over his head. She called out, "Need a hand?"

He looked up and grinned. "I need many things right now, but getting out of here would be good."

"If it's all right with you," Josh said, shivering, "I'm changing back to wolf form. I'm freezing my ass off."

"No problem," Avery said. By the time she'd turned back to Alex, he was already dragging himself out of the hole in the ground, and Avery extended a hand, giving a final pull.

"Are you okay?" she asked, checking him over for injuries.

He tied his hair back in a half-ponytail, and rolled his shoulders as if ready for a fight. "Fine. Just pissed off. If they're going to throw stuff like that at us, we'll be in trouble later."

"We'll be fine," she said, giving him a big hug. "We just need to get more creative. We're a great team, remember?"

"I remember," he said, stealing a quick kiss. "Now, let's get out of here. I feel like Indiana bloody Jones."

Once they were safely back in the car and headed back into Ambleside, with the heating turned up full blast, they decided on their next step.

Josh was mulling over their options. "It's pointless going to Cooper's. We may well find the same problem, and we've wasted over an hour already. But, maybe I'll call my mate, Evan. I'd like to see what he thinks of all this."

"One of the Shifters who supports you?" Avery asked.

"And he fancies Holly," Piper said, raising an eyebrow. "You may find him more willing to help than you think, Josh."

He groaned. "He fancies her. It's not bloody Romeo and Juliet."

"You have no romance in your soul," Piper chastised him.

"Neither has he," he answered.

"I like this plan," Alex said, grinning. "Where to?"

"Keswick. The centre of all things Wolf in Cumbria."

"Is it?" Avery asked, feeling she was learning something new every second.

"That's where Castlerigg is, and where Cooper lives, as well as a few other Shifter families."

"But you're right, there's no point in going to Cooper's place," Piper said, adamant.

"Why's that?" Alex asked, twisting to look at her in the backseat.

"We may find ourselves trapped at Cooper's forever. He lives in what's near enough a bloody castle. We could end up in the dungeon."

"A castle?" Avery said, incredulous.

"Yep. With security."

With that, Avery's stomach emitted a large growl. "I have a small request. Before we do anything else, let's go to the pub. I'm starving, and sick to death of sitting in a car and eating motorway service food."

"My thoughts exactly," Josh said, finding a parking space on the side of a busy road. "And then we plan our attack."

17

The Unicorn Inn was a small stone building painted white, tucked in the middle of a row of shops along a one-way street.

They headed inside to find a cosy pub with a low-beamed roof, a long wooden bar, an array of local beers, and a gin display. There were a couple of spare tables, and once they had drinks and ordered food, they headed to the table in the corner, glad of the privacy.

Now that they were inside in the warmth, their experiences in the Devices' garden seemed like a nightmare.

"The good thing is that at Castlerigg, they won't be able to plant booby trap spells," Josh said, cheering up as he sipped his pint. "The whole pack will be there."

"But they could try to stop us from getting there," Piper pointed out. "The road is remote."

"Not if we time it right," he answered.

"How long to get there from here?" Alex asked. It was already nearing eight.

"Half an hour. But we'll leave as soon as we've eaten. Which reminds me, I'll call Evan." And with that, Josh slipped out to make the call.

"What's Keswick like?" Avery asked Piper, her expression already returning to her normal scowl.

"Busy, old, and full of tourists most of the year. It's popular with walkers."

"And Shifters," Alex added.

"Yeah, those too. There are forests, moors, lakes—all wild and remote, if you leave the towns far enough behind."

"And the stone circle is close?"

Piper nodded. "Just out of town."

They paused while the waitress delivered their food, just as Josh returned looking pleased. As soon as she left, Alex asked, "Good news?"

"Very," Josh said, grinning. "Evan and another couple of mates have decided to help."

Piper looked suspicious. "Who? And how?"

"Ollie and Tommy."

Piper frowned. "Tommy is a brawler! He just wants a fight."

Josh pointed his fork at her. "Exactly. And so do Ollie and Evan. I pointed out that Evan may actually stand a chance with Holly if he can get Cooper out of the way."

"You used Holly as bait?" she asked, outraged.

"No! Not like that," he said, looking equally outraged. "Will you shut up and let me finish?"

Piper grimaced and waved him on while Alex and Avery watched, amused.

"It turns out that in the last few months, Cooper's been pressuring them and a few others to support his business, whilst threatening theirs."

"What *is* his business?" Alex asked.

"Real estate. Don't ask me the details, because I have no idea. Anyway, they've had enough and with this latest incident with Hunter, and they have finally decided it's time to act." He turned to Alex and Avery. "If you can control the witches."

Avery looked at Alex with a smirk and then turned back to Josh. "I can't guarantee control, but we can probably work something out. But what's your plan?"

"Hunter will fight Cooper. I need to tell him he must submit once he's got a good way into the fight—we have to get to him to let him know—and then I will challenge, as will Evan, Ollie, and Tommy. All at once. We tell him we take him on, one at a time. He can't beat all of us. Whoever beats him becomes Alpha. He will have to capitulate."

Avery felt the faintest stirring of hope within her. "Until he capitulates to what?"

"Everything. Keeping his nose out of other people's business. His claim on Holly. His bullying tactics. He only remains Alpha if he agrees to those terms."

"And if he doesn't?" Alex asked.

"We fight," Josh said, shrugging. "And he will lose."

"Bullies don't like to be cornered," Alex said softly. "And he has the Devices to render you impotent."

"Not in the open, in front of everyone. Everyone knows they support him, but have never suspected them of manipulation using magic. The Devices have, in fact, sworn to us many times that they would never subvert our will or Cooper's leadership in that way." Josh was looking excited now as his plans began to take shape. "Wolves are swift and deadly. The Devices can't watch their backs all the time. They know they have to keep us sweet. They will need to agree. And you need to bind them to it."

"We need to *what*?" Avery asked, almost choking on her drink.

"Bind them. You can do that, right?"

It was Alex's turn to smirk. "We know all about binding."

A sudden memory of a spell flashed into Avery's mind as Alex spoke. "We can use a word binding."

"We can?" he asked, confused.

"Trust me. It's tickling my brain. I need to check my grimoire." She was itching to leave the table right then, but she forced herself to finish her meal and listen to what else Josh had planned.

"Excellent," Josh said, carrying on regardless. "We're heading to Evan's place in Keswick. We can leave the car there and walk to the stone circle when we're ready."

Alex asked, "Do we enter the stone circle with you, or loiter undercover nearby?"

"This fight will be witnessed by pack members and Devices only," Josh said, tucking into his pie and chips. "But the circle is surrounded by stone walls, so you should be able to hide behind one of them. At the right time, we'll call on you. Sound good?"

"And that means you can monitor them in case they decide to use magic anyway," Piper added, buzzing with anticipation. "But you'll need to disguise your scent, or stay a long way back. Wolves, even in human form, have a strong sense of smell."

"No problem. We'll think of something, won't we, Avery?" Alex said, winking at her.

"Nothing a cloaking spell won't solve," she answered. Despite her worry, she was curious to see a Shifter meeting, especially in a stone circle. Then she asked something that had been on the tip of her tongue all night. "Do you fight as wolves or humans?"

Piper answered, pushing her plate away. "Humans—most of the time. By mutual agreement, the last time Cooper and Hunter both shifted at the same time. It got ugly. That's why Hunter was injured so badly."

"Which brings me to my next point," Josh added, reaching forward for his pint. "For the last couple of days, he's kept a low profile. Rumours are he was pretty badly injured himself. We didn't see it because we fled. Only the ministrations of Rose Device have helped him so quickly. That's another reason he can't fight us all. He's not fit enough."

"So why fight now?" Avery asked, incredulous.

"Appearances are everything," Josh said. "Especially to an Alpha. And he thinks he'll only have one challenger to fight. He's in for a big surprise."

***

The group followed the A591 to Castlerigg Village, and then on to Keswick without incident. It was a small market town on the northern end of Derwentwater Lake. They passed through its quiet streets, and then scoped out the area around the stone circle before going to Evan's house, so that Avery and Alex could get a feel for the place.

The night was getting colder by the minute. Castlerigg Stone Circle lay at the bottom of Skiddaw and Blencathra hills. It was situated on raised ground, and the wind rolled across it relentlessly. A crescent moon rode high above them, and the sky was filled with stars. Dew lay heavy on the ground and soon it would frost. Already patches of white sparkled in the muted light, and snow speckled the hilltops above them.

The circle itself was large, formed by 38 tall, misshapen standing stones that went back millennia—at least 5,000 years. On the way, Avery had Googled it, fascinated by its history. There was a break in the stones on the left of the circle, indicating the possibility of a ceremonial entrance, and a small rectangle of stones in the centre. Like many stone circles, it was believed to have astronomical significance, as well as burial purposes.

Piper was right. Low stone walls edged the surrounding fields, including the one the stone circle was in. They discussed their approach and the best place to stand, and then Josh turned the car around, heading back along the lanes and snaking through the outskirts of the town, before finally drawing to a halt outside a small stone cottage at the end of a row of identical cottages. It backed into a small copse—the perfect place for a Shifter to live.

Josh bounded up the path, Piper behind him, but Alex and Avery reached into the boot for their magic supplies, and then stood for a moment, looking over the street. The air was crisp, and the hoot of an owl drifted across the still night air. Nothing else stirred.

"Are you sure we can do this?" Alex asked Avery, his hand resting slightly on her arm. "I don't want a war with the Devices."

"I'm sure. I don't want one, either. If I work this properly, we come to a truce. A mutual binding that will satisfy both of us."

"I don't think I want to be bound to *them*."

"It's not that kind of binding," she said, smiling up at him. "Come on inside and I'll explain. I'm really hoping there's some kind of hot toddy waiting for me."

The front door was still partially open, and they entered a small, narrow hall. Shutting the door behind them, they headed to the light at the end of the passage, and found five people clustered around a fire burning fiercely in a huge, old-fashioned range. A mismatched series of armchairs and an old, worn sofa battled for space around it. The other half of the room featured a very old kitchen that probably hadn't been updated since the 1950s.

Josh looked up and caught their eye. "Hi, guys. Let me introduce you to the troops." He indicated the three very large men in the room. *Now this is what I thought Shifters would look like*, Avery thought.

Ollie was tall with an athletic build, short-cropped hair like Josh, and pale hazel eyes. Evan was average height, wiry and lean. And well, Tommy was just huge. He looked exactly like what Piper had called him—a brawler. He had shaggy brown hair, a full beard, large muscular arms and legs, and piercing baby blue eyes, which were most disconcerting. Those baby blues were frowning, his sleeves were rolled up, and he looked ready to take on anyone.

After quick handshakes all around, Tommy resumed his conversation in a broad northern accent. "I swear I'll rip his head off, given the chance. I will not let Holly get trapped by that bastard. I've had enough of him. He thinks he's better than the rest of us, and I can put up with some stuff, but not this!" He banged his fist on the range, and Avery jumped.

"You don't need to rip his head off! Just threaten to. He won't want to fight you, Tommy. In fact, I'm surprised he's even attempted to rope you into his crap," Josh said, trying to calm him down.

Tommy looked slightly guilty and glanced away, into the fire. "He might have something on me."

Josh looked at Ollie and Evan, and then back to Tommy. "Like what?"

"Just a bit of under the table selling of building supplies."

"Don't tell me you nicked off Cooper's site?"

Tommy scratched his ear. "It was a small error on my part. It won't happen again."

"He's threatened you with the police?"

"Might have," he said sheepishly.

Josh frowned. "So why the change of attitude?"

"I don't like that bastard having something over me. This is one time when violence is the solution."

Ollie remonstrated with him. "The *threat* of violence, Tommy. The *threat* of him losing Alpha status. That's all!"

By now Avery had eased herself into a chair and was warming her feet and hands on the fire. Alex leaned against the wall behind her, arms crossed, an amused expression on his face as he watched the exchange.

Tommy caught him looking and said, "And what will you do, pretty boy? Here to tame the witches?"

"You don't tame witches," Alex said drolly. "They're not wild animals."

"Well, that Alice needs a leash. Mad cow. Interfering in our business."

"So are we, but I gather that's okay?"

"It depends what you're going to do," Tommy said, assessing Alex with an even gaze.

Avery could feel Alex's power building. If Tommy didn't watch his mouth, he'd find his tongue bound.

Piper intervened. "Oh, shut up, you great pillock. Alex and Avery are here to help."

He looked at Piper, frowned, and then laughed. "You've always got a big attitude for a little thing."

"And you're full of shit. Shut up."

Avery laughed out loud, and that set everyone off.

"So," Josh said, after wiping his eyes, "can someone give me a bloody drink before we have to traipse up to that place in the freezing cold?"

Evan grinned and headed to a cupboard in the kitchen, bringing out whiskey and glasses. He poured and handed everyone a shot, before turning to Alex and Avery. "So, what's your plan?"

"We're here to stop Alice from using her magic to either confuse or glamour you, or to influence the fight," Avery said. "We'd like to be there in the circle right at the start so they know we're there. It will make our life easier, and yours. They won't tamper because they know that we will know."

Tommy shook his head. "No way. The pack won't allow it."

"In that case, we work behind the scenes to prevent them from interfering in the fight. But at some point, we'll have to reveal ourselves."

"Why?" Ollie asked, speaking for the first time.

Alex explained. "Anything Cooper promises you could be subverted by the Devices at some point. You could have nasty *accidents*, your businesses might fail inexplicably…" He shrugged. "Anything might happen. If Cooper agrees to your terms, you need to demand proof the terms will be abided by, and that's when Josh or Piper have to invite us in."

Ollie looked suspicious. "And how will you manage that? They have influenced things for generations—we all know it. It's an open secret."

"We offer a reciprocal binding," Avery said. "We agree never to interfere here again, and they agree not to break their word by attacking you or seek revenge on us. They have violated Sanctuary already. Hunter can demand terms, and so can we. And the Cornwall Covens will support us."

"And that will hold how?"

"By magic. Binding spells are exactly that. They can be used in all sorts of ways—to bind someone's magic, tongue, actions—but also they can be used to maintain trust. And we will bind their whole family, No loopholes."

"I don't like magic," Tommy said suddenly, glaring at them. "I don't trust it."

"So trust me," she answered.

"How will we know you're there?" Evan asked.

"We'll be cloaked, but I promise you we'll be there. We won't let you down."

Ollie sipped his drink. "Tell me about the binding. Can anyone do one?"

Alex frowned. 'What are you thinking?"

"If something goes wrong. Can we do one?"

He nodded. "A blood oath. All witches will abide by that. It's the oldest and strongest binding there is—outside of actual magic. But you must make your terms very clear."

"Good to know," Ollie said, nodding thoughtfully.

Avery stood and knocked her drink back, shook her head at the sharpness of it, and then turned to Alex. "Let's get out of here and prepare. Can we use another room, Evan?"

Evan ushered them to a small front room, muggy with central heating, and as soon as they were alone, Alex shook his head. "I don't like this. There are too many variables."

"I know, and obviously Ollie thinks the same. But what other options do we have?"

"We can get in the car and leave them to it."

"You don't mean that," Avery said, looking incredulous.

Alex sighed. "No, I guess not. But I want an advantage. I have another idea."

Avery raised an eyebrow. "Go on."

"We protect these guys with a charm, so they can't be influenced by Alice."

"That's a good idea."

Alex grinned. "And I think we offer them a strength potion."

"Really? Isn't that a bit, well, cheat-y?"

"Do we trust *them* to allow a fair fight?"

"No."

"So we really are just evening the odds," Alex pointed out.

Avery grinned, too. "Well, when you put it like that… And we need something strong for the binding."

Alex nodded. "Bindings like this work best with something sympathetic. This place backs on to a wood. What about using ivy?"

"Excellent. You get it, and I'll start preparing the rest."

18

It was close to 11:30pm and Avery stood with Alex overlooking Castlerigg, cloaked in shadows. They had left Piper and Josh in Keswick so they could make their own way to the circle with the other Shifters.

Avery looked up at Alex's strong profile that at the moment, only she could see. His hair was tied back in a half-ponytail, and his jacket collar was high around his neck. It was freezing, but she had once again whispered the warming spell that enveloped both of them. It felt like they were the only people in the world.

She thought back on what he told Josh in the car, when he said he'd do anything for her and anybody else he loved, and she desperately wanted to ask him if it was true. She half-wondered if she'd imagined it, or if she'd exaggerated what he meant, because she realised now, looking at him under a huge sky full of stars and the faint crescent of the moon, that she loved him and needed him to love her. Desperately so.

Just as she was summoning her courage to ask, a sweep of car headlights in the distance caused Alex to look away, and she followed his gaze. Two men made their way to the stone circle. They were just barely visible as black shapes against the grey of the night sky and the faint line of the stone walls. One raised his nose to the sky and turned in their direction for a second, and then turned away.

Alex stiffened next to her. "They can smell us."

"No, they can't," Avery reassured him. "We cloaked sight, smell, and sound. And we're downwind. He can smell something, but it's not us."

The men walked to the very middle of the circle and huddled together, talking. Alex pulled her arm. "Let's get closer, then."

They edged away from the stone wall and trod silently across the grass, stopping when they were a few meters away. The wind carried the gruff male voices to them, and for a moment, Avery struggled to understand what they were saying. Their accents were so strong, but as she got used to the cadence of their tones, she started to understand the conversation.

"Alice will be sure they arrive last," an older man said. "She doesn't want him to get sympathy from the others."

"And Holly?" A younger man spoke, but he was bearded and had a wool hat on so Avery couldn't see his face.

"She'll be here. She needs to understand this is the way of the pack."

The younger one laughed unpleasantly. "She should know that already. That's why she ran."

"She won't run tonight. Alice will see that Cooper wins, and that Holly promises herself to him."

"What has Alice arranged?"

"Some potion or another." The older man shrugged. "Nothing too obvious, but it will give him the edge. Hunter injured him badly the other night, though he's kept it quiet. But he has to act now. Others are restless. Hunter has been busy on the phone, seeking support, and he's getting it."

Ha! Vindicated. Avery turned to Alex with a sly smile.

More voices broke the silence, and they retreated quickly, watching as others arrived in groups of twos and threes. They all gathered in the centre of the stone circle, until eventually—over the next ten minutes, Avery estimated—there were about 30 Shifters present, and other than three or four women, including Piper, they were all men.

The clear, ringing tones of a bell sounded from beyond the stone circle, and a tall man led a group into the middle. It must be Cooper. He carried himself with arrogance and command, and everyone turned to him as he arrived. The change in the energy was interesting. Avery sensed both excitement and dread.

Behind Cooper, Hunter and Holly were escorted between Alice and Jeremy, and behind them were another woman and three men all carrying long poles. The woman bore a distinct resemblance to Alice, and Avery guessed it must be Rose, her daughter, the one who'd been helping Cooper to heal.

As soon as everyone was present, Cooper turned to Alice. "Please seal the circle."

Immediately, Alex and Avery realised what was happening. They were watching from the walls at the edge of the field again, and if she sealed it before they reached the stone circle, they would be locked out and unable to help in any way.

Alice acted quickly, drawing her Athame out, and went to the ceremonial entrance, where she started to walk around the back of the standing stones, chanting the spell to consecrate the ground.

Alex and Avery raced to the far side of the stones, stepping inside far enough to remain away from the Shifters, but also well enough inside that Alice wouldn't stumble over them. *Thank the gods Castlerigg was big.*

Alice passed them by, her expression calm with a hint of triumph, as if she had already won.

Within another minute the circle was complete, and with the sound of wind through grass, a veil fell on the outside world. Josh looked around nervously, as did Piper, clearly worrying about whether Avery or Alex had made it, but there was no way to reassure them right now.

The three men who had entered last walked around the perimeter, placing out the torches they had brought with them. Once they were all in place, Alice lit them with a clap of her hands, and they flared into flames. Everyone's features came into focus, revealing expressions of worry, confusion, or excitement. Avery's unease heightened. She felt she had stepped into some kind of primeval gladiatorial arena.

Cooper spoke, his deep voice carrying in the clear night air. "Welcome. Tonight we finish what began two weeks ago, before Hunter was dragged from our midst before the fight was complete."

A rumble of laughter came from a few members, but not many. Most just watched Cooper with stony gazes.

He continued, "The rules remain. Hunter must defeat me to become the new Alpha. I will not yield. I want to make it clear to everyone that he has to kill me to do so. I, however, will not demand death." He turned to Hunter, his eyes cold. "You only have to yield to *me* and promise fealty."

Hunter was bristling with anger and determination, and he didn't flinch as he looked at Cooper. Avery wouldn't have imagined he was recently so grievously hurt had she not seen it herself. He looked fit and eager to fight. "And if I don't yield?"

"Then it will be a fight to the death," Cooper said, smiling unpleasantly.

Josh stepped forward from where he had been hidden within the circle of his friends, Piper behind him. "I would like to speak to my brother before the fight."

Cooper looked at him, surprised, as did Alice and the other witches. "I was not sure you would return after running away," Cooper sneered.

"And miss watching my brother win?" Josh said, baiting him. "No chance. Now, I believe I can speak to Hunter."

Hunter's hands had been tied up until now; Cooper leaned forward, pulled a large knife from a sheath on his belt, and cut the ropes. "You have two minutes to talk some sense into him. And don't think you'll be able to pull the same stunt as last time."

While the rest of the pack formed a circle around what Avery presumed would be where they fought, Josh and Piper took Cooper and Holly aside.

Alex pulled Avery up on one of the smaller standing stones that formed the inner square, well away from the edge of the circle, allowing them a view of the fight. Alice and Jeremy looked around Castlerigg with narrowed eyes. They might suspect they were there, but they didn't know for sure, and there was nothing they could do now.

Within minutes, the mutter of conversation fell silent, and Hunter and Cooper stepped into the makeshift fighting ring, both wearing only jeans. Their feet and chests were bare, and the flickering light revealed that both had livid red scars. After formal bows from each, the fight began.

It was bloody and brutal, a mixture of punching, kicking, and martial arts. The pair were evenly matched. They traded blow for blow, and several times it looked as if Hunter had the upper hand, with Cooper stumbling back over uneven ground. But he always got back up again.

By now both were bloody, lips were split, and one of Hunter's long scars, barely healed, had already opened up and was bleeding again. The smell of blood was thick in the air, and Avery noticed that several Shifters had taken on distinctly wolfish features, their eyes ringed with yellow fire.

Avery grimaced as Hunter sustained his biggest beating yet, and as he fell to the floor, Cooper kicked him in the ribs before he could roll away.

"Submit?" Cooper asked with an evil grin.

"Never," Hunter grunted before launching at Cooper again.

Avery whispered to Alex, "Why doesn't he submit now?"

"Because he's trying to wear Cooper out. If he takes him right to the edge before submitting, he'll struggle more in the second challenge."

Avery nodded and looked away. This was horrible and brutal.

The fight went on and Avery could hear grunts, thumps, and brutal cries, and then a gasp from the Shifters as a crack resounded.

Avery reluctantly looked, and saw Hunter lying on the ground, more blood than man, holding his left arm.

"Yield?" Cooper asked, triumphantly standing over him, and also dripping with blood.

It was clear that Hunter could not continue to fight.

Hunter nodded, pain visible in every movement, and someone ran forward, helping him to his feet to hobble away.

Cooper surveyed the crowd. "Is anyone foolish enough to challenge again?"

Despite being bloodied and bruised, with a thick lip and cuts to his face and the rest of his body, Cooper looked like he could keep going, and the crowd fell silent long enough for Cooper to grin as if he'd won. But then Evan stepped forward.

"I challenge. Same terms, same conditions—which means that if I win, you relinquish your claim on Holly."

The light in Cooper's eyes dimmed for a moment. He risked a glance at Holly's mutinous face, and then he nodded. "It seems like some people don't know when they're beat."

"And it seems you don't know when you've been rejected," Evan shot back, fists clenched at his side and a snarl starting in the back of his throat. "Why don't you act like a gentleman for once in your miserable life and revoke your claim on her?"

"I'll revoke my claim when she has the nerve to reject me." He looked at her once more, but she remained silent, and once again he looked triumphantly at Evan and the other Shifters. "Anyone hear a rejection, then? No, I thought not. Now, let's get this over with."

Cooper wiped the blood from his face with the back of his hand and stepped back, inviting Evan in. And then the next fight began.

Evan was shorter than Cooper and Hunter, and his fighting style was different. He was wiry and fast, and managed to get a few quick punches and throws in. But Cooper drew on an inner strength, and soon had the upper hand. But he was tiring, that was obvious. He took a second longer to recover after blows, and a second longer to stand, and his wounds opened up even further.

Avery watched for only a short while before turning aside. "How can you stand to watch?" she whispered to Alex.

"Because one of us has to. I'm making sure the Devices aren't using anything, and so far, so good. Just the potion."

But Evan didn't push his luck too long. He made sure he was bloodied and bruising too, and that Cooper was breathless, lasting just long enough to look convincing before he yielded.

Cooper's victory stance was more unsteady this time, but he threw his head back as he snarled out, "Anyone else?"

Cooper's supporters were moving through the crowd, and heads were dropping. It was clear some were intimidated, despite Cooper's weakness, and were genuinely terrified of him. Others, however, had clearly had enough, and some of the older Shifters who were too old to challenge successfully looked around with an anticipation that wasn't lost on Cooper or the witches.

"Do you think my time has come?" Cooper asked defiantly. "Because I don't think anyone else has the nerve."

Ollie stepped forward. "I do."

Cooper narrowed his eyes at him, and then at the half a dozen Shifters gathered behind him, and he looked wary.

"Taken leave of your senses, Oliver?"

"Come to them, more like," he answered as he peeled off his shirt to reveal a muscled physique covered in tattoos.

Alice stepped forward. "Cooper should have a break first."

"No, he shouldn't," Ollie said, glaring at her. "These are the terms of challenge, Alice. You know that. Don't interfere."

Avery felt her magic start to manifest as Alice prepared to retaliate, as did Alex next to her, but Jeremy laid a hand on her arm.

"We will not interfere," he agreed, and shot Alice a warning glance as he pulled her back to the edge of the watching crowd.

At this point, Avery expected Tommy to step forward, too, to warn him that he would challenge next, just as they had planned, and offer Cooper a chance to release Holly now, but that didn't happen. They were going to push him to the brink.

By now the atmosphere in the crowd had shifted, and it was clear that whatever the outcome many had thought there would be tonight, it actually might prove to be very different. It was as if a thrill of electricity ran through everyone, and the energy in the circle spiked in anticipation.

One of Cooper's supporters rounded on Ollie, and Avery recognized him as being one of the two men who had arrived first. "Ollie, you don't want to do this. We'll all have much to lose if you win—yourself included."

The threat was clear, and if some had forgotten Cooper's influence in the excitement of the challenge, they all remembered now.

Ollie smiled slowly. "It's threats like that, Garret, which remind me why change is good." He rolled his shoulders, and started to turn away.

"If you win, I will challenge *you*." Garret's voice was low and threatening, and once again the mood changed.

Ollie grinned and his eyes lit up. "Is that so?"

At which point, Tommy shouted, "And if you win, I'll challenge *you*, Garret, you little prick. And I promise to break your scrawny little neck, and then I'll take on the next." He swung around to face Cooper and pointed. "I'd love for that to be you, but anyone will do."

Cooper snarled, and the pack dissolved into shouts as small fights began to break out.

Alex looked at Avery. "I think our plans have gone awry."

Alice shook free of Jeremy and raised her hands as if to use magic, but someone shouted, "Beware the witch!" She turned abruptly as a dark shape launched from the crowd and took her down, landing on her chest and snarling in her face.

Alice lay frozen, understanding dawning that everything hung in the balance of this moment, and Cooper looked panic-stricken as he realised he was losing control.

A shout broke through the air. It was Holly. "Enough!" She threw back her head and howled, and every hair on Avery's body stood on end.

Silence fell, thick and heavy, as all eyes turned to her. "If you want to remain Alpha, you release me right now, Cooper Dacre, from all commitments, with no repercussions for anyone who has helped us. I reject you, and I expect you to comply."

He glared at her, snarled, and then despite everything he had to lose, leapt at her. But before he could get near her Ollie charged, tackling him to the ground, and all hell broke loose.

Avery and Alex leapt down, fighting their way to the witches, who were now casting spells in any way they could to aid the fight. Alice had thrown the wolf off her chest and was back to back with Rose and Jeremy.

Despite the torches flickering within the standing stones, the light was low, and long black shadows stretched across the ground. Alex and Avery cast their shadow spell aside, deciding it was too hard to maintain, and went head to head with the Devices.

Alice shrieked. "You! How dare you interfere with this?" She sent a fireball at Avery that she caught and threw back, and then threw flashes of bright white energy in rapid succession, knocking Alice off her feet. She heard a snarl as a wolf leapt at her throat, and she pulled the sword free of its scabbard. Flames licked along its length as she slashed at the wolf, sending it rolling past her.

Alex was fighting his own battle with Rose and then Jeremy, as both ganged up on him.

Josh came running to her aid. "She's with me!" he yelled, as an unknown Shifter turned to her, fists raised.

And then there was another howl, this time guttural and vicious.

Most fighting came to a halt as Ollie triumphantly lifted Cooper's head—and only his head—above the watching pack. A gasp rippled around the crowd, and Alice visibly paled.

"Does anyone want to challenge me?" Ollie roared.

A small spat broke out as Garret, Cooper's clear second in command, struggled to rise from the ground. Tommy was sitting astride him. "You move one more muscle, and I will end you now."

"Screw you!" he shouted in Tommy's face, and without hesitation, Tommy ripped his throat out with his bare hands, and Garret fell back, dead.

"Anyone else?" Ollie yelled again.

The silence was deafening.

"Are you accepting me as your Alpha?" he shouted as the crowd drew back, revealing him to be covered in blood and gore and standing above Cooper's now headless body.

Josh answered first. "I do. If you agree to run the pack *without* the Devices."

Ollie looked at the others and shouted, "Is this what you all want?"

The muted rumblings of "yes" became louder and louder as the Shifters realised the position of power they were in, and then the cries of agreement were deafening.

Ollie nodded and turned to Alice and her children. "From this moment, you no longer have any affiliation with us. I demand your word that you will agree to this."

Alice stuttered, "But we have been loyal to this pack for generations!"

"You have been loyal to the Dacres. They are gone now. Do you agree? If you do not, you will not leave Castlerigg alive, regardless of your magic."

Jeremy and Rose looked to their mother, and Alice nodded, knowing they were defeated.

"Swear it," Ollie demanded. "No repercussions. I will allow you to remain in Cumbria, but our business is separate."

Alice's eyes were hard, but she nodded reluctantly, and Jeremy and Rose nodded as well. "I agree. No repercussions."

"Then swear it on a blood oath," Ollie demanded.

Alice's voice was harsh. "We need to do no such thing."

"Yes, we do."

Ollie held his hand out, and Avery passed him El's sword, the flame now quenched. He ran the blade along his palm, and blood dripped onto the grass. He passed the sword to Tommy, who now stood next to him, and then to Hunter, who stood supported by Piper and Josh. Each cut their palms, and then passed the knife to Alice.

All swore the oath, palm to palm, repeating, "From this day forth, all Devices, from generation to generation, swear that they will leave the Cumbria Pack to manage their own affairs. The pack in return swears not to interfere with the Devices. To break the oath invites death."

Once it was done, Ollie roared to the Shifters, "You are witness?"

"We are witness," they agreed as one.

"And now we must also swear an oath, Alice," Avery said, determined to protect herself, Alex, and the others. She didn't trust Alice at all. "We promise not to interfere with your business here, and you promise not to pursue us in White Haven." Alice narrowed her eyes as if she was about to complain, but Avery pressed on. "You broke Sanctuary. I demand your oath."

Jeremy and Rose shuffled in discomfort, but Alice held her gaze. "A blood oath?"

"A witch-binding oath," Avery answered.

Alex reached into his backpack and brought out the spell's ingredients. Watched by the Shifters, all five witches repeated the spell Alex and Avery had prepared, and while saying it, Alex wrapped the long piece of ivy around their wrists, binding all of them together. As the spell finished, the ivy ignited and then turned to ash, leaving a sooty mark.

Alex smiled, but it didn't reach his eyes. "It is done." He turned to Ollie and Hunter. "You are witness?"

"We are witness," they agreed.

Ollie addressed Alice, his eyes alight with victory. "Leave now, Alice. Dissolve the circle and be gone."

He didn't speak again until Alice lowered the protection spell, and the normal night noises flooded into Castlerigg as the witches walked across the fields and left.

One of the other Shifters looked at Alex and Avery, and then back to Ollie. "Care to explain who these are?"

A ripple of curiosity and fear ran around the crowd, and Avery wondered if they were going to have to fight their way out. Over half the pack had changed into wolves, and as she looked around, she realized some of the wolves were grievously injured. Cooper's supporters, she hoped.

It was Josh who answered as he stood next to them. "They gave Sanctuary while we recovered. Alice defied it, taking Hunter and Holly hostage for Cooper. They came here to see that Alice did not interfere in tonight's meet."

The Shifter nodded. "Fair enough. But it's time for you to leave now. We have much to discuss."

Alex and Avery nodded their agreement, and Avery said softly to Josh, "See you later."

He smiled a silent thanks as they headed to the road. Alex shook his head in disbelief. "So much for us needing to do a binding spell for them."

She laughed. "I prefer their version, although it was hideously bloody. I knew they'd be stronger than the average man, but to rip someone's head off…" She shuddered at the memory of Cooper's bloody head.

"I like this Ollie guy. He'll make a good Alpha!"

Avery stroked his cheek and smiled. "Let's head back to Evan's place and await their return. If I remember correctly, there's a bottle of whiskey and a fire to keep us company."

***

It was at least another hour or two before the others returned, and Alex and Avery were dozing on the sofa, full of the comfort of whiskey when they heard the key turn in the lock and the others come in.

Evan led the way, a bounce to his step, and he grinned to see Alex and Avery in front of the roaring fire. Hunter was walking behind him with a limp, leaning heavily on Piper. He was bleeding from at least half a dozen cuts. His right eye was swelling, and he held his left arm carefully.

Josh and Holly followed, and Josh wasn't looking much better than Hunter. Holly, however, was grinning like the Cheshire Cat.

Alex and Avery scooted out of the way to allow Hunter to sit. He gave them a weak smile. "Do you think Briar will fix me again?"

"I think she'll give you an earful of abuse," Avery said, bending to look at his many wounds. "But yes, she'll fix you. As long as you promise no more fighting, at least in the near future."

He winked, leaned back, and closed his eyes.

Holly hugged Avery. "Thank you for helping, both of you."

Alex shrugged. "We really didn't do much in the end. Looks like Ollie had a better plan."

Evan topped their drinks off as he said, "It was a very last-minute change of plan when we realised we could actually win if we kept pushing."

"What happens now?" Alex asked, sitting and pulling Avery onto his lap to make more room for everyone else.

"Ollie has plans," Josh said, sitting with relief. "I didn't realise he wanted to be Alpha."

"I don't think HE did until seconds before it happened," Piper said. "At least now we can stay here."

"Not right away," Hunter grunted as he opened half an eye. "I'm heading back to White Haven to heal, and you're coming with me."

Piper looked outraged and appeared as if she might complain, and then she thought better of it. "All right."

"What about you two?" Avery asked Josh and Holly.

"We'll head back to our house," Holly said, smiling. "Resurrect our business! Do you think the Devices will retaliate?"

"No. Not after a blood oath," Alex said with certainty.

Avery added, "Not unless they're insane. There'd be huge repercussions, and they know it." She frowned, remembering the deaths of Cooper and Garret. "Er, what are you going to do with Cooper and Garret's bodies?"

"Their bodies have been dragged a long way away and hidden. They'll be found eventually, but not before the local wildlife has picked over their bones."

Avery paled as she realised that probably, hopefully, no one would know what had really happened. *What was she thinking? She was becoming a monster.*

"Great," she said weakly.

"So now you just have your rogue witch to worry about," Holly said, as if hiding bodies was an everyday sort of thing. She cradled a drink as she huddled in front of the fire, and every now and again she cast shy glances up at Evan.

"Yes, we do." Avery said thoughtfully. "And it won't be easy."

"But we'll help if we can," Hunter said earnestly. "We owe you."

19

Everyone arrived back in White Haven late on Friday night after what seemed to Avery like the longest car journey ever.

They'd had a few hours of sleep at Hunter's house in Chapel Stile before they headed out in the late morning, each of them taking a turn at driving. Avery had phoned Reuben to let the others know when to expect them, and they'd dropped Hunter and Piper off at their rental house, promising to visit the next morning with Briar. Whatever injuries needed fixing would have to wait, and once again, Hunter had refused to go to the hospital.

By the time they arrived at Reuben's house, Avery was exhausted. Fortunately, the aroma of food hit her, and they walked through to the back of the house to find all three witches and Newton in the snug, snacking on chips, drinking beer, and keeping half an eye on the TV, which flickered quietly on the wall. For the most part, they were surrounded with spell books, history books, and Avery recognised some of Anne's papers. They looked up and grinned as the weary travellers entered, and Avery's cats emerged from their hiding spots around the room, meowing loudly and rubbing her ankles.

"Circe and Medea," she exclaimed, reaching down to give them a big fuss. "I've missed you."

"You're back!" Briar said, leaping up. "Sit down, you look dead on your feet. I'll bring through some food."

Avery looked at her gratefully. "You don't have to," she said, trying to protest, but Briar shushed her away.

"It's pizza, won't take two minutes."

"Had a fun two days, then?" Reuben said sardonically.

"Yes," Alex said dryly, as he dropped into a large, squashy armchair. "Mutiny in Shifter packs, wolf fights, interfering Devices, and lots of blood. Loved it!"

Newton held his hands over his ears in mock protest. "I don't want to hear if anything serious happened."

"Like decapitations?" Alex asked, sipping his beer.

Newton glared. "I'm bloody serious! I'm a policeman!"

"Cornwall's finest *paranormal* policeman, too!" Reuben added with a smirk.

El laughed. "Leave him alone!"

Newton scowled. "Piss off, all of you."

Briar came in with two plates loaded with food and passed one each to Avery and Alex. She looked at Newton's grumpy face and grinned. "Oh no, I think we're baiting Newton again."

"If it's any help," Avery said before she took a bite, "the two affected Shifters were pretty vile people."

Newton held a hand up. "Stop right there."

Briar sat on the rug in front of the fire. "Are you talking about Hunter? Is he okay?"

Alex nodded. "Beaten to a bloody pulp once more, but he's okay. He's back here and wants your help to heal again." He raised a quizzical eyebrow at her. "Interested?"

Briar flushed. "Of course I'll help. But he better stop fighting. I'm not a miracle worker."

"Are you any good at healing broken bones?"

"Are you kidding?" She looked horrified. "Not particularly, but I suppose I'd better learn."

"Good." Alex pushed his plate away with a satisfied look. "Because there's no way he's going to a hospital." He filled the others in on their trip and the outcome of the fight. "And now that they're back, Hunter wants to help us—well, once he's healed."

"So, how are things here?" Avery asked. "How are you, El? You look better than when we left."

She smiled. "I am, thanks. The curse left me pretty weak for a while, and it really knocked my mood. I couldn't shake off this horrible feeling of oppression and sadness, but it's going. I went into work today, which gave me something to focus on."

"No attacks on anybody else?" Alex asked.

El shook her head. "No, and the protection spell on this house is working well."

"Any updates on Old Haven?"

"Bloody Halloween horror hunters are flooding up there," Newton grumbled. "Gabe has his work cut out."

"Really?" Avery said, astonished. "I didn't think that many people would actually bother to go."

Reuben threw his head back and laughed. "It's the latest attraction! Stan's really excited. Thinks it will be the best celebration we've had yet." He was referring to their resident occasional Druid. "He's contemplating moving the bonfire."

Avery gasped. "Please tell me you're joking."

"No. But James has put his foot down, and so has Gabe, who, as you can imagine, is very firm when he wants to be."

"Thank the gods," Avery said, relieved. "That could have really complicated things."

"But there's a change up there," El said. "The witch has cast another spell around the area again. It's a sort of revulsion spell, makes your skin crawl just to get close. It's very effective—we couldn't make a dent in it. But the good thing is, it's putting off our Halloween hunters."

Alex frowned. "She got past Gabe and the other Nephilim?"

"She can do witch flight, remember?" Avery pointed out.

Reuben nodded. "I went up there today. The whole place is bristling with power, and it's still building."

"Less than a week to go until Samhain," Avery said thoughtfully. "Have you found any new information?"

"Yes, we have," Reuben said, pleased with himself. "Have you heard of Ley Lines?"

"Sure. They're hidden lines of supernatural energy that connect across the Earth, and where they cross, their power is amplified."

"Exactly." Reuben gestured at the papers around him. "And on them we find ancient places of power, such as stone circles, cairns, mounds, dolmens, henges, hill forts, long barrows."

Newton scoffed. "Sounds like hocus pocus to me."

Briar just looked at him. "After all you've seen, you'd dismiss this?"

"Well, hidden lines of power. Sounds loopy."

Her gaze hardened. "And yet you've seen us wield magic. Seen Shifters, Nephilim, Mermaids… Why wouldn't these lines exist? Just because you can't see them!"

Newton looked away, slightly chastened.

"Anyway," Reuben continued, "Cornwall has a Ley Line running directly through it, right from Glastonbury and Stonehenge to St Michaels Mount. And a small line runs off it to Old Haven."

Alex and Avery looked at each other and back to Reuben. "Really?"

"Really. And in this book," he gestured to an old history book on Druids at his feet, "are listed places where Druids were known to be more prevalent. This area is one of them. Druids liked their groves of trees. They were natural places of worship and magic. Old Haven is one of them. Or rather, the grove of trees with the yew tree at its centre is one of them."

"What better place," Briar said, "to build a church than in one of the old pagan places of worship?"

El smiled. "The usual tale. We all know it. Buy good will off the pagan community who follow the old gods by co-opting their place of worship."

"And their celebration dates on the calendar," Alex added.

Avery frowned. "Isn't there another name for Ley Lines? Spirit ways or death lines?"

"Death roads," Reuben corrected her. "The roads that the dead were carried along. People were very specific about how they were walked and how you would carry your dead. And they're also called Faery paths—you have to respect them, or bad things happen." He rummaged through the books around him, pulled one free, and passed her a page with a map on it.

The map showed Britain with lines running across it, many intersecting. On these lines, and particularly where they crossed, were places of historical and supernatural significance. Stonehenge, Glastonbury, Anglesey, and the Lake District in particular were places where many of these lines intersected, as if they were hot spots of power.

"Strange," Avery mused. "We spent last night at Castlerigg Stone Circle in the Lakes. It was ancient and powerful. It's the Shifters spiritual home—I think that's what Piper called it."

"I would say it's had a lot of blood spilt there over the years," Alex mused. He'd moved behind Avery so he could see the map.

Reuben continued. "Anglesey, as you can see, is another hot spot, and well known for its Druid worship. It was supposedly covered in trees at one point, but the Romans cut them down as they executed the Druids and destroyed their religion. It's another place that is believed to be have been a source for Avalon—the island out of the King Arthur tales. Its ancient name was Ynys Mon."

Newton had been listening silently to all of this new information. "Were there Druids in Cornwall?"

"Yep. Where do think Stan gets his ideas from? Cornwall was a Celtic nation once, and Celts and Druids go hand in hand."

"Wow." Avery leaned back, deep in thought. "So the grove at Old Haven is on a Ley Line, and was a Druid centre of power?"

El ran her hands through her white blonde hair, ruffling it thoughtfully. "Looks like it. And maybe a gateway to the Fey."

"Hold on a minute," Newton said, looking confused. "Fey? As in Faeries? You're talking like these really exist!"

"We keep talking about gateways for a reason, Newton," Briar explained patiently, as if she was talking to a child. "Faeries live in another reality—supposedly—one that runs parallel to our own, but used to be accessible years ago, when the paths between worlds were thinner. The Druids and Fey exchanged knowledge."

"Druids and Fey have always been linked," Reuben added. "Druids worshipped trees and nature, and were connected spiritually to the Earth, just like the Fey. There's nothing more magical than the Faeries and their mounds, where the myths suggest they live beneath the visible world."

"Heard of Merlin?" El asked Newton.

"Of course I bloody have. I'm not an imbecile."

"Merlin was a Druid, and all of the King Arthur tales were linked with the Fey. Arthur's half-sister, the dreaded Morgan Le Fay, was half-Fey and a witch—hence the name."

Reuben continued to explain, "The yew, remember, also represents—" He held his fingers up one at a time. "Death, rebirth, a guardian to other worlds, a symbol of the Triple Goddess, and is linked to Samhain, the time of the year when the veils between worlds are at their thinnest. That's a pretty powerful combination."

Briar shivered and wrapped her arms around herself. "Well, now we know why she picked that place."

Alex exhaled heavily. "Well, we guessed it must be something of the sort, but it's good to have some tangible evidence. But this doesn't really tell us why."

"And we still don't know how to stop it or close it," El pointed out.

"Or how bloody big it might get!" Newton said. "What if this thing blows up and takes over most of White Haven?"

"It's not a bomb, Newton." Briar looked at him, exasperated.

"How do you know that?" he said angrily. "It's a big hot spot of concentrated energy up there, and it's building by the day. And what's going to come out of it?"

"We have to find out who she is," Alex said, looking around at them all. "I know it seems impossible, but it might help."

"I don't give a crap who she is," Newton answered, popping the cap on another bottle of beer. "I just want you to stop her. The last time a doorway opened, we ended up with the Nephilim. I don't want some raging Goblin King like David Bowie coming out of it next."

The room erupted in laughter, and even Newton sniggered. "Well, you never know."

20

After the best night's sleep she'd had in a long time, Avery headed to Happenstance Books, looking forward to catching up on work gossip.

Saturdays were always busy, and she was hoping for a welcome distraction from Old Haven. In the end she hadn't gone to see Hunter. Briar was happy to go on her own, and Avery wondered if she liked Hunter more than she was letting on. It was hard to know with Briar; she liked to keep things to herself. She did notice, however, that Newton was very grumpy about Hunter being back, which she thought was pretty funny. Maybe he'd changed his mind about pursuing a relationship with a witch.

The shop was still closed when Avery arrived, but she found Dan and Sally in the backroom, starting on their first coffee of the day. Sally ran over and hugged her.

"So glad you're back! I've been worried sick," she said, looking at her carefully for signs of injury.

"Things were weird, but I'm fine, and the Devices are neutralised, for now," Avery said, trying to reassure her. "How have things been here? Did the story time go okay?"

Dan preened himself. "Brilliantly. The kids loved it, and there's another session this afternoon. Sold oodles of books, too, you'll be pleased to know."

"And were the costumes a success?"

"Of course! Looking forward to seeing yours, Avery." He grinned as he passed her a coffee.

"Can't wait, either," she grumbled into her drink.

"Excellent, I'm going to get changed." He grabbed his costume off the back of the chair and headed for the staff bathroom.

"I'm so relieved things have been okay," Avery said, sinking into a chair. "I was worried something might happen."

"All good so far. Just Stan and his niece waxing lyrical about our shop and costumes. The local press is visiting at some point today."

Avery groaned. "You're kidding."

"No. It's good for the town, promotes tourism, and very good for the shop, too," she pointed out. "They're visiting a few places. The Witch Museum is first on the list, I think."

"I suppose you're right," Avery answered.

Sally looked nervous. "Oh, and before I forget, I need to warn you that Stan's niece, Rebecca, is coming back today. She loves this place, loves everything about it, especially the tarot cards, and Dan accidentally let it slip that you read them."

"He did *what*?"

"Nothing witchy mentioned," she said, trying to reassure Avery. "Just tarot. So she's coming back for a reading. We said she'd have to ask nicely."

Avery groaned and stood up. "I suppose I could do one." She headed to the door of the shop with her coffee. "In the meantime, I'm going to try to cheer myself up by spelling us up a little Halloween magic."

"And then your costume!" Sally wagged a finger at her at her retreating back.

Avery smiled with pleasure as she spelled the lights on in the shop. The place really did look magical, and that was all Sally's doing. Halloween-themed strings of lights were festooned over the shelves and walls, and pumpkins, grinning skeletons, witches, and ghouls were propped everywhere. The reading corner looked especially good, with rugs and cushions spread over the floor.

Avery reinvigorated her special spell that helped her customers find the book they never knew they'd always wanted, and lit incense and fake candles as she progressed around the shop. She took a deep breath as she glanced around. Today was going to be a good day; she just had this feeling, despite the fact that she was going to have to dress up.

Her thoughts were disturbed by the arrival of Dan in a sweeping black cloak, black suit, and slicked black hair popularised by film Draculas. "Oh, nice! You look good in a suit, Dan. You should wear one more often."

He winked. "Thanks. And the cloak?" He picked up one side and held it dramatically over the lower half of his face.

"No. Not the cloak."

"I'm crushed. Now, off you go to get changed." He shooed her out and she headed back to the kitchen to see Sally emerging from the bathroom in a long, empire line gown with the beginnings of zombie make-up on her face.

"That's not a zombie costume!" Avery said, looking with bewilderment at her dress.

"Er, yes it is! *Pride and Prejudice and Zombies*! Come on, Avery. Know your popular culture, please. This is a book shop, and *Pride and Prejudice* is a national classic."

"Ah! Very good. I stand corrected. Give me five minutes to join the fun."

Avery's costume was where she'd left it on the bed in her flat, and she changed quickly, laughing at herself in the mirror. Despite her misgivings, it looked good, and as she strode through the attic swishing her long skirt, Helena appeared in front of her, a wry smile on her face.

Avery smiled and twirled. "Morning, Helena. Like it?"

Helena reached out, and Avery felt Helena's cool hand stoke her cheek.

Holy crap, what was that? And was Helena being affectionate?

She stepped back. "You shouldn't be able to do that!"

Helena shrugged and smiled mischievously.

"Is this a Samhain thing?"

Helena shrugged again.

"Any other surprises?" Avery asked warily.

Helena merely smirked and disappeared.

With chills running down her spine, Avery picked up the large, pointed witch's hat with a broad brim and headed back downstairs and into the shop, stopping to grab an ornate fake wand from a display shelf. Witches didn't really need to use a wand, she never had, but popular convention liked them, so she decided to add one to her costume. If she was going to do this, she may as well commit to it.

Dan howled with laughter when he saw her. "I love it!"

Avery pulled the hat on and posed. "Do I look the part?"

"And then some!"

"Where's Sally?"

"I'm here!" she yelled from behind a large bookshelf. She emerged, fully made up as a zombie, fake blood artfully placed on her face and arms.

Avery laughed as she unlocked the front door. "*What we must look like!* Come on, let's get this show on the road!"

The customers started arriving early, and kept coming in a steady stream all morning, lingering a long time. Sally had placed bowls of Halloween sweets around the shop and on the counter, and these encouraged loitering and chat, so that when the press arrived, Avery was shocked to find it was already late morning.

Stan beamed as he shepherded them in, greeting them all with hearty hellos. Avery was surprised to see the blonde news reporter who'd been at Old Haven. She was accompanied by a middle-aged man who carried camera gear, and a young girl bringing in lighting equipment. Avery struggled to remember the reporter's name, but she introduced herself anyway as she extended her hand. "Sarah Rutherford. So pleased to meet our resident witch!"

Avery stuttered, "What?"

"Your costume! You look fantastic!" She turned on a wave of perfume. "And Dracula and a Zombie Miss Bennett! Perfect!" She gestured towards her cameraman. "This is Steve." He waved a silent hello, pre-occupied with setting up the camera and scanning the room.

A young voice said breathlessly, "I'm Becky, and I'm so excited to meet you!"

Avery turned in alarm to see the girl who'd arrived with them at her elbow, gazing up at her in admiration.

"Hi!" Avery said, slightly bewildered at this young, breathy creature who looked so excited.

Stan swooped in. "My niece, Becky. She's been dying to meet you after hearing about your skills with the tarot. And she just loves your shop, don't you, Becky?"

"I do! And I love your costume, too!"

Faced with this enthusiastic teen who could barely be older than 14, Avery blinked and tried to be polite. "That's lovely, thank you." She reached for a bowl of sweets. "Would you like an eyeball?"

"Yum!" she said, reaching in and grabbing a couple. "I love these." She lowered her voice and pulled Avery aside while the news team decided where and what to shoot. "Dan said you might be willing to read the tarot for me later. Would you, *please?*"

Avery hesitated for a second, having rehearsed all morning ways to say no, but found in the face of such pleading it was impossible. "Of course. We'll go into the back room after the news team has finished. But I'm not that good, really," she said, lying horribly. "I wouldn't get too excited."

But it was as if she hadn't spoken. "I can't wait. Dan said you're the best."

"He's being polite because I employ him." She looked up and caught his amused glance with a glare that said, *I will kill you.* She turned back to Becky. "You know, lots of people do tarot reading around White Haven. You could try some of them if you like."

"But none of their shops are as cool as this. I'd like to buy my own cards too."

Avery smiled. "You should never buy your own cards. They should be given as a gift."

Her face fell. "Oh, why?"

Avery lowered her voice. "It's the rules of magic. They work better that way."

Becky widened her eyes with surprise, but Avery turned away, caught by the commotion by the till.

"So," Sarah was saying, "who's best to interview?"

"Sally!" Avery said, heading over. "She's my shop manager, and is the one responsible for all of these amazing decorations. Without her this wouldn't be anywhere near as good."

Sally looked surprised but actually quite pleased, and Avery smiled. She deserved it. And besides, she didn't want to be interviewed at all.

Sarah seemed happy. "Excellent. I've never interviewed a zombie Miss Bennett before."

Avery hated to tell her Miss Elizabeth Bennett was never a zombie, she was a zombie hunter, but decided to let it go and kept out of the way while the news team did their shoot. They didn't take long, and Sally was a natural.

While the cameraman set off around the shop to take some more footage, Sarah warned them that only a snippet might make it onto the news. "We've got a few other places to visit, so we'll see how much time they give us. It will all probably be edited down to a few minutes at the most. But all this activity at the church has created a lot of interest in Halloween and White Haven. The story might even go national!"

"Really?" While Avery thought that sounded horrible, Sarah looked pleased at the thought.

"Yes. It will be great for me, and you'll get more tourists. Good all around, don't you think?"

"So, you think everything happening at Old Haven is a hoax?" Avery asked, feigning ignorance. "You were the reporter up there the other day, weren't you? I think I saw you on TV."

For a moment, Sarah looked worried. "It was odd, if I'm honest. The vicar just flew off those ladders, and the camera was already playing up. It gave me a hell of a shock, too." And then she laughed. "But of course it was a hoax! A good one, I admit, and we couldn't work out how they'd done it, but—well, what else could it be?"

Stan had been listening with interest and he joined in. "White Haven is well known for its old religions and witch history. Someone's just decided to take it a step further." He turned to Sarah. "I agree with you, it just adds to the fun of Halloween in White Haven. Fortunately James is okay, so no real harm done."

"Well, Steve had a few burns, and our camera was destroyed, but the insurance will cover that," Sarah added brightly, as if Steve's burns didn't matter at all. "And of course the place is well protected now by that lovely Gabe and his team."

Avery nodded. "So I saw. Have you been back?"

"Not yet, but I'm hoping to go later this week, just to report on updates before Halloween, talk to some of the locals who are staking out the place, and interview Gabe. Anyway," she said as Steve returned. "We better get to the next place. Where's that, Stan?"

"Angels as Protectors," he said, mentioning one of the many new age shops closer to the quay.

"Okay. Lovely to meet you all," she said, heading for the door.

"Uncle Stan," Becky said quietly. "Can I stay here and I'll meet you later?"

"Sure thing," he said, patting her head like she was a dog. "See you at Cakes and Bakes in an hour."

As soon as he'd gone, Becky turned and looked expectantly at Avery, and Sally smiled.

"Come on, then," Avery said, leading the way to the back room. "Let' see what your future holds!"

Avery sat Becky down at the small table with a cup of tea and headed up to collect her own tarot cards from the attic. She'd been tempted to use a fresh pack, but the results wouldn't be as good, and she felt she owed it to the young girl to give her a proper reading since she was so excited.

By the time she returned, Becky was already looking at some of the tarot packs they kept as stock. Avery asked, "Is there a pack that speaks to you?"

Becky frowned. "What do you mean?"

"Well, usually as you look at or handle a set of cards, you might get a warm feeling, or a sense of familiarity with one. That's the one you should work with."

Becky was wide-eyed. "Really? I don't know! I need to check them again."

Avery smiled. "That's okay. We'll do the reading now and you can do that later." Avery lit a small white candle on the table and unwrapped her cards from the square of silk she kept them in. She fanned them out, blew on them gently to cleanse them, and then gathered them back together and knocked on the top of the pack. She handed them to Becky. "Now shuffle them for me."

Still wide-eyed, Becky did as instructed and when she'd finished, Avery split them into three piles and placed them on the table. "Choose a pile." Becky tapped one and Avery placed it on top of the pack and started to lay them out in the Celtic cross.

"This is so exciting," Becky said, watching her every movement.

"What do you want to know?"

"Anything. Will I travel, will I meet a handsome man? You know, stuff."

"A specific question sometimes works best," Avery advised her. "But that's okay, I can do a general reading today."

The first few cards seemed fairly straightforward, and Avery talked through them as she placed them. Avery saw a strong male influence, some chaos in her past, and Becky nodded. "My parents have split up. Uncle Stan has been really sweet. Will they get back together?"

"Your parents? I can't really see what will happen for them, this is about you," Avery said, smiling.

As Avery turned the cards, preferring to see all of them before she made predictions, a heavy feeling flooded into her, but she kept her face neutral. This was not a nice, light reading for a teen; it was edged with darkness. The Wheel of Fortune sat poised on her outcome at the top of the ladder, below it the reversed High Priestess, and beneath that the Queen of Swords, and below that the Moon. There was a powerful woman in this girl's life, and she did not mean well. But there was also a protector, Avery's own card, the Queen of Swords. As Avery concentrated on the cards she had a vision of blood, and she closed her eyes for a second, trying to see it more clearly, but it went as quickly as it arrived.

"What can you see?" Becky asked, watching her closely. "Is it bad?"

Avery looked up, schooling her face into calm neutrality. "No, of course it's not bad, but there's a strong woman in your life, see here, The High Priestess?"

"She's upside down."

"Yes, someone maybe who is a negative influence on your life. Is someone pressuring you at the moment?"

Becky looked alarmed. "No. No one. Maybe my teacher at school? She says I should concentrate more—stupid cow."

Avery shook her head. "No, that's not it. How's your relationship with your mother?"

"It's fine, I suppose," Becky said, shrugging. "She's left my dad, which is crap, but you know…"

Avery fell silent. It wasn't her mother, she just knew. She had an intuitive feeling for the cards. Why would Avery need to be her protector? She didn't even know Becky. A horrible thought kept returning.

"Have you met anyone recently? A new female friend?"

Becky shrugged. "There's Uncle Stan's new girlfriend. She's pretty cool, I guess. A bit weird sometimes—intense, you know? But he likes her."

"How long has he been seeing her, Becky?"

"Couple of months, I don't know." Her enthusiasm was wearing off. "What's this got to do with my reading?"

"Absolutely nothing," Avery said, lying through her teeth. "Let's get back to your reading. The cards say that you have been through some unsettled months, and you have some difficult decisions to make. These decisions are blocking a long-term reading, sort of clouding your future. I think in another month your reading will be much clearer."

"So it's a short-term reading, no plans for the future, a hot man, travel?"

"Not that they reveal yet." Avery could feel disappointment coming off her in waves. "The cards reveal what they want to. It's my job to interpret them. Sometimes that's tricky." *And dangerous. Becky might not even have a future.* "But you also have a powerful woman on your side. That's cool—someone mysterious. Call her a guardian angel. She's telling you to choose wisely and listen to your intuition. If something feels bad, then it is bad."

"A guardian angel is cool, I guess."

"Better than cool," Avery said, leaving the cards on the table for her to examine at her leisure later. She placed out the half dozen new packs of tarot cards on the table. "Now. Have another feel of these and see which one speaks to you. I will give you whichever you choose."

Becky immediately brightened up. "Wow. Will you? That's great." She returned to the cards and examined them all in silence for the next few minutes, closing her eyes as she concentrated.

Avery waited, quietly examining the spread. Could the High Priestess be their mysterious witch? If she was, she was close to Becky. Too close. What did she want with her? Why did she see blood?

Becky chose her pack, sliding it in front of Avery. "This one, please."

"The Aquarian Tarot Deck. Nice choice!" Avery took it from her, blessing it quickly, and then wrapped it in a bag. "Just spend some time getting to know them," she suggested as she headed back into the shop. "I'm sure you'll have lots of fun with them. By the way, Becky, I'm wondering if I've met Stan's girlfriend. What does she look like?"

She shrugged. "Oldish, like him—well, older than you anyway, and long, reddish hair. Darker than yours. Pretty tall, really."

"Does she live with him?"

"Nah. I don't know where she lives." She grinned at Avery suddenly, making her look even younger. "Thanks for the cards and stuff." And then Becky headed out of the door, leaving it swinging behind her.

By three that afternoon the children's area was full of excited kids and parents ready to hear another spooky Halloween tale. Sally had handed around fairy cakes with icing made to look like witches and grimacing pumpkins, and they had disappeared in minutes.

"What are you reading today?" Avery asked Dan, as he pulled a book from his bag.

"I thought I'd keep it local, by popular request. The kids want Cornish tales, so we've got a doozy. It's very Halloween!"

"Go on," Avery said, intrigued.

"I'm reading a story about the Devil's Dandy Dogs."

"The what? Doesn't sound that scary. What are Dandy Dogs?"

Dan grinned. "Avery. You should know this. It's what our Shifter friends do." He looked at her expectantly.

Avery looked at him blankly. "Change to wolves?"

"Hunt! It's the Cornish version of the Wild Hunt. You know, unearthly warriors summoned from the Underworld to come and claim more souls. It used to be seen as a way to cleanse a place—clear out the bad folk." He looked up dramatically. "If you look up at the sky on Halloween, you can see the Wild Hunt racing across the night sky—mad horses and wild dogs!"

Avery frowned. "I've heard of the Wild Hunt, but never the Cornish version. Who leads it?"

"Odin, Herne the Hunter, sometimes Diana, sometimes Hecate. It varies depending on the tale. But essentially they cross from the Underworld," he shrugged, "or Otherworld. The Fey come to hunt humans as sport—and hunt until dawn. Lots of bloodshed, death, vanishing people, and mayhem. Fun, eh?"

But Avery wasn't grinning. She'd just had a horrible idea.

21

After work, Avery headed to The Wayward Son, and found Alex hard at work behind the bar.

It was almost six, and the pub was busy. Zee was also working, and he headed over as Avery sat at her usual corner of the bar. She hadn't spoken to him often, and still couldn't place which of the Nephilim he was from her first impression in the mine.

He spoke softly for his size. "Hey, Avery. What can I get you? It's on the house."

"Hey, Zee. A large glass of the house red, please."

She settled herself comfortably and waved to Alex when he looked up and saw her. He winked and continued to pull pints. She'd left him in bed that morning, and was looking forward to having a lie in with him tomorrow.

Zee slid the glass in front of her and before he disappeared, she asked, "So, how's life in the twentieth century?"

He smiled, revealing gleaming teeth. "Pretty good, if different."

"I bet. Do you like it?"

"I'm getting used to it. Humanity has progressed in interesting ways. Not always good, I have to say, but to be quite honest, humans often indulge their baser instincts."

She lowered her voice. "So you don't think of yourself as human at all?"

"No. I have wings. Do you?"

She smirked. "What? Think of myself as human, or have wings?"

He laughed. "Have wings."

"No. Your perspective is interesting."

"So is yours, witch," he said quietly.

"What do you think of Old Haven?"

"It is steeped in old magic and ancient rites. Blood rites. The ground is soaked with it."

Avery put her glass down in alarm. "Is it? How do you know?"

"I feel it. We all do." He glanced up and saw a waiting customer glowering at him and called over, "One second." He lowered his voice even more. "Old magical places are often built on blood. It creates power, but you know that. Druids loved their blood sacrifices."

"You knew Druids? I thought that they were too recent for you."

He shook his head. "They have been around for a long time, only their name changes. They believed the Earth demanded sacrifice—she does sometimes, that is true—and so they gave it. The grove was once a dark place. The magic that's up there now was started with blood and will end with blood—if that doorway is to open properly."

"Have you seen the witch who has triggered it?"

"No. We feel her sometimes. She passes like the wind and feels like the Carrion Crow. We cannot stop her or follow her. But that's not what we're there for. We keep the locals back, and they are safe while we are there. For now."

And with that ominous warning, he returned to his job.

Avery sipped her wine, thinking on what Zee had said. He must have discussed this with Alex, so she'd be curious to know what he thought of it. And she wanted to share her tarot reading.

As soon as Alex was free he came over, his dark eyes warm and admiring. "How's my gorgeous girlfriend?"

"Feeling better by the moment. How's my gorgeous man?"

"Missing you." He leaned over the counter and kissed her. "Why aren't you wearing your costume?"

"Funny! It's back in the shop where it belongs."

"Shame, I'd have liked to peel you out of it later."

She blushed. "Alex! You're very naughty. You can peel me out of this instead." She gestured to her jeans, top, and boots.

"That will be my pleasure," he said with a grin. "You want some food while you're here?"

"It depends, could do, but what are the others doing back at Reuben's?"

"No idea. Why don't we go out for a meal and then head back?"

"Sounds great. I'll let him know."

But no sooner had she said that than Briar breezed in and sat next to Avery. Her cheeks were flushed and her dark hair tumbled around her shoulders, complimenting her dark red coat. "You beat me to it, Avery. I've been hanging out for this all afternoon." She eased her coat off and waved at Zee, and within seconds a glass of wine appeared in front of her. There were definitely perks to knowing the owner.

"That bad?" Avery asked.

She sipped her wine. "Just busy. Stock is flying off the shelves, which is great, but it means I'll have to spend all day tomorrow making new stock and filling the shelves. Eli said he would help. All this healing has drained me and sucked my time." She looked guilty. "Don't get me wrong, I'm happy to help, but I need to spend time in my shop, and although Eli and Cassie are great, they can't do what I can."

"I get it. You've been great though this week. We're lucky to have you. So is Hunter. How is he?"

Briar sighed. "Charmingly dangerous, and in need of a lot of healing."

Avery leaned on her hand, watching Briar. "Charmingly dangerous? Sounds interesting."

"He keeps asking me out. He's covered in bruises with a broken arm, and that won't keep his libido down." She giggled. "Imagine what's he like when he's fit?"

Avery almost choked on her drink. "I'll leave *you* to imagine that."

"That's not what I meant! Anyway, he wants to take me out to dinner later."

"Why not go? You said yourself you'll be hard at work all day tomorrow, and have been all week. Take a break tonight and have some fun. It's just dinner. And it's Saturday."

Avery glanced up and saw Newton come through the door, and Briar followed her gaze. "I think he's still interested, too," Avery said.

Briar rolled her eyes. Just then, her phone rang, and she glanced at it. "It's Hunter."

Avery mouthed, "Go on!"

As Newton grabbed a stool, Briar said brightly, "Hi, Hunter. Okay, sounds good. Where?" She looked at her watch. "Sure, I'll meet you there. "No. No lifts. Bye."

"Plans?" Newton asked Briar.

"Yes. Dinner with Hunter." She stood up, knocked back her wine, and grabbed her coat and bag. "See you later, Avery."

"Have fun," Avery said, grinning as she turned back to Newton.

He scowled. "I don't know what she sees in him."

"He's single, hot, and fancies her. And she needs some fun in her life right now."

"Is he staying In White Haven?"

"Don't know. Does it matter? Didn't think you were interested anymore."

Newton shrugged and ordered a pint.

Avery took pity on him and changed the subject. "So, what else have you been up to, Newton?"

He let out a world-weary sigh. "This old guy, a tramp who used to sleep rough around Truro, has disappeared. It's a bit weird. Everyone knew him—the shop owners, locals, police, local services, you name it. We all spoke to him, checked in on him, encouraged him to go to the night shelter, but he was a law unto himself. He sat outside shops, begged, slept in alleyways, drank." Newton looked into his pint. "You know, he had a job once, a wife, children, a life. And then—poof! Gone. Just like him."

"You can't find him at all?"

Newton shook his head and looked at Avery, sadness filling his eyes. "No, and he's been gone a couple of weeks. He couldn't have moved to another town, because we've asked—he's done that before. He has literally disappeared. We can't even find his dead body."

"I'm sorry. That sucks. Poor old guy. Maybe someone took him in?"

Newton shook his head. "He stank. No one would take him in. And he wouldn't go, anyway. Hundreds of people have tried to help him, and everyone has failed, because he didn't want help. So, I can only conclude that we'll find his body somewhere—rotting, probably, in a few months' time."

Time to change the subject again. "Well, let me tell you about my day, because I bet you didn't have to wear a costume for Halloween!"

***

Over dinner at a local Thai restaurant, Avery told Alex about Becky's tarot reading. "I think we need to find out who Stan's girlfriend is."

"You think she's our witch."

"Don't you? The timeframe fits—after all, she must have only arrived here recently. She's the right age and description, and I just get bad vibes about her. And she's INTENSE."

"Maybe," Alex said thoughtfully. "She could also be a regular intense person who is dating Stan. I would imagine he'd make you intense."

Avery laughed. "Really? You think about Stan often?"

"All the time," he answered, deadpan.

"Well, I think we should try to see if she's the same woman who appeared in your lounge. If she's not, then back to square one."

Alex frowned. "It's just that I find it hard to believe our time-walking witch would shack up with Stan, of all people."

"Why not Stan?" Avery was slightly affronted on his behalf. "He's a nice older guy with a good job, and he's open-minded and culturally sensitive. He's grown on me recently. He was very sweet today with Becky." She thought for a second. "What if it's the fact that he's our town's pseudo-Druid that led her to him?"

"Maybe. And I guess at the moment we have no other leads. But why take up with anyone? Why not just keep her head down, know no one, and talk to no one? This way she has tangible links. She's traceable."

"Maybe she needs him for something." Avery had a horrible thought. "Have you chatted to Zee about Old Haven?"

"Not really. He's had a couple of days off, and today's been busy."

"He said that blood had opened the spell in the grove, and that blood will close it. Maybe she needs Stan as a sacrifice." And then Avery gasped. "Maybe it will be Becky? She's younger, easier to handle, more impressionable. That fits my reading!"

Alex looked at her, astonished. "A blood sacrifice! As in, she's going to kill someone?"

"Yes. That's what Druids did. We know that. They believed in it. But if you were desperate enough…"

Her words hung on the air and Alex sat back, perplexed.

And then things dropped into place as Avery remembered her conversation with Newton. "And a tramp has disappeared. Vanished. What if he was the sacrifice that started the spell?"

Alex just watched her for a second. "That's quite a leap! Anything could have happened to him!"

"I know, but it's unusual. And as Newton said, if he'd died, they'd have found his body by now."

"Human sacrifice is pretty old school—and extreme!"

"So is she. She cursed El. *She could have died*! She would have, without Caspian's help! So could *you* if I hadn't been there! This woman is a killer. She will do anything to open that gateway to *wherever it is!*"

Alex had finished his meal and he pushed his plate away. "I guess it makes sense. Horrible, gruesome sense."

The more she thought about her theory, the more sense it made to Avery. "Think about what we found under Reuben's mausoleum—evidence of demon traps and blood sacrifice. There are spells involving blood magic in our grimoires, and you had to use it just to get to your grimoire. This is in our past, too!"

"There was no evidence of human sacrifice," he pointed out. "Just blood magic, which is very different."

"True, but it indicates a different mindset—a different way of approaching magic."

Alex exhaled heavily. "So, you want to check her out tonight?"

"Yes. We have to. And if she IS Stan's girlfriend, than I am willing to bet that either he or Becky is the next planned sacrifice."

"If that's her plan—we don't know that, remember?"

"As much as I hate my theory, I'd put money on it. And Dan said something today that made me think about what our witch could be summoning. Have you heard of the Wild Hunt?"

"Yes, vaguely."

Avery gave him a brief summary. "What if that's what she's trying to do?"

Alex took a long drink of his beer before looking at her. "I think your imagination has gone nuts."

"I know how it sounds, but it feels right."

"Why would she want to summon the Wild Hunt?"

"I don't know."

"For just some random weirdness?"

"No. There'll be a reason. We just have to find what it is."

***

After some Googling and looking through a phone directory, Avery found Stan's address. He lived in a large Victorian semi-detached house in a small suburb of similarly-aged houses, and they drove slowly down the street, identifying his, before parking several doors down.

It was an average suburban road, lined with trees and with cars parked along the kerb. Like most houses of that age, there were no garages, and everyone had to park on the road. The houses all had three floors, with small front gardens and large back gardens. Tonight the road was busy, and they were lucky to squeeze into a small space. Fortunately, they were in Alex's Alfa Romeo.

They cast Avery's favourite shadow spell and settled in to watch the house and the road. It was after nine and cold. Stray leaves whirled past on the biting wind that set the bare branches skittering together. Some of the houses were well lit, and they could see TVs on in the front rooms of some houses where the curtains hadn't yet been closed. Stan's house was in darkness, other than a light over the front door and in one of the third-floor dormer windows.

"Maybe they're in a back room?" Avery suggested.

"Or, maybe Becky is in and Stan's out with his girlfriend? Or Stan and his girlfriend are snogging on the sofa and Becky's left them to it. I bet that's Becky's room." Alex pointed to the third floor room.

"They might all be in watching *Strictly*."

Alex grimaced. "Ugh. Sounds hideous."

She sniggered. "I bet you're a great dancer."

"Well, of course! But I wouldn't sit and watch *Strictly*, thanks very much."

Avery laughed again, and then wriggled further down in the seat to get comfortable. For the next half an hour, nothing much happened. A few people walked down the street, a few more lights went on, some went off, and then, close to ten, Stan appeared at his front door with a woman. It was difficult to see her at first. The light from the hall was behind Stan, and she was in his shadow.

"She looks tall," Avery observed.

"There are a lot of tall women in the world."

Stan leaned forward and kissed the woman on her cheek and then she turned and walked down the path to the road and turned right, away from them, walking to an old, black VW Golf. As she walked beneath a street light they could see her long, auburn hair and slim figure. She was wearing a stylish woollen coat and leather boots. For a second she hesitated, and then turned to look down the road. Instinctively, Avery and Alex hunched lower in their seats, even though a spell cloaked them completely.

The light showed the arrogant expression of the woman who'd appeared in Alex's flat. She narrowed her eyes as she looked around, and then turned back to her car and got in.

"Well, that looks like her." Alex looked annoyed. "Why did she have to be Stan's girlfriend? That sucks."

The car's headlights flashed on as the engine started, and she pulled out, driving towards them. They had a glimpse of her as she passed, a malicious, satisfied expression on her face as she accelerated away.

As soon as she passed, Alex started his car and he pulled out, with the intention of following her. "Crap, there's nowhere to turn around." He sped down the road looking for a gap to turn in, but reached the intersection. He turned right. "I'm hoping we can pick her up this way."

Avery fell silent for a moment. Something was troubling her, and she couldn't quite place it.

Meanwhile, Alex kept driving, turning once and then again, hoping to find her on another side road, but after a few minutes of cruising up and down, he slammed the wheel in frustration. "Bollocks. She's gone."

Crap! "Oh, no. I know why I recognise her."

"Er, she was in my flat!" He looked confused.

"No. I mean she looks like someone. The look on her face as she drove away. She looked like Helena. That's her expression when she's malicious and sneaky."

"You have to be kidding."

"I'm not."

"What are you suggesting? That Helena has possessed her?"

"She looked so pleased with herself this morning. What if she has?"

"You really know how to ruin a perfectly good night out," Alex groaned.

22

Avery woke on Sunday morning wrapped in Alex's arms, and with the weight of a cat on her stomach and one between her feet.

She smiled in satisfaction as Alex stirred next to her, and she stroked his bicep, her fingers tracing his tattoos. *He is so delicious.* Medea and Circe stirred too, meowing softly, and then Medea padded softy up to her chest and began to lick her face and then Alex's.

He groaned. "Avery, don't lick my face."

She giggled. "Idiot. It's the cat."

He nuzzled her neck. "Ah. I didn't think your tongue was that rough."

She giggled again. "You're a silly bugger."

The house was quiet, and the outside world seemed a million miles away. She stretched luxuriously and the cats meowed, demanding food, so she wriggled out of the bed to feed them. She'd set up their bowls, bedding, and litter tray in the corner of their large bedroom, so the cats would have a safe space. Not that they seemed to care; they both wandered all over the house and congregated where people were, mainly in the snug.

Alex roused, too, and they pulled on jeans and t-shirts and padded down to the kitchen where they found El and Briar sitting at the large wooden table, sipping coffee. Outside the sky was a leaden grey, and the sea beyond the garden matched it.

"Morning guys," El said, her eyes sleepy. She was wrapped in a large bathrobe that dwarfed her, and Avery presumed it was Reuben's. "There's a fresh pot of coffee over there."

"Awesome, I'll get it," Alex said as he fished two mugs out of the cupboard.

Avery sat next to the others. "You look loads better, El!"

She smiled. "Feeling loads better, too. I finally feel like my magic is surfacing again. I think your potions are helping, Briar."

Briar nodded, looking bright-eyed and alert, which made Avery feel even more knackered. "It's one of my favourites, and very effective."

"How was your night?" Avery asked her with a grin. "Have fun with Hunter?"

"Fine, thank you," Briar said primly. "We had a lovely meal."

El grimaced. "She's giving nothing away! Spoilsport."

Alex joined them, plonking a coffee in front of Avery. "Good for you, Briar. I think Newton's jealous."

"I don't care what Newton thinks! And I didn't do it to make him jealous." She looked at Avery. "You were right. It was just a meal, and why not? He wants to help us find our witch."

"We have found her—sort of," Avery said, and she updated them on what they'd found.

"Stan's girlfriend?" El looked perplexed. "And blood sacrifices? What does she *want* up there?"

Alex sighed. "Avery has had another crazy idea. Tell them about the Wild Hunt, and the fact that you think she's been possessed by Helena."

"Dan gave me the idea," Avery said, as she told them about his storytelling, and then the strange witch's expression that reminded her of Helena.

El raised an elegant eyebrow. "Did you guys do some serious drugs last night?"

"No!" Avery said, affronted.

"It's quite a leap," Briar added. "You actually think Helena has possessed someone again?"

"She liked it last time. What if she's found a way to do it again?" Avery felt panic starting to bubble up inside her as she talked it through. "Crap. She really could have! What am I going to do?"

"We are going to calm down and think about this logically. After breakfast." Alex rose from the table and headed to the fridge. "I can't think on an empty stomach. Where's Reuben?"

"Surfing, of course." El looked outside and shivered. "Looks freezing, but you can't keep him away when it's calm like this. But he went really early, so he might be back soon."

"I'll do enough breakfast for him, then," Alex said, starting to gather bacon, eggs, tomatoes, and bread.

El sipped her coffee. "Yeah, let's park this discussion until Reuben is back and I've had a least a gallon more coffee."

Avery felt slightly put out that everyone thought she was mad, but she sighed in agreement. "All right. So what did you and Reuben get up to last night?"

"We had a thrilling Saturday night looking at our family histories. We had this theory that maybe the reason the witch is here is because she knew the town well at one point."

"Interesting," Avery said thoughtfully. "You think she's one of our ancestors? Did you find anything?"

El shook her head. "No. Not yet. It's just a theory. I prefer it to yours, if I'm honest."

Avery grinned. "So do I. I want to head to Old Haven first though this morning, and then I'll help with research this afternoon."

"I have to work," Briar said. "But remember to call Hunter. He wants to help."

***

Full of English breakfast, Avery headed to Old Haven where she'd agreed to meet Hunter. The Old Haven car park had half a dozen cars parked on there, including Gabe's big shiny SUV, and within seconds of her arriving, Hunter pulled up in his old Volvo.

Hunter winced as he got out of the car, but nodded at the SUV. "Nice ride."

Piper exited from the other door, and gave a half-smile of greeting towards Avery.

"Yeah, I have no idea how he can afford that," Avery said, inwardly marvelling at Gabe's enviable resources and negotiation skills. "Are you sure you shouldn't be resting? You look like you're in pain."

"No. I'd just get bored. Besides, Briar's healing skills are great."

"But you look terrible," she said, looking at his split lip, black eye, scratches, and his arm in a sling. "Did you get a proper plaster on that arm?"

"No. It would mean I couldn't shift. Briar's not happy."

"She's the only one he'll listen to," Piper said, annoyed. "But not even she could persuade him to do that."

Hunter grinned. "I like it when she shouts at me."

"You're gross," Piper said, leading the way across the car park and along the path to the church.

Gabe was standing at the end of the path, dressed in black fatigues with dark shades on. He nodded in recognition as they approached. "Hey, guys. You come to see the freak show?"

"Just like everyone else," Avery told him. She was glad she sort of knew him, because he looked really intimidating. She looked past him where she could see a few people milling around the graves. "Are they here for the cemetery or the grove?"

Gabe grinned. "They say the cemetery, but they just keep prowling around, taking lots of photos."

Hunter narrowed his eyes. "You don't throw them out?"

"Makes it too interesting not to let them in at all. We let them wander around, but the new spell the witch has put on the place means no one wants to venture beyond the trees. Dread creeps into your bones when you get too close. But there's another couple of my guys closer to the grove, just in case. You'll see when you get there."

Avery frowned. "A protection spell, is that right?"

"Of a sort," he said enigmatically.

Intriguing. "Okay. I have to see." Avery headed down the path, followed by Hunter and Piper. Her breath caught as she saw the grove in the overcast autumn light, and her blood chilled.

A line of witches-signs hung from the trees on the edge of the grove, twisting in the biting wind that blew in off the sea, and marking a very distinct boundary. She could see dark red marks daubed on some of them, and close up her suspicions were proven correct. It was dried blood.

Hunter and Piper lifted their heads and inhaled deeply, and both recoiled.

And then Avery felt it. A wash of dread and creeping terror that made her want to turn and run. She stepped back and shuddered. WHAT WAS THAT?

One of the Nephilim strolled over. "Avery. You've brought friends."

"I have. Hunter and Piper. I'm afraid I don't know your name." She held her hand out and he engulfed it in his large one.

"Othniel. Niel for short." He turned and greeted the other two.

Niel, like the other Nephilim, was tall, broad-shouldered and olive-skinned, but unlike the others, he had white-blond hair and bright blue eyes. He'd kept his hair long, but had tied it back, and he had long sideburns and stubble.

Avery asked, "Have you been in the grove beyond the witch-signs?"

"Once or twice when I thought I heard someone in there. I wouldn't advise it."

"Why not?" Piper asked.

"Because, small wolf, it affects you here." He pointed to his head and his stomach.

"I can take that," she said, lifting her chin.

"I doubt that." His blue eyes bored into hers.

Piper pouted in annoyance. "How do you know what I am?"

He smiled with a predatory grin. "I have many special skills."

"Did you find anyone in there?" Hunter asked. "The noise?"

"Just the rustle of dry tree branches and the scent of Carrion Crow. It was her, I'm sure. She comes with the wind and adds to her spell."

Avery took a deep breath, hating what she was about to suggest. "I need to enter. I'd like to try and work out what she's done."

"Be my guest, but I'll come with you."

"Is she there now?" Hunter asked, lifting his head and sniffing again.

The Nephilim shook his head, turned, and ducked beneath the rattling bare branches, into the trees.

Avery followed him, yet every instinct she had urged her to run. Dread settled into her stomach as heavy as a stone and she started to shake. *This is a spell, only a spell,* she whispered to herself as she followed Niel further into the grove, Hunter behind her.

A small voice shouted, "I can't!"

They looked around to see Piper frozen in fear.

"It's okay," Hunter said, reassuring her. "Go back and wait, we won't be long."

She turned and fled, and they watched her until she was clear of the trees.

Avery fought down the desperate urge to follow her. "Are you okay?" she asked Hunter.

"No, but let's keep going."

With every step that brought them closer to the yew, the feeling of terror rose, and Avery cast a protection spell in a bubble around them. Immediately the sensation eased, and she started to breathe more easily.

Hunter sighed with relief. "If that was you, thank you."

She nodded and kept going, the bare branches clicking above them impatiently. Niel stood waiting in front of the yew, its huge trunk cracked like an open mouth, screaming in pain. Its gnarled branches loomed over them, one of the only trees still to have its dark green, needle-like leaves.

"This place has changed in the days since we were last here," Avery observed. "The magic is deeper and darker. The trees, the ground, the air—it's all saturated with growing power." She cast her awareness out, seeking the magic beyond the spell, and all of a sudden felt their own magic they had released from the binding spell. She was drawing on it; it was subtle but unmistakable. She looked at Niel. "You can feel her spell?"

He nodded, his eyes wary. "It chills my blood, too. *She* chills my blood. She is not like you."

Hunter had been looking suspiciously around the small clearing surrounding the yew, but he now looked at Niel. "You look human, but you obviously aren't. You're a bit like the witch—there is something ancient about you."

Niel was silent, so Avery answered for him. "You're right there, but I'm not sure Niel wants to share." She turned to him. "You called her the Carrion Crow earlier, so did Gabe. Why do you call her that?"

"She reeks of death, feeds on death, and rejoices in it." He pointed across the grove to a bundle of feathers on the ground. "Every day for the last few days she kills a small creature, mostly birds, but it could be other woodland creatures. And always there."

Avery stepped a little closer, trying not to gag as the smell of decay grew stronger. Small animal bones and the rotting bodies of birds lay in a pile next to a cairn of stones covered in blood. The Carrion Crow. *The Crone.* She frowned. The Crone was an aspect of the Goddess, associated with age and death, but not necessarily cruelty. But there were other aspects of her nature, such as Hecate the Goddess of Death. *Was that what she could sense, what the Nephilim could sense?*

Avery retreated from the bundle of death and turned back to Niel. "The Mermaids' call did not affect you, their Siren call. Why can you feel this?"

"We heard their call, but we could resist it, as we can resist this. Our uniqueness gives us added strength, but we are not impervious. I feel it well enough. The darkness invades my dreams. Have you seen enough?"

As he spoke, wind ripped through the trees, setting the branches rattling and the witch marks spinning, and the scent of decay intensified. "Yes." She turned and all three ran as if the Devil was at their heels.

***

Avery drove back to Reuben's place, and Piper and Hunter followed.

The snug next to the kitchen was warm and bathed in weak autumnal sun that struggled to get through the clouds, but Avery could still feel the sullied air of the grove clinging to her like a second skin. Only El was there, tucked into an armchair in front of the fire, and she looked up as they came in.

"What happened to you?"

"Why?" Avery asked. "Do we look odd?"

"You look haunted. What happened?" She uncurled and put her book down.

Avery sank on to the sofa, her legs suddenly weak. "The grove feels horrible. You're right about that spell. It spills out terror and dread."

Piper sat on the floor next to the fire, looking ashamed. "I couldn't even go in. I wanted to scream."

"There's no shame in that," Hunter said, looking at his sister fondly. "That's exactly what the spell is meant to do."

"But you managed to cope with it," Piper protested.

"Not for long," Avery said. "I had to cast a protection spell once we got close to the yew. It was the only thing that stopped us from running."

El leaned forward. "Is it just a spell, or is something else going on there?"

"Oh, there's plenty going on." Hunter ran his hands through his hair. "The stench of blood and decay was overwhelming, and with my sense of smell, I'm used to being more sensitive. But that was something else."

"She's making blood sacrifices now, daily. Killing small animals and birds." Avery shook her head. "I went in there trying to work out what spell she might be using, or just to try to detect what's happening, but the feeling of terror was so overwhelming it just drowned everything out—even with my spell as a buffer."

"Damn it!" El exclaimed, leaping to her feet and joining Hunter's pace around the room. "Who IS she?"

"Gabe and Niel call her the Carrion Crow. She even scares them."

"That's not a good sign," El grumbled.

"You know, I think I'm wrong," Avery said thoughtfully. "I was worried Helena was doing this, but she isn't. I just know it. Maybe you're right. Maybe it's someone who knew the town well in the past. Have you found out anything?"

"Well, we've scoured our family trees and histories, but nothing particularly odd stands out. We considered Rueben's mad uncle, Addison, but he doesn't fit for many reasons, particularly because he's a man. But we thought maybe a descendant?" She shrugged and sighed. "Anyway, we realised the only family history we didn't have here was yours, so Reuben and Alex have gone to fetch them from your flat."

"It took two of them?" Avery asked.

"Research isn't Reuben's strong point," El said, grinning. "I think he needed a break. And they needed more beer."

At that moment, the front door slammed and their voices arrived ahead of them. Alex headed into the snug carrying a huge box, while Reuben stayed in the kitchen, yelling, "Who wants a beer?"

"Me!" a chorus of voices called back.

Alex took one look at Avery and his face fell. "What's wrong?"

"So many things," she said, groaning. "But I'm fine. I'll tell you both over a beer."

She headed to his side and helped him unpack Anne's files, placing them on the floor within easy reach of the sofa and chairs. As soon as Reuben came in with the beers and they were all settled, she filled them in on what had happened at the grove.

Reuben frowned. "This is all sounding very bad. The Crone and the Carrion Crow?"

"I keep coming back to the Wild Hunt," Avery said. "It just got stuck in my head, and I can't shake it."

"It's just a myth, surely," Hunter said. He'd finally sat down next to his sister on the rug in front of the fire, and he sipped his beer, listening carefully.

"So were Mermaids, until they attacked White Haven," Alex pointed out.

Piper looked shocked. "And I thought our life was weird."

"Stick around White Haven some more and you'll realise what weird is," Reuben said dryly. "What did your super noses pick up?"

"Blood, death, and decay. Always a winning combination," Hunter said.

"Pass me one of your books on myths," Piper said suddenly. "I'll look up the Wild Hunt."

"And I'll start searching my history, again," Avery said, settling back on the sofa with Anne's research.

For the next hour, the room was relatively quiet as they poured over papers and books, even Hunter helping as he looked at some of the maps of White Haven and histories of Ley Lines. She could hear him, Reuben, and Alex discussing where the lines fell across Old Haven, but she tried to block them out as she studied the tiny writing spread across several pages of her family tree. Although Anne had concentrated on Avery's main line from a couple of generations before Helena, there were lots of names to study.

And then she saw it, buried deep on a line in the centre of one big roll of paper. A name with no date of death—just like Addison Jackson. The name was Suzanna Grayling, and she was descended from Ava, Helena's older daughter.

Avery's pulse raced as she scanned the names above and below, but Suzanna was the only one not to have a date of death. *Why couldn't Anne find it? Was she their mysterious time-walker?* She looked up at the others. "I've found something. Suzanna Grayling, one of my ancestors, has no date of death."

El's mouth fell open in shock. "Wow. When was she born? I mean, age-wise would it fit?"

"She was born in 1780, and she married a David Grayling when she was…" Avery quickly did the maths. "Nineteen years old."

"Does it say anything about her?" Alex asked.

Avery fumbled for the book of notes Anne had made. "I don't know. Anne sometimes commented on certain people and anomalies, but often they were nothing much, just odd snippets she'd found out about what they did and where they lived." She shook her head. "Her research was phenomenal. Give me a few minutes and I'll let you know."

Anne's notebooks were carefully numbered and annotated, and Avery briefly wondered if she'd spent so much time on the other witches' history. She presumed Helena's special status as the only one to be burned at the stake made her more interesting, in a gruesome way.

It was another ten minutes before she found what she was looking for, and she lifted her head to tell the others. "Suzanna Grayling was the first of Helena's descendants to return to White Haven."

"No way!" El said, wide-eyed. "That has to be significant!"

"Who's Helena?" Piper asked. "You keep mentioning her."

Awkward. "She's my ancestor who was burned at the stake, and now haunts my flat as a ghost."

"Right." Piper nodded with a grim smile.

Alex asked, "What else does it say?"

"The man she married, David, bought the house that I now live in..." She checked the document. "In 1801. Two years after they got married. Well, he bought the middle house. The others were bought later."

Alex smiled. "So after two hundred years, your family returned to White Haven. That's amazing."

"Do any of you know when your ancestors returned here?" Avery asked thoughtfully.

"Well, mine never left," Reuben said, gesturing around him at the house.

El nodded. "True. Is there anything in your notes, Avery, that says anything about our families?"

"Not that I noticed, but then again, I haven't really looked for that."

"What was the date for your *new* grimoire?" Alex asked.

It wasn't a new grimoire, but Avery knew what he meant. It was the grimoire that wasn't Helena's. She hesitated for a second as she scrabbled to find her grimoire under the documents. "1795."

"And who is the first name in your new grimoire?"

Her gaze met his. "Suzanna Grayling."

"So, she was fifteen years old when she decided to assert her witch roots. That's pretty young. Who's the next name?"

"Ava Helen Grayling." She looked at the others in shock. "Her daughter, who she named after Helena's oldest child and Helena herself!"

Piper had watched their conversation with interest. "She was a woman on a mission. She obviously knew her own history very well. "

El agreed. "Your family might not have been living here, but they certainly passed down their heritage. And Suzanna was keen to practice the craft again. She started the book before she moved here with her husband."

Alex sat next to Avery and pulled Anne's notebook from her hands. "Didn't Helena say that Ava was already strong as a child, and that's why Octavia wanted her?"

Avery narrowed her eyes as she looked for the original grimoire, and quickly thumbed to the back where the note had been written next to the binding spell. She read, "*Ava already shows signs of power well before one would expect it.*"

"So," Alex said softly, "it would be reasonable to assume that Ava's strong abilities passed down to her descendants, and that Suzanna had been honing her magic for some time. Maybe she even pushed her husband into coming here."

"It must have been a wonderful feeling to have finally come home," Avery mused. "Maybe though, once she was back, she got annoyed and wanted to make White Haven pay for Helena's burning all those years ago. I mean, it wasn't really the town's fault, but I guess they didn't stop it."

"They couldn't," El pointed out. "Our families fled, too, except for Reuben's, and they were rich and influential enough to stay."

Reuben winced. "Sorry."

El held up her hands. "Wait a minute. If it's her—Suzanna—why is she here NOW? After all this time?"

Alex sighed. "Because she's casting the mother of all spells, and to do that you need a lot of magical energy, and guess what's floating over White Haven right now?"

"And she's using it, too," Avery said, realising that she hadn't told them what she'd sensed. "She's drawing on it *right now*. When we released the binding spell she must have known. But why the delay?"

"A spell this big needs preparation," Alex said thoughtfully. "It seems that she's drawing on the power of the Crone and is trying to open a portal to, what?" he hesitated. "The Underworld? The world of the Fey? To allow the Wild Hunt into this reality, to kill, seek vengeance, and generally cause chaos? She's using our own magic against us!"

"It's her magic, too," Reuben pointed out.

Avery rubbed her hands over her face. "Wow. Are we really suggesting that for over two hundred years she has bided her time in order to seek revenge on White Haven?"

"It seems so," El mused.

Alex said, "So, she knows the power of the White Haven witches has been released, and she has to use it as effectively as possible. She waits for the best possible time for her plan—Samhain. And chooses the most affective spot to centre her magic—the Grove. And within two weeks of Samhain, she starts her spell."

Hunter looked at them as if they were mad. "So she makes herself a time-walker, biding her time for revenge, and lucky us, now's the time!"

"And then uses her spare time to target others she considers responsible for Helena's death," Avery said. "Maybe that's why she targeted you, El. Not for trying to stop her spell, but for your family's perceived betrayal of hers."

"And maybe that's why she didn't want to see you at Alex's flat, Avery," El said. "She must know who you are."

"It didn't stop her from trying to kill me though, once she knew I was there," Avery pointed out. "I'm not entirely sure she's rational."

"You were in her way," Hunter said. "At that point, her loyalty to you went out the window."

"Rational or not," Reuben said, "she's powerful, and is prepared to kill to get what she wants. So, let's be logical. We think she killed the tramp to start the spell—the timeframe fits—and she's planning a final human sacrifice to seal the deal—Stan or his niece. How do we stop her?"

Avery became excited. "I've got her blood. I can make a poppet."

"Awesome," El said. "But we need more. We need the Council."

23

Avery walked across Reuben's wide patio enjoying the afternoon sunshine, which had finally triumphed over the clouds, her phoned pressed to her ear.

The sunshine couldn't really be called warm, but it was a bright spot in what was proving to be a dark day. They had talked for a while about whether to involve the other twelve covens of Cornwall. Avery wasn't sure it was worth asking after Genevieve had declined to help with the Mermaids, but Reuben had argued that Suzanna was a much bigger threat to everyone, and she had to try. And he was right.

Genevieve answered the call, her voice bright but abrupt. "Avery, I hope you're not ringing to cancel Samhain."

"Actually, no," Avery said, biting down the urge to tell her to get stuffed. "We have a problem, a big problem, and need your help. We would like to offer Reuben's house as a meeting place for the Samhain celebrations. It's large and private, and everyone could comfortably fit in."

"Why on Earth would we want to change from Rasmus's house?'

"Because we need your help to stop the Wild Hunt from ravaging Cornwall."

There was silence for a moment. "*The what?*"

"The Wild Hunt, which although mythical, does have roots in reality—" she broke off as Genevieve interrupted.

"I know what the bloody Wild Hunt is! Why would it be released on us?"

"We have a rogue witch, who I believe to be a time-walker and one of my ancestors, who is seeking vengeance for Helena's death. We think." Avery went on to explain what was happening, and by the time she'd finishing, Genevieve was spitting.

"You should have told me sooner. This is huge! It has repercussions for all of us."

Avery took a deep breath, reminding herself that they needed the others. "I know, but we didn't fully understand what was happening until today. And quite frankly, Genevieve, you haven't really given much of a crap about our predicaments before."

As usual, the angrier she became, the more the wind was whipping about Avery, and she funnelled it away into the garden, watching it pick up leaves in a whirlwind and carry them across the lawn.

Genevieve's tone was icy. "Well, unlike last time, this situation will affect all of us. The Wild Hunt is deadly and vicious, and once released will be uncontrollable."

"Which is why I'm calling you. We know where it's going to happen. We need to stop the breach between worlds. And if not, we need to form a protective ring around the grove to contain it. And then we have to send it back."

"Can't you seal off your escaped magic?"

"No! You know we can't, or we would have. And besides, she's already using it. But that doesn't mean we can't use it, too."

"And you couldn't feel her using it?" She sounded annoyed. "Don't you have a connection to it?"

"Not 24 hours a day! It's not like a battery we're plugged into! When it was released it flooded into us, but then it was as if our bodies had enough and just—" She struggled to find the right word, "Disconnected! I can't explain it better than that."

Genevieve fell silent for a moment, and Avery could feel her anger crackling down the phone. "I can't come tonight, but I will come tomorrow. And if it's as bad as you say, then yes, I will convene the coven."

She rang off and Avery headed back inside, smiling triumphantly.

"Good news, then?" Alex asked, watching her.

"You could say that. Genevieve's coming to assess the situation, but I know she'll say yes."

"Wow," Reuben said, grinning. "Go Avery. And I get to host the coven. Lucky me."

El came in from the kitchen with bowls of chips and dips. "We need to tell Newton, too."

"Someone else's job," Avery said immediately. "I do not want two people moaning at me today."

Alex rose to his feet. "Fancy another trip, Reuben?"

"Why?"

"We need to ward Stan's house and protect him and Becky. Something to stop Suzanna using either of them as a sacrifice."

"A glamour?" Reuben suggested. "Make them leave for a few days?"

"Brilliant!" Alex looked at him in admiration. "Let's go."

"Can I come?" Hunter asked. "I'd like to pick up her scent again."

"Sure. Road trip! More the merrier."

"Stay here, Piper," Hunter said. "We'll head home once I'm done."

She nodded, watching them silently as they strode out the door, full of energy and intent.

In the silence of their departure, El said, "He's pretty bossy, isn't he?"

Piper met her gaze. "And then some. He's a natural Alpha, which has its pros, but also cons." She stood up and stretched her legs. "I need to run. Okay if I change here?"

"Be my guest. I'm going back to the spell books, and then I'll cook something, enough for everyone." El patted her non-existent stomach and reached for the crisps. "I'm starving. I only had nibbles for lunch."

"And I'm going to go make my poppet," Avery said. "Well, Suzanna's actually."

"There's a sewing room somewhere upstairs," El said, gesturing vaguely. "There'll be plenty of material there, and the herbs are in the attic."

"Laters then," Avery said, and she grabbed her grimoire and swiped some crisps from the bowl before heading for the stairs.

***

After hunting around for a while, which included getting lost in Reuben's vast house, Avery eventually found some material and chose a small square of plain cotton cloth. She'd never made a poppet before, and didn't relish doing one now.

A poppet was a small doll made to resemble the person you wished to cast a spell on. It could be made from cloth, clay, or wax, but using cloth allowed her to fill it with herbs and the tissue with the blood on it, which she'd carefully stored in a small wooden box. Magic should not be about controlling someone's actions, but in this case they had no choice. In order for it to be effective you needed something of the person, like hair, or nail clippings, or blood—so even the tiny drop of blood should make the spell work. There was no way they could get anything else from her.

Avery cut two pieces of fabric out in the shape of a gingerbread man and started to stitch it together, and then added rudimentary eyes, a nose, and mouth. She fashioned some clothes to put on it, to make it look female, and used wool to make long hair. The actions were soothing and contemplative and she focused on Suzanna, envisioning her clearly: her body, her hair, and her face.

When the doll was nearly complete, she took it upstairs into Reuben's attic workshop. Although he lived here alone now—except for El visiting—he still kept most of his magical gear there. She lit candles and incense and then once she'd found the herbs she needed, she mixed them together in a bowl, pounding them down just slightly. Satisfied, she stuffed the doll with the herbs, placing the blood-stained tissue in the centre, then completed the stitching, sealing the ends completely.

Now what? Should she work a spell now, or would that be too soon? Should she try to bind her and weaken her magic, injure her, mute her? Whatever she chose, it had to be effective. If she used it too soon and Suzanna was able to resist it, it would be a valuable resource lost.

Avery closed her eyes, hoping for inspiration. *Was this woman really Suzanna?* It seemed insane.

The warmth of Reuben's attic wrapped around her, folding her within its space that had seen so much magic worked over the years. She inhaled the soothing incense, relaxing her shoulders, the candlelight barely visible through her closed eyelids. She focused only on her breath, and then cast her awareness out, trying to feel Suzanna. She was her blood, like Helena, but she'd got lost somewhere along the way, possessed by revenge and darkness. How would it feel to walk alone through the years with all your loved ones gone? Had she watched them die? Her children and husband? Her friends? Her grandchildren and their grandchildren? She would have had to leave White Haven, she'd have been recognised otherwise, her unnatural lifespan discovered. Perhaps she returned from time to time?

And Helena? Did she know who she was? What she had planned? Did she approve? Avery remembered Helena's sneaky smile. *Yes. She probably did.*

As she sat quietly, listening to the beams creak and settle around her, she became aware of another presence close by, something dark and predatory. She tried not to panic, and kept her eyes closed. It wasn't a physical presence she sensed; it was something else.

A voice rang out suddenly, in her head. *I sensed you earlier, at my grove. You're too late.* The voice was strong, certain of herself. It was the witch.

Suzanna. Is that you? Avery asked, her question silent, in her mind only.

There was moment's hesitation. I haven't been called that in many years.

Yes! It was her. Avery desperately squashed her elation, hoping she couldn't sense it, and schooled her mind carefully.

So who are you now?

There is power in a name. You know that, she chided.

But I know your real one, that's powerful enough.

I won't tell you. All knowledge is power.

Yes it is, and we have knowledge, too. We know what you're doing.

I doubt that.

She was so sure of herself, so confident.

Would it hurt to spell it out? Probably not.

You're summoning The Wild Hunt.

More silence followed, and for a second, Avery thought she'd gone. *Well done. You're brighter than I thought. But it matters not. The spell is too far advanced for you to stop it.*

Why are you doing this, Suzanna? These people had nothing to do with Helena's death.

Her voice dripped with scorn. *They are the descendants of those who did. They walk and talk and act as if nothing happened. They celebrate the old ways without fully understanding them. They celebrate their festivals and make their bonfires, but they know nothing.*

They try. Isn't that better than nothing? These are different times.

Suzanna laughed bitterly. *They are no different. People still betray each other out of fear and anger and greed. Trust me. They would betray you in a heartbeat.*

Was she right? Would they? They had told James. Was that a mistake? No.

Your age has corrupted you, Avery said sadly. *You have learnt nothing. You see everything through a veil of the past.*

So would you if you were in my shoes. You, of all people! You only found our grimoires this year! So much secrecy and lying. So much betrayal. You did well to break the spell. I admire you. Her voice dropped, low and seductive. Are you sure you don't want to join me?

Yes. It's pointless to ask.

Then it is pointless to talk to you. You can try to stop me, but you will fail. Our magic will help me, and my spell is too strong. I have prepared for this for a very long time. You should leave now while you have the chance.

I'm not leaving!

Then you will die with everyone else.

And then she was gone.

Avery opened her eyes and looked around the room, and then down at the poppet. She had banished the making of it from her mind, and hopefully Suzanna would not have been able to see it. She wouldn't use it right now. It was too precious. She'd save it and talk to the others first.

Unfortunately, she hadn't seen anything of where Suzanna was living. She had been a voice in the void.

When Avery returned to the snug she found it empty. She could smell cooking; El was in the kitchen.

Audioslave was playing loudly, and El was singing as she chopped and prepared. A glass of wine stood on the counter. She looked up as Avery entered. "You look like you've seen a ghost."

"Heard one, more like. No, not a ghost. Suzanna."

El put the knife down and gaped. "You've spoken to her? How?"

She gestured around her head. "One of those weird head conversations."

"Wow. And what happened?"

"She basically told me I'd die with the rest of White Haven because I wouldn't join her crazy crusade." Avery headed for the wine rack and pulled out a bottle of red wine she'd put there yesterday. "I need this."

"The whole bottle?"

"Eventually," she answered, as she poured a glass.

"Is she Suzanna?"

"Yes. And she's summoning the Wild Hunt. We're right, but it doesn't make me feel any better. And it doesn't make it any easier to try to stop her."

El stirred the pot of whatever she was cooking—something spicy. "Did you make the poppet?"

"Yes. But I don't know what to do with it, or when. I want to use it at the most opportune moment."

El nodded. "Makes sense. We're up against it this time."

"We were last time as well, but we succeeded in the end. Hopefully Genevieve and the coven will help."

***

It was another couple of hours before Alex and the others returned, but when they did, they looked pleased.

"Success?" Avery asked.

"Yes," Alex answered as he headed to the fridge, grabbed three beers, and handed them to Hunter and Rueben. "We successfully glamoured Stan and Becky, and they're heading away for a few days."

"And," Reuben added, "we've added protection to their house with a few well-placed runes around the home."

"That's great news," El said, relieved. "I feel better knowing they'll be away from harm. Will Suzanna be able to find them?"

"Even if she does, we've glamoured Stan enough to resist her charms. Unless, of course, she decides to just grab them and force them against their will, which is highly possible," Alex pointed out.

Avery frowned. "It's great, and I'll sleep easier knowing they're gone, but I can't help but think she'll just use someone else. Did you get her scent again, Hunter?"

"Yeah, it's faint, but there. But of course when she gets in the car, it disappears and I can't track her." He looked frustrated, and the wild power of the wolf hung around him still; his eyes had a strange yellow light to them. "Where's my sister?"

El pointed out to the garden. "Out there, somewhere."

"I'll go and find her, and then we'll head off." He paused for a moment. "I'd still like to help you, so we'll come to the grove for Samhain. I'm calling to get Ollie, Evan, and Tommy to come, too."

"I don't think it's a good idea—you could easily get hurt. We all could, and you don't have magic to protect you," Avery said, frowning. "You don't owe us anything, either."

He gave her a cocky grin. "But I'm a wolf and I hunt. What better help can you get when the Wild Hunt comes to town?"

El agreed with Avery. "You're injured! And you're already in harm's way. We should protect your place, too."

"Already done," Reuben said, sitting down and joining them at the table. "We have been fast, efficient, and effective today!"

El raised an eyebrow. "Go you!"

Hunter headed for the door into the garden. "See you later, guys. And keep me informed!"

24

It was halfway through Monday afternoon when Genevieve strode into Happenstance Books. She looked around imperiously, and when she spotted Avery, she pushed through the customers to get to her.

Genevieve lowered her voice as she approached. "That's a fine mess up there!"

Avery tried to smile, but failed. "How lovely to see you, too."

Genevieve had no time for pleasantries. "You should have told me about this sooner."

"I had no idea how bad it was going to get, or what was going on!"

Customers started to stare, and Avery headed to the back room, Genevieve on her heels. She slammed the door behind her.

"The magic in that grove is very dangerous!"

Avery glared at her. "I know! Why do you think I called? Will you help us?"

"I'll have to. It will need all of us to contain it, and I still think we'll struggle."

Avery sagged into a chair with relief. "Thank you. I really appreciate it. Would you like a drink? Tea, coffee?" Seeing Genevieve's unamused face, she added, "Whiskey?"

"No. I have to get back and start organising things for Samhain. I'll have a think about how we approach this, but essentially I will be the High Priestess leading whatever spell we do. I shall be channelling all of your energies."

"That's fine with me, whatever you need us to do. Do you want to go ahead with our Samhain celebrations at Reuben's before?"

Genevieve shook her head. "No. We'll meet at Reuben's to discuss our plans, and then we'll head straight to the grove. This will be a hell of a way to celebrate." She paused, looking thoughtful. "We haven't performed a spell this big as a coven for many years. Not in my lifetime, anyway."

"Really?"

She sat in the chair opposite Avery, all of her bluster gone. "It will scare some of the witches, the more inexperienced ones. They will need our support. Our strength and our ability to act as one is paramount."

"How many are there in the whole coven?"

She ran through the numbers in her head. "Thirty-seven, I think."

"Quite a few then, really."

"Yes, plenty of energy to draw from, but also a lot to control. And if one person falters…" She trailed off, the implications clear.

Something struck Avery. "Does this mean that you haven't channelled all of our energies before?"

"Not quite so many, and certainly not for an event such as this." If she was worried, she didn't show it.

"I hate to ask, but are you sure you can control all of our power?"

"I was chosen as High Priestess of the Cornish coven for a reason. I am one of only a few who could handle all of that energy, so yes, I can do it. But it will drain me afterwards, for days probably. But that's okay, it needs to be done."

"And who else has the power? I'm just curious," Avery explained.

"Rasmus, Jasper, Claudia, and Caspian. Probably Eve. And in time, maybe you."

Avery couldn't have been more shocked if she'd slapped her. "Me?"

"Surprised?"

"Of course! I'm not strong enough to control the power of so many witches."

Genevieve watched her thoughtfully. "I didn't say now, but you already wield power well, and your focus is good. And importantly, your heart is positive. So yes, I believe one day you could." She rose to her feet, ready to leave. "The road you travel on is long, and the knowledge we gather is never-ending. As long as you're open to that journey, you will always be in a position of power, Avery. I'll be in touch."

She smiled and left, shutting the door behind her softly.

It was almost five when Caspian came in. He glanced around and then headed to the counter. Avery sat behind it on her own, counting down to closing time. The shop had been busy, and she couldn't wait to go home. Well, to Reuben's.

"I didn't think you could get many more Halloween decorations in here, and yet you've managed it," he smirked.

"It's festive. I like it. Have you just come to criticise?"

"No. I've heard from Gen," he said.

Avery looked shocked. "I've never heard anyone call her that before."

"I'm not sure she has, either," he said, winking. "Anyway, she's told me about the grove and the need for a collective spell. All of my family will be present."

"Really?" She squirmed, not really comfortable at feeling she owed so many people her thanks, especially the Favershams.

"They have no choice. Gen orders it, and I endorse it. Besides, we all know of the danger of the Wild Hunt."

"It sounds crazy," Avery confessed.

"It will be. Everyone will be affected, everyone in danger. And besides, it's not your fault."

"Well, actually it is. Our rapidly diminishing cloud of magic over White Haven has given Suzanna the power to do this. So it is my fault."

"You're not responsible for a mad woman's desires. Anyway, that's all I wanted to say. I shall see you on Thursday."

"Before you go, I have a question. I forgot to ask Gen earlier."

"Sure, ask away."

"I've made a poppet with her blood in it. When's the best time to use it?"

He looked impressed. "You have her blood?"

"From when we fought."

He nodded. "Probably on the night itself, but ask Gen. As High Priestess, she will now control the how's and when's."

"All right, thanks, I'll ask her."

He smiled and left, and Avery wasn't sure what was the most unnerving. The Caspian she hated, or the Caspian she was beginning to like. How weird was *that*?

***

Before Avery headed back to Reuben's she had one visit planned. She wanted to see James.

His wife, Elise, answered the door for her and narrowed her eyes. "You're back."

"Any chance I can speak to James?"

"He's in the church." She closed the door in her face with a *slam* that made the frame rattle.

Avery realised that James had shared what she was with her, and that she didn't like it one bit. She shrugged and headed up the path to the church's side door, reflecting on the fact that she couldn't please everyone. She just hoped James's wife would be as discrete as James.

The passageway beyond the door was slightly warmer than the chill air outside, but not by much. She shivered and shouted, "James?"

Silence. She headed to the nave, noting low lights in that direction, and saw James kneeling in prayer before the altar. Feeling guilty for disturbing him she turned away, deciding she could speak to him another time, but he lifted his head. "It's all right, Avery. Come in."

He looked drawn, his eyes shadowed.

"Sorry, I didn't mean to disturb you."

He rose to his feet. "I've finished. What can I help you with?" His voice was cool, and overly polite.

"I just wanted to see how you were."

"As you can see, I'm fine."

No, he was far from fine. She felt so awkward. "Good. Have you been to Old Haven over the last few days?"

His expression was hard. "I went there yesterday. It's an abomination. I felt evil, TRUE evil there."

"Yes, we feel it, too. But by Friday it will all be over. You need to stay away from the place on Halloween. Well away."

He walked up to her, challenging her. "Why? Have you found out what's going on there?"

Avery wanted to tell him, but feared it would be too much. "We have, and we can stop it." *Or at least try.* "It will be a very dangerous place, so you must promise me you'll stay away."

"It's my church. I should be there."

Avery's blood ran cold. "No. You shouldn't. You won't like what you'll see."

"Why? Do you plan to desecrate the place further?"

"Of course not!" she said, recoiling at his suggestion. "We plan to free it from the magic that possesses it now. Will you stay away?"

"I think I need to understand more about you and magic, and White Haven's weird happenings, not less."

"Not by going there," Avery insisted.

"What are you hiding?" He watched her for a moment as she schooled her expression to neutral. "You said magic was good. That was a lie."

"Like anything, it can be subverted. The person behind all of this has carried revenge with her for a long time. Suspicion and hatred of others who do not understand her and who have betrayed her family have led to this. Don't perpetuate it."

"How can I do anything else when you still keep things hidden from me?"

He was right, and a war raged inside her as to how much to tell him. So far, his knowledge of what they were and what they did was not really working in their favour. "Once this is over, I will share some more. But until then, please listen to me. Stay away from Old Haven."

He shook his head. "I can't promise anything. You should go now, Avery. I'll see you soon. "

She took one long look at him and then turned and left. *Maybe they should glamour him on Thursday, too.*

25

All Hallows' Eve arrived all too quickly. The sky was a brittle blue and a chill wind sliced down the streets, reaching inside coats, slapping cheeks, and biting fingers and noses.

Avery looked out of the window and shivered, despite the warmth of the shop and her cheery surroundings. This should be a day of harmless fun, trick or treating, and scary stories, not worrying about the battle they would face that night.

Sally nudged her. "You're miles away. Cheer up."

Avery hadn't told her much about the threat they faced. She hadn't wanted to scare Sally or Dan. She'd contemplated glamouring them and trying to make them leave, but had decided against it. It wasn't fair to make someone do something against their will. Glamouring Stan had been a last resort because they knew he was directly involved. Sally and Dan were not.

She smiled. "Sorry. Just thinking of tonight."

"Ah. The coven meeting and the grove. I know you're keeping stuff back, Avery."

"Not really. I'm looking forward to meeting the whole coven. It's long overdue."

And it was true. She wasn't lying about that.

"Well, at least you're wearing your costume today. Thank you."

"Of course I am! It is Halloween."

Sally grinned. "I'm making hot chocolate. Want one?"

"Yes. Sounds fantastic." She headed back to the till while Sally went to the back room. Dan was somewhere in the shop, probably setting up for the storytelling event later. There would be two. One in the mid-afternoon, and one at six as it was late-night opening. But not for her. She'd be at Reuben's by six, waiting for the covens to arrive.

Her phone rang—*Alex*. "Hey, how are you?"

"I've got bad news."

Her heart skipped a beat. "What?" When they left the house together this morning, everything was fine.

"I can't get hold of Newton. He's not answering his phone, and he called in sick at work."

Relief rushed through her. "There you are, then. He's probably in bed, sleeping."

"You know Newton. He's reliable, a workhorse. His colleagues are worried, I could tell—although they didn't tell me anything. I just wanted you to know I'm heading round to his place to look for him."

"You shouldn't go alone," she said, immediately worried. "I'll come with you." She looked down at her witch costume and groaned. She'd have to get changed.

"No. Stay there. I'm going with Hunter. I want to know if SHE'S been there. And if he answers the door, grumpy, then at least I know he's okay."

Avery's mouth was suddenly dry. "You're kidding me. You think Suzanna has something to do with this?"

Alex's voice was grim. "All morning I've been feeling this creeping dread steal over me. My neck is prickling, and something is happening at the corner of my vision. It's what triggered me to call him in the first place."

"Oh, no." She slumped against the wall, thinking. "Did we protect his place, or him?"

"No—not recently, anyway."

"Bollocks. Let's hope he's sick… As horrible as that is."

He sighed. "I hope so too, but I don't think he will be. I'll let you know, okay?"

"Okay. Stay safe, Alex." It had been on the tip of her tongue to say, *I love you,* but she couldn't. Ever since that journey in the car, she'd been meaning to bring up that conversation with him, but she'd shied away, terrified she'd misunderstood and he'd look at her like she was mad. He hadn't said a word about it, either. Instead, she repeated, "I mean it. Don't do anything stupid. I'm already worried sick."

She heard the smile in his voice. "I'll be fine. Be careful yourself." And then he hung up.

She could feel her nervous energy starting to build and the air began to eddy, teasing her hair. She caught a customer's double-take, and she quickly quelled it, taking deep, calming breaths. Half of her wanted to race through the day so they could get tonight over with, and half of her wanted the day to last forever.

Sally headed over, precariously carrying three cups. She handed one to Avery. "What else has happened?"

"Newton has disappeared."

"That nice policeman?"

"Yes. Crap! We should have protected him. Of course she'd target him!"

"Slow down!" Sally remonstrated. "Explain."

"I can't. I need to speak to Helena."

Avery headed up to her flat, leaving her drink behind. Once inside, she shouted, "Helena! Where are you?"

Silence.

She missed her flat. Reuben's estate was great, and she'd really enjoyed spending more time with the others, especially Alex. But it wasn't home. Tomorrow, all being well, she would be back here.

"Helena!"

Still silence.

She marched up to the attic where Helena was more likely to appear and sent out her magic and a summons. "Helena. I command you to come to me right now! I mean it!"

With a faint stir of air, Helena manifested, a challenge in her eyes.

Avery glared at her. "You know who's behind all this, don't you?"

Helena's gaze was coolly calculating. She was shockingly tangible. Was that Suzanna's doing, or Samhain, or both?

"Helena, I know that what happened to you was terrible, but that was a long time ago, and the people in White Haven now are not responsible. You have to stop Suzanna. You are the only one she will listen to."

Helena's gaze gave nothing away.

"One of my friends, *a very good friend,* is in danger. If you're helping her and he dies, I shall do my utmost to banish you forever!" She stepped closer so that they were almost nose to nose. "I will do it. This freedom to move between planes will go. You will be locked away forever."

Helena leaned forward, her mouth brushing Avery's ear, and she whispered, "Trust me."

Avery stumbled back in shock, but Helena had already vanished. She held her hand to her ear, still feeling Helena's icy touch.

She headed to her table, ready to start a banishing spell straight away, and then she hesitated. *Newton. The grove. The Wild Hunt.* There were so many uncertainties, and Helena's part was not clear. If she banished her now, would that benefit them, or harm them?

Damn it! She had to wait.

***

Avery was on the verge of calling Alex when he finally phoned her. "Have you found him?"

"No. His place is a mess. There was a fight, so he didn't go quietly, but her scent is all over the place, as is the strong stench of magic."

Avery felt tears prick her eyes and headed to a quiet corner of the shop, facing the wall. "We have to find him. If he dies, I will never forgive myself. We should have protected him. He should have been at Reuben's with us."

"We won't find him, you know we won't. Hunter's been all over that place, and there's not one single scent outside of his house."

"There must be something we can do."

"We can do nothing until tonight. She'll keep him alive. He'll be her sacrifice."

"If she kills him, I will kill her."

Alex's voice was grim. "We'll find a way. Stay safe."

As soon as he rang off, Avery called Ben. "I hope you're planning to stay away from Old Haven tonight."

"Actually, we were planning to come. It's Samhain, Avery, and the biggest event in Cornwall will be at Old Haven. Of course we want to be there."

"No. I'm serious. Stay away. All of you. I will tell Gabe to keep you away, and you know he will."

Avery heard resignation in Ben's voice. "From a distance, then?"

"Like the moon?"

"Funny, Avery. All right, we'll avoid Old Haven, but we'll be in the town. Our spookometer's been picking up some enhanced readings over the last couple of days. If we can't be in Old Haven, the town is the next best place."

"Your spookometer? What enhanced readings?"

"My EMF meter, obviously. The town's reading is rising."

She was incredulous. "You've been wafting that thing around town?"

"Discreetly, yes."

She sighed heavily. "Please try not to rile the locals."

"Trust me. We're all about discretion." He paused. "You sound stressed. I've not heard you sound like this before."

"We've not encountered this amount of crazy before. I'll call you tomorrow."

I hope.

***

The White Haven witches were at Reuben's house and pacing the large front sitting room in nervous anticipation by half past five. They were all dressed in black, much as when they broke into The Witch Museum a few months before.

Briar was far more upset than Avery expected. She stood stock-still and glared. "What do you mean? She's kidnapped Newton?"

Alex nodded, watching her carefully. "I'm afraid so. We should have protected him. I've been thinking on it all day long."

Briar's hands shook. "Yes, we should have. But that's our entire fault. I've been so mad with him lately that I…" She broke off. "I should have put it behind me."

"Well, tonight," Alex reassured her, "he's our first priority."

They were interrupted by the arrival of Genevieve, and Reuben escorted her into the room. She looked calm and commanding, far calmer than any of them. She took one look at them and said, "What else?"

They updated her on Newton's disappearance, and she swore profoundly. "It doesn't matter. I knew she'd have someone. I'm just sorry it's him. I've already decided we need two teams. An inner team, and the witches who will form the main outer circle."

"What do you mean?" El asked. "Why two teams?"

"The bulk of the coven will support me. We'll form a circle around the entire grove. I've decided that the simplest option is the best. Our intention tonight, and the one that we will focus on collectively, is to stop the Wild Hunt escaping from the grove and running riot. The spell will be for that alone. Containment, and then sending them back where they came from. "

Avery was horrified. "So you're anticipating that they *will* break through into our reality?"

Genevieve nodded. "Yes, unless we can stop Suzanna. But at this stage, she's far too prepared and clever for that to happen. I'm taking the broad approach."

"But what about her final blood sacrifice?" Briar asked, squaring up to her. "Are you saying we just let her kill Newton? I won't do it!" Her voice rose in fury.

"Of course not!" Genevieve snapped. "The second, smaller team will be in the grove. You will have to rescue him, but as I said, I don't anticipate that saving him will stop the spell. She will spill her own blood, or any other if she has to. It could well be that at midnight the magic is so great that the Wild Hunt can break through on their own. Once you have him, you need to get back to us, on the perimeter. But it won't be easy."

Reuben nodded. "We're the second team, right?"

"Right. Can you handle it?"

"Of course we can," El said, flexing her hands in anticipation. "If the boundaries between worlds fall, how long before the Wild Hunt arrive?"

Genevieve shrugged. "A second? A minute? An hour? I have no idea. No one in our lifetime has seen anything like this, ever! But if they break through quickly, you'll be in there when they arrive. You could all be killed, you must know that."

They fell silent, glancing at each other, and Avery slid her hand into Alex's, squeezing it gently. He squeezed back, and said, "We know. We're prepared to take that risk."

"And where is the poppet, Avery?"

Avery had told her about it after she'd spoken to Caspian, and she pulled it from her jeans pocket and gave it to her. "How do you plan to use it?"

"I have a few options, so I'll see what the occasion needs." She tucked it into her bag.

Briar was still annoyed. "Why don't we use it now? Bind her tongue, paralyse her—kill her, even. She then can't kill Newton, or complete the spell."

Genevieve held Briar's gaze. "Do you know where she lives, or where Newton is?"

Briar faltered. "No."

"If I maim her now, she could kill Newton this instant out of spite. Or she'll be so incapacitated that if Newton is trapped by a spell, or locked somewhere inaccessible, we may never find him, and he'll still die. Is that what you want?"

Briar's shoulders dropped. "No."

Genevieve patted her arm gently. "And that is why I can't use the poppet now. Personally, I find them inaccurate and haphazard to use. I would rather see the effects of my magic firsthand. Now, can someone direct me to the bathroom? I need to change into my ceremonial robes. I always wear them when I lead the coven in magic such as this."

"Sure, follow me," Reuben said, leading her out of the room.

Avery looked at the others. "This is going to be far bigger than facing the Mermaids. Maybe just a couple of us should go in to get Newton. I'll go. Who else?"

"No way," Alex said firmly, hands on his hips. "We all go together. We're a coven now, and we work better together. Don't go all gung-ho on me, Ave!"

"All right." She smiled weakly. "I do feel stronger with you guys around."

Outside, cars were starting to pull up, and she saw the familiar figures of Eve and Nate exit the first one. "Awesome. The troops have arrived. I'll go and get them."

For the next couple of hours witches arrived from all over Cornwall, and as each coven showed up, they filled each other in on the events of the last weeks and the plans for the night. There were young and old witches in the covens, and Avery understood what Genevieve had meant by some of them being nervous. They were eager to help, but Avery sensed their inexperience.

Some of the witches wore formal robes—long-sleeved gowns or cloaks. Others wore their normal clothes, wrapped up in thick coats with sturdy boots and hats. Claudia wore a sweeping gown and cloak, and she looked regal and imposing, her magic rising to the occasion. Eve and Nate wore their usual clothes, and the White Haven group spent time chatting to them privately and filling them in on the details.

Jasper greeted them warmly, a long thick cloak over his jeans and boots, and Avery was pleased to introduce him to Alex, El, and Briar. "You guys are certainly shaking up our quiet existence," he said, smiling.

"I'm sorry," Avery said. "We really didn't mean to."

He reassured her. "As big as tonight will be, and maybe deadly, for us to practise together is a good thing. Other than celebratory rites, we haven't done anything like this for years."

Oswald and Ulysses arrived together, Ulysses dwarfing everyone. He wore combat gear and a thick coat, but Oswald, like Jasper, wore a thick cloak over normal clothes. The last to arrive was Caspian and his family, and they drove up in two cars. Caspian was the only one to greet them; the others ignored their presence, but like them they wore their regular clothes.

Genevieve was undoubtedly the High Priestess. She looked stunning. Her hair was elaborately bound on her head, and she wore a long, dark green dress with a tight bodice and flowing skirt, and a long black cloak over it. All heads naturally gravitated towards her and she walked around the room, having private chats with everyone.

Reuben had organised platters of food that had been dropped off earlier that afternoon, and Avery and El helped bring them in. They all needed to eat, but heavy food was not advised before magic of this magnitude. Some of the witches refused to eat entirely, preferring an empty stomach and purification.

At length Genevieve addressed them all and the room fell silent, the tension palpable. "Tonight will be a test of our strength. We will see something that people have not seen for hundreds of years. Some of you may doubt that this will happen. I do not. The Wild Hunt *will* arrive. I have seen the grove at Old Haven and sensed the blood magic there. It is an old place of worship that sits atop a crossroad of Ley Lines—a gateway to the Other, not used in centuries. The yew tree at its heart guards that gateway, and the power is building. The boundaries between worlds will crack tonight. The Wild Hunt is vicious and bloodthirsty, and I believe that Suzanna Grayling has channelled the Crone to make this spell so effective. As to who will lead the Hunt—" She shrugged. "We will see. The myths suggest many leaders. But if they break free of the grove, many souls will be lost."

A young, male witch who had accompanied Jasper cut in, "Lost as in dead?"

"Lost as in either dead or kidnapped, taken to the lands beyond ours without a choice."

"What land? Where?"

"The lands of the Fey. Tonight you will experience wild magic, terrifying and chaotic. You must hold firm." She looked at each and every one of them. "You will be frightened, but you must concentrate only on them not escaping. It is a simple spell. We will raise a cone of power and build a wall between them and us, and I will make it impenetrable. And when the time is right, I will cast them back from whence they came. The White Haven witches will be in the grove—they have a friend they need to rescue. When that is done they will join us. But *no one* must flee!"

"Will we link hands?" another witch asked.

"No. The area is too large. We will link mentally, not physically, but you know how to do that. You will be in sight of others, though. We will be on the edge of the grove. No one goes in except myself and the White Haven witches. Is that clear?"

They all murmured their assent.

Avery spoke up. "I should warn you that Hunter said he'll turn up tonight with some other Shifters. He wants to help."

Genevieve glared. "If they get in the way, they're on their own. I can't take care of everyone. Understood?"

Avery nodded, hoping that Hunter wouldn't turn up. She didn't want him hurt too.

"One last thing," Genevieve said. "The Nephilim will be there behind us, but they will not take part in the spell. They may, however, have a part to play in this yet. Any other questions?"

The room was silent.

"In that case, let's meet at the grove, and hope Gabe has kept the onlookers away."

26

Old Haven Church squatted like a troll against the night sky. The air was crisp and clear and a sprinkling of stars shone overhead, but already a ground mist was rising, snaking over the paths and gravestones, and winding amongst the trees.

The witches made their way to the grove, witch-lights illuminating the path. Some of the witches had set off in other directions, heading to the fields behind the church at the back of the grove, to encircle it. Genevieve placed them all carefully, leaving Avery, Reuben, Alex, El and Briar to summon their courage at the edge of the trees.

"Bloody Hell," Reuben exclaimed. "I haven't been here in days. This place is vile!"

Briar shuddered. "I can't believe another witch would desecrate the Earth in this way. She's a monster."

Gabe stood at their side. "She is the Carrion Crow, bringer of death and destruction. You are foolish to step in there tonight."

Briar was resolute. "We have no choice. We have to get Newton."

Avery looked at Gabe's strong profile as he gazed into the wood. "Don't let anyone else in. I have told Ben and the others to stay away, and Hunter, too, but I have a feeling he's already in there with the other Shifters."

He nodded. "None will pass."

"Are there any onlookers trying to get in now?" Alex asked.

"No. Although some may come later—it's inevitable. Eli will stand at the end of the lane just in case. The other Nephilim are around the grove." He frowned. "What will you use to protect yourself?"

Avery answered first. "A protection spell, similar to one I used the other day, enough to numb the worst of her spell."

Gabe nodded and headed off to patrol the grounds.

For the next half an hour they waited, shuffling restlessly and discussing tactics, and time crept on as Genevieve prepared the circle. The stronger witches were interspersed with the weaker, and to her right Avery saw Caspian, his face lit from below by the pure white candle he held in his cupped hands. He caught her eye and nodded and she nodded back.

It was now half-past eleven, and finally Genevieve reappeared at their side. "We will start. Good luck."

"You too," they murmured as the larger group stepped within the outer ring of trees.

As soon as they entered the grove, a shudder ran through Avery, and she heard the others gasp.

"By the Goddess," murmured Briar. "The Earth bleeds. I feel it."

"I feel the air tainted with blood," Avery said.

"And the waters are stained with it," Reuben added.

"Fire will cleanse," El said with determination as she pushed through the overhanging branches. She had unsheathed her sword and held it steady, sweeping it before her, a shimmer of white fire running along its blade.

Alex said nothing, silently following.

Ahead of them, luring the group onward, was a yellow glow that got stronger and stronger as they reached the clearing with the yew at its centre. Suzanna had already been here. The place was filled with candles. They were on the ground, hanging from trees, and wedged into branches. One sat in the yew's hollow trunk, and the red wood seemed to bleed in the rosy glow. It looked both beautiful and deadly, and the smell of blood hit them like a wave.

Alex fell to his knees, clutching his head and breathing deeply. Avery dropped down next to him. "Alex, what's wrong?"

He blinked and gathered himself. "I can hear screaming."

She looked around, alarmed. "From where?"

"Everywhere."

Reuben, El, and Briar stood around him, watching the clearing and protecting him while he was weak, but nothing stirred.

Alex took a few deep breaths and leaning on Avery, rose to his feet. "I'm okay. I've blocked it enough so that I can think."

"What is screaming?"

His eyes were dark and troubled. "The Earth and the trees. The spell affects them, too. It violates everything. The animals have fled."

Reuben gripped his shoulder. "I think we should draw back and cloak ourselves, so she won't see us when she arrives."

"She'll know we're here, though," Avery said, feeling despondent. "She's too good."

Reuben tried to cheer her up. "We have a good plan. We'll spread out around the clearing as we planned—she can't attack all of us at once. As soon as she's here, I'll run for Newton, and you have to cover me. Agreed?"

They all nodded. "Agreed."

Before they separated, Avery said to Alex, "If you have another psychic moment, get out of here—don't risk yourself."

"If you think I'm leaving you, you're mad. I'm fine now. It's under control," he reassured her. "Don't you do anything stupid, either."

She nodded and they hunkered down, crouching behind trees and bushes, biding their time.

Suzanna's spell was making Avery's skin crawl. It was as if something evil had burrowed beneath her skin and was wriggling about. Goose bumps had risen on her arms, and she felt as if the blade of a knife was running up and down her spine. She wanted to scream. It must be some kind of repulsion spell on a huge scale. The power to maintain that over days was impressive.

Avery could also feel the power of the coven begin to grow, a subtle awareness that pricked at her consciousness, and it reassured her. Every now and then she caught a glimpse of a distant flame through the trees, marking the spot where a witch stood. So far, so good.

Without warning, the air in the centre of the grove started to whirl, leaves lifting from the ground and flying around like a mini-tornado. They spun in an ever-widening vortex as more leaves were sucked into the maelstrom, blinding the witches to what was happening in the centre. Avery leapt to her feet as every single candle went out, plunging them into darkness. A scream rent the air, and just as Avery was about to hurl a witch-light into the sky, the candles relit in an instantaneous blaze, and she fell back, almost blinded.

Newton was on his knees at the base of the tree, bound and gagged, and next to him stood Suzanna. Her hair was wild, lifting around her, and she wore black trousers, a tight black bodice over a white shirt, knee-length boots, and a cloak. But Avery only briefly took that in, her attention drawn by the long, jagged knife in her hands and the triumphant sneer on her face.

Avery was vaguely aware that several things were happening at the same time. She lunged forward, whipping air like a lasso in an effort to wrench the knife from Suzanna, and she saw Reuben sprint towards her, weapon drawn. Tree roots thrust up beneath Suzanna's feet, trying to throw her off balance, at the same time that a ball of flames hurtled towards her from the trees. But they were all too slow. Suzanna drew her knife along Newton's throat and blood surged out as he fell to the ground, blood pooling around him as she yelled a furious incantation that Avery couldn't understand.

They had all agreed not to blast her with too much power for fear of hurting Newton, but as she saw him fall, Avery sent a bolt of lightning at Suzanna. Alex was beside her as they sprinted into the clearing, but Suzanna was on her feet, deflecting the lightning around the clawing tree roots, and she rolled free.

Alex, El, and Avery continued to throw everything they had at Suzanna forcing her away from Newton, and Reuben and Briar darted forward, reaching Newton's side. But it was as if Suzanna no longer cared about him. She had spilt his blood, lots of it, and that was all that mattered.

She stood at the edge of the clearing, raising a wall of crackling energy in front of her, and then she started to chant again, raising her hands into the air.

Avery began her spell to bind Suzanna's tongue, but the ground beneath them started to buckle and lift and she fell, unable to complete it. She felt Alex grab her around the waist and pull her backwards at the same time as El sank into the earth, waist deep.

Avery struggled against him. "El, go help El!"

Alex let her go, and together they ran to her aid. Behind them, Avery was vaguely aware that Reuben and Briar were at Newton's side, trying to stem the blood flow.

Suddenly, howling snarls filled the air, and Avery looked up to see half a dozen wolves launch themselves at Suzanna from out of the trees behind her. She was caught completely unaware, and she crashed to the ground. The Shifters must have been hiding, biding their time. They all rolled together in a blur of teeth, fur, and skin.

Unfortunately, Avery couldn't help them. El was uttering a spell in a desperate attempt to free herself, and Alex and Avery grabbed her hands, pulling together.

El screamed. "I can't get free. It's like something is biting me!"

"Wait!" Avery shouted. She laid her hands on the ground and sent a pulse of power deep down into the earth, churning it up as her power sank deeper. Alex continued to pull, and with a reluctant pop, Alex hurled her out and then pulled her backwards. El's jeans were torn and her legs were bleeding as she struggled to rise. In the end, Alex picked her up.

He yelled over his shoulder, "Get back beyond the clearing! I feel it. They're coming!"

Avery glanced back at the wolves. Suzanna was already struggling to her feet, the wolves flung from her as if they were toys, but her arms were dripping blood, and blood was smeared across her face. As much as Avery wanted to attack Suzanna, it was pointless. Her shield between them was still strong, and they needed to get out of there. She shouted, "RUN!" But they didn't, and instead snarled and snapped at Suzanna as she struggled to fend them off.

Avery dropped to Newton's side next to the other two witches. Briar had her hand over the wound on his neck. She was covered in his blood, her arms and clothes slick with it, but she ignored it, repeating a spell over and over, her concentration absolute.

Avery looked at Reuben. "We need to move him."

"She won't let me."

Avery turned to Briar. "Briar, we have to go, now!"

A wild wind rushed around them, and the candles' flames eddied, throwing shadows across them.

Avery turned to look at the yew. They were only feet away, and she saw a crack of light within its centre, as if reality itself was tearing apart.

"Briar!" she yelled.

Reuben didn't hesitate. He lifted Newton in one monumental effort, and Briar was forced to follow, and then all three ran into the trees, as far from the yew as they could get, following Alex's path with El.

The grove's edge was now glowing with a bright white light, throwing the trees ahead of them into sharp relief. The coven had raised the shield.

At the edge of the clearing, Avery risked a look back and saw the yew tree split in two as light blazed from its trunk. The air was rent with the sound of horses screaming, dogs barking, and the long, haunting bellow of a horn carried across the night.

She turned and ran, fear in her throat, her stomach twisted with panic. Wild magic surged outwards, obliterating the revulsion that had filled the grove, and replacing it with something far scarier.

Thudding hooves filled the night, and Avery staggered and fell. She looked back and saw the light shimmer as a huge, black horse emerged, hounds at its feet, on its back a man with antlers on his head and a bow in his hands.

She froze, filled with a mixture of terror and fascination. The horse cantered into the clearing, and behind him more and more horses emerged, the riders shining with a strange spectral light and mad, wild music surging around them. The horn sounded again, and more dogs ran through, all huge, with gaping jaws dripping with saliva as they snarled and snapped.

Avery shuffled backward, hiding within the darkness of the trees and bushes, well away from the gusting candlelight. Not that it was needed anymore. The Wild Hunt brought their own light.

She watched the figure that had entered first. She knew who he was, from a myth; the partner of the Goddess, Herne the Hunter, come to ride through the night. The figures behind him were not of this world, either. They looked like men, but they weren't. They must be Fey. Even on horseback she could tell they were tall, and they emanated magic. They were bewitchingly beautiful, a mix of masculine and feminine; fierce, strong warriors, dressed in dark mail, with swords in their hands and bows at their backs. Their horses were decorated with feathers and plumes, and the saddles and harnesses jingled with silver.

Herne turned towards Suzanna, who stood triumphantly watching. Her face was transformed. She was no longer Suzanna; she was the Crone, bringer of death.

In a voice that transcended time, Herne said, "Ride with me, my queen!" He held his hand out and as she took it, he pulled her up behind him.

His horse whinnied and pawed the ground, and he turned and stared right at where Avery crouched in the undergrowth. He threw back his head and laughed. It echoed over the grove and the ground trembled beneath her feet, and then he pointed at her, and the hounds at his feet raced towards her, teeth barred.

Suddenly, Alex was at her side, and pulled her upright. "Avery, run!"

As she turned, she saw Hunter the wolf launch himself at the hound, and they rolled into the undergrowth. Then all hell broke loose as the Hunt reared on their horses as one and raced out of the clearing in all directions, charging through the trees towards the edge of the grove.

The wolves emerged from their hiding spaces and attacked.

Alex and Avery ran, pursued by Herne himself. They scrambled, half falling and mad with fear, the hounds howling. Together they turned, and while Alex hurled balls of fire and energy at their pursuers, Avery lifted the leaves up to form a wall and sent it rushing towards Herne, buying themselves seconds only.

The grove was alive with the thunder of hooves, the bark of dogs, the howl of the wolves, and the frustrated shouts of the Hunt as they pulled up against the circle of protection the witches had created. A couple of Fey charged at the perimeter, but were thrown backwards by the projected force of the coven.

The wolves continued to attack the dogs and horses as they raced through the grove, but they were horribly outnumbered, and the Fey slashed at them with their swords.

Avery and Alex stumbled to the edge of the woods, seeing Genevieve ahead of them. She stood a few feet clear of the wall of light. Behind her Newton was prone on the ground, Briar next to him, desperately trying to heal him as his life ebbed away. Reuben and El stood next to Genevieve, ready to fight.

Genevieve looked as spectral as the riders. She was bathed in the pure white light of the protection spell, her arms outstretched. She called to Alex and Avery. "Join me, now!"

They stood next to her, raised their energy and joined it to hers, backs to the circle, facing the Hunt, and Avery felt the protection spell envelop her, too, wrapping her in its warm embrace.

Herne came to a halt, a few of his riders spread behind him, each one eager to probe the spell that sealed them inside. Herne's horse pawed the ground in fury, desperate to start the true hunt, but Herne laughed.

Avery tried to focus on his face, but it was hard. His features almost repelled memory. He was handsome, cruel, dark-eyed, long-haired, and broad-shouldered, his feet ended in hooves, and his many-tined antlers rose several feet above his head. His eyes seemed to glow with a feral light.

His deep voice rattled the earth. "You seek to stop me, witch?"

Genevieve's face was fierce. "I seek to send you back from whence you came."

"It is our time now, leave while you still can."

"You underestimate my power, old one. Your time has long gone. You have new hunting grounds now. This place is not for you."

He threw back his head and laughed again as if they were a joke, and the riders behind him laughed too. "You challenge the immortals?"

"I do." Genevieve took a pace forward and pushed her power out towards him. The circle stepped forward, too, and she continued to advance on him, one step at a time, and against his will, he was forced back, the circling tightening continuously.

Herne pulled his bow free, raised it, and fired an arrow at Genevieve.

Avery's heart faltered in fear, but she kept her magic raised, feeling the coven's powers surge with hers, as Genevieve swatted the arrow away like a fly.

Suzanna leapt from behind Herne, her face contorted with fury. She pointed at Genevieve, releasing a stream of fire at her, but it was pointless, as Genevieve deflected it easily.

Avery had experienced the joined power of witches before, but nothing compared to this. She felt it lift her hair, and elemental air lifted her off the ground as magic swelled through everyone.

Herne lost patience. He raised his bow, aimed at Genevieve, and released another arrow at her, but again, she batted it away, her concentration absolute. She stepped forward again, and Herne raised his hand for a moment. Every single rider raised their bow and the air crackled with tension. And then Herne dropped his hand again and the air was alive with flaming arrows, all desperate to penetrate the shield. They failed, and the arrows fell uselessly to the ground.

Avery heard a scream to her right. A young, unknown witch stood the other side of Caspian; she looked terrified. She sank to her knees and the wall wavered. A rider immediately spurred his horse and charged at the weakened spot, punching through it as his horse left the ground, leaping over the fallen witch and escaping into the night, closely followed by a few others.

Genevieve didn't falter, she strengthened the wall, sealing the breach, and Avery heard the riders engage with the Nephilim beyond them, their cries piercing the night.

Genevieve kept advancing and the coven followed her, moving ever forward as they tightened the circle. She paused momentarily as they stepped over Briar, leaving her and Newton behind, and then they pressed on.

As they advanced the wolves attacked again and again, snapping at the legs of the horses, dodging swords and arrows, and harassing the dogs so that they howled with frustration and pain. Herne turned and raced back towards the yew tree.

The coven was advancing quickly now as they reached the clearing around the yew, and soon they were within feet of each other. The wolves paced before them, many of them bleeding and limping as they watched Herne and his Wild Hunt forced back to the gateway between worlds.

Suzanna was spitting with fury. She launched many spells at the coven, but none of them worked. She screamed, "You cannot end this! I will not allow it!"

Genevieve pulled the poppet from one pocket and a knife from another. Her voice boomed out, "You have no choice, Suzanna. You, like Herne, are out of your time. There is no place for you here. I banish you from this world forever." She plunged the knife into the heart of the poppet and Suzanna staggered back, her hand to her breast.

Half of the Hunt had already retreated back through the open doorway to the land beyond. As Suzanna stumbled, Herne's horse reared up, Herne's wild eyes furious in defeat as he glared at them, the only part of his face visible with the light behind him. Then he whirled around straight into the light, the remainder of his Hunt following him with a jangle of spurs, the flashing of silver, and malevolent stares of regret.

Genevieve threw the poppet in after him and in the blink of an eye Suzanna disappeared. With an almighty rumbling sound the light between worlds shrank and then closed with a deafening crack, and the grove was once more filled with silence.

Genevieve slowly lowered her hands, releasing the power of the coven back to the witches, and with it, the bright white light of the protection spell.

With a word, the remaining candles flared into life.

Most of the coven collapsed on the ground, Avery one of them. She felt so weak; she could hardly lift her head. She held her hand out and felt for Alex's, grasping it firmly. He squeezed back. But Genevieve didn't stop. She turned and raced back towards the edge of the grove.

Newton.

Alex pulled her to her feet. "Come on."

El and Reuben had risen too, and together they ran, finding Briar still crouched next to a barely alive Newton, Gabe on the other side, and now Genevieve, as well. She placed her hand over Briar's and sent her the last of the coven's power she still carried.

The blood flow had stopped, though Newton was horribly pale. But at Genevieve's touch, his eyes fluttered and he groaned. Avery sighed in relief, unaware she'd been holding her breath. But it wasn't over yet. He was still just clinging on to life.

Briar was crying, tears streaming down her face. "I wasn't good enough," she said, her voice cracking.

"Oh yes, you were," Genevieve reassured her, "or he'd already be dead." She turned at the sound of someone approaching, and saw Caspian had arrived. "Caspian, take Briar and Newton to the hospital. Do whatever you need to do."

Caspian looked as cool, calm, and collected as always. He crouched down, a hand on Newton's shoulder, and then extended his hand to Briar. In seconds they disappeared.

Genevieve looked at others, clearly exhausted. "I think I'm going to sleep for a week. That's the most magic I've drawn on for some time."

Avery felt a rush of guilt as she remembered how snappy she had been with Genevieve at times. "You were amazing. We couldn't have done it without you."

She smiled weakly. "It's okay. I understand. Life gets frustrating sometimes." She gathered herself with determination. "Come on, we're not done yet. We need to cleanse the grove, tend the injured witch, and ensure that doorway is closed forever." She looked at Gabe. "Did you catch the escaped Hunters?"

He nodded grimly, and Avery realised he was holding his shoulder stiffly. "You've been injured," she said.

"I will live, and the fey are dead. But you need to go into White Haven."

Avery looked at him and then the other witches, confused. "What do you mean? We need to cleanse the grove."

"Ben has phoned. The spirits have risen. They walk the streets of White Haven, your Helena among them."

She looked at Alex, Reuben, and El in shock, speechless.

Alex gathered himself first. "When did this happen?"

"Before midnight." He gestured around him. "They rose from here and other places as you started to battle with the Hunt. Go, *now*!"

They looked at Genevieve, but she only shooed them on. "Go. We will finish here, and then we'll talk later."

***

As Reuben drove recklessly into town, Avery called Ben, and it took him a while to answer.

"How bad is it?" she asked, finally connecting.

"Pretty bad from your point of view, but great from ours!"

"What do you mean?"

"There are ghosts flitting all over the town and we've got some great footage—I hope. You survived the Hunt, then?"

"Only just." She looked around her at the exhausted faces of El, Reuben, and Alex. They were streaked with dirt and blood, and were covered in bruises and cuts from their pursuit through the woods. Reuben was driving with fierce concentration, taking corners way too fast, and Avery bounced around in the backseat. "We're almost there now. Where are you?"

"Bottom of High Street. Prepare yourselves, because—"

Ben's voice crackled, and the line was broken.

Avery looked at the others. "I think this is going to be big."

Reuben turned onto the main street and continued to race down the road. It was now almost two in the morning and the roads should have been deserted and dark, but instead lights were on in upstairs windows, front doors were wide open, and a few people were running down the street, pulling on clothes as they ran.

"This is not good," El said, worriedly.

They were close to the bottom of the town now, and as Reuben rounded a corner, he mounted the pavement and screeched to a halt, and they were all thrown forward. El's hands slapped the dashboard. "Bloody hell, Reuben—" she started but didn't finish, because in front of them was utter chaos.

In the middle of the road was a procession of ghosts, their spectral forms giving off a pale blue light, and what looked like half the town watching with shocked faces, some at the edge of the main street, some down side streets and others half hanging out of upstairs windows. All of them had phones in their hands, recording and snapping frantically. Shop windows were lit up, displays of pumpkins, jack-o-lanterns, and strings of lights a backdrop to the craziness of the spirits.

And there was a lot of screaming.

While some of the spirits were walking slowly, seemingly oblivious to their onlookers, others raced around, disappearing and re-appearing in the blink of an eye, running down streets, appearing on roofs, and manifesting in the middle of huddles of people who then scattered and ran away screaming, only to turn around and run the other way as spirits raced towards them.

"Holy shit!" Reuben exclaimed, and he started to laugh.

Alex groaned. "How the hell can I banish ghosts with half the town watching?"

Reuben laughed again. "There is bugger all that we can do about this! And look, no one's getting hurt!"

He was right. The spirits were like naughty children. They pulled hair, baited people, ran around, ransacked rubbish bins, and actually seemed to be having fun. And despite the palpable fear, sometimes terror, and general excitement of the crowd, Avery had to agree and she turned to the others, grinning. "Wow! This is mad!"

The witches moved in, circling slowly, and now that they were closer, they could see the ghosts' old-fashioned dress and their strange hairstyles as they progressed their mad carnival march towards the harbour.

And then Avery saw her—*Helena.* She led the procession, a look of delight on her face, as her spectral being gave off reams of smoke that billowed around her. She looked around and saw Avery watching. For a brief second their eyes met as Helena grinned in triumph, and maybe a look of relief, too, at seeing Avery unharmed after their battle at Old Haven. And then she turned away, leading the mad carnival onward.

As they reached the harbour, the crowds were swelling, and Avery saw Ben, Cassie, and Dylan perched on the harbour wall. Dylan was filming, while Ben and Cassie were fiddling with their other equipment. A short distance away, Avery saw Sarah Rutherford and Steve the cameraman.

Avery pointed them out to the others. "Crap. This is going to be all over the news!"

Reuben was still laughing. "This is going to be all over the Internet, all over the world!"

El was giggling, too. "This is awesome!" She turned to Avery. "This is what Helena's been up to. You suspected she was up to something!"

Alex snaked his arm around Avery's waist. "Maybe this was her way of keeping people from Old Haven."

"Maybe it was," Avery said, watching the spirits enjoying their freedom. It was infectious, and she felt like running with them. Some people actually were. It was like a collective madness had infected the town. She starting laughing, too, feeling her tension ebb away. Helena never ceased to amaze her. "You know what? I'm going to call Genevieve. I think the coven would enjoy this."

"So would Briar and Newton," Alex said sadly.

"No, he would not," El corrected them. "He would be furious with the publicity and the paranormal tag the town will get." And then her voice trembled. "If he survives."

"He'll be okay," Avery said resolutely. "He has to be."

27

At dawn, after no sleep at all, Avery and the others went to Truro Hospital.

The mad rabble of spirits had finally disappeared as the night edged to a close, by which time Avery was convinced most of White Haven and the surrounding countryside had flocked to the town.

When they were convinced it was safe to leave and that nothing more sinister was going to happen, Avery and the others left the scene and drove straight to the hospital, still in their dark clothing and filthy with dirt, but they didn't care. They wanted to see Newton and Briar.

Newton looked awful, and Briar didn't look much better. He was in a side room, hooked up to drips giving him fluids and a blood transfusion, and a large dressing was on his neck. He was pale and sleeping, but he was alive. Briar was sitting next to him, half asleep in a large chair next to the bed. She had washed the blood off her hands, but her clothes were stiff with it. She stirred as they entered, and El and Avery rushed over to hug her.

"How are you?" Avery asked.

At the same time, El cut in, "How's Newton?"

Briar nodded as tears welled up again. "He's okay, I'm okay. He'll make it."

Alex came over and enveloped her in a huge hug, and Reuben gave her a squeeze of the shoulders as they all crowded into the small room.

Alex smiled. "You did good."

She shook her head, doubting herself again. "Not good enough."

"Briar, none us were that great," Avery said regretfully. "We were there to stop Newton from being hurt, and we failed. Suzanna was too quick, and in the end we weren't prepared enough. But if we hadn't have been there, he'd have bled out. So…" She shrugged.

El sat on the edge of the bed, trying not to disturb Newton. "What happened last night with Caspian?"

Briar rubbed her eyes and sat up. "He was amazing—hard to believe, I know. First he saves you, El, and now Newton. He brought us to the doors of the accident department, using witch-flight obviously, and then ran in for help. He said he'd found Newton on the street close by and just brought him here." She shook her head again, clearly stunned by the events. "No one questioned him. They just whisked us in, and it was fine. The police came and took statements, but we said we hadn't seen anything. If I'm honest, it sounds completely implausible, but Caspian was together enough to use some glamour, and well, here we are."

"Damn it," Reuben exclaimed. "I should like the guy, but I'm still struggling, to be honest."

Avery felt the need to defend him a little. "We have to give him a break, despite what happened to Gil. He's clearly trying to make amends." She felt Alex watching her, and she smiled. "Right?"

He nodded silently, and Avery had the horrible feeling he was mulling something over. She reached forward and squeezed his hand and he gripped hers back, fiercely possessive all of a sudden.

"What happened after I left?" Briar asked, breaking into Avery's thoughts.

Reuben answered. "Unfortunately, the young witch who had collapsed and let the wall break was trampled by one of the riders. She's in a pretty bad way. She's also here, on another ward. Gabe brought her in—once he and the other Nephilim had stopped the riders from escaping the grounds."

Briar's face fell and she sat up. "No! That's terrible. Will she be okay?"

El nodded. "We think so. We looked in on her before we came here. Broken bones, internal injuries, and a fair degree of shock. She's from Jasper's coven, and he was there with her. Her name is Mina."

"Did the riders cause any more problems?"

Reuben grunted. "Depends what you mean by problems. They fought viciously. Eli was injured. He ended up with a spear through his wings, and cuts down his arm, but he'll heal. One of the advantages of being a half-angel is that you have great healing powers apparently, as well as being supernaturally strong."

"Zee, too," Alex added. "A sword almost took his eye. Now he has a scar down his cheek."

"And Hunter and the Shifters?"

"A few injuries there, too. Mainly bites and mauling. They're at Hunter's house now, but they'll be heading back to Cumbria later today. We'll catch up with Hunter later."

"He's okay?"

Alex laughed. "No. But he'll survive. He was worried about you."

Briar dropped her eyes. "Tell him I'm fine."

"You can tell him yourself, he'll be visiting later."

Avery noticed Briar's constant checks on Newton, and how close she sat to the bed. She was pretty sure Hunter wasn't going to like what he was going to see or hear. But it really came down to Newton. *What did he want from Briar?* Avery was pretty sure her feelings hadn't changed for him at all.

"Something else happened, too," Reuben said, a wicked glint in his eye. "Something BIG!"

"Wasn't the Wild Hunt big enough?" Briar asked, looking worried.

He laughed. "There was a mad carnival of spirits in White Haven!" And then he started to describe what happened.

At that moment, Newton stirred in his bed. He peeled an eye open and grimaced. "You lot make such a racket."

"Hey, Newton!" Alex grinned. "You must be better, you grumpy git."

"Sod off, Bonneville. I better have drinks on the house for a year."

"Maybe a month! Don't push it."

Avery sighed with relief. He was going to be okay.

***

After visiting the hospital, Avery collected her gear from Reuben's house and took everything back to her flat, including the cats. It was great to be home, and she turned up the heat, relishing a night in front of the TV, doing nothing.

There was no sign of Helena after her antics of the night before, so trying to convince herself she didn't need to sleep, Avery headed into work to reassure Sally and Dan that everything was fine. To make up for the crazy week, she bought coffees and pastries, and spent time catching up with them—mostly gossiping about the night before, which they had witnessed, too. In fact, it was all the town could talk about. The story was on the news, on the radio, and all over the net. There was a stream of people in the shop all day long, and they didn't want books.

By the time Avery and Alex got to Hunter's house it was late afternoon. Hunter opened the door, once again covered in fresh bruises and with another black eye, and now bite marks scored his arms.

"Wow. You look terrible," Alex greeted him.

Hunter grinned and let them in. His grin split his lip, and it started bleeding again. "Ouch. Thanks. Don't make me laugh. Why aren't you battered and bruised like me and Piper?"

"We have mental scarring, as well as plenty of cuts, scratches, and bruises, thanks."

Avery added, "And enough memories to give me nightmares for a lifetime."

"True that!" He led them into the kitchen. "Beer or tea?"

Alex snorted. "Beer! It's almost five."

He handed them a bottle each and cracked one open for himself. "That was probably the weirdest night of my life. And that says something, after what happened at Castlerigg."

Piper joined them, her hair now a violent crimson, which matched the long cut running down her arm. "Last night was insane! My skin is still tingling with all that magic." She pinched her arm. "It's right here! And those spirits in the town! I still can't believe it."

Avery agreed. "You're not the only one. There was too much magic *everywhere.* Ours, Suzanna's, the magic of the Wild Hunt … Who cut you?"

Piper shook her head. "Some rider guy with a huge sword. I managed to bite his ankle. Hard."

Avery looked around. "Where's the rest of your crew?"

"Headed back at dawn. They didn't want to stay away too long, in case of insurrection," Hunter explained. He leaned against the counter, thoughtful. "Were they Faeries in the grove? Fey? And who was the guy with the antlers?"

Avery answered. "It was Herne the Hunter. The God of the Hunt, the partner of the Goddess. And yes, they were Fey with him, and yes, they brought a wild, chaotic magic all of their own."

Alex agreed. "Too wild. It was unpredictable, uncontrollable for us."

"I could feel it here." Hunter tapped his chest and his head. "Took all of my strength to resist running."

"It's easy to understand why normal people would have no chance when faced with the Wild Hunt tearing through the countryside and streets," Alex said. "They'd go mad, die of terror, or simply become frozen in fear waiting to be cut down or carried away. Without our own magic and supernatural abilities, we'd have stood no chance." He exhaled heavily. "The more I think about it, the luckier I realise we were."

"Don't you guys worship Herne and the Goddess?" Piper asked.

Alex groaned. "Worship is an interesting word. Sometimes we appeal to them to aid our magic, but not worship. Witchcraft does not involve bowing to gods. Magic works all on its own."

Avery agreed. "We possess and wield elemental magic, no gods needed, but we sometimes like to satisfy the gods. They're out there—in everything, if you adhere to pagan beliefs. But they have their own agendas, as you saw last night."

Piper was still confused. "So, Suzanna became the Crone?"

"She had taken on the Crone aspect of the Triple Goddess, but subverted it for her own ends, and yes, Herne recognised the Goddess in her. Gods have many faces. And I probably won't ever appeal to Herne again," Avery said with certainty. "It's easy to give them human emotions, but they're not human, and last night was a good reminder of that. They can be cruel and indifferent to our brief lives."

Piper said, "Your High Priestess, she made all the difference. And the Nephilim. Otherwise, those escaped Hunters would have caused enough chaos on their own."

They all fell silent for a moment, contemplating their great escape, and then Hunter laughed. "But what a thing to see! It was insane, but amazing—something out of a storybook! Definitely something to tell the pack about over drinks and a fire. At least *that* hasn't made it on to the news."

Avery had to agree. "True. It's better to have ghosts on the news than a huge coven of witches spelling away the Wild Hunt."

Alex gestured to the boxes in the room. "So, you're going, then?"

"Seems so."

"We'll keep in touch, though," Piper said, smiling. "If you ever need a pack, just call."

"Same goes," Avery said, smiling back. Despite her snark, Piper had grown on her, and she'd actually quite miss seeing them around. "You're not taking Briar with you?" she asked, half wondering if she'd go.

Hunter shook his head sadly. "I know when I'm beat. That sodding Newton guy just had to get injured, didn't he? She's all cut up about him."

"Hunter!" Piper was outraged. "He's their friend and he almost died!"

"Don't get me wrong, I'm glad he's okay, but well, you know." He shrugged and then grinned. "All's fair in love and war. He better treat her right or I'm coming back to try again."

As Avery watched him, with a wolfish glint in his eyes and Alpha swagger on display, she knew he meant it. *Newton better sort his feelings out, or he'd lose Briar forever.*

***

On Saturday night, Avery was at a very different Halloween celebration. It was the night of the town's bonfire, and she was in the crowd at the castle grounds, waiting for Stan to begin the ceremony.

She leaned into Alex's side, her arm wrapped around his waist, and pulled him so close he complained. "I can't breathe, you crazy woman." He kissed the top of her head.

She looked up at him, admiring his smile, his dark eyes, and gentleness. "Sorry. I can't help it."

"Hugs are good, but breathing's important."

She laughed and nuzzled into him again. Ever since the other night, when they'd all almost died, she felt she was so lucky to have him as her partner. It was only really four months since they'd got together, but it felt like a lifetime, and she meant that in a good way. He made her laugh, looked after her, and kept her grounded. He had simply changed her life. She kept thinking about the conversation in the car when they drove to Cumbria, and was annoyed with herself that she still hadn't brought it up. *What was she so scared of?*

Avery was disturbed by a shout from the front, and then she saw Stan stand on the small raised platform that served as a stage. He and Becky had returned from their short trip, slightly confused as to why they had gone away in the first place, and also wondering why Suzanna was no longer answering his calls. He was also utterly disappointed he'd missed the ghosts. She and Alex had been around to see him, just to check that they were okay, and offered lame excuses on behalf of Suzanna. Now, however, he was again dressed in his Druid robes, and after he'd made his speech and performed his libations, the fire was lit, and the party got underway.

They wandered through the crowds and visited a few stalls that were offering apple bobbing competitions, hot food, donuts, and mulled wine, and then found a good spot to watch the fireworks. Halfway through the *oohs* and *ahhs*, Avery summoned her courage and turned to Alex.

"Did you mean what you said in the car the other day?"

He looked at her thoughtfully. "What did I say? When?"

"You said to Hunter that you would move anywhere and do anything if it saved me or anyone else you loved."

He gave her a half smile. "Yes, I did mean that."

She swallowed. "You love me?"

He pulled her to him and looked down into her eyes, his hand stroking her cheek. "So you heard that? I wondered, because you didn't say anything, and I thought maybe you didn't care." He looked troubled. "But of course I love you. I'd do anything for you."

All of a sudden, Avery was flooded with overwhelming joy. She beamed at him. "I was terrified I'd misheard and didn't want to make a fool of myself. I love you, too. So much." She laid her hand over his, and then rose on tiptoes to kiss him, the noise of the crowd disappearing as she savoured his heat and his kiss.

When he finally released her, he was grinning. "I thought you were planning on letting me down gently, like some hideous 'we're just friends' crap."

She punched him on the arm. "Idiot."

"So no second thoughts about Caspian? He's obviously just waiting for the right opportunity."

And then she realised why he'd been looking worried lately. "No! He'll never have the right opportunity with me, Alex Bonneville!"

He grinned again. "Awesome. Let's talk about a trip I want to take you on." And then he nuzzled her neck and started whispering in her ear, and Avery couldn't stop giggling.

UNDYING
WHITE HAVEN WITCHES (BOOK 5)
MAGIC
TJ GREEN

1

Avery took a deep breath and uttered the spell that she now knew by heart. Within seconds she blacked out, and when she woke up, she found herself on the floor, her cheek against the thick wool rug.

She gingerly pushed herself upright, checked for injuries, and then looked around the room. She had no idea where she was, but the room was beautifully decorated with antique furniture, a huge bed, and expensive Persian carpets.

A moment later she heard a voice, faint but clear. "Avery! Can you hear me?"

She sighed, hating the fact that she could not master witch-flight. "Yes. I'm in a bedroom, somewhere."

A whirling black cloud appeared in front of her, manifesting into the tall, dark-haired Caspian Faversham. He raised an eyebrow. "You seem to have found my bedroom."

She glared at him. "I can assure you it was not intentional."

He smirked. "The bed would have been a softer landing." He stretched out his hand, and Avery accepted it as he pulled her to her feet.

"I'd settle for landing on my feet," she said archly.

"Perhaps you'd like me to demonstrate with you this time? I *did* suggest it was the best way to learn."

Avery sighed heavily. She had been at Caspian's house—the huge one he had inherited from his father, Sebastian—for the last two hours, and was no closer to mastering the skill than when she had arrived.

Ever since Caspian realised Avery needed help, he had offered to teach her, but she had resisted. Partly because Avery knew Alex was uncomfortable with the idea once he learned Caspian had made a pass at her, but also because she didn't really want to spend time with Caspian alone. Although, she couldn't fault him. He'd been the perfect gentleman. But he was also still

Caspian, and therefore infuriating. He'd said the best way to learn was to experience witch-flight with him, but she didn't want to. Until now.

Caspian spoke again, echoing her own thoughts. "Avery, I realise you're a stubborn and independent woman, but you really are no closer now than when you first arrived." He frowned in thought. "Are you still saying that spell?" He was referring to the spell she had found in the old grimoire.

"Yes. Why?"

"Because, as I told you, I don't use one, and neither do most other witches. The spell you found was most likely for witches who are not masters of elemental Air, and was therefore designed to help them achieve witch-flight. Clearly it's flawed, and you shouldn't use it again. It's hampering your natural ability." He held out his hand again. "Let me demonstrate."

Avery stared at him for a few seconds, assessing her options, but had to agree that he was right. She extended her hand and he held it in his cool one, pulling her closer.

"What are you doing?" she asked, resisting.

"Not seducing you, just making life a little easier," he said with a smirk.

He placed his arm around her waist so her back was pulled against his chest, his chin an inch above her head. She held herself stiffly, uncomfortably aware of his closeness.

"Now, I want you to feel as I gather the air. You do what you normally do—pull it towards you, and use its energy for yourself. But you need to become a part of it, Avery."

She grimaced. "Yes I know, but…"

"But you're rushing it. You must control it. I've seen you lift off the ground before. This is a similar process. We are going to the kitchen, which I am envisaging very strongly. Do not resist me."

Avery felt Caspian's power reach out and the air begin to gather. He pulled it closer until they were wrapped within it, and then she felt its elemental force start to rush through her, her body dissolving into it. However, with the process slowed by Caspian, she was better able to feel how it worked.

With a snap, the bedroom disappeared and was replaced by a kitchen. More importantly, she was still standing and conscious.

Avery pulled away from Caspian, who still held her lightly, and looked around the room. "Wow. We made it!"

He sounded impatient. "Of course we made it! I'm an expert."

She turned to look at him and resisted slapping his arrogant face. "You're right. I could feel how to do it better with you."

He smirked. "Everything's better with me, Avery."

She snorted. "I doubt that."

He still looked insufferably pleased with himself. "Suit yourself. Now, once more. But this time, I'll do it slightly quicker."

She backed into his embrace once more, wondering at what point double-entendres with Caspian had become normal, but within seconds the room disappeared again. This time they reappeared in the garden overlooking the large lawn that spread to the shrubs and trees bordering the grounds.

She shivered as she stepped away. "Bloody hell. It's freezing! Did we have to come outside?"

He grinned. "I thought it would motivate you to get back inside again. Ready to try on your own?"

Avery nodded. "Yes. I can definitely feel where I was going wrong before."

"Good. See you back in the kitchen." And with that, he disappeared.

She took a deep breath and closed her eyes, clearly envisaging Caspian's kitchen, and then she summoned Air, dissolving her being into it. The now familiar but uncomfortable sensation overcame her, and this time, she landed in the kitchen, fully conscious, but on the floor again.

"Bollocks," she exclaimed.

Caspian was leaning against the counter, watching her. "But you're here, and awake! I really am a great teacher."

Avery just stared at him as she stood. "Can you stop being quite so irritating? I'm going to try again. Put the kettle on."

***

Avery drove back into White Haven after leaving Caspian's place and headed to The Wayward Son, Alex's pub, ready for some lunch.

She smiled as she navigated through the streets. It was a Thursday in mid-December, and the entire town was now groaning under Christmas decorations. A large Christmas tree had been erected in the square, shop fronts and restaurants were lit up with fairy lights, and the streets were adorned with giant baubles and snowflakes.

Avery loved Christmas. She didn't believe in God or Jesus, instead celebrating the pagan Winter Solstice, but nevertheless, she loved the way everyone came together to enjoy each other's company and to give presents.

The winding streets were full of shoppers huddled in heavy woollen coats or puffer jackets. The skies were grey and heavy with clouds, and a biting wind sliced through the streets. It looked as if it would rain, and Avery mused, it might even snow. Although, on the coast, snow never seemed to stick around for long.

As she rounded the corner onto the quayside, the view opened up and she saw the sea stretching to the horizon. The sea was as grey as the sky, and fishing boats bobbed on the heavy swells. Avery shivered, despite the warmth in her van. She pulled around the back of the pub and squeezed it into a parking spot. When she entered the pub, the chatter of the lunchtime crowd hit her, and she headed toward the bar to her usual spot.

Alex, another witch and her boyfriend, was pulling pints, and he grinned as he saw her. He was working with Zee, one of the Nephilim, and a young woman who Avery had never met before. This must be either Grace or Maia. Alex had told her he'd employed some extra bar staff for the Christmas and New Year period. The young woman was blonde, and looked to be in her early twenties. Alex had said they were both students at the university. Zee caught her eye and nodded before continuing to serve customers, and Avery smiled. Zee now had a scar running down his left cheek after his encounter with the Wild Hunt a few weeks before on All Hallows' Eve. With Briar's salves and his own unnatural ability to heal, it had already faded considerably.

Avery perched on a stool, and looked around the pub at the crowded tables. A large Christmas tree stood in the corner of the room, decorated with lights and baubles, and tinsel was strung up over the bar. She recognised quite a few faces, but there were new ones, which was unusual at this time of year. It was well out of the summer holiday season, and the school holidays were another couple of weeks off. But she knew why the place was busy. It was the same reason the whole town had been busy for weeks.

Ever since Samhain and the Walk of the Spirits, as the press had called it, paranormal lovers and ghost hunters had arrived in droves. They had booked up hotels and Bed and Breakfast places, and the whine of EMF metres sounded along every street. The event had put White Haven on the map. The footage—admittedly sketchy—had been on national news, and interviews with the locals had dominated headlines for over a week. Ben, Dylan, and Cassie, the paranormal investigators, had also been interviewed, and they were now getting referrals from all over Cornwall. National reporters had descended for a few days, and then finding that nothing else of interest was happening, had disappeared again. But the steady stream of other visitors had remained.

Avery allowed herself a smile. The Walk of the Spirits had been fun, especially after the horrors of the Wild Hunt in Old Haven Church. Although, not a single ghost had appeared in the centre of White Haven since. Except, of course, for Helena, her own witch ancestor who'd been burned at the stake. She was now a ghost who appeared from time to time in her flat. Avery strongly suspected that Helena had organised the spirit walk in order to keep everyone's focus away from Old Haven Church, if ghosts did such things as *organising*. It was a surprisingly magnanimous gesture from Helena if that was the case. Avery presumed that with the passing of Samhain, the time when the veils between worlds became thinner, the opportunity for such a mass event had gone. However, there were still spirit sightings, hauntings, poltergeists, and other unusual spirit activity in certain places.

Avery was disturbed from her reverie by Alex placing a glass of red wine in front of her. His dark brown, shoulder-length hair was loose, and as usual he had stubble across his lower jaw and chin. "Hi, gorgeous. How did your witch-flight go?"

She smiled. "Very well. I can do it! I hesitate to use the word *master*, but I don't pass out anymore."

He grinned and leaned closer. "Awesome. I knew you'd do it. And I expect you to show me later."

"Of course. How is your new staff?" Avery nodded to the blonde.

"That's Grace. She's a bit slow, but she'll pick it up. She's very charming, and I'm pretty sure very capable of telling the overeager punters to back off." He frowned, changing the subject. "How was Caspian?"

"Very helpful. I actually didn't need the spell from my grimoire, but I did need his guidance."

"Did he try anything with you?"

Avery knew Alex was annoyed at Caspian for his over-familiarity with her, and she tried to reassure him. "No. He was the perfect gentleman, and as usual, very annoying."

"Good." Alex looked relieved, and he pulled a menu off the bar. "Go and grab a seat and I'll join you in a minute."

"Are you sure you can spare the time? I don't mind if you're too busy." She looked around at the room again. "There are a lot of people in today!"

"And my bar staff are very capable of handling the crowd," he said with a wink. "Besides, I have news."

Avery headed to the small back room that Alex had spelled to remain quiet, a haven for the locals, and found a table under the window looking out on the small courtyard garden that was deserted today, except for two hardy smokers who sat under a string of colourful fairy lights.

Avery had barely had time to decide on her lunch of soup and garlic bread when Alex reappeared, placed their orders, and then sat down opposite her with a pint.

"So, what's your mysterious news?" Avery asked, thinking it was something about the pub or their Christmas plans. They hadn't decided how to spend it yet, but were debating whether to go to Reuben's, their surfer friend and rich witch who lived at Greenlane Manor.

He sighed and stared at the table for a second, and then looked up, his eyes meeting hers. "You know how we thought Gabe, Zee, and the other Nephilim had killed the two fey who broke through the protection circle?"

"Yes." Avery hesitated. "Well, not so much presumed. Gabe said they had."

"Well, he lied. One of them was killed, the other one survived."

Avery almost dropped her drink in shock. "What do you mean? A fey is alive, here in White Haven!" She looked around as if she would see it sitting in the bar, casually sharing a drink with the locals.

Alex laughed briefly before looking deadly serious. "No, she's not here. Gabe's keeping her prisoner up at that old, creaky farmhouse they live in on the edge of the moor."

"The fey is a *she*? And how do you know?" Avery's heart began to pound with worry and annoyance.

"Zee told me. He's not happy about it. He wants me to 'do something.'"

Avery frowned and took a big glug of wine in an effort to steady her thoughts. "But it's been almost six weeks since Samhain! He's been keeping her prisoner all that time? That's terrible!"

Alex shrugged. "Well, yes and no. Would you rather she was dead?"

"Well, if she was killed during battle as I expected, yes. She was attacking us! She was part of the Hunt!"

"Well, according to Zee, she's not attacking anyone anymore. She just wants to get out and try to salvage her life."

Avery's thoughts were reeling and she leaned back in her chair. "Does Gabe know that you know?"

"Not yet." Alex watched her, his dark eyes thoughtful. "But I'm going up to see him this evening, when Zee finishes his shift. Want to come?"

"Hell, yes! I've been dying to get up to their place. Gabe has been very secretive."

"That's why I'm going with Zee," Alex explained. "I want to be sure of a warm welcome."

"He still may not let us in. In fact, he may be furious with Zee."

"Zee's a big boy. I'm sure he can handle it," Alex said, and then promptly shut up as their food was delivered by a nervous Grace.

She smiled as she placed their plates in front of them and Avery introduced herself.

Grace nodded, saying, "Good to meet you, Avery. I've heard all about you! See you next time."

As she disappeared back to the bar, Avery said, "I presume she doesn't know we're witches."

Alex shook his head. "She doesn't know she works with a Nephilim, either. Not many do." He winked. "There are some things I like to keep secret."

2

Avery and Alex followed Zee up the winding country lane to the house he shared with the other Nephilim.

Zee rode on an old Enfield motorbike at unnerving speed, and Avery found herself gasping every time he rounded a corner. In the end, Alex gave up trying to keep up, and they cruised along behind him, knowing he'd wait for them before he went inside the house.

After navigating a series of winding lanes in the darkness of the crisp, cold December evening, they finally found the turn off to the old farmhouse. The road quickly became rutted, and Alex cursed as his low-slung Alfa bounced along. "Bloody stupid dirt lanes," he muttered under his breath as he slowed to a crawl.

The headlights picked out a wide, steel gate that was swung back against the wall of an outbuilding, and they entered a paved courtyard. The main, two-storey building lay ahead, but numerous small outbuildings surrounded the courtyard on all sides. It was easy to tell it had once been a working farmhouse.

Zee was leaning against the wall of the house, and he pushed himself away as they exited the car. He was dressed in motorbike leathers, and he carried his helmet in his hand. A single light shone overhead, casting his features in shadow, and Avery shivered. She didn't know anything really about the Nephilim, other than they were the sons of Angels and women who had lived and died in biblical times, killed by the great flood, and unwittingly released by their magic the previous summer.

Seven of them had been released from their otherworldly plane, and they now lived in White Haven, co-existing peacefully with the town. Somewhere, magically hidden, each of them had a pair of huge wings that they could unfurl at will, and all of them were well over six feet in height, muscular in build, and had a keen intelligence. Apparently, they were reasonably impervious to magic, and had great healing powers. Avery had a feeling there was a lot more about them they didn't know. More importantly, Avery still wasn't entirely sure they could trust them. Although to be fair, they'd supported the witches when the Wild Hunt attacked at Samhain, and had given them no reason to doubt them so far.

Gabe, short for Gabreel, seemed to be their leader, and was the only one that Alex had made a psychic connection with. Gabe was the spirit that had lurked within the Church of All Souls and had killed the verger, Harry, in order to regain physical form. Despite Gabe's leader status, Zee was clearly not happy with his current decision.

"Is he expecting us?" Alex asked as he glanced around the yard.

"No. I didn't want him to think of a good reason to stop us, or to just not be here."

Alex looked surprised. "Would that be likely?"

"Yep." Zee didn't elaborate, but he turned and led the way through the wide oak front door into a passageway lined with broad flagstones. Avery looked around and grimaced. The place was plain and unadorned. There were no pictures on the wall or rugs on the floor, and there was a chill to the air.

Avery exchanged a worried glance with Alex, and then followed them both to the back of the house and through a long, rustic kitchen to a rear passage that led to the back door and other rooms. The passageway was lined with boots and coats, and halfway along was another thick wooden door on an inside wall.

Zee shrugged his jacket off and placed his helmet on a small side table, and then opened the door. "She's down here."

"Is Gabe there?"

"Probably." Zee was trying to be impassive, but Avery detected tension around his shoulders and behind his eyes.

Alex stepped closer. "Zee, you're being very mysterious. Is this safe?"

Zee sighed and nodded. "I'm just worried about Gabe. She's safe enough."

He headed through the door, and as Avery followed him, she realised there were stairs leading down to a basement. A low light burned, and as they descended, Avery felt warmth creep towards her. The basement was heated, and was far warmer than the rest of the house.

Zee shouted, "Gabe! I've brought visitors."

Gabe's voice sounded muffled. "Who? Zee, I warned you!"

"Too late," Zee replied, completely nonplussed.

Zee led them into a low-roofed, brick-walled room with a slabbed floor. A large cage that was ceiling height took up most of the space, and in it paced a distinctly otherworldly creature.

Avery froze as her gaze met the startlingly violet eyes of a fey woman. She was slightly taller than Avery and lithe, and she paced her prison with a catlike grace. She was dressed in figure-hugging black trousers, a short jacket, and knee-length boots of soft leather. Her hair was long and shot with silver and gold, her skin was clear and almost luminous, and she emanated magic. And she was furious.

Their eyes met for only seconds, but it seemed to Avery that the moment lasted for far longer. Her gaze passed from Avery to Alex and then back to Gabe. "You invite people to stare now? Like I'm some kind of amusement?"

Her voice had a soft lilt to it, an accent that Avery couldn't quite place.

Gabe had short hair and a military demeanour. He was well over six feet and bristling with muscle, and had been sitting on a chair to the side of the room staring at his prisoner, but as soon as they entered he stood and swiftly turned, eyes narrowed. "Zee! What the hell are you doing bringing *them* here?"

Zee crossed his arms, unperturbed. "Doing what I should have done days ago. Someone needs to talk some sense into you."

Gabe looked between Zee, Alex, and Avery. "And you think these two will do it?" He frowned. "And I am perfectly in control of my senses, thank you."

Zee huffed. "You're keeping a fey prisoner in our cellar. How long do think you can do this?"

"As long as I need to!"

"I will live a long time," the fey said, sneering. "And sooner or later, I'll break out of this prison."

Gabe rounded on her, looking huge in the small room, his dark eyes narrowing. "Not from an iron prison you won't."

Of course. Folklore said the fey didn't like iron. Avery had wondered how Gabe could contain one.

Alex sighed. "Gabe, please. What's going on? You said you'd killed the two escaped fey."

Gabe grimaced. "I thought we had. And then, after you witches had left Old Haven Church, we went to collect the bodies, and one of them had gone. I decided not to tell you and find her first."

"And now you have. Well done," Alex said, looking between Gabe and the fey. "And what now? Do we open the doorway and send her back?"

The fey stepped forward, inches from the bar, looking excited. "Can you do that?"

Alex's shoulders dropped as he met her gaze. "No. I'm sorry. I was being sarcastic. That portal has long gone, and the magic that created it, well," he shrugged, "we can't create it again."

"Neither can I. And believe me, I've tried." She obviously detected his sympathy. "So, I'm stuck here, without my kind, in a world far from my own. A prisoner to this gigantic oaf." She glared at Gabe.

"I am not an oaf, woman," he growled.

Avery tried to suppress a giggle. Calling Gabe an oaf was pretty funny. "So, what *is* your plan, Gabe? Zee is right. You can't keep her locked up forever."

Gabe glared again. "I don't know what to do with her! Other than kill her."

"You couldn't before," the fey shot back. "Changed your mind?"

Avery's head was whirling with confusion. "Can you explain how you caught her, and where you found her?"

"We found her trail and tracked her for days. We eventually discovered her in Old Haven wood. She's very skilled at hiding."

"Of course I am. I am fey," she answered smugly.

Gabe continued. "While we tracked her, I had this cage made. I knew iron would contain her and her magic. Long story short, we caught her in the grove, trying to reactivate the portal in the old yew."

"And you didn't kill her. Why not?" Alex asked.

"Because I promised *you* that we wouldn't kill anyone, remember?" Gabe said, frowning. "It was part of our agreement for staying here. When I make a promise, I keep it. And besides, it is one thing to kill in the heat of battle; it is another thing entirely to kill in cold blood."

Alex smiled. "Thanks, Gabe. I appreciate that, difficult though our situation is now."

Zee was leaning against the wall. "Doesn't give us a solution, though, does it? What do we do with her now?"

Avery looked at the fey who was watching their exchange with interest. "Sorry, I hate to call you *her*. What's your name? I'm Avery, and this is Alex. We're both witches, and we're responsible for these guys being here."

"Not your finest moment then, Avery," the fey replied, deadpan.

Avery laughed. *This fey could be a handful.* "No, but they have their redeeming features."

"I have yet to see them." The fey relaxed slightly. "My name is Shadow Walker of the Dark Ways, Star of the Evening, Hunter of Secrets. You may call me Shadow."

Wow. "That's quite the name. Nice to meet you, Shadow."

Shadow narrowed her eyes. "I wish I could say the same. Maybe under other circumstances."

Avery nodded. "Agreed. You arrived here as part of the Wild Hunt. You were trying to kill us, and would have if not for our magic. And you would have killed many more if you had escaped. How can we justify releasing you?"

"I've been here for a while now, Avery. Well over a moon cycle. I haven't killed anyone since, have I?"

Avery held her gaze. "That's an excellent point. Why didn't you?"

Shadow shrugged. "There is no need. The Hunt's purpose is sport—like all hunts. It is a spectacle of courage and skill, and..." She paused for a moment. "Herne enjoys it. It releases his blood lust and reinforces his power over mortals. The witch who created the portal between worlds reminded him of his past glories, and he felt the loss of them greatly. To stride as a God amongst mortals is something in which he revels, and to retreat so soon that night would have cost him dearly. I was one of the chosen when we felt the pull of the portal. You do not refuse Herne." She stood straight and lifted her chin, her eyes flashing with a challenge. "And besides, it was a great honour. But now…" She shrugged. "Why kill? It has no purpose."

Avery looked briefly at Alex, considering Shadow's words. "I hate to break this to you though, Shadow, but you do not look entirely human. How will you survive in our world?"

Shadow smiled in a predatory manner. "I can live under a glamour. It will be easy for me once out of this cage, which restricts my magic." She turned to Gabe, who watched her speculatively. "This is a discussion we have had many times over the past few days, Nephilim. You know this. Why do you hesitate to release me?"

"Yes, good question," Zee added, meeting Gabe's grim stare.

Gabe flexed his huge shoulders. "Because it was I who failed to kill you in the first place. My failure sits heavily on me."

Shadow grinned suddenly, a flash of white teeth glinting in the dim light of the basement. "Will it help if I tell you that you wounded me? I limped away from that battle. And you have my horse."

Of course! Avery hadn't even thought to ask about them. She presumed they'd been killed, too. "Where are the horses being kept?"

"In the fields behind the house," Zee replied, admiration creeping into his tone. "They are amazing creatures—beautiful, intelligent, and fast. Faster than any horse I have ever ridden."

Alex rubbed his face thoughtfully. "Zee's right, Gabe. You can't keep her locked up forever. And, Shadow has a point. For almost six weeks she was free, and no deaths." He looked at her, puzzled. "It's freezing out. How have you survived?"

"I am fey. I can conjure magic to keep me warm, although it saps my strength. That's why *he* was able to catch me. And I can hunt to survive. My bow and arrow are over there, along with my other weapons." She pointed to the corner of the room, where an impressive array of weapons was stacked: a sword with an intricately carved pommel and hilt, a dagger, and a bow as tall as Avery, with a bundle of arrows next to it.

"And I presume your magic helps you speak our language?"

"Yes, it does. Although, our races have long intermingled, and our language is close to yours, anyway." She turned to stare once more at Gabe, whose bulk loomed over her slender frame. "Now, let me out!"

Gabe groaned. "I don't like this at all."

Zee strode forward and patted his arm. "You knew that once you imprisoned her, it couldn't last forever. You have to release her. And you," he turned to Shadow. "Behave yourself. You are superior to mortals, you know that. Don't take advantage."

She gave a shifty smile. "I'll try."

Gabe pulled a key from his pocket and reached for the sturdy padlock and chain that was wrapped around the bars and door to the cage. He unlocked them with a *snick* and pulled the door wide open. The fey quickly crossed through before he could change his mind, and took a deep breath in relief at being free.

Avery felt Shadow's magic swell around her, and stepped back a pace, watching her with curiosity. She might have been human in shape, but her violet eyes glowed from within, and her movements were swift and graceful. Her hair looked as if actual silver and gold were in it throughout. As if she was aware of Avery watching, she shimmered slightly and her magic swelled again, and within seconds the glow within her eyes disappeared, and her hair changed to natural caramel tones, soft and tumbling around her face. "Better?"

"Better," Avery agreed, nodding.

Shadow strode across the room and picked up her weapons. She attached her scabbard to her belt and sheathed her sword, strapped her dagger to her thigh, and heaved the bow over her shoulder, then turned to face them as they watched in silence. "Time to go."

Gabe looked uncomfortable. "Where will you go? It's freezing out."

"I'm inventive," she shot back.

"Stay here," he said.

"*What?*" Zee asked, stepping between them. "Are you insane? When I said release her, I didn't mean invite her to stay."

"I feel responsible for her," Gabe said, his tone short. "We have plenty of room."

Avery watched him, trying to hide her amusement. She was pretty sure Gabe had more than a passing interest in Shadow. And why not? She was seriously hot, and a warrior to boot. If Gabe had a type, Avery was willing to bet that she was it.

Shadow didn't wait for Zee's response. "Excellent. I accept."

3

"Are you serious?" Reuben asked. He lounged on Alex's sofa, beer in one hand and a slice of pizza in the other, paused halfway to his mouth.

Avery knew that not much stopped Reuben from eating, so he must have been shocked.

"Yes," Alex answered, reaching for a slice of pizza, too.

Briar edged forward on her seat. "Really? A fey woman is here, in White Haven?"

"Yes. Staying with Gabe and the other Nephilim. It's like some twisted version of Snow White and the Seven Dwarves."

El sniggered, almost spitting out her beer. "I wish I had been there! Newton is going to be so pissed when he finds out!"

Avery laughed. It was Friday evening, the day after they had been to see Gabe with Zee, and they were sitting in Alex's flat, relaxing on his comfortable tan leather sofa and armchairs that were clustered around a blazing fire, eating pizza. The lamps were lit, candles placed in dark corners, and incense smoke drifted across the room. It had started to rain, and the steady drumming cocooned them.

The five White Haven witches had gathered together for one of their regular catch-ups. Reuben, a tall blond surfer and Water witch, was partnered with El, a leggy blonde Fire witch with the ability to make magic-imbued jewellery. Briar, small, dark, and petite, was an Earth witch, known for her ability to heal and make great balms, lotions, and candles. She had an enigmatic relationship with Newton, their friend the Detective Inspector who had almost died at the hands of Suzanna Grayling, one of Avery's witch ancestors. It was Suzanna who had summoned the Wild Hunt on Samhain. For a while in the summer it had seemed like Briar and Newton might start dating, but then Newton declared he couldn't be in a relationship with a witch. However, after his brush with death, it seemed he might be reconsidering that idea. He'd have to be quick, however. Briar had many admirers, not least Hunter Chadwick, the Wolf-Shifter who'd since returned to Cumbria, but Avery knew he was still in touch with Briar.

Avery curled up in the corner of the couch, sipped her beer, and observed, "They could do with a woman's touch in that place. It's so stark and cold."

Alex just looked at her. "I'm not entirely sure that Shadow is the homemaking type. She was packing some serious weaponry."

"I think Gabe fancies her."

"Really?" Briar asked. "What makes you think that?"

"He had this way of watching her," Avery told her. "And why invite her to stay? That's nuts. She could murder them in their sleep."

"I doubt that," Reuben said. "The Nephilim have very heightened senses. And they're quick. I reckon they'll balance each other out."

Alex shrugged. "Well, it's not our concern. They're adults. They can sort it out."

"It will be our concern when things turn shit-shaped," Reuben pointed out as he reached for another slice of pizza.

They were interrupted by a knock at the door, and Newtown stuck his head in. "It's only me. Room for one more?"

"Talk of the devil," El said, grinning. "Come on in."

He looked suspicious as he came in carrying a couple of beers, and he joined them around the fire. He must have just finished work, because he was still wearing his suit. "Why are you talking about me?"

Alex grinned. "Well, let's just say that life keeps getting more interesting in White Haven."

Newton groaned. "Why? What's happened now?"

"A fey woman survived the Wild Hunt, and is now in residence at *Chez* Nephilim."

Newton looked like he'd been slapped. "What? Is this a joke?" He looked around at them all, dumbfounded. "It's not funny."

"Not a joke. Sorry, Newton," Avery said, patting him on the arm. "Gabe had been hunting for her for over a month, ever since Samhain, and he found her last week."

"She's one of the two who escaped? Gabe said they were dead!" Newton said, still incredulous.

"One is, but she isn't," Alex explained, stretching in front of the fire like a cat. "Her name is Shadow. But, from what we can tell, she isn't about to set out on a mad rampage across Cornwall, so she's just one more weird resident."

Newton took a long pull on his beer before he loosened his tie and took it off, opening the top button of his shirt. His grey eyes looked tired. "I can do without this right now."

"Why? What's happened?" Briar asked, looking worried.

He ran his hand through his hair and paused for a moment. "A student has been found dead on the grounds at Harecombe College."

"Oh no!" Briar said, her hand flying to her mouth.

"That's terrible," Avery agreed, feeling dread creeping through her. "What happened?"

"She was found on the campus this morning, almost frozen—her lips and skin were blue, and there were no obvious wounds."

Alex frowned. "So, how did she die? Hypothermia?"

"Nope," Newton said, and then he sighed as if reluctant to voice his next words. "As I said, there were no obvious injuries, but there were the faintest marks on her neck. Two puncture wounds."

"Puncture wounds!" Avery exclaimed.

He nodded. "The initial autopsy made it clear she lost a lot of blood."

"How much?" Reuben asked.

"We're not sure at the moment, but well over half of her body's capacity. I'll know more tomorrow."

They looked speculatively at each other, but it was El who said what they were all thinking. "I can't believe I'm about to suggest this, but it sounds like a vampire."

Newton glared at her. "Oh, don't you start. That word is being whispered everywhere at the police station."

"What do you think it is then?" Reuben asked, cocking an eyebrow. "Some weirdo who drains people of their blood for some macabre reason?"

"I'd rather it were that than a bloody vampire," Newton said, annoyed. "I've become accustomed to witches and Nephilim, and now I'm supposed to accept fey and vampires?"

"I think once you open up that particular can of worms, Newton, it just keeps on giving," Alex said with a sad smile. "You can't *un-know* this stuff."

Avery noticed Briar's eyes drop to the floor, and she realised this was another reason for Newton not to get involved with her. Not because it was Briar's fault, but because she was part of that otherworld—the paranormal world beneath the everyday. And unfortunately, whether he liked it or not, so was Newton. He just didn't want to admit it yet. He thought he was on the periphery, but he was wrong. Avery inwardly sighed. *Sometimes life was too hard.*

"Who's in charge of the case?" Avery asked him.

"Me, of course. It's already got the weird label, and we know that means me now."

Much to Newton's annoyance, he'd become the go-to investigator for what the police referred to as the strange occult happenings in Cornwall.

He sighed deeply. "I had to see her family today. It was horrible. Her mother couldn't stop crying, and her father sat there like he'd turned to stone." He looked at his beer. "I should have brought more of these, but I have to drive home."

"Have my bed," Alex offered. "That way you can have a few. I can go to Avery's."

Newton shook his head. "I have to get up early anyway and head back to the crime scene."

"Sorry, Newton," El said. "It's a crap way to welcome in Christmas."

He shrugged. "It's just the way it is. Tell me about this fey woman. Should I worry?"

"No," Alex said. "She seems reasonably well-behaved for a powerful immortal. She liked to remind us of that. And besides, if anyone has to do anything, we'll sort it out, together with the Nephilim. You have your hands full. What are you doing over Christmas? I think we've decided we're all heading to Reuben's for the day. You could join us."

Reuben nodded. "Sure, you should. Take your mind off work."

"I'll see. I might be working, if this carries on."

Briar frowned. "You already think there'll be another?"

Newton drained his bottle and cracked open the next. "There always is, Briar, you mark my words."

***

When Avery opened up her shop, Happenstance Books, the next morning, she tried to banish Newton's grim news from her mind as she looked forward to the day ahead.

They would surely be busy with Christmas shoppers, and they had plenty of stock to replace from yesterday. The increased traffic that White Haven was getting following the publicity from the Walk of the Spirits was translating to great sales.

After she'd been up to her flat above the shop to feed her cats and give them plenty of fuss, Avery entered the small back room and put the kettle and the coffee machine on ready for when Sally and Dan came in; surprisingly she'd arrived before Sally, who was usually in first. Sally was the shop manager and Dan was an employee, although both were good friends.

Avery then headed into the shop and inhaled with a dreamy expression on her face. The smell of cinnamon and nutmeg from the oil burner behind the counter lingered from the previous day. The strings of fairy lights that had been put up for Halloween remained, but the pumpkins, witches, and ghouls had gone, replaced with a large Christmas tree in the front window, and sprigs of green pine branches and mistletoe on the shelves and displays. Giant baubles hung in clusters from the ceiling, and the whole place sparkled with Sally's decorative touches.

She'd just arrived back in the kitchen to grab her second coffee of the day, when Sally struggled through the back door carrying two large Tupperware containers. Avery ran to hold the door open for her. "Hold on, let me help!"

"Cheers, Avery," Sally said, looking flushed. "I've been baking for today." She placed the containers on the table and shrugged off her coat. "I can't believe you beat me in!"

"Don't worry, it probably won't happen again." She peered at the boxes, trying to make out the shape of the cakes inside. "What have you made?"

Sally answered with a wicked glint in her eye. "Mince pies, baby ones, and clotted brandy cream."

"Wow! For us?"

"Us and our customers."

"Nice," Avery said, eying them appreciatively. "Have you heard about the death at the college yesterday?"

Sally nodded, her face grim. "Yes, Dan told me yesterday afternoon. Poor girl, and her poor parents. Is Newton looking into it?"

Avery nodded, but their conversation was disturbed by Dan's arrival. He appeared, wrapped in a large heavy coat and wearing a cap that he pulled from his head as he came in, revealing a thick shock of dark hair. "Ladies," he greeted, as he slammed the door behind him. "It's cold enough to freeze my bollocks off out there." He lifted his head. "Mmm, but fortunately I smell coffee, and are those your delicious mince pies, Sally?"

Sally shook her head at him. "When it comes to my baking, your olfactory senses are uncanny."

"I know. It's fortunate you're married, or I might have to woo you."

Sally laughed at that. "Idiot. We were talking about that poor girl who died at the college yesterday."

Dan's mood immediately changed. "Yeah, that's horrible. I caught up with one of my mates who teaches there. Understandably the whole place is talking about it, and it's put a bit of a damper on people's moods."

Avery nodded. "Any thoughts on how she died?" She assumed the news about the body being drained of blood wasn't public knowledge yet.

Dan watched her. "No. Why, what do you know?"

"It just sounds a bit unusual, that's all."

"Well, I presume you know more than we do, courtesy of Newton. I do know she was found sitting upright on a bench."

"What?" Avery almost stepped back in shock. "I didn't know that!"

"Yeah, very strange." Dan nodded thoughtfully as he headed to get a coffee. "I saw Dylan yesterday, too. He's pretty gutted. He knew her."

Dan was referring to his friend, Dylan, one of the three paranormal investigators that helped the witches.

Sally and Avery glanced at each other in shock, and Avery fumbled for her phone. "I'll call him. Poor Dylan. This just gets worse."

Dan stayed her hand. "Not now, Avery. I think he had a late night, a few drinks to help him sleep. Maybe call him later?"

She put her phone away and wondered if some magic would help him, but then she rejected the idea swiftly. Magic wasn't useful for anything like that. It would only mask grief, or slow the healing process. Best to let him grieve naturally. "Sure, I'll phone later. In the meantime, let's stock the shop and get ready for the day."

***

By mid-morning the shop was busy, and a steady stream of customers were coming in, bringing a blast of cold air with them every time the door opened. Outside the day was overcast and dark, making the Christmas lights in the shop even brighter.

Sally brought a batch of mince pies out and handed them around, cheering the customers and Avery and Dan alike. Avery was nibbling on her pie behind the counter and absently looking out the window when she saw Cassie head into the shop. It had been a few weeks since she'd seen her, and Avery left the counter to speak to her by the Christmas tree.

"Hey, Avery," Cassie said, reaching forward to hug her.

"Hey yourself," Avery replied, returning the welcome. She stepped back to appraise her. "You look different. I can't quite work out why." Cassie certainly looked the same physically; her pale brown, shoulder-length hair hadn't changed, and she wore her usual skinny jeans, flat leather boots, and a three-quarter length jacket. It was her manner that seemed different. "There's something a little meaner about you. I don't mean that in a bad way!" she stressed, apologetic.

Cassie laughed. "No, that's fine. I get that a lot. I think it's because I'm more self-confident than when you first met me a few months ago."

Avery nodded. "Yeah, that's it. You looked terrified of all those spooks and ghosts for a while, and now you look like you could seriously kick their ass."

Cassie leaned forward conspiratorially. She was of average height, a little shorter than Avery. "That's because I probably could—if they were corporeal! We've all been learning to fight."

Avery's mouth fell open in shock. "Fight! Like proper fighting?"

"Yeah. For months now, since the summer, and more in recent weeks. Facing spooks and other weird paranormal stuff needs strength of character, but you need to back that up with physical fitness, strength, and agility. Me, Dylan, and Ben have all been training together."

Avery glanced around the shop, and seeing that Dan and Sally seemed to have everything under control, she pulled Cassie to the back room, her de-facto meeting place. As soon as the door was shut, she asked, "Were you attacked or something? Is this why?"

Cassie reached for a mince pie from the supply in the second container. "Yes and no. Just the usual spirits rushing at us, falling objects, thrown objects, weird smoke, apparitions, and tricks. You have to be on your game, Avery. But you know that!"

"I guess so," Avery mused. "But I have magic to help me."

"Hence the training! We all started in the summer, a month or so after we met you guys and realised what was really out there." Cassie helped herself to another mince pie. "These are delicious! Anyway, it's been pretty intensive, but over the past few weeks, I've really started to feel the difference. I mean, clearly I'm no expert after so few months, but I have enough skills now to defend myself. With, of course, the aid of some of your magic."

"Wow! Go you. I'm so impressed," Avery said, admiring Cassie's lean form. "So, you're ready to face anything now?"

"I wouldn't say *anything*...but that brings me to what I'm here for. We've been thinking about items you could help us with."

"Go on," Avery said, intrigued. She vaguely remembered having a conversation a few weeks back about objects that could be imbued with magic.

Cassie looked excited. "We've been asked to investigate this old house in West Haven, the little village on the road between White Haven and Harecombe. The house has an occult history, and the couple who have recently bought it want us to investigate it, although I don't think anything is really happening there. We're setting up recording equipment and a few cameras in some key spots, but..." She paused, mulling over her next words. "After our initial inspection of the house, I've just got a bad feeling about it."

"The house, or the people who've hired you?"

She shrugged and frowned. "Both, really. Something's not right. We've accepted the job, and the money is good, but I was discussing it with the guys. We need magical support."

Avery was worried. None of them had ever expressed concern about an investigation before. "Do you want me or one of the other witches to come with you?"

Cassie shook her head. "No, we can do this on our own. It'll be a week or so of monitoring, and then we might stay overnight. It will be a longish job, time you won't have. Besides, we can't rely on you all the time."

"You've been pretty self-sufficient for a while," Avery pointed out. "All those spirit sightings you've been following up on."

"I guess so, but this feels different, and I can't explain it."

Avery thought for a moment. "So, going back to magical objects, you mean like a ring that could release a spell, or energy balls or fire balls?"

"Yeah," Cassie said, her expression bright. "Exactly. Alex has taught us some simple banishing spells. Briar has taught me some basic potions that I've put into these salt bomb kind of things, and El said she could definitely work some magic into jewellery or a knife. So, can you help with anything? Fire balls sound good!"

Avery grinned. "They do, if I can work out how to make them so that you can use them! Leave it with me. I'll see what I can do." And then she had a thought. "Teaching you some simple wards would also be useful—you know, to protect yourself with. I use a shadow spell a lot to hide with. I might be able to package that up in something. But that would be a onetime use. Once you release it, it's gone, until I make you a new one," she warned.

"That would be amazing," Cassie said, looking relieved.

"I'm glad you're here, anyway," Avery said, heading to the counter and putting the kettle on. "Have you heard about the death at the college?"

Cassie's face fell and she sat heavily in the chair. "Oh, that. I can't stop thinking about it. You know Dylan knew her—sort of?

"Dan mentioned it."

"She was the cousin of one of his mates, I know that much. They found her on a bench!"

Avery nodded. "Yeah, Dan told me that, too. That's just weird."

"There was a big party last night, a sort of end of term thing."

Avery pondered whether to tell Cassie about what Newton had said about the blood loss, and then decided she should. Cassie was a friend and could be trusted. "Newton said she'd lost a lot of blood, and there were two faint puncture wounds on her neck." She poured them both a cup of tea and joined Cassie at the table.

Cassie visibly paled. "Like a vampire?"

"Yep, but not exactly bite marks. It's particularly worrying because Harecombe is so close to White Haven, and I think a lot of kids from here attend there."

"Isn't that where Caspian lives?"

"Yeah, in the massive house he inherited from his crazy father." Avery realised she had no idea who Cassie lived with. "Where do you live? With Ben and Dylan?"

"Not bloody likely," Cassie said, incredulous. "Ben is so messy, it's unbelievable. No, I live with a couple of girls in Harbour Village, Penryn. Ben and Dylan live together, though, in Falmouth, not too far from me. We ended up setting up our business there, after we got booted out of that room at the Uni. They managed to get quite a big place. It needs a lot of work, but it's perfect for our needs. "

"I remember you saying that might happen," Avery said, sipping on her tea. She and Alex had visited their office at the Penryn campus during the summer. They had an impressive range of equipment that they used to monitor ghosts and poltergeists, as well as to test subjects who declared themselves as having psychic or telekinetic abilities. "Shame it didn't work out."

"Probably for the best. They wouldn't like all this extra attention we're getting at the moment from the Walk of the Spirits."

"I thought they'd like that!"

Cassie wrinkled her nose. "Sometimes there is such a thing as too much publicity!" She drained her cup, and then stood. "Anyway, I'd better go. I'll be seeing Dylan later. I'll ask him if he's heard anything else. Cheers for the tea and mince pies!"

Avery stood, too, and walked with her to the door. "Okay, and I'll conjure up some charms and magical aids for you. But ask if you need us. And if for some reason we can't help, we have witch friends who can."

As Avery watched Cassie leave, she reflected that she didn't want her, Ben, or Dylan getting hurt.

4

After work had finished, Avery headed up to her flat, the smell of fresh pine from her Christmas tree soothing her senses. She breathed deeply, letting the cares of the day drain away from her. The shop had remained busy all day, which was great, but exhausting.

Night had already fallen, dark by 4.00pm at this time of year, so Avery closed all her blinds, blocking out the chill night, lit the fire with a spell, turned on a couple of lamps, and headed to the kitchen to feed the cats.

Medea and Circe wound around her legs, glad to see her, and she tickled their silky ears. Once she'd fed them, she poured a glass of wine, and then headed up to the attic, her favourite part of the house, and the place where she worked her spells. Avery had been pondering on Cassie's request all day, and she had finally decided how to capture the shadow spell. She lit the fire in the attic, too, spelling on lamps, candles, and incense, and then sat at her large wooden table and pulled her grimoires towards her.

The familiar feel and smell of the pages tickled her senses, and she sensed the spark of magic beneath her fingers, wrapping around her arms and drifting across the room. When she opened the books, it was as if a sigh escaped them, a palpable excitement at their pages being turned. A witch's relationship with her grimoire was a special one. It linked her to her ancestors, and bound their thoughts, feelings, and knowledge together. She never felt more like herself than when she was performing magic, and she knew the other witches felt the same. She smiled as she stroked the pages, softened by years of use, and protected by a spell that saved them from the ravages of time.

She flicked through the first few pages, remembering her encounter only a few weeks before with Suzanna Grayling, her witch ancestor and Helena's direct descendant, and unfortunately the witch responsible for summoning the Wild Hunt on Samhain. Suzanna had started this very grimoire and the new line of White Haven witches, picking up after Helena's death a couple of centuries before. *So much death, so much anger.* Avery sighed as she ran her hand across Suzanna's name written in her script at the front of the book. She still couldn't believe that Suzanna had managed to time-walk to the present day. The things she must have seen and experienced; Avery had never even had a chance to speak to her about them. Her spells were meticulous, annotations made in tiny writing in the margins, with corrections and recommendations. Nothing had been written in here to indicate her mindset or intentions. *What a waste.* Avery dearly hoped that whatever may happen to her in the future, she wouldn't be tempted into such rash and destructive actions.

She shivered, feeling as if a darkness has settled into her attic space, and she roused herself, turning to the shelves behind her to find a couple of black candles to ward off negativity, and a smudge stick to cleanse the room.

Once that was done, Avery returned to the grimoire and searched for a containment spell, pausing every now and again to examine illustrations, archaic writings, and the occasional journal-style entries. Realising she could search for hours, she said a finding spell, and watched as the pages started to move on their own, as if an unseen hand was searching the book. She smiled as the pages fell open at the right place. *There it is.* A spell that enabled the user to put an enchantment in a box, bottle, or other receptacle. First, she needed to find an object that was suitable.

Behind her on the shelf was a selection of bottles and jars of differing sizes. Some were made of glass, others were ceramic, and she also had a couple of small wooden boxes that might work. She decided to try a petite glass bottle with a screw cap. She placed it on the table, following the spell exactly. She needed to use wards to protect it, and she also needed wax to seal it when the spell was inside.

She worked intently, not even noticing the time until Alex called up from below. She shouted back, "I'm up here!"

He ran up the stairs and smiled, no doubt amused by her very messy workspace. The table was now strewn with objects. "What are up to?" he asked, watching her finish the spell.

Avery grinned. "I have successfully placed a shadow spell into this bottle for Cassie and the others. Something to help with their work. It's good for stealth, but now I need something with a little more punch!" She showed him the bottle. An inky blue smoke writhed inside, the lid sealed with black wax.

"Ah yes. Spells to help them with things that go bump in the night!" He picked up the jar and examined it. "Very cool. I taught them a couple of simple banishing spells, as well. What else were you thinking of?"

"Maybe an energy bomb, in something like a salt ball. Something that would smash easily when thrown to blast an attacker away." She frowned. "I'm struggling, actually. It's a different way to think of using my magic."

He kissed her as he put the bottle back on the table. "Maybe you should bottle some of that tornado wind you control so well."

Her mouth fell open. "That's a brilliant idea!" Her mind began working overtime as she started to plan how to do it.

"No, no, no. I don't mean now! I've brought Thai food, and it's downstairs waiting to be eaten. Come on. I'm starving." Alex grabbed her hand and pulled her down the stairs.

Her stomach grumbled as she followed him, and she realised she was starving, too. Alex had set out half a dozen cartons on the counter, and as she started to dish food onto her plate, she asked, "Did you see Zee today?"

Alex smirked as he loaded his own plate. "Yes, I did, and it's all fun and games at *Chez* Nephilim."

They headed to the sofa with their plates and drinks, Avery desperate to know what was going on. "Don't leave me hanging! What's happening there?"

"Fey magic can do some interesting things!" he said enigmatically.

"Like what?"

"Shadow is living in one of the outbuildings, and it's covered in climbing plants in the middle of winter." He grinned. "Sounds fascinating, but Zee didn't seem too impressed."

"Why not?"

"I have no idea. He just grunted."

Avery chewed thoughtfully. "I think we should go tomorrow. We're both off, and I'd love to see what's going on!"

He looked at her with raised eyebrows. "That might not be a good idea. They may think we're prying."

"I am!"

"You're shameless."

"I know, but so are you." Avery returned to eating, wondering how to persuade Alex they should go.

"Well, in that case, we better take the others, because Reuben dropped in today for a pint, and he wants to come, too, so I said we'd go together tomorrow morning."

Avery threw a cushion at him. "So you'd already arranged it!"

Alex laughed. "Actually, Shadow wants to see *us*."

"She does? Why?"

"I don't know, but I guess we'll soon find out."

***

Reuben collected Alex and Avery in his VW Variant Estate the following day. El and Briar were already with him, looking very excited. The drive to the farmhouse seemed to take far too long, and by the time they pulled into the courtyard, Briar and El had explored a dozen scenarios of what Shadow could want with them.

It was easy to tell which outbuilding Shadow had moved into. It was a long, low building set back to the left, and looked like an old stable block. The building was made of solid stone and brick, with rudimentary windows and multiple doors, but now it was smothered in a rustling wall of green leaves, and the roof was covered in moss. The greenery hadn't stopped there, either. Tendrils of growth had appeared on the farmhouse, small shrubs and greenery were thrusting their way through the flagstones, and a delicious honeysuckle smell filled the air.

Avery's mouth fell open in shock. "Wow. This place did not look like this two days ago. Nothing grew here—at all!"

Briar was wide-eyed in admiration. "Her magic must be very strong to produce so much growth in the middle of winter."

"Could you do this?" El asked.

Briar shook her head. "No way. I could make one plant bloom for a few hours, but I couldn't sustain it, and not on such a large scale. But the fey are of the Earth. It is their element."

"Very true," a voice said from their left.

They all turned swiftly, hands raised for either defence or attack. For a second, Avery couldn't see where the voice had come from, and then a tree to the side of the courtyard shimmied slightly, and Shadow stepped out from behind it, her grey and black clothes blending with the stones in the yard. She walked across the courtyard to join them, and once again Avery had the sense of how Otherworldly she was, even though she looked so human.

"Neat trick," Reuben said, watching the fey intently.

"I know," she answered. Shadow tipped her head to the side and fixed Reuben with a long, intense stare.

He glared back, refusing to give her any ground. "*What?*"

"Water. That's your element. I can sense it moving through you." She moved closer, lifting her head as if sniffing. "It is untapped, as yet. You've barely touched it."

Reuben frowned. "Yeah, well, I've avoided it for years. Go figure."

"You shouldn't be scared of it," she said, before turning to look at El, and leaving Reuben glowering at her. "And you manipulate fire—very well." She smiled at El, and if anything, it made her look even more Otherworldly. "Sister, I smell metals upon you, and jewels. You wield the old magic into weapons?"

El laughed. "And jewellery, and a few other things."

"You must show me how," she said, clearly fascinated by El.

Avery mused on how Shadow called her 'sister.' It was strange to hear, but physically they were similar, and she obviously loved her own weapons.

But Shadow was already moving on, turning to look at Briar. "And you are of the Earth. Small and grounded. It wells within you, gathering around your feet, and moving through your sinews and bones. You are stronger than you look."

Everyone was now staring at Shadow, intrigued by what she might say next, and Avery almost forgot how cold she was, standing in the courtyard with a bitter wind slicing across the moors and fields beyond.

"Alex." She turned to look up at him and closed her eyes slightly. "You have the Sight, spirit-walker. And you banish those who trespass into this realm." She shuddered. "You sometimes tread a dark path."

Alex looked startled, but Avery had barely time to react before Shadow turned to her. It was unnerving to have those violet eyes turned upon her, set within her sharp face with its pointed chin. Her little ears had a slight point to the tops, just visible behind her long waves of silky hair. Avery felt she was being mesmerised. She certainly hadn't experienced this when Shadow was in the basement only two days earlier. "Mistress of Air, and seeker of arcane knowledge. Interesting," she said, before swiftly turning, leaving Avery dazed.

"It is cold," Shadow announced to the group. "Follow me."

She marched to the door of the outbuilding, leaving the others to trundle in her wake, looking at each other, mystified and slightly confused. Alex mouthed at Avery, "*What was that?*"

She shrugged and gave him a half smile, hooking her hand into his arm, and squeezing it. The inside of the building was lined with rugs, blankets, and furs, and a few chairs and other rudimentary items of furniture had been brought in from the main house. A smokeless fire burned in a pit in the centre of the room, and Shadow gestured them to the seats placed around it. "This is my home. Welcome."

Briar sat down, warming her hands over the crackling flames. "Why are you out here instead of in the main house?"

"Here, the space is all mine, and the winged men do not trouble me."

"And why are we here?" Avery asked, and then worried she might have given offense, added, "Lovely though it is to see you!"

Shadow's eyes flashed with a challenge, but also curiosity. "You and your kind banished mine. It shouldn't have been possible. We were stronger, our magic more powerful. We were led by Herne himself, and the finest warriors of our land stood with him. I wanted to know how you did it."

"We combined our magic," Avery explained. "The High Priestess of our Coven harnessed our energies to hold you back."

"If it makes you feel better," Reuben said dryly, "it wasn't easy."

"It does not make me feel better. I am here, alone, cut off from my world and my people."

Reuben was belligerent. "Well, if you hadn't punched through our wall—injuring a witch, by the way—you wouldn't be stuck here, would you?"

A surge of magic filled the air around them, and Avery looked about in alarm, noting Shadow's hands were clenched.

"Reuben," Alex said, a warning tone in his voice.

Reuben glanced at him and nodded, dropping his shoulders and taking a deep breath to calm himself down.

"You killed one of my brothers," Shadow said accusingly.

"Not *us*," Alex answered quickly. "One of the Nephilim did, and only to prevent him from killing others. You *did* come here on the Wild Hunt, Shadow. We protected our own."

Shadow fell silent for a moment, and the tension rose.

Avery's pulse sounded loud in her ears, and she gathered her magic, ready to strike in self-defence if she needed to. *What is going on here?*

Briar spoke next, leaning towards Shadow. "I'm sorry, Shadow. No one anticipated that one of you might be stranded here. That wasn't our intention. If it was the other way around, and I was stranded in your world, I'd be terrified and very lonely. And I would want a friend, someone to trust. If that's what you want, we can help."

"I'm not terrified, I am fey," she said with an air of superiority that was infuriating. "But, yes, I am alone. I want you to open that doorway again so I can go home."

Briar lowered her eyes briefly with regret. "It's impossible. The witch who opened that doorway had planned it for years. She waited for the opportune time, used reserves of our magic, and cast a potent spell to achieve it. We cannot recreate it, and neither can she—we banished her to your world."

"We told you this the other night," Avery said softly. "It wasn't a lie."

Shadow leapt to her feet, her eyes wild. "There must be a way! I cannot stay here with these half-Sylphs!"

"Half what?" El asked, confused.

"Sylphs. They are fey who fly—creatures of the skies. That is what they are!" She gestured behind her to where the farmhouse stood.

"But they're Nephilim," Avery said. "The sons of Angels and humans, born thousands of years ago."

"I don't know these words, and I don't know what Angels are. But I smell fey magic upon them. They are part fey!"

Avery's mind was whirring with questions. "Okay, half-Sylph, fine, whatever. Isn't that good? They are half fey—part of your kind!"

"Not *my* kind. I am an Earth fey." She softened slightly. "But yes, at least part fey. But they have never known their real land. They are trapped here in this shadow-land, like me." She sat down again. "You have magic, all of you. They have not. You must help me get home."

The witches looked at each other, clearly perplexed, and El answered. "We don't know how, sister. The gateways that opened between our worlds have closed long ago."

Shadow's expression was mutinous. "But there must be something! In our world, in the Summerlands, there are special places that can be opened with words of power. And there are artefacts that possess that power, too, held within their metals or pages. That was what I did—well, one thing among many." She looked shifty, as if whatever it was had been dodgy. *Were there any laws in the Summerlands? Were her activities illegal?* Avery wondered as her mind went off on a tangent. Shadow continued, "I was a treasure seeker, a hunter of such things. Hired by others sometimes, at other times I searched for me. There *must* be some of those things here!"

Reuben looked exasperated. "Maybe there are. Through the centuries there have been rumours of arcane objects—mysterious books with unknown powers, and objects that wield incredible magic, but they are probably lost in time, buried beneath the earth. They are myth and legend only!"

"Neither myth nor legend!" Shadow insisted. "They are real, and they are here somewhere. I will find them, and you will help me."

5

The witches sat around a table in a pub on a country lane on the way to White Haven, eating lunch and discussing their conversation with Shadow.

"She's nuts," Reuben said, sipping his pint. "I'm not going to hare off across the country looking for sodding artefacts for her to return to the Summerland!"

"I sympathise with her," Briar said, "but you're right. We have businesses to run! What she's asking is impossible."

Avery sighed as she gazed into her pint. "I don't mind doing some research for her. It might actually be pretty interesting! But, it could take ages. There are thousands of references to strange mythical objects and arcane books that hold secrets. Some of it will be utter rubbish! The difficulty will be finding the nuggets of truth amongst the crap."

"You're talking about a lifetime's search, Avery," El said, thoughtfully. "But we don't know how long her lifetime is. She's not human, her magic is different, and the fey are supposed to be close to immortal—if the myths are true. She could well have much longer to search than us."

"I think it's a good thing she's with Gabe," Alex said. "For all we know, they'll have a much longer lifespan, too. And what did she say about Sylphs?"

"They're mythological Air spirits," Avery said, frowning. "I've heard of them. I've never thought of them as fey, though."

Reuben laughed. "Well, I've never believed in God or angels. They are all part of the Christian religion, which, let's face it, none of us believe in. It's a religious construct that's all about control. And Christians hijacked all sorts of pagan beliefs and festivals. Why not Sylphs? If the borders between worlds really were so indistinct years ago, they could well have been in our world. And how weird would they have been!"

Alex shrugged. "God, angels, or Sylphs, what does it matter? They're just words at the end of the day. Whatever they are, the Nephilim are half-human, half-something. And if Shadow senses fey?" He shrugged. "I trust her to know. And what does she gain by lying? It means nothing to her."

"It doesn't help us with how to help her though, does it?" Briar said, frustrated. "Imagine that one of us had been sucked into the Otherworld? I'm horrified just thinking about it!"

"All myths suggest that we would be used as slaves. At least she doesn't have to suffer that," El pointed out. "I was wondering if I should invite her down to my shop. She seemed pretty interested in what I do."

"Yeah, she did, sister!" Reuben said, grinning. "She's going to be bored senseless. It might keep her occupied and out of trouble."

Alex drained his pint. "If Gabe's got any sense, he'll use her in his security business. That will keep her busy, too." His phone rang, and he picked it up. "Newton, how's it going?" He frowned. "Another? Where?" He nodded. "No problem. We'll meet you there." He looked at the others as he rang off. "There's been another death at Harecombe College. He wants us there now."

***

By the time the group arrived at the college it was nearly three in the afternoon. The sky was heavy with clouds and the day was already darkening. Avery could smell snow, and she predicted that by this evening, the moors would be covered in it.

Newton met them in the car park looking harassed. He wore a heavy wool coat over his suit and had a thick scarf, but he still looked cold. And no wonder, the wind was bitter. "We haven't got long. The coroner has, fortunately for us, been tied up with another death, and we only have one on over the weekend. So, before SOCO get stuck in, I want your opinion."

"You want us to look at a dead body?" Briar asked, her face pale.

Newton nodded. "If you don't want to, stay in the car. I know it's grisly. But I wouldn't ask if I didn't need your help."

"I'll go, if no one else wants to," Alex offered.

"No. If something weird is happening, I want to know about it," Avery said, and El and Reuben agreed.

"It's fine, I'll come," Briar said, not looking at all certain. "Just wanted to prepare myself."

"Thanks," Newton said, looking at all of them. "I really appreciate this. As soon as we get close to the scene, I've got shoe covers for you to wear. And don't touch anything!"

They followed him across the college grounds, to a building on the edge of the sport fields. He headed around the back to where a couple of big bins were half open, full of rubbish. Officer Moore, Newton's partner, was standing guard, and a uniformed policeman stood at the other end of the building. Moore nodded at them, and then walked away, leaving them to it. As usual, he said nothing.

"She's here," Newton said, lowering his voice with sadness. He handed them the plastic shoe covers, waited until they had all put them on, and then led them to the huge square bins. He pointed between them, and on the ground, sitting upright, was a young woman. Her eyes were wide open, staring into space. Her skin was pale, almost blue, and her lips were parted as if she was about to speak.

"Oh, no!" Briar said, shivering. "This is horrible."

Newton looked grim. "Yes, it is. Welcome to my world."

"What are we looking for?" Alex asked, his eyes never leaving the young woman's body.

"She's very pale, as you can see. Almost blue. It could be because it's bloody freezing, but I think it's because she's had significant blood loss. She has tiny puncture wounds on her neck, just like the other one. Can you see if there's any sign of magic? Or can you detect a vampire? Just don't move her!"

Alex looked at him. "Having never met a vampire, I have no idea what signatures they leave. And it's tricky, without touching her, Newton."

He sighed. "I know. But I just want your opinion."

Briar looked as pale as the dead girl, and El said, "Help me search the area, Briar."

She nodded, looking grateful. "Sure."

They walked away, talking softly together, and Alex crouched next to the body, Avery and Reuben crouching on the other side.

Avery looked up at Newton. "Did you say the other one was posed? Sitting up, too?"

"Yeah, but on a bench, where everyone could see her."

Avery held her hands above the girl's body, trying to sense magic, while Alex and Reuben examined her clothing and skin as carefully as they could without touching her. Avery closed her eyes to help her focus. She sensed *something.* It was hard to place, though. It was like she felt *darkness.* But it was very faint. She sighed, exasperated. "I can't feel anything. Not really."

"'Not really' sounds like something," Newton said, an edge of hope entering his voice.

"I don't know how to explain it, other than I sense darkness—almost like a void, I suppose."

"But you can see the wounds on her neck," Alex said. He pointed to the pale round marks over her carotid, almost two inches apart, the skin already looking scarred rather than raw and new.

Reuben grunted. "There's not many things that would leave marks on the neck like that."

"So, you *do* think it's a vampire," Newton said, pulling his scarf around his neck as if to protect it.

Avery had to agree. "It's possible."

"Let me see what I can feel," Alex said, frowning.

They watched for a few seconds, and then Alex jerked back, sitting heavily on the floor. "Wow. That was intense!"

"What?" Newton crouched, too, looking worried.

Alex shook his head. "I had a vision, almost a snapshot of her final moments, and it was just as you said, Avery. I felt I had dropped into a void." He rubbed his face. "Shit. I wish I hadn't done that. That was horrible. I felt her despair and confusion."

Avery reached out and squeezed his arm. "Sorry you had to feel that."

"I'm sorry *she* had to feel that," he answered.

Reuben watched silently, and then, almost regretfully, he closed his eyes and held his hands above her, too. He nodded. "Yeah, I obviously haven't had that psychic connection, but I feel the blackness, too. But that may just be death, as she loses consciousness." He opened his eyes again. "And yes, there's a lot of blood loss. I don't sense violence, though."

"How can her death not be violent?" Newton exclaimed. "That doesn't make sense!"

"It feels gentle, a sort of slipping away," Reuben said, trying to find the right words for it.

Avery nodded. "Yes, that's just like what it feels like. How do you know about the blood loss?"

"I've been harnessing my water elemental powers, practising with El. I can feel water and fluids in the body—it's something I noticed when we lifted

El's curse. And consequently, I know she has less blood than she should have."

Newton stood and walked away, and the others followed him, joined by El and Briar who had completed their search. "Have you two found anything?"

"Nothing at all," El reported. "Nothing magical, anyway."

Newton ran his hands through his hair, looking weary and worried. "So, we know this must be something supernatural, and most likely is a vampire. What do you know about them?"

Avery looked baffled. "Not much."

"Well, I suggest you do some research, because if this is a vampire, I'm going to need your help in finding it, and then killing it. And if it's not a vampire, I want to know what it is."

Reuben looked sceptical. "Have you mentioned this theory to your colleagues? Officer Moore, for example?"

"No." Newton glanced over to where Moore stood chatting to the PC. "But, he knows I consult you about the occult, and whispered rumours are already circulating around the station." He looked uncomfortable. "They don't know what I do, and I want to keep it that way, so the quicker we stop this, the better."

***

Avery and Alex spent the rest of Sunday together at Avery's flat, talking about the two deaths and vampires.

"This is not how I envisaged spending my day," Alex said, as he looked through the books on Avery's shelf in the attic.

"Nor me," Avery said, frowning as she had a thought. "While you search those shelves, I'll run down to the shop and check my stock on the occult."

"And maybe find some books for Shadow's problem, too?"

Avery nodded. "Of course. I'd almost forgot about that."

Alex looked at her, confused. "Why are you running down? Why not use your witch-flight?"

"Of course!" Without another word and before she had a moment to doubt herself, Avery wrapped elemental Air around herself like a cloak and envisaged her shop, and within a second she was there, swaying unsteadily. But she didn't fall over, and she wasn't unconscious. *Yes!*

The shop was dark and gloomy, illuminated only by the glow from the lights on the Christmas tree in the front window. Rather than put a light on, Avery spelled a witch-light over her shoulder, safe in the knowledge that at the back of the shop and behind a large bookcase, no one outside would see.

She had a large stock of occult books, some new, but many were old, collected from house sales over the years. She started to pull books, aiming to keep her search wide. There were a few titles that she didn't remember seeing before, but Sally had been to a house sale only a few weeks before, so maybe they were from there. As she pulled a few out, a mark showed up on the cover of an old leather volume—a mark only visible because of the witch-light. She held her breath for a moment in shock. *Where had this come from?*

The book looked ordinary enough, if old. It was about the size of A4 paper, and an inch or so thick, with a worn leather cover and faded lettering that said, *Mysteries of the Occult.* Avery flicked through the first few pages and then scanned through the contents that included psychic phenomena, tarot readings, and runes and their uses. *It isn't a grimoire, but this is a witch-mark,* she mused. *Maybe there are more witch-marks inside? Maybe it was previously owned by a witch?*

After scanning through a few more books, she gathered up the pile and flew back to the attic, arriving in front of the fire. Alex let out a cry of surprise when she manifested. "Bloody Hell! I don't think I'll get used to you doing that."

"Should I ring a bell next time?" she said cheekily.

"Yes, please. I almost spilt my beer!" He handed her a glass of wine as she put the books on the floor next to the sofa. "Something to lighten our mood."

"Cheers, I think I need it." She sank down next to him, sipping with pleasure. "I found an interesting book with a witch-mark on it."

His eyes widened with surprise. "A grimoire?"

"No." She pulled it from the pile and handed it to him. "This. It looks like an ordinary, if old, non-fiction book on the occult. The mark is on the front, but there may be more inside. I didn't inspect it that closely."

With a whispered spell, Alex extinguished the lamps, leaving them only in fire and candlelight, and then with a flick of his wrist, he magicked a witch-light above them both. "*Mysteries of the Occult,*" he said, reading the title. "Not exactly exciting. But that is an interesting mark." He lifted the book closer and squinted at it.

"I don't recognise it. Do you think it means anything?"

He shook his head. "It may be just a way to mark a book of interest." He turned it this way and that, feeling the cover carefully before he opened it and turned the pages gently. "I don't feel magic on it, either." He handed it back to her. "It's your discovery. Maybe you should ask if Sally remembers where she got it from. Anyway, I'll leave it to you while I sort through these I found on your shelf. Just be careful, in case something leaps from between the pages."

"Idiot," she said, laughing.

For the next half an hour they were both silent as they searched through the books. Avery was frustrated. "There isn't one other single mark in this book."

"Maybe it needs another spell to reveal them?"

"Maybe. Have you found anything?"

"Just the usual history and lore on vampires—garlic and holy water to repel them, and a stake through the heart, burning, or beheading to kill them. I've had a horrible thought, though." He turned around to look at her. "What if these bodies *have* been bitten by vampires and start to turn?"

"You mean they become vampires, too?" She rolled her eyes. "Have you been watching old Hammer House films?"

"It's in the lore, Avery! They might." Alex looked very serious.

Avery shuddered, and the sudden flurry of hail against the window made her jump. "Now I'm spooked!"

Alex grinned and reached out to stroke her foot that was on his lap. "I'm going to go to the kitchen and cook us up a feast, something garlicky, because I'm starving, and a bulb a day keeps vampires away. You can keep reading. Will you be okay on your own?"

She threw a cushion at him. "Yes, I'll be fine!"

"Maybe you should ask Dan tomorrow if there's such a thing as Cornish vampires," he said, as he rose from the couch and headed to the stairs. "Or, of course, ask Genevieve and the coven."

6

Dan frowned at Avery on Monday morning. "Do you go out of your way to find trouble?"

"No! Trouble just seems to find me, thanks," Avery answered, affronted.

It was just after nine, and the shop was still quiet. Outside it was bitter cold, and it was still dark, the light dulled by thick clouds. Hail lay on the ground from the night before, and the pavements were slippery. Avery had just updated Sally and Dan on the events over the weekend, and Sally looked horrified. "That poor girl. I saw it on the news. I didn't think you'd be involved!"

"Newton wanted our opinion," she explained. "And although it was horrible, we had to help."

Dan sat on the stool behind the counter, his chin on his hand as he gazed into space. "I can't think of any particular tales about Cornish vampires, but they don't have to be Cornish, do they? Say these deaths *are* caused by vampires. They could have recently arrived. Or arisen."

"Arisen?" Avery asked, startled. "You mean like it's just woken up?"

"I don't know! You're the witch. Where's it been all this time, if killings have just started?"

"That's an excellent point," Avery admitted. "Are there any other creatures that cause death by exsanguination?"

"None that spring to mind."

Sally looked at them with her mouth open. "Are you both seriously having a discussion about the real possibility of vampires?"

"Yes, we are," Avery answered. "There's a whole, big paranormal world out there. Surely you can't doubt it?"

She sighed. "No, not really. I just don't want to have to acknowledge it. It's Christmas, and I'm feeling jolly. Or was."

"Me, too," Dan said. "If I'm honest, Avery, this is not the conversation I expected to be having on a Monday morning. And no, I don't know anything about magical objects that may open doorways to the Otherworld, either. However," he said, holding his finger up. "There are many strange objects mentioned in British folklore, and in fact, world folklore. Objects that belonged to mythical beings that possessed great powers. But these are objects of myth, and if they once existed, they are long since lost."

"Objects like what?" Sally asked, clearly relieved not to be talking about vampires.

"Well, for example, there are the thirteen magical objects of Britain, commonly called the Thirteen Treasures, often mentioned in the Arthurian tales and other legends."

"What type of treasures?" Avery asked.

Dan thought for a few seconds. "There's a sword that would burst into flames all along the blade, if it was drawn by a worthy man. There's a halter that was owned by a man who could wish for any of his horses and it would appear in the halter, and there's a pot that would contain any food you could wish for. Merlin collected them all together, and placed them in his tower of glass, ready for the return of King Arthur."

Sally looked unimpressed. "Well, that's not a very exciting group of magical objects."

"They would be if you were starving and needed a horse," Dan said. "There's more, of course, but I'll have to look them up."

"What about rings of power?" Avery asked.

"I think you're confusing that with *Lord of the Rings*."

Avery glared at him. "No, I'm not. Cheeky sod. I know the difference between myth and fiction, thank you."

'I'm glad *you* do, because it's all starting to blur for me," Dan said, rubbing his head. "Have you asked Caspian, or the lovely Genevieve? Or maybe Jasper? Didn't you say he was interested in that kind of thing, too?"

"I'd forgotten about Jasper," Avery said thoughtfully. Jasper was a member of the Cornwall Coven, and one of the witches who lived in Penzance. "I'll ring him later. In the meantime, can you investigate for me?"

"Absolutely. I'm sure I can squash it in between pub and football."

They were interrupted by the arrival of their first customer, and they went their separate ways, Avery mulling on ancient objects and vampires. She returned to the stacks, wondering if she might have missed any books that might be useful. She browsed through the arcane and occult shelves, lost in thought, and nearly jumped when Ben's voice disturbed her.

"By fire and earth! Bloody Hell, Ben, you almost gave me a heart attack."

He looked apologetic. "Sorry, Avery, didn't mean to scare you." His cheeks were red from the cold, and he pulled his woolly hat off and rubbed his dark hair to stop it sticking to his head.

"It's fine, I'll live. Have you come for those spells Cassie asked for? I've only done one so far."

"No, although I'll take it if it's ready. I thought I'd show you this." He pulled an old bottle out of his pocket and shook it gently. The bottle was old, the glass a murky blue, and stoppered with an old cork sealed with wax, much like what she'd prepared for Cassie. But instead of being filled with smoke, it contained a collection of needles and nails, and some dried, dark fluid.

"It's a witch-bottle!" she exclaimed, taking it from Ben's hand. She moved from behind the shelves and headed to the window to examine it under the light, Ben following her. "Where did you find this?"

"It was found in the house we've been asked to investigate. The one the couple are renovating. They lifted some damaged floorboards, and found this. It was used to repel curses, wasn't it?"

Avery nodded, still examining the bottle. She turned it under the light, hearing the *chink* as the nails and pins turned in the bottle. She saw tiny bits of skin and fingernails shifting among the metal. A faint wisp of magic clung to it still, like the remnant of perfume on clothes. She smiled with pleasure. "Wow, this is interesting. Fancy finding one in that house!"

"How old do you think it is?" Ben asked, watching Avery turn the bottle, as fascinated by it as she was.

"A hundred years old probably, maybe older, but the witch museum could date it better than me." She looked at Ben. "How old is the house?"

"Late eighteenth-century I think. It's surrounded by an old garden, probably not half as big as it once would have been. I think the land has been sold off over time. Anyway, Rupert and Charlotte are restoring it."

"And is anything going bump in the night?" Avery asked thoughtfully.

"No. It's weird. We've never been asked to investigate a house *before* it shows signs of being haunted. Do you think this suggests it might have been in the past?"

Avery shrugged, puzzled. "This bottle protected the then owner from a curse or a hex or other negative energies. It gives protection. So, it suggests that at one point something unpleasant may have been directed at the owner in the past, but this does not tell us what."

"And the stuff that's in there is common?"

"Common enough. The nails and skin are probably from the person in the house, and the dried liquid is likely menstrual blood. It would have conferred a lot of power."

Ben grimaced. "Yuck. And how does it work?"

"By placing something of the owner in the bottle, like skin and blood, they would attract the curse away from the person themselves—sort of a misdirection—and the pins would burst the evil, or impale it. They often placed it outside, actually, or under a hearth—the heart of the house. Sometimes sprigs of rosemary were used, or urine, or wine. It depends on the witch casting the spell, the person who needed protection, and the nature of the threat. Sometimes a person would make their own to protect them *from* a witch."

"Do you use them now?"

She smiled. "This is fairly rudimentary—a simple spell. I'm using something very similar for Cassie and you, actually. A bottle that contains a spell for your protection, but much more sophisticated."

Ben fell silent for a moment. "Finding this makes me wonder if they know more about the house and the previous owners than they've told us."

"What have they told you?

"That it was owned by a medium, and her reputation suggests she was genuine. Rupert seems to think that spirits may have left their mark on the house in some way." Ben frowned, and Avery sensed he had the same misgivings as Cassie.

"You look as worried as Cassie did."

He shrugged. "I know. I can't explain why, either. Dylan's the same."

Avery was intrigued. "I'd like to check it out—just to see if I can sense something. Is that possible?"

"Certainly. I'm sure I could explain you away as a consultant."

"Great. When are you next going?"

"Tomorrow afternoon, to pick up some of the recordings. Cassie probably told you we're surveillance-gathering for now."

Avery nodded. "Great. I'll see if one of the others can come with me. I'd like a second opinion. But come and grab this spell before you go."

Avery let Sally know she was leaving the shop for a few minutes, and then led Ben to the attic in her flat. Ben looked around with a big grin on his face. "Oh, wow! Look at this place."

Avery looked at him, perplexed for a second. "Oh right, I'd forgotten you hadn't been up here before." She laughed. "It's my inner sanctum that only the privileged few get to see."

"Lucky me, then," Ben exclaimed. "It's quite the spell room, isn't it?" His gaze travelled around the room, and for a moment, Avery saw her sacred space with fresh eyes. The grimoires on the wooden table were open where she had left them earlier, revealing their archaic writing and illustrations, and were enough to give the uninitiated a thrill of the strange. Above the table hung bunches of herbs, and their gentle aroma filled the room with the promise of earthy magic. Lining the walls were several deep shelves filled with bottles of more dried herbs, roots, leaves, powders, tinctures, dark and clear liquids, gemstones, and other important ingredients for spell casting. Next to them were her books, baskets of candles, pots of living herbs, scales and bowls, a pestle and mortar, and other arcane objects. Her Athame lay on the table, next to a small, silver cutting knife and silver bowls containing salt and water. She always had something seasonal in there, too, and at the moment there were bundles of pine, ivy and holly. Yes, this was most definitely a spell room, and every time Avery came here it renewed her soul and filled her with joy.

"This is so you," Ben said, wide-eyed. "I forget when we chat downstairs and in pubs about this side of you, strange though that sounds. I mean, I know you're a witch."

Avery was amused, but she was kind, feeling his discomfort and wonder. "It's not a *side* to me, Ben. It's just me—all of me."

"I know that, really I do." He grinned again, childlike. "Go on, do your thing."

Avery laughed. "You mean this?" The candles on the table flared into life as did the fire in the fireplace, and she sent a breath of wind around the room, ruffling the pages of the grimoires and setting the herbs swinging from the beams.

"Awesome," he murmured as he wandered over to the table, his hands running along it. He paused to look at the books. "Can I touch them?"

"Of course. They're protected from wear and tear by a spell, but even so, be gentle."

He turned the pages as Avery reached for the bottle containing the spell she had made for them. "Here you go. It's for defence, not attack."

Ben turned and took it from her, watching the smoke curl lazily in the bottle. "Awesome. What does it do?"

"It's my shadow spell. When you need to hide, pull the cork and release the spell. It will last for about half an hour without me there to renew it. The wax seal is thin, so it will open easily, and the bottle is sturdy, so shouldn't break." Ben nodded and pocketed it. "I should add that it's more effective at night and in poorly-lit buildings. It will not work in broad daylight."

"Thanks. We're assembling a spell kit, so this is great."

"So I gather," Avery said thoughtfully. "I've going to bottle a mini-tornado for you, too, and a pulse of energy—enough to create a diversion. I'll make a few bottles of each, now that I know I can."

He smiled, "You're the best. Anyway, I better go. I'll text you the address."

She nodded and followed him down the stairs and out through the shop, and felt a chill settle over her that had nothing to do with the weather.

***

After work, Avery headed to The Wayward Son to spend some time with Alex, who was working behind the bar. Within minutes of her arrival, Reuben and El turned up, too, easing themselves onto barstools next to Avery. The pub was an unofficial meeting place, and most nights after work one of the witches or Newton stopped by for a drink to unwind after the day.

"Oh good, I'm glad you two have arrived," Avery said. "Are either of you interested in coming with me to the house our friendly ghost-hunters are investigating? It's tomorrow afternoon, and Alex can't come."

Alex grimaced as he placed a pint in front of El and Reuben. "Unfortunately, my new staff are sick, and we're too busy to leave the rest of the bar short-handed."

"I'm busy, too," El said, reaching for her drink. "Sorry, Ave."

"I can come," Reuben said brightly. "The business ticks along well enough without me. And I need to get out and see something new. What time?"

"About two," Avery said.

"Perfect. I'll drive—your van's a bone shaker."

Avery was mildly affronted, but had to agree. "Fair enough." She looked across to the far side of the bar where Zee was serving a customer. "Any news on our new friend?"

Alex grinned. "I think she's stirred up a hornet's nest. Apparently, she's very determined. Over the last few days, as she's observed their activities, she's realised that for now, she is very much stuck here. Gabe is busy building up his business and making money, and she knows that for now, she has to play it our way."

Avery frowned. "What do you mean, *our way*?"

"Jobs, money. Zee said Niel accused her of being a freeloader, and if he had to pay bills, so did she."

Avery remembered Niel from Old Haven Church. His full name was Othniel, and he was blond and bearded, with very impressive side-burns.

Reuben almost choked on his pint. "Freeloader! That's hilarious. So, she's working with Gabe?"

"For now." Alex caught Zee's eye as he finished serving and called him over. "Tell the guys what Shadow's plan is."

Zee groaned. "She's trying to recruit one of us to help her with her artefact-finding business. She's promised big money. It's what you call bullshit." His face creased with annoyance. "She's causing arguments."

"So some of you must be interested," El speculated.

"A couple. Barak and Ash."

"Ash!" Reuben said, his face falling. "But he works for me! And he's bloody good, too."

"Don't worry," Zee said. "Gabe is having none of it. I don't think he can bear anyone else to work with her, which is worrying in itself. And Caspian's just offered him a contract."

The witches looked at each other in shock, even Alex. "You didn't mention that! Doing what?"

Zee shrugged. "Apparently, the contract with the security team who look after his warehouses has just run out, and he decided he'd rather replace them with us. It makes sense. We know what he is."

Avery sipped her wine thoughtfully. "Wow. Yes, it does make sense, but I'm still surprised. That must be a big job."

Zee nodded. "I might have to do a few less shifts, Alex, if this works out."

Alex shrugged. "I hate to lose you, but you're wasted here. Just give me some notice."

"I'll be here over Christmas, so I'll let you know in January."

"Awesome, that will be great," Alex said, relieved.

Reuben turned, suddenly distracted, and his face fell. He nodded towards the TV screen, muted on the wall. The news had started and headlines scrolled across the bottom of the screen, stating, *Girl found dead in Harecombe.*

Their collective mood fell. "Not another," El said. "They have to be linked."

Avery voiced something she'd been wondering for the last couple of hours, ever since she'd seen Ben. "I'm hoping it's not linked to that house."

"The medium's house?"

"Yep. It's between here and Harecombe. Ben and the others all think it's weird, and they have good instincts, and well, we all know there's no such thing as coincidence."

Alex held her gaze for a moment. "Be careful when you go there tomorrow. Reuben—make sure she stays safe."

"I'm not a child!" Avery protested.

Reuben patted her head jokingly. "Of course I will! Don't worry about me, though," he said, mock-offended.

"You stay safe, too," El said, placing a hand on his arm. "No bravado, please."

Alex frowned. "Three deaths in Harecombe. I wonder if we'll hear from Caspian."

As he finished speaking, Avery's phone rang. "It's Genevieve." She answered, "Hey, how —" But before she could say another word, she fell mute and nodded. "Yes, I'll be there."

"Let me guess," Reuben said. "Another meeting?"

"Tomorrow, at her place in Falmouth. Reuben, you're coming, too."

7

It was a blustery day, and the wind carried the promise of snow. The moors were already covered with a sprinkling of white, and thick clouds blanketed the sky.

Avery felt the solstice creeping towards her; the longest night of the year. Another night associated with the Wild Hunt, but that couldn't happen twice, surely. But more than that, it was a time of celebration marking the symbolic death and rebirth of the sun and the turning of the wheel. Once that night had passed, summer was once more on its way. For the pagans it marked Yule. This year it occurred on the 22nd of December, and the witches would celebrate its passing together, with a fire, candles, and stories. Much like the summer solstice, it would be a time to reconnect to the earth and each other. But Avery shuddered. It was dark and cold, and girls were dying. Someone was hunting them.

They passed a few scattered houses, and then the road turned inland. Locally, it was called the Coast Road, but that was deceptive; the village was a good way back from the closest beach. At one time there'd been a post office there, but now there were a few dozen houses, a popular pub called *The Sloop* on the main road, and a small shop.

Reuben spoke as he drew close to West Haven. "You're quiet. Are you okay?"

"I'm just thinking about those poor girls, and hoping it's not a vampire doing this."

"What else would drain blood through puncture wounds on the neck?"

She turned to face him, twisting in her seat. "I don't know what to think. It's suspicious, certainly, but there are many twisted people in this world."

He glanced at her with a small shake of his head. "Yes there are, but this is something different. Maybe it has something to do with this house. Maybe something has been disturbed. Why else would you get paranormal investigators in? It's a good thing we've been making spells for them. They could be at risk."

Avery glanced at the bag on the back seat. They had brought spells packaged in bottles, potions, salt bombs, and even jewellery. "Do you think there's such a thing as an occult black market?"

"What a weird question! Why are you asking that?"

"Well, all that stuff we've made. I bet they'd fetch good money, if someone stole them and wanted to sell."

Reuben nodded. "Yeah, they would, and yeah, there is undoubtedly one. People will traffic anything. And that stuff is solid magic, undiluted and potent. They should probably keep it all locked up. Do you know that El has spelled a knife that will slice through most things—even some metals—like butter?"

Avery was amazed. "No. You mean like rope or chain?"

"Yep. As long as the chain isn't too thick. And she's spelled a key that will unlock anything, and placed a hex inside a locket."

"Wow. She's so devious! I wish I'd thought of that stuff. What about you? What have you made for them?"

"Nothing. I'm still not as good at this stuff as you guys. I'm good at controlling water, especially when I surf—"

"Yeah, I remember that time when you raised that huge wave." She was referring to a day just after Gil's death when Reuben was so furious and grief-stricken that he'd almost drowned himself and El on the shore. It had been a dark time for their relationship, and for a while, El wasn't sure it would recover. Reuben knew it, too.

"Not my finest moment," he murmured.

"You were grieving."

"That's no excuse for my behaviour." He paused, thinking. "I'd like to remember Gil at Yule. I know that's traditionally more of a Samhain thing, but it didn't feel right for me then. Now it would."

Reuben's brother, Gil, had died in the summer while they were searching for their grimoires. He'd been killed by Caspian Faversham—accidently, according to Caspian. Avery smiled. "That's a great idea. What do you want to do?"

"I want to head up to the mausoleum at Old Haven and wait for the dawn to rise there. It's a weird way to celebrate the solstice, I know, but…"

"But we celebrated the last solstice with him, so why not this? He'll be there in spirit. I think that's a brilliant idea." *And creepy and cold, but Reuben needed this.* "As long as we can have a fire."

"Deal," he said, throwing her a grateful glance as he pulled in front of an old house at the end of a long street, behind Ben's van. "Here we are."

Avery exited the car, pulled her coat closed, and tucked her scarf tighter around her neck. Reuben joined her, and they looked at the house that was positioned on the outskirts of the village. It had three storeys and was made of red bricks with a heavy stone portico over the front door creating a small porch. A large window was to the left of the front door, but several windows stretched away to the right, and a short tower rose from the roof on the left side of the house. The front garden was neglected and overgrown with weeds.

"It looks normal enough," Reuben said, squinting at it.

Avery nodded. "I can't sense anything weird from here." She looked down the street, and then back at the house. "Why is it bigger than the others? Has it been converted from something?"

"Didn't Ben say it probably had a lot more land before? Maybe it was built before the others." He led the way to the house. "Come on; let's get out of the cold."

Avery hesitated just before the porch and pointed towards a plaque on the stone portico. "Holy crap. Have you seen what it's called? House of Spirits."

"Didn't Ben say the owner was a medium? That's good advertising!" Reuben declared as he bounded up the steps. The front door was ajar and Reuben knocked loudly as he pushed it open. "Hello? We're here!"

Silence.

Reuben raised his eyebrows quizzically at Avery and headed inside, shutting the door behind them.

The house was warmer than Avery had expected. The long, wide hall was covered in Minton tiles, wood panelling covered the lower half of the walls, and the ceiling had ornate architrave running around the edges. Doors led to large rooms on either side, and Avery caught a glimpse of old, wooden furniture and out of date décor. Reuben walked down the hall, shouting greetings. The house went back farther than they expected, but they hadn't gone far when they heard a shout from above.

Ben appeared at the top of the stairs, hanging over the banisters. He looked dusty. "You made it."

"Wouldn't miss it," Reuben said dryly. He hefted the bag he was carrying. "And we bring gifts."

Ben grinned. "Brilliant. Come on up."

They headed up the stairs and followed him down a dimly lit corridor, passing several doors on either side. Avery was itching to see inside the rooms they passed, but Ben hurried along, not allowing Avery a chance to look around properly, until he finally halted outside double doors at the far end.

"This is the master bedroom," Ben said, pushing the doors open in a grand gesture. "It's quite impressive."

Avery gasped as she walked in. "Wow! You weren't kidding." It was a huge corner room with two big windows to the rear and side of the house, giving expansive views of the fields and garden behind them. Like the rest of the house it had all of its original features, and the walls were covered in green Chinoiserie. The furniture was solid oak, and old, worn rugs covered the floor. "This is seriously cool."

"Even the crazy bird wallpaper?" Reuben asked, perplexed.

"Particularly the crazy bird wallpaper," Avery said. "Your crazy bitch dead sister-in-law would like it." Alice, Gil's dead wife and demon-summoning witch, was also an interior designer before she was killed by her own demons. "Crazy, but she had great taste. She would *love* this place."

Cassie and Dylan were fiddling with some camera equipment by the bed, and Cassie paused for a moment. "I agree, Avery. This place is seriously cool. I feel like I'm stuck in time. Wait until we show you the rest of the place!"

Reuben adopted a sly smile as he walked over to join them. "Why are you filming in the bedroom? Is it some sort of porn gig?"

Avery sniggered as Cassie looked at him open-mouthed. Dylan winked. "I wish. No, we're just filming regular old ghost stuff. Or something like that."

Ben pointed to another camera mounted on the wall on the other side of the room. "Luckily for us, after days of experiencing absolutely nothing, Charlotte announced yesterday that she'd been having strange dreams. She thought something was in here, standing over her. Obviously we haven't been filming in here, until now."

Reuben edged closer to the camera, trying to see the screen where Dylan was replaying the footage. "Found anything?"

Dylan grimaced. "Not sure. This is a few minutes of the recording of last night. I'll examine it better once we get it home, but I just wanted to see if we'd caught anything. It's all in thermal imaging, because of course it's dark."

They crowded behind Dylan and watched some very dark footage for a few seconds, before Avery made out shapes in the thermal imaging. She could see the bed very faintly against the blackness of the room, and two shapes beneath the sheets. She heard what sounded like laboured breathing and a weird rasping noise. Avery's skin immediately erupted in goose bumps.

"Is that breathing?" she asked, alarmed.

Dylan raised his eyebrows. "Sounds like it, but then there's that horrible rattle."

"Like a death rattle," Reuben observed, frowning at the screen. "But there's nothing there. Does that mean it's a ghost?"

"But there's no spectral form, and clearly it's nothing human or we'd see *something*. You can't disguise body heat—even if it's cooler."

He was right. The Nephilim had shown up quite distinctly when they'd filmed in the church, and humans had very clear imaging.

Cassie frowned at the screen. "Well, we might not be able to see anything, but we can hear something. What is it?"

Reuben shrugged. "Maybe it's something we haven't come across before."

"Maybe it evaded this camera, but will be on that one," Ben said, pointing to the other camera.

"I'll study the footage properly later," Dylan said, changing the data card. "And I'll listen to the audio again."

"But I don't feel I'm being watched," Ben pointed out. "I've got used to spirits being around now, and it's like there's a presence lurking just at the edge of your vision. Here—*nothing*!"

"Not now," Dylan said. "But I bet if we were here all night we'd sense something."

Ben grimaced. "I'm really reluctant to be here overnight until we know what we're facing. I have a strong sense of self-preservation."

Dylan collected his gear together and placed it all in a large holdall. "We may have no choice."

While he packed, Cassie headed for the door and asked Avery, "Fancy a tour?"

Avery grinned. "You know I do!"

Reuben and Avery followed the other three through the house as they showed them the rooms. There was a thick, musty odour that permeated everything, and dust seemed to hang on the air. The wallpaper was old and peeling in places, glamorous once, but now faded and sad, and the carpet underfoot was threadbare. It was clear that renovations had started in some places, but other rooms, including the hallway and stairs, hadn't been touched at all.

"Hell! This is a massive job," Reuben exclaimed as he looked around, appalled. "The whole place needs gutting."

Cassie nodded. "I know. But it will be amazing once it's done."

"But it *is* creepy," Avery said. "I know what you meant the other day. It feels…strange."

"Madame Charron should have called it the House of Secrets," Reuben suggested.

Ben led the way, and he pushed open a door to a room at the rear of the first floor. "There are a couple of rooms we think may have been used for séances. This big one has a central table, and the wallpaper is quite opulent. It *was*, I should say."

He was right, Avery thought as she looked around. It had a faded glamour to it. The lower half of the walls were panelled, the upper half covered in wallpaper. The curtains were heavy brocade, dull now, like everything else, and full of moth holes, there was a huge floor-length mirror, and an ornate chandelier hanging in the centre of the room. "Did they buy it fully furnished?"

"Yep. Apart from some books that Joan, the housekeeper, sold off a few weeks ago, pre-sale," Ben explained. "Rupert was not impressed. He wanted *everything*!"

Avery remembered the book she had found on her shelf, the one with the witch-mark in it that she hadn't seen on her shelves before, and a strange, unsettled feeling materialised in the pit of her stomach. "Do you know who bought the books?"

Ben looked at her, frowning. "No idea. Why?"

"Just wondered," she said vaguely.

Reuben started to press areas of the wall around the fireplace. "Have you found any hidden panels in here?"

"No, but if I'm honest, we've been concentrating on the other stuff," Dylan said, watching Reuben's progress with interest. "I'm pretty sure that Rupert has searched this place very thoroughly and found nothing."

Reuben grunted with disappointment, and after some more fruitless attempts, Cassie led them downstairs to the kitchen, which like many homes, was at the back of the house. It was a building zone, with just the hob and cooker left in position, a freestanding fridge, and a basic kitchen sink under the window. Cassie filled the kettle and turned it on, rummaging for clean cups among the debris.

Reuben grimaced as he took in the room. "Are the guys who own this seriously living here?"

"They can't afford not to," Ben said. "They sank all their money into this place."

Avery looked out of the glazed double-doors that led to a paved patio area. The garden was a mass of overgrown shrubs and weedy borders. "It's been neglected for a long time."

"There was one old lady living here for years, and one housekeeper," Cassie explained. "It was much too big for them to manage."

Avery leant against the frame, looking around the kitchen again. "What do you know about the previous owner?"

Dylan handed Avery a steaming cup of tea. "The lady of the house was the daughter of the medium. She inherited the house from her mother, and lived here alone ever since—well, except for the housekeeper. Her mother, Madame Charron, was well known for her ability to talk to those who passed…" Dylan adopted a spooky voice, "*Beyond the veil.*"

"But she must have been a charlatan, right?" Avery asked as she sipped her tea, savouring its warmth.

"Not according to what I heard," Ben said, referring to his conversation the day before.

Dylan shrugged. "It's hard to know, but she was very famous in the 1920s and '30s."

Reuben leaned against the counter. "When did you find that out?"

"Rupert told us," Cassie said. She'd cleared some space on a counter and sat there, swinging her legs against the old units. "It turns out they're occultists, or rather they study it. They couldn't wait to get their hands on this place when it came on the market. Hence, sinking their money into it."

"But they love it," Ben said. "They are fascinated with every single thing—bumps in the night, witch-bottles, everything. Dynamite wouldn't move them. Especially now Charlotte has experienced her strange dreams and the feeling that someone is watching her."

Reuben looked puzzled. "So, potentially, say Madame Charron had some ability, she *could* have summoned something and now it's here, stuck in the house. Did she use a Ouija board, or a crystal ball?"

"Not sure," Dylan mused. "But I'll make some enquiries. I guess she could have been the real deal. I mean, we try to debunk this stuff, because let's face it, most people do fake it, but *you're* the real deal."

"I couldn't summon spirits," Reuben said emphatically. "I'm a witch and I can shape elemental magic, do spells, and make wicked potions if I try really hard, but I couldn't summon a spirit if I sat there for a whole year, nor could Avery. That's a different sort of skill—the type Alex has."

Avery shook her head, feeling perplexed. "We could be making too much of this. You've found nothing in the house, except for the bedroom. It could be her spirit. Or her daughter's. *Or*, Madame Charron might have summoned something deliberately, for some nefarious purpose, or summoned something accidentally and couldn't get rid of it again. Or, whatever it is, has been around for a long time, before the medium arrived."

"Bollocks!" Ben exclaimed. "So many possibilities!"

"Do you think it has anything to do with those deaths of the young girls?"

Dylan's voice was low. "Don't say that, Avery. One of those girls was my mate's cousin."

"Why should it?" Cassie asked, looking between them. "Surely that's completely unrelated."

Reuben laughed. "Avery's got a thing about coincidences. We all do, I suppose. And the deaths seem to have a supernatural cause, and here you are investigating a house with an occult history."

Avery shot him a troubled glance. "And this house is close to Harecombe and the college grounds."

Dylan groaned. "Damn it. If I'm honest, it crossed my mind, but I've been trying to tell myself I'm imagining it."

"Always listen to your gut," Reuben said. "I don't give advice often, but that one's a given. We all have a sort of second sight—a flash of knowing what's right or wrong. Don't ignore it."

"I wish we could analyse *that*!" Ben said, looking regretful.

Avery sighed. "I hope the students are taking precautions on the grounds."

Cassie nodded. "Classes are over now."

"And let's not forget the witch-bottle," Avery added. "That was placed here for a reason."

"Just more crap to confuse us. Where are the owners of the house?" Reuben asked, frustrated.

"At work," Ben said. "They trust us to come in here, and sometimes workmen are here, too."

Avery swilled her empty cup in the sink. "Show us where they found the witch-bottle."

Ben led the way to the large room on the right of the front door. The walls were covered in old, peeling wallpaper, underneath which the plaster work sagged and cracked. A large fireplace was in the centre of the far wall, and a few tiles in the hearth were lifted up. "The hearth stones are cracked, and, as you can see, they lifted some to repair them; it was under there."

Avery and Reuben crouched down and saw the hole that would have contained the bottle. Avery held her hands over it, sending out a tendril of magic, but all she felt was the remnant of an old spell. When she'd finished, Reuben reached inside as far as he could manage. Avery heard a rustle as he triumphantly pulled something free.

In his hand was a small, yellow piece of paper, dry as bone and brittle. He gingerly peeled it open to reveal a row of runes across the middle.

"What do they mean?" Cassie asked, breaking the silence.

"Something to do with the moon, and runes for protection, I think. I'd have to look them up," Reuben answered.

"I recognise them," Avery said, taking it from Reuben. "It warns against the night, as if it's a curse, and the rest is a protection spell." She looked up at the ghost-hunters. "Can we borrow this?"

"Just be careful with it," Ben cautioned.

Reuben rocked back on his heels. "I think there was something weirder going on in this house than just séances, guys. You might want to get familiar with that bag of spells we brought you."

The front door banged open, disturbing them, and a man shouted, "Ben, are you here?"

"It's Rupert," Ben said, and headed out the door, the rest of them following. "I'm coming, Rupert."

Rupert stood waiting for them in the hallway. Avery estimated he was in his late thirties or early forties, and was of average height and build, but there was an intensity to him that was unnerving. His eyes were deeply set back, with heavy lids that made him look like a hawk, and he peered at Reuben and Avery with interest as Ben introduced them. "These are my friends I mentioned. Avery owns a bookshop in White Haven, and has an interest in the occult. I thought she might know something to help us with this house."

Rupert held on to her hand a fraction longer than was comfortable as he shook it. "And *do* you?" he asked. "Know something about this house, I mean?"

"No more than you do, I'm afraid. But it is fascinating." Why did she have the feeling that she needed to hide as much of herself from him as possible?

He turned to Reuben. "And you? Do you work at the bookshop, too?"

Reuben shook his head. "No, I'm a friend of Avery's. We should probably go, and leave you to it." He looked at Avery quizzically, and she nodded.

They said their goodbyes, the ghost-hunters promising to get in touch, and all the while Avery felt Rupert watching them, and that feeling didn't stop until they'd left the house and were driving down the road.

8

"Can't we go to the pub instead of the meeting?" Reuben asked, looking hopefully at a quaint country pub on the way to Genevieve's house.

"No! Although, maybe we've got time for a quick glass of wine so we don't arrive early," Avery conceded.

Reuben grinned at her. "That's what I love about you, Avery. You're always up for a drop of the good stuff."

"Idiot! You started it," she said, smirking as she got out and almost ran to the pub. It was freezing, and twilight had fallen, bringing with it plunging temperatures.

They ordered drinks and snacks from the bar menu, and settled in a corner by the fire, surrounded by twinkling Christmas lights and the sound of Michael Bublé singing "Rudolph the Red-nosed Reindeer" in the background.

Reuben peered at her over the top of his pint of Guinness. "How much do we tell the coven about the House of Spirits?"

"I think we have to tell them everything," Avery said. "Three women have died under mysterious circumstances. We have to."

Reuben groaned. "I suppose you're right. But as soon as we say something, Genevieve and the others will be all over it. We won't get a minute's peace."

"But they'll probably know something we won't," Avery said, sipping her red wine thoughtfully. "Rasmus has a huge store of knowledge, as does Oswald. They may already have some ideas about what might be causing this."

"They may even know something about that house," Reuben said, and then fell silent as the bar maid brought them their food order. "That place must have been fairly notorious in its day. And Rasmus must be nearly a hundred by now."

Avery threw her head back and laughed. "Don't be ridiculous! He's not *that* old!"

Reuben winked. "Maybe not. But I bet he's an old gossip underneath that fusty exterior."

"You're so naughty, Reuben."

"I know. But if I didn't joke, I'd go mad. I mean, seriously, a house with an occult history, occult owners now, a hidden witch-bottle, strange noises, women drained of their blood…" He trailed off, and they both fell silent for a moment.

After a few mouthfuls of chips, Avery said, "I wonder what those runes really mean?"

"The ones on the paper? I thought you said it was a warning against the night?"

"Maybe." She shrugged. "It was a sign for the moon, but I may be wrong. We'll let El and Alex look. They're better than we are at that kind of thing."

"Vampires don't need a full moon," Reuben said, dipping his chip in mayonnaise. "That's werewolves."

"I'm pretty sure it's not a werewolf. I think they'd be messier."

"I bet Hunter could tell with that nose of his."

"I bet he couldn't. We're chasing shadows right now. They don't have a scent."

"But it breathes—albeit in a raspy, weird way. Therefore, not a shadow." Reuben pointed his fork to emphasise his point.

"Well, whatever it is, if it carries on in the same manner, there'll be more deaths this week. It's pretty terrifying."

"But Charlotte, or whatever her name is, was unharmed, and so was Rupert. What's that about? Maybe the raspy-voiced invader isn't linked with the college deaths after all."

"If we don't get any more concrete evidence, we either need to stake out the house or the college."

Avery was stunned into momentary silence. "Stake out the college? That sounds horrendous."

"But we may see something. And we're witches. We have more protection than most. There is one good thing about all this, though."

"Really? What?"

Reuben grinned triumphantly. "This has nothing to do with our magic."

***

Genevieve lived in an elegant Georgian house on a quiet side street in Falmouth, and it suited her perfectly. And surprisingly, it was full of toys. Avery could see toys on the floor of the hall, and a box full of them in the room to the right of the front door.

Genevieve must have noticed Avery's puzzled expression. "I have three kids," she explained. "They're in there, watching TV."

"I had no idea," Avery said, feeling terrible that she didn't know this detail about her life.

"That's because I never mentioned it," she explained, without adding any other information about them. Avery presumed she wanted to keep her private life private, and that somewhere around the house was the children's father, or she couldn't have left them alone.

Genevieve shrugged apologetically as she took their coats. "I'm sorry this meeting was called on such short notice, but it's important. And, I've only invited a few of the coven. I decided to keep numbers down, which may potentially annoy a few of our members, but it's tough. Head upstairs and take the first right. We're meeting in my spell room."

"Hey, you're the boss," Reuben said. "Sorry if I gate-crashed, but we were together all afternoon anyway."

"That's fine," she said, brushing off his apologies. "I'll grab snacks, and meet you up there."

Genevieve looked rattled, which was unusual. Avery was used to her being abrupt and rude, but this was a side she hadn't seen before. She watched her head down the hall, and then followed Reuben upstairs.

Genevieve's spell room turned out to be a long room at the rear of the house, lit with corner lamps, candles, and filled with the scent of vanilla. It was carpeted with soft coir matting on top of which were colourful rugs. The whole of the long interior wall opposite the windows was lined with shelves filled with magical paraphernalia and books, and just inside the door was a large worktable crowded with documents. At the other end of the room, next to the fireplace, were a chaise longue and a table filled with a selection of drinks, but there was no other furniture at all except for lots of large floor cushions and low, round tables. Avery felt it was like a scene from the Arabian Nights.

Rasmus and Eve were already there. Rasmus stood with his back to the fire, his hands nursing a small glass of what looked like sherry. He was again wearing one of his dark velvet smoking jackets and straight black trousers, and his shock of white hair stood up on his head. He looked grumpy, lost within his thoughts, barely acknowledging their arrival.

Eve was browsing Genevieve's bookshelves and she smiled when they arrived, clearly pleased to see them, but once they'd exchanged greetings, her smile dropped.

"I hoped Genevieve had invited you. These deaths are horrible."

Avery agreed. "The worst. We're looking forward to seeing what everyone thinks about the cause."

"I have no idea," Eve confessed. "All I know is what I've seen on the news, and they're not saying much. And neither did Genevieve."

"Newton told us what little we know," Avery said, taking a glass of gin and tonic from Reuben after he'd mixed drinks from the stand in the corner. "The victims appear to have been partially drained of blood, which suggests something supernatural. I presume Genevieve must know that, too."

"Any ideas, Rasmus?" Eve asked, catching his eye.

"None that I want to share right now," he grunted. His face creased with lines of worry.

Avery was about to ask him more when Oswald, Caspian, and Jasper arrived, carrying in a waft of bitter cold air.

"I wish I'd known you were coming," Oswald said to Avery and Reuben. "I'd have grabbed a lift." He looked chilled and tired, dark circles beneath his eyes, and he immediately headed to the fire to stand next to Rasmus.

"Sorry," Reuben said. "We haven't been in White Haven all afternoon. Drink?"

"Whiskey, and make it large."

Reuben suppressed a grin as he fixed his drink, but then Oswald immediately fell into a hushed discussion with Rasmus, and Caspian and Jasper raised quizzical eyebrows at the others. They joined Eve and Avery, while Reuben played barman.

"It seems we must again meet while under stress," Jasper said in his low voice.

"At least we're not facing the Wild Hunt," Caspian said, accepting a whiskey.

"How's the young witch who was injured?" Avery asked Jasper.

"Mina has made a good recovery, thank you, but I will leave her out of whatever's going on here. She's not ready." He shook his head regretfully. "I think the events of Samhain have troubled many members of the coven, and that's why Genevieve has left some out of tonight's meeting."

"Very true," Genevieve said as she swept into the room, followed by Claudia, who, to Avery's eyes at least, looked like a mad bohemian in her long, flowing dress with a bold print. She caught Eve's wide-eyed expression and turned away, trying to not to giggle. Genevieve carried on, regardless. "This series of murders is not for the faint-hearted. I need witches I can rely on."

"I'm glad we meet your expectations," Caspian drawled.

"You might not be when I tell you what I think we're facing." She looked grim as she and Rasmus stared at each other for a long moment. "Sit, all of you."

They arranged themselves in a rough circle, each finding a comfortable cushion to sit on, and Avery slipped her boots off and crossed her legs as she settled herself in. This felt like things may go on for some time.

Genevieve placed a tray of biscuits and cheese on the floor within easy reach of everyone, and then also sat cross-legged on a large cushion. "I'll let Claudia explain."

Claudia began without preamble. "We have seen this before."

"What? The murders?" Eve asked, confused.

"Yes, three girls to start with, and then there'll be more—men, too."

They glanced at each other, alarmed.

"Who's *we*?" Avery asked.

"Myself, Rasmus, and Oswald. We're the only ones old enough." She closed her eyes briefly, as if to suppress a memory. "We didn't know what we were hunting then—at first—and we didn't even know if the deaths were linked. They were spread all over Cornwall, in small communities. News wasn't as instant as it is now. We were slow to act then, but now…" Her words hung on the air.

"I'm not sure I have the energy for it," Rasmus said, his gravelly voice full of sorrow. "Hunting takes energy I haven't got."

Genevieve's tone was strident. "There's nothing wrong with your magic, Rasmus. It's better than most."

He made a gesture with his hand as if to brush her off, and a wave of magic washed around the room, carrying a note of regret that hung sorrowfully on the air. "It's not my magic I doubt."

"Can you get to the point?" Caspian said, narrowing his eyes. "It's a little late in the day for games."

"I hate to say the word," Rasmus said, distaste written all over his face.

Oswald huffed impatiently. "It's a bloody vampire. I hate the damn things. They bring death wherever they go."

Avery's breath caught in her chest. It was one thing to speculate about vampires, but another to have it confirmed.

"Are you sure?" Reuben asked, leaning forward, his hand gripping his glass.

"The last time this happened, ten people were killed before we could stop it, and all ten rose from the dead."

"*Rose from the dead*?" Eve was incredulous. "But how do you know? What did you do with all of them?

Claudia answered, her tone flat. "We had to kill every single one of them."

"How?"

"A mixture of beheadings and stakes through the heart." Her voice was so matter of fact that Avery couldn't quite comprehend it.

"And I burnt one," Oswald added, looking only into his drink. It was as if he couldn't bear to look them in the eye. "Don't forget that. I can't."

The room was silent for a moment, the younger witches all wide-eyed in shock.

Genevieve took a hefty slug of her drink. "Now you know why I only need witches I can rely on."

Caspian frowned. "Was my father involved?"

"Yes," Rasmus said. "He was one of our most effective hunters. He killed four of them."

Caspian nodded vacantly, and Avery realised he was having as much difficulty absorbing this as the rest of them.

"But not mine, I presume," Reuben asked. "We were *ex-communicado*."

"No one from White Haven," Claudia confirmed. "There were other witches involved, of course, across Cornwall, but they have since died, or moved from here. And a couple of our members were killed in the fight. It was a horrible time."

Reuben looked alarmed. "Witches *died*?"

"Oh, yes. Make no mistake," Rasmus said. "Vampires are a deadly enemy. This is not *Twilight*. They do not take humans as lovers. They have no emotion. They are killers, monsters, bloodsuckers, evil parasites—" His voice broke and he sobbed, bringing a hand to his face.

"Old friend," Oswald said, patting his shoulder and looking very tearful himself. "We should have left you out of this."

"No." Rasmus's head shot up, his expression fierce. "I will not back away." He looked at the other witches defiantly. "You should know that my wife was killed by one of these things. We had been married for only a few years. We were trying to have children." His voice broke again. "Sorry. I shouldn't have said."

Shock rippled around the room, along with the murmur of condolences, and Eve said, "I'm so sorry, Rasmus. I had no idea."

"I don't speak of it," Rasmus confessed. "It's far too painful, even now."

"Our biggest regret, and there were many, trust me," Claudia said, finally lifting her gaze from Rasmus. "Another, of course, was that we never found the vampire who'd turned them all."

"Ah," Reuben said, comprehension dawning. "And now he's back."

"It seems so."

Reuben's pale blue eyes, normally so teasing, had darkened like a stormy sea. "Apart from a stake through the heart, beheading, and fire, are there any other ways to kill a vampire?"

"Holy water will slow it down," Claudia said. "Stabbing, maiming, and shooting it will also slow it, but to my knowledge, only those three things guarantee death. I also burnt them after staking, anyway. I like to be sure."

This is a nightmare. Avery tried to imagine Claudia doing such things, but it was impossible to envisage this exotic older lady, and the very dapper Oswald and Rasmus, as being vampire killers. *I'm going to wake up and laugh about this.* But then Avery met Reuben's troubled gaze, and knew it was very real.

"How do we find it?" Caspian asked. "And why did it stop the last time?"

"Unfortunately," Oswald said, rising to his feet slowly and heading to the table to top up his drink, "we have no answer to either question."

If the mood was grim before, it now felt worse. A wind whipped up outside and rattled the window, causing every single one of them to jump.

"And the victims? Once they've been bitten and killed, is there a way to prevent them from turning?" Caspian asked.

"Not that we know of, but for us it was too late, anyway," Claudia said.

Genevieve spoke for the first time in a while. She had been listening, and Avery could see her calculating possibilities and strategies. "How long until the dead walk again?"

Claudia thought for a moment. "I think it was about four days. That's when they disappeared from the morgue."

"In theory, then, the first girl will disappear tonight?"

"Yes."

She exhaled and seemed to shrink, cowed by the news. "By the holy Goddess. This is a disaster."

"But we know what we're fighting now," Oswald pointed out, "unlike before. We can start the hunt sooner, and hopefully prevent more deaths."

"Right," Jasper said decisively. "We need a plan. Potentially, we should split up tasks to make our attack more efficient. I will do whatever you need me to. Genevieve?"

"Thank you, Jasper. I have been giving this some thought. We need to do several things, the most important being to find its lair. It cannot walk in the day, therefore it must be somewhere dark and secure."

"We are *sure* it can't walk in the day?" Eve asked. "It couldn't be disguised as something human?"

"I'm pretty sure not," Jasper said. "I have researched vampire lore, and there is nothing that suggests they can overcome their inability to walk in the sun. It will kill them instantly."

Oswald agreed. "Yes, that's what we believe, too, and nothing suggested otherwise all those years ago."

Eve looked relieved. "Good. That's something, at least."

Genevieve continued, "So, we will of course have the advantage if we can find it in the day and kill it where it sleeps. But that potentially means we have to track its movements, and that's very dangerous. At night it is strong, fast, and deadly. But, the deaths are all in Harecombe at present, on the college grounds. This suggests it's close by. The deaths must be opportunistic."

Avery put in, "We have a theory as to where it may be—or at least where it's linked to." She updated them on the house that Ben and the others were investigating. "It has a strange past, and a few recent odd occurrences there seem too coincidental not to be connected."

A palpable air of excitement lifted the room. "That's very interesting news," Genevieve said, "and definitely worth investigating."

"Unfortunately, I've never heard of the place," Oswald confessed, his brow furrowing.

Claudia shook her head, puzzled. "Me, neither."

"We're already working with Ben, so we can continue to help," Avery suggested.

Genevieve looked pleased. "Agreed. But Jasper, can you look into the background of the house, too? See if there is any chance it could be connected to those events years ago."

"Of course. Can you give me a date?" he asked.

"1979," Claudia said, immediately. "At just this time of year. Forty years ago, exactly. I will never forget it."

"Any chance you can introduce me to the ghost-hunters?" Jasper asked Avery and Reuben.

"No problem," Reuben answered. "I'm sure they'll be glad of the help. I'll call Ben tomorrow and set it up."

"Before we go on," Claudia said, "just who else in our own covens will get involved? Genevieve, you are on your own here, of course, and Jasper has already ruled out Mina, understandably."

"I will keep my other witch, Bran, out of this, too," Jasper said. "I would like to keep him free to keep an eye on Mina—and Penzance, in general. I will of course keep them both updated."

Avery leaned forward, hating to be involved but knowing there was no way anyone from White Haven would want to be left out. "All of our coven will help."

Genevieve looked relieved. "Good, I thought you would. Caspian?"

"My sister will, and possibly my cousins. I'll check." He looked grim. "If we need them, I will make them help."

"Eve?" Genevieve asked.

"Nate will help, of course. We'll do anything you need."

Genevieve's face softened momentarily. "Good, thank you. And Claudia?"

"I have two other witches in Perranporth, but I'll leave Lark out of it. She too is young, and like Mina, was overwhelmed at Samhain. But Cornell will help, if needed. He's fast and strong and to be honest, I'll have trouble keeping him out of it."

Avery had a vague recollection of Lark and Cornell. Lark was in her late teens, and certainly skilled, but yes, she was still unsure of her strengths.

Cornell, however, was several years older and almost overconfident, if Avery remembered correctly.

Oswald had stood and was pacing up and down, listening, and he added, "Count Ulysses in, of course."

Rasmus looked thoughtful. "My daughter, Isolde—from my second marriage, just in case you're wondering—will want to help, although I'm not sure I want her to. But, well," he glanced at Genevieve. "You know Isolde! And Drexel will, too, although he's barely twenty. My coven is very headstrong," he muttered.

Avery smiled. She'd forgotten Isolde was his daughter. She'd met her and Drexel at Samhain, but the whole coven was there, and it was difficult to keep track of who was who. Rasmus seemed to have cheered up as everyone confirmed their involvement, and despite the risks, Avery was also starting to feel positive about the battle ahead.

Genevieve turned to Avery and Reuben. "You have good links to Newton. Perhaps you can find out more about the deaths? Access the bodies?"

Caspian grunted. "We could all do that. A simple spell will get us into the morgue."

Genevieve looked at him, annoyed. "I know that. But I want to know what the police know!"

Caspian gave a barely perceptible nod to her.

"What do you want us to do with the corpses?" Reuben asked. "I mean, if we behead them now, will it stop them rising from the dead?"

Avery's mouth fell open. "Reuben!"

He shrugged. "One less vampire is a good thing, right?"

Oswald was once again warming his hands by the fire. "It may work. But there's only one way to find out."

Reuben rose to his feet. "If the first victim will rise tonight, that means we need to go to the morgue now, and kill it before it does. I'll call Alex, El, and Briar. They can meet us there. I presume it's in Truro."

"I'll join you," Caspian said. "It's on my way home, and we'll need the numbers. We have no idea what may happen."

Reuben looked at Caspian, his expression almost unreadable. "Thanks. That would be good."

It seemed the meeting was at an end as everyone now rose to their feet, stretching out their limbs.

"Would you like me to come, too?" Eve asked.

"No. It's out of your way," Avery reassured her. "Go home and update Nate, and maybe make some preparations."

"And I will start researching." Jasper checked his watch. "It's not late. I'll start tonight, if you're sure you don't need me?" He looked to Avery, questioningly.

"No. There'll be six of us at the morgue."

"Besides," Reuben added, "if we all die, you lot will have to finish the job."

Avery swatted his arm. "Reuben!"

He rolled his shoulders. "I'm kidding. We're going to be just fine."

"I should come," Oswald said. "I'm going that way, too, and I've at least seen a vampire before."

"No," Caspian said emphatically. "You're a powerful witch, Oswald, but you're old and physically slow—no offence. I'll worry more about you, and that will distract me. There'll be enough for you to do another time."

Reuben nodded. "Agreed. You guys strategise, and we'll act. I think your battle with them last time means you get to sit this one out. And for now, that includes you, Genevieve, as our High Priestess."

Oswald nodded, a mixture of relief but also disappointment on his face. "You're right. We need to find out why it's happening now, and if there's a link to the last time. Knowing about this occult house may give us the advantage."

"Agreed," Claudia said. "We may remember something about the last time that helps us now."

Avery had a thought. "You didn't say where you caught up with the newly turned vampires. You mentioned you killed them all. Where?"

"We managed to track down a couple of places they'd used," Rasmus explained. "We cornered one and it fled to a barn as day was breaking. It thought it had lost us, but we found it, covered in hay in a hole in the floor, and we staked it."

Oswald nodded. "We found one in a cave, hidden at the back. Again, we'd tracked it one night and struck in the day."

"And we found three in an abandoned mineshaft," Claudia said, her gaze distant. "That was tricky. The place was a death trap—fallen beams, trapped gases, twisting passageways…" She trailed off, lost in thoughts of the past.

"Gave me nightmares for a long time," Oswald admitted. "There were another couple, but I can't remember where we found those. I'm sure it will come back to me."

"Wow," Avery said, looking at them in admiration. "You're amazing."

Claudia smiled. "We had no choice, and I genuinely hoped never to face them again."

"You'll need weapons," Rasmus said, all business as he picked up a holdall next to the bookcase and placed it in the centre of the room. He rummaged in it for a moment and produced a stake with a flourish. It was about one foot long with a long, sharp point. "Take the bag. There are about half a dozen of these in it, and a mallet."

Reuben took it from him, twirling it in his hands like it was a drumstick. "You're a dark horse, Rasmus. We'll take three. Keep the rest for yourself—just in case. We can make more later."

Rasmus straightened his shoulders, as if squaring for a fight. "Fair enough. I'd better start practising."

"I think we all should, and begin finding spells that could help. Our magic will give us an advantage, but…"Claudia looked intently at Avery, Caspian, and Reuben. "Do not underestimate the strength and speed of a vampire. They are superhuman, preternaturally strong, and vicious. Never forget that. I hope to see you all at the next meeting."

Hope. The word hung on the air.

Reuben said, "I'll get El to bring a sword, too. And besides, there'll be plenty of knives in the morgue."

"Be careful! Wear gloves—you may be witches, but we still leave fingerprints—and do not take risks," Genevieve warned. "If it escapes, so be it. I'd rather have you all alive, and we'll get our chance again. And protect your friends and family—and that applies to all of us. There are tough times ahead, and there'll be more blood spilt before this is over."

9

As soon as Avery and Reuben got in the car, Avery called Alex to update him on the plan, and she asked him to call El and Briar. She could hear the shock in his voice, but he didn't hesitate. The last thing he said was, "Don't you dare go in without us," and then he rang off.

"I'm going to call Ben, too," she said to Reuben, as he steered them out of Falmouth and on to the A39 to Truro. "They need to know the danger they're in. They *cannot* stay at that house overnight. What if that was a vampire standing over Charlotte?"

He nodded. "Using her as a regular blood bank? Agreed. But it makes me wonder why they're still alive, if it's linked to this business. "

"I'll worry about that later," Avery said. She was relieved to find that Ben and the others were not at the house, and made them promise not to go at night until they had more information.

She glanced over to the back seat and pulled a wooden stake out of the bag, feeling its weight. "You need a lot of strength to drive this into someone's heart."

"Hence the mallet."

"But they'd need to be sleeping for that to happen—in the day. It would be tough if you were fighting one."

"Buffy managed it," he said, grinning.

"Yeah, well, I'm not Buffy. She was a Slayer."

"But you're a witch. You can punch it in with a well-timed blast of wind."

She considered his suggestion. "That might actually be possible."

"Of course it is. You just need practice. "

"There are many things I need right now. Maybe I should ask for a mannequin for Christmas."

"What I need right now are directions to the morgue. Can you look it up?"

"Of course," Avery said, reaching for her phone again. "All I can think about is what to do when we get there. I can't believe we're actually going to face a vampire—*tonight*!"

"Hopefully we won't. Hopefully all we'll encounter is a dead girl that needs beheading. Maybe three dead girls that need beheading."

"We should tell Newton."

Reuben sounded alarmed. "Not bloody now, we shouldn't! And I hope Briar doesn't, either."

Avery quickly found the directions to the Cornwall Coroner. "Bollocks. It's not in Truro. It's just outside, off the A39. And there are a few buildings onsite, including a crematorium. I'll tell the others." Behind them she could see the lights of Caspian's Audi, so she phoned him first before telling Alex. "My hands are shaking," she confessed to Reuben.

"It's the adrenalin," he reassured her. "You'll be glad of it when we get there."

They arrived at the Coroner's office all too quickly. It was in a secluded area of countryside, surrounded by fields, and it was bigger than Avery expected. The place was in darkness, apart from some security lights, but Reuben pulled into the rear of the car park and killed the lights, and Caspian pulled next to them.

A heavy frost covered the ground, and rather than wait outside, Caspian joined them, getting in the back of Reuben's car. "I don't like it. It's isolated, and the vampire could be out there, watching us right now."

"On the plus side," Reuben said, twisting to speak to him. "It's well away from public places and from where people could get hurt. Although, if the girl rises and gets away, there's no way we'll find her out here."

Caspian grabbed a stake, hefting it much as Avery had done. "I've done many things, but I've never encountered a vampire before."

"Did your father ever tell you what happened all those years ago?"

"Never." His eyes glinted in the dim lights of the car. "And I have no idea why he never spoke of it, either."

"Maybe," Avery suggested, "it was such a nightmare that none of them ever wanted to think of it again. Rasmus lost his wife!"

"We should work in pairs tonight," Reuben said. "No one should be alone."

Caspian and Avery nodded, and then they fell into an uneasy silence, waiting for the others to arrive.

It was another fifteen minutes before they saw the headlights approach in the distance, and Alex phoned to check where they were. A minute later, El pulled up in her Land Rover, and they all piled out of their cars, stomping their feet for warmth, their breath billowing around them in clouds.

Alex leaned back against El's Land Rover, arms crossed in front of him, leather gloves on his hands. "What the hell happened today? Avery's given me some details, but why are we at the morgue?"

Reuben twirled the stake. "We have a vampire to kill."

Briar's eyes were wide with surprise. "Really? Because when Alex called, I thought he was joking. The whole journey here, we've been debating what you found out at the meeting."

"It's not a joke," Avery reassured her. "I'm going to make this quick, because it's freezing and I don't want to stand in the dark, knowing we could be attacked at any moment. Claudia and the others are sure that this is a vampire, because it's happened before. We think that the first girl who was attacked and killed will turn into a vampire too, tonight, and we need to stop it happening."

El, Alex, and Briar regarded them silently, looked at each other, and then back at the other three. El gave a dry laugh. "You know you sound nuts, right?"

Caspian huffed with impatience. "I can assure you, if you heard what we did, you wouldn't question this. And when Avery tells you everything later, you'll understand. In the meantime, let's get on with this. If she turns tonight, that big ol' vamp that turned her could be waiting for her. Out there!" he jerked his head to indicate the surrounding fields.

"Right," Alex said decisively. "Do we know where her body is being kept?"

"No idea," Reuben said, shaking his head. "Mr Google does not provide online maps of the facility."

Briar was clearly struggling with their plan. "Hold on. How will we know which girl is which? It's the Cornwall morgue. There could be dozens of dead bodies in there. And when we do find her, what if she's lying there, looking completely normal? Are you actually suggesting we desecrate her dead body? That's appalling!"

"Can we address this issue once we're inside?" Caspian asked, growing impatient, and he turned and led the way across the car park.

"Brought your sword, El?" Reuben asked, as they followed him.

She patted the scabbard strapped to her left side. "Two swords. One for me, and Alex is carrying the other one. Briar declined. Why do I need it?"

"You may have to behead her."

El stopped dead, and Briar walked into the back of her. "I might *what*?"

Reuben paused, too. "I only said *might*."

El sighed and started walking again. "Maybe you should carry the sword, because I'm not sure I can do that."

Reuben nodded. "I'll do it if we need to."

As they closed in on the main building a security light activated, but within seconds it was off, shorted out by Caspian's magic. He quickly turned to the other lights over the entrance and on the far corner and spelled them off, too. Avery noted the security cameras and quickly deactivated them, and then the group huddled together in front of the glass doors.

Caspian suggested, "Before we go in, I want to scope the perimeter."

"Agreed," Reuben said. "I want to know our exits, and the general layout."

Avery nodded. "The only thing I could make out on the map is that the crematorium is to the right." She pointed to a square building with a separate entrance a short distance away.

"This place is bigger than I thought," Briar said, hugging herself for warmth. "I'll come with you, Caspian. Are we sure her body won't be in the hospital morgue?"

"Very. I checked," Caspian answered. "Only those who die in hospital will be in the hospital's morgue, and that's just a holding place. She'll be here. They all should be. Reuben, if we go right, you go left. We'll meet around the back. There'll be a rear entrance, and we'll get in that way. Alex and Avery, are you happy to go in through the front?"

"Anything to get out of the cold," Avery said, starting to shiver.

"It'll be just like the museum, Avery," Alex said softly.

"Let's hope there aren't security guards here." She remembered when they shorted out the security system at the Truro museum, and guards had arrived to investigate.

Alex nodded. "With a bit of luck, there won't be."

Caspian checked his watch. "Ten minutes should cover us. We'll see you inside. Phone us if you need to explain where the morgue is. And don't do anything rash."

"Nor you," Alex said, resentment creeping into his voice.

Within seconds, the other four had disappeared, leaving Avery and Alex alone. Alex deftly released the lock on the door, and they slipped inside, the heated air warming their chilled skin.

The silence surrounded them like a blanket, and it was completely dark, other than the alarm system blinking to their left on the wall. Alex took care of it, and the lights winked out.

"Where now?" he asked, his voice low.

Avery could just make out a reception desk on the left, a long corridor leading to the back of the building, and doorways to the left and right, but she was reluctant to send up a witch light because the door behind them was made of glass.

"I'm sure the morgue must be toward the rear of the building, but we should check every room as we go," Avery suggested.

"Agreed." Alex quickly checked the door to the right, and Avery to the left. "It's an office," he called, softly.

"Here, too," Avery answered.

Alex moved down the corridor, past the reception desk, and Avery sent up a witch-light as soon as they were out of sight of the entrance. The corridor arrived at a T-junction, with another corridor running from left to right.

Avery whispered, "It would be logical for the morgue to be close to the crematorium, in which case we should try right first."

Alex nodded and led the way, and Avery listened intently for any noise, but it was still silent, and that made it creepier. They passed several offices, but there was no sign of the morgue until Alex found a door leading to another corridor. Satisfied they hadn't missed anything he headed down it, and quickly came to a door with swipe card access and a sign saying *Morgue.*

"Bingo," he said, running his hands across the panel and whispering a spell. The door released with a *click*, and they entered a small anteroom with a desk and a large whiteboard. Numbers ran down the side and columns were next to it, listing names, investigations, time arrived, and other details. There was a door in the rear wall.

"What was the first girl's name?" Alex asked as he searched the board and then opened the other door. The witch light illuminated another short but wide hallway with a couple of doors to the right.

Avery quickly pulled her phone out, searching for a news report. "Bethany Mason, aged eighteen." She looked up, searching the board. "There. Number 4b."

"That must coincide with the storage number. Come on." He continued down the corridor, lined with stark white tiles. The first room on the right was very long and filled with stainless steel work surfaces and cupboards, and had three gurneys in the centre of the room. Various jars and stainless steel objects were laid out on the counters. "This must be the autopsy room," Alex guessed.

The next room was also large, but on the right-hand side were rows of doors, three short doors to each row, and each numbered. There were no windows in any of these rooms, so Alex flicked the light switch on; they both blinked as a bright white light banished the shadows.

Alex pointed to a square door situated in the middle of the fourth row. "There's 4b. She must be in there."

"There's no way you could get out of that on your own," Avery said. She patted her backpack, double-checking the stake was there. "It locks from the outside. Even if she turns, she couldn't get out."

"Maybe you could if you had superhuman strength," Alex said, grimly. "We should wait for the others. Let's see if the other girls are here, too."

Avery searched for their names in her phone again, while Alex headed back down the corridor. Avery followed him absently, half watching him while searching in her phone. He found a few more offices, a room lined with lockers, sinks, showers, and toilets, another wide anteroom, and a set of double doors. "That must be the rear entrance," he murmured. He quickly checked that all the alarms and cameras were disabled, and then pulled the door wide open. The cold night rushed in from the parking bay. A couple of vans were parked out the back, but it was otherwise empty.

"Where the hell are they?" Alex muttered, and stepped out to look around. A black shape swooped past the entrance, and Alex disappeared.

Avery blinked, thinking she'd missed something. "Alex?" She ran to the back door and looked out, but nothing moved, and Alex was nowhere in sight. *Shit.* Avery's heart thumped and her mouth went dry. She wanted to shout, but she bit back the urge, instead pocketing her phone, dropping the backpack, and pulling the wooden stake free. Her magic rose instinctively, surging into her hands.

An explosion of bright white light emanated from the corner of the building and Alex dropped onto the floor, landing in a crouch. Avery heard a shout, and Reuben and El ran around the corner. El had drawn her sword, and the blade flashed with white fire, the only thing illuminating them in the darkness. There was another swoop of blackness, a deeper shadow against the night sky, and Avery rocked backwards as a wave of air buffeted her, bringing the stench of death and rotten meat with it. She had barely time to look up when a figure collided with her from the left. Caspian. She landed on the floor, winded, with Caspian sprawled across her. She peered over his shoulder and saw Briar running towards them, throwing a ball of fire into the air.

Caspian rolled away and threw a jagged bolt of lightning up towards the swooping figure, and it disappeared.

"Get inside, now!" Reuben yelled, as he, El, and Alex pelted down the side of the building towards the rear entrance.

Avery jumped to her feet, stepped just inside the entrance and grabbed the door, ready to pull it closed. Caspian waited outside, searching the skies. Briar ran through the door first, followed by El, Reuben, and then Alex, and Caspian whirled in after them. Avery pulled the door shut with a resounding *thud.* A shudder passed through the door as something hit it from the outside. She shot all three bolts across at once with a wave of magic, and sighed with relief as she leaned against the wall.

Avery was happy to see all of them in one piece, but particularly Alex. "Are you all right?" she asked, concerned. "What happened? Did it pick you up?"

He nodded, his face pale under the witch light. "Shook up, but unharmed. I never even saw it coming. It's quick and strong." He felt his neck. "I can still feel its grip, and its smell—ugh! It certainly didn't expect me to fight back." He looked at the others. "How are you?"

"Annoyed," Reuben said, brushing himself off. He'd skidded across the floor as he entered the building, colliding with the opposite wall, almost taking down El in the process. "That thing is bloody quick."

"And it *stinks*," El reiterated, wrinkling her nose. "But I'm fine."

"Briar? Caspian? Are you okay?" Avery asked, turning to them.

"Just about," Briar said, still breathless. "It ambushed us by the crematorium. Caspian witch-flew us out of there with mere seconds to spare."

Caspian looked as annoyed as Reuben. "I didn't even hear it! I could only bring us as far as the corner of the building—I had no idea where we were going!"

"It bought us precious time," Briar said, reassuring him.

Another *thud* on the outer door interrupted him, echoed by an answering *thud* from down the hall.

They fell silent, listening with dread, and then heard another *thud* and a blood-curdling scream.

"Shit. She's awake," Alex said, drawing his sword and racing back down the corridor without a backward glance, El and Briar hard on his heels.

"I'll hold this door," Caspian shouted. "Reuben?"

Reuben nodded, gripping the stake firmly in his right hand. "I'll stay with you. Avery, go with Alex. We'll shout if we need you."

Avery skidded into the morgue seconds after the others to see the door labelled 4b being dented from the inside, crumpling as if it were a cardboard box.

Great. A vampire outside, and one inside. We're trapped.

Before any of them could act, the door burst open and a snarling Bethany dropped onto the floor, squinting in the bright light. Her skin was pale, almost blue, and her bloodless lips were pulled back, revealing two long, curved canine teeth either side of her mouth. Her eyes were like dark pits, and for a brief second she was unfocused, but as she saw them, her mouth opened, her jaw unnaturally wide.

Everything became chaotic, Avery barely able to register what was happening, it was all so quick.

The newly-turned vampire leapt at Alex and he threw her back against the wall where she crashed to the floor, before jumping again to her feet. Briar hurled a stream of fire towards her, but Bethany ran at her, evading the fire with catlike reflexes. El and Alex slashed at her with their swords, but she dodged effortlessly through them.

The vampire wrapped herself around Briar, the force of her lunge carrying them both to the floor, Briar underneath, her arms pinned. Briar looked terrified as Bethany opened her jaw wide, revealing the long curve of her teeth, ready to strike her neck. Avery ran forward, braced herself, and plunged the stake into the middle of the vampire's back. The vampire rolled off Briar and lunged to the doorway, effectively blocking them in. She hissed and snarled, the stake hanging uselessly from her back.

How the hell had that happened?

Despite being in shock, Avery noticed the girl moved in an odd way, her limbs stiff, and her hands grasping like claws. Her lack of humanity was startling. She reached behind her and wrenched the stake out of her back, throwing it to the side,

A series of shouts sounded from the corridor, followed by a tearing, groaning sound, and then they heard plaster falling, along with noise like a roaring wind. A lean creature landed on its feet behind the girl, and rose to its full height of over six feet. Its shoulders were broad, and it wore the semblance of dark clothing, but its skin was grey and leathery, and its eyes glinted like dull metal. It scooped the former girl towards it, encasing it in his scrawny limbs, and then it was gone, leaping up through the hole it had made in the roof, and silence fell.

10

Reuben and Caspian skidded to a halt, and Reuben stood under the hole in the roof, looking up. "I didn't see *that* coming."

"So much for blocking the entrance," Caspian said angrily.

Alex turned quickly towards the freezer storage doors. "We haven't got much time. We need to kill the other two girls before we leave." He hesitated. "Not kill, they're already dead. You know what I mean. But that *thing* may come back, and I do *not* want to hang around."

"I agree." Briar patted her neck with a trembling hand, clearly shaken, although she was trying to hide it.

Caspian nodded as he stepped into the storage room. "There's an excellent chance of it returning if it has somewhere close by to store its new friend."

"Did she hurt you?" Avery asked Briar, struggling to call Bethany an *it*, despite her lack of humanity.

Briar shook her head. "No. You saved me."

"We all saved each other," she answered.

Reuben was still standing in the corridor. "I suggest three of us get the cars and bring them outside the rear entrance while we still have time. I don't want to be attacked again."

Caspian immediately volunteered. "I'll go."

"So will I," El said, joining them. She too looked shaken, and that was unusual for El. "I know what I've just seen, but I can't behead someone. Yet."

"I can do it," Alex said, looking at a second whiteboard on the wall. "Names, Avery?"

Reuben answered instead. "Amy Warner and Clara Henderson. I checked earlier."

"5c and 3a," Caspian noted, eyeing the doors warily, especially the one that was dented and hanging loose. "Are you sure we should go?"

"Yes." Alex's dark eyes met Caspian's, and he glanced at Reuben and El beyond. "Be quick, and be safe. We'll deal with this."

They nodded and ran, leaving the other three to stand staring at each other bleakly for a few seconds. If Avery was honest, beheading a dead girl was the last thing she wanted to do, but it had to be done.

"Plan?" she asked, the stake once again in her hand, poised to strike.

Alex looked decisive. "Briar, grab the gurney, and we'll slide the next body straight out and onto it to give us plenty of room. Then—" He paused and swallowed, looking at the floor as if strength would flow from it to him. "I will use the sword to cut her head off." He looked up at Avery. "Stand ready with the stake—just in case."

They had only one stake between them as Caspian and Reuben had taken the other two.

They nodded in agreement, and while Briar fetched the gurney, Alex opened the freezer door. 3a was in the section at the top of the freezer, and the body was covered in a white sheet. As soon as the gurney was in position and raised to the correct height, they slid the body clear of the freezer on a long, white tray and then rolled the gurney to the centre of the room, lowering it to waist height. Alex peeled the white sheet back, revealing the victim's head. She'd already had a post-mortem as they could see the stitched incision that ended at the base of her throat.

Briar looked at the young girl's pale face and sighed. "What a way to go."

It was the first time—other than seconds before, and Avery didn't really count that—that she had seen a dead body. She felt overwhelmingly sad more than anything else.

"Well, at least she's not moving," Alex observed. He raised his arms high above his head, sword extended, and took a few deep breaths.

"Are you sure we have to do this?" Briar asked, looking between Avery and Alex.

Alex didn't hesitate. "Yes." He brought the sword down so quickly that there was a *whoosh* of air and then a solid *thunk* as he sliced through the girl's neck, beheading her in one, clean sweep. Her head rolled to the side, turning towards Avery, and even though she was expecting it, she jumped.

She met Alex's eyes across the body. "Well done."

He looked pale. "One more to go."

They pulled the sheet back over the girl, slid her body back into place, and shut the door, before turning to the next. They worked quickly, listening for any sign of movement from outside or in, but all was still silent.

This girl was as young as the others. Her dark hair was swept back from her head, her skin was an icy blue, and her eyes were closed. Alex once again raised his arms high, ready to bring his sharp blade down on her neck, but without warning her eyes opened, revealing pupils as black as night. She snarled low in her throat and started to rise, her right hand shooting up to grasp Alex's arm.

"Shit!" Alex instinctively tried to jump back, but he couldn't. She was too strong, and he couldn't bring the sword down, either. "Avery!"

Briar was standing at the end of the gurney, and she leaned forward, her hands on the girl's legs to stop them from kicking up. She whispered a spell, momentarily pinning her down.

Avery's heart was in her throat, but she leapt forward and brought the stake down over the girl's heart, thumping into her body with a sickening *crunch* as she hit the rib cage. She used her magic to force it down harder than her normal strength would allow, and the stake plunged through her body with such force it went through the plastic tray beneath her, as well. The dead girl loosed her grip on Alex and tuned to Avery. Her black eyes focused with a hungry intensity, and she snarled again, showing her sharp, white teeth and her extended canines. Alex didn't hesitate.

"Get back," he yelled at Avery and brought the sword down, severing the girl's head, the sword's tip missing Avery by inches only.

The head rolled to the side, eyes frozen open. In seconds her eyes reverted to their normal human state, her teeth retracting.

"Holy shit!" Alex exclaimed. "Let's get the fuck out of here."

Briar ran to the doorway. "The cars are here—I can hear them. And something else."

A howl carried on the still night air.

"We haven't got time to put her back," Alex said. "They'll know what's happened soon enough, anyway. Let's go."

Avery hurriedly pulled the stake free, and Alex swept the room, ensuring they had gathered everything, and then they ran to the back door, wrenching it open.

The cars were lined up, engines revving, ready to flee. Reuben leapt out of his car and ran to El's Land Rover. "I'm going with El. Alex, you take my car. Caspian will make his own way home."

"No!" Briar said immediately, running straight to Caspian's passenger door. Caspian leaned half out of his window, peering into the sky above. "I'll go with Caspian. He may need me. You can find me a bed, right?"

He looked grateful, even if he didn't voice it. "No problem. Jump in."

Alex slid behind the wheel of Reuben's car, and Avery had barely shut the passenger door when he revved the engine and raced across the car park, following the other two past the Gardens of Remembrance and onto the country lane.

Alex glanced over at Avery. "Are you all right?"

"As much as I can be after encountering three vampires in one night." She noticed Alex's hands were gripping the wheel, his shoulder's stiff, as he concentrated on the road. "Are you?"

"I'm not sure I'll ever forget cutting someone's head off, but I'll survive. Better that than being bitten."

All three were driving fast—too fast for these lanes—but it was now well after midnight, and hopefully no one else would be on these back roads. A howl sounded again, and Avery saw a blurred figure as something leapt out of the fields to the right, over the hedge, and onto the top of El's car. It crouched, gripping the sides, and then started to punch the roof as El's car veered across the road.

"What the—" Avery's voice trailed off as she wound the window down, wiggled halfway out of the car, and aimed a blast of wind towards the vampire. Alex put his foot down, bringing them closer.

Avery's aim went astray as El's car kept veering across the road, but an explosion of light from within the car pulsed up through the roof, knocking the creature off balance. Avery aimed again, directing a vortex of swirling air at the dislodged vampire and tossing it high in the air. She grinned to herself. *I've got you now!*

She slowed her breathing and focused, trying not to let her underlying panic throw off her natural control. The wind whipped the vampire around and around, turning it in the air, where it hung helplessly for a few seconds. Avery raised her hands, lifting the creature higher and higher before sending it spiralling to the right, far over the fields.

Alex had slowed down, keeping the car steady, and Reuben had done the same, all three cars moving together and staying close. The main road was ahead, the lights of the junction bright against the night sky. *Safety…hopefully.*

Avery made sure the vampire was still being carried on the fierce wind and then ducked back in the car, just as they reached the junction. Barely slowing, they turned left and headed towards Harecombe and White Haven.

"Do you think we've lost it?" she asked, peering behind them.

"I think so." Alex took a deep breath in and out. "Well done."

"Do you think it can fly? Like a bat, I mean?"

"Isn't that Dracula?

"I don't know! My vampiric lore is shaky."

"Maybe it can. Can they change into smoke or something? You should call Genevieve, let her know what happened. She'll be worried. But I think we're safe. For now."

"For now," she echoed ominously as she stared ahead, vacantly. Just how long would *for now* last?

11

Happenstance Books seemed unnaturally bright and festive after the events of the night before, but Avery was glad for it.

She'd had a bad night's sleep—they both had. Images of dead girls and snarling vampires filled her head, and even Alex's warm arms couldn't dispel those. Before sleeping they'd reinforced Avery's protection spell, but they'd agreed they would need more—something more specific to the undead. The others had also arrived home safely, but they'd agreed to meet again later that day, and invite the ghost-hunters. They would catch up with Genevieve and the others another time.

Sally took one look at Avery over their morning coffee and asked, "What happened?"

"You don't want to know."

"Yes, I do."

Avery fell silent for a moment, thinking. Sally was right. She did need to know, if she was to protect herself. But equally, this would terrify her, and did she really want to inflict that on her—and Dan—before Christmas?

"Spill!" Sally insisted, cradling her cup of coffee as she leaned against the shop counter. "I can cope."

"What's going on?" Dan asked warily, as he joined them.

Avery looked at him and sniggered. "What the hell are you wearing?"

He looked down. "What? It's my Christmas t-shirt. I'm being festive!"

His t-shirt was bright red with white lettering and it read, *I'm not Santa, but you can sit on my lap.*

He grinned. "I have several that I shall wear from now until Christmas. Hope you approve, boss."

"Of course—as long as you don't offend anyone too much."

Sally interrupted. "Don't distract her, Dan! Something has happened. Look at those bags beneath her eyes!"

Avery grimaced. "Thanks!"

"Ah. More mayhem in White Haven." He bit into a mince pie. "What now?"

Avery glanced around, checking the shop was empty. "We encountered a vampire last night. Well, two actually, and *almost* a third."

Dan almost spit out his pie. "Are you serious? I foolishly assumed that conversation we had the other day was purely theoretical. "

"Yes! And it wasn't. I wouldn't lie about that."

"So those girls *were* killed by a vampire?"

"Yes. Without a doubt." Saying it now, in the cold light of day, sounded ridiculous, but last night had been only too real.

Sally visibly paled. "Is it here? In White Haven?"

"No, not quite. We think it's halfway between here and Harecombe. Close enough." Avery looked sheepish. "We broke into the Cornwall Coroner's office last night and it attacked us there."

Dan whistled. "Wow, Avery, you just keep surprising me. And what did you do that for?"

She filled them in, and noticed them both looking at her, slack-jawed. When the door chimes rang to announce a customer, they all jumped. The customer nodded in greeting and headed to the shelves, browsing the stock.

Avery concluded in a low voice, "I need to enhance my protection spells, for this shop, and you two, so I'm going to spend a few hours doing that today, if that's all right."

Sally and Dan exchanged an uneasy glance, and Sally said, "That's fine. Do I need to start wearing garlic bulbs?"

"Maybe. I'll let you know when I've done some research. Hopefully I can think of something more sophisticated than that."

Dan waved her away. "Go now. I'll call you for elevenses. And you better have made progress!"

"Yes sir!" Avery saluted him and headed up to her flat.

***

Avery laid out her grimoires and started hunting for spells to specifically protect against vampires. In order to cheer herself up she put on some Christmas music, lit the fire, burned some incense, and turned on the fairy lights that she'd placed around her walls and across her shelves.

Satisfied she'd banished some gloom, she began searching her grimoire methodically. She found all sorts of interesting spells that she'd missed before, some of them quite unpleasant. There was one to give someone warts, one to cause uncontrollable sweating, and one to cause 'the pox.' She shuddered. Her ancestors seemed really quite unpleasant sometimes. She could only hope they hadn't really used them.

One spell made her pause, excited. A spell to bottle sunlight. That would be perfect—not only for them, but for the ghost-hunters, too. She marked the page, and started to list all those she thought would be useful.

She found another spell that detailed how to make a wooden stake. It specified the type of wood to use, suggesting that ash or hawthorn were the most effective. The stake she had from Rasmus was made of hawthorn. It sat across the table where she'd left it the night before after cleaning it and blessing it, banishing the negative energies. The newly turned vampire might not have bled, but nevertheless, the stake had been covered in gore, the point dented from where she'd driven it through the plastic tray beneath the body.

She turned back to her grimoire and found several spells that used garlic. One made a useful potion, and there were herb bundles that incorporated it and other protective plants. That was a brilliant idea. She could make Christmas wreaths for the all the doors and windows, or she could just bundle the plants together to make posies. And maybe she should see James for holy water. While she didn't believe in the value of it, clearly a vampire did if the lore was to be trusted.

Avery had a hawthorn hedge at the rear of her garden, and plenty of holly and bay. All offered protection. She'd already brought in branches of holly to decorate the shop and her flat. If she visited Old Haven Church, she could cut some yew and oak, as well. And they'd need ash to make more stakes—the more the better. She picked up her cutting knife, grabbed some garden gloves, and headed outside.

The day was dark, the sky full of heavy grey clouds, and it was bitterly cold. Most of the garden was bare, as all of her summer flowers had died back, but the shrubs still struggled along, and there were bright berries in places. She'd only been working for an hour when she heard a shout, and looked around to see Newton marching towards her, looking furious.

Avery braced herself as she turned to face him, and dropped her cuttings of hawthorn into the wheelbarrow next to her.

He didn't bother with pleasantries. "Are you responsible for that horror show in the Coroner's building last night?"

"I'm afraid so."

"You beheaded young, dead girls! Do you know what that will do to their parents?"

She squared her shoulders. "Better that than they become vampires! I presume you've noticed that one of the girls is missing?"

He paused. "That wasn't you?" He looked around suspiciously, as if he would see the girl propped up in the corner somewhere.

"By the great Goddess, Newton!" Avery glared at him. "I'm not a bloody body snatcher! She turned last night and became a vampire!"

He looked apoplectic. "Why the hell didn't you tell me?"

Avery took a deep breath in an attempt to calm herself down. Sometimes Newton was infuriating. "By the time we left the morgue—pursued by a vampire, by the way—it was very late. I presumed you wouldn't want to be disturbed. I phoned early this morning, but it went straight to voicemail. Don't you check your messages?"

He looked slightly chastened. "I was called into the morgue at six. I went by Briar's house, actually, but she didn't answer." *Interesting!* Avery raised a quizzical eyebrow, but Newton rushed on. "I was worried. Is she okay?"

This should be fun. "She should be. She stayed at Caspian's last night."

Newton's face darkened. "Caspian's? Why?"

Avery explained what had happened at the morgue and on the way home. "It was probably a good idea to go with him, not only to have two of them in the car, but also to save Briar sleeping at home on her own."

Newton nodded, and a calculating expression settled behind his eyes. "I could stay at hers for the next few days, or weeks, until this is over."

Avery crossed her arms in front of her and glared at him. "What are you *doing*, Newton? Stop messing her about! You seemed to make it very clear a few months ago that whatever you two had going on was over, and now you seem to be hedging your bets! Either walk away and stay friends or actually commit to a relationship! You can't have it both ways."

"I am not trying to have it both ways!" he protested poorly.

"So what are you doing?"

He seemed to deflate, like a popped balloon. "She saved me, and I liked it." His hands moved to the scar on his neck, caused by Suzanna's blade on All Hallows' Eve. Newton had been seconds from death, and only Briar's magic had saved him. She hadn't moved from his bedside for over 24 hours, and had been tending him for days afterwards, helping to reduce his scar and regain his strength. Up until then, Briar had been blisteringly impatient with him for months after the summer when he'd backed away, but now she'd calmed down, and Avery had the sense that she was waiting, again—for him.

"So *do something*! Ask her out, take her for dinner, or make it clear you're just friends. Briar is hot! She doesn't deserve to have to wait for you to make your mind up. I don't even know why she *is* waiting! I bloody wouldn't." Avery's exasperation came flooding out. "Hunter fancies her, and he's still in touch! He may even be coming down over Christmas. I hope they get together."

Newton looked like she'd slapped him. "He's coming back?"

"He might be."

Newton abruptly changed the subject. "Are you all meeting again for a debrief?"

"Yes, tonight, at my flat. You're welcome to come. Just don't be a dick." She turned her back on him and went back to her cuttings, and she heard Newton leave. *Men!*

By the time she'd finished gathering wood from her garden, she was cold and hungry, and her cheeks were glowing. She staggered into the small kitchen behind the shop carrying an armful of branches, dumped them on the table, and went back for the rest.

Dan was waiting when she brought in the last load, and he handed her a cup of steaming hot chocolate. "You've been busy."

"I'll be making wreaths and posies. Lots of them. It will take me a few hours, but magic will help speed up the process. You can have a couple to put by your front and back door. By the end of the day I'll have something basic for you to take home."

He looked worried. "This is just a precaution. Right?"

She started sorting through her cuttings, not meeting his eyes. "Right."

"I bet you haven't heard the news."

Her head shot up. "No. What's happened?"

"A young man has been reported missing. He was last seen outside a night club in Truro, and his jacket has been found in an alleyway behind it."

Avery closed her eyes briefly, as if she could block out the news. "Crap."

"Didn't Newton say anything? He was here earlier."

She shook her head thoughtfully. "No, he didn't, but maybe he didn't know." She rubbed her face, exasperated and overwhelmed by what they faced.

"This isn't going to go away, is it?" he asked, sadly.

"No. It's only just beginning."

***

As soon as Avery had finished her hot chocolate, she headed to Old Haven Church.

As usual it was deserted, which gave it a haunting beauty. Frost lay thick on the ground, and clung to the branches and decaying vegetation, and as she crunched along the path to the wood behind the cemetery where they had encountered the Wild Hunt, she found her gaze drifting to the mausoleum where Gil lay. So much had changed since he died. She wasn't sure Gil would have liked the changes at all, but he would have enjoyed being part of the coven.

She plunged under the trees and made her way to the clearing and the huge, old yew tree in the centre. There was nothing left to remind her of that terrifying Samhain. The space had been cleansed of the ritual blood magic, and once again it was a peaceful place, the silence broken only by the occasional bird song.

And there was something else. A flickering movement on the edge of her peripheral vision caused her to whirl around, hands raised, her heart beating wildly in her chest. Shadow stepped out from behind the trees, as if out of thin air.

"Shadow! You scared the crap out of me. What are you doing here?"

Shadow gave a slow, calculating smile that chilled Avery's blood. "I always come here, human. It's where I arrived, and where I keep trying to return to the Summerlands."

Avery kept her distance, taking a pace backwards, and summoning her magic. Shadow was dressed all in black: skinny jeans, black boots, and a fitted leather jacket. *Where had she got them from? Not her problem.* "But you can't return, you know that. The doorway is closed."

"Maybe I should try some blood magic."

Was that a threat? "You'll fail." Shadow stepped forward again, and Avery raised her hands. "Take one more step and I'll freeze your faery blood until you explode into shards of ice."

Shadow gave a hollow laugh. "I'd like to see you try."

"Take one more step and you will."

She held her hands up in surrender. "Sorry. It was a joke. I was wondering what you'd do if I threatened you, and now I know."

Avery narrowed her eyes. "I don't think you understand the word *joke*. Besides, you asked for our help. I won't be much help if I'm dead."

"True. Does that mean you've found something to help me?"

"Not yet. I've been a little side-tracked." *Understatement of the year.*

"With what?"

"A small matter of the undead."

"The undead? Spirits or night-walkers?"

"Vampires."

"What's that?"

"They were once human, but now suck human blood to survive. They are fast and deadly."

Shadow walked towards Avery, her threatening posture gone. "So, what are you doing here?"

"I'm collecting supplies to make a spell," Avery said warily, still not trusting Shadow.

"I'm no threat to you. Maybe I can help?"

"I can manage just fine on my own. I just need some branches of the yew, oak, and rowan, and then I'll be gone."

Shadow pulled a long, thin knife out of the scabbard on her belt. "I can help. I will feel useful." She nodded behind her to where a couple of oak trees stood. "I'll get some oak." She ran over to the tree and began to climb it nimbly and effortlessly, and Avery turned to the yew.

The sooner I do this the better. She laid her hand upon the yew's trunk and blessed it, asking to take only what she needed. She worked quickly, until she had a small pile of skinny branches covered in tiny needles at her feet, and then found the rowan tree and did the same, cutting some branches that still had a cluster of bright red berries on them.

She'd just finished when Shadow reappeared with her arms full of cuttings, and a swath of mistletoe on top. "What do you need these for?"

"Protection. All of these plants have special properties."

Shadow shrugged. "I'm not a healer. I'm a hunter, a treasure seeker. Are you hunting this creature?"

Avery nodded, wondering where Shadow was heading. "Yes, we need to stop it as soon as we can."

Shadow flashed a huge smile. "Good. I can help."

12

Avery's open-plan living area was full of people. The White Haven Coven was there, the three ghost-hunters, Newton, and Caspian had arrived last with a bottle of wine, as if attending a meeting to decide how to hunt vampires was something he often did on an evening after work. They were seated on the sofa and chairs, around the dining table, and others were standing and talking.

Avery had gone back to work for a few hours after meeting Shadow in the wood, mulling on her offer, but it was something she wanted to discuss with everyone else, and she'd told her that she would be in touch. She'd spent most of the afternoon in her attic making wreaths and posies for protection, and sent Sally and Dan home with two each, and then started to prepare food for everyone—platters of cheese, ham, fresh bread, olives, pickles, and a tray of mince pies.

By the time the other witches started to arrive she felt exhausted. Alex greeted her with a kiss. "Busy?"

"Too busy. Especially after last night. How have you been?"

He headed into the kitchen to deposit a six-pack of beer, and she followed him. "Exhausted and depressed." He popped a cap and took a long swig of beer before he spoke. "A bloody vampire! I keep trying to tell myself I imagined last night, but then I remember how that sword felt, and well, it makes me feel sick."

Avery tried to reassure him. "You did what you had to do. What we couldn't."

"But I feel like a monster."

"You're not the monster."

"I know, but—" He shrugged, unusually despondent.

"You're sleep-deprived and tired. Come and eat," she said, leading him back to her dining room table that groaned with food. "You'll feel better."

The news was on the TV, and Reuben stood watching it, absently eating. "That vamp must have gone hunting as soon as you threw it off our tail, Avery."

"You think the vampire's behind the missing man, then?"

"In Truro? Last night? Sure. The timing's right."

Newton nodded. He was still in his suit, but he'd pulled his tie off and opened the top button of his shirt. "I agree. I mean, I have no proof, but you did deprive him of two victims."

"We had to," Avery said, feeling guilty.

"I know. It would have probably done it anyway if what your coven says is true." He sipped his beer, half an eye on the TV. "Is he making some kind of undead army?"

"It takes more than two to make an army," Reuben pointed out.

Newton sighed. "I think there have been more victims."

They all looked confused, and Briar paused mid-bite to ask, "More disappearances?"

He nodded. "My colleagues have been investigating some for weeks. All adults, nothing suspicious, other than they have just gone!"

"Doesn't that automatically raise questions?"

"People go missing all the time, for all sorts of reasons. Often they're alive, but are hiding from domestic abuse, parental abuse, or are using drugs, or there's trafficking at play. It's huge. You have no idea. But these particular disappearances are clustered together," he admitted.

Alex exchanged a worried glance with Avery and asked, "If the disappearances are linked, why would the vampire overtly kill some, while others have just disappeared?"

Newton sighed. "Maybe he's stronger now, and wants to scare people. Vampire psychology is not my thing. Cassie? Isn't that your area of study?"

"Not exactly," she answered, dead-pan. "But killers thrive on power, and the more they get away with the more confident they get. I'm not sure if that's a useful comparison, but it's all I've got." She shrugged apologetically.

"Hold on!" Ben said, holding his hand up. "Before we all start speculating, can you recap us on everything that happened last night? All we've been hearing are terrifying snippets. Remember, some of us weren't there."

"Thankfully," Cassie added, her face grim.

Dylan agreed. "From what I've heard so far, I'm wondering if we should drop this job."

Ben looked shocked. "No way! This will be the biggest thing we've done—for money, at least!"

"My life is worth more than money." Dylan was annoyed, and it sounded like their conversation was the continuation of an earlier argument. "Remember, my mate's cousin was one of those girls."

The six witches glanced at each other, a warning in their eyes. *Shit!* Avery had forgotten that. They were going to have to tell him that she was the one who'd turned.

Alex sat heavily in one of the chairs next to the table. "Actually, we really need your links to this house. We think this is all connected. Everyone settle in, we have a lot to share."

For the next fifteen minutes, Avery, Caspian, and Reuben updated them on the meeting with the coven, and then the other witches joined in and shared what had happened at the morgue.

Dylan looked at them all, stunned. "Are you seriously telling me that *dead* Bethany escaped the morgue?"

"I'm afraid so," Briar said. She was sitting next to him on the sofa, and she squeezed his arm in sympathy.

He flinched. "Are you sure it's her?"

"Very sure," Alex answered. "We'd just identified which freezer she was in."

Dylan fell against the back of the sofa and closed his eyes. "This is a nightmare. Beth is a *vampire*."

Ben looked sceptical. "Seriously?"

"I've never met one before," Reuben answered sarcastically, "but yes, I think so. I don't know anything else that causes people to rise from the dead."

"It could be a zombie," Cassie said, as if that might be better.

Reuben was emphatic. "It's not a zombie. It had big canines, perfect for sucking your blood!"

Cassie shifted uncomfortably in her seat on the sofa, glancing at the others in a way that made Avery think they knew something they hadn't yet shared. "And you still think it's linked to the house we're investigating?"

El nodded. "It seems too much of a coincidence. But maybe we're wrong. What have you found out?" she prompted.

Dylan exhaled, opened his eyes and sat up. "Lots of weird shit. I'll start at the beginning. The House of Spirits was built in the early nineteenth century, but was bought by Madame Charron, as she became known, in the late 1920s. Her real name was Evelyn Crookshank. Her husband had died in

1923 by suicide, after his experiences in World War One, leaving her with a daughter, Felicity. She'd have been about two at the time. Suicide was pretty common, unfortunately, for war veterans. At about the same time there was a resurgence in interest in the spirit world and mediums. There's lots of research about it. People speculate that it stemmed from a need to contact their loved ones, and charlatans took advantage of that. It seems Evelyn became interested in spiritualism just after his death, and in a short time became a medium."

Avery leaned forward, fascinated. "Was Evelyn a charlatan?"

"Hard to know for sure. That's partly why we're investigating the house. I think I told you that Rupert and Charlotte are fairly obsessed with this kind of thing, particularly Rupert. Apparently, he's wanted to buy this house for years."

"How do you know?" El asked.

Ben shrugged. "He told us. He develops this fervent glint in his eye when he talks about the house. Makes him look feral."

"Anyway," Dylan continued, "from what I could find out through various sources, she bought the house in 1928. By then she had a reputation, she'd made good money, and she moved in. It's big and imposing, good for impressing people, as you saw. It wasn't called the House of Spirits at the time. She named it later, had renovations done. For years the business did well, up until about 1938, and then something happened." He paused dramatically.

Caspian had been silent for a while, listening intently, almost an outsider in the group, but then he said, "She disappeared."

"Sort of. She retreated into solitude with her daughter. She stopped all her séances, all her private work, and wasn't ever really seen again."

"And her daughter?" Caspian asked.

"She'd have been a teenager by then. But no one saw her much, either. They dismissed the servants, and apart from the daughter who went out for shopping, they pretty much became recluses. They both died in the house—several years apart, of course."

"Wow," Avery said, feeling sorry for them. "Imagine living in a house for so long and never going out!"

Briar looked shocked. "Felicity never moved out? Never got married, never did anything?"

Dylan shook his head, looking as perplexed as Briar. "No. She inherited the house from her mother, who died in 1979, and just stayed there, letting it decay around her."

"She'd have been, what—97, 98 when she died?" Reuben speculated. "Living on her own?"

Cassie stirred from where she'd been listening in the corner of the sofa. "She had a cleaner for the last twenty years or so. She inherited *everything.*"

"But," Dylan said, "she sold the house as soon as she could—to Rupert. It was a very quick sale."

"What was the cleaner's name?" Newton asked, pulling out his notebook.

Ben looked frustrated. "Joan Tiernan. We've tried to contact her, but she hasn't responded to our calls, yet."

"She could know quite a few things about that house," El speculated.

Ben nodded. "That's what we think, too."

"Have Rupert or his wife, Charlotte, spoken to her?" Alex asked.

"It doesn't sound like it," Cassie said. "They only dealt with the estate agent for the sale. They're just focusing on renovating the house, and finding out its secrets."

Briar frowned. "Secrets?"

"Hidden panels, mechanisms, tricks—anything that could indicate Evelyn was a fraud. Or better still, the real deal," Ben explained.

Newton stood and paced the room, looking very policeman-like. "I need to get this straight. Felicity dies, leaves the house to Joan, and she sells it to Rupert, Mr Occult. At what point do they employ you?" he asked Ben, Dylan, and Cassie.

"Right after they start renovating," Ben explained. "We were on the news because of the events at Samhain, and they thought we could investigate the house—even though nothing was really happening, as far as hauntings go. We agreed…the house sounded interesting."

Newtown stopped pacing and stood, deep in thought. "But what links the house to these disappearances and murders?"

Ben gave a wry smile as he looked at Avery. "Witches don't like coincidences. And now there's timing. From what you've just said, the disappearances started at the same time as Felicity died. And then Charlotte told us that she's been experiencing strange dreams about someone standing over her in the night—for a while, by the way—not just the last few nights. She came clean about that today."

"Did you have a chance to examine the footage?" Reuben asked.

Dylan nodded. "Yes, and it's looking really odd. At about two in the morning she gets out of bed and heads to the window, opens it, and returns to bed. Then for a few minutes we lose part of her image as something comes between her and the camera. We can hear a strange breathing noise, and a rasping sound, but we can't see anything on thermal imaging. *Nothing.* And then we see her again. And that's it." He spread his hands wide, perplexed. "We'll keep filming, obviously."

Avery had a horrible thought. "Is she wearing a scarf around her neck?"

Cassie met her eyes, fear lurking behind them. "All the time. Silk ones, of varying designs."

"Holy shit!" Reuben exclaimed, looking at Avery. "We talked about the possibility of that in the car. The vampire has his own blood bank."

Cassie almost shrieked. "And she lets it in?"

"Just like Dracula," El murmured. "He was very persuasive."

"And there's nothing in the rest of the house?" Avery asked.

"No. But we found something else," Ben added.

"What?" Newton asked.

"All that poking about with panels has paid off. Rupert found a panel that opens to a hidden staircase that leads up to the tower room, and there's all sorts of weirdness up there!"

At that point, anyone who wasn't paying full attention was now, edging forward on their seats.

"Go on," Alex prompted.

Dylan elaborated. "Well, from the outside it's a square tower, but inside there are painted wooden panels that make the room circular instead. There are sigils and signs on the floor, too."

Avery shuffled in her chair. "What kind of paintings?"

"Demons, and what look like tarot images," Cassie told her.

"We need to see it," Reuben said immediately.

Ben nodded. "Yes, you do. I'm wondering if the attic is the seat of power in the house, actually."

"Although," Dylan added quickly, "there are no EMF readings up there at all at the moment. We checked it out today."

"That reminds me," Reuben said, reaching into his jeans pocket. "We found this yesterday afternoon." He pulled an envelope out and then from inside that, the yellowed scrap of paper with the signs of the moon on it.

"When we were at the house yesterday, we found this under the hearth where the witch-bottle was found."

Caspian took it and examined it, and then passed it to Alex. "I didn't know there was a witch-bottle."

"Ben showed it to me," Avery said, and Ben nodded. "I presumed Evelyn had felt threatened and needed to protect herself from some curse or something. I must admit, I thought it was older, initially—maybe a couple of hundred years, but I must be wrong."

Caspian looked at her speculatively. "Maybe not. The house is old. It could have been there from a long time before. Maybe there's always been something about that house. Maybe something that predates Evelyn. Was there anything unusual about the bottle?"

"Not that I could tell. It contained nails, sharp objects, blood, skin, human nail cuttings—the usual." She turned to Dylan. "Did you film in the tower?"

"No, just ran the EMF metre around it."

Newton huffed impatiently. "Did you test the walls?"

Ben looked disappointed. "We did, but they all sounded the same—hollow. But that's not surprising. There must be a gap between the panels and the walls."

"Maybe they hide a passageway?" El suggested.

Reuben grinned. "You need to get us back in the house."

13

By unspoken agreement they took a break, some refreshing drinks and topping up on food, while others clustered in small groups to discuss their findings.

Alex was in the kitchen getting another beer, and Avery was bringing more cheese out of the fridge. "Before we do anything," Alex said to her, "we need to do some more homework. I don't think any of us should be blundering into that room without knowing more about that house or vampires."

"Agreed," Caspian said, joining them to refill his red wine. "There's a vampire out there—well, two now, that we know of. I do not want to stumble into their resting place unprepared."

Avery sighed and rolled her shoulders to try and release her tension. "I agree, but we haven't got a lot of time. I mean, the deaths and disappearances have happened so quickly, to wait even a couple of days will inevitably mean someone else will die."

Alex nodded. "Then we divide up, cut the work in half, just like Genevieve suggested to the coven. Come on, let's get this done with." He turned and led them back to the living room.

Newton was partway through a conversation with Reuben and looked agonised. "Well, yes and no. But, that thing has kidnapped someone, for all we know. It could be out again tonight. We have to stop it quickly."

"I agree," Reuben said, leaning against the wall, looking nonchalant despite the risks they faced. "But we need a plan." He called over to Ben, "Did you hear from Jasper today?"

Ben straightened up from where he'd crouched, talking to Briar and El. "Yes, sorry, meant to tell you. He's coming over to our place tomorrow. He and Dylan are going to get geeky over research."

Dylan wagged a finger at him. "That research may just save your miserable ass, my friend!"

Caspian frowned. "Check as far back as you can. If that witch-bottle is old, then maybe something dark has been happening around that house for a long time."

"And what can I do?" Briar asked, looking around the room. "I feel useless at the moment."

"You're far from useless," Newton said, his eyes shadowed. "You weren't useless last night."

"I wasn't the one beheading vampires-to-be. That was Alex."

"And I'll never forget it," Alex said, regretfully. He smiled at Briar. "Don't worry. There'll be plenty to do when the time comes. Ben, when can we get in that house?"

Ben rubbed his forehead. "I don't know. I'm not sure Rupert will want you in there. He was a bit annoyed to find Avery and Reuben there, actually."

"We've glamoured people before," Reuben reminded them. "We glamoured Stan out of White Haven for a few days before Samhain, and I'm sure we can do the same with Rupert."

"No," Newton insisted. "Not a chance."

"Spoilsport," Reuben said, looking annoyed. "You like us breaking the rules if you need us."

Cassie brightened. "I know when! They're away this weekend—don't you remember them saying so, guys? Charlotte told us they have to go to her sister's birthday party. They leave Saturday morning!"

"That's right," Dylan agreed, excited. "They're back on Sunday. They know we'll be in there checking the cameras, so you could come with us. They'd never know."

"Excellent," Reuben said, stretching to his full height and grinning like the Cheshire cat. "We have three days to find out the secrets of that house—well, you do," he said, looking at Dylan. "And we have three days to try to figure out what we're facing, and to track missing, newly-turned vamps, and one lair."

"Or several lairs," Alex reminded him, looking thoughtful. "We could check out likely dark and secure places within a reasonable radius."

"Three days to hone my vampire hunting skills and spells," El said, not looking half as excited as Reuben.

"By the way," Avery said, "Shadow wants to help with this. I haven't given her an answer yet."

Alex shook his head. "I don't want her help. I don't trust her. I don't *know* her!"

"I'll call her," El offered. "My *sister* may be able to help make vampire-killing equipment. That way I can get to know her, and suss out her motives."

"Have we missed anything?" Newton asked, pacing again.

"Yes," Caspian said, as he put his glass down and pulled his coat on. "Get us the autopsy report, and check Rupert and Charlotte's background. I agree with Avery. He sounds dodgy."

Newton rubbed his hands through his hair, and absent-mindedly stroked the scar on his neck as he did so. "Yes, I could see if they have a record of any sort, or check where they came from. It shouldn't be too difficult."

Caspian frowned and paused. "What happened when the people at the morgue discovered the mess this morning?"

Avery had been meaning to ask that all evening, but had become distracted by everything else, and so had the others by the look of their reactions. Everyone focused on Newton.

He exhaled heavily. "There was utter hysteria from a couple of people, a few who thought it was a sick prank, but most were just shocked. We shut the whole place down for the day while we investigated. They'll have to get the roof repaired, and that freezer door, and we've all had to have some horrible conversations with family members. It was like a horror show in there."

"You should have been there last night," Alex said. He'd sat down again and was watching Newton with tired eyes.

Newton nodded. "The morgue has a 24-hour police watch on it now, and will have for the next few days—until we can decide if it might happen again."

"Is anybody linking the deaths with vampires?" Caspian asked.

"Only in a jokey, unbelievable kind of way. No one really thinks there's a vampire on the loose. Although, as you can imagine, there have been a lot of questions as to why someone would behead dead girls and steal a body. And it hasn't gone unnoticed that the freezer door was kicked off from the *inside*."

"And the press?"

"I give it until tomorrow," Newton answered. "That Sarah woman from Cornwall TV will be all over this, I guarantee it."

"No links to us, though, right?" Reuben asked.

"None. And it will stay that way." He looked around at them all, frowning. "I still wish you'd told me what you were planning."

Avery tried to reassure him. "There was no time. And besides, you can't get involved in this. You know the rules. You're a policeman. We're protecting you…your job."

"I know." Newton sighed. He looked across at Ben, Dylan, and Cassie. "Make sure you don't go anywhere alone at night, especially around that house."

Cassie shuddered. "Don't worry, we won't."

"Take some of my protection wreaths with you." Avery walked over to the table where she'd stacked them up. "Hang them on your front and back doors, and don't let anyone in that you don't know."

Alex agreed. "That thing we saw last night looked distinctly inhuman, but it could have a sort of glamour to look human when it wants to."

Briar looked up, her face drawn. She'd been in quiet conversation with El. "What if it tracked us after last night?"

As one, they all looked towards the windows. Avery had drawn her blinds against the night, but they were all aware how cold and dark it was outside, and the night was a vampire's friend.

"You can stay with me again tonight if you want," Caspian said to Briar, pausing by the door.

Ever since Briar and Caspian had teamed up to save El from the curse, they seemed to have reached a new understanding. Briar hadn't hesitated to help Caspian the night before, and he didn't have a problem with her staying at Faversham central. Avery couldn't believe how things had changed since the summer and after Sebastian's death. Apparently, Newton couldn't either, because he released a barely-suppressed huff of annoyance at the suggestion. He needn't have worried, as she declined.

"Thanks, but I need to stay at home tonight. I'll be fine."

"I pity the vampire who tries to attack you," Caspian said, laughing briefly. "I'm going to investigate the area for possible places for them to hide. I'll be in touch." And with that, he left.

Dylan started to get ready to leave, too, addressing his partners. "Come on, guys. I want to go home and try to sleep. I have a feeling that sleep is something I'm going to miss over the coming days."

"I'll be interested to hear what you find out about that old place," Reuben said, reaching for another beer.

Cassie rose to her feet, grabbed her coat, and headed to the door behind Dylan. "Me, too. I'm starting to wonder what we've got ourselves involved in.

Thanks for the food, Avery, and good to see you all again. We'll call with updates."

Newton picked his jacket up from the back of a chair, and as he followed the ghost-hunters out the door, he looked back at the witches. "Don't take any chances. And please, try not to behead any dead bodies again."

Avery wondered if she was reading too much into how he looked at Briar, and how she returned his glance, but she decided that whatever was going on between them was none of her business.

Once the witches were alone, Avery started to feel the weight of their situation sink in. It felt huge. A vampire on the loose that was killing and creating new vampires; they could all be at risk.

Reuben had been energetic during the meeting, standing for most of the time and leading much of the discussion, but once everyone had left he sank into a chair, his shoulders bowed.

"Are you all right?" El asked, sitting next to him.

"I'm fine, just daunted at what we're facing."

She squeezed his arm. "It's no worse than what we've faced before, it's just…different."

Briar laughed, dryly. "That's one way of putting it."

Alex and Avery joined them on the sofa, and Avery felt herself relax finally, comfortable with her coven. It had taken her a while to acknowledge the other witches as that, but tonight, finally, she felt they were, and she trusted them with her life. She turned to them, smiling shyly. "I'm glad I got to know you all properly. My life is better because of it."

El grinned. "Thanks, Avery. So is ours."

Reuben snorted. "Snowflake."

"Sod off, Reuben," Avery retorted.

He laughed. "Kidding. So is mine, although it took Gil's death to make me see it."

"You're my family," Briar said, tearing up slightly. "I love you all, and I'm terrified that something will happen to you. This thing has got me genuinely scared. It's like nothing we've ever faced before."

Alex looked at all of them, one by one. "We're not all going to die, you depressing bunch of gits! We're facing a vampire here. We're bigger, badder, and more powerful. And we're going to kick its scrawny, undead ass. We gave it a serious setback last night. Don't underestimate what we did."

Avery looked at him, wishing he were right. "But, Rasmus lost his first wife to one. They were young and powerful, just like us. One of us could die, too!"

"No, we won't. I won't allow it." He looked stubborn and annoyed and Avery loved him all the more for it. "Evelyn and Felicity would have known exactly what was going on. That first attack in 1979 coincided with Evelyn's death. What if Felicity was the one to stop it? You said Rasmus and the others never found the original vamp. Maybe her death has released whatever hold she had on it?" He started to get excited. "They both lived there for years, and although their spirits may not be roaming the house, they must be there *somewhere.* I want to speak to one of them. Whatever secrets that house holds, whatever they know, I aim to find out."

"On Saturday?" Reuben asked.

"Yes. I'll check with Ben first, see which room will give me the best chance, and that will be the room I'll try. In the meantime, I'll have a think about the best way to connect."

14

A persistent scratching sound woke Avery from a restless sleep. For a few moments she lay quietly, trying to discern what the noise was, and trying to work out the other noise that was competing with the scratching. She realised she could hear her cats growling, their throaty rumbles coming from deep within their chests.

Avery sat up, trying not to disturb Alex, and in the pale light that filtered through her blinds, she saw Medea and Circe sitting up at the end of the bed, staring at the window on the far side of the room. She followed their gaze, mystified. *What were they fixated on? Why were they growling?*

She edged forward to reach the cats, stroking them to try and reassure them, but their fur bristled, and they ignored her, transfixed.

The steady *scratch, scratch, scratch* perplexed her. There were no trees by the window, nothing natural to scratch in such a persistent manner. She slipped out of bed, heading to the noise, and the cats increased their deep, throaty rumble as if in warning. As she reached towards the window, a shudder ran through her. *Something was on the other side of the window, something strange. Something that shouldn't be there.*

As if she couldn't control her movements, she reached forward and raised the blinds.

A face was pressed against the glass, and fingernails tapped and scraped downwards. Avery faltered and stepped back, almost stumbling, a cry caught in her throat. The figure on the other side of the window was clearly Bethany Mason. Her long hair floated around her head in a halo, her face was pale, and her dark eyes were fixed upon Avery with a fierce intensity.

This shouldn't be happening. Avery was three floors up, and there was no way to her window other than climbing up a straight wall or by flying. And yet Bethany was there, her fingernails scraping the glass. Avery made the mistake of looking into the dark abyss of her eyes, and she was lost.

She needed to open the window. Bethany was cold. She must come in.

Avery reached forward towards the latch, ready to release it and let her inside. Alex slept next to her, unmoving, his sleep almost unnaturally deep.

With an unearthly howl, Circe leapt towards her, launching on to her arm and sinking her claws deep into her skin, and at the same time, the door to the bedroom flew open, banging against the wall.

Pain cleared Avery's head. She backed away from the catch and clutched her scratched arm, retreating as the reality of the situation dawned. She turned to the door of her bedroom where Helena stood, a spectral wind whirling about her. Her eyes blazed with fury, but she couldn't come in; Avery had cast a spell that banned her from the room. But it wasn't Avery that she was glaring at—it was Bethany.

Avery stepped back again, terror rising. Bethany locked eyes with Helena and for a few seconds neither of them moved, and neither did Avery, frozen with fear. And then Medea howled, spurring Avery into action. She uttered a spell that banished Bethany from the window, causing her to skitter away down the wall like a lizard. Avery ran to the window, watching her leave, her stomach twisting with horror at Bethany's unnatural movements, just like the night before in the morgue. She glanced up once, giving Avery a malicious look that suggested she would be back.

Avery shuddered and turned back to Helena, who watched with her equally dark and hollowed-out gaze. "Thank you."

Helena nodded, her expression softening, and then she vanished.

Medea had returned to the end of the bed, next to Circe, and both watched the window more placidly, their tails swishing across the quilt. Alex was still in a deep and soundless sleep. *How could he have slept through that?* She considered waking him, but in the end, Avery decided that it was pointless. There was nothing he could do now. At least one of them would get some decent rest.

***

When Alex finally woke the next morning, he was groggy and heavy-headed. "I feel like I have a hangover, and after only a couple of beers, that really seems unlikely."

Avery rolled over to face him, watching as he squinted in the dim light of the room. "I think your groggy head is because you had some weird, vampire mojo on you last night."

"*What?*" he turned to her, frowning. "Are you kidding me?"

"No. I had a visitor, and Helena and the cats saved me." She told him what happened, and Alex's expression changed from confusion, to worry, to complete panic.

"But I didn't hear a thing!" He propped himself up on an elbow and stared at her. "Nothing. I was in a really deep sleep."

"Yep, vampire mojo." She was making light of it, but she wasn't fooling anyone.

Alex pulled her towards him, his arm around her waist. "Are you sure you're all right? You should have woken me."

She reached up and stroked his cheek, feeling his stubble beneath her fingers. "There was no point."

"Yes, there was. That's what I'm here for, to look after you."

"I'm a lucky girl."

"Yes, you are," he said, grinning. And then his smile faded. "But what if Bethany tried the same on Briar or the others? They haven't got a helpful ghost or cats to save them." He sat up and reached for his phone.

Guilt flooded through Avery. "Sorry, I didn't even think of that. The whole thing had me so freaked out." She sat up, too, watching him call, reassured only when they all answered and confirmed they were okay.

"I need to put those bundles of protection around my windows," she said, getting out of bed. "I didn't consider that vampires could scale walls like Spiderman."

"Dracula did," Alex pointed out as he pulled his clothes on. "You must have read it. Poor old Jonathan Harker watched him crawling the walls in the castle."

Avery headed into the bathroom for a shower. "Great. Transylvania has come to White Haven."

***

Avery was not looking forward to updating Sally and Dan on the latest events, but she had to. Dan had entered the shop that morning reeking of garlic, and wearing another Christmas t-shirt that was painfully unfunny. Sally had arrived with mince pies.

Sally's hand flew to her neck as Avery told her of her encounter the night before. "She was here!"

"I'm afraid so. I don't want to panic either of you, but you need to know to take this seriously. With luck she will only be targeting us, but who knows where the main vampire is, and who he is—rather, *was*." Avery shook her head perplexed. "I never know whether to call them an 'it' or a he or she. They're so inhuman they seem to have lost their gender. Anyway, you need to be careful."

"And that's why I'm already taking steps to protect myself," Dan said, sipping his coffee.

"With garlic, yes, I can tell." Avery wrinkled her nose, keeping her distance. "Did you put the protection bundles up?"

Dan mock-saluted. "Yes ma'am." He looked around the bookstore and dropped his voice. "I even made a stake last night. Just in case. Not that I want you to involve me in any other way."

"Wow! Good to know you're prepared. Which reminds me, I need to prepare some stakes, too. I have the wood. I'll put in a few hours here and then head outside, if that's okay with you?"

"No problem," Sally said. "As far as I'm concerned, that's your number one priority."

Later that morning, Avery headed out to the garden with the harvested wood from Old Haven and a sharp knife, and using a combination of magic and the sharp edge, fashioned several stakes. As she worked, she cast a spell into them, too, something to enhance the accuracy of the user when it came to finding the heart. As she'd found out only too well, the stake was hard to use, and to combine strength with accuracy was difficult. She'd only managed it the other night with the aid of her magic.

She looked around the garden in the bleak winter sunshine and again found it hard to believe that only the night before Bethany had scaled the wall of the building. She looked up to her attic window and shook her head. *Unbelievable.*

And then she thought of something else. *They needed holy water.*

***

The Church of All Souls was decorated with pine branches, holly, ivy, poinsettia, and candles. Not only did it look pretty, but the pine scented the air and Avery inhaled deeply, enjoying the refreshing smell.

She hadn't bothered going to the vicarage as the church doors were wide open, inviting parishioners in, and quite a few people were sitting quietly in the church, praying or enjoying the colours of the light through the stained glass windows, and the Christmas cheer.

Avery passed them all, heading to the sacristy where James, the vicar, wrote his sermons, hoping he would be there. A new verger had started since Harry's death in the summer, and Avery passed her doing some Christmas preparation by the altar.

The last time she had seen James was at Samhain, when he had taken the press to Old Haven to watch him take down the witch-signs that had been hanging in the trees. The magic they contained had blasted him off the ladder, and he'd broken his arm and suffered a concussion. The cameraman had also been injured, as had the reporter. Avery and Alex had visited James at home and shown him the true nature of their magic. It was an attempt to warn him of the dangers of other witches in the hope that he'd be more careful, but she knew they had scared him, and if anything, the knowledge had made him unsure of Avery. She hadn't seen him since.

The door to the sacristy was open, and James was at the desk under the window, writing. He turned at the sound of her footsteps, but when he saw who it was, an undisguised apprehension filled his eyes. He stood and came to meet her at the door. "Avery. It's been a while. What can I do for you?"

She pondered how to broach this request, and knew he would leap to assumptions, but there was no way to ask this any differently. "It's a strange request, but important. I need some holy water."

He flinched. "Holy water? I presume it's not for a christening?"

Was that an attempt at a joke? Doubtful. "No, not a christening."

"You're not converting to the faith?" His tone was light, but scathing.

"No."

He watched her for a few moments, silent, and she could tell he had a million questions he was trying hard to push to the back of his mind. "Should I know why?"

"Probably not, but I'll tell you if you want."

His eyes dropped to the floor, and when he lifted his face again, his lips were pursed. "I think that if I'm to supply you with my services, then I should know what they are being used for."

"Then I should come into your office and close the door."

His eyes flickered with fear for the briefest of seconds before he backed away, allowing Avery inside. He retreated to his desk, and she shut the door behind her and leaned against it, giving him lots of space.

"Are you sure you want to know?" she insisted.

He folded his arms across his chest, resolute. "Yes. If I'm to protect my flock, I need to know from what. And there's only one thing I know of that can be defeated with holy water."

Here goes. "There's a vampire in Cornwall—well, two now, actually—and potentially there will be more."

His hands flew to his neck, in that unconscious gesture she'd seen a few times now. "Here? In White Haven?"

"Close enough," she said, "and one paid me a visit last night."

"A visit?"

"At my window, on the third floor. Fortunately, I was able to send it away."

He paled. "*Vampires*! And what do you plan to do about them?"

"Kill them, of course. Holy water will be one of our weapons in the fight."

He straightened his shoulders and nodded. "Yes, of course. The church will be a safe haven should any need to come here. It is open to all, regardless of faith."

She smiled, relieved by his support. "Thank you, James, I appreciate it. How does this work?"

"You bring me a large container of water, and I will bless it. Then you can use it as you see fit."

"Thanks. I can get one now, if that's okay?"

He nodded. "Yes, that's fine." He sat in the chair and despite the chill in the stone room that was inadequately heated, a light sweat broke out on his forehead, and he wiped it with the back of his hand. "I never expected to hear that word here, especially in the quiet, small towns of Cornwall. Vampires are more associated with big cities."

Avery's mouth dropped open. "Big cities? Has this happened before in somewhere you know?"

"Reports of suspicious deaths and disappearances are common in towns. Sometimes people choose to disappear into the underbelly of places, some reappear after a while, changed, older, worn out by poverty and crime. Others have no choice, and they are taken by drink, drugs, traffickers—you know." He looked at her, his eyes dark. "But there are those that return in unexpected ways. My colleagues in other parishes report such things, and well," he hesitated, summoning his strength. "They sound suspiciously like vampires. They love the underbelly of cities. The crowded streets, the anonymity. It's hard to track who is where, or what has happened to them."

"Wow. You're actually admitting they exist? I did not expect to hear you say that." She sank into the only other chair in the room, feeling her legs go weak beneath her.

He smiled, breaking the tension in the room. "So, finally I have surprised you."

She laughed, grateful to have him actually talking to her like she wasn't a monster. "Yes, you have. Although, I am pretty disturbed to hear about vampires elsewhere, like it's a normal thing."

"Oh, I wouldn't say normal."

"You must have tips about how we can get rid of them."

"No more than you already know, I'm sure. Holy water, a stake through the heart, beheading, burning. The church and vampires have a long history. They cannot cross consecrated ground."

"But why?" she asked, leaning forward. "I don't understand."

He shrugged. "They are the undead, and as such reject the rules that govern everyone else. Call it God's will, or your elemental magic—the magic of the wind, the rain, the sun. All of it is natural. The undead are not. Maybe that's why holy water and consecrated ground burns them. I'm sorry, it's only conjecture. I believe the real reasons will lie in the mists of time, because they have been around for that long. As have witches, spirits, and other things that exist which are considered abnormal."

"Witchcraft is not abnormal," Avery corrected him. "It's just unconventional. And some of us happen to be more skilled than most." She frowned. "If you were aware of the existence of vampires, why was the existence of witches such a shock to you?"

"I have known that vampires exist for a long time. They are associated with the church, in an unnatural way, but to acknowledge their existence as something other than abstract is something else. It's the same with witches. Of *course* I know about them—Wiccans, that is. But your type of magic, the covens you talk about, seem darker to me, more frightening," he explained. "Even though I know that was not your intent."

"But lots of people call themselves witches now. It's accepted."

"But they're not witches like you are, are they?" he asked gently. He considered her for a moment. "I confess I was wary of you for some time,

Avery, especially after Samhain and the strange events there. And of course when you revealed your skills. I've been avoiding you."

"And I, you. But I was trying to protect you from the witch at Old Haven. I needed you to know how dangerous magic can be."

"When wielded by someone with dark intent." He nodded. "I understand. But, seeing you again today, I know that's not you. And I know you protect others like you, which is sensible. I can live with that."

Relief flooded through Avery. She hadn't realised how important it was to hear that from James. He was a good man, and while they had their differences, both had good intentions. "Thank you. I appreciate that."

"Which means," he said, rising to his feet, "that I will help you in any way I can to get rid of the vampires. If you need me to bless a swimming pool, I will."

"Not necessary yet," she said, grinning. "I'll be back with a few litres for now."

15

Avery lined up several large bottles of holy water in the back room of the shop, and then returned to work to spend the last few hours of the day chatting to Dan and Sally. Dan had changed the music from Michael Bublé's Christmas album to pop Christmas specials, and the 1970s band Slade rang out around the shop.

Stan, the local councillor and pseudo druid was leaning against the counter. He was middle-aged and balding, and took great pleasure in all the town festivals. "Once again, you've outdone yourself." He looked around the shop with pleasure.

"Sally has," Dan corrected him. "This has nothing to do with me."

Sally grinned. "Thanks, Stan. And how are the Yule Parade preparations going?"

On the day of the solstice, a Sunday this year, there would be a Yule Parade through the town, ending at the harbour. Lots of schools and local businesses took part, and everyone dressed up. There'd be a mixture of Christmas and pagan figures in the procession, and all of the costumes were elaborate, some macabre.

"Exhausting," he said, but there was still a twinkle in his eye. "This will be the biggest year yet, and the most visitors to watch, too. White Haven is becoming quite the place to visit! Especially after Samhain."

"How's Becky?" Avery asked, referring to his niece who had been visiting at the time of the last major celebration.

He wagged his hand. "So, so. Not coping well with her parents' separation. She'll probably visit for a few days. Anyway, must press on." He grabbed a mince pie and headed for the door. "One for the road."

They watched him head to the shop next door, and Dan said, "He'll have doubled in size by Christmas day if he has a mince pie in every shop."

Sally smirked as she watched Dan help himself to a chocolate. "Look who's talking."

"But I have youth on my side," he pointed out.

Avery checked that the shop was still quiet, and customers were nowhere close by. "Any idea of suitably dark and secure places that our new friends may like to stay in during the day?" She sipped a strong coffee while perched on a stool behind the counter.

"Tin mines," Sally suggested. "There are plenty of abandoned ones around, and they stretch for miles underground. Didn't you say you found the Nephilim in one?"

Avery nodded. "Yeah, but I don't know which one. However, they would offer a good, safe place, especially as most of them are unsuitable for visitors. I could ask them, hopefully they'd remember."

"I can't see them holing up in the Poldark Mine." Dan was referring to the tourist attraction a few miles away. "But I think your best bet are caves. I'm sure there are some beneath Harecombe and White Haven, leading to the sea. Old smuggling routes that lead out of cellars."

"True. And there might be a passage beneath the House of Spirits. They've found a hidden panel that leads to the tower, and it sounds really odd."

"Wow!" Sally said, looking excited. "So there could be a hidden passage down through the house, behind the walls! That would make sense, if she was a fake."

"You're right. It would explain how she would have performed tricks and illusions!"

Dan reached for a mince pie from the plate on the counter, took a meditative bite, and then said, "But that doesn't make sense. You can't build hidden passages into a house that's already been built. The work would be extensive! Whatever passages or hidden panels there are would surely have been put in by the person who built the house in the first place."

Avery's excitement completely disappeared. "Damn it, you're right. I didn't think of that."

"If anything, though," Dan continued, "surely that's *more* exciting. It means that house was built for a purpose—not just for a medium who wanted to trick her punters."

"You think the house keeps an older, darker secret?"

He shrugged. "Maybe. Why else build hidden panels and passageways? But, I know nothing. I'm just trying to be logical."

"They found a witch-bottle, is that right?" Sally asked.

Avery nodded. "Yeah, under the hearth, which already suggests something was happening years before Madame Charron."

Sally looked doubtful. "But does it really link the vampire to the house—originally, I mean? I still can't see that they're related."

"But when Evelyn died in 1979, the vampire killings started," Avery explained. "And again when Felicity died. You know I don't do coincidences."

"I'll be interested to see what Dylan and Jasper find out," Dan said, dropping his voice as a couple of customers came in. "Sounds like that place should have been called the House of Secrets, instead."

***

Avery perched on her usual stool in The Wayward Son, her cheeks glowing after her brisk walk down through White Haven. It was already dark, and the streets glowed beneath the Christmas lights, filled with the hustle and bustle of visitors and locals alike.

Zee greeted her with a glass of mulled wine, and she took the opportunity to ask him about Shadow. He rolled his eyes. "She's nothing but trouble."

Avery laughed. "I get that. What's she done now?"

"What hasn't she done? Gabe watches her like a hawk. He's trying to get her involved in the business, particularly with security for Caspian's business, but she's obsessed with finding a way back to the Summerlands."

"And some of you are still interested in helping her, I suppose."

He raised an eyebrow. "Yes, and Gabe's starting to get interested, too, ever since she pitched it as a side business."

"A side business?"

"Recovery of rare artefacts, for a high price. Let's face it—we have special skills that most don't have. It would help a lot."

"You're starting to sound interested, too, if I'm not mistaken, Zee." She sipped her wine and watched him over the top of her glass. There was energy about him that she hadn't seen before. An air of excitement.

He shrugged. "To be honest, it sounds far more interesting than endless security jobs and bartending forever."

"I don't think anyone expected you to bartend forever. We all know it's a side gig until you all get on your feet. Reappearing after years in the spirit world, a few thousand years after your past life, was never going to be easy." She thought for a moment. "But you're right. This could be a great business for you, if risky. And probably illegal."

He frowned. "Why illegal?"

"Buried treasure or found treasure normally goes to the government or museums, with a finder's fee. If you declare it. I think, anyway. It's not something I know a lot about. There would be a lot of black market interest. But I have a feeling you wouldn't care about breaking the law."

"Maybe not. But it could compromise the security business."

"Well, you'd have to keep them very separate, wouldn't you? And besides, I'm sure there would be times when for a certain customer, those jobs would go hand in hand," Avery suggested.

A speculative gleam entered Zee's eyes, and he looked into the middle distance, transfixed. "You know, this could actually be a good idea."

Avery laughed, nervously. "Oh, dear. What are you going to get up to? It was only a couple of days ago I wondered whether there'd be a black market for magical objects." *Was it really only two days ago? It felt like a lifetime.*

"You want to sell magic?" Zee asked, confused.

"No! Not at all! That would be a terrible idea. I was thinking about how to keep magical objects off the black market, actually!"

Over Zee's broad shoulder, Avery saw Alex emerge from the kitchen behind the bar, and noticing her, he joined them.

He looked between them, frowning. "Why do you two look as if you're up to no good?"

"*Zee's* up to no good," Avery corrected him.

"It was your suggestion," Zee said.

"Oh, no. You're not blaming that on me. It's Shadow's suggestion that I merely speculated on, and you got excited about."

"Now I'm really worried," Alex said.

"No need, boss!" Zee turned and nodded to a woman who was looking at him with a speculative gleam in her eye, and Avery was pretty sure she was thinking about more than her next drink. "I'll let Avery fill you in, while I serve a few customers." He headed to the other side of the bar, leaving them alone.

Avery laughed and filled him in on the conversation. "I wonder what they'll call their new business."

"I'm not sure I want to know," he said, leaning over to kiss her. "How was your day?"

"Interesting! I talked to James today, and he's blessed lots of water for us."

Alex looked surprised. He'd been with Avery when they revealed their powers, and they'd both worried that they had shown him too much. "Really? He talked to you?"

She nodded. "We seem to have come to an understanding. And guess what? He's not shocked that vampires exist—only that one is here in Cornwall. He says his colleagues have long believed they are dwelling in cities. It's easier to hide."

Alex leaned on the shiny wooden counter that ran between them. "Is there no end to the unexpected behaviours of people today? Zee wants to become a treasure hunter, and James knows about vampires. I feel something has shifted in my world."

"I haven't," Avery reassured him. And then she noticed Newton heading through the door, Briar next to him. "But Newton is here with Briar. It *is* a day of surprises!"

They both turned to watch the pair approach, Avery wondering what had brought them here together. She didn't have to wait long. As Briar slid onto a stool next to Avery, Newton leaned on the bar and said, "I collected Briar on the way here, so I wouldn't have to tell you all what I've found several times. A pint of Doom and a chardonnay, please."

"You look pleased with yourself," Alex noted as he poured the drinks.

"And he's keeping quiet about it, too," Briar said, taking her glass from Alex. "We have to wait for El and Reuben."

Avery looked hopeful. "At least give us a clue."

"It's about Rupert, nothing too exciting, but that's all you're getting. Any chance you can put the footie on while we wait?" he said to Alex, nodding to the TV mounted on the wall.

Alex switched the channel over and then headed off to serve some more customers, while Newton sipped his pint and silently watched the highlights of the mid-week matches, refusing to be drawn.

Briar turned to Avery and kept her voice low. "How are you after last night? It sounds terrifying."

"Ah, my vampire visitor." Avery shuddered. "It was, actually. I was mesmerised by her, and I knew it, but all I wanted to do was open the window. I'm lucky the cats and Helena saved me. I've hung my protection bundles outside the windows now. I suggest you do the same."

Briar looked shaken up. "Already done. Another reason for me to get a cat."

"You could always take Caspian up on his offer to stay there again."

Briar shook her head. "No, I'd rather not. He was great, but his sister wasn't, and I'd rather be in my own home, anyway."

Avery whispered back, although she probably didn't need to, Newton was so transfixed by the football. "Maybe Newton could stay with you?"

Briar narrowed her eyes. "No, definitely not. We're friends, and that's the way it's going to stay."

Avery was surprised. "Really?"

"Yes, really."

"You don't look sure," Avery persisted.

Briar appeared suddenly coy. "Hunter has called again. He wants to come down after Christmas. I said sure, why not?"

Avery let out an undignified squeal. "Go, Briar! He's staying at your place?"

"Yes, I have a sofa bed."

"Sofa bed! Yeah, right."

Briar looked prim. "That's all I'm saying. We were talking about vampires."

Avery snorted. "No, no, no! Has he been phoning a lot? He must have. You're a dark horse, Briar."

"Yes, he's phoned, we've chatted, he's coming to visit. That's it! So, vampires. Discuss."

"Don't think this subject is dropped for good. It's merely on a hiatus," Avery warned. "Moving on, you tell me, have you done any vampire-related stuff?

"Not really. I've been busy in the shop. Everything's selling out. Which is great, but keeps me busy restocking. And Eli is side-tracked by Shadow, which means he's not as onto it as he usually is."

"Did Eli tell you why he's distracted by Shadow?"

"He's the strong, silent type, but he did say something about treasure hunting services." Briar looked at Avery, amused. "Do you know more?"

"It seems Shadow's expanding on her idea for searching for something to get her back to the Summerlands, and she's trying to persuade the Nephilim to help. I think it's working."

They chatted quietly for a few more minutes until Reuben and El arrived, striding through the now crowded pub to their side. Alex lifted the hatch that was set into the counter and joined them. "Let's head upstairs, away from prying ears," he suggested, and he led the way up to his flat.

As soon as they were through the door, Briar burst out, "Come on, Newton, don't keep us waiting."

Newton pulled his notebook out of his pocket and flicked through the pages while the others settled themselves. "It seems Rupert has a reputation."

"For raising vampires?" Reuben asked, looking surprised. He'd dropped into the closest chair, his legs hanging over the armrest.

"No, idiot," Newton answered scathingly. "Buying creepy old houses, and doing them up. Houses with their own reputation."

He had everyone's attention now.

"What sort of reputation?" El asked.

Newton referred to his notebook. "Houses that have had people killed in them. Over the last fifteen years he has bought six houses, all of them old, large, and with an unusual history. But, that's it, Nothing has happened, nothing macabre or occult, and no other deaths."

Reuben groaned. "Nothing! Well, that's boring. So, he's just a nutter who likes creepy houses."

The witches glanced at each other, confused, and El asked, "There's nothing to suggest he's on a vampire hunt? That he's raising an undead army?"

"No!" Newton looked annoyed. "I think even the police with no paranormal background would have noticed something like that!"

El glared at him. "No need for sarcasm."

"Now, now," Briar said, trying to smooth troubled waters. "It seems as if he's interested in the occult, just as Ben suggested. Ghosts, poltergeists maybe, vampires, troubled spirits of some kind that may be easy to manipulate. He sounds harmless." She paused for a moment, thinking. "To me, this suggests a man who maybe likes using Ouija boards and trying to summon spirits. Maybe his lack of success was what made him involve the ghost-hunters."

"And if he was hiding something, he wouldn't hire Ben, would he?" Avery asked. "Plenty of people like the occult, there's nothing wrong with that."

El mulled over Avery's suggestion. "He hired them before Charlotte's strange dreams, right?"

"Right."

Alex lay flat on his back on the rug in front of the fire, and stared up at the ceiling. "He's interested in the House of Spirits because of Madame Charron's reputation. But, unbeknownst to him, there's something *else* attached to this house. He thinks it's all about spirits. It's not."

"And now they've discovered the tower room," Reuben said. "I wonder what that hides."

Newton's phone started to ring, and he headed to the kitchen to answer it, his voice low.

Avery watched him for a second, and then said, "I'd love to know if Dylan or Jasper have found out something about that house. I was thinking about hiding places for vampires earlier, and I think they must be hiding in old smuggling caves. There are no mines that are that close to White Haven or Harecombe, but they both have a smuggling history. There's probably a warren of tunnels that everyone's forgotten about."

"Or the sewers," Reuben suggested, wrinkling his nose. "That will be a fun place to hunt them."

"Excellent suggestion," Alex said.

Newton finished his call and stated to pull his heavy wool coat back on. "I have to go. There have been two deaths in Harecombe. A couple found together on a side-street in the middle of town." He looked grim. "Their throats were ripped out."

All five witches sat up, alarmed.

"Ripped out?" Briar asked, eyes wide.

"Yep. This will be a long night." His phone went again, and he picked up. "Newton here… *Another* one? Give me half an hour." He hung up. "And another at the Royal Yacht Club Marina. Those bastard vampires are hunting, right now, in Harecombe."

Reuben jumped to his feet. "Then we'd better come, too. This could be our chance to kill them. And we should tell Caspian."

16

The centre of Harecombe was busy, with holiday crowds still milling about the streets as Reuben navigated them through the main roads towards The Royal Yacht Club Marina. It was private, and the largest of Harecombe's two marinas, sited on the west of the busy harbour that Kernow Shipping, Caspian's business, overlooked.

Bars and restaurants were busy, and the streets looked bright and festive, but it was hard for Avery to appreciate it as they were discussing strategies, and the most effective spells to use to fight vampires. There was a bag of stakes in the boot of the car, along with bottles of holy water.

Briar sighed. "I don't feel prepared at all."

"Nor me," Avery agreed, "but we have to try. Three people are dead in one night."

"Three people who may become vampires," El pointed out.

Alex turned around to look at them from the front seat. "I doubt it. Their deaths are more violent than the others, their throats ripped out. The others didn't die like that." He shrugged. "I don't know anything about vampire motivations, but the viciousness of their deaths suggests to me that they won't transform."

"I agree," Avery said, meeting his worried gaze.

Briar looked at the crowded streets with sorrow. "Maybe that's one positive thing to take from tonight."

"What did Genevieve say?" Reuben asked, glancing over his shoulder. Avery had phoned her before they left.

"She agreed that they're unlikely to turn from their injuries, but she can't help us tonight. I told her that was okay and that Caspian will help."

For the past few days Avery had kept her up to date with their findings, and Genevieve had been coordinating with the older witches, too. But so far, she hadn't had much to share.

"I'm going to park at the back of the marina," Reuben said as he slowed down to navigate the lights. "This is where Newton said the last body was found."

Newton had left a good half an hour before them, as they had needed to gather equipment.

"I wish the shifters were still here," Alex said, twisting to look out of the window. "If anyone could sniff out a vampire, it would be them. It might give us the upper hand."

Avery glanced at Briar, who returned her glance slightly sheepishly and said to the group, "Hunter is going to come and visit after Christmas, but I could see if he's free before."

El leaned forward to look at her. "Really? That's great! You kept that quiet."

"There's not much to say," she said nonchalantly, but looking pleased.

"Sounds bloody brilliant," Reuben said as he parked. "I like Hunter. If you can ask him to come, why not?"

Briar nodded. "I'll call him tomorrow."

They all exited the car and clustered around the boot, each of them taking a stake, and Reuben pulled out a large water gun loaded with holy water.

El stared in disbelief. "I cannot believe you've got that."

"You'll be glad when it works. I think I should get you all one."

"Give them to the ghost-hunters. I'll stick to my sword, thanks," El answered as she patted the scabbard that hung at her side.

"Good idea," Reuben said, slamming the boot shut. "I spot Caspian, over there on the corner."

Caspian's tall, distinctive profile was highlighted against the streetlights, his shoulders hunched against the cold.

They crossed the road to join him, Avery calling, "Caspian, thanks for helping."

He looked pale. "This is bad news for all of us. Unfortunately, my family is out of town on business, so it's just me."

"Six are better than five," Reuben told him.

"Maybe. But our chances are better in the day. Tonight will be ugly."

"It's already ugly," Briar said, looking at the police cars lined up along the road, their flashing lights garish.

Alex shouldered his backpack. "We should split up. We'll cover more ground that way."

"I'll scope out the marina," Caspian suggested, "or as much of it as I can get to." He pointed to the uniformed officers patrolling the area. "They'll be crawling all over this place for hours."

"Which means the vampires will have moved on. It's too bright and busy here now," Avery put in. "They could be prowling the back streets of the main centre, or they could be in the harbour. There's too much area to cover and not enough of us."

Alex was eager to get moving. "We have to try. Me and Avery will head to the square by the harbour, all the main streets join that, and we'll check out the smaller Clearwater Marina while we're there. Briar, you search this marina with Caspian. El and Reuben can head to the harbour. We'll check in with each other in thirty minutes."

They separated, and Alex and Avery hurried down the dark streets, their stakes hidden in their backpacks. There were less people around once they left the quayside, and they were alert and watchful as they walked.

"This is insane," Avery said. "I don't know what we're thinking."

"We're thinking that we don't want any more people to die," Alex answered.

Avery zipped her jacket closed, and wrapped her scarf tightly around her neck. She had decided to wear her leather jacket rather than her wool coat, but it wasn't really keeping her warm. The night was clear and cold, the stars above bright pin pricks in the sky. She considered using the warming spell she had used before, but the brisk walk soon warmed her.

They entered the square and gasped. The square was surrounded on most sides by large, wooden buildings that contained shops and restaurants, the space in the centre reserved for bands, markets, and other gatherings. Tonight a Christmas Market was in full swing. Lights glowed and customers strolled through the narrow aisles between the stalls. She could hear a brass band playing somewhere, and delicious smells filled the air. Had they not been hunting vampires, Avery would have liked nothing better than to stroll and shop, but Alex pulled her to the edge of the market as if reading her mind. "No time for shopping, Ave. We'll come back next week when we're not in danger of being dinner."

They walked to the less well-lit areas looking for anything unusual, and then on through the square to the streets on the far side where Harecombe Museum sat. It was quieter there, and Avery could hear the sea. They explored around the museum but again saw nothing suspicious, and headed towards Clearwater Marina. The entrance was secure but they passed through it, unlocking the gates easily with magic as they headed to the yachts bobbing on the water. Lights illuminated the area in patchy spots, and for a moment Avery stood silently, watching the shadows, hoping to see or hear something. However, all was still, other than the gentle lapping of the waves against the wall.

Alex waited behind her, staring at the wharf over the water, part of the main harbour. He called softly, and pointed. "Avery. I can see something moving along the quay. Over there."

She ran to his side, and saw he was right. "Are you sure it's not a dog?" The creature looked low down, but they were too far away to see details.

"It's keeping to the shadows around the shipping containers. A dog or a cat wouldn't care. We need to get over there."

"We'd have to walk right around the quay, and by then we might have lost it," Avery pointed out. "There's no direct access from here. But I could fly us there."

"Witch-flight?" Alex asked, glancing at her briefly, unwilling to take his eyes from the creature. "Can you take us both?"

Avery hesitated. She'd been practising a lot, and had no problems on her own now. She travelled without nausea or passing out, and had landed where she wanted to all the time. From here, she could see exactly where she was going, too. *But could she manage Alex?*

"I think I can. We should let the others know what we've seen before we go." She pulled her phone out and called Briar first. "Have you found anything?" she started without preamble.

"Nothing," Briar said. "We've seen Newton, discretely, but there's nothing in this marina now. We had to break in around the back just to make sure."

"Head to the harbour," Avery instructed. "We think we've seen something. We'll liaise when you arrive." She described the spot as best she could, and then phoned El and Reuben, who should already be there.

"That wharf is big," Alex said as she was waiting for El to answer, "and very secure. They might have had trouble getting in." And then he paused, worried. "Shit. I can't see it anymore. I think it's moved further in. We have to go."

Before Avery could respond, El answered, her voice low. "They're here. We can see Bethany. She seems to be stalking a couple of dock workers."

"We're on our way," Avery said, starting to panic. "We'll find you, stay safe."

"Alright we'll—"

El's voice broke off with a muffled cry, and the line went dead.

"Bollocks," Avery said forcefully as she pocketed her phone. "Something's happened. We need to go now. Hold on tight."

Alex looked like he was going to protest, and then he hugged her close, pulling her so that her back rested against his chest as she gazed out across the dock. Avery tried to remain calm. *This will be fine. Absolutely fine.*

There was a rushing sensation as both she and Alex were swept up into a vortex of air. She was aware of his presence next to her, part of her almost, and then it was over and they landed next to a huge container, both falling into a heap as Alex dragged them both down.

Avery struggled out of his grip. "Alex! Are you all right?"

He lay on the floor, white and breathing heavily. "I feel as sick as a dog."

Avery glanced around nervously, aware they should be running to find El, not crouched on the ground, vulnerable to attack. She grabbed Alex's hand. "Can you stand?"

"Give me a minute."

Sweat beaded on his forehead, and she knew exactly how he felt, but when Caspian had transported her before she had felt fine, and so had Briar on Samhain. She must be doing something wrong.

A scream broke the silence, making her skin crawl. "Alex! Get up!"

Alex dragged himself to his feet, and leaning on her arm, they ran as best they could down the dark passages between the stacked containers. Echoes of their footsteps reverberated around them, and when the scream came again, Avery froze at a junction, unsure of which way to go. It was a maze. Another shout resounded to their left, and they ran again, finally stumbling to a halt as they came upon carnage. A man lay on the ground ahead of them in a space formed on three sides by the containers, the fourth by the sea. Blood poured from his neck, and in front of him Bethany snarled, like a cat over its prey. El stood a short distance away, her sword raised and blazing with a fiery white light, while in her left she held a fireball. She hurled it at Bethany, who easily dodged it, leaping out of the way with inhuman speed, before running towards El.

El crouched, ready for the attack.

Alex turned to Avery, his voice low. "Bethany hasn't seen us. Call Briar, and I'll distract her."

Before Avery could protest, Alex sent a force of white-hot energy at Bethany, which slammed into her back and smacked her against the side of one of the containers. Bethany slid onto the ground, dazed.

Avery called Briar, glancing around to make sure another vampire wasn't close by.

Briar answered, "We heard a scream, where are you?"

"Over on the far side of the harbour, behind some containers and next to the sea. I'll send up a witch light. Come as soon as you can."

She hung up and sent half a dozen lights high into the air, not caring who else would see them at this moment. Hopefully the area was poorly staffed, although no doubt that scream would get someone's attention.

Bethany was already rising to her feet, as if smashing into a container was nothing, and she raced at Alex. He and El sent more fireballs towards her, but she rolled with freaky agility, dodging all of them.

From her position in the shadows, Avery saw a coil of rope lying on the pavement. She lifted it with a gust of wind and hurled it at Bethany. The vampire didn't see it coming and it dropped on her, sending her sprawling.

Alex still looked pale, but he pulled a wooden stake out of his pack and ran towards Bethany; she didn't stay down long enough. She threw the rope aside and leapt to her feet again.

Where was Reuben? Avery glanced around anxiously, and saw him crumpled against a wooden crate on the edge of the harbour, a large cut on his head. Just as she was considering how best to reach him, he struggled to his feet, and raised his ridiculous water cannon to his shoulder.

Bethany leapt at El, but she defended herself by slashing the vampire's stomach with her sword. Unfortunately, it was as if Bethany hadn't been stabbed at all. She side-stepped and snarled again. For the first time, Avery could see the vampire's face clearly and her breath caught in her throat. Her skin was white, almost translucent—what she could see of it anyway, beneath the smears of blood over her chin and cheeks. Bethany's eyes were dark pits, devoid of any humanity, and her jaw opened wide to reveal long canines that dripped with blood.

Before her courage faltered, Avery sent a blast of wind at the vampire that swept her up and pinned her to the side of the container. She extended her power, closing her hands like a vice, and the vampire struggled to break free. Reuben followed up with a blast of holy water that he enhanced with his magic, the water spreading like a fan. It hit her face and body, steaming and hissing as it bit into her skin. The vampire screamed and writhed, but still couldn't break free of Avery's grip.

Alex hurled the stake, and it arced through the air, his magic holding the aim true, but inches from its target another vampire leapt over the side of the container, moving so fast it was a blur of motion. It snatched the stake out of the air, landing on its feet with unnatural strength and grace. It turned to face the group, grimacing and snarling, its long teeth exposed.

There was a momentary pause in the fight as they all stopped in shock, assessing each other for the briefest of seconds.

It was the vampire from the other night, the older, male vampire. Tonight, the monster more closely resembled a human, dressed in a black shirt, trousers, and a three quarter-length coat. It was old-fashioned clothing, from a century or so ago at least, although the clothes themselves did not seem old or damaged. The vampire's hair was dark, falling over its face, making its pallor more marked. Its skin was stretched across its skull like a cadaver, and its limbs looked equally thin, but with the strength of steel. It stalked up and down in front of Bethany, guarding her, and assessing them.

Avery's hand was still outstretched, pinning Bethany to the container several metres above the ground. The old vampire focused on Avery, and she felt as if its cold, dark eyes penetrated her soul. For a moment, it felt as if time stood still, and then it hurled the stake at her. In order to protect herself, she raised her other hand to knock the stake away with magic, but the distraction was enough for her to lose her hold on Bethany, who dropped to the floor in a panther-like crouch.

Two of them. We can take two, she reassured herself. And then a third vampire entered the fight, slipping out of the shadows like a nightmare incarnate, and Avery's blood ran cold. It was a young man; it must be the man who'd gone missing. *They couldn't cope with three.*

The older vampire smiled at her with a strange, rictus grimace, and then charged across the ground so quickly that she barely had time to respond. Neither did the other witches, as Bethany raced towards Alex, and the other male vampire charged at Reuben and El.

Avery hardly knew what happened next, other than she saw movement as Briar and Caspian ran around the corner of the farthest container and joined the fight.

Powerful blasts of magic surged across the space as they fought to repel the attack. Avery raised a wall of fire in front of the old vampire who was closing the distance between them, but it passed through unscathed, threw her to the ground, and straddled her with its powerful legs as it pinned her down. It opened its mouth, its teeth bearing down upon her neck. She could smell its foetid breath, foul with the stench of rotting meat and the metallic smell of blood.

No one could help. They were all fighting for their own survival. Avery couldn't throw it off, but she could use witch-flight, and in a flash she vanished, re-appearing on top of the closest container. The vampire squirmed on the ground, bewildered at her disappearance. While it was still confused, Avery pulled the stake from her backpack, smothered the point in fire, and hurled it towards the creature, using her magic to make the blow more powerful. It pierced its back and it screamed with anger, flailing wildly as the stake immobilised its body temporarily. She followed it up with a huge, swirling fireball, and it ignited in flames, screaming with an inhuman howl.

The scene below was chaotic. Bursts of fire and pure energy zigzagged across the space, but as the old vampire howled and burned, the other two vampires immediately disengaged from the fight, their eyes narrowed with hate and confusion, and running to the side of the burning vampire, they all fled down a narrow passageway.

Avery had no urge to follow; she was exhausted and injured. Her chest ached from where the vampire had straddled her, her shoulders felt bruised, and her head throbbed from where it had hit the ground. She looked down on the other witches and saw they were all bleeding and dishevelled, too. The concrete had been torn up by Briar's magic, and ropes, oil drums, and tools were strewn around as if a tornado had hit, water sloshed across the ground from where Reuben had pulled it from the sea, and the sides of the containers were dented where the vampires had hit them.

The dead man still lay in the shadows at the edge of the area, a pool of blood beneath him.

Alex looked around, shouting, "Avery?"

She materialised at his side. "I'm here."

He jumped as he saw her. "I don't think I'll ever get used to that. Are you all right?"

"Bruised and battered, but I'll survive. You?"

Alex's hair was wild and tangled around his face and his pallor had gone, his skin now flushed red with cold and action. "Annoyed as hell, but fine."

Shouts and running footsteps sounded in the distance. "Time to go," Caspian said, running a dirty hand across his face. "We snuck in, and can leave the same way. Follow me." He ran, and the others followed without a backward glance.

Although they used magic to escape, and were deeply cloaked in a shadow spell, it was still a close call. The witches emerged on to the busy road outside the harbour, breathless and nervous. They took a moment to gather themselves, and then slowed to a walk, stakes stashed back in their packs, looking as if they were out for an evening stroll. Police cars were already whizzing past them, the darkness broken with bright blue and red lights.

Avery wanted to go home, but Caspian headed to his business headquarters, calling, "Follow me."

They entered the warm, dark lobby and backed away from the glass doors, watching the scene of chaos outside. While some people seemed oblivious to what was happening, others were running away, looking panic-stricken.

Alex's eyes narrowed. "They probably think there's been a terrorist attack."

"I'm not sure what would be worse," Briar answered.

Caspian turned to them, his shoulders bowed. "There's no point in searching for the vampires. They could be anywhere by now. Besides, they're too strong to tackle at night—by choice, anyway. I just hope they're not searching for us."

"You're closer than we are," El pointed out.

"I'm well protected. Don't worry about me," he reassured them. "I've got tricks up my sleeve and magic traps all over the house." He looked at Avery, his glance too intense to be comfortable. "I feel we were lucky back there. If you hadn't managed to set the oldest one on fire, Avery, I don't think they'd have retreated."

Avery shuddered. "No. It was close to ripping my throat out. Just promise me that we'll stick to hunting them in the day."

"I'll call Jasper tomorrow," he answered. "Let's hope they've found something out about that house."

"Are you coming to the House of Spirits on Saturday?" El asked him.

"Yes. And we better tell Genevieve in case she wants to come."

"I can do that," Avery said, trying to stifle a yawn. "And now I want to go home and sleep for a week. If I ever sleep easily again."

17

"Please tell me you've found some good news out about that house," Avery said to Dylan.

It was Friday morning, and Avery had risen late, exhausted by the fight the night before, and she hadn't long been in the shop. For the millionth time, she thanked her lucky stars that Sally and Dan were so understanding.

Dylan leaned on the counter of Happenstance Books, his expression both pleased and perplexed. "Sort of."

"What's *sort of* mean?"

"It means," he said, his voice weary, "that weird stuff has been associated with that house for a long time, well before Madame Charron, but there's nothing concrete—although Jasper is looking into another couple of things today."

"Bugger," Avery said, groaning. She sighed, stretched, and winced. "Ouch."

Dylan frowned. "Why are you *ouching*?"

Avery hadn't told him what had happened the night before. She guessed now was as good a time as any. She lowered her voice as she described the battle, and Dylan's eyes opened wider and wider with shock.

"You set it on *fire*?" he hissed. "Did you kill it?"

"I doubt it. It ran off, trailing flames, smoke, and the stench of burnt skin. Although, its breath stank like death, anyway."

Dylan looked around to make sure no one was close by, and then glared at her. "You should have called. We'd have come."

"I know you would have, but it was too dangerous. Only our magic got us through unscathed."

"Not completely, Ms Ouchy. You know we've been training?"

"Yes, Cassie told me."

She assessed Dylan's frame. He was tall and lean, and although he'd always had an edge that Cassie hadn't, he held himself with more conviction now, a threat lurking behind his eyes. She wondered if they all had that, a result of knowing about the paranormal world and the threats they faced.

"And so?" Dylan looked very annoyed, and Avery knew he was desperate to do more than just monitor paranormal activity.

"Dylan! It was very dangerous. They killed four people last night! *Four*! Their throats were ripped out and they were left on the road like litter." Avery started to get angry, and wind whipped up around her, making Dylan step back. She took a deep breath and calmed down. "Sorry. I don't want my friends to die. And besides, you might not have liked what you'd have seen. Bethany was there."

Dylan's shoulders dropped. "She's hunting now?"

"She is a fully fledged vamp, and needs blood to survive. When we found her, she was crouched over her victim."

"Bethany's a killer." Dylan slumped against the counter, his fight gone. "This is horrific. There's no way back for her—er, *it*—is there?" He looked agonised. "Is she a *she* or an *it*?"

"She's whatever you want to call her. And no, there isn't."

They were suddenly interrupted by Dan, who knew Dylan from Penryn University. "What's up, Dylan?"

"Everything," he said, shaking Dan's hand. "Good to see you again. You know all about what's happening, I presume?"

Dan nodded. "Need a drink? It's my lunch soon. We can head to the pub."

Dylan brightened. "Yeah, that sounds good."

Avery smiled. That was just what they both needed. Dan made light of her magic, but she knew that underneath it all he must be worried by the supernatural weirdness that was going on. He and Dylan could support each other.

"Boss?" Dan said, raising an eyebrow at Avery. "Now okay?"

"'Course it is. Take your time. And Dylan, we might be meeting tonight. I'm waiting to hear from Genevieve."

"I'll hang around, then, and let Cassie and Ben know."

Avery watched them leave, wondering how she could advance their investigation and protect her friends. Her gaze drifted to the shelf under the counter where she'd stacked a few books in case she had a spare moment.

She pulled out one called, *Cornish Smugglers: Truth is Stranger than Fiction*, and settled down to read, disturbed only by the occasional customer.

When she finally looked outside again, she was shocked to find snow was falling. No wonder it felt cold, and no wonder the shop was so quiet. Dan hurried past the window alone, and burst through the door, shivering. "God's bollocks, it's freezing out there."

"No Dylan?" Avery asked.

"Nah, he's gone to my place, actually. He's a bit upset about Bethany." Dan looked worried. "I've never seen him like this before."

"He's never had a mate's cousin become a vampire before," Avery pointed out with a sigh. She placed her book back beneath the counter, thinking she was no further forward than she'd been hours earlier. "I'm heading for lunch, and I'll be back soon."

***

During her break, Avery received two calls. The first one was from Briar, her voice heavy with tiredness. "You sound as shattered as I feel," Avery said, putting the call on speaker as she pottered in her kitchen and made lunch.

"I dreamt of vampires last night," she answered. "And every time I heard the slightest noise I woke up, convinced a vampire was at my window. I got up at five. It was pointless trying to sleep."

"You should have stayed at Reuben's." Reuben had almost begged Briar to stay at his place with him and El, but she'd refused.

"I like my own bed, as lovely as Reuben's place is. And it's handy for work." Briar lived within walking distance of her shop, in a lovely old cottage full of vintage charm. She hesitated for a moment. "And Newton called just after I got home."

Avery fell silent for a moment. "Just a call?"

"He dropped by at about half past two."

"In the *morning*? So it wasn't just vampire dreams that kept you awake. How was he?"

"Shattered. Four deaths in one night. Everyone is depressed and frightened. And he's angry. We need to stop this, Avery."

"I know," she said, feeling the weight of responsibility settle even more heavily on her shoulders. "Did he stay?"

"No. He was just checking that I was okay."

Avery could hear the tightness in Briar's voice, and was that regret she could hear? She softened her tone. "What's going on with you two?"

"Nothing. *Absolutely* nothing."

"That's not true. He wouldn't be around if he didn't care about you," Avery remonstrated.

"He's conflicted."

"Hunter isn't."

She started to protest. "Avery—"

Avery cut her off, very frustrated. She took it out on her toasted sandwich, slicing it in half with a vicious cut. "You know I'm right. You could be waiting forever, and as much as I like Newton, that's exactly where he wants you—waiting and hoping while he works his shit out. Hunter is a threat, and Newton's trying to buy himself time. Don't let him." Briar was silent, so Avery continued. "You know I'm right."

Briar groaned. "I know."

"And as much as Hunter is a cocky Alpha, literally, he likes you—*really* likes you! Prepared to drive seven hours to see you-likes you. What does that say to you, Briar?"

"I know," she repeated softly. "And I like him, too. But Newton's stuck in my head, and I'm so annoyed with myself, because I know that what you've just said is right. *I know it.*" Her voice rose with frustration. "I'm an idiot. A hot, male shifter wants me, and what am I doing? Pining after someone who can't move past the fact that I'm a witch. And I want what you have with Alex, and what El has with Reuben. I want someone to be there for me. To hold me when horrible things are happening, and to laugh with me when things are great."

Avery could have whooped with joy. Finally, Briar was opening up. "Yes, girlfriend! What are you going to do about it?"

"I don't know."

"Liar. What are you going to do?"

"Call Hunter?" she asked tentatively.

"With conviction, please."

Briar's voice got stronger. "I'm going to call Hunter and ask him if he wants to visit earlier, maybe stay over Christmas."

"Yes!" Avery shouted, startling Circe, who was cleaning herself with great thoroughness on the floor. "He'll be down by tomorrow."

"Don't be ridiculous. It's almost one already."

"Next round's on you if I'm right—which I am. You *will* owe me a drink."

"He might say no."

Avery snorted. "Bollocks he will. He'll break land-speed records to get here."

"He might. He does call a lot." Avery could hear a smile creep into Briar's voice.

"Oh, you are so going to get lucky this Christmas."

"Avery!"

"Once we get rid of the vampires, of course."

"You know, I didn't actually ring to talk about this at all," Briar said.

"You so did. But what else is on your mind?"

"Have you heard from Genevieve? I wondered if we might be meeting with the coven tonight?"

"No, not yet, but I'll let you know. If anything it would make more sense to meet tomorrow, when we're at the house."

"Good point. All right, I'll leave you to it. Speak soon."

"And ring Hunter now!" Avery shouted quickly before Briar hung up. Then she'd gone, leaving Avery hopping with excitement about Briar's love life.

She immediately rang Alex, and he answered quickly, the noise of the pub in the background. "Hi, gorgeous. Are you okay?"

"I just wanted to hear your voice, and tell you I love you."

His voice was warm and velvety, even down the phone. "I love you, too. What's brought this on?"

"I'm lucky, that's all. I wanted you to know."

"You are lucky, I am awesome," he teased. "But what else?"

"Briar's inviting Hunter down today."

He laughed. "I knew it, you gossip. Good for Briar. Any news from Gen?"

"Not yet."

"Okay. I better go—it's insane here. See you tonight at yours?"

"Please."

He rang off, and within seconds, Genevieve phoned.

"You've been busy," she said brusquely. "I've been trying to get through for the last ten minutes."

"Just chatting to Briar," she explained, trying not to be annoyed. She did have a life outside of vampires.

"Jasper has some more leads to chase up, so he wants to see us tomorrow. I told him to meet us at the House of Spirits. Ten o'clock okay? Ben assures me that Rupert and Charlotte will have left by then."

"Sure," Avery said, pleased that her Friday night would be uninterrupted.

"Fine. Tomorrow then," Genevieve answered, and hung up.

Before Avery did anything else, she texted Dylan in case he wanted to leave Dan's place and go home, and told him they'd meet tomorrow instead, and then she turned the TV on, watching it absently as she finished her sandwich that was almost cold. The news was on, and it was filled with reports on the four brutal murders. Sarah Rutherford, the news reporter who had been in White Haven over Samhain, was on the broadcast, managing to look simultaneously Christmassy and grim all at the same time. She wore a bright red coat and deep red lipstick that highlighted her blonde hair and pale skin, and she stood on the main street in Harecombe, with shoppers hurrying past her. She talked with sorrow about the deaths and how the police had no leads, but she also speculated that the attacks looked as if they were caused by an animal, and said there would be a press conference later.

Avery turned the TV off. Although the news had depressed her, it also spurred her on. She had research to do.

***

By late afternoon, Avery had read everything she could about smuggling on the Cornish south coast.

She knew the names of the pubs that were known to store smuggled brandy and gin, as well as silk, muslin, china, and tea. Some of those pubs in Harecombe still existed now. The ships that anchored off the coast usually came in carrying coal, with casks of brandy and gin hidden in the hold. There was no mention of hidden passages, though. Maybe they should try to investigate some of those pubs after they'd been to the House of Spirits the next day. Or maybe try to access the sewers. The vampires could be sheltering down there. *In fact*, she mused, *there was a strong possibility the passages and the sewers now intersected.*

Avery thought back to the summer when they were still searching for their missing grimoires. Gil and Reuben had found a smugglers' passage beneath their glasshouse and had hoped their grimoire was hidden there. The passage had led to caves and then out to Gull Island off White Haven coast; it was the cave that Gil had died in, when they were attacked by Caspian. The fight had eventually led to Faversham Central, their nickname for Sebastian's house, where Helena had killed Sebastian and they had reclaimed Reuben's grimoire.

After all of that, they were almost friends with Caspian now. He had saved El from Suzanna's curse and taught Avery how to use witch flight, and offered Briar shelter at his house. She wasn't sure if she should feel regret for all of their actions, or ashamed for making a truce, or whether it was a good thing they were now working together. And Caspian had made a pass at her, but that was something she wasn't going to think about, *at all.*

The sounds of jazz lulled her thoughts, and she drifted over to the window of the shop to look at the street. It was almost dark, and the snow had stopped, leaving a light covering over the road and footpath that reflected the Christmas lights. The shop was quiet, and she'd sent Sally and Dan home for the day. She should be looking forward to Christmas, but all she could think about was vampires, necromancers, and mediums.

Avery sat behind the counter again and opened another book, wondering if it was too early to close the shop up, when the door chimes jingled. She looked up in surprise, and then felt a stone settle in her stomach. It was Rupert from the House of Spirits. He wore a short jacket over a jumper and dark jeans, and his shaved head was bare. In the light she could see faint pock marks on his skin, old acne scars.

Avery forced a smile. "Hi, Rupert. What a surprise to see you here!"

For a moment he didn't answer, instead pausing at the entrance of the shop to glance around, his hooded eyes taking everything in. It was a cool gaze that assessed and judged, and Avery became acutely aware that they were alone.

He turned to her finally, and headed to the counter. "Avery, isn't it? Good to see you again. Where is everyone? Your customers, I mean."

"I think the snow has kept them home, but my shop assistant's out back, cataloguing books," she said, lying. "I'm surprised you're here." She glanced at the windows and the snow beyond.

"Oh, the main roads are not too bad," he said, fixing her with an uncomfortable stare. "Besides, I really wanted to see you today. I went to see Jean, who sold us the house. She tells me she sold the books from my house to your shop. I'd like them back, please."

Avery was completely flummoxed. She'd been meaning to ask Sally all week about the book with the witch-mark in it, and where it had come from, but with everything that had happened, she'd completely forgotten. In fact, she'd even forgotten to examine the book again.

"I'm sorry, Rupert. I have no idea which books are yours. From what I understand, you said they were sold months ago. I'd have to ask Sally, my manager. And besides, we bought them in good faith."

"I'll rephrase it," he said, still pinning her under his gaze. "I'll buy them off you."

"But as I said, I don't know which ones are yours. I'll have to check with my manager, and she's not here right now."

"I thought you said she's out the back?" He glanced across the room toward the door to the back room, as if he might march over and find out for himself.

"I said my assistant was in the back room, not Sally."

"Can you call her?" He stood immobile and implacable, and it infuriated Avery.

Who the hell did he think he was?

"No, I'm afraid not. She's finished for the day." Avery refused to be intimidated. "And besides, we buy lots of books. She might remember the purchase, but she won't remember the inventory. Fortunately, she keeps excellent records, and we can check them tomorrow. But of course, it's likely we'll have sold some."

He narrowed his eyes, annoyed. "Do you keep records of who would have bought my books?"

"No, there's no reason to." And they're not your books. In fact, for all she knew, the book with the witch-mark wasn't from his collection.

He leaned over the counter, intruding on her personal space, and watched her silently for another moment. Avery stared right back. If he took one more step, he'd find himself the victim of a very unpleasant hex.

As if he'd sensed her annoyance, he stepped back and looked around once more. "This is an occult shop."

"Sort of," she admitted. "We're a book shop that sells some occult things, but we have a wide range of all kinds of books."

He swept his hand up and around. "But the incense, tarot cards, divinatory equipment, and witchcraft items all suggest the occult. Not common objects for a book shop."

"I'm not a common book shop owner."

"No, you're not." He frowned. "Remind me why Ben wanted you to see my house again? And that big blond man you arrived with? Reuben, was it?"

Shit. What had Ben said she was? A consultant, that was it.

"I have an interest in the occult, as you've noticed." She gestured around vaguely. "Ben knows this. He, Cassie, and Dylan often visit, and Ben wanted my opinion on the witch-bottle found under the hearth. I suggested a site visit might be useful." She smiled, trying to be as charming as possible. "Thank you for agreeing."

"And what did you think of my house?"

"It's fascinating. I think its name references its history. What do you think?"

His lips were tight with annoyance. "It's the most likely explanation, I agree. But the spirits of the house are keeping their secrets very close."

What a strange admission. "Do you speak to spirits? Are you a medium?"

He blinked as if he'd said too much. "No, not really. I meant as in, I can't find out much about Madame Charron and whether she was real or a fake."

"But you employed Ben. What are you hoping he will find?"

"Something that proves Madame Charron was authentic." He looked excited, fervent almost. "I'm so tired of fakes, and now with Charlotte experiencing strange dreams, we hoped it might indicate something was awakening… That she might be there in the house, waiting to speak to us. But so far, things are proving elusive."

Avery persisted. "And is that good or bad? Most people don't want ghosts in their house."

He smiled, but it didn't reach his eyes. "I like old houses because of their ghosts, so no, it doesn't bother me. Anyway, I must go. My wife will be waiting for me. Please speak to your manager and let me know how much you want for those books. It's very important. I suspect there may be personal items in those books that could be relevant to my research." He held out a business card. "Call me as soon as you can."

Avery went to take the card from his hand, but his hand closed over hers with a vice-like grip. "Don't let me down, Avery."

She resisted the urge to blast him through the window, and instead settled for a mild magical current that made him release her hand immediately. His eyes opened wide with shock.

"Must be static electricity," Avery explained blandly. "I'll be in touch."

He narrowed his eyes at her and then turned and left the shop, leaving the bells jingling in his wake. *Wanker.*

Avery hurried to the door and locked it. She checked that the bundle of herbs and wood above it was intact, and uttered another protection spell on top, and then she lit a sage bundle and walked around her shop, cleansing it of Rupert's very negative energies. Meeting him again confirmed her earlier suspicions. He was odd—dangerous, even. She could sense it. Was he a necromancer? Necromancers raised spirits with the intention of controlling them. Surely he would have been able to raise the spirits in the house easily if that were so. Maybe there was another level of protection on the house that was stopping that. And how did this connect to vampires? Were they wrong? Were the house and the arrival of the vampires completely unconnected? She needed to speak to Sally.

Sally answered the phone after half a dozen rings. She could barely hear her above the shrieks in the background. Sally's kids were either in deep distress or having the best fun ever, and she couldn't quite work out which. "Is everything all right, Sally?"

"Oh, God. It's mayhem here. The kids are so excited. I wish I'd stayed at work. Are you okay?"

"Yeah, fine. Look, I have a quick question. You bought some books from a house sale a few weeks back, a house in West Haven. It turns out they're from the House of Spirits, the one Ben is investigating. Do you remember what books we bought?"

The sound dulled as Sally obviously moved rooms. "I do vaguely remember, but check the online inventory for August, maybe September. I'd have noted it there. I don't think there was anything that I thought you'd be particularly interested in. You know I flag them for you if I do."

"Thanks, Sally, you're a star. Remind me what file the inventory's in again?"

As Sally talked her through the electronic filing system, Avery headed to the back room and sat at the computer. When she found it she rang off, leaving Sally to her chaotic household, and then started to scroll through the list. Sally had grouped the books together under general fiction, and then detective novels, thrillers, and romance. *A lot of romance*. Avery presumed that Felicity had developed prolific reading habits after living alone for years. Sally didn't name the titles for these, just added the numbers. After these were the arcane and occult books, of which there were about a dozen in total. Sally did add the titles and authors for these, because they were of interest to Avery. She recognised a couple, especially *Mysteries of the Occult*, the book with the witch-mark on it; the book that was now in her flat. She printed the list off and headed back to the shelves in the shop. It was fully dark outside now, and the only light in the shop came from the coloured Christmas lights that were strung up around the shelves. Of the books they had purchased, only four were left, five including the one upstairs. *The others must have been sold,* Avery thought.

There were three books on witchcraft, one on runes, and another on divination. The missing books were of a similar mixture. Avery decided to pull all of the ones she still had and take them up to her flat. Alex was coming around later, but not for hours. That would allow her time to research.

Once she'd fed the cats, turned the lights on, and made the place cosy, she spread the books out on her attic table and threw a couple of witch lights above her, and then started to methodically examine them.

An hour later, she'd still only found one witch-mark, the original one on the first book. The witchcraft books contained simple spells, nothing that you couldn't find in many books on the craft, or at least variations on themes. The book on runes was more interesting. There were notes along some of the pages in scrawling script, and the pages about runic divination were heavily marked, which was curious.

She was so absorbed that when her phone rang in the silent flat, all outside noise muted by the snow, she jumped, startling the cats who slept beside her. It was Sally.

"I've just remembered something," she started breathlessly. The noise behind her was still deafening. "I found a book that wasn't a book in that collection."

"What? I don't know what you mean." Avery said, puzzled.

"You know, a fake book. The spine looks like a book, the cover looks like one, but actually, it's a box. I found it and put it aside for you."

Avery's heart started to race with excitement. "Where?"

"I'm not sure. I think it was under the kitchen cabinet with the biscuits. I wanted to make sure it didn't get mixed up with the other books and I think you were busy hunting Mermaids at the time. I'm really sorry."

"No, it's fine," Avery said, getting ready for witch-flight. "Was there anything in it?"

"A little pouch of something. I didn't look. I left it for you."

"Great, thanks, see you tomorrow." Avery hurriedly ended the call, and within seconds she was down in the kitchen. She ferreted in the kitchen cupboard, pulling biscuits and teabags out of the way, and then she saw it. *A book that was a box.*

At the same time that she pulled it free, her protection spell on the building started to toll like a bell, and a deep reverberation ran through Avery's body. Someone had triggered her protection spell.

Within seconds, she threw the book back under the cupboard. Now she could concentrate.

She pushed out her magical awareness, trying to feel where the threat was coming from. If it was the windows, it could be a vampire, but immediately she found it. Someone was trying to get in through the back door.

Avery knew her protection spells by heart, and as the reverberation grew stronger, she added to the strength of her spell, uttering the words with power and conviction.

She hadn't got time to be afraid. Instead, she was furious.

She turned the lights off with another whispered spell, plunging her flat and shop into darkness, and simultaneously cast a shadow spell and cloaked herself. She opened the door to the small hall that led to the rear entrance. The external door had small panes of milky white glass in the top half, but nothing was discernible through them at all as it was pitch black outside, and her security light hadn't come on.

She stood still, listening intently. The door handle rattled slightly, and she smiled. She ran back into the kitchen and grabbed a handful of chamomile teabags. They weren't as effective as the bundle of chamomile in her attic, but they would do. She ripped them open and threw them in the air, whispering a spell that sent the chamomile spinning in a gentle vortex towards the door. Avery whispered the final incantation meant to lull and confuse, and the chamomile vanished through the door to the other side. There was a muted cry outside and the handle stopped moving, and then she heard footsteps retreating down the alley behind her house.

She raced through the shop to the front window, hoping to see someone emerge onto the street, but it was snowing heavily again, blurring everything into swirls of white and muting all sound. With a sinking heart she realised she had no idea who her attacker was, but she strongly suspected it was Rupert. He was annoyingly persistent, and clearly naïve as to her powers, but was he a threat?

Only time would tell.

18

Avery spelled the Christmas lights back on, and walked back to the small kitchen to retrieve the box disguised as a book.

She checked to make sure everything was locked and her wards were in place and then headed upstairs. She walked instead of using witch-flight, needing the security of seeing her home intact rather than heading straight to the attic. The Christmas tree glowed with light in the corner of the living room, and her jumble of scarves, throws, cushions, and books made the place look warm and chaotic, but nothing seemed out of place. Reassured, she carried on to the attic, stoked the fire, and placed the box on the worn wooden table.

It was quite obvious that it was a box, but if she'd looked at the spine in the midst of a row of books, it wouldn't have stood out at all. The title was the *Esoteric Mysteries of Divination*, and the box was made of wood covered in thick paper, but when Avery lifted the lid, she found the interior was lined with black velvet. A cloth of soft white linen was folded at the bottom, and a pouch of black silk lay in the centre. She held her hand over the box, feeling for any magic, but instead she felt a presence. It was faint, but it was there.

She picked up the pouch and pulled out an old, well-used pack of tarot cards, and then unfolded the square of white linen, thinking that it would likely be for reading the cards on. *These must have belonged to Madame Charron.*

Just as she was wondering why they were in a box disguised as a book, she heard the door open below as Alex arrived. He shouted hello, and within a minute arrived in the attic, covered in a fine sprinkling of snow. He stood behind her, wrapped his arms about her waist, and nuzzled into her neck. "You smell delicious."

She leaned into him. "Thank you. You smell of snow."

"That's because it's snowing, smarty pants." He dropped his head on her shoulder. "What have you got there?"

"Tarot cards."

He laughed. "Er, yes, I can see that. Where did you get them from?" He released her and picked up one of the cards. "These are nice. Unusual. And I feel a little bit of magic in them."

"Me, too, although I thought it was more of a presence than magic."

Alex placed the cards down, and slipped his jacket off. His cheeks were flushed from the cold, and he headed to the fire to warm his hands. "Where did you find them?"

"It's a long story." She told him about how Rupert had visited, prompting her to call Sally.

Alex's hair was pulled back into a half-ponytail, but he released it and ran his hands through it. "So, they're from the House of Spirits?"

"Yes. They must be Madame Charron's. But I can't decide why they were tucked away in this box."

"Maybe for safety," he suggested.

Avery looked at them, frowning. "This case just gets weirder and weirder."

"Case? You sound like a detective," he said, laughing. "Do you think Rupert knows these exist?"

"I doubt it, but even if he did, how would they help him? And what the hell have these got to do with vampires?"

"God damn blood sucking vampires," he exclaimed, quoting the 1980s film, *Lost Boys*. "I must admit, I've never worried about walking through White Haven before, but I did tonight. Every sound made me think one was behind me. I hate feeling like that. Your protection charms feel stronger tonight. Is it because of the vamps?"

"No." Avery didn't really want to tell him about the attack, she knew he'd worry, but equally, she couldn't lie. "I think Rupert hung around and tried to break into the shop when it was closed."

"What?" He'd been absently gazing into the fire, but now his head whipped around to look at her. "Why didn't you phone?"

"There was no time. Besides, I dealt with it."

She described what had happened, and suddenly felt vulnerable all over again. She'd never felt scared in her home before, but recent events had changed that. She felt a rush of gratitude that Alex was here. He was solid, reassuring, and as a bonus, a very sexy presence. He was watching her, his hands on his head, which lifted his t-shirt, revealing a sliver of toned stomach, and her own stomach flipped in response.

"In the future, call me. I don't care how busy the pub is, you're more important."

"Thank you," she said softly.

He crossed the room swiftly, pulling her close. "I mean it." He kissed her, and warmth and desire flooded through her until he grabbed her hand and pulled her to the bedroom. "The cards can wait."

***

A long time later, and after food, Alex and Avery returned to the deck of cards.

"They're just a regular pack," Alex said, examining them and the white linen cloth. "Maybe they weren't hidden, and were just put on the bookshelf for safekeeping."

"Maybe. I think this is a dead end." Avery picked up the book with the witch-mark. "I've double-checked this. There are no other marks in it, or the other books. There's nothing special about them at all."

"Have you checked the box under a witch light?"

Avery looked at him, eyes wide. "No."

He threw a light up above them and turned the lamps off. Within seconds, a series of runes appeared on the inside of the box. "Abracadabra! It's a message."

"Bollocks! Why didn't I think of that?"

He smirked. "Because I'm awesome." He picked up the box, squinting at the rune script. "You got a rune book handy?"

Avery had already opened the book of runes from the House of Spirits. "*Voila*! And a pen and paper."

For the next few minutes they worked through the runes, translating each one for a letter until they had deciphered everything.

The centre of the mysteries is beneath the full moon.

"Well, that's interesting," Alex said. "What the hell's it mean?"

Avery grabbed the pack and shuffled through it impatiently. "Maybe it's the Major Arcana card!" She found the card called The Moon and examined it under the witch light, but there was nothing on it. "Damn it. Why would she leave some random message written in runes in a box?" She looked at the books on the table. "The marked book is called *The Mysteries of the Occult.*" She picked it up again, quoting the line. "'The centre of the mysteries is beneath—'"

She broke off and flicked through the book until she reached the centre.

"And?" Alex asked, leaning over her shoulder.

"The middle of this book falls in the middle of a chapter about demonology, and using demons as spirit guides."

"Really?" he said, tickling her ear with his breath. "Using a demon as a spirit guide sounds very risky."

"And it would take a lot of power," Avery said, lifting the book to eye level. "There's only one name on this page—Verrine." Avery twisted in Alex's arms, turning to look at him. "Okay, this is what I think this means. Madame Charron may have been running scams for ordinary people, but I think she also had a gift. She really could summons spirits, and liked to experiment with using spirit guides. I think at one point, and maybe lots of times, who knows, she used this demon as a guide. Maybe she delved too deep and found something she didn't want to? Maybe that's why she had to stop her business. Perhaps she woke a vampire?"

Alex frowned as he thought. "It sounds crazy. Do vampires even have spirits to wake?"

She shrugged. "I don't know. But if you're roaming the spirit world, talking with demons, you're risking all sorts. Demons are there to tempt and trick."

"You're presuming it was an accident. She might have done it deliberately. She could be evil to the core."

"But why retire and lock yourself away? Perhaps she had to control whatever she'd unleashed. Maybe it scared her so much that she could never be a medium again, real or fake."

"Hopefully we'll find something out tomorrow."

***

The next morning, the journey to West Haven was slow. The roads were covered in snow, and although the main streets had been cleared and gritted, the smaller side roads were less accessible. Alex and Avery had opted to travel together in Alex's Alfa Romeo Spider, because Briar informed her that Hunter had arrived that morning, and Reuben and El were picking them up.

"I knew he'd come," Avery said, excited. "Apparently, he arrived at about ten last night, after an epic trip on icy roads. That's dedication."

Alex grinned at her before turning his attention back to the road. "You're such a matchmaker."

"I want Briar to be happy, and I think Hunter will do that. Newton will certainly not. And Caspian just texted. He'll meet us at the House of Spirits, too."

"Full house, then. Let's hope Rupert really has gone away for the day, or this will be one big, fat waste of a trip."

Alex and Avery arrived at the same time as Eve, and she greeted them with a grimace. Her long, dark dreads were wrapped up under a thick wool scarf, and her eclectic clothes were bright against the snow. "I wish I was seeing you guys under better circumstances."

"Me, too," Avery said, hugging her. "No Nate?"

"Not today, but he'll help when needed."

Ben ushered them inside, and the smell of coffee hit them like a wall. "Hey, guys. We're in the séance room," he said, after greeting them. "Come on up. We've got plenty of coffee."

"They've definitely left, then?" Alex asked, shaking snow from his boots.

"Bright and early!"

Avery looked around, admiring the high ceilings edged with elaborate cornices, and the decorative architraves around the doors and windows. She watched Alex as he closed his eyes and concentrated. She knew he was feeling for any signs of spirits, or a presence of any sort, but he took only a moment before following Ben up the stairs.

With everyone seated around the table, it looked as if they were about to have a real séance. Alex and Avery were the last to arrive, and they acknowledged the others with a brief nod. Avery could feel Hunter's Alpha male presence resonating across the room. He wore his black leather jacket and dark jeans, and radiated testosterone.

Hunter sat next to Briar, and he could barely keep his eyes off her, although he did meet Avery's gaze and grinned, a flash of victory lurking behind it. Briar looked flushed and slightly furtive. Avery glanced at El, who raised her eyebrow speculatively, and Avery tried hard to subdue a smile. Looking around the room, Avery saw that only Jasper, Eve, and Caspian were there from the other covens.

Genevieve, also present, caught her questioning glance. "I told Rasmus, Oswald, and Claudia that they didn't need to come today. I'll update them later." She turned to Jasper. "Do you want to start?"

Jasper cleared his voice with a cough. "It was difficult to find out some of the more colourful history of the House of Spirits until I resorted to magic."

"You make it sound like that's a bad thing," Caspian noted curiously.

"No, not at all." Jasper shook his head, and pulled his notebook onto his lap. "It just meant I had to use subterfuge and engage in a rather risky break-in to the council buildings."

"Good work," Reuben said. He leaned back in his chair, his long legs stretched out in front of him. "Didn't think you were the breaking and entering type, Jasper."

Jasper shuffled uncomfortably. "I'm not, but it was important. I needed to find out who had owned that house before, and they're not public records." He gestured to Dylan. "We've both been busy. Tell them what you've found, first."

Dylan flipped open a small notebook, too. "The house was built in 1810 and was originally a large private house with extensive gardens that took up most of the existing street. The family must have been pretty wealthy, but a chunk of the grounds were sold off in 1854, and that's when some houses were built along the street. Fifteen years later more land was sold, and more houses were built. By the time the First World War rolled around, the house belonged to another family, and the road appeared much as it looks today." He paused and looked up. "Before the land was divided up in 1854, there were a couple of deaths in the area. Two female bodies were found close to the grounds. There were also a number of disappearances, men and women, whose bodies were never found."

Caspian edged forward on his seat. "When they built on the grounds, did they ever find any remains?"

"No. But," Dylan pointed out, "it's remote, and the land is surrounded by trees and fields. There was a lot of speculation in the press, but they never found out who did it."

"What years were the deaths and the disappearances?" El asked.

Dylan consulted his notebook again. "On and off over forty years, between 1820 and 1860, approximately."

A collective murmur ran around the room. Avery was astonished. "That long!"

"I know. And this isn't something *I* discovered," Dylan said. "I found this out from a book on unexplained Cornish deaths. It's pretty old, written in the 1960s, and it saved me a lot of work. The author, some guy called Ralph Nugent, speculated it was a local serial killer, and that the disappearances and murders stopped when the killer died. Of course the police never connected them, and perhaps they *weren't* connected, but it's suspicious, especially as they're in the same area." He shrugged. "We'll never know. The murders stopped, apart from the usual ones whose perpetrators were found and arrested. Then time passed and all was well, until—" He paused again, looking at them ominously. "In 1938, a spate of unexplained disappearances started again, lasting just over a year. And of course World War II started in 1939, bringing chaos and disruption."

"Evelyn bought the house in the 1920s and retired from the world in 1938," Alex said. "Everything adds up. So, who owned it originally?"

"And that's where I come in," Jasper said, placing his coffee cup down. "The first owner, the one who built it, was from Eastern Europe—Romania, in fact."

"As in Transylvanian Europe? Dracula-land!" Reuben declared, incredulous.

Jasper didn't even laugh. "I can't give you specifics, because the owner didn't provide them, but Transylvania *is* in Romania."

Once again the room fell silent as everyone glanced nervously at each other and Jasper continued. "His name was Grigore Cel Tradat. Other than the fact that he arrived with his wife and four children, and owned a successful business, I know very little about him. He rented for a while, and then built the house. He traded silks and other materials and did very well, but when he got older he made some bad investments and had to sell some land. According to my notes he'd have been 84 at that point. His wife was much younger. She was not the children's mother, or certainly not of the oldest ones. She would have been too young."

Alex leaned forward on his chair, listening intently. "How old was the oldest child?"

"He was a young boy of sixteen when they arrived. Grigore's wife, Sofia, was only ten years older."

"And the other children?"

"A girl of fourteen, and then two younger girls, aged five and two."

"So the two youngest must have been Sofia's children. It was a second marriage," Genevieve said.

"Well, that's all very interesting," Caspian said dryly, watching Jasper, "But was there anything suspicious about them? Anything other than they built the house that links the family to this current nightmare of vampires and death?"

"Other than the deaths around where they lived? No. But," Jasper's eyes held a gleam of excitement. "The oldest boy was called Lupescu, and he was never seen *anywhere*. He didn't join the family business, not that I could find, anyway, and I checked the census several times. I found the other children, but not him. He never married. He never had children. It's as if he never even existed."

Ben had been watching and listening, frowning between Jasper and Dylan until he finally spoke. "You think it's him, don't you? Our mysterious killer. The vampire."

Jasper spread his hands wide. "It would make sense. Although in Romania, the more common name for vampire is Strigoi. Their mythology describes them as troubled spirits that cause havoc when they rise from the grave. They can become invisible, and transform into an animal. They are what Bram Stoker took his inspiration from. The word is fascinating," he went on, revealing his love of research. "It has also been associated with witches, through various etymological means, and is linked to the word *striga*, meaning scream."

"What about Vlad the Impaler?" Reuben asked. "I thought he was part of the legend too?"

"Ah yes, Vlad Dracule," Jasper replied, nodding. "A man known for his cruelty to his enemies. His reputation was conflated with the vampire myths. Dracul means the devil, or dragon in old Romanian."

Eve looked at them as if they'd gone mad. "As fascinating as that is, Jasper, and great job on finding all this out, nothing about this makes sense. You're suggesting that Grigore brought his vampire son to Cornwall. Why? To hide?"

"Perhaps. Why not? He was a wealthy businessman with a reputation to protect, and his son has become a Strigoi. He needs to get the family out of Romania, and go where no one knows them."

Eve just looked at him. "This is pure speculation!"

"Eve, we're just reporting what we found in the records," Dylan explained. "It's dry—words and records only. Yes, we're speculating, but the missing son is weird! Oldest sons don't just disappear. And there's no record of his death. Grigore died in 1859, and his wife inherited the house. And if you remember the date, that's when the disappearances stopped."

Eve still looked confused. "So you think Grigore had something to do with the deaths, too?"

Dylan leaned forward, his eyes bright, and he raised his index finger to emphasise his point. "No, I think his death freed Sofia to do what Grigore couldn't or wouldn't let her do. She was able to stop Lupescu."

As the events started to slide into place, Avery smiled. "Of course. Grigore wanted to protect his son, despite the fact he was a vampire. Or else why bring him here, where no one knew him?"

"And he built this house to protect him," Caspian said darkly.

"But how did Sofia stop him?" Avery asked.

Jasper shrugged. "That is still to be determined."

"Don't forget the witch-bottle," Caspian said. "You said it was old. That would fit the time period."

Avery nodded slowly as she added things together. "She hired a witch to help, and the witch-bottle was part of that. But who?"

Caspian looked across to Alex. "Your family's magic is the strongest as regards controlling spirits and demons, and they weren't linked to the Cornwall Coven. It's most likely to have been one of them, and that's why we have no knowledge of it. And they would have been close by."

Alex leaned back in his chair, his eyes staring blankly into the middle distance until eventually he looked at Caspian. "You're right. Maybe my family did help. I'll see if there are any clues in my grimoire."

"But there's more," Dylan added. "The children all married and moved out, and then had their own children. But they stayed close." He looked at Jasper. "Do you want to tell them?"

Jasper grinned. "Evelyn…aka Madame Charron, was Grigore's great, great, something granddaughter. When she bought this house, she was going home."

They stared at each other, mute with shock, the silence so great that Avery wondered if she'd gone deaf until Alex groaned. "Now it makes sense! Evelyn was trying to contact the spirits of her ancestors. She was in the house where they had lived for years!"

El nodded in agreement, excited. "Her husband was ill, probably unrecognisable after the war, and she wanted to be somewhere safe."

Cassie frowned as she glanced at the notes Dylan had made. "Do you think she knew about the mysterious Lupescu?"

"Maybe, maybe not," Reuben said, reaching for a pastry from the table next to him. As usual, nothing dented his appetite. "It's hard to know at the moment. You would have hoped she wouldn't have gone poking about with that family history, though."

"We found something else last night," Avery said, placing the box-book on the table, and the book called *Mysteries of the Occult*. "I found these. They're from this house." She outlined everything that had happened, including the attempted break-in. "There's a message in this, written in runes, which says, 'the centre of the mysteries is beneath the full moon.' We think it points to the centre of this book—there's a witch-mark on the cover. The chapter is about using death deities and demons as spirit guides. The page focuses on demons of the First Hierarchy."

"The first *what?*" Ben asked, perplexed.

"According to demonologists of the 16th and 17th century," Avery explained, "there was a hierarchy of demons, much as there was a hierarchy of angels. There's a first, second, and third hierarchy, as well as many lesser demons. The hierarchy denotes importance and power, and they have traits."

"Christian theology," Caspian said disdainfully.

"There are many belief systems in this world," Jasper admonished him. "Any demon in particular, Avery?"

"Verrine, who tempts men with impatience—apparently."

Reuben snorted. "What kind of demons did we face in the summer?"

Avery stared at him, incredulous. "I have no idea! If you remember, we really didn't have time to ask."

"I think demons are demons are demons," Alex said contemptuously. "I don't hold with this hierarchy crap. As Caspian said, it's Christian theology, and was designed to aid with hunting witches—that was the original reason to name them. In my opinion, Evelyn was looking for a spirit guide, and she found one. And a malevolent one, by the sound of it."

Briar looked thoughtful. "But the runes say beneath the full moon. Is it a reference to vampires? They don't need a full moon, do they? Is it relevant?"

"There's more to this, I'm sure," Genevieve said, worried. "Madame Charron's name is a play on *Charon*, the ferryman who takes souls to the underworld in Greek mythology. I'm sensing a deep obsession."

Hunter finally spoke. "We still don't know if she really was genuine though, do we?"

"There's only one way to know for sure. I aim to try contacting some spirits myself, preferably Evelyn's," Alex said, resolutely.

19

While Alex set up his crystal ball, remaining in the séance room as he tried to detect the presence of ghosts, the others split up to look around before Ben showed them the tower room.

Avery wandered through the ground floors of the house, checking for signs of spells or magical protection, but she felt nothing untoward, which reassured her. Rupert puzzled her, but she thought it unlikely that he had any magical ability.

The first time she visited the house, she had been taking in so much that she failed to see details in the decor, but now that she had time to look, Avery observed many occult symbols. This included a large sigil embedded in the plaster above the front door, small symbols in the cornices of the ceiling, and the roses around the light fittings.

The rooms on either side of the hallway were large and imposing reception rooms that stretched to the rear of the house. The one on the left of the main entrance had symbols and sigils around the fireplace, and even the paintings were occult in nature—dark, brooding fantastical landscapes. They were symbols she was familiar with, but for anyone coming into the house for a séance, they would have been striking, and probably intimidating. They suggested a house of power and mystery. Perhaps this room was intended for those participating in séances, while the other room was for daytime visitors. The colours were lighter, and decorated with nothing occult at all. No doubt she would find more as they explored.

Avery paused in front of the fireplace and looked up at an oil painting hanging above it. The subject was a striking woman, dressed in velvet and silk, all purples and reds. Her black hair was arranged in an elaborate chignon, and her dark eyes stared down at Avery, imperious and challenging. *Was she Madame Charron?*

Avery found Cassie in the kitchen, pulling the EMF metre out of their equipment bag, and asked, "How long did you say they'd be away for?"

"Overnight. Back by midday tomorrow." She looked annoyed and slammed the metre on the table. "Rupert is getting pretty cranky. He wants to know why we can't find the spirits that he *knows* are here. I've told him we don't raise spirits, just read them! He's being really unreasonable. We're as frustrated as he is that we can't identify whatever it is in their bedroom."

Avery stood by the window, gazing out across the large garden, currently covered in snow, as she listened. At the end of the garden was a brick wall, and beyond was a thick strand of trees that must lead to the reserve. On the far right of the wall was a wooden gate, padlocked. She could see it glinting in the weak sunlight from here.

"I'm still wondering why he hired you in the first place," Avery said, turning to face Cassie. "Everything this man does confuses me. Why is he so obsessed with spirits? It makes me wonder if he's toying with necromancy. A weird hobby."

"No weirder than ours," Cassie said with a wry smile.

Avery heard Eve and Caspian's voices in the hall, and went to join them, leaving Cassie to finish setting up her equipment.

"Interesting place," Caspian noted, looking around, his gaze finally falling on Avery. "It's quirky. I like it."

Eve moved past him, staring at the architraves, as Avery had. "I'm surprised. You don't strike me as the quirky type."

A smile crept over Caspian's face and his gaze swept down Avery from her head to her toes. "Quirky is growing on me."

Is that directed at me? Avery thought, feeling her face flushing with annoyance. Fortunately, no one seemed to notice as Jasper and Genevieve came down the stairs to join them.

"First impressions?" Jasper asked them eagerly.

"Fascinating," Briar said as she exited the room on the other side of the hall with Hunter, El, and Reuben. "And creepy."

Avery caught Hunter's eye. He looked a lot better since the last time she'd seen him. The cuts and bruises he'd received from his fight with Cooper, the old Pack Alpha, and from his encounter with the Wild Hunt had healed. He looked strong and his usual cocky self. "Hey, Hunter. Good to see you back here. I didn't think you were coming until after Christmas."

He smiled, his eyes mischievous. "Good to see you too. When Briar called I grabbed my bag, jumped in the car, and drove like the clappers. I don't like the thought of her being alone with a vampire on the loose."

"How long you staying?"

"At least until the New Year." His gaze followed Briar's retreating back. "Maybe longer."

Avery grinned. "What about work?"

"Josh and the girls can handle it for a while."

Reuben was close, listening to their conversation, and he lowered his voice. "Staking your claim?"

"Something like that," he murmured, watching her as she chatted with Eve. Briar definitely had a glow that morning, Avery decided. Briar looked up and saw Hunter watching, their eyes locking for a moment as something unspoken passed between them.

"Come on, guys, time for the tower room," Ben called from the first floor landing. Alex was standing next to him, looking distracted.

"Hold on," Avery replied. "Can I ask you about this painting?"

She led the way to the left reception room, the rest of the group following, and pointed to the picture above the fireplace. "Is that Madame Charron?"

"Wow," Eve said, softly. "She's impressive."

Ben laughed. "Yes, glad you reminded me about this. It is her. Charlotte found it in an upstairs room and decided it belonged here instead. She's imposing, isn't she?"

"She's in her full regalia, too," Genevieve observed. "It's good to see her in colour. Many of the photos from that era are in black and white."

"I like her," El declared. "She's got a lot of style. The whole room has. It's so dark and mysterious. Do you think that knowing what she looks like will help you find her spirit, Alex?"

"Let's hope so," he said, continuing to examine the picture minutely. "She's holding a card in her hands. You can just see the edge of it. Is that The Moon card?"

Avery stepped closer. "I think it is. How amazing."

"Will you tell Rupert what you've found?" Caspian asked Avery.

She squirmed. "Eventually."

Ben turned away, ever the tour guide. "Come on. Upstairs is more atmospheric."

The group trailed behind him as he showed them the other rooms, many of which Avery and Reuben had seen before.

They lingered in the master bedroom for a few minutes. "This is where we've been filming," Dylan said, heading to one of the windows. "And this is the window Charlotte opens, letting her blood-sucking visitor in."

Briar looked down to the garden. "He'd have to scale the wall. But I guess we know that's not a problem."

"What a stunning room, though," Eve noted.

Briar shuddered. "Beautiful or not, I wouldn't be sleeping in here knowing that something was standing over me at night."

"Let's have a look at the tower," Alex said, already heading to the door.

Cassie had been standing in the doorway watching, and she spun on her heel and led the way down the passage, stopping at a dead end. A panelled wall was in front of them, a series of carvings around the edge. She reached to the side, pressing an ornate moulding of the moon, and the panel popped open, revealing a door. She turned to look at them, a wry smile hovering on her lips. "It's only just registered that it's the moon carving that releases the door." She headed through, leading them up a long narrow staircase. She called back over her shoulder, "There's a third floor for servants and storage. The rooms are much smaller and quite bare, as you can imagine. We'll show you them later. But this set of stairs bypasses that floor and leads you to the square tower you can see from outside."

The stairs turned on to a small landing, and Cassie pushed the door open into the tower, lit from above by a dusty sky light. They all crowded in, hot on each other's heels, and Avery gasped and shivered. She was not the only one.

"Holy crap. This is creepy," Reuben exclaimed.

The room was lined with long, dark wooden panels, making the room circular in design. Nothing could be seen of the square brick bones of the tower. The ceiling was vaulted with an ornate, circular glass pane at the apex. But it was the decoration on the wooden panels that was so chilling. Paintings of demons filled some of the panels, with glowing eyes, horns, and hooves. Spectres and ghouls also jostled for space, and there were several depictions of Major Arcana cards, including The High Priestess, The Moon, The Tower, Death, The Devil, and The Hermit. The floor was decorated with a large pentagram, and surrounded by various runes and sigils, the edges crowded with candles. A small, round table covered with a long, black velvet cloth that reached the floor sat in the middle of the space, a chair on either side.

"Wow," Jasper exclaimed. "This room radiates power."

"I agree," Genevieve said, her hand stroking one of the panels. "This suggests she had real ability. Look, that's her image again as the High Priestess."

Caspian grunted. "I'm not so sure. She seems to be trying very hard to impress."

"But you'd need to surely, for your customers," El reasoned, her eyes narrowed.

If some of them were baffled, Eve was pleased, grinning with delight. "These paintings are stunning. Look at the detail, and the light. I admit, some of the subjects are gruesome, but they're good! Someone spent a lot of time on them."

"Can you imagine seeking a private audience with Madame Charron?" Briar said, turning slowly. "You're probably paying good money, and you're brought *here*! I've got chills just looking at the pictures, and I'm a witch. I know magic and power. But if you didn't—"

"You'd be overawed and seriously impressed," Hunter finished, moving next to Briar, his hand resting on her lower back.

"And impressionable!" Caspian added. "You'd believe anything."

Cassie was staring up at the glass roof, grinning broadly. "Has anyone noticed what the inscription on the glass says?"

"What inscription?" Dylan asked, looking up.

"There, all around the edge. It's hard to make out because of the italics."

Avery's mouth fell open as she deciphered the writing. "Bloody Hell. It says '*The Centre of the Mysteries*.'"

Alex laughed. "The runic script!"

Avery swivelled towards the panel with the moon on it. "And a full moon panel."

"Another hidden doorway?" El asked. "The door release mechanism downstairs was a moon."

"And one of the symbols on the paper found with that witch-bottle was a moon, too," Reuben added.

"So," Genevieve said, hand on hips. "Time is marching on. What first? I suggest that Alex, you try to reach Madame Charron, or Felicity, or whoever else may want to say hello, and that we try to find out if there really is a hidden door in here."

"I wonder if Rupert thinks there is?" Briar mused.

"I guarantee you," Ben said, starting to test the panels for release catches, "that Rupert and Charlotte will have tested every single panel in this room, because they did the same all over the house. That's how they found this attic room in the first place."

"Jean didn't tell them, then?" El asked.

"Nope."

"It would explain why he wants to find the books," Avery said, placing her hand on one of the panels. "I bet he thinks there are instructions somewhere."

"Well, there is, just not the type he probably expected," El answered.

"I have a feeling this may be the best space to try to connect to a spirit," Alex said, "but I agree, you should focus on that door. I'll use the séance room on the first floor."

"Can we film you?" Ben asked.

"Sure," Alex nodded. "But at this stage, I'll work better without any other witches. If something starts to happen, I trust you to get someone, sound good?"

"Perfect," he and Dylan said together, both looking excited.

"I'd like to explore the house a bit more, if that's okay," El said, shouldering her bag. "I would hate to think we'd missed something."

"Good idea," Genevieve said, already looking weary at the task ahead of them.

"I'll come with you, El," Reuben said.

Eve nodded. "Me, too. This place is fascinating. It's like a time capsule. Nothing seems to have changed—not obviously, anyway."

"Rupert has been very keen to preserve it," Ben told them. "At least until he unlocks its secrets. I'd love to talk to Jean, the cleaner who inherited it."

"Remind me to ask Newton about that later," Avery said. "I'll stop here and help with the door. And call me if anything happens to Alex!" She said this specifically to Ben and Dylan. "*Anything*!"

"We will, don't worry," Dylan reassured her.

Alex kissed the top of her head. "Be careful."

"You, too." She leaned into him affectionately.

Eve was already heading out the door. "And call us when you find something!"

20

Caspian, Genevieve, Briar, Avery, and Jasper stared at the panels, and started to discuss their options. Hunter and Cassie stood back, watching.

"We should try some opening spells," Caspian suggested.

"But that would suggest that Madame Charron was a witch," Briar pointed out. "We're pretty sure she's a legitimate psychic, but that doesn't mean she's a witch. Those are two very different things."

Jasper shook his head, frustrated. "This house was constructed long before Madame Charron took up residence. She is not responsible for these panels. She may have painted them, she may have found out this room's secrets, and she may have left clues to find them, but she didn't make them or conceal the room." Jasper's eyes now burned with excitement. "The tower is separate from the rest of the house, the access hidden behind a panel. And there are more panels, one of which must be a door. Grigore did this to hide Lupescu. This *has* to be the way to his hiding place. Grigore would have wanted to protect him from being hunted, and his family from Lupescu's blood lust. As he grew older, he would have grown stronger."

Caspian frowned. "Good point, Jasper." He spun on his heels, looking around the room. "And if I wasn't a witch, I wouldn't want a door to be sealed with magic so that I could never access it. I'd want a mechanism. Where would I choose?"

Avery's head hurt with the layers of time and complexity. "But there *was* a spell at some point—the disappearances stopped."

"True." Briar stared at the panels intently, as if they would reveal their secrets under scrutiny. "But somehow we think the spell, or whatever you want to call it, was broken, because of the deaths in the late 1930s, the 1970s, and the ones that have started now."

"Deaths that coincide with the homeowner dying," Genevieve reminded them.

"Maybe a binding spell of some sort, something to bind the vampire to the owner?" Cassie suggested. "Is that how they work?"

"A binding spell can work however you want it to," Caspian said, looking at Avery. "As we know only too well."

She met his eyes briefly and looked back at the panels, puzzled. "We're missing something. Grigore dies, his wife, Sofia, takes over the house, the deaths stop. And when she dies, *nothing happens*. No resurrection of the vampire until Madame Charron disturbed it in the 1930s."

Genevieve sat on one of the chairs next to the table in the middle of the room, her fingers drumming the surface. "We think she broke the spell that trapped the vampire using Verrine, the demon spirit guide, and then had to trap the vampire again."

Briar nodded. "Two different spells, then. One cast by Sofia, or the witch she employed, and whatever means Madame Charron and her daughter used. A binding spell of sorts, linked to their lives, broken by death."

Cassie frowned, marched over to the panel, and started feeling the edges again. "So, in theory, we're back to square one. If one of these panels is a door, it should just pop open with a mechanism."

"In theory," Jasper echoed, joining her in the search. He ran his hands over the surface, his palms flat, moving in an orderly manner, left to right, right to left, as he moved downwards.

Caspian brushed his fingertips across his lips. "Maybe we need a full moon to see it? Or it could be a play on words." He looked around the room again, scanning the other panels. "There are a least three other panels with moons on them. The High Priestess, The Tower, and The Hermit. The verse could refer to those." He strode across to the closest one, The High Priestess, and started to examine it.

Avery became excited as an idea began to form. "The Major Arcana representations here aren't typical of any particular style of deck. They're rich in symbolism, of course, but look at what's at the feet of The Devil. Normally, there's a male and female figure at its feet, but on this one, there's only a man."

Genevieve frowned as she stared at the painting. "You're right. A man dressed in black and wrapped in chains, with blood on his face." She turned to Avery, a smile spreading across her face. "Well spotted. What else?"

"The Tower is normally depicted with flames coming from the roof, and lightning striking it. That one is set against a night sky with a full moon above it, and there's a cave of some sort, a dark hollow beneath it."

Hunter had been watching and listening, hands thrust into his jeans pockets as he leaned against the door frame, but now he came to life, stalking across the room. "Holy shit! You're right. Does that mean there's a cave beneath this one? Well, the house?"

Avery raised her eyebrows. "Perhaps. It fits our theory."

They were all paying close attention now, glancing back and forth between Avery and the paintings.

Avery continued, "The Hermit is numerologically linked to The Moon. He's an old man, as commonly depicted, but his guiding light is the moon in his lantern, not the star as it normally is. The Hermit shows thought, introspection, isolation…like Madame Charron." She turned to the High Priestess image. "The face is already Madame Charron, we can see that. She depicts wisdom of the world beyond the veil. But again, a full moon hangs above her, which isn't normally represented in many standard decks, and this card is astrologically linked to the Moon, too."

"And Death?" Hunter asked.

Avery exhaled heavily. "Death is normally depicted as a soldier, with a skull for a head. He charges into battle, usually on horseback, so the imagery is medieval, one of the Four Horsemen of the Apocalypse. Sometimes people are at his feet, as he brings judgment to all. But the card doesn't mean actual death; it represents a spiritual death and rebirth. There's usually a setting sun in the background—the end of day, the end of life, or a time in life. In this panel, he stands on a bloodstained field, a tower in the background, but the sky is dark, and it's a moon rising, not a sun setting."

"Wow!" Cassie said, looking at her in shock. "How do you remember all of that stuff?"

"I read the cards," Avery explained. "They are old friends that whisper to me, revealing past, present, and future. Not all witches use them, but I always have."

Genevieve watched her speculatively, and said, "I rarely use them."

Cassie frowned. "Do they predict things—like this?"

Avery frowned, trying to explain. "It's not that straightforward. They offer a personal reading, not broad predictions. In the summer, I certainly read there was a change coming to me, danger that threatened my life in some way, but it depends what you ask them. I certainly haven't predicted *this*!" She spread her hands wide, encompassing the room and the house.

Briar studied her for a moment, frowning. "Do these images match the ones in the deck you found?"

"Shit! I don't know." Avery reached into her bag, pulled the book-box out, and rapidly thumbed through the pack. While she looked, there was a flurry of activity, as Briar, Hunter, Cassie, and Genevieve started to examine the other panels, leaving Jasper to finish examining The Moon panel.

Avery was annoyed with herself, because she knew when she found the pack that they weren't a typical deck, but she hadn't stopped to examine them properly. She'd assumed they were an old design, one she'd not seen before. She found the cards represented on the panels and laid them out in a line on the table. *Damn it.* They weren't the same at all. Not even close. The pictures on the panels told a story, certainly, of a vampire bound in a cave beneath a tower, a High Priestess who navigated worlds beyond the veil, and who sat in lonely contemplation. *But why paint them?* A warning maybe, or perhaps a clue, in case things went wrong, as they have done now. A way to track the vampire. *Bollocks! I'm missing something!*

Avery stared into space, watching shadows move across the room. It brought her back to the present. Time was passing. She looked up at the glass pane set into the roof. The light coming through was muted, filtered by a covering of snow, which earlier had given the room a weird, spectral light. Now it seemed darker, as if the clouds were once again gathering outside. She stared at the words painted on the glass, pondering their many meanings. *The centre of the mysteries lies beneath the full moon,* she repeated to herself. In this light, the circular glass roof looked like a full moon. *The floor!*

Excited at her discovery, she examined the runes that circled the pentagram beneath her feet. The design was painted on, the paint now a faded white, almost yellow, but it was relatively undamaged, sealed beneath a layer of varnish. She couldn't see images of moons, full or otherwise. And then she turned and stared at the table in the middle. What was that hiding? She removed the cards and candles, placing them on the floor by the door, and then pulled the heavy velvet cloth away, dust rising in clouds and making her cough.

"What are you doing?" Caspian asked, turning to watch her. He funnelled the air away with a gesture, and it streamed out of the door and down the stairs.

"I think we're looking in the wrong place. Can someone help me move the table?"

Hunter shooed her out of the way, lifting the table up on his own, and moving it next to the door. By the time he turned round, Avery was already on her knees. In the centre of the pentagram, woven discreetly into other symbols, was the sign of the Triple Goddess, with the waxing, full, and waning moons next to each other.

Briar crouched next to her, watching Avery run her fingers over it. "This must be it. Can you feel anything?"

Avery touched it gently, terrified she might do something before they were ready for it, and then looked at Briar, triumphant. "I can feel a faint line all around the full moon."

They both twisted to look up at the others who surrounded them in a tight circle.

"What now?" Avery asked. "Do I press it?"

But before anyone could answer, they heard footsteps racing up the stairs. It was Dylan, breathless with excitement. "Alex has found Madame Charron! Come quickly."

"Go," Genevieve said, assuming control. "I'll wait here until you're back. No one is pressing anything until we're *all* ready."

Avery rose to her feet, and ran to follow Dylan. "Thanks!" she called over her shoulder.

"I'm coming, too," Briar said, trailing her out the door. Without hesitation, Hunter followed.

***

They skidded to a halt in front of the door to the séance room, and Dylan paused, hand on the handle. "You should know that he was about to use the crystal ball when he started to examine the large, full-length mirror that rests on the floor against the wall."

"I remember it," Avery said, barely containing her impatience.

"It has an ornate frame. Alex noticed arcane symbols around the edges, a sigil denoting a doorway. He decided to try mirror scrying."

Without another word he pushed the door open, and they entered silently, Dylan shutting the door behind them.

It took a moment for Avery's eyes to focus, because the room was as dark as night. They had drawn the heavy curtains, and the only light was from the fire in the fireplace and a single, black pillar candle placed on the floor in front of the mirror. The room was warm, adding to the sense of claustrophobia. The candle flame burned with unnatural stillness, and behind it, staring into the mirror, sat Alex, cross-legged and immobile. He was oblivious to their arrival.

It was hard to see his face at first, only his deeply shadowed reflection, all hard angles and planes from the firelight. They moved closer, behind and to his right, careful not to disturb him.

His lips were moving, and Avery could hear him murmuring, but was unable to make out the words. She was focused so completely on his face and the flame that it was with a shock that she realised the rest of the mirror was completely black. Nothing of the rest of the room was reflected at all. It was a void. A chill raced down her arms and she shivered, despite the heat.

Avery lowered herself to the floor, staring at the mirror intently. She slowed her breathing and stilled her mind, willing herself to focus. A figure emerged from the darkness. A woman, her face pale and thin, the rest of her body swathed in layers of voluminous clothing. Her lips moved in response to Alex's murmurings. Back and forth they went, their conversation impossible to follow. It seemed to last an age; her face became impassioned, and then furious. And then her eyes widened with shock as a huge, clawed hand appeared on her shoulder, dragging her backwards. She vanished in a cloud of billowing smoke.

Another face appeared, and Avery jumped, suppressing the scream that bubbled in her throat. A demonesque figure filled the mirror, huge and terrifying, and she felt a ripple of fear run through the room. It was nothing like the formless, writhing shapes filled with flames they had encountered in the summer. This assumed a man's shape, but its face was a skull from which thick, grotesque horns protruded. Fire burned from within, lighting his eye sockets and jaw with flames. It fixed Alex with a questioning glare and started to speak, and the most hideous, unearthly sound boomed around the room. This time Avery yelped, jerking back in shock. Her heart pounded so hard she thought it would leap out of her chest.

Simultaneously, a howl filled the room, emanating from behind her. She turned, dreading what she would see, but found that Hunter had changed into a wolf, partially ripping his clothing in the process. He snarled, head lowered, glowering at her, but Briar intervened, a hand on the wolf's head, utterly fearless. Hunter dropped onto his belly, his head in Briar's lap, and she stroked him, her hands buried deep in his soft fur. She met Avery's gaze, eyes solemn.

Avery glanced at Dylan and Ben, and saw them both sitting on the floor, transfixed on the mirror; reassured that they were okay, she turned her attention back to Alex.

He was still immobile, sweat beading on his brow as he murmured a response to the demon. It didn't seem to like what it heard, because it threw back its head, opened its jaws wide, and shot flames out into the void, until nothing could be seen except fire; then it was gone, and the mirror was just a mirror again.

Alex fell backwards onto the floor with a *thump*, and the candle extinguished, a thin stream of smoke rising into the air. Avery untangled her legs and crawled to him. She couldn't have walked if her life had depended on it.

"Alex! Alex, are you all right?"

Fear gripped her like she'd never experienced before. It wasn't like the terror of facing the Wild Hunt. This was something deeper, more personal. *What had he done?*

He stared vacantly at the ceiling for what seemed like endless moments, and Avery was aware of the deep silence around her. She reached forward, wanting to shake him, but knowing that might shock him too much. "Alex! Please speak to me."

And then he blinked, the trancelike state leaving his eyes, and he turned his head towards her and smiled weakly.

"Thank the Goddess," she whispered.

"*Water*," he croaked.

She looked around, and Dylan's hand appeared, thrusting a water bottle in her face. She took it and passed it to Alex, and after taking a deep breath, he eased himself upright and took a long drink, before finally meeting Avery's stare. "Well, that was pretty fucking scary. Remind me not to meet Verrine again."

Thankful he still had a sense of humour, Avery laughed, and the tension in the room dropped.

"Can I open these curtains?" Ben asked, his voice shaky. "I'd really like to see daylight."

"Me, too," Alex called over his shoulder. "Go ahead."

"In a moment," he answered. "I've just realised my legs won't move."

Avery raised her hand, twitching back the curtains with a gesture, revealing the three long windows backed by swirling snow. She then turned her attention to the fire, where the flames had burned down to embers only, and with a word, she reignited it.

Light and heat flooded the room, and Alex sighed.

"Please tell me you didn't promise that *thing* anything?" Avery asked, fear coursing through her again as she remembered their exchange.

He smiled, her usual, adorable Alex, his jaw covered in stubble, his hair falling around his face, and his dark eyes holding her with warmth she never wanted to lose. "I'm not a nut job. He didn't like the fact that I was talking to Madame Charron. Apparently some secrets should stay hidden. I was warned off, and told not to contact her again. I told him I'd do what I wanted and he could get lost. He didn't like that."

Relief rolled through her, and she felt weak all over again. Just as she was about to ask more, she heard the sound of thudding feet as if a herd of elephants was stampeding down the hallway, and the door flew open, Reuben standing at the head of the group. His hands were raised, fire balled in his palms. His eyes swept the room, and when he registered they were okay, he lowered his arms. "What the hell have you been doing? We heard a howl—and we were down in the cellar!"

"You got into the cellar?" Dylan asked, incredulous. "It's out of bounds for us. What's down there?"

"Necromancer shit. What have *you* been doing?"

"Raising demons," Alex answered. "Do you think someone can make some coffee before we get into it?"

21

Avery leaned against the window frame, holding a hot cup of coffee, and watched the snow. In the last fifteen minutes, since Cassie had made coffee and tea and rustled up a pack of biscuits, the snowfall had become thicker, muting the outside world. Avery felt that some time in the last hour she had stepped back in time. The house was getting to her. Its layers of history and secrets lay on her spirit as thick as the snow on the ground.

She turned away, watching Briar lean against Hunter, his arm protectively wrapped around her. Hunter had returned to human form looking shocked and unsettled, his clothing ripped, and told them that the demon Verrine's voice had literally forced the change to his wolf. "That has never happened to me before, and I hope it never happens again. That was *horrible.*"

"Are you sure you're okay?" Briar had asked him, her eyes roving over him as if he was nursing a hidden injury.

"I'm fine. Lying in your lap was worth it."

Briar had flushed with pleasure.

Avery allowed herself a smile. It was good to see Briar happy. She turned her attention to the roomful of people as they listened to Genevieve finish telling them what they had found in the attic.

El whooped. She was sitting next to Reuben, her short sword on the table next to her, glinting in the icy cold light from outside. "Well done! So we've found a way to open the hidden door."

"In theory," Caspian said in his low drawl. "The proof is yet to be found."

As Genevieve finished pouring her second cup of tea, she said, "You better tell us what happened here, Alex."

Alex was still sitting on the floor in front of the fire, sipping on super strength coffee. "I was going to try to reach Madame Charron with my crystal ball, as I said, but before I started, I decided to check the room again. I realised that the mirror had symbols all around the frame that reference doorways and safe passage. I had an idea that perhaps she used this mirror to talk to spirits. Mirrors are a popular way to enter the spirit world. I hoped this would be a hotline to her. I was right." He paused, taking another sip of coffee. He still looked pale, as if the communication had taken much of his energy. "Within only a few minutes of me searching the void, I found her. It was as if she was waiting for me—well, someone. But she was nervous, her spirit flitting away and back again. Anyway, long story short, she confessed that she was told by her mother about how her family had arrived here from Romania, and how Grigore had built the house, and that there was a dark and terrible family secret. But she didn't know what it was. She thought it was related to her own psychic abilities that had been passed down to her. Her mother and her daughter had them, too. She thought that maybe something had gone horribly wrong and that someone's spirit was trapped in the void, so she decided to investigate, like a spiritual detective. She became frustrated with her failure, and in her effort to succeed, she reached too far. She found Verrine. He promised to help her."

Verrine. Avery shivered again. His unintelligible, screeching voice still echoed in her head, and his appearance… She doubted she'd sleep well for a while.

Alex continued. "By then, Madame Charron was an accomplished medium, but she also embellished her séances by either toning them down or enhancing them, depending on the group. She was confident in her ability to manage spirit guides, and had used them before. But Verrine was different. He certainly didn't present himself to her as he appeared to me. Not at first, anyway. He offered to show her the family's dark secret, and he led her to Lupescu's chained spirit—metaphorically speaking. He encouraged her to set him free, so she did."

"And unleashed a monster," Eve said. She sat at the table, watching Alex with fascination.

Genevieve edged forward in her seat. "So that's how the witch did it. They *chained* his spirit. That would have meant separating it from his body." She looked astonished. "That's hard, dark magic."

"And surely," Caspian asked, also leaning forward in anticipation, "that means Madame Charron broke a spell, without having magical ability. As you said, she's a medium, not a witch."

"She broke it because Verrine helped her," Alex explained. "I have no idea about this hierarchy of demons crap, or whether it really exists, but he's powerful, able to transform himself into any feature he chooses. He saw what she needed and manipulated her. A witch chained Lupescu's spirit, but he helped her break it."

"So, Verrine couldn't break it free on his own?" El surmised.

"Perhaps the original spell bound it to a family line. Maybe that's why when Sofia died the spell remained, passing down the generations, until Evelyn broke it, and his dark and twisted spirit fled back to his body. And the deaths started."

Jasper nodded solemnly. "Demons love chaos. They would love the chaos that a vampire would bring."

"When did she realise what she'd done?" Avery asked.

"As soon as she released him. She saw Lupescu for what he was. From that point on, she had to try to find a solution."

Dylan was sitting at the table, fiddling with his camera while he listened. "It took her a while, obviously—over a year, during which time Lupescu ran rampant."

Alex nodded. "She had to find a witch to help her, and it wasn't easy. Let's face it—you can't exactly advertise that sort of thing."

Caspian asked the question that everyone was thinking. "Did one of our ancestors help her? And if so, why don't we know about it?"

"White Haven again," Eve suggested. "The witches that were isolated from the rest of the coven. There was no one to tell—except descendants."

Alex, Reuben, and Avery all snorted, and Reuben said forcefully, "No one told us!"

Genevieve shuffled impatiently. "Did she tell you who she used, Alex? It may help us now."

He grimaced. "No, I'm afraid not. But it was another sort of binding spell. They bound him to her, but she was bound to the house. And when she died, Lupescu was released and went on the rampage again until Felicity contained it. Don't ask me any more details, because I don't know them. I don't know what Felicity did, or who with. She was about to tell me more—I asked about the hidden panel—but Verrine dragged her away before she could answer."

Reuben started drumming his fingers on the table. "We can debate this later. Can we get on with opening this door?"

"Not yet," Genevieve said, as everyone started to rise. "What did you find in the cellar?"

El answered that as she slid her short sword in to its scabbard. "A necromancer circle to summon spirits, and a demon trap. That's why Rupert kept the door locked. It's pretty fresh, drawn in chalk, salt circle and the works. We can show you later."

"Good," Genevieve said, rising to her feet. "Let's get on with this, then. Grab whatever vampire-killing kit you need. This could get ugly."

***

The group assembled in the tower room, and Avery pressed the moon symbol in the centre of the floor, depressing it by a couple of inches.

Nothing happened.

"Bollocks. What now?" she asked, looking around at the others.

"Maybe it's a double mechanism?" Eve suggested. "You always need someone else to help."

Jasper looked weary and frustrated as he rubbed his hands across his short hair. "Let's check the other moon images again."

"It's pointless," Cassie said, echoing his frustration.

"We haven't checked the rising moon image of Death, have we?" Caspian pointed out as he strode to the panel. He examined the half-moon visible over the tower on the horizon, and ran his fingers over the edge. He turned to them and grinned. They didn't often see Caspian grin; it transformed him, making him look ten years younger. "Bingo. On the count of three, Avery? One, two, three!"

They both pressed the images together and with a loud *click*, the panel of The Moon swung outwards, revealing a passageway.

Whoops of joy filled the room, and Caspian rolled his shoulders and stepped inside first. "Here goes," he murmured and threw a couple of witch lights ahead. "There's a passage running between the panelling and the wall for a few feet, and then it disappears into the wall."

They filed in after him, and he led the way through the musty, cobwebbed passage, dust rising around them. It was narrow, with just enough width for one person to pass comfortably. The wall was straight on one side, and the curved panelling lined the other. A dark opening appeared in the wall and they turned into it. Immediately, a set of steps appeared and ran downwards, turned left and then heading down again.

Caspian called back over his shoulder. "We must be next to the outside wall, and I think this goes directly to ground level."

The stairs were steep, the steps small and slippery underfoot, and Avery started to sweat. It was hot in here, stuffy, and the dust kept rising, getting in her hair, her eyes, and up her nose. She sent a waft of air around them, and immediately felt better. Eventually, they reached a small landing on what they estimated was the ground floor, and the stairs turned again. Avery was now completely disorientated, unable to work out whether they were at the front, middle, or rear of the house. The air became damp and musty and Caspian stopped, causing everyone to stumble into each other.

"A little warning, please," El grumbled.

"Sorry. I think we're under the house now. We've reached a flat area."

Avery was at the back, still on the steps, and light bloomed down below as Eve and Alex immediately threw more witch lights above them, throwing the room into stark relief. Avery stumbled down the last few steps, glad to be out of the narrow passage.

The room they were in was made of stone, plain and unadorned, and the floor was packed earth. On the far side were two heavy wooden doors, enormous bolts keeping them locked.

Caspian strode toward them, rattling the wood. "These are still solid."

"Do you have to do that?" Ben asked, looking horrified. "You might wake what's behind it!"

Cassie visibly shivered and gripped her stake hard. "Don't say that. Do you really think the vampires are there?"

Genevieve stood next to Caspian, her pupils huge in the low light. "If we're in luck, they will be. We can kill them and get this over with. Are we ready?"

"No," Cassie answered.

"You can leave if you like," Genevieve said. "I understand."

Cassie shook her head. "I'm just nervous. I have a few spells in my pockets, as well as my stake. I'll be fine."

Eve patted her arm. "I am, too—you're not alone."

Everyone was nervous, it was obvious from the general air of tension in the room, and level of fidgetiness that everyone exhibited as they readied themselves, Avery included. She hadn't forgotten how quick the vampires were when they'd encountered them before, and she took deep breaths to calm herself.

Genevieve looked them all in the eye. "Are we ready?"

Reuben pulled a torch from his backpack and lit his face up from under his chin, pulling a ghoulish expression and announcing in his best Vincent Price voice, "Time for the crypt! Ha ha ha!"

"You're such a doofus," El said affectionately.

"I'll take that as yes," Genevieve said dryly.

"Wait!" Jasper called. "What's the time?"

Alex checked his watch. "Half past three, why?"

"Not long until sunset," Jasper noted. "If they're in there, they should be sleeping, but we're cutting it close."

"I'm not turning back now," Genevieve said, and together she and Caspian released the bolts and pulled the doors open.

It was pitch black beyond them, and they launched a flurry of witch lights, illuminating another passageway, but this one was as wide as the double doors. At the far end was another set of doors.

"It seems Grigore was keen to keep the vampire from his own door," Hunter said, wryly. He started to shed his clothes. "I'd rather proceed as a wolf from now on."

Within seconds he changed into a larger than average wolf, and he loped to the passage entrance, Briar next to him, her hand buried in the fur of his neck. She'd slipped her shoes off, and she wriggled her toes in the dirt. "I can't feel any magic ahead."

"Me, neither," Caspian agreed.

The passage was again lined with brick, and they progressed slowly, as if they were expecting booby traps. Avery felt like she was in an Indiana Jones film.

Alex nudged her. "You okay?"

She nodded. "I think so. You?"

He raised an eyebrow. "As I'll ever be."

The next set of doors was as solid as the first, but they were ornate, covered in sigils.

Genevieve ran her hand over them gently. "These had a spell on them once. There's just a trace of it now, but the sigils warn against intrusion."

Once again, everyone raised their weapons or their hands, magic summoned, as she and Caspian released the bolts and opened the doors, sending witch lights through at the same time.

They illuminated a bedroom. This time, the walls and floor were made of large stone blocks, and it was filled with wooden bedroom furniture—an ornate, four-poster bed, a chest of drawers, a mirrored dressing table, and a wardrobe. But it was an imitation only. The place was a wreck, the furniture broken, as if smashed in a rage, and the mirror shattered. The bed was the only intact item in there, but it was covered in rumpled and rotten linen that tumbled onto the ground, and it was soaked with stiffened, dark blood. But worse was the pile of bones that lay ankle deep in places, and the skulls lined up along the deep shelves cut into the wall; the stench was horrific. On the far side of the room was the entrance to another passage.

Avery heaved, and she heard a few others doing the same.

Briar's hand flew to her mouth, and she said a quick spell; within seconds, the smell disappeared, replaced by the scent of roses and honeysuckle.

For a second there was silence as they all stared aghast at what lay before them, and then Hunter headed in, padding stealthily towards the bones, the rest of them fanning out as they explored.

"Over a century of death," Jasper said solemnly as he looked at the devastation. He raised his hand, and immediately the candles placed around the room flared to life, and if anything, the warm light made the horror of it all so much worse.

Alex advanced slowly, the stake raised in his right hand, a ball of fire in his left. He kicked at the bones by his feet. "But nothing recent, by the look of it. These bones are old."

"No wonder they never found bodies," Dylan said as he swept his camera around the room. "He brought them all here. What an animal."

The room fell silent as they advanced, and Avery shivered. Although Briar had disguised most of the stench, it was still there, faint and rancid, and Avery sent a gentle wind ahead of her, carrying it away. She reached out a hand to touch the broken mirror. "Grigore must have been trying to make his son more human."

"Well, that was a big fat failure, wasn't it?" Cassie said. "I can't believe what I'm seeing."

El extended her sword ahead of her as she looked around. "Well, it's clear there's nothing here. So where are they now?"

"The recent bodies, or the vampires?" Avery asked her.

"Both."

Genevieve rubbed her face with her hands, her lips pinched tightly together. "I can't believe we haven't found them. Where the hell do we look now?"

Caspian pointed to the passageway ahead. "We keep going."

Hunter was still sniffing around the room, and he jumped on the bed, his head lowered as he sniffed the sheets. A snarl rumbled in the back of his throat, and he snapped at the sheets, grabbing them between his strong teeth and pulling them back. Before he could do anything else, an arm emerged, knocking him off the bed and sending him crashing into the wall.

Everyone whirled around, as Reuben yelled, "Shit!" One of them's here!"

Instantly everyone was ready, and Alex raced towards the bed, stake raised. Before he could get close, the vampire sprang up to the ceiling, its long, claw-like fingers grasping a wooden beam. It hung upside down, and still looked dazed, if that's what you could call it, struggling to open its eyes against the daytime pull of sleep. The struggle didn't stop its strength or viciousness, though. Its eyes were completely black, skin grey, and its teeth elongated and sharp, dried blood already crusted around its mouth.

For a second it seemed everyone was frozen in shock, and then Reuben and Ben raised their water guns and blasted the vampire. It screamed as its skin blistered, but it barely slowed it down. It dropped to the floor and charged Reuben.

Before he could take more than a few paces, Hunter leapt towards it, jaws wide. The vampire raised its arms, stopping Hunter from reaching its throat, and he bit hard on the vampire's arm instead, his weight carrying them both to the floor.

With superhuman strength, the vampire tossed Hunter aside, though Hunter took a good chunk of its arm with him.

Once again the vampire sprang to its feet, but a powerful blast of magic swept it back against the wall and pinned it there.

Half a dozen stakes were raised, ready to attack, but Dylan was closest, and he charged, leaping over the piles of bones and driving the stake into its chest. The vampire roared, the noise terrifying. The stake was only partway in.

Dylan looked around wildly, desperate for something to hammer the stake in with as the vampire struggled to break free, but instantly every single witch sent a wave of magic that pushed the stake home with such force it went straight through its chest and cracked the wall behind it.

The vampire went limp, but Alex took the sword from El's hand and decapitated the body, as well. "Just making sure," he said, grimacing.

The room fell silent, and then Reuben quipped, "Holy shit. Who would have thought this lurked beneath West Haven?"

"Is everyone all right?" Genevieve asked, arms still raised and magic dancing at the tips of her fingers.

She was answered by groans and nods, but Caspian and Alex were silent, both of them standing at the entrance to the passage on the other side of the room. Alex turned, his finger to his lips gesturing silence, and Caspian sent half a dozen witch lights ahead, illuminating another narrow passage.

They all listened, and Hunter padded forward, sniffing the air.

After a minute of absolute silence, Alex said, "I think we're okay. The others aren't here. Hunter?"

Hunter looked at them and gave what could only be interpreted as a nod, and then he padded forward again, ears pricked.

"I think we should get out of here," Jasper said, looking worriedly at the others. "His death may have alerted the others, and they could be on the way right now."

"But we may not have the opportunity to come down here again," Caspian pointed out. "Let's press on, at least see what's down here. We have the chance to end this. *Tonight.*"

He was right, and everyone knew it, but nobody liked the idea.

He marched on regardless, Alex at his side, as Hunter led the way, and they hurried behind him, their footsteps echoing around them.

The passage was narrow, carved out of natural rock, the ground a mixture of earth and sharp stones. After a few minutes they came across a ladder leading up to a heavy metal door.

"Let me," Reuben said. He clambered up and inched the hatch open, allowing a sliver of dim light to illuminate his features. "We're in the wood behind the garden. I'm going out."

Alex leapt onto the ladder. "I'm going, too."

Avery followed, eager to see where it led, Genevieve right behind her. They emerged into undergrowth, trees growing closely around them, the ground speckled with snow and thick with leaves and rotting vegetation.

Reuben stood nearby, peering through the bare tangle of branches. "This is a natural dell," he said. "Kids might use it for a camp, but probably not in years."

Avery walked over to his side, and squinted through the trees, noting that there was nothing else in sight. "This was how he hunted then. No one would find him in here."

Snow was still falling, and it was almost fully dark.

"Damn it," Genevieve said, hands balled at her sides. "Let's get back inside. There's nothing else we can do here."

The group was arguing when they joined them, Jasper annoyed. "It would be madness to continue. We have no idea how long this passage is, or how many vampires we may find at the end of it. There are definitely two, and one is older and much stronger than the other."

"Agreed," El said, raising her sword and watching the white flame flicker along its blade. "As much as I want to finish this, when we encountered them the other night at the docks, they were too strong for us. We got away only because Avery got the upper hand."

Avery nodded. "El's right—I was lucky."

Caspian glared at her. "But there are more of us now! This is our chance."

Genevieve intervened. "Not our only chance. The entrance above means we don't need the house. We could come back tomorrow in the daylight."

Caspian's expression was bleak. "And what if there are more deaths tonight?"

She looked away, her expression conflicted, and Avery knew exactly what she was thinking. As much as none of them wanted to continue now that it was dark, Caspian had a point. She'd never forgive herself if someone else died, and from her quick glance at the others, despite their misgivings, she knew they thought the same.

But Genevieve was their coven lead, and she didn't want to argue with her again.

Fortunately, Alex was prepared to. "I hate to agree with Caspian, but he's right. We have the chance to end this. Now."

Caspian glanced at him with the barest flicker of appreciation, and maybe annoyance.

Reuben added his support. "I agree. Those who don't want to come should leave now. I won't hold it against anyone. Especially you three," he said, looking at Cassie, Ben, and Dylan.

"Not a chance," Dylan said, squaring up to him. "I staked the last one, didn't I?"

Reuben high-fived him. "Yes, you did!"

"I'm staying, too," Cassie said, dropping her shoulders as if preparing for a fight. "Don't you dare tell me to go!"

"Genevieve?" Caspian said softly. "I know you don't want to lose anyone like Rasmus did last time, but we have to move, now!"

Hunter changed into human form, completely naked but seemingly impermeable to the biting cold around them. "I got a good scent of Lupescu.

It was the strongest scent in there, which makes sense. I can smell him now—it's faint, but there. I'll lead you straight to him."

Genevieve smacked her hand against the earth wall, a wave of magic punching a hole into it. "Damn it! When did you get to be so rational, Caspian?" She turned to the others. "All right. Let's do this. Who wants to leave?"

Jasper sighed. "If you insist on this madness, of course I'm coming."

Everyone nodded, resolute, and Genevieve sighed. "Let's get on with this then, before we freeze to death down here."

22

Hunter turned back into a wolf and led the way again.

El was just behind Avery. "I don't like this. It's too narrow. If anything happens, those at the front are on their own."

"As are those at the back," Avery said softly. She could see Ben ahead, but not the other paranormal investigators, and she looked back over her shoulder, hoping it wasn't one of them, but she couldn't quite see. She raised her voice. "Who's at the end?"

"I am," Jasper called back. "All good so far."

"Thanks," she shouted, relieved, and then fell silent, concentrating on the path ahead.

After endless minutes they reached an intersection with three passages running off in different directions, and they waited while Hunter sniffed the ground. Avery was now completely disorientated. She had no idea where they were, or what direction they were heading in. After a moment, Hunter headed down the right-hand passage, and Eve marked their path with a streak of white luminescence against the wall. "Just in case," she said to no one in particular.

Several more times they encountered other passages, some wider than others, some with the distinct stench of sewage emanating from them. They would never have done this without Hunter, Avery reflected. His nose was saving them hours.

As they hesitated for a moment at another crossroads while Hunter sniffed the ground, they heard a skitter of footsteps behind them that immediately stopped when they fell silent. They turned as one.

We're going to die down here.

A blast of fire hurtled down the passage from the direction they had come from, briefly illuminating the people behind her, and Jasper yelled. "Get a bloody move on!"

Hunter howled and raced ahead, and they ran, too. A scream echoed around them, and Avery stopped to look behind her. El was sprinting away. *Shit.* Avery followed, and almost stumbled over figures wrestling on the ground.

Jasper was pinned down by Bethany, her teeth inches from Jasper's throat. Cassie clung onto her back, desperately trying to pull Bethany's head away. Eve was lying dazed on the floor, a cut on her head, and Dylan was nowhere in sight.

"Move!" El yelled at Cassie, and with a well-timed blast of magic, propelled her away from the vampire. Bethany's head lifted, her lips peeling back as she snarled at El, fire blazing behind black eyes. El bounded forward, sword ready, and sliced with clinical precision, beheading Bethany in an instant.

The body slumped on Jasper, and thick, viscous blood pumped over him, and spattered across the wall as Bethany's head rolled away into darkness.

"Where's Dylan?" Avery yelled. She threw up another witch light, showing Cassie, insensible against the wall, and Dylan another few feet beyond.

Leaving El to help Jasper to his feet, she raced to Dylan's side, her heart pounding in her chest. *Please be alive.*

His left arm was lying at an odd angle, but his neck was unmarked, and he was still breathing. She heard running from the other direction, and saw Alex and Reuben in the dim light.

"Avery!" Alex shouted.

"I'm okay," she called back. "Dylan's unconscious and I think his arm's broken, but he's alive."

Avery held her hand against his head, feeling for bumps or cuts. She whispered a healing spell that Briar had taught her, and Dylan's eyes flickered open.

He groaned. "What the hell…"

"Careful," she warned him as he sat up.

"Bollocks, my arm." He cradled it, stiffly.

"You need to leave."

She turned and saw El helping Cassie to her feet, Eve and Jasper already standing.

"What the fuck happened?" Reuben asked, walking over to examine Bethany's head.

"She snuck up on us, even through the fire ball," Jasper explained. "She moved too quickly, and took me down first, but Dylan jumped on her, and she threw him like he was nothing. She leapt around the walls like a damn spider."

"Where are the others?" Avery asked, looking behind Alex and Reuben.

"We told them to go on. We'll catch up."

"They won't," Avery said. "Everyone's injured, especially Dylan."

"I'll be fine," Eve reassured them. She brought her hand to her cheek and wiped away the blood, healing the cut as she did so.

"But Dylan won't be. Or Cassie. She smacked her head against the wall, too."

"Sorry," El said to Cassie. "My fault."

She grimaced. "At least I still have my head. Poor Bethany. What an end."

El wiped her sword on a cloth from her pack. "Better dead than killing us."

Jasper watched Avery help Dylan to his feet. "I'll escort them out, and get Dylan to a hospital."

"No!" he protested weakly.

Cassie looked defeated. "You can't fight like this. Neither can I—I can barely focus."

"That settles it, we're going." Jasper looked at the other witches apologetically. "I'm sorry; we'll leave you short-handed."

Avery brushed off his concerns. "There are still plenty of us, but one of us needs to go with you. What if you're attacked by other vampires? You'll all die."

"I'll go with them," Eve said decisively. "You guys should stick together. I have a plan, but it will get hot. I'll surround us with fire for the entire journey. If I make it big enough on either side, they won't be able to penetrate that."

Alex frowned, looking between her and Jasper. "It's a long way to hold that spell. You'll be exhausted."

"But we'll live, hopefully."

Avery hugged Eve. "Stay safe, and we'll see you soon."

The White Haven witches watched them walk a safe distance away and fire ignite around them, and then they ran to catch up with the others.

***

The group raced through the twisting passageways, and after a few minutes heard shouting and the familiar blasts of magic.

"What now!" Alex said, sprinting ahead.

They burst into a low-roofed cave, and Avery's feet immediately crunched into old bones that littered the floor. At least a dozen vampires were fighting with the three witches, the wolf, and Ben. It was mayhem, and without hesitation, they dived in to help.

Genevieve, Caspian, and Ben, were back to back, fighting furiously, battling either hand to hand or with magic. Ben kicked, punched and rolled to defend himself, swinging an axe viciously as one vampire tried to get close enough to take him down. Another scuttled over from above, clinging to the roof like a spider, and Avery picked it up in a flurry of wind, smacking it repeatedly against the far wall until it fell, unconscious. Alex readied his stake and ran to it, plunging it into his chest. Avery directed the wind to another vampire and smacked it so hard against the cave walls that it was almost swallowed by them. Ben threw his axe and it embedded into its chest with a *thunk*. But it wasn't enough, and it struggled to break free, ripping the axe out. But Ben hadn't finished. While Avery still had it pinned to the wall, Ben grabbed a stake and drove it into the vampire's chest, then picked up a heavy rock and smacked the stake, forcing it deeper. The vampire fell to the floor, dead.

At the same time, Briar had opened the earth beneath a vampire and it sank into it, desperately trying to free itself, but it was waist-deep, and although its arms clawed wildly, it couldn't move. Hunter raced forward, and ripped out its throat, and then followed that up by ripping her head off.

El and Reuben were together, both wielding swords as they attacked two vampires with grace, severing limbs as they went, but although that slowed the attack, it didn't stop them. The witches were quick, but the vampires were quicker.

One vampire had Caspian cornered, and he was losing the fight. The vampire's long, talon-like nails had sliced Caspian's chest open, and the smell of blood enraged it. Just as the creature was about to sink its teeth into Caspian's neck, Caspian disappeared in a whirl of Air, appearing right behind it, and he plunged his stake through its back, into its heart.

Genevieve was fighting her own battle, fending off a vampire with fire streaming from her fingers.

They must have found their main cave.

"Ben!" Avery yelled, "Did you bring the spells I gave you?"

Ben was busy fighting yet another vampire. He ducked, swung his axe, missed, and rolled to face the vampire again. "The bag at the side," he yelled back breathlessly.

Avery turned swiftly, spotting his rucksack near the entrance. Only days ago she had made the sunlight spell. She hoped they'd brought it, and she hoped it would work.

She was steps from the bag when a vampire attacked from above, lifting her off her feet, its teeth inches from her neck. Avery was so annoyed, she didn't hesitate. She punched him and his head snapped back, and then she pressed her hand into his ice-cold skin and burned through his flesh, hearing it sear and pop beneath her fingers as its eyeballs exploded. He screamed and dropped her, and she used Air to cushion her fall. The vampire fell at her feet, blind and vulnerable, and she plunged the stake through its heart, and set fire to it at the same time.

Avery ran to the bag, fumbling through the contents, vaguely aware of the mayhem around her. She found bottle after bottle and cast them aside, until she found the right one—a black bottle, sealed with yellow wax.

She needed to be in the middle of the room for the best effect, and she used wind to lift her to the roof, rising above the carnage. She uttered the simple words of the spell and smashed the glass against the roof.

A wave of energy knocked her to the ground as sunlight streamed through the cave, bringing with it screams, fire, and then silence. For a few more moments the sunlight warmed them, cleansing the cave of vampires, and then it was gone, leaving them with only the pale, white witch light.

Within seconds hundreds of candles were burning as someone's magic lit them, and the witches, wolf, and Ben stumbled to their feet. Avery could see Alex, covered in blood, but he was standing, and seemed otherwise okay.

"What the hell was that?" Genevieve asked. Her clothes smoked from the fire spells she had been casting.

"My sunlight spell. It worked better than I thought," Avery confessed.

Reuben looked around warily. "Let's talk about that later, and instead get the hell out of here."

Caspian stumbled, and Briar ran to him. "You've lost a lot of blood."

"I'll live," he said. "I'm just dizzy." Blood poured from the wound down his chest, and he winced. "It's burning."

As Briar pressed her hand to it, Hunter growled softly at her side, and she glanced at him. "Behave." He sat and watched, his eyes boring into Caspian.

Avery surveyed the room. "How many do you think there were here?"

"Probably a dozen." Genevieve shrugged. "More or less. I didn't see Lupescu, though."

Reuben twirled a sword like a Samurai and looked appreciatively at El. "But Bethany's dead. El killed her."

Genevieve suddenly realised the others weren't there and she looked panic-stricken. "Where is everyone else?"

Avery tried to reassure her, hoping that what she was about to say was true. "They're okay. Dylan's broken his arm, and there were some minor head injuries, but hopefully they're all safe now. We need to get out, too." She looked around for the closest exit, but there were too many; at least half a dozen passageways left the cave.

"We'll go back the way we came," Alex said, already striding towards it. "Quick, in case reinforcements come back."

***

It was relief to be out of the dark, narrow tunnels, although the house felt strange, somehow expectant. They shut the hidden panel, and left the tower room as they had found it, and after gathering their gear, they congregated in the hallway, ready to head their separate ways.

"Wait," Reuben said, halting by a small door beneath the stairs. "I need to show you the cellar, Alex. I'm pretty sure it's all hooey and no doey, but I'd like your opinion."

Alex nodded, weariness etched across his face. "Sure. Let's make this quick."

Reuben turned on the overhead light, and led them down the stairs to a long cellar, lined with brick. Dozens of candles lined the edges of the room, and in the centre of the floor, drawn in chalk, was a rudimentary series of sigils and signs within a circle. The witches walked around it, and Alex crouched, examining some of the signs carefully. Caspian echoed his movements, and Avery remembered that Caspian's family also had a history of demon raising and necromancy, particularly Alicia.

Alex looked up and grinned. "This is useless. A façade."

"I agree," Caspian said, rising to his feet. "It looks pretty, but it has no power. Idiot."

Alex stood, too. "It's a worrying occupation, but essentially harmless."

Reuben looked relieved. "Great. Just wanted to check."

They filed back upstairs, Avery sure her legs would collapse beneath her at any point.

"We need another plan of attack," Genevieve said, her face grim, once they were in the hall again. "Lupescu is still out there. Have we heard from the others?"

Avery nodded. "I spoke to Eve; she's on her way home."

Ben held his phone. "Cassie texted. They're at the hospital. I'll meet them there."

"Maybe have a shower first," Reuben suggested, gesturing at his clothes.

They were all covered in blood.

"Right, shower."

Relief flooded Genevieve's face. "Good. Let's go home, I'm too tired to think now. I need space, and I want to see my kids."

Briar's expression was gentle as she said, "I think we all need space to think. This feels like a house of horrors. I don't know how Rupert and Charlotte can bear to live here."

"Because they don't know what's under them," Alex answered. "I hope. Let's talk again tomorrow."

"It's the solstice tomorrow," El noted. "The longest night of the year."

"Let's hope that's not bad news for us," Caspian said, clutching his coat to his chest.

Briar noted his wince. "Who can heal you?"

"My sister has passable skills. Thanks, Briar."

"Even so, come and see me tomorrow," she insisted. "I'm better than passable."

He nodded, and as Ben locked up, they called their goodbyes.

Avery turned to watch the house as Alex drove away. Within seconds, it was swallowed by the swirling snow, as if wrapping itself in its secrets once again.

23

The Wayward Son was a welcome haven of warmth, cheer, and noise, after a tense journey in heavy snow on hazardous roads. Only the use of magic had helped them get back so quickly.

Once the witches had arrived in White Haven they headed home to shower, and then met in the quiet backroom that overlooked the courtyard. No one wanted to be alone, needing the normality of a crowded pub to cheer them up. And besides, it was still only 9:00pm. They had been in the tunnels under the house for all of four hours, although Avery felt like it had been much longer.

Avery sipped a glass of wine while she looked out of the window. The snow was still falling thickly, which was unusual so close to the coast. She would have enjoyed it, had she not been so worried. She caught her reflection in the glass and wondered how she could look so tired and still be awake. She ran her hand through her hair, trying to look more presentable.

"Cheer up," El said, chinking her glass. "At least we found out a lot more today, and managed to kill some vamps."

Avery turned to face her, amazed that El could still look so cheerful after all they had seen today. Her long, blonde hair was swept up into a messy knot on her head, and her red lipstick was bright against her pale face. "How come you always look so good?" Avery asked her. "Even when we're fighting vampires, you manage to look cool."

El winked. "It's a skill. Besides, you always look pretty good yourself. So do you, Briar." She nodded to Briar who sat next to her, her dark hair tumbling about her face. She was looking particularly pretty tonight, and Avery was sure she knew why. El continued. "Stop changing the subject."

Avery sighed. "Sorry. I'm trying to distract myself from that horror show we've just experienced."

"So am I. Wine helps." She looked behind her to where they could see Reuben at the bar, ordering food. "So does he, even with his stupid water gun."

Briar laughed. "It is stupid, but it works."

"True dat," El said, nodding. "And unfortunately, I'm sure he'll have to use it again."

"We need to tell Newton what we found," Avery pointed out. "There's nothing he can do, but even so."

"There's plenty he can do," Briar said, frowning. "They need to collect all those bones down there and give them a proper burial."

"Not yet he can't," El replied. "It means letting Rupert know what we've found, and we can't let that happen yet. We have no idea whose side he's on, or what he's prepared to do. Finding that necromancy stuff was weird."

The arrival of Reuben, Alex, and Hunter interrupted them, and they all sat down with fresh pints. Alex sat next to Avery, nudging her arm. "Cheer up."

"That's what El said. I can't help it. Lupescu is still running around, and we have no idea where he is."

"I can rip his throat out," Hunter said nonchalantly. "I've got Lupescu's scent now. It will give me great pleasure to hunt him down."

"It's a bit weird that he's called Lupescu," Reuben said. "Is that something wolfy?"

Hunter shrugged. "Maybe. But it's just a name. He sure didn't smell of wolf—just death and rotting flesh." He tapped his nose. "I'll be able to find him again, if we can narrow down where he is."

"How can you distinguish him from the other smells?"

"They may be vampires, but they all have their own distinct scent, beyond the decay."

Avery watched him thoughtfully. "Had he been in that cave?"

He nodded. "Yep, but it wasn't as strong in there as in his 'bedroom,'" he said, making air quotes. "We were close to the sea in that cave, though. I could smell it."

"Smugglers' caves again," Briar said. "As we thought."

Avery persisted. "But how do we find him?"

Reuben took a long drink of his beer, as if bracing himself. "We go back tomorrow, in the daylight, through the hatch in the woods. We don't need the house now."

Avery rubbed her face, annoyed with herself. "Of course. I'm so tired I'd almost forgotten it. Could you find it again?"

"Easily. But I think only we should go. Eve, Jasper, Dylan, Cassie, and Caspian, were injured, and Gen has three kids! She can't risk her life with them at home."

"I'm not sure she'd agree with you," Briar said, glaring at him. "She's our coven's High Priestess, and will want to be there. She saved us on Samhain."

"But that was different," he argued. "It was a huge coven spell. This is us hunting vampires. We have agreed we aren't going to try and bind Lupescu—who it seems is the lead vamp. We're going to kill him, and end this once and for all."

They were interrupted by the arrival of their food, and they fell silent for a moment, as Grace spent the next few minutes bringing their plates. The young blonde woman looked as knackered as Avery felt.

"Anything else, boss?" she asked Alex.

He smiled at her. "No thanks, Grace. You can start taking out the rubbish, if there's time."

She nodded and went back to the bar, and Avery's stomach growled with hunger. No wonder she was tired. She was starving. For a few minutes everyone was silent as they ate, and then Avery asked, "But what if there are *another* dozen vampires?"

"I don't think there are," Reuben said. "I'm pretty sure we killed all of them except Lupescu. It was only just after dark. They wouldn't have had time to leave."

El frowned. "Unless there was another base. There was the last time."

He shrugged. "Maybe, but the deaths and disappearance have all been local, which makes me think they are only based here."

"True," Alex agreed. "But I was wondering where they came from. There were more there than I was expecting."

"I was wondering that, too," Hunter said, pushing his plate away. "They've probably been accumulating over years of disappearances, probably from long ago. I think Felicity's spell not only sealed Lupescu, but all of his progeny. That would explain why they've been inactive for so long. And why they've woken so hungry that they've caused such obvious devastation."

Briar looked at him, admiringly. "Good point. There have only been a few recent deaths that we think have turned. The others are accounted for."

"But there have been quite a few disappearances," El reminded them. "They may not all be dead."

Reuben picked his glass up. "I need another pint. Anyone else?"

The others nodded, and Avery drained her wine. "Yes, please."

He headed back to the bar while they discussed their options, and then a scream sliced through the hum of conversation. Something fell with a *thump* into the courtyard, blood splattering against the windows. They all leapt up so quickly that their chairs scraped back and fell to the floor.

A woman's body lay on the ground of the courtyard, her limbs spread at unnatural angles, her throat ripped open. Blood spread around her, staining the snow. It was Grace.

Without hesitation, Hunter rose to his feet and headed to the back door.

Briar shouted, "Wait! What are you doing? You can't go out there. It's a crime scene! And you'll get hurt."

Hunter's eyes were already developing a molten yellow glow. "I'm going to find him. Wait here!" And then he was gone.

***

Newton stood over Grace's body, looking furious. The coroner was next to him, and they had a few hurried words before Grace was lifted up and carried out of the side gate. The place had been cordoned off by SOCO, and blue and red lights were flashing, making the blood on the floor look black against the snow. He looked up at them watching through the window, scowled, and turned to speak to Detective Moore.

The Wayward Son was now empty of everyone except the witches and the bar staff, and everyone was upset. The bar staff were sitting together by the fire in the main room, but the witches stayed by the courtyard window, watching the police. For a while, Alex had sat with his staff, but now he sat next to Avery again, looking white faced and grim, his hands clenched. He stared at the blood staining the snow, unmoving.

Avery sat next to him, squeezing his arm from time to time, and feeling ineffectual. She was horrified by the events of the last few hours, worried about Alex, and *very* worried about Hunter. She watched Briar's taut face, and the way she kept looking behind her to the door. El and Reuben sat apart from them, talking quietly, no doubt hatching some plan, but Avery was too tired to think coherently.

Eventually, Newton came in through the rear door, at the same time that Hunter reappeared through the main doors, and their eyes met across the pub, both of them glaring at each other. Newton glanced at Briar and back to Hunter, and his grim expression soured further. Avery noticed that Hunter didn't push it; he just sat next to Briar quietly.

"Where have you been?" Newton asked Hunter.

"I was out, trying to get his scent."

"Really? Because the victim's throat is ripped out, and wolves do that, don't they?"

A low snarl started in the back of Hunter's throat as he said, "I was sitting here when it happened. Everyone saw me. I went out afterwards."

Briar glared at Newton and clenched her fists, and the pot that the indoor plant in the corner was sitting in exploded in a shower of earth and plastic.

Avery spoke quickly before Briar could do anything else. "Newton, Hunter was sitting here with us. All of us were in here for at least 20 minutes, together, when that happened." She gestured to the window, swallowing hard, and then back to him, imploringly. "You *know* the vampire did this. She was dropped from a height."

"And how did she get to the roof?"

Alex looked up at him, finally. "I checked with Simon—he's the bar manager tonight. She was putting the rubbish out, as I asked her to do, heading out the kitchen door to load the rubbish bags in the main bin. It must have been waiting. It would have lifted her up before she could do anything." He paused. "This is my fault. If I hadn't asked her…" He trailed off, unable to finish his sentence.

Avery squeezed his hand. "Stop it, Alex. It's not your fault. It's Lupescu's."

"And who is Lupescu?" Newton asked, seething.

"The vampire we've been chasing. The one who has been responsible for the recent deaths—well, some of them," Avery explained.

"Nice to know you're keeping me in the loop," Newton said, glaring at them all as if they'd betrayed him.

Avery could feel her eyes filling with tears. "We only found out today, and it's been *a very long day*. Of course we would have told you."

Reuben butted in. "Newton, calm down. We'll tell you everything we know. We're not the enemy here."

Newton blinked, with what might have been reassurance, but then he turned to Hunter. "And when did *you* arrive?"

"Last night. Briar asked for my help." He tapped his nose. "This is good for tracking."

"And have you tracked it?"

"I found its scent a few roads down. It took me a while. It must have cut across the roofs. I followed him back out of town, and then lost him—he must be up high again."

Newton stared at him for a moment longer, and then addressed everyone. "I need statements from all of you, and the staff. Moore will take them."

"That's fine," Avery said. "And then is that it for tonight?"

"Yes," he said abruptly. "Where can I find you later?"

"I'll be here, with Alex."

Briar bristled with defiance. "I'll head home. Hunter is staying with me."

They were back to this now, were they? Avery thought, looking between them.

Newton could barely look at her. "And you, El?"

"We'll be at my flat," she answered.

"Fine. I'll be in touch." And then he turned and left, the door slamming behind him.

***

However, they didn't head home straight away. After they'd been interviewed, and Alex had locked the pub up and ensured the rest of his staff weren't travelling home alone, they all headed to Alex's flat to discuss their options.

As soon as they were through the door, Reuben said, "I need whiskey."

"In the cupboard next to the TV," Alex instructed him. He slumped in the armchair, immobile. "Make mine a large."

"Whiskey all around?" Reuben asked, as he reached for the bottle and glasses.

"Yes, please," Hunter said. He'd never been in Alex's flat before, and he paced around, curious.

Avery declined. "Not for me, thanks. I'll have more wine." She lit the fire and the lamps, and then peeked through the blinds. "It's still snowing. I haven't known it to fall this heavily for years. Do you think Lupescu will hunt again tonight?"

Briar stood next to her, watching the swirling snow. "I hope not, but I doubt snow will stop it."

El was curled in her favourite place on the sofa, her long legs tucked beneath her, and she stared into the fire, swirling the whiskey around the glass. "I feel guilty sitting here when it could be out there now, attacking others."

"Me too," Alex said, as he took his glass from Reuben. "Grace is dead, and more could be tonight, and what am I doing? Sitting here by a warm fire, drinking sodding whiskey." He downed it in one go and held it out again. "Another, please."

"Yes sir." Reuben topped him up, and then stood with his back to the fire, looking at them all. "Let's do something about it!"

El's head shot up. "Now?"

"Yes, why not?"

"Because there's a bloody great blizzard out there, and we can't see Lupescu. The night is *a vampire's* friend, not ours."

"Where's your sense of adventure, El?" he challenged.

"Buried beneath my sense of self-preservation!" She looked at him as if he'd gone mad.

"Just hear me out," he said, appealing to everyone. "I don't mean we run around like loonies chasing him in the snow. That *would* be suicide. And pointless. No, I suggest that we find Lupescu's lair and wait for it, and then when it comes back—*boom*! It will *not* be expecting that! It will think we're lying in terror in our beds."

Hunter had stopped pacing, and he leaned against the wall, sipping his drink. "I could smell Lupescu's scent particularly strongly in one of the tunnels leading away from the main cave, and there were very few other scents with it. I think that particular tunnel led to its very own den of horrors. Lupescu is the head vamp. The king doesn't slum it with the rest of them." His eyes developed a molten glow again. "And we smelt the sea, remember? I bet that his lair is close to the beach for easy access. I've got a very good sense of direction—it's a wolf thing. If you pull a map out, I can tell you which way we were moving underground, and I can narrow down where the cave will exit."

Reuben frowned. "You're saying that we don't have to use the hatch in the wood?"

Hunter shook his head. "No—I don't think so, anyway. Show me a map, I'll show you where we should exit, and you tell me what's there. We'll see if it's possible."

"Hold on," Avery said, confused. "It's probably not in its cave. It's out here, hunting innocent people. And, sorry to keep reminding you of this—it's *awake*! That means it's *dangerous*! What happened to the plan to stake it when it's asleep? And—" she added, "it could well move to another sleeping area. Our scent will be all over that main cave. It knows we've been there. That's why Grace is dead—for revenge!"

"Which is why we should act tonight," Reuben argued. "It could be heading back to grab its vampire backpack of death and escape right now!"

El rolled her eyes. "Now I know you've gone mad. *Vampire backpack of death*?" She looked at Briar and Avery. "When I said earlier that he keeps me sane, I was clearly delusional. Remind me of this in the future."

Reuben batted his eyelashes at her. "I keep you sane? That's so sweet."

"And wrong!" she retorted.

"Actually," Hunter said confidently, "I think Lupescu has no idea that we know where to find it. I sniffed out every single exit in that place, making sure to smear my wolfy scent everywhere. I even started down the wrong passage. I made it seem I was going the wrong way." He grinned, smugly. "And besides, it's arrogant. It underestimates us."

Talk about arrogant. If only Newton could see him, it would be all out war.

Alex was suddenly alert. "I like this idea. I like it a lot. I've got a big map here, somewhere. I know I have. It'll be better than using a phone." He jumped up and ran to the bookcase, shuffling through books and throwing a few on the floor. "Here!" He triumphantly pulled an A4, dog-eared folder out, filled with folded maps, and rustling through them produced one of the Cornish coast. "These belonged to my uncle." He headed to the table and spread it out, turning the overhead light on at the same time, and the others crowded around. He pointed to a spot on the map. "Madame Charron's, and there's the woodland where the hatch is."

They fell silent while Hunter studied the map, running his finger over it while muttering to himself.

Half of Avery wished that he wouldn't have a clue and they'd give up this ridiculous idea, and the other half wanted him to be absolutely sure so they could go and get this over with.

"Look," Hunter said, his finger stabbing the map. "There's the hatch. We continued on for a while, west, then we turned south, then east, then south, and east again. We smelt sewage in a few places here, which would make sense—it's right under the village. Then east, then south again, and that's where I think the main cave is." He jabbed the map emphatically.

Alex frowned. "It's closer to White Haven than I expected. Are you sure?"

"Yep. I'd bet my life on it."

"What's that squiggle under your finger?" Briar asked, as she leaned in closer.

"It's one of the old Second World War bunkers, called a pillbox, I think," Alex answered. "I didn't think those things had tunnels."

"What were they for?" El asked.

"They were part of the coastal defences that were erected when we thought the Germans were going to invade at the start of the war," he explained. "Pillboxes are concrete boxes dug into the ground with slits for weapons. Some were linked together by huge trenches for tanks, but they've long since been covered in weeds and undergrowth. You can't even see most of them anymore."

"Maybe when this one was constructed, it opened up an existing tunnel," Reuben suggested.

Alex nodded in excitement. "Maybe." He looked at Hunter. "You're sure about this?"

The molten glow fired in Hunter's eyes in anticipation. "Yes."

"Are you sure it wouldn't be safer to go through the tunnels?" Avery asked. "We know that way."

"But it's long. This will be quicker," Alex reasoned.

Briar looked worried. "But it will scent us, surely."

Reuben looked exasperated. "We're *witches*! We can disguise our scent, hide ourselves, and set up a trap. We're allowing ourselves to be frightened by this thing! We are stronger combined than Lupescu is." He looked around, appealing to them. "We have stakes, swords, fire, holy water, and magic. We have spells that can immobilise it! Come on! Are we witches or wimps?"

They looked at each other, slow smiles spreading.

Avery felt hopeful once more. "You're right, Reuben. Let's do this."

24

Avery's van crawled along the coastal route towards West Haven, the blizzard ensuring no one else was on the road, and shielding them from prying eyes.

Briar sat up front, next to Avery and Alex, and used magic to clear the snow from their immediate path, creating a pocket of calm in the storm, while Reuben and El erased their path from behind. Alex consulted the map.

"Are we close?" Avery asked, her hands gripping the wheel.

"I think so. GPS says we are, anyway."

Hunter called from the back of the van. "Let me out and I'll check."

Avery eased to the side of the road, and within seconds Hunter had shed his clothes and disappeared, a flurry of snow settling in the van as he left.

Reuben grinned at Briar. "I like your new boyfriend. He's very useful."

She glared at him. "He's not my boyfriend."

He sniggered. "Yeah, right. He thinks so, and so does Newton. He was *not* happy tonight."

"Well, Newton has no say in what I do," she shot back.

Reuben continued, undaunted. "In my opinion, you made the right choice. Newton will never really get his head around witchcraft, no matter how much he likes you, whereas Hunter doesn't give a crap." He smirked as he added, "And clearly can't keep his eyes off you."

El prodded him. "Reuben, behave."

"Just saying! I have a brotherly love for you, Briar. I approve."

"Thanks so much," Briar said, a dangerous edge to her voice.

He grinned again. "My pleasure."

"Could we maybe get back to our plan to kill a vampire?" Alex asked, watching with amusement from the front seat.

Reuben held his hands out, palms up. "We have a plan. Trust me."

They jumped as Hunter landed on the bonnet with a *thump*, and then ran around the side. "He's back," Avery said.

El opened the door and Hunter bounded in, shaking snow from his fur, and then changed back to human form.

"It's bloody cold out there, even with my wolf fur to keep me warm. But I found it. Another couple of hundred metres up the road."

"I don't know how you can find anything in this," Briar said, and even in the tension of the moment, Avery noticed how her eyes travelled across him almost hungrily.

"We have a lot of snow in Cumbria," he answered. "I'm used to it. But someone will have to wipe my prints…I went a few different places before I found it."

Reuben grabbed his backpack. "That will be me. Let's erase those first, and then we'll go."

They both disappeared for another few minutes, and the others waited in anxious silence. Then Reuben stuck his head in the back door. "Ready everyone?"

They nodded, and slipped out of the van and into the night, Avery casting a spell to hide the van, before following Hunter.

Avery's jacket was zipped up tight, and she wore a scarf and a hat, but even so it was bitterly cold. Hunter led them away from the road, a bubble of stillness around them as Briar kept the snow away, and Reuben erased their tracks from behind.

It was hard going despite their magic, and they slipped and stumbled through the deep snow. Avery could hear the sea, the waves crashing onto the beach and the cliffs somewhere beyond them, but she couldn't smell it. The snow blanketed everything. After a few minutes they passed through some scrubby bushes, bent over by years of wind, and stumbled into a ditch. A low, concrete wall appeared in front of them, cracked and pock-marked.

Hunter led them around the small building. The walls were only a few feet high, and at intervals Avery could see long, dark slits in the concrete. They must have been for the lookouts and their guns. The ground dropped as they reached the other side, and a rotten wooden door appeared, partially open. Inside it was pitch black, and a musty, sour smell escaped from it.

Hunter slipped inside and they followed him. Avery hesitated a moment, watching Reuben as he wiped their prints, the snow smoothing under his magic, and then she slipped inside, too, Reuben behind her.

A witch light hung in the air, revealing cracked walls and chunks of concrete on the broken floor beneath them where weeds were pushing through. At the rear of the small room, a black hole yawned in the ground, and Hunter sniffed at its edges, Alex next to him.

Hunter changed back to human form as he crouched next to the opening, shivering in the cold, and once again Avery tried to ignore the fact that he was completely naked. "This is it. The scent is really strong here, only hours old. But I'm pretty sure Lupescu's not here."

Alex nodded. "Good. Are we covered outside?"

Reuben nodded. "All trace has gone, including our scent. Briar will take over in here—she's better with Earth spells."

Briar was already taking her shoes off and putting them in her backpack. "I'm ready."

"Won't your feet freeze?" Avery asked, worried.

"The Earth generates her warmth for me," Briar reassured her. "Go on. I'll be right behind you."

Alex threw another witch light into the hole, revealing a metal ladder set into the wall. It led to a brick-walled room beneath the bunker, but a passageway went out of it on their right and left, running parallel with the coast.

"Was this part of the defences?" El asked.

"Must have been," Alex said. "Storage for weapons, I guess. They must have dug into the tunnel that was already here. Smugglers' tunnels, I bet. They probably link caves to cellars. Like at your place, Reuben."

Reuben nodded in agreement. "This place never ceases to surprise me."

Hunter, already a wolf again, was sniffing around the passage entrances, and led them down the passage heading west. It sloped downwards, and the lower they went, the louder the sound of the sea became, until suddenly the tunnel ended in a small cave.

The ground was a mix of sand, earth and rock, but the roof was high, disappearing into utter blackness. The walls were made of rock, except for the side closest to the sea, which was a jumbled mass of earth and huge boulders of rock with the occasional tree roots thrusting their way through. Another tunnel headed north, away from the coast. But most importantly, the cave had bones in it, blankets on the floor, the remnants of a fire, candles, and the limp but unmistakable form of a teenage girl against the far wall.

Hunter was already sniffing her gently, and Avery ran over and felt her pulse. "She's alive, but only just." Puncture marks scarred her neck, and she was thin and pale. "We need to get her out of here."

"Not yet," Alex said. "Lupescu will know. We have to just try and keep her out of the fight."

Briar pointed to the mass of boulders and fallen debris. "A cliff collapse. This place has probably been hidden for well over a century."

El had already unsheathed her sword. "What now? There aren't many places to hide in here."

Reuben pointed upwards. "There are natural cracks in the rock face…some of them look pretty big. A couple of us can hide in them. The rest can hide down the tunnel."

Alex nodded. "I want to check down there, make sure nothing else is lurking behind us while you investigate the cave."

"I'll come, too," Avery said.

She followed Alex down the narrow passage, which was sculpted by water and difficult to navigate. They had to crouch and wiggle through in places, and Avery hated it. She felt suffocated, and for one horrible moment, thought she was going to be trapped forever. Then it opened out into the main cave they had found earlier that day; it already seemed like a lifetime ago. They spent a few minutes exploring it thoroughly before Alex said, "I think we're good. You?"

"Yep, all good. That's one win for us."

They squeezed back through the narrow tunnel again, and Avery turned to Alex at the entrance to the Lupescu's lair. "Once we cast the shadow spell we'll be completely invisible, but I'm worried we won't have a good view of Lupescu until he's in the middle of the cave."

"But we will," Reuben noted from above their heads. "I'll see it the moment it arrives."

"And once it's in," El said, from the other side of the cave, "I'll seal the tunnel behind it."

Avery looked up to see her lying in another natural rock crevice, almost invisible in the shadows.

Alex still looked worried, but he said, "All right. Where will you be, Briar?"

She stood next to the rock fall. "I'll pull some of this earth and plant debris around me. There's room within the gaps between these boulders…enough for Hunter, too."

"So now we just have to wait," Reuben called down.

"Take your places, and I'll erase our scent again. But we could be waiting some time," Briar cautioned.

"So be it," Alex said. "It will be worth it. Good luck everyone—and let's stick to the plan!"

***

Once the lights were extinguished, the cave was pitch black. Avery stood immobile for what seemed like an age. She felt utterly alone. The shadow spell was so effective that even though Alex was only a short distance away, she couldn't feel him at all. She started to get anxious, and willed herself to complete stillness, using her magic to help keep her warm. Just when she began to think Lupescu would never arrive and they'd got everything wrong, she heard a noise.

It was the sound of footsteps, slow and deliberate. And then they stopped for a moment, and Avery could sense its doubt and caution. She willed it onwards, and with relief heard the footsteps again. Then there was a *thump* as something hit the floor.

At the same time as the vampire started to light candles, Avery felt the gentle *whoosh* of magic as El placed a protection spell on the tunnel, sealing Lupescu inside. It walked into view in the centre of the cave, dragging a body behind it, then lit the fire, allowing Avery to see its cruel, hard face. The vamp was young looking, far different than the other night when its skin had looked grey and was wrapped tightly around its skull. The blood it had consumed must have plumped up its skin. Its hands were almost elegant, had they not ended with long, curved nails. Lupescu might have been handsome before he became a monster.

As planned, Briar opened the earth beneath its feet, swallowing Lupescu up to its chest, and the fire disappeared with it. It roared, its jaw opening unnaturally wide and showing sharp canines, stained with blood.

Avery was just saying her spell to immobilise it when with unexpected swiftness, it disappeared in a streak of smoke up towards the roof and the tiny vents in the rock.

They had talked about whether it could do this, and they had a plan just in case. Avery and Alex linked hands, sending another protection spell around the cave and sealing it with a rippling blue wave of magic. Lupescu veered course, flashing towards Reuben, who rolled out of his hiding place and sent out a shockwave of power, effectively blocking him again.

Meanwhile, Alex ran out, and he grabbed the unconscious young woman Lupescu had brought in, and pulled her out of the way.

Lupescu remained in smoke form, streaking around the cave, desperately seeking a way out.

Briar and Hunter stayed hidden, biding their time, as did El, but Avery sent a blast of wind around the cave in ever stronger circles, sweeping the vampire up, and herding it into the centre of the room. It landed on its feet, in physical form again, and, full of rage, launched itself at her so quickly that Avery had barely time to react. But Briar did, opening the earth beneath it again, and this time tree roots snaked towards it, grabbing its limbs and pinning them tight.

It smiled at Avery, a terrible, rictus grin that made it look more dead than alive, and spoke with a horribly wheezing, raspy voice that grated her nerves. "I can hear your heartbeat now, witch. You're scared, like they all are. I'll enjoy your blood." It pulled free of the roots, snapping them in seconds, and with superhuman strength, it leapt out of the earth, ready to attack. But she was ready for its speed this time, and didn't hesitate.

She commanded wind and using it like a giant hand she pinned the unnatural creature to the ground, watching it squirm. Roots again sprang from the earth, and Hunter raced across the cave, snarling, his jaws wide, at the same time as Alex raced towards it with his stake raised.

But again, Lupescu changed into smoke, evading all of them. It headed toward Reuben, who stood on a narrow ledge, watching it. Reuben again blasted it with a shield of magic, and Lupescu shied away. El rolled free of her hiding place and raised another magical shied, reducing the places that Lupescu could run to.

Briar stepped out of her hiding spot and placed a silver jar on the ground, covered in runes and sigils. She raised her arms in front of her and started the spell that would bring the vampire down into the jar they had prepared to seal it in. When they had discussed this earlier, they were pretty sure it wouldn't work. It would likely change again before it would risk that happening.

El and Alex closed in, Alex with his stake, and El with her raised sword. They edged closer and closer as the witches closed the protection circle, trapping the creature in an ever-smaller space. It flitted about like a crazed, dying bluebottle.

Briar's spell was working. Lupescu was being pulled towards the jar, the runes and sigils on it now blazing with a white light. Just as they thought they might trap it after all, it transformed into its physical form again, and Hunter launched, leaping metres across the floor and landing with a *thump* on the vampire's chest. He ripped into its skin and took a chunk out before Lupescu flung him off like he was a toy, but El was close now, and she swung with her sword, cutting off its right hand.

Lupescu was enraged, its eyes blood red with fury. It leapt to its feet, snarling and hissing, as black veins rose on its skin. But no matter how furious it was, it was clear that Lupescu was running out of options. Hunter jumped, and his huge paws landed on Lupescu's chest again, propelling it to the ground. But this time as they rolled, the vampire pinned Hunter to his chest with its right arm, and forced its left hand into Hunter's jaw, as if to rip it out. It happened in a split second, and for one heart stopping moment Avery froze, unsure of what to do. But Hunter was as unnaturally strong as the vampire, and he bit down hard on Lupescu's remaining hand and twisted as he leapt free, ripping the hand clean off and leaving a ragged stump. Lupescu fell awkwardly, unable to defend itself.

Alex seized his chance and ran in, plunging the stake into its chest, but it wasn't in deep enough to kill, and Avery used a blast of powerful wind to hammer it in.

Lupescu was motionless on its knees, looking helplessly down at the stake protruding from its chest, its arms ending in bloody stumps. It looked up at them, unnaturally still as it became clear there was no escape.

"Move!" El yelled at Alex, and as he stumbled backward, El swung the sword and cut Lupescu's head off, and its twitching body collapsed to the ground. She raised her hands and cast a fireball at it, consuming the corpse in flames.

The witches and Hunter stood back watching it burn until nothing was left.

"And so ends over a century of violence," Briar said softly, her left hand once again buried in Hunter's thick fur.

There was no quiet moment from Reuben; instead, he whooped. "See! I told you it would work."

El just looked at him. "Oh, shut up, bragger!"

The rest of them laughed as their remaining tension seeped away, and Hunter howled so loudly that Avery winced as her ears protested. And then a groan disturbed them.

Avery whirled around. It came from the young girl Lupescu had dragged into the cave. She ran to her side, Briar next to her, but before the girl could rouse further, Briar cast a spell that sent her to sleep. "Best she doesn't remember this," she said gently, before heading to the other girl.

Alex said, "We need to get these girls out. Looks like the other one is still unconscious."

"That's because she's almost dead," Briar said, her fingers feeling for her pulse. "I can stabilise her, but then we need to drop them somewhere close, where they can be taken to a hospital."

"Why don't we call Newton?" Avery suggested as she hefted her pack. "He can say he'd had an anonymous tip, and he can organise it."

"Great idea," Reuben agreed. "It means they can get into that other cave, too, and hopefully start to identify the bodies."

Briar finished healing the young girl, and as her breathing started to improve, she wrapped an old blanket around her. "She'll need a blood transfusion and lots of fluids, but that should keep her going."

As the witches gathered their things, Avery looked at the cave and the old bones littering the floor, and she shuddered. "I'm glad to see the back of this place. Can you imagine being one of his victims, dying here? Horrible."

"Well, we've ended it now," Alex said, wrapping his arm around her waist and pulling her to his side.

"Are we sure we've killed them all?" she asked, worried.

El walked to the tunnel entrance, ready to leave. "After the noise we made tonight, any other vampires would have rushed in. I'm sure we got the lot."

"If they have any sense, any survivors would have taken off, in my opinion," Reuben said. "But there's nothing we can do about that now."

Avery just looked at him. "Oh, thanks for your reassurance, Reuben!"

He winked. "My pleasure." And then he turned and led the way out of the cave.

When they exited the pillbox, they stopped with surprise. The storm was over; snow lay thick upon the ground, and it was utterly still and silent, other than the sound of the waves crashing onto the beach below them. A full moon was low on the horizon, and the snow sparkled in the light. Hunter howled again, and everything seemed perfect.

25

The solstice parade started at midday and the main road that ran through the centre of the town down to the harbour was lined with excited crowds that had been gathering for the last hour or so. Hundreds of children crowded to the front.

The deep snow, which was unusual in Cornwall, made White Haven postcard-picture perfect, and after the previous week of horror, it warmed Avery's soul. She'd given the shop an extra zing of magic, and it smelt of cinnamon and frankincense. The parade didn't pass by Happenstance Books, for which she was very grateful. Stan and the town council had insisted that the shops open for a few hours, and it would have been madness to close anyway, as it was a good day for business. Although, she had trouble keeping her eyes open. She didn't work well on three hours of sleep.

She'd opened the shop at ten, and Alex had decided to spend an hour or so with her, before he walked down to his pub. Sally wasn't due in for another hour, and Dan had gone to fetch hot chocolate. They were sitting behind the counter, each eating a bacon sandwich and idly chatting, when Stan bounded in. He couldn't have been happier, and he grinned at Avery and Alex with delight. "The gods have smiled on us today! Look at White Haven. It has never looked more magnificent!"

Magnificent was a stretch, but Avery smiled. "It is beautiful, Stan. I'll try and sneak out to see some of the parade. We're going to take it in turns once Dan and Sally are here."

Stan sidled closer to the counter, his voice low. "Is the snow anything to do with you two?"

Avery almost choked on her coffee, and Alex froze. "Us?" Avery said, shocked. "No! How can we make it snow?"

He wiggled his eyebrows. "You know. You have a certain something we've all grown to trust."

She was momentarily stunned into silence and glanced nervously at Alex, but she had to answer his expectant look. "I have many skills, Stan, but I can't make it snow."

"Neither can I," Alex said with a shrug, as if being asked if he could make snow was the most normal thing ever.

Stan's face fell slightly and then he smiled. "Oh, well. We all have our limitations, I suppose."

Avery tried not to laugh. "Are you in the parade?"

"Of course! I shan't be wearing my druid's robe today. Instead, I shall be the Oak King," he said proudly. "I have a cape of oak leaves, an oak crown, and an oak staff to carry."

"Who's the Holly King?" Alex asked.

In Celtic legend, the Oak King and Holly King vied to rule over the year's turn. The Oak King conquered the Holly King at the winter solstice and ruled until midsummer, when the Holly King is victorious and rules until midwinter.

"Phil from accounts. We'll have a bit of banter and fight before I declare victory. I can't wait!"

They laughed, and Avery said, "Fingers crossed I'm there in time to see that!"

"Anyway, I must run," Stan said. "I'm just doing my rounds before the parade begins. Your shop looks great." And with that he was off, leaving just as Dan arrived with their drinks.

Dan joined them behind the counter and sipped his drink, his eyes half closed with pleasure. "This is exceptional. All I need now are Sally's mince pies, and my morning will be complete." He was wearing another Christmas t-shirt, reading *Santa Does It Better*. "Now, would you two like to tell me why you look so awful?"

"We had a very busy night killing a vampire," Alex explained. "And day, actually. In fact, there was a lot of vampire killing all around."

"I love how you say that so casually," Dan said, raising an eyebrow. "Like it was just a regular Saturday for you."

"Yeah, right," Avery said, grimacing. "I hope we *never* have to do that again. Although, the way James was talking, it sounds as if vampires are not that uncommon in cities. They can stay there."

Alex grunted, his mouth full of sandwich. "James is full of surprises."

"And what about that Rupert guy?" Dan asked. "Is he something to worry about?"

"I don't think so." Avery pulled a stack of books from under the counter. "I phoned him this morning and told him he can come and get these."

Dan frowned and picked up the box-book. "You're letting him have them?"

Alex shrugged. "They're of no use to us, and to be honest, they belong with the house."

Avery agreed. "He won't be able to read what we can, anyway. There's hidden runic script in the box that he can't possibly see."

"You don't think he's a necromancer?"

"He'd like to be," Alex answered, "but I had a good look at the stuff in his cellar. It looks cool, but it's harmless. He's just a regular guy who's a bit obsessive over the occult. And a bit of a creep."

"A lot of a creep, actually," Avery corrected him. "But essentially harmless."

Alex grinned. "I'd love to see his face when he gets a visit from the police about the crypt under the house."

"Ha! Me too. How much will he love that?"

They were interrupted by the jingling of the bell by the door. Shadow strode in, dressed completely in black, which made the shine of her silvery hair stand out even more. Dan hadn't met her before, and his mouth gaped open.

Shadow was oblivious. She stood in the entrance looking around the shop for a moment, and then marched over to them. "You did not tell me that you had so many books!"

"It's a bookshop—of course I have lots of books!" Avery said, already irritated. Dan was still gaping at her. "Shadow, this is Dan, he's a friend and works here. Dan, Shadow."

She smiled at him, and a strange, otherworldly light seemed to shine from her. She held her hand out, and Dan stood and grasped it as if she was a queen. "Dan. So good to meet a friend of the witches." She was only a fraction shorter than him, and she leaned forward, as if she was going to sniff him. Dan leaned in, too, and Avery wondered if she needed to snap him out of the sort of trance he'd fallen in. "No, you are not a witch. Just human."

"Er, yes, just human," Dan stuttered. "And you are what, exactly?"

Alex seemed to be trying very hard not to laugh, so Avery intervened swiftly. "She's our new arrival, the fey from Samhain."

Dan stepped back in shock. "You're the fey from the Wild Hunt! The one who wants to find all the artefacts and get back to the Otherworld."

Shadow held a finger to her lips. "Our secret." Then she put her hands on her hips and said to Avery, "So, are you going to let me help with the night walker?"

Awkward. "Sorry, too late. It happened quicker than we thought, and we killed it last night."

"Mmm. How convenient. You don't trust me!"

Alex narrowed his eyes. "We don't know you. And you did try to kill us. It gives me trust issues."

She sighed in true drama queen fashion. "So long ago! And I told you, that was Herne's request. I'm a good soldier. Besides, that's over now. I'm going back to treasure seeking."

"To return home?" Avery asked.

"To try to. And to make some money. That's what I used to do."

Dan frowned and managed to speak. "You hunted treasure for a job?"

She wiggled her shoulders. "A sort of job. I teamed up with others occasionally. It could be lucrative. My friend, Bloodmoon, was very good at it."

Dan gaped again. "*Bloodmoon*? Is that the name of a person?"

"A fey," she corrected him. "One of the best thieves I know. In fact, you'll like this story—he helped your old king."

Avery was starting to wonder if Shadow had lost her mind. "What old king?"

"King Arthur. He was a king here, is that right?" They looked at her, baffled, but she carried on regardless. "Bloodmoon actually stole a Dragon Blood Jasper—one of *the* rarest and most expensive gemstones *ever*—from the private collection of one of *the* richest men in Dragon's Hollow for his cousin, Woodsmoke, his friend, Tom, and the displaced King Arthur, to help them break a curse. Now that's impressive!" She looked proud and took a moment to bask in Bloodmoon's glory. "Unfortunately, he's not here to help me now, but Gabe and the others said they can."

Dan held his hand up imperiously. "Wait! You said King Arthur. *The* King Arthur?"

"Your old king, so I understand, yes." She shrugged, in a what-of-it sort of way.

Now they were all looking at her like she was mad, but it was Dan who spoke first. "King Arthur is dead, and has been for well over a thousand years, if he even existed at all."

"Well, he's not dead now. He's well and truly alive in the Other. Now, can you show me the books you have? Avery said you could help." She turned and walked away. "Where do I look?"

Dan stared at Avery and Alex, and said quietly, "Are you sure she's sane? And why didn't you tell me she was so hot!" And then he vanished into the stacks, shouting, "This way, Shadow."

Avery looked at Alex. "*King Arthur*?"

"She's clearly nuts."

"And what about Dan? You'd have thought he'd have learnt his lesson after Nixie."

He looked at her, doe-eyed. "True love knows no bounds."

"You are so full of shit, Alex Bonneville."

"You have no romance in your soul."

Avery was tempted to throw her hot chocolate over him, but it was too good, so she changed the subject. "So, what now?"

He kissed her. "I'm going to the pub, but we're not opening today. I've asked all the staff to come in so I can talk to them about last night, and I'm going to try to speak to Grace's mother. I'm not looking forward to it."

Lupescu's last victim. Avery closed her eyes briefly in regret. "I hope it goes okay. I don't envy you that job."

His eyes darkened. "At least I can tell them it won't happen again."

She nodded. "I'll try and get hold of Newton. And I'd better phone Genevieve, too. All I managed to do was send a garbled text last night to her and Ben. See you at your place later, before we go to Reuben's?"

"Perfect."

He kissed her again, leaving her breathless, and she watched him saunter down the street, wishing they could stay in bed all day instead of having to work. She picked up the phone and started her round of calls, waving at Sally absently as she came in with more mince pies. Genevieve and Ben were predictably annoyed at missing the fight, and relieved at the same time. Genevieve was going to hold a coven meeting in the New Year to update everyone, but was planning on otherwise spending a quiet Christmas at home. Ben told her that Dylan was okay but had broken his arm, and Cassie had mild concussion. She then phoned Eve and Jasper to update them, and was about to call Newton, having left him until last, because she knew he was going to be the most difficult, when Caspian walked in, holding himself stiffly.

"You look sore," Avery told him.

He grimaced. "Never underestimate the sharp talons of a vampire."

"Have you come to see Briar?"

"Yes, she's right. She's much better at this than Estelle."

"I bet Estelle hated hearing that."

He allowed himself a small smile. "Yes, she did. I heard from Genevieve you killed Lupescu last night."

Avery had a flash of guilt that she'd forgotten to call him. "Wow. News does travel fast. You were next on my list to call."

He watched her for a moment. "I think you were mad to go with so few of you, but well done."

"You were injured, so we weren't going to ask you. It seemed quicker to just get on with it. It was Reuben's crazy idea."

He nodded. "Fair enough. Just be careful, Avery." He looked as if he were about to say more when Dan and Shadow arrived at the counter. Caspian's eyes widened as he looked at her, and then he looked quizzically at Avery. She nodded and introduced them, hesitating to announce he was a witch, but Shadow could tell.

The fey's sharp eyes appraised him. "You're the one who Gabe now works for."

"I am. I think we met briefly on the night of the Hunt. You created a lot of damage that night."

She smiled, but it didn't quite reach her eyes. "Herne's orders. That's over now."

His cool, calculating gaze appraised her and clearly found her wanting. "I hope so." He turned back to Avery. "More interesting company in White Haven. See you soon." And then he left, a cold draft swirling in his wake.

"He's a prickly one," Shadow said, dropping a pile of books onto the counter. "Powerful, too."

"Very," Avery agreed, as she started to charge the books. "Interesting selection you have here."

"Dan's been very helpful." She flashed him her biggest smile, and Dan grinned goofily back. She continued, "I have much to study before I start my hunt. I may need your help."

Avery considered her next words carefully. "If I can, I will, but I am very busy in White Haven. The Nephilim will be of far greater help I'm sure."

She pinned Avery under her intense stare. "Maybe. But they aren't witches. See you again soon."

Avery watched her leave, then looked at Dan and said, "Bollocks."

***

White Haven glistened in the winter sunshine. The main street was shut off from traffic, and crowds thronged the pavements. The sound of drumming filled the air as the parade made its way down to the harbour. The participants were dressed in all manner of strange costumes; the Holly King and Oak King led the way, but behind them were adults and children all dressed and masked as various woodland creatures, goblins, elves, and a man dressed up with huge antlers on his head—Herne, the winter king. He looked far less terrifying than the real one. Jugglers and fire-breathers strolled along the edges, and Avery could smell hot chestnuts and mulled wine from the various street stands that had been set up. She smiled and clapped in time with the drums, feeling the beat in her blood.

She watched for a short time before heading back to her shop, and was almost there when Newton fell into step beside her. He looked shattered. "I've been looking for you."

"I've been trying to call you," she explained.

"Can we have coffee before you go back to the shop?" he asked her. He pointed to a cafe on the opposite side of the road.

"Sure." She followed him in, and sat at a small table in the corner. He spent a couple of minutes ordering coffee and food and then he slumped into the opposite seat. He looked pale, his shirt was rumpled, and his hair was messy. "Long night?" she asked.

He grunted. "Exhausting. All those bones, and those two girls." He shook his head. "It will take weeks to go through. Probably more. The forensic team have barely started."

"But at least they are found now," she said, trying to comfort him. "That's a huge amount of cases you can close. All those people will be able to be buried properly, and all of their loved ones will know what happened to them."

"Thank you, again. And sorry about last night. I was angry."

"It's okay. You're allowed to be."

He rubbed his face. "I know this is a good thing, but it's been an exhausting night. It's been an exhausting few weeks, actually. Are you sure it's over?"

"Yes. We watched him burn, and the others—including Bethany." She filled him on the details of the night, and the history they had found out about the House of Spirits. "Some of those bones will be very old. Did you find the other room? The crypt with the smashed furniture?"

He nodded. "Only a few hours ago. I'm paying a visit to Rupert and Charlotte tomorrow. I know they aren't a part of this, but we have to interview them, anyway. And then of course, search the whole house."

"I bet Rupert will love it," Avery said thoughtfully. "But how will you explain the deaths?"

"Serial killer, probably. It seems to be my only recourse when these weird deaths happen—although, I have no idea who we'll blame it on." He paused while their coffees were delivered, and a huge plateful of English breakfast was placed in front of him. He had a few mouthfuls, and then asked, "How long's Hunter here for?"

Avery sighed. She knew he'd ask this. In fact, it was probably his only reason for wanting to see her. "I'm not sure, but he'll be here over Christmas, maybe longer. Why do you care? It's not like you and Briar are together."

He tensed slightly. "I know, but I like her. I don't want her to get hurt."

Avery wanted to throw something at him. "The only person who's been hurting her is *you*, Newton."

He glared at her. "That's bullshit."

"Is it? You like her, that's clear, but you can't get around the fact that she's a witch. You've admitted it yourself."

"I don't have a problem with witches. I'm sitting here with you, aren't I? You're my friend, so is Alex, Reuben, and El. I respect what you do. I helped you recover the grimoires!"

"I know that, and I know that you keep our abilities a secret. But you still struggle with the decisions we make sometimes—especially about the Nephilim. And that's okay. You're a detective. Your priorities are different from ours. But Briar is a witch, to her core, and you clearly can't handle that in someone who might be *more* than friend," she said abruptly. "So, she's moved on, to someone who can deal with that. He'll make her happy, so you need to get used to it." Newton grunted again and continued to eat, refusing to meet her eyes. "Newton, seriously, stop it. You can't have it both ways, with her waiting and waiting until you change your mind—which you will never do. If you want to keep her friendship, respect her decision."

He grunted again, and she finished drinking her coffee in silence. *Men!*

***

The full moon shone over Old Haven Church, and snow glistened around the old headstones spread across the cemetery.

The witches and Hunter sat around a brightly burning fire in the cleared space in front of the mausoleum steps, wrapped up in layers of jumpers, coats, and scarves. They had placed rugs, cushions, and fur blankets on the ground to sit on, and Avery sipped a mulled wine, heated with a spell. She smiled at Reuben. "This was a great idea."

"Thanks, Avery. I've been thinking about Gil a lot lately. He was with us on the summer solstice, when we were attacked by demons in your garden. Remember?"

"Of course. I don't think I'll ever forget it."

"Although I am trying to," Briar put in with a shudder. "I hope we don't have to face those again in the coming year."

El nodded. "It has been pretty eventful. Sad at times, but also good." She squeezed Reuben's arm. "At least this place feels much better than the last time we were here."

Instinctively, they all looked up and across to the wood at the rear of the grounds where Suzanna had summoned the Wild Hunt.

Hunter stretched his legs out, wiggling his toes in front of the fire. "The pack enjoyed that story!"

"And now you can tell them about vampires!" Briar said, smiling.

"You can tell them yourself," he said, with a cheeky grin.

"What do you mean?" she asked, and even in the firelight, Avery could see Briar's cheeks flushing.

"We have a wild party on New Years! In the Castlerigg Stone Circle. You have to come." He watched her, his eyes molten gold again, and not with anger this time. They challenged her to refuse.

"I might be able to spare a few days away from my shop," she said hesitantly.

"Good," he replied, and looked back into the fire, a ghost of a smile on his face.

Avery grinned at El across the fire, which she swiftly hid when Briar scowled at her. She decided to change the subject. "At least James is happier now—well, since Samhain."

"Have you seen him today?" Alex asked.

"No, but I'll try and see him tomorrow. I thought today would be too busy for him. At least he doesn't have to worry about vampires in White Haven any longer."

"None of us do."

"For now," Reuben added ominously. "We might have them again. I'm still sure there'll be another one or two out there."

"Preferably not half-starved, vengeful ones," El said grimly. "I wonder if Charlotte will be okay. Hopefully her neck will heal and her weird dreams will stop. I wonder why he didn't kill her."

"Convenience," Avery suggested. "For when you don't want to go on a killing spree for food."

Alex sighed. "Today was horrible for me. The bar staff are shaken up and upset. But Simon is a good manager, and Zee's been pretty good, too. I think his sheer size is a comfort. I can't help but wonder, if Zee had have been working last night whether that would have changed anything. If he'd have gone outside instead of Grace, Lupescu wouldn't have been able to kill him."

"You can't start the what-if thing," Briar told him. "That will take you down a rabbit hole you'll never get out of."

"Are you open tomorrow?" Hunter asked.

"Yeah, life goes on, and the staff need to get paid. We'll go to Grace's funeral, though."

"I'll come, too," Avery said, nudging him gently. "I have news. Shadow came to visit today. She's borrowed a load of books to start her artefact search. She's going to be trouble."

Reuben laughed. "Sounds fun to me."

"We can handle her," Alex said, wrapping his arm around Avery and pulling her to his side.

El agreed. "We can handle anything together."

"True," Avery murmured, looking around at her friends. Six months ago she wouldn't have dreamed that she'd be such close friends with all of them, and that she and Alex would be together. It had been quite the journey. Avery smiled, raising her glass to the group. "Here's to the next six months. Happy Solstice!"

CROSSROADS MAGIC

WHITE HAVEN WITCHES (BOOK 6)

TJ GREEN

1

A fire blazed brightly at the centre of the clearing, and figures weaved a dance around it as they passed candles between them. The light cast a warm, gentle glow on the faces of the participants, many of whom were laughing as they trod the well-known path in the centre of the woods.

It was midnight at Imbolc, and the entire Cornwall Coven was celebrating the festival together.

Avery was there with the White Haven witches, all of whom had travelled together to Rasmus's estate on the edge of Newquay. After the horrors of the vampire attacks before Christmas, they hadn't seen the coven since, so it was a chance to celebrate the festival and their victory over Lupescu, the Romanian vampire who had caused so much destruction only weeks before.

However, it was freezing cold. Imbolc fell on the second of February, and frost lay thick upon the ground. When the coven completed the circle, they stopped and turned to watch Genevieve, their High Priestess, raise her hands to the sky. She invoked the Goddess, giving thanks and asking for protection for the months to come, and then she turned to kiss Rasmus gently on each cheek, and handed him a besom broom. Rasmus accepted it with a small bow, and then walked around the circle, brushing it along the ground as he did so, symbolically chasing away the old in a cleansing ritual. Once completed, he gave it back to Genevieve, who invited the others to join in, and then there was a frenzied few minutes as they all grabbed their own brooms and repeated the ritual.

Avery laughed as she furiously swept the ground. It was an old rite, but fun, and the symbolic cleansing really did feel as if they were getting rid of the toxic time they had all experienced. *And at least the snow had gone*, she reflected, as she swept past Reuben and laughed even harder. He looked so out of place with a broom in his hands, but he participated with good grace, even though he had moaned about it on the way over.

When they all finally stopped, they were breathless and hot. Genevieve clapped her hands, her smile beatific, and called a halt to the proceedings. She said a few final words before lifting a chalice of wine from the altar next to her. "And now, it's time to eat and drink!" She gestured to the table on the far side of the clearing, filled with food, and with that the circle broke apart and they headed to fill their plates.

Avery fell into step next to Nate and Eve, the two witches who lived in St Ives on the north coast of Cornwall. Both were artistic and unconventional. Nate was dressed in scruffy combat trousers and an old flying jacket, and Eve had long dreads. "How have you been?" Avery asked them.

"Pretty good," Nate said. "Better than you, by the sound of things."

Avery shrugged. "At least I didn't get a head injury like Eve. Are you better now?" she asked her.

"I'm fine, thank you," Eve answered, with a rueful rub of her scalp. "It soon healed. It was scarier getting out of those tunnels surrounded by fire. I was more worried I'd burn us all. No more news of vampires though, I hope?"

They had all been worried that some vampires had escaped, but if they had, they'd been quiet, and there were no other disappearances or strange deaths that had been attributed to them. "No, fortunately, which is good because we now have a headstrong fey on our hands."

They arrived at the long table, and Avery filled her plate as Nate frowned. "Ah yes, the survivor from the Wild Hunt. I'm intrigued."

Avery laughed, or at least tried to laugh. "Her name is Shadow, and she's driving us mad, the Nephilim included. She's an absolute force of nature! She's using Dan, who works in my shop, as her own personal myth-ometer." She rolled her eyes. "He loves every minute of it. I guess it's good that someone does!"

Nate studied her for a moment. "Eve mentioned her to me, but what's Shadow trying to do? Get back to the Otherworld?"

"And treasure hunt at the same time. You know, find ancient artefacts and sell them for a high price."

"And will the Nephilim help her?"

"I think so. They're trying to find their way in our world, and to make money. They think this will be lucrative. And let's face it, they're supernatural creatures. They have a natural interest in this sort of thing."

Nate looked troubled, and Eve said, "Nate's worried, because he thinks she could find things that are best left hidden."

"You're probably right, Nate," Avery said, worry stirring within her again. "But there's little we can do to stop them. I think we'll just have to manage the consequences."

"But those consequences could be big," he pointed out. "Any black market for art, drugs, or guns will always attract the worst kind of people. A market for mythical objects won't be any different—except for maybe having supernatural buyers. She may even want to steal what's already been found for her own uses."

Avery had a sudden image of Shadow breaking into museums and raiding their displays. Nate was right. She could definitely see that happening.

"Although," Eve countered, "the Nephilim and Shadow are very capable of looking after themselves. If you ask me, anyone who takes them on would be an idiot."

Avery sighed. "True. An even better reason for us to remain on their good side."

Avery spent the next hour or two mingling with the other witches, glad of the chance to talk to Ulysses and Oswald, and then Jasper, Claudia, and a few others. The fire was now blazing, and they sat around it on old deck chairs and logs in an effort to keep warm. They were nearly ready to return to the warmth of Rasmus's house when Caspian arrived at her side. Caspian lived in Harecombe, the town next to White Haven, and like Avery was an elemental Air witch. His relationship with their coven had started badly, but over time things were improving.

"Avery," he murmured, his dark eyes appraising her. "How are you?"

"Pretty good," she replied. "How's your wound?" She was referring to the deep cut on his chest caused by a vampire.

He rubbed it absently. "Better now, thanks to Briar. It felt like it had poison in it for a while—maybe it had. Let's face it, we don't know much even now about vampires, do we?"

"No, and if I'm honest, I'd like to keep it that way." She remembered that Gabe was now working for Caspian. "How's it going with the Nephilim as security guards?"

"Good, but I'm not surprised. Gabe has a strong work ethic, and they're imposing. No one argues with them."

Avery was curious. "Your company doesn't work with occult goods, does it? Why did you want Gabe?"

"We hide enough of ourselves in everyday life, don't we? I thought it would be good to have honest conversations with as many people as possible. Life can be lonely otherwise." He held her gaze for a moment before returning back to the fire.

Avery knew Caspian seemed to have developed an interest in her, but she refused to be drawn in, instead deciding to tease him. "You need to find a girlfriend. You're a catch, surely, with your wealth and big house. I'd have thought you'd be battling them away."

"Is that all I am? Money?" he asked, his eyes narrowed.

Avery had been flippant, and certainly hadn't meant to cause offence, but this was a topic she wanted to steer clear of. "No, of course not. And anyone who is interested in only that clearly isn't worth your time."

"You don't care for money, do you?" he asked, watching her.

"Not particularly." Avery started to get annoyed. He was being a flirt, and she didn't like it. "And stop it, Caspian."

"Stop what?"

"You know what. I'm with Alex. I love Alex." As she said it, she glanced up and saw Alex across the fire, deep in conversation with Genevieve. As if he sensed her looking, he glanced her way and smiled, before turning away again.

Caspian stared at his feet. "I know."

Immediately, Avery felt terrible, which annoyed her even more. "Maybe you should turn your attention to someone who's free."

"But where's the fun in that?"

Now she knew he was baiting her. "I'll stop talking to you if you keep this up."

"Oh, please don't, we have so much fun!"

She was about to say something unpleasant, when she felt a tap on her shoulder, and she turned to see Reuben's large frame looming over her. "We're heading back to the house, and then home. Coming?"

"Sure," she said, grateful for the interruption, and swiftly rose to her feet. "See you soon, Caspian."

He nodded and turned back to the fire, and Avery fell into step beside her coven, feeling Alex's arm slide around her waist. Alex's strength was spirit-based, and he was able to banish demons and ghouls, and use his intuitiveness to scry, spirit-walk, and communicate with ghosts. He was also skilled with elemental Fire, and as an added bonus for Avery, he loved her, despite all her quirks.

Reuben and El, both tall and fair-haired, walked just a few steps ahead. Reuben was an elemental Water witch, who was still coming to grips with his powers after neglecting them for years. It had taken the death of his brother, Gil, to bring him back to magic. El was skilled with fire and metal work, wore lots of jewellery, and like Reuben, had several tattoos. Briar, the fifth member of their coven, was petite, with long dark hair, and a natural affinity for Earth magic and healing. She was a caring, gentle soul, who had just started a relationship with Hunter, the wolf-shifter who lived in Cumbria, and she was keeping very quiet about it.

Being with them brought Avery more pleasure than she could describe. She had resisted joining a coven for so long, but now these four amazing people were family. They completed her. She smiled and nestled against Alex, feeling a sudden flash of guilt about Caspian's behaviour, even though she hadn't done anything wrong.

"What's Caspian done?" he asked. It was as if he'd read her mind, and she loved him for it.

"Nothing, really. Just flirting, even though he knows it's useless."

A trace of annoyance flashed across Alex's face. "Doesn't stop him trying though, does it?"

Avery hugged him harder. "I ignore it, and so should you."

"I try. Don't worry, I'm not about to get violent."

He pulled her to a halt and kissed her, and Reuben grimaced as he glanced at them. "Oh, you two, get a room."

Alex flipped him off. "Sod off, Reuben."

Reuben just laughed, and El punched his arm. "Stop being naughty."

"You normally like it," he teased, as he increased his pace.

The house came into view, as did Rasmus, greeting them on the broad patio that stretched across the back of his old home. His place wasn't as old as Reuben's, and it was made of faded red brick rather than mellow stone, but it was eccentric, just like he was.

Avery broke away from Alex and went to his side, hugging him. "Thanks, Rasmus. It was great to finally be here and celebrate Imbolc with you. You have an amazing home."

Rasmus smiled, his old face dissolving into wrinkles. "Thank you, Avery. You're welcome anytime. Are you sure you don't want to stay? I have room."

When she'd first met him, Avery had thought him gruff and quite scary, but now she was incredibly fond of Rasmus, especially knowing now what she did of his past. "No, it won't take us long to get home. And besides, we all have to work in the morning." Newquay was on the north coast of Cornwall, and their trip to White Haven on the south coast would only take about 45 minutes.

Briar hugged Rasmus, too. "I'm sure after having to put up with us all, you'll be glad to have the place to yourself."

"I wouldn't offer if I didn't mean it," he remonstrated. He turned to Alex and gripped his proffered hand. "Alex, thank you. The White Haven witches have been a welcome addition to our coven."

"And we're glad to be part of it," Alex replied.

While the others talked, Avery looked back towards the trees, noting the feeling of peace and gentle magic that came from them. Rasmus's family and the Cornwall Coven had celebrated there for years, and the wood seemed to have absorbed the positive energy. A line of lanterns lit the way to the clearing, but the fire itself was lost to view. She was about to turn away when she felt a prickle run down her spine, as if she was being watched. She stared into the darkness and saw a figure standing a short distance away from the path, just at the edge of the wood. Avery blinked. She could have sworn the figure hadn't been there a second before. She stared on, waiting for whoever it was to come fully into view. It must be one of the other witches; although, it was odd that they wouldn't have followed the path. The undergrowth was thick in places.

The figure didn't move. Whoever it was just stood there, watching her. Avery could see a pale face, but it was impossible to tell if it was male or female. And then, as quickly as the person had appeared, the voyeur went. Avery squinted and blinked again. *Was she seeing things?*

"Are you okay?" Briar said to her, following her eye line. "What are you looking at?"

"I could have sworn I saw someone at the edge of the trees, but they've just vanished!"

Briar frowned. "It's dark, and the lanterns throw uneven light, or maybe it was one of the witches enjoying the solitude."

"Maybe." Avery finally turned away. "And it's late and I'm probably overtired."

But as they said their goodbyes and finally left, Avery couldn't help but look over her shoulder again, convinced that someone had been silently watching them all.

2

The sound of shouting, and the honking of horns broke the silence in Happenstance Books on Monday morning, and Avery groaned.

She hadn't slept well because her mind had buzzed with memories of their rites, and she sat behind the counter, nursing a hot coffee and a chocolate biscuit.

Dan headed to the shop window, grinning. "Yes, the circus has arrived!"

"What circus?"

"The Crossroads Circus!" He looked at her incredulous, as behind him a high-sided van drove down the road, large letters spelling the Crossroads Circus painted on the side. Behind it were a couple of outlandishly dressed performers, who ran up and down the street shouting loudly as they darted into shops with flyers, and handed them out to pedestrians.

A young woman burst into Happenstance Books, her hair a bright green, and wearing a skin tight green Lycra costume covered in leaves. She thrust some flyers into Dan's hands, and said, "The circus opens on Saturday! Come and see myths become real!" And then she left in a whirl of energy, leaving Dan looking after her appreciatively.

Avery groaned again. "What *is* the Crossroads Circus, and why should I be excited about it?"

Dan smacked his forehead with the palm of his hand. "Are you kidding? You must have heard of it!"

"Er, no," Avery admitted as she racked her brains trying to remember if she had. "Aren't you a bit old for one?"

"No one's too old for a circus, especially this one!" He placed the flyer in front of her and pointed at the text. "Look - The Crossroads Circus brings the old myths to life! The Green Man, the Raven King, giants, dryads, King Arthur, dragons, and much, much more!"

Avery was still perplexed. "Seriously, I have not heard about this."

Dan grabbed the local paper that was folded on the counter top, flicked through the pages and then placed it in front of Avery. The headline announced, "*The Crossroads Circus is coming to the supernatural home of Cornwall!*"

She almost spit her drink out. "Where's the supernatural home of Cornwall? Is that supposed to be here? White Haven?"

"Where else, my dear witch, descendant of the famous Helena, who most likely orchestrated the Walk of the Spirits?" he answered with a smirk. "We're on the map now."

Avery skim read the rest of the article, which described how England's most famous circus of myth and magic had worked its way down the country wowing visitors and building an impressive reputation.

She looked at him, slack jawed. "Well, I guess that does sound impressive. I must admit I've been avoiding the news lately. I've been trying to avoid all that speculation about the deaths, bones, and vampires." As much as she wanted it to, the news would not stop reporting on the police finding the hidden caves beneath West Haven, and the link to the House of Spirits, even though it had happened well over a month before.

"Ah, fair enough. Well it's a big thing. Everyone's saying it's the best circus ever - maybe barring Cirque Du Soleil. The theme is mythical figures and magical creatures, and that's what all the performances are based around – hence Crossroads." Crossroads had a reputation in myth as a place where boundaries between worlds weakened allowing in the strange and otherworldly.

"Are you going to go?"

"I think so. It might even distract our new friend."

"Shadow? You'll think she'll like a circus?"

"Why not?" Dan picked up the paper, and examined the article again. "I think it sounds great. I'll offer to go with her, keep her company." Dan was about to finish his master's in something to do with folklore, Avery could never remember exactly what, but he took an avid interest in magic, myths and legends. He also took an avid interest in Shadow. He was trying to look relaxed and nonchalant, but Avery knew him only too well.

"Yes, I'm sure you'll love that." She dropped her voice, even though the shop had no customers, and looked at him worriedly. "Dan, she's *fey*! Please don't forget that!"

He gave a very undignified roll of the eyes. "How can I forget that? She reminds me of the fact every time we talk. And, so what! There's nothing wrong with some cross-species' lovin'."

"Hasn't Nixie put you off?"

He frowned. "Nixie was a mermaid who hid her true nature and tried to drag me to the depths of the ocean. I know exactly what Shadow is!"

"But we don't know anything about her. She's fey. She might look like us, but she isn't." Her voice softened. "I just don't want you to get hurt. And I definitely don't want you being sucked to the Otherworld accidentally, if –" Avery wagged a finger, "she ever discovers how to get back, which is seriously unlikely. And, if she starts to try and sell mythical objects, that could involve some very dodgy people. In fact, that's probably a bigger risk to your health!"

Dan's shoulders sagged. "Yeah, I know. It's something I've tried to warn her about, actually, but she's seems to like the risk." He leaned forward. "I think she's finding life a little boring so far. That's why I think this circus is a good thing. February is cold and drab otherwise."

Avery leaned against the shelf behind her, sipping her drink. "I'm enjoying boring. It makes a nice change."

They were interrupted by Sally who joined them from the back room, where she'd been doing the accounts. She looked between them. "What are you two in deep discussion about?"

Dan showed her the newspaper. "We're just debating Shadow's interest in this."

Sally skimmed the page, and laughed. "It's here already. Cool! I'll take the kids. It sounds amazing. And I think we should set up a table of themed books - circuses, carnivals, and crossroads stuff." She looked very pleased with herself, and her eyes darted around the room as she looked for the best place to set it up.

"Dan thinks it will distract Shadow from her quest, but I seriously doubt that. She's obsessive about the Otherworld and portals." Avery tried to shrug off her worry. "But maybe I'm just sleep deprived and it's making me paranoid."

Dan squirmed. "Maybe not completely paranoid. You should know that she's planning to check out some old sites around Cornwall, just for starters."

"Like what?"

"Castle an Dinas, the old iron age hill fort. It's linked to King Arthur, like lots of places across Cornwall and the UK, including Tintagel, King Arthur's birthplace if you believe the legends. His history crosses over with the Otherworld — you know, the Green Knight, Excalibur, Avalon, the Lady of the Lake, she thinks that places linked to him will perhaps have links to her world."

Sally folded her arms across her chest and narrowed her eyes. "So, I presume she'll check out Glastonbury, the Tor, and Stonehenge too."

"Yep. And a few other places. I offered to take her to a few, but she's thinking on it." He looked miffed. "I think she wants to go with Gabe."

Avery tried to console him. "Maybe that's a good idea, but at least she comes to you for research."

"What myths does the Crossroads Circus focus on?" Sally asked.

"It mentions a few on this," Dan said, passing her the flyer. "But I know the Green Man plays a major part, as does the Raven King. That's who the Ring Master appears as."

"Sounds great," Avery conceded. "Something to cheer us up after vampires. I'll have to take Alex, although I'm not entirely sure he's a circus fan. No live animals I hope?"

"None. Just the mythical kind."

"Well, that's alright then."

***

During her lunch break, Avery decided to head to El's jewellery shop, the Silver Bough. She was curious to see if Shadow had mentioned any of her planned search to her as she knew El saw more of her, and she wanted to know if she'd heard about the circus, too.

She strolled down the streets, huddled within her coat. It was a grey day, the sky low with heavy, sullen clouds, and it was cold. The wind carried the smell of the sea, and as she rounded a corner it came into view between a gap in some buildings, and she paused to watch it. The heavy swells beyond the harbour were as grey as the sky. The fishing boats were out, and she was glad she wasn't with them.

Avery picked up her pace, nodding greetings to a few locals as she passed. The town had finally emptied of all their visitors, but that wouldn't last now that the circus was here, which was a shame because it was nice while it lasted. The tourists would return, and the place would be full of the performers from the circus too; that would be different.

As Avery made the final turn onto the main street that ran down to the harbour, she ran straight into a familiar figure. Rupert, the owner of the House of Spirits. She hadn't seen him since before Christmas.

Rupert stepped back, giving her space, and looked down at her. He wasn't a tall man, but he was imposing and ever so slightly sinister, an impression exacerbated by his hooded eyes that seemed to pin her to the spot. "Avery, I'm glad to see you. I've been meaning to thank you for those books." He was referring to the books that had been sold from his house to Happenstance Books, and that Avery had willingly returned.

"Hi Rupert, it's fine. I hope they were interesting." There was nothing unusual about them that Avery could find, other of course than the one with the witch-mark on it, but she doubted Rupert could see that.

"They're excellent. I've placed them in pride of place on the book case in the main living room."

"The one with Madame Charron's painting in it? That's a good place." It wasn't until she'd said it that Avery had the horrible realisation that Rupert didn't know she'd been back to the house with the other witches while he and Charlotte had been away. *Crap.*

He frowned. "You know about the painting? How?"

She lied quickly, startling herself with its smoothness. "Cassie told me. She loved it, and she knew I would want to hear about it." She met his eyes, smiling lightly.

"Of course, Cassie," he murmured, doubt lurking behind his eyes. "The house is looking a bit different now. We've started to do some of it up. Not too much of course, we want to keep its character."

"Did you ever find a ghost?"

Again, he narrowed his eyes, and then his chest swelled as a gleam of excitement fired. "No, but you might have heard the police visited us — it was on the news. They found a passage beneath our house—that actually *starts* in our house! It leads to caves and piles of bones."

Of course she knew, she wanted to shout, *they'd* found the passage and tipped the police off, but she held her tongue. Rupert knew none of it. However, it had been all over the papers. "Of course, I've been reading about it. Didn't you have Sarah Rutherford visit you as well, from the news?"

He smiled, but she didn't like it. There was something challenging about him. "Yes, we've had lots of interest. We've decided to run small tours of the house, a sort of paranormal experience."

Of course you have. "Well, it is in keeping with the theme of the town I guess."

"You weren't entirely honest with me though were you, Avery?" he said.

"In what way?"

"Your ancestor? Helena, the witch who was burned at the stake. You never said."

She laughed outright whilst simultaneously wanting to punch him. "It's not a secret, Rupert! But equally it's not something I announce to everyone as I introduce myself. That would be a little odd, don't you think?"

He persisted, almost glaring at her. "You knew I had an interest in the occult."

"So, does everyone in White Haven. Anyway, I must get on. I'm meeting someone. I'll see you again sometime," she said, forcing herself to be polite as she pushed past him and headed down the street. She could feel his eyes on her back, watching her leave, and she resisted the urge to hex him.

By the time she entered El's shop she was seething. Zoey, the Immaculate Guardian of the Shop, was, as usual, looking, well, immaculate. Her dark hair was cut into a blunt bob, and this time the tips ended with deep purple dye. Her eye makeup and nail polish matched, and as usual she made Avery feel woefully underdressed.

"You look furious," Zoey noted as she lifted the counter to let her through to El's workroom.

"Stupid Rupert from the House of Spirits is a ginormous ass," Avery told her.

"Oh him. Yes, he is."

Avery stopped, surprised. "You know him?"

"Everyone's getting to know him. He likes to visit announcing his paranormal house tours." She put the counter back down behind Avery. "Don't worry; he's annoying the crap out of all of us."

She turned away as a customer entered, and Avery passed through the door to see El bent over the counter, a small soldering iron in her hand. She was perched on a stool next to the bench, her white blond hair piled on her head, wearing a pair of scruffy jeans and a jumper, and the most enormous goggles over her eyes. She was concentrating on soldering an intricate piece of jewellery, and Avery hesitated to disturb her. And then she noticed the buds in her ears, and realised she couldn't hear her anyway.

Rather than startle her, she moved around to the side so she appeared in El's peripheral vision. While El was concentrating, she looked around the room, noting the rings, earrings, nose rings, belly-button bars, and necklaces in various stages of completion along the bench. She was obviously working on a new range, because these looked slightly different to the designs she'd seen before. Tiny black gemstones littered the bench that Avery was sure were jet; it was commonly known as a protection and purification stone. To the side of the bench was El's oldest family grimoire, the one she had found in the cellar of Hawk House. A hum of magic floated from it, and she realised that El was working a spell into the object.

Avery's gaze drifted around the room, taking in the huge cabinet with the glassed front. It contained hundreds of jars of different gemstones, and they sparkled in the light, making Avery want to pick them up and run her fingers through them. There was also an organised collection of tools, many of them tiny, and an array of magnifying glasses. It was stupid to only realise now, but watching El, Avery realised how intricate and skilled her work was.

After another few moments, El looked up and Avery waved, gesturing her not to rush, and she sat in the chair in the corner, but it was only another moment before El turned the soldering iron off, and pulled her buds from her ears.

"Sorry, Avery, didn't see you there for a minute, and then I just became aware of someone hovering. I thought it was Zoey." She looked at her watch. "No wonder I'm starving! Look at the time." She pushed the goggles on to the top of her head, and smoothed her hair.

"What are you making?" Avery asked, rising to her feet and moving to the bench for a better look.

"A Crossroads Collection to coincide with our visitors. I thought it was too good an opportunity to pass up."

"You've heard about the new arrivals then? I hadn't."

El laughed. "Avery! Where have you been? They've been in all the news recently, and everyone's saying how inventive they are. That they're breathing life into old tales! We should go."

"I was just talking to Dan and Sally about it actually. I'm game. I just hope there won't be some dodgy woman pretending to look into a crystal ball, and asking me to cross her palm with silver."

El laughed even harder. "I think it's going to be a little bit more inventive than that. And it's set in the castle! What a back drop that will be." She rose from her seat and headed to the percolator sitting on the end of the bench top. "Want one? It's strong."

"Yes please."

El poured them both a cup, and then headed to the fridge in the corner and pulled out a large round cake that already had half missing. "Do you want some?"

"Go on then," Avery said, hearing her stomach growl.

"There was more," El explained, "but Reuben popped in." She didn't need to say anything else. Reuben ate like he had hollow legs, and he never put on a pound.

"Don't tell me he's surfing in this weather."

"Of course he is. It's like breathing to him." El placed a large slice on a chipped plate and pushed it in front of Avery, and then took a large bite of her own. In between chews, she asked, "Is there a reason for this visit? Not that there has to be, obviously."

"I wanted to stretch my legs, but yes, just wondering if you've heard about Shadow's plans."

El nodded. "Of course. I even offered to help. I figure, the more she has to try, the less frustrated she'll feel."

Avery licked her fingers. This really was a great cake, sticky orange if she wasn't mistaken. "I guess you're right. It's better than us blocking her at every turn."

"We can't do that. Remember what I said last night. This is part of my management strategy. Although it's inevitable that she'll do her own stubborn thing eventually."

"Dan thinks the circus will distract her. I think she's just distracting Dan."

"Yeah, but he enjoys it. You coming around later anyway? Newton phoned and said he wants to talk. I thought he'd already phoned you actually."

"I haven't heard from him, but this morning I have been very distracted." Avery pulled her phone from her bag and checked her messages. There was nothing. "I think I've upset Newton."

"No, you haven't." El stood and brushed crumbs off herself. "He's probably just smarting a little after finding Briar has hooked up with Hunter. You do give him heaps about his *issue*."

Avery felt guilty. Yes, she had told him off several times, but hadn't wanted to upset him, not really. "Maybe I should apologise."

"Maybe. He's just confused, and that's okay. And Briar's happy." El sniggered. "She has a glow."

"And then some," Avery agreed. Getting together with Hunter had certainly lifted her spirits.

El looked even naughtier. "What do you think shifter sex is like? I reckon he'd be very hot in the sheets. He smoulders every time he looks at her."

Avery shrieked. "El! I don't want to think about that!" Although it had crossed her mind, briefly, before she banished it forever. And now it was back in her head again.

"Well I'm going to ask her."

"We don't ask you what sex is like with Reuben!"

"You could!" El raised a wicked eyebrow. "But I wouldn't tell. Just know that it's good. *Very* good."

"That's it, I'm out of here!" Avery said, laughing. "Are we meeting at yours then?"

"Yep, and Reuben's bringing curry. Aim for seven."

***

After work, Avery headed to The Wayward Son and had a drink at the bar, before she and Alex headed to El's place where they'd arranged to meet Newton.

They walked briskly through the chilly streets, and Alex hugged Avery to his side. "Any idea what Newton wants with us?" he asked.

"None, but it will be good to see him. He's been so busy lately."

"Which is our fault. We must have given him a massive headache. Imagine having to legitimately investigate that?" He was of course referring to the mass of bones found in the cave system beneath West Haven.

"Those bones need to be identified," Avery pointed out. "And Newton will want to do it."

They entered the lobby of the building where El lived, a converted warehouse next to the harbour, and used the lift to reach her flat on the fourth floor. They were greeted by a welcome blast of central heating, which thawed Avery's chilled extremities.

They were the last to arrive. Briar and Newton were already there, chatting quietly next to the fire. Despite their differences recently, both seemed civil. Newton was in his mid-thirties, dark-haired, and grey-eyed, and a descendant of another old family in White Haven. He struggled with magic and the paranormal, but he was a good friend regardless, and firmly part of their world. For a while it seemed something may happen between him and Briar, but not anymore.

The smell of curry filled the air, and Reuben was already placing out containers of food down the centre of the dining table, which sat in the open-plan living area. He looked up and grinned. "Good timing. I couldn't have guaranteed much would have been left if you hadn't arrived soon."

"There's enough there to feed a small army, so I'm sure you couldn't have eaten it all," Alex observed, as he and Avery shed their coats and joined him.

El strode to the table with a bottle of red wine in her hand, and poured Avery and herself a glass. "But you know he'd have tried!" She called over to Briar and Newton, "Come and sit, you two. I'm starving."

They sat around the table, filling their plates as they exchanged pleasantries, until Avery eventually asked, "Are you making much headway with the bones?"

Newton shook his head regretfully. "No. The forensic pathologists have just started, really. They have to organise the bones before they even start analysing them. This is going to take months, and that's a conservative estimate. Meanwhile, we're looking at missing persons files going back years, and then we're collecting DNA samples from relatives who are still alive." He shook his head. "It's something I've never done before on this scale, so there are a few people involved."

Briar smiled. "Well done. That's quite an achievement."

"Or an absolute nightmare, depending on the moment," he confessed. He looked tired, Avery noticed, now that she was sitting closer to him. He wasn't as cleanly shaven as usual, and dark shadows circled his eyes.

Avery shifted in her seat and faced him. "Has something happened?"

Newton looked up, his eyes haunted. "Well, the word *vampire* won't go away, and my superiors have decided it's something we can't ignore." He shuffled uncomfortably. "I know that I've joked about this, but they really do want me to investigate any deaths that look remotely paranormal. This latest debacle has forced their hand."

They all paused, forks lifted halfway to lips, but Alex spoke first. "Is that a good or a bad thing?"

He sighed. "I don't know. If you guys are remotely involved, it could be bad, but obviously I'll try and keep you out of it."

"But we're never involved in deaths," El pointed out, indignant. "We're the good guys."

"Well, I know that, but they don't. And frankly, it's hard to explain away magic without me sounding like a fruit loop."

The witches looked at each other furtively, and Avery said, "Thank you. We want to be kept out of things as much as possible."

Reuben waved his fork. "Do you mean they really believe the deaths were caused by vampires, and it wasn't someone playing a sick prank?"

Newton exhaled heavily. "Initially it was thought to be a joke, and for a while people laughed it off, but not anymore. With the marks on the victims' necks, the blood loss, and what happened at the Coroner's office, everyone had to take it seriously. My superiors consulted with some bigger town divisions, and what they heard made them reconsider their position." He looked at Avery. "What James said to you was pretty much what the police said, you know, about vampire activity being more easily disguised in a big city environment. So, yes, they are being considered as a probable perpetrator in these deaths. And the presence of ashes as remains supports that theory."

Avery looked down at her plate as she remembered when they burned Lupescu, and when the sunlight spell destroyed the vampires in the main cave. All of a sudden, her appetite retreated. They may have been vampires, but it was a horrible thing to have done.

Newton continued, "That leaves us in an unusual situation in that we've had a few big city activities we wouldn't normally see in little ol' Cornwall, and that has raised suspicion. At least no one knows we have seven Nephilim and a fey living here as well."

Alex frowned. "Does this mean there are other paranormal activities going on out there that we don't know about?"

Newton's grey eyes darkened. "Outside of Cornwall? Yes, without a doubt. Which leads to my next subject. The Crossroads Circus is coming to town, and I need a favour." His eyes scanned them, gauging their reaction.

El groaned. "Don't let it be bad! I'm making a Crossroads Collection."

Avery's stomach sank. "What's wrong with the circus? We were talking about that today."

His lips pressed into a thin line. "I don't know yet. That's what I want you to find out."

Reuben leaned forward. "Something must have happened."

"We've been advised that strange occurrences seem to follow the circus. It could just be a coincidence, or—" he spread his hands wide. "It might actually be something. You're the best people I know to find out."

Alex glanced at Avery before he spoke. "But how do you get around asking us? I mean, what happens if we find something? I presume we don't come into it?"

"Absolutely not," Newton said, shaking his head vehemently. "You just tell me what you find, as you've done before. And of course, we'll be keeping a close eye on them anyway."

"Your friend, Officer Moore, has seen us show up a few times. What does he know about us?" asked Reuben.

"Rob? He knows that you have occult interests and that's why I consult you sometimes. But he's quiet and discrete, and I trust him."

"He's beyond quiet!" El exclaimed. "He's utterly silent. I've never heard him speak at all."

Newton grunted as he forked some more chicken biryani onto his plate. "He speaks when he needs to. He likes you lot, actually."

Avery was surprised. Most of the time, it seemed as if he barely noticed them. It looked like no one else expected to hear that either, as they all looked puzzled.

Alex brought them back to the subject. "You said, 'strange occurrences.' We need more than that, and I presume it needs to be more than that to trigger a police investigation."

"True," he admitted, "which is why this is nothing as formal as an investigation. There are no grounds for one quite yet. There have been a few disappearances—but there are always disappearances, you know that. However, a body was found on the outskirts of the last town they visited, just outside Torquay in Devon. There was no obvious cause of death, the person was young, and there were no signs of drug or alcohol use, and no visible injuries." Newton sighed and ran his hands through his hair. "But the post-mortem report showed his organs were old, too old for his body. Atrophied and withered."

A trickle of fear ran through Avery. *Atrophied organs?*

Alex said, "That is weird. But why connect that to the circus?"

"Because some bright spark decided to look at where the circus had been and see if anything else had shown up. And something did." He paused for a moment and took a slug of beer. "That's when we found out that at intermittent points on their tour, the same thing has happened. Not every stop—they have been working their way down the country since September—but at least one in three. All found with atrophied organs, all young men, and all with no reason to be dead."

Briar's hand flew to her mouth. "That's horrible. What could do such a thing?"

Newton shrugged. "We have no idea."

"But there's nothing to link the deaths to the circus at this stage?" Reuben asked.

"No. There is nothing to link the deaths to anyone or anything!" He looked frustrated, and he rubbed his stubble before leaning back in his chair and pushing his plate away.

Avery shook her head, incredulous. "But surely you're too busy to look into this? You're still following up the vampire deaths."

"Well, technically there's no investigation to complete. Yes, we're trying to match bodies to victims and find existing family members, but I'm not looking for the perpetrator, am I? He's dead. While the press have been all over this, we've essentially said the killer is a man with a vampire fixation, and he was found dead at the scene, burnt in some freak accident. They've run with it. We're going to have to release a name soon, so we'll probably use one of the victims."

Avery had followed the early news reports before it had depressed her, and had been relieved to know that they were reporting it was a freak and not an actual vampire. The whole thing was turning into a sort of Jack the Ripper-type affair. No one knew who the offender was, but the press kept speculating.

"What about the two girls that we found?" Avery asked. "Have they remembered details?"

"No, and that's a good thing," Newton said, obviously relieved. "As you know, one of them, Alice, was barely alive at the time. She's made a good recovery since then, physically, but mentally—" He shook his head. "She remembers darkness, shadows, pain, cold, thirst, and starvation. The second one, Daisy, who Lupescu had just taken, she remembers someone attacking her from behind, and that's it. She spoke to the press, briefly, and that's all she told them. She just wants to be left alone now, to get on with her life, poor kid."

"Let's hope they both make a good recovery," Avery said, her mind a jumble of thoughts. "Are you saying that the police, your colleagues, now believe in vampires?"

"A small group of us do. The rest believe what the press are saying. I'm now the head of a small paranormal division. There's me, Moore, a detective called Walker, and my boss. It's very under the radar."

Reuben snorted. "Like black ops? That's seriously cool!"

Newton just stared at him. "Not so cool if you ask me, I'd rather they give the job to someone else."

Avery started to feel very uncomfortable. "I know we've talked about this, but just to come back to it again—how honest are you being?"

Newton's grey eyes met hers. "I'm going to be reasonably honest about everything except you five, and the Cornwall Coven, obviously. As for the rest, I have no choice. These things that have been cropping up cannot be ignored."

"By things," El asked, "you mean the strange behaviour of the men down on the beach with the mermaids, in the storm? And the events at Old Haven Church at Samhain?"

Newton nodded. "Yes, but not the deaths at All Souls and the other churches when the Nephilim arrived. There's still no solution to those, and that's how it will remain. I can keep them out of the paranormal bracket. They were violent deaths, easy enough to explain. But the latest stuff, impossible! My boss on this is perceptive and open-minded. A dangerous combination."

"Where are you based?" Reuben asked.

"At the station in Truro. Our main office, where the Major Crime Investigation sits, is in Newquay, but I've always been based in Truro. We've been given our own office there. I think they like us out of the way of the main team. I'll still investigate *normal* murders—if you'll forgive the word—but I'll get the weird stuff, too."

Reuben looked suspicious. "And what's the new guy seem like? I mean, does he have paranormal experience?"

"Woman, actually," Newton corrected him. "I've only just met her. She's come from Major Crimes, too. She seems a bit intense, but open-minded. Let's face it, you have to be to investigate this stuff."

El stood and started to clear the plates, and Alex helped her, but Avery remained seated, thinking. "So, this circus mystery, this is something your paranormal team are investigating? No one else?"

"No one else," he parroted. "And, as I said, it's not even a proper investigation, it's just something that's on our radar. With luck, the circus will leave and nothing will happen."

"Where do they go after us?" Reuben asked.

"Further south—Penzance. Final show before they take a break." He rubbed his jaw absently again. "If there *is* something going on and they're connected to these deaths, and we don't find out who's responsible, they'll disappear for months, or even go abroad, and we might not have the chance to investigate anytime soon."

"And potentially, people will start dying again, elsewhere," Briar pointed out. "So, we have to find out if they're responsible, quickly."

"Happy to help?" Newton asked them.

"Of course," Avery said, answering for all of them, wondering what on earth they were getting themselves into. "Have you got some background on any of the people there?"

"Just coming to it," he said, pulling his notebook from his pocket. "I'll start with the owner, or rather the main owner. His name is Corbin Roberts. He took the circus over from his father. It's been in the family for years, travelling a lot in Europe. It was just a regular circus then. However in the last few years they've been struggling financially, and Corbin has had to find new backers. He's 55 and seems a straight-up guy who runs an honest business.

"For years, Corbin co-owned the circus with a man called Alec Jensen, but he bailed out last year, and within months Corbin teamed up with a younger married couple, Rafe and Mairi Stewart, who are Scottish, originally from Inverness. They were with another circus for a while, but not as co-owners, just managers."

"So this couple invested money?" Reuben asked.

"Yep, and must be responsible for the new direction the circus has taken, because in the summer last year the entire circus headed to the shores of Loch Ness, outside Inverness. I've checked the dates. They didn't have any performances for about three months, and when they re-emerged, they were called the Crossroads Circus."

Briar picked at her naan bread while she listened. "Interesting name. It has all sorts of connotations, especially with boundary magic."

Avery nodded. "Just what we were talking about in my shop. Perfect for their theme."

Alex called over from the kitchen, "Anything suspicious about Rafe and Mairi?"

"Nothing," Newton answered. "Mairi has family in Inverness, Rafe doesn't. But again, there's nothing suspicious about them. I've done background checks on the performers, but to be honest, there are a lot of them. It's a big circus. Again, some of the performers have been with Corbin for years, others are new, and joined them in the summer." He shook his head, puzzled. "They must have been confident of the new show to take on more performers when they were struggling. They are from the UK and all over Europe, with diverse backgrounds. A few convictions for fighting for some of them, speeding tickets, but again nothing too dramatic."

"So no one we should focus on in particular," Briar observed. "That makes it tricky."

Reuben cracked open another beer. "I take it that there were no deaths associated with the circus before, though? Not in Europe?"

Newton loosened his collar. "That's trickier. Not that we know of, but to track all over Europe would be a nightmare, especially based on so little information. We don't think so."

El joined them again after finishing the tidying up. "So, in theory, whoever is responsible is new."

"In theory," Newton agreed. He reached into his pocket and fished some papers out, covered in a list of names. "I wish I could tell you more, but I've got the list of employees here. If you find someone suspicious you think we should focus on, let me know."

"Let's just hope you're wrong," Avery said to him. "I was looking forward to some peace, but I guess we need to start investigating them soon."

"The sooner the better."

"Let's go tomorrow night," Reuben suggested. "We'll wear full Ninja-witch gear. I like feeling like I'm in special ops. We'll meet down the lane, out of sight." He rubbed his hands together in happy anticipation. "I can't wait!"

3

Halfway through the next morning, Avery left Happenstance Books to buy coffees and pastries from their favourite place just down the road, when she heard shouts, drumming, and the sound of wild piping coming from the centre of town.

Curious, she walked to the high street that snaked down to the sea, and paused to watch the spectacle. Some of the performers from the Crossroads Circus had arrived to promote their show, and they capered down the pavement in their bright costumes. They reminded Avery of their own Yule Solstice parade.

There were about a dozen people, led by a man in a green costume covered in leaves, with a big nest of leaves and twigs on his head. His face was painted green, he carried a staff crowned with leaves, and his boots were made of sturdy brown leather. Avery presumed he was the mythical Green Man, the pagan symbol of fertility and rebirth. He was grinning and waving at the pedestrians, shouting about the opening of the circus. He caught Avery watching and waved, and she laughed, his enthusiasm infectious.

Behind him were a couple of drummers, dressed in shades of green and brown, their hair wild and uncombed, and a piper followed them, skipping, in a jester's costume. A couple of slender acrobats dressed in the skimpiest of Lycra costumes tumbled down the street, doing hand stands, flips, and cartwheels.

A woman trailed behind the acrobats, wearing a long, shimmering blue dress, medieval in design, and she carried a huge sword in her hand. She shouted, "Come meet the true king! Arthur has returned." It could only be the Lady of the Lake.

By her side was a woman dressed completely in straw and corn, a braid of corn around her face. *Was she a corn doll, to celebrate Imbolc?* Avery wasn't sure. And finally two men followed breathing fire, and wearing costumes covered in scales, in bright yellow and reds. *Dragons, perhaps*. One thing was certain—they were all causing a stir. They handed out leaflets, running in and out of shops, and shouting in cackling voices as they entertained the onlookers.

Avery was ready to return to the coffee shop when another woman caught her eye. She looked to be in her mid-thirties, with long, wavy auburn hair, and she wore a mixture of loose clothing in earth colours. The woman paused on the pavement, transfixed as she looked at Avery, and as their eyes locked, Avery felt the strangest sensation, as if she'd been seen completely, inside and out, before the woman broke their connection and continued down the street without a backward glance.

Avery shuddered. *What was that?* As she turned away, slightly flustered, she stumbled into the broad chest of man dressed in dark grey and black. He righted her, his hands on her arms, and she was acutely aware of his steely grip. He glanced at her, his eyes narrowing, before he looked over her shoulder to the woman with the auburn hair. He nodded, and muttered a brief, "Excuse me," before hurrying on down the road. Avery watched as his long stride carried him out of sight.

When she returned to the shop, Dan and Sally were behind the till, talking quietly. Dan was distracted, and he leaned on the counter, looking through a book as they chatted. A Blues album was playing in the background, and the shop felt mellow and welcoming. He looked up. "Finally! I thought you'd forgotten us." His appetite was almost as legendary as Reuben's.

Sally rolled her eyes. "You weren't gone that long, Avery, don't worry."

Avery set the coffees down and pulled an almond croissant out of the bag for herself, before passing it to Dan. "Sorry, I was distracted by the mini-parade. The circus is drumming up trade on the high street."

"Really? Does it look good?" Dan asked.

"The costumes were great. I saw the Green Man and the Lady of the Lake, and there were some fire-breathing men dressed as dragons. I think the acrobats were dryads—they were very energetic. It's a good thing it's warmed up a bit, they weren't wearing much." She paused for a bite of croissant, spilling crumbs over the counter.

Sally watched her over the rim of her coffee cup. "What aren't you saying? You look odd." Sally was surprisingly perceptive.

"There was a woman behind the procession, and she sort of made eye contact with me, and it was the strangest sensation. I felt like she saw right through me and knew everything about me. It was spooky."

"Are you sure she didn't fancy you?" Dan asked, smirking.

"No, you pillock. Our eyes did not meet across a crowded room!"

"Is she a witch?" Sally asked. "Newton's worried about that circus, isn't he?"

Avery had filled them in on Newton's concerns. "He is, but she's not a witch. I don't get that feeling from any other witch. This was different." Avery gazed into the middle distance, shuffling through the possibilities, before she shrugged in frustration. "I don't know, it's weird. And then I bumped into a man who seemed to be watching her, but I must have imagined that. He was probably watching the circus folk. I think he was American."

"Why? Dan asked. "Was he wearing stars and stripes?"

"Oh, you're very funny today! He said 'excuse me' in an American accent."

Dan finished his pastry and wiped his hands on his jeans. "Could it all be related to the deaths, or could she be?"

"It's too soon to say. I'm seeing the other witches later, though." Avery looked behind her and lowered her voice, even though no customers were too close. "We're going to go to the circus tonight, hidden by my shadow spell. We're hoping to see or hear something that might give us a clue."

Before she could say anything else, the bells chimed over the door announcing a new arrival, and Avery glanced behind to see Stan, their pseudo-Druid and town councillor, enter with a couple in their thirties.

Stan beamed when he saw them. He marched across the shop, his tie askew and his hair wind-blown, with the couple close behind. "Excellent, I've got all of you! I'd like to introduce you to Rafe and Mairi from the Crossroads Circus. They are part owners, and I've been telling them what a special place White Haven is! This is Avery, our Mistress of the Occult, Sally and Dan, her occult assistants!"

Avery tried to keep her expression polite as she shook their hands, and forced herself to remember what Newton had told them. "I think you'll find that Stan is exaggerating a bit. I'm not nearly so interesting as to be a Mistress of the Occult, but welcome to my shop."

"And to White Haven," Sally added, and they all shook hands. "Your circus sounds fascinating. I'm going to take my kids."

"I'm sure they'll enjoy it," Rafe said, smiling. "We're certainly enjoying your beautiful town." Rafe was of average height with short, reddish hair, and ruddy skin. Avery could hear his Scottish accent, but it wasn't strong, probably because he'd travelled around. "We debated setting up near Truro, but your town has such a wonderful reputation for ghosts and witches, it seemed like the best place to stay."

Stan rubbed his hands together and looked gleeful—if a fifty-plus man could be said to be gleeful. "I couldn't believe it when you approached us," he said. "The castle will be an amazing backdrop for your show!"

"It certainly will be," Mairi agreed. She was shorter than Rafe, with shoulder-length, wavy hair, and again, a soft Scottish accent. "Hopefully our tales and your history will make a good fit."

"Your circus has been very popular! It makes me wonder why no one has thought of your theme before," observed Dan.

Rafe laughed. "Sometimes, you just need inspiration to strike."

Avery listened and nodded politely as they chatted, but she was watching Mairi, who was the quieter of the two. Her eyes were darting everywhere around the shop, her gaze speculative and unsettling. "Do you like books, Mairi?"

Mairi looked startled, not realising she was being watched. "Yes, of course, but I don't get a lot of time to read. Managing a circus keeps us very busy."

"I'm sure it does. It looks big. You must have a lot of performers. I saw some of them today in the town—very impressive."

She nodded, seeming slightly distracted. "Thank you. Yes, it takes a lot to organise setting up, moving on, booking where to go. It takes months of planning."

"Well, while you're here, feel free to look around."

Before Mairi could answer, the doorbell rang again, and Avery looked up to see Rupert striding in. *Crap.* "Ah! There you are, Stan! I heard you were taking a tour of the town with our guests." He nodded at Avery, a vicious gleam in his eye. "Should have known he'd have been in our favourite witch's shop."

Mairi whipped around to gape at her, and Rafe stilled slightly as he too looked at her, his eyes wide.

Avery's heart thumped in her chest, but she replied calmly, "I think you mean my witch ancestor, Helena, who was so cruelly burned at the stake."

Stan leapt in with a melodramatic shudder. "Terrible business! Terrible! Fortunately, we embrace magic, witches, and the paranormal now, not like back then. I love our pagan celebrations. It's what makes us so special, and Happenstance Books is a part of that. And Avery is so good at dressing her shop for those occasions."

"Sally is, actually," Avery corrected him. She pointed at the table close to the entrance that Sally had filled with a selection of circus and myth-themed books. "She's responsible for our Crossroads theme, as well."

Stan winked at Sally. "Of course. Forgive me, Sally! Did you want me for something, Rupert?" Remembering he hadn't introduced them, he explained to Rafe and Mairi, "Rupert owns the mysterious House of Sprits in West Haven, and he's planning on running some ghost tours of the area. Excellent idea!"

Rafe and Mairi nodded encouragingly, but Avery was aware of Mairi's glances at her.

"Yes, I wanted to discuss my plans with you," Rupert said, smoothly. "However, you're busy, and I'll catch up with you another time. I'd like to add Happenstance Books to the tour actually, Avery. Any objections?"

She had plenty, but she wasn't about to say so. "Absolutely not. It would be great for business. Just as long as you remain outside the shop, of course. Readers like a quiet bookshop to browse and read in. I'm sure you understand. But I guess it depends if you're running them in the day or at night."

Sally backed her up. "Very true, Avery, but so kind to include us in the tour, Rupert. Thank you."

Stan again leapt in before Rupert could answer. "Excellent news! This tour will be a great success, Rupert."

While Stan and Rupert continued their discussion, Rafe smiling politely and nodding, Mairi's phone buzzed, and she pulled it from her bag. She answered it immediately, heading to the far side of the shop to talk, and when she returned, her eyes gleamed.

Stan noticed her return and immediately changed the conversation. "You two must be eager to get on, and we should leave these good people in peace." He started to usher them from the shop, but Mairi pulled a handful of tickets from her bag, thrusting them at Avery.

"You must come to our opening night. I think you would love it! Do you think you can?" She stared at Avery, and then as if she realised she was being intense, glanced at Dan and Sally, too. "All of you, of course!"

Avery stuttered as she took the tickets. "Er, that's very generous of you, and yes, I'm sure we'd love to come!"

Sally rushed in, too. "Absolutely. I can't wait!"

Stan beamed again and winked. "How very generous! Let's hope there are a few more in that bag of yours!"

He escorted Rupert, Rafe, and Mairi out of the shop as they called their goodbyes, and Avery couldn't resist throwing a hex at Rupert. She watched with pleasure as he tripped outside on the pavement, but was careful to turn away when he looked up furiously, brushing himself off.

She waited until they had moved out of sight, then asked, "Why do I loathe that man so much?"

"Rupert? Because he's an arrogant prick," Dan said. "I don't think he likes you, either. I think he's jealous of your ancestry. He's a wannabe."

Sally nodded. "I agree. I'm not sure I like that Mairi woman, either. There was something about her that rankled—despite the free tickets. And she couldn't take her eyes off of you when she heard the word *witch*."

"I noticed," Avery said, feeling unsettled. "Let's just hope it was idle curiosity."

***

At lunchtime, Avery settled herself into her usual spot at the end of the bar in The Wayward Son, and Zee, one of the seven Nephilim, slid a glass of red wine in front of her.

"All alone?" he asked her.

She nodded. "Just a quick lunch. I needed a break from the shop, and I wanted to see Alex about tonight. We're going to investigate the circus."

He frowned. "Is something wrong with it?"

"Maybe, that's what we're trying to find out. How's Shadow? I gather she's been busy."

Zee looked amused. "Busy keeping Gabe on his toes. She sets off on her horse most mornings, heading across the downs to shoot rabbits and investigate *the wild places*. When she's not working security at Caspian's warehouses, anyway."

"She's settling in then?" Avery asked, in between sips of wine.

"She's settled in just fine. Got a few of us roped into her research."

"Does that include you?"

"When I have time, and the inclination." His face creased with amusement, rippling the faint scar down his cheek. "At least I'm still able to put a few hours in here."

"I remember you saying you might not have time after Christmas," Avery said, thoughtfully. "Caspian's not keeping you too busy, then?"

"Not yet. It's just standard security at the docks." He broke off suddenly, and looked towards the door, grinning. "Speak of the devil—as you say. Look who's here."

For a second, Avery thought he meant Caspian, and then she turned and saw Shadow just inside the door. She looked around the pub, drawing a few double-takes from the customers, not surprisingly. She was still an arresting sight. Today her long hair was a tumble of soft caramel tones, and her high cheekbones and violet eyes added to her unusual beauty. She glanced towards the bar, and seeing Avery, advanced with a speculative gleam in her eye.

"Ha! You've been spotted." Zee waited for her to reach them, and while Shadow pulled up a stool, he asked, "And what trouble do you bring today?"

She gave him a snide look. "No trouble, thank you, Zee. Now, fetch me a pint of Heligan Honey, please."

"Yes, ma'am," Zee said sarcastically, and turned away to grab a bottle of the local beer from the fridge behind him. He plonked it on the bar with a glass, and said, "I'll let you to pour it yourself. No doubt I'll pour it incorrectly."

She arched an eyebrow. "Someone's sensitive."

"Someone is sick of being criticised." He nodded to Avery. "I'll leave you to it. Shout if you want another."

Avery placed a hand on his arm, "Before you go, where's Alex?"

"In the kitchen, chatting with the chef. He'll be out in a minute." And then he headed to the other end of the bar to check on another local.

Avery watched Shadow pour her beer. "Are you upsetting your housemates?"

Shadow pursed her lips. "Not intentionally. I have high standards. I am fey."

Avery inwardly sighed. *That was wearing thin really quickly.* "Poor you. You're just going to have to get used to us, now that you're stuck here." She sipped her wine, as they assessed each other.

"Yes, you may be right. I'm sure I'll get used to all of you."

"And us, you," Avery pointed out. "So, why are you here? You haven't visited the pub before."

"I thought I should investigate where you spend a lot of your time. And besides, I wanted a drink."

"Is that all?"

Shadow looked away briefly, a guilty look flashing across her features. "Maybe not all. As you know, I've been spending some time with Dan, and he has suggested places that may offer gateways to my world."

"You know that's highly unlikely, though? I'd hate for you to get your hopes up."

Shadow looked into her drink, despondent, and suddenly all of Avery's compassion came rushing back, and she realised Shadow had come to the pub out of more than idle curiosity.

"I know," Shadow admitted. "But I have to try. The longer I am away, the harder it gets. I'm lonely without my kind. I feel…" She stumbled for words, showing a vulnerability Avery hadn't seen before. "Untethered. I still don't know what to do with myself."

"I understand that. But you have to give yourself time. Working with Gabe and the others will help. Don't antagonise them. They offered you a place to live and work. I wouldn't take that offer lightly. I'm surprised by Gabe's actions. I think he's surprised himself, too."

"The thing is," Shadow said, "those sites that Dan has suggested, most of them probably only have power at certain times of the year, like solstices and equinoxes, sunrises and sunsets. It's hopeless."

"Perhaps you can help us, then, when you're not on security duties?" Avery suggested in a rush, before she could think through the consequences. She filled her in on the Crossroad Circus and the deaths possibly associated with it. "We're going tonight, but that's probably a bit too short notice."

Shadow's face lit up. "Sounds great to me. I know you don't completely trust me, but I will help. I have unique skills, after all. And frankly, if we need to use weapons, I can handle most things."

"All right. But don't go off and do anything on your own. We have no idea what we're dealing with."

Alex exited the door leading to the kitchen and walked over to join them. He leaned over the bar to kiss Avery lightly on the cheek and nodded at Shadow. "To what do I owe this pleasure?"

"I thought I should investigate this pub, I hear it's where you all hang out. I like it. I'll bring Gabe here." She frowned. "I don't know why he doesn't come anyway. He works too hard. It makes him a dull boy."

Avery intervened. "Shadow is going to help us investigate the Crossroads Circus. She's coming tonight."

Alex looked at her, trying to hide his appalled expression. "Really? Great."

"She needs something to do, Alex, and she'll be a great help." Avery wasn't sure who she was trying to persuade more.

"Of course," he said begrudgingly. "The more the merrier."

Shadow's enthusiasm returned in a rush. "Excellent. Do you need to disguise yourselves?"

Avery nodded. "There's a spell we use."

"Good. We need to eavesdrop. That's my favourite form of reconnaissance."

"Of course it is," Alex said, groaning.

Shadow grinned and then stared at the mute TV screen on the wall. "Look. They're talking about the circus."

Avery turned to look at the screen, and Alex flicked the sound on low, just in time to hear Sarah Rutherford, the reporter who had covered White Haven events a few times, talk about the arrival of the circus. Behind her was the castle and the Big Top.

Alex frowned. "The tent is covered in Green Man images!"

"Fits the theme," Avery said. "He was one of the figures in the town today. The costumes are really good! I saw a strange woman, though. She gave me the shivers." Avery told them about her intense stare and that she thought a man was following her.

"This place never gets any quieter, does it?" Alex reflected. "Let's hope it knocks the caves under West Haven off the top spot on the news."

4

That evening, five witches and Shadow met at The Wayward Son, and then split into two cars, agreeing to meet in a lay-by, just down from the castle's car park.

It was just after 8pm by the time they arrived on the edge of the castle grounds, and a low mist was already rising from the ground. The lights that lit the castle walls were veiled by more coiling streams of mist, and it pooled in corners and swirled around their ankles. The Big Top squatted in the field to the right of the castle, and beyond that, in a large grassy area edged by hedgerows, were the rows of caravans and camper vans that the performers lived in. Wood smoke hung on the air, and the blinking motes of cinders curled on the faint breeze.

"What's the plan?" Reuben asked, dressed like the rest of them in black clothing, what he called their Ninja-witch gear.

Alex adjusted his gloves. "We mingle, listen to conversations, and see if we can hear them discuss anything odd. We should try and find Rafe and Mairi, and Corbin, too." It seemed Stan had introduced Rafe and Mairi to most of the shop owners, so they all knew what they looked like, but Corbin was still unknown. He looked at Shadow. "This is reconnaissance, nothing more. No heroics or grand gestures."

Shadow blinked once, dripping with disdain. "I am quite capable of following the brief, thank you."

"It's what I always expected of one of Herne's hunters," he replied, dryly.

Before Shadow could respond, Briar asked her, "Do you want us to include you in our spell?"

Shadow's face softened. "No, I'll be fine. I am fey and can conceal myself."

Alex continued with his plan. "Let's split into three groups. I'll be with Avery in the field with their caravans. Briar, you go with Shadow into the set-up in the castle, and then Reuben and El can cover the Big Top. Let's meet back here in an hour. Sound good?"

They nodded, but El asked, "What if we hit a problem and need support?"

"Phone us, or scream." Alex smiled slowly. "Phone would be better."

"No shit, Sherlock," El said sarcastically.

Alex flipped her the bird and El laughed, and then Avery said the spell that draped them in darkness. With a blink, the others disappeared, their appearances turning wraith-like and insubstantial. Had Avery not known where they were, she wouldn't have seen them.

Avery and Alex were able to see the details of the tent as they drew closer. A large archway with the words *Welcome to the Crossroads Circus* framed the path to the tent's entrance, flanked by two enormous imitation standing stones. A large raven was perched on one, and his black eyes stared down at them. For a second, Avery thought it was fake, until it cawed loudly, and she jumped. The sound of voices drifted towards them, and music, low and tinny, filled the air.

"Is that coming from the tent?" Avery asked.

Alex nodded. "I think so. Maybe they're practising."

Figures strode to and fro, some quickly, others slowly, usually in groups. The door of the tent was lifted and light poured out, giving Avery a glimpse of seats, ladders, and performers swinging on a trapeze. However, they didn't loiter, instead skirting around it to the field housing the performers' living quarters. They reached a gate in the hedge, jumped over it, and sticking to the dark shadows, walked into the campground.

The smell of cooking and wood smoke was stronger here, and the voices were louder. They edged their way through the mobile homes, noting some had lights within them, and others were dark. The hum of generators filled the air, and with it the smell of diesel, quickly overpowering the scent of food.

Little had caught their interest so far. The occasional figure drifted past in scruffy jeans or combat trousers, boots, trainers, t-shirts, and jackets. The passed a lone juggler, a middle-aged man with long, wild hair, throwing half a dozen balls into the air and catching them with grace and dexterity. He was mesmerising, and Avery dragged her gaze away as Alex pulled her towards the inner caravans. The light was brighter here, and as they peered around the corner of a van, they saw a small, central area with a blazing fire in the middle, and a muddle of seats around the edge in which a few people were sitting, chatting, and eating. They seemed comfortable and familiar with each other, which wasn't surprising, and so far there was nothing untoward happening, just the usual hustle and bustle of a crowd of people who knew each other well.

They walked on, heading to the outskirts, passing more vans grouped together around other fires, and it reminded Avery of music festivals, as every group sounded different; different music, different languages, and different types of performers. Eventually they reached the vans tucked beneath the furthermost hedge. An old gypsy caravan was set apart from the others. It was beautifully decorated, the door open to reveal a colourful interior lit with lamplight. It had its own small wood burner in there, and smoke poured from a tiny chimney, but there was a small fire burning outside, too. As she watched, the woman who she'd seen earlier that day in the town dressed in earthy colours walked down the steps in the same clothes, but with a large jumper and an old parka, too. She was rolling a cigarette between her fingers, but she paused and looked up towards Avery, and Avery quickly slipped back into the dark shadows next to a van, pulling Alex with her.

Alex looked puzzled, but she said nothing, watching the woman and wondering what she would do. For a moment she stood, looking perplexed, and then glanced around quickly as if unsure of her surroundings, but after another brief moment, she carried on down the steps and settled into an old wooden deck chair, propping her feet on a log as she smoked her cigarette and watched the flames.

Avery was rattled. For a moment, it felt as if she'd been seen. She raised herself up on tip-toes and whispered in Alex's ear. "Sorry. She's the woman I saw in town earlier, the one I thought looked into me."

Alex watched the woman. "Are you feeling anything from her now?"

"No, but for a second there, I thought she'd seen me through my spell, but I must be wrong."

"Interesting," he murmured. "I wonder who she is. I also wonder if I'd have had the same feeling if she'd seen me today, too."

"Like maybe she's some kind of witch detector?"

"Maybe."

They watched for a short while, but she remained alone, unmoving and remote.

"I wonder why she's set apart from the others?" Avery mused. "I'm too worried to get any closer to her. I feel as if she has an Avery-radar."

"I'm sure she doesn't, but let's not take any chances and check out the vans further along the hedge. Some of these look bigger than the others—maybe they belong to the managers."

They kept to the shadows, moving between the cars, vans and caravans, hearing snatches of conversation, usually about what crowds to expect, complaints about rehearsals, and relief the weather was warming up. And then they saw a tall, gaunt, middle-aged man exit a large camper van that had been converted from an old army vehicle. He bristled with authority and strode through the vans with purpose, but rather than follow him, they tiptoed up the steps to look into the interior.

It was dimly lit with one small lamp, and it illuminated a sitting area, a small kitchen, and large bed at the rear behind the driver's compartment, and it was a mess. Dirty glasses and plates crowded the surfaces, the bed was unmade, and clothes were strewn everywhere, but what was more interesting was the costume that draped over a chair. It was a cloak of black feathers, and a mask hung next to it—a feather hood and large beak.

"This must belong to the owner, Corbin, aka the Raven King," Alex suggested. "Isn't he the Ring Master?"

Avery nodded. "That's what Dan said. It's an amazing costume, but so were the ones the performers wore in town today. It's going to be quite the show."

"It doesn't tell us anything about who could be responsible for these deaths though, does it?" Alex headed for the exit, but before they could leave, they heard voices, and the man returned with another man behind him. It was Rafe. They walked up the shallow steps, shutting the door behind them.

Avery quickly reinforced their spell and they retreated to the back where it was dark, squashing next to the bed behind a row of clothes. If necessary and they were spotted, they could glamour them so they could escape, but Avery hoped it wouldn't come to that.

Corbin rounded on Rafe. "How is she? Is she keeping it at bay?"

He nodded. "For now. But it grows stronger, and I have a feeling that soon she won't be able to control it for much longer, despite the sacrifice not being complete. It will hunt, regardless."

Corbin punched the wall and swore. "Damn it, Rafe! I thought we'd get away with one more show."

Rafe drew himself up and looked him squarely in the eye. "And I told you we couldn't. It will feed before the first show, it's inevitable, but we'll make sure it happens away from here, as usual. Just stick to your end of the bargain. Caitlin's arrangement feeds this place—and you, don't forget that. Your costume wouldn't be half so impressive without it."

"You didn't fully explain the consequences of this," Corbin said, almost snarling.

Rafe laughed grimly. "Don't give me that crap. We did, but you just heard what you wanted to hear—money and success. You just let Caitlin do what she needs to, and we'll be fine. Hold your nerve, Corbin."

With that, Rafe pushed the door open and left, and Corbin watched him go, his hands clenched and his expression furious. He stood for a moment, breathing deeply, no doubt in an effort to calm himself down, and then he strode to a small fridge, grabbed a beer, and headed out again, slamming the door.

Avery let out a breath she hadn't even realised she'd been holding. "Wow. What did *that* mean?"

Alex was already untangling himself from the clothes. "I don't know, but we need to follow Rafe. He clearly knows more about this than anyone."

Unfortunately, by the time they stumbled down the steps into the night, Corbin and Rafe had both disappeared. For the next half an hour, they hunted between the cars, caravans, and camper vans, desperate to find Rafe, but he'd gone.

Avery scanned the crowd looking for Mairi, but couldn't see her, either. "If Rafe knows about this, Mairi must, too. They're married, so they must all be in this together. But who's Caitlin?"

"Good question," Alex said, as they left the field, frustrated that they had more questions than they'd had before.

They met the others back by the cars. Reuben leant against El's Land Rover, his arms crossed, and his hands tucked under his armpits. His long legs were stretched out on the road, and his head was tipped back, looking up at the stars. El sat inside, the engine running, trying to keep warm. Briar and Shadow were nowhere in sight.

"Any joy?" Reuben asked, straightening up as El joined them.

"You could say that," Alex replied. "Although, what we heard raises more questions than answers. You?"

"We sat on the seats in the dark at the back of the tent, watching the performers. They've already set up the high wires and trapeze, and a couple of acrobats were in there warming up. They're still decorating the inside, though."

El said, "It looks so cool. They're decorating the inside like the out. The walls are covered in paintings of leaves and images of the Green Man, but they're hanging thick curtains of leaves and feathers over the walls, too. The whole place felt like it was rustling, like it's alive, and that there are things watching you. Only half the stuff is up at the moment, but it will feel like we're in the middle of a wood when it's done."

"Any sign of magic?" Alex asked.

"None. Not yet, anyway," Reuben said. "At this stage, I just think it's well put together."

El agreed. "It will be interesting to see what it's like on a performance night, though. I certainly didn't pick up on any magic from the performers. And we didn't hear anything strange, either."

Avery placed her hands on the warm bonnet of El's car, which was still running. "We didn't feel any magic either, but after what we heard, something strange is definitely happening there." She looked beyond Reuben's bulk, up the slope to the castle in the distance. "I'm starting to get worried about Briar and Shadow, though."

Alex checked his watch. "They get five minutes, and then we go and find them."

"Tell us what you heard," El urged them.

Avery had only just started to tell them when they heard footsteps, and Shadow and Briar emerged out of the darkness, Briar glancing nervously behind them.

"Is everything okay?" Avery asked, alarmed. They seemed unsettled, even Shadow.

Briar's eyes were bright with excitement. "Ancient magic is happening up there. I felt the Green Man. Did you?"

"No!" Avery said, startled. "What about you, Shadow?"

Shadow also looked excited, and a bit furtive, which was worrying. "He's here, and he's bringing spring with him. Things are going to get very weird."

"Let's head to my place," Avery said immediately. "See you there."

***

"How come you could detect ancient magic when we couldn't?" Reuben asked Briar. He sat on one of the chairs that were placed around Avery's dining table, but he'd turned it around so that his legs straddled the seat as he leaned forward on the raised back of the chair.

Briar pointed to her bare feet that were currently flexing on Avery's rug. Her back was to the fire, and she faced the rest of the room, her hands cupped around a mug of tea. "These feet are very sensitive when bare and connected to the earth. Although it was freezing, I decided it was worth trying, and I immediately felt the connection, stronger than I've ever felt before. The Green Man is powering the earth up there. The actual Green Man! The strongest nature spirit of all is truly here! And now that I've felt him, I can't un-feel him. He's here—he's everywhere!"

Avery's stomach fluttered with worry. "Please don't say it's like what happened at Samhain in Old Haven Church." The earth in the wood had been saturated with blood magic, and with the aid of a powerful spell had enabled the opening of the portal. The earth had been tainted, and they had needed to cleanse it after they banished the Wild Hunt.

Briar shook her head vigorously. "No, absolutely not. This was very different. No blood magic, just good, strong Earth magic."

Shadow agreed. "I did what Briar did, and dug my feet into the earth, not expecting to feel anything really, beyond what I normally would, anyway." She shrugged. "As a fey I always have a connection with the earth. It sings to me, responds to me, like it recognises me. But," she paused, her violet eyes darkening to a stormy blue, "something else recognised me. He recognised me." She gazed into the fire and whatever visions lay in there, and her hand flew to her heart. "It felt like home."

The witches exchanged worried glances, and Avery said, "Forgive me for saying this, Shadow, but in the short time I've known you, you seem pretty impervious to anything, and yet, you look upset tonight."

Shadow just stared at her, unflinching. "You would be too if something had tugged at your soul."

"It must have been good to feel your home, though," El said to her gently. She turned to Avery and Alex. "What did you find out while you were hanging around their vans?"

"We found Corbin," Avery told them. "It seems he wears the Raven King's costume, which means he's the Ring Master. Well, that's what Dan told me, anyway." Between them, Avery and Alex related what they had seen and heard, and immediately the collective mood dipped even further.

Reuben reached for another beer and repeated what Avery had told them, "'It grows stronger, and I have a feeling that soon she won't be able to control it for much longer, despite the sacrifice not being complete. It will hunt, regardless.' Have I got that right? What the hell does it mean? Sacrifice sounds ominous."

"But who is Caitlin? And what is her arrangement that gives Corbin's costume power?" Alex asked.

"Whatever it is must be responsible for the Green Man's presence, too," Briar mused.

El brightened. "At least we know there's some kind of magic going on up there, enough to attract the Green Man, and maybe the Raven King—if that's what Rafe meant."

Briar was playing with the ends of her hair as she sat, thinking. "Maybe the circus is named after crossroads magic? Maybe that's what Rafe was talking about?"

Reuben's eyes widened. "Ooh! This sounds fun. Enlighten me."

Briar just looked at him. "Don't you read anything?"

To his credit, he was completely un-offended. "No. You know that. I surf, practice magic—which, admittedly involves some reading of grimoires—and work, when I have to. I'm not the research type."

Alex laughed and toasted him with his beer. "I love your honesty, Reu. You'd better educate all of us, Briar."

Briar settled on the rug, cross-legged, and pushed her long, dark hair back over her shoulders. "I know a little bit. Crossroads are liminal places, and offer a bridge between this world and the Otherworld." She noted Shadow's excited face. "But what the Otherworld is, is debatable. It could be the world of fey, or Hell, or where the spirits live. Common myths talk of being able to summon the Devil at the crossroads, or that the Devil will appear unbidden, promising you your heart's desire in exchange for your soul. They're a powerful place to perform magic, too. Offerings of food or wine can help you make decisions at important times of your life—when you're at a metaphorical crossroads."

"Do these myths occur all over the world?" Alex asked.

"I believe so, all with their own legends and interpretations. In Britain they're commonly linked with standing stones."

Avery sat up straighter. "Is that why there are standing stones at the entrance to the circus?"

Briar shrugged. "I guess so. Crossroads mark thresholds, keep the fey from our doors, and maybe show places where mythical creatures are buried.

Like many thresholds, they are more potent at dusk, dawn, and midnight. And of course, they're more powerful on Samhain."

El agreed, adding, "One of Hecate's many roles includes that of the crossroads witch, which I guess fits with her guarding the thresholds of the dead."

The room fell silent for a moment as they thought through the implications, and then Reuben spoke up. "So, the fact that the circus is named after crossroads means what?" He waved his half-empty beer bottle. "It's a good fit for British myth and magic, especially as their performances are based on myths, but is there a deeper meaning?"

A smile hovered on Alex's lips. "Of course there is, because..." He trailed off, looking at them expectantly.

"There's no such thing as coincidence," Avery finished for him. A heaviness settled in her bones and the pit of her stomach. The circus was bringing more than performers to White Haven. She turned to Shadow. "Are there crossroad myths in your world?"

Shadow's face broke into a smile. "We have many stories, old legends that stretch back years—well before I was born—but we would call them less myths than just old tales. The creatures that exist only on the periphery of your world walk about in mine, as real as the sun. But crossroads myths, I'm not so sure."

"What sort of creatures?" Briar asked, her face becoming animated.

That was a good question, Avery reflected. Shadow was a fey; she was a treasure of stories they hadn't even started to unpack.

"There are so many. This world feels only half-alive to me. So many things should be here that aren't." Her eyes dulled as she looked into the fire. "The trees and rivers have spirits—dryads, nymphs, water sprites—all of them are visible, with their own special magic. Satyrs, animal spirits, shapeshifters..."

"We have those," Reuben pointed out. "Briar's boyfriend is a wolf-shifter."

Briar rounded on him. "He's not my boyfriend."

Reuben smirked. "Liar."

Shadow smiled. "I would like to meet him. It's nice to be around creatures with blood from the Other."

Briar looked startled. "What?"

"Of a sort, surely? I told you that Gabe and the Nephilim are half-sylph. These Angels you speak of," she shrugged, unimpressed. "Sounds suspicious to me."

Avery rubbed her face. "This is great, Shadow, but we need to get back to the topic and find out if it is crossroads magic in that circus."

"And if it is, how it works," Alex added.

***

Newton looked at Avery bleakly. A frown creased his face, and he pulled at his tie, loosening it slightly. "Are you sure?"

"Yes, that's what we heard, and that's what Briar and Shadow felt."

They were in the back room of Avery's shop, which was her stock room and meeting place, and it was just past nine the next morning. Avery had forgotten how energetic Newton was at this hour; he sipped his tea with furious concentration, looking alert and calculating. She, however, felt barely alive. Avery hated mornings.

"But you have no idea who this mysterious Caitlin is?"

"None. We tried to find her, but Rafe had disappeared." She'd told him about the woman who was dressed in earth colours, and she referred to her now. "She might be Caitlin, or she could be unrelated."

"But someone, a woman, controls *it*, whatever that is," Newton pointed out. "And *it* needs to feed. That has to be our killer."

Avery mulled over his suggestion. The woman was perceptive, with an uncanny *knowing* about her. "The woman I saw could be her, but I'm not sure. It's just too soon to say."

After another moment of silence, Newton smiled, and his entire demeanour lifted. "Brilliant work, though. Thanks, Avery, and thank everyone else for me. It's unfortunate to know that we were right, but at least we know *something* about what's going on. I'm going to look into this Caitlin woman, and I think we need to get Ben and the guys involved."

He was referring to the three paranormal investigators, and Avery was startled. "Ben! Why?"

"If they can set cameras up, they might be able to read a weird energy signature."

"But where can they do that? That's nuts. The whole place is buzzing with people."

"On the hill somewhere? Dylan's clever, he'll think of something." He put his mug down. "I'm keen to stop a murder. If we can find whatever it is first, we could save a life."

"Yes, of course, but I'm not sure it's possible with a camera."

Buoyed with positive news, Newton headed for the door. "Can you contact them and let me know? I'm heading back to deal with vampire fallout." He grinned. "Thanks, Avery."

The door banged in his wake and Avery groaned. This was the most cheerful she had seen Newton in weeks, and although it was horrible news, it was also good news. They had an edge. She wasn't particularly pleased about being his deputy, though. She sighed and reached for her phone and tried Dylan first, but he didn't pick up, and neither did Ben, so she called Cassie, who answered quickly.

"Hey, Avery! How are you?" Her voice was warm and welcoming, but she also sounded tired.

"I'm fine, how are you?"

She sighed. "Busy with finishing our papers. We graduate this year, hopefully, so we're trying to get back into coursework after all that vampire madness."

Immediately Avery felt guilty at distracting them with another request. "Of course, I forgot you were in your last year. Have you and Dylan fully recovered now?" They had both been injured after Bethany the vampire had attacked them in the tunnels below West Haven.

"We're fine. Dylan's back to being his annoying, bouncy self, and my head injury cleared up really quickly."

"Good. Well, in that case, I'll leave you to it."

Cassie leapt in quickly. "But you must have called for something?"

"It's fine, you're busy, and you need to graduate."

"But what did you want?" she persisted.

"Newton wondered if Dylan could do some filming for him." She went on to explain what was happening at the circus.

"Of course he can," Cassie said, "and we'll do anything else you need."

"No, you're too busy."

"It's a bit of filming. Dylan will do it." Cassie hesitated for a moment, and Avery could hear other people around her. "I'm heading into lectures now, and then I'll find him and we'll call you. Sound good?"

"Great, but only if you're sure—"

The line went dead, and Cassie was gone.

Avery headed into the shop, taking a plate of chocolate biscuits with her.

Happenstance Books was quiet, with just a few customers browsing the shelves, and the place had a calm, reassuring feel to it. That morning she had reinforced her protection spells, and she felt soothed as she strolled through the shelving units to join Dan and Sally at the counter.

However, as soon as Sally saw Avery, she stood and grabbed a biscuit. "Great, have you finished in the back?"

"Yes, why?"

"I'm going to do a stock take of our children's section, and handle some accounts while we're quiet. That okay?"

Avery shrugged. "Of course, you don't need to ask me."

Sally disappeared, leaving Dan and Avery alone. Dan crunched into a biscuit, and speaking through a mouthful of crumbs, he said, "You look like you have the weight of the world on your shoulders."

"Do I?" She peered into the glass at the front window, hoping to catch her reflection. He was right; she did look slightly dishevelled. She rubbed her hair, pulled a lip salve out from her pocket, and ran it around her lips. "Better?"

Dan squinted. "Only if I look at you like this."

Avery looked over her shoulder to check that they weren't being watched, and then flicked her fingers at him, making a little *whoosh* of air ruffle his hair. "Cheeky sod."

He laughed. "I'm kidding. You look great. Apart from the weighed down-thing. What's happened now?"

Avery explained what they had found the night before, and what Newton wanted Dylan to do.

Dan whistled in surprise. "Wow. So the Crossroads Circus really has crossroads magic? There are lots of myths associated with that."

"So I gather. Got any to add to the list?"

He held up a finger and then pulled out his phone, scrolling through Spotify. In seconds, the music that was playing in the shop changed to an old Blues tune, and an achingly smooth voice filled the shop. "This is Robert Johnson," Dan explained. "Heard of him?"

"No."

"He's an American Blues musician who performed in the 1930s. One day his guitar playing became phenomenal, and when asked about it, he said he'd sold his soul to the Devil at the crossroads in exchange for musical talent."

Avery's coffee cup stopped halfway to her lips. "Really?"

"Really. He was very honest about it. And then he died at that spooky age when all great musicians die."

"27?"

Dan nodded. "The Devil came to claim his soul! This track is actually called 'Cross Road Blues.'"

The Blues guitar and Johnson's haunting voice filled the room. Avery shivered. "Well that's just spooky."

"I'll try and find some more stuff for you later. In the meantime, I'll line up his album."

The bell ringing above the door disturbed them, and Avery turned to see Caspian enter the shop. He paused and listened.

"Delta blues. I like it." He joined them at the counter. Caspian looked smart, dressed in a formal suit and three-quarter length woollen jacket.

"To what do we owe this pleasure, Caspian?" Avery asked him, suddenly self-conscious of her appearance.

"Gabe told me we have a new problem."

'News travels fast!"

"Need my help?" he asked, raising a quizzical eyebrow.

"I'm not entirely sure what we need help with right now. We're just starting to investigate."

Dan waved them away. "Off to your meeting, Avery. I've got this."

Avery wasn't really sure she wanted to spend time alone with Caspian, but this certainly wasn't a conversation for the shop floor. "Fair enough. Follow me, Caspian."

Sally was in the back room, on the computer, and she looked up as Avery entered. Her face fell as she saw Caspian. Reformed character or not, he had kidnapped Sally months before, and she hadn't forgiven him. She went to stand. "I'll leave you to it."

"No, you stay here," Avery said, gesturing for her to sit down. "We'll talk upstairs."

She led Caspian up to her flat, and as soon as they were alone, Caspian took his jacket off and draped it across the back of a chair. "Crossroads magic is complicated, Avery."

She perched on the arm of the sofa. "So I gather."

"We should tell Genevieve."

"But nothing's happened yet."

"Even better."

"I'd like to keep this small. The vampire thing became huge!"

"It needed to be. Vampires are deadly."

"Well, hopefully this thing isn't as dangerous. I think we can handle it."

He watched her silently for a moment, and Avery's living room began to feel very small. He finally spoke. "You're very stubborn."

"It's part of my charm," she shot back.

"I know." His eyes drifted to her lips and then back to her eyes, and a smile crossed his lips.

Shit. Wrong thing to say. Caspian did not need any encouragement. "Behave," she warned him. "Have you some gems of wisdom to share?"

"Not yet, but I'd like it if you'd tell me what's happening."

Avery sighed, and for what felt like the hundredth time, explained what had happened at the circus the night before, and the suspicious events around the country that made them suspect the circus in the first place.

He nodded. "A circus is a good place to hide a supernatural creature. Circuses already have a reputation for odd characters, and they travel frequently."

A thought struck Avery. "True, but although this circus is named after crossroads, it's not actually on a crossroad, is it? So why has it got crossroads magic? It's a travelling circus. They're not even on crossroads up at the castle!"

"Interesting point." He smiled again. "It's a good thing we like a puzzle, isn't it? Are you going again?"

"We're going to go to the opening night, on Saturday, and we'll probably go with Dylan if he agrees to set up cameras. That might be tonight."

"Good. Keep me informed. I can help if you need me." He picked his coat up and headed for the door.

"Thanks, hopefully we'll be fine."

"Hopefully." And then he left, smiling at her enigmatically.

As the door clicked shut, Avery's phone rang. It was Dylan, and he didn't waste time with pleasantries. "Hey Ave, of course I'll help. Let's do it tonight. I can go alone."

"No, you can't. We don't know what might happen. Where are you thinking of putting cameras?"

"I don't know yet, but I'll think of something. I'll come around at eight tonight. Laters!" And then he was gone, and once again Avery felt as if her life was spiralling slightly out of her control.

5

Avery, Alex, Dylan, and Ben stood on the ridge of the hill looking down on the castle, which had become an apparition of itself; the yellow lights that illuminated the walls were webbed by a heavy mist, which had become steadily thicker as night fell, draping the landscape in veils of illusion. They had pulled onto the verge of a road further away from the castle and trekked across the fields, approaching well away from the grounds.

Once again, the circus tent was lit up, and fires burned sporadically across the campsite next to it, but like the castle, they were ghostly. Avery glanced around and shivered. It was eerie here, surrounded by darkness and the sticky fingers of mist. She imagined she could hear things moving beyond her vision and stepped closer to Alex.

"Where are you thinking of putting the cameras?" Alex asked, shuffling on his feet to keep warm.

Dylan pointed to a black shape further down the hill. "That tree will be great. Close enough to get decent images, but far enough away for them not to see it. Besides, I'll put it up high. But I'm not sure about the other two."

"Something will suggest itself," Alex said, setting off down the hill. "Let's get this one in first."

The wet grass was spongy, and Avery was glad she'd worn Wellington boots. The others, however, wore trainers or short leather boots, and their jeans were already wet around their calves when they reached the huge oak in the middle of the field.

Dylan opened his backpack and scrabbled around, pulling out a small, lightweight camera. He checked the batteries and the settings, while Ben pulled a wooden box out of his own pack and a cordless drill.

"This is what we'll house it in," Ben explained. "We've used them before at Old Haven Church and other places, and it means the camera is fixed and protected from the weather, at least for a short time." He looked around, worried. "However, it's cold and damp out here, and I'm worried it will affect the camera's performance. The box is insulated, though."

Dylan grimaced. "It wasn't too bad at Samhain, but I'll have to come in the morning to get it, in the light. I should be far enough away that no one really notices what I'm doing, but I'll leave it to tomorrow night if it looks risky."

He took the box, drill, and screws from Ben, put them in a much smaller pack that he had pulled from the larger one, and started to climb the tree. He was quick and agile, and he swung up through the branches effortlessly. After another few minutes Ben's phone buzzed, its volume muted, and he read the text aloud. "He's ready."

Alex said a small spell designed to muffle sound, which would stop the noise of the drill from echoing across the fields. After another few minutes, Dylan reappeared, exchanged the drill for the camera, and headed back up the tree.

Avery and Alex watched the castle and their surroundings, wary for any intruders. However, everything was silent, other than the rubbing of bare branches overhead, clacking like disapproving old women. Avery could see movement around the campsite, and people going in and out the circus tent, and there were a lot of smaller stalls now erected within the castle walls. A few shouts reached them, but nothing that could be understood. Avery closed her eyes and reached her awareness out, feeling for magic. She didn't take her shoes off; that would be pointless. She couldn't feel Earth magic as strongly as Briar, but the wind could carry things to her. She reached out, pulling air towards her from the campgrounds, and all of a sudden, the faint noises grew louder. She stepped away from Alex to allow her to concentrate on the snatched conversations: questions about performances, complaints about someone's noise, an argument about costumes.

And then she felt *her*—the mysterious woman.

Avery was momentarily startled, but rather than retreat, she shielded herself and the others with a protective spell, blocking her probing mind. She was pretty sure she'd detected her first, before the woman became aware of her presence. She waited, feeling her mind like the gentle brush of a feather, as it moved past her and the others, moving up the hill and out across the fields. If she had detected them, she would have loitered, pushed harder to try to find out who they were. Fortunately she didn't, and Avery relaxed.

Now that Avery had detected her, she could follow her easily. She was searching for something, but what? And then she vanished. *Damn it.* She'd gone too far, past where Avery could follow her. *How did she do that?* Avery wasn't sure she could send *her* mind so far from her body, not without spirit-walking anyway, and this wasn't spirit-walking; she was sure of that. Unfortunately, there was nothing that would tell her more about who she was, or what her powers were, but Avery was sure she wasn't a witch. After another few moments, Avery turned her concentration back to the circus below.

Alex disturbed her, gently taking her right elbow in his hand. "Are you okay? You're miles away."

"That woman has been here, searching for something."

"Did she detect us?"

"No, I don't think so. I shielded us, and she passed on, across the fields." She nodded in the general direction that she had gone.

"I felt your magic flare, and I wondered what for. I thought you were searching."

"I was. It was good timing."

Dylan landed on the ground behind them with a *thump*. "Done. On to the next." He looked between them. "What's happened?"

"Someone's *essence* is out here, searching for something," Avery told him. "But don't worry, we've got it covered."

"Good, let's get a move on," Ben said decisively. "I want to get to the far outer wall of the castle. There's no one near there. We can mount a camera on that."

He turned and led the way to a large bulk of blackness that was dense against the grey of the sky. There was no moon or stars to guide them, and it was tricky going, especially in the mist. Avery stumbled in rabbit holes and over patches of gorse, until eventually they reached the outer wall, which stood a good distance away from the main part of the castle. It enclosed a smooth, grassed area that ran to the edge of the castle's interior.

"Do you want me to focus on the campsite, or the circus tent?" Dylan asked as he pulled another camera from his pack.

"Campsite," Avery said immediately. "There are all sorts of things going on there."

All the while they had been walking, Avery had kept the protective shield around them, and now she focused on trying to feel the woman's presence again, while Dylan climbed the crumbling wall, and Alex and Ben supported him. The mist was growing thicker, and its cold fingers stroked Avery's cheek and reached down her neck. She felt moisture on her eyelashes and skin but ignored it, as she concentrated on the campsite and the surrounding area.

Then she felt the beat of wings, low overhead. Their span felt unnaturally large, and the wave of air threatened to push her into the earth. She felt Alex jump besides her as he felt it too, and they crouched to avoid being hit. A presence loomed above them, silent and oppressive, and she felt an unknown power smother her, silencing all other night sounds. Then it magnified a hundred times, and the sensation of one single span of wings exploded into hundreds of birds, all flapping above her as they streaked away across the land and over the sea.

They leapt to their feet as the oppressive feeling disappeared, and looked to the horizon.

"What the hell was that?" Alex asked her in urgent, hushed tones.

"I've no idea. What is happening here?" Avery felt breathless with panic.

But before he could answer, she felt a surge of *something*, and the unmistakable feeling of malevolent glee. She grabbed Alex's hand and felt the flutter of wings return overhead, back to the campsite where they vanished to a single point, and normal night sounds returned.

"It must be the Raven King," Avery suggested. "Did you feel wings, too?"

He nodded, looking as bewildered as Avery felt, but Ben's voice disturbed them. "What is going on with you two?"

Ben and Dylan were watching them from the shelter of the wall, both wide-eyed.

"Didn't you feel it?" Alex asked them in a low voice.

"No," Dylan said. "Why were you both crouching?"

"It felt as if there were hundreds of birds flying overhead, and I had this feeling of doom," Avery explained, for want of a better word.

Ben and Dylan exchanged a confused glance, and Dylan said, "*Birds*? We didn't feel a thing."

Now it was Avery and Alex who were exchanging worried glances. "Not surprising, really," Alex finally said. "It's a magic thing. You done here?"

Dylan nodded. "You want me to place the final camera?"

"Part of me wants to say yes. The more we know, the better. But most of me just wants to get out of here," Alex answered.

Avery nodded in agreement, and looked back over her shoulder to the campsite, where everything looked surprisingly normal. "I agree. Forget the last camera. Let's get back to the car. Are you sure they're set up?"

"Absolutely," Dylan said, reassuring them.

They headed back across the fields, but within a few minutes the light from the castle grounds disappeared behind them, and they were in pitch darkness, surrounded by mist that was so thick, they could barely see each other.

Avery faltered, gripping Alex's hand tightly. "Are we going in the right direction?"

He paused, too. "I think so, but I can't see a damn thing. Dylan, Ben? What do you think?"

Ben's voice was tight with worry. "I don't know where we are, but we're heading uphill, so we must be going the right way."

"Let's stay close together," Dylan suggested. "No wandering off!"

They trudged onwards, and the field seemed to go on forever. Alex gripped Avery's hand as they stumbled over uneven ground, and with unspoken agreement they quickened their pace. Suddenly, an unexpected wind rustled the grass beneath their feet, and the scent of loamy earth surrounded them, rich and overwhelming, almost cloying as it filled their nostrils.

They stopped again. "Feel that?" Alex asked Dylan and Ben.

They nodded and Ben said, "I can *smell* that."

"I don't know if that's a good or a bad thing," Alex admitted, perplexed. "Let's keep going."

They pushed on as the rustling sound and the smell of earth became more insistent, until Ben said in a panicked, whispered tone, "Why aren't we coming to a hedge? We should be at the boundary by now. We only crossed one sodding field."

"Things seem further when you can't see where you going," Avery said, trying to be logical in the face of increasing panic. She strengthened the protection spell, and as she did so, felt the unmistakable presence of the woman again. She suddenly started to doubt herself. *Were they as protected as she thought? Was this a game? A ruse?*

Avery's voice was strained. "I think we're being hunted."

"What?" Dylan hissed, whirling around.

"I can feel something stalking us—despite my spell," Avery said, almost stumbling over her words.

Alex squeezed her hand. "I feel something, too. We need to think smarter. I think we're being led astray. This smell of earth is bewildering, and the rustling all around us is misleading."

Avery thought of the spells she could say without needing her grimoire. "What about a finding spell on Ben's van?"

"Try it," Alex urged.

Avery turned to Ben. "Give me some of your hair and the keys."

Without question, Ben yanked a few strands free and placed them and his keys in Avery's hand. Trying to block out everything else, she said the spell, and within seconds a blue light appeared before them, and then set off across the grass, barely visible in the mist.

"It's going the wrong way, I'm sure," Dylan said, watching it go.

"Trust it. Go now!" Avery cried, and ignoring their instincts they virtually ran after it, stumbling and falling occasionally in their haste.

Avery could feel it now. Something was behind them, gaining ground, but just as Avery was prepared to turn and fight, they ran headlong into the break in the hedge, the van appearing in front of them. It beeped as Ben unlocked it, and he slid across the bonnet in his haste to get to the door. Dylan dove for the passenger door, and Alex and Avery threw themselves in the back. The doors were barely shut as Ben sped away, tires squealing.

Avery pressed her face to the glass, watching as another face manifested out of the swirling mist. She fell back in shock, but a wave of magic exploded from Alex's outstretched hand behind her, and he sent a spear of concentrated power at the mysterious entity. It exploded into fragments as Ben put distance between them.

"Anyone want to tell me what happened back there?" Dylan said, turning around in his seat to look at them. He sniffed his jacket. "I think I can still smell that composty stench."

Avery and Alex exchanged a troubled glance, and Avery said, "I think we were pursued by the Green Man, the Raven King, and the unknown woman. One of them was threatening us, and I'm not sure who it was."

"Me neither," Alex agreed.

Ben drove recklessly through the country lanes, glancing back at them to ask, "Just back up a moment. I thought the Raven King was just a costume, and the Green Man was the theme of the circus. How they can now be *real*?"

Alex spread his hands wide, shrugging. "We don't know, but Briar and Shadow are convinced the Green Man is here, courtesy of boundary magic, which must apply to the Raven King, too. And don't ask us how that works when the circus isn't on a crossroad either, we have no idea. I'm very confused right now."

"Essentially, you're saying something is bringing those myths to life?"

Avery nodded as she remembered what Rafe had said in the camper van only the night before. "And we know *something* is inhabiting *someone* and its hunger is growing, and it will hunt."

Alex looked at her, perplexed. "Did you feel that pulse of power, while we were sheltering under the castle wall? That feeling of pleasure that something had?"

"Yes. Why?"

"Maybe *it* already hunted. Maybe someone is already dead."

Ben groaned. "Bloody brilliant. Maybe we were next on the list. We were in the middle of that field, alone, unseen, and being shepherded away from safety, until you did that spell, Avery."

"But I had put a protection spell around us. Does that mean it was useless?"

"Maybe not," Alex said. "We're still here, aren't we?"

"But whatever it was, it was gaining ground on us. We all felt it."

"We need to hit the books again, soon," Alex suggested.

"Yes, that's a good idea. If you guys do pick up those cameras tomorrow," Avery said, "don't go alone."

Dylan laughed dryly. "You don't need to worry about that. We'll go early, as soon as it's light, and change the card and batteries. I'm betting circus folk aren't early risers."

"Don't take any chances!" Avery warned them.

"We won't, and with luck, the mist will cover us," Dylan said, as Ben pulled into the outskirts of White Haven and made his way to The Wayward Son.

"You two coming in for a drink?" Alex asked.

Ben twisted around in his seat as he stopped outside the pub. He still looked damp from the mist, and his hair was tousled. "I'd rather get home. Then I can have a hot shower and several stiff whiskeys."

"I hear that," Dylan agreed.

"All right," Alex nodded. "We'll be in touch. And stay safe."

6

"Whatever was chasing us somehow got through my protection spell," Avery murmured to Alex as they curled in bed, holding each other.

"Not true," he said, his warm breath tickling her ear. "It's not meant to hide us, not like your shadow spell. It did as it should—it protected us. Whatever was chasing us couldn't get close."

She snuggled against him. "I suppose you're right. But I did shield us earlier, when I felt that woman's presence in the field. She couldn't find us then."

"But then other things happened, and you probably dropped it unconsciously." He rolled on top of her, a forearm on either side of her head supporting his weight as he looked down at her. "I think it's a good thing they know we're watching. It might make them hesitate."

Her hand traced the contours of his face. "They didn't seem too worried to me. They chased us across the field. The Green Man was around us! It had to be him! I just wish I knew what it all meant."

"We'll work it out, we always do," he said before kissing her and leaving her breathless. "Now, I think we have better things to do than talk about that damn circus." And as his hand trailed down her body, Avery blocked out the night and their pursuers, focusing only on Alex, his touch, his lips, and the delicious heat spreading from her stomach.

Unfortunately, Avery didn't sleep easily. She dreamt that she was in the field again, and this time the mysterious pursuer was closer and Avery was alone. The mist was once again wrapped around her, and the rustling of the hedges and grass beneath her feet was vividly real. For a second she stood her ground, and then as she felt the strange presence grow closer, Avery ran as fast as she could, but she had no idea where she was running to. Something was close. She thought she heard breathing behind her, and a whisper of some undecipherable word, and she stumbled as something on the ground wrapped around her ankles. She fell heavily, her breath knocked out of her, and she felt the wet grass against her cheek and beneath her palms. She struggled to rise, but she couldn't get up. Something was smothering her, suffocating her, and she tried to scream, but she couldn't do that, either.

She was going to die, and she couldn't summon her magic. She couldn't do anything. With a monumental effort she pushed her attacker away and her eyes flew open, and suddenly she was back in Alex's bedroom, sitting upright, eyes wide open.

Her heart was pounding in her chest, and she took some deep breaths. Alex was asleep at her side, oblivious to her panic. It was just a bad dream, she told herself. But she couldn't shake the ominous feeling the dream had brought with it, and she shuddered as she tried to go back to sleep.

When Avery woke the next morning, she smelt bacon, and she slipped out of bed and headed to the kitchen, pushing the strange dream of the night before to the back of her mind.

"You're cooking! Thank you."

Alex smiled, his hair tangled around his face and stubble creeping across his cheeks. He pushed a cup towards her across the counter. "My pleasure. Here's your coffee." He watched her for a second as she took a sip and said, "Have you ever considered if we should move in together? We're at each other's place most nights anyway."

She paused as she met his eyes, feeling a flush of pleasure. "I had, actually. But I guess it's tricky with us both living above where we work. And I have my cats, so…"

"You'd rather be at your place than mine." He smiled as he moved closer. "For the record, your place is bigger, as well as the fact that you have two cats, so it would make sense to me, too."

She grinned. "Are you saying you want to move into my place? Properly?"

"I guess so. Sound okay?"

"Sounds great," she said, a warm, fuzzy feeling filling her. "But your flat is gorgeous. What will you do with it? And all of your lovely furniture?"

"I'll keep it empty for now and we'll see how it goes. You never know," he teased her, "your mess might start to drive me insane."

"My mess!" she said, wanting to throw something at him. "I'm not messy. That much."

He laughed and kissed her. "You know you are. But that's okay. It's part of your charm. Now, let me finish breakfast, because we have somewhere to be."

"Where?"

His face fell and he became serious. "Newton just called. Someone found a body on the beach this morning. He wants us to look at it."

Last night's activities came flooding back to Avery. "Oh, no. It's not a natural death, then?"

"Maybe not. Get dressed, food will be ready in a few minutes."

***

The beach was silent, other than the steady lap of waves on the shore. The sea was oddly calm, but so was the weather. There wasn't a breath of wind, and although the mist had lifted slightly, there were still ribbons of it undulating across the sands and winding up the steep cliff face.

They were at the same beach where Avery had first met Caspian. A set of rickety wooden steps led from the car park on the hill to the beach below, and rock pools edged along the far side, under the cliff. Avery wrinkled her nose as she looked around, wondering what felt so different. And then it clicked.

It felt like early spring. Shadow was right about the Green Man's influence.

Avery and Alex reached the bottom of the steps together, and Newton walked over to join them, a woman next to him. She was in her mid-thirties and had olive skin and very dark hair, and she looked curiously at both of them. Avery felt uncomfortable under her direct gaze. It was something the police did well, and she assumed she had to be the new detective, Walker.

Newton greeted them. "Thanks for coming. This is DCI Inez Walker, the detective I was telling you about."

Inez shook their hands. "Good to meet you. Newton has told me how you help his investigations sometimes, although I feel he's not telling me everything." She gave Newton a long, sideways glance.

"This way," Newton said, not rising to the bait, "and wear these." He handed them plastic overshoes, watched while they put them on, and then walked over to the man's body, which was on the dry sand, just above the tide mark.

Officer Moore was a short distance away, watching them silently, and a dog sat next to a policeman who had it on a lead. It whined and pawed the ground, agitated.

Avery eyed it regretfully. "Is that the victim's dog?"

Newton sighed. "I'm afraid so. It seems they went for a late night walk and never came back. Someone jogging on the cliff path," he paused and pointed over their heads, "saw him lying here, and called it in."

Avery looked at the man at her feet. Other than being dead, he looked normal, nothing to indicate how he'd died. "Is there anything you want us to focus on?"

He shook his head. "Just see if you can detect any magic, or anything odd. The coroner will be here soon, and SOCO. I'll tell them that you two were here to consult. I was given clearance for it."

Avery thought she detected Inez flinch when Newton mentioned magic, but she recovered quickly. Alex had already crouched and he held his hands out above the body, so Avery sent her magic across the beach, trying to feel anything further afield. She shook her head. "I can't feel a thing," she said regretfully. "What about you, Alex?"

He looked up. "I sense a powerful type of energy I haven't felt before. You try."

She'd hoped to avoid this, but she crouched next to him, echoing his movements. He was right. "Yes, I feel it. It's like that oppressive power we felt last night."

Inez narrowed her eyes. "A power?"

Avery nodded. "Malevolent. Well, that's how it seemed to me."

Newton intervened. "Alex mentioned something has happened."

Avery rolled her eyes in disbelief. "Lots of weird things. We can tell you later. We might know more, too, if Dylan had success with the camera."

"Good. Can you narrow down this sense of oppression?" Newton asked. "Would you recognise it again?"

Alex and Avery exchanged glances, and Avery shrugged. "Probably."

"Good."

It looked as if Inez wanted to ask more questions, but the noise of cars from the car park above disturbed them.

"That will be the coroner," Newton said. "We'll see you later." And with that, they were dismissed, and Alex and Avery headed up the steps, aware of Inez watching them all the way.

"Well, it's clear Newton hasn't told her that much about us yet," Alex noted as they reached his car.

"No. But that won't last long, and then it will be interesting to see just how open-minded she is. He didn't say if he'd found out who Caitlin was, either."

"I guess this has side-tracked him," Alex said. "I'll ask him later."

***

Sally's hand was already at her mouth as she listened. "You had to do *what?*" She closed her eyes briefly. "Please don't tell me something else is happening here."

"Sorry," Avery said, feeling inexplicably guilty. "It seems someone at the circus is responsible for those deaths after all."

Sally's expression changed as she spat out, "Bollocks. The kids were so excited about that circus. I can't take them now!" She looked at Avery, outraged. "No one should be taking their kids there."

Avery's mouth fell open and she looked at Sally, shocked. "We can't announce this! We have no evidence. And besides, everyone who has attended the circus in other towns has been fine! The performance will be safe enough."

Sally continued to glare. "I don't care. I'm not taking the kids."

"That's fair enough, but it's not my fault, you know."

Sally deflated like a popped balloon. "I know, but I was just hoping life would get back to normal around here, or at least relative safety. I'm fine with magic, just not the deaths."

"No one's fine with the deaths, Sally, you fruit loop."

The shop was quiet, and Sally, Dan, and Avery were chatting around the counter in a lull between customers.

"Someone needs a chocolate biscuit," Dan said, holding out the open packet.

Sally glared at him, too. "It will take more than a digestive biscuit to make me feel better."

"But it will help, right?" he said, wafting it under her nose. "I'm as upset as you, Sally, but we're here to stop this. It's our job now."

Avery looked at him, surprised. "That's very sweet of you, Dan."

He puffed his chest out. "I'm Team Witch all the way, you know that. I'm tackling Raven King and Green Man myths for you later. "

"Thanks," she said, taking a biscuit for herself. "I should call Genevieve."

"Why are you putting it off?"

"I just think it's something we can handle, that's all."

"But she has collective knowledge, and you've got Oswald and all the oldies to ask. Although, you do have me, and I'm awesome."

"True, so awesome," she said, sarcastically. "I'll call her soon, before Caspian beats me to it, and outs me like a grass."

"However," Dan continued, jabbing his half-eaten biscuit, "I have been thinking about the Green Man and his connection with the crossroads, and I would argue that he's another liminal figure. He sits on the boundaries of earth, nature, growth, decay. He's a nature spirit, essentially, and here we are, blind and unknowing in the presence of nature's true face. It's there, just beyond our understanding, a wild force we can't control."

"Holy cow. Have you drank extra strength coffee this morning?" Avery asked, looking at him, amazed.

"Master's in Folklore," he said, poking at his chest. "Almost. By the way, I'll need a few days off to finish up soon."

"Sure," Avery agreed, not fully focusing on what he was saying.

"That's pretty cool, actually," Sally said, her expression softening. "The Crossroads Circus has all sorts of crossroads figures in it. Maybe I will go, after all."

Avery leant on the counter. "I just wish I knew who the other woman is, the one I saw behind the procession, and at the campground. I wasn't sure she was with them at the time, but she has to be. She's camped with them, admittedly a little bit separate from the rest. I wonder what her role is? I felt she looked straight through me, and her mind—her awareness—travelled far beyond where mine can." She thought through the attack in the field. "I'm convinced she was the presence I felt."

"Maybe she's the conduit for the crossroads magic," Sally suggested. "As you said, the circus isn't on an actual crossroads, so if the name refers to the magic from a crossroads, maybe she's it. She carries it within her."

Dan and Avery blinked at her, and Avery said, "That's quite brilliant, Sally."

Sally looked pleased. "Is it? Oh, good."

Dan continued to theorise. "She could be that Caitlin woman."

Avery's voice filled with excitement. "Rafe said 'Caitlin's arrangement feeds this place,' but it didn't make sense at the time. That could be what it means—an arrangement to get crossroads magic. I feel something is just beyond our reach, though."

Dan nodded. "Yeah, we're not quite there yet, but it will all drop into place."

"But when? We're running out of time. They've killed once already. What if once isn't enough this time?"

"Let's hope Dylan's film suggests something," Dan said, before falling silent as the doorbell chimed, announcing a customer.

"I'm hitting the books," Avery announced, aware they'd know exactly what books she was referring to.

They nodded, and Sally called, "Good luck!" as Avery made her way up to her flat

***

As Avery walked into her lounge, she looked around, wondering how her home would feel once Alex moved in. She smiled. It would feel great. *As long as he didn't try to make her tidy too much.*

She glanced at the sofa. Hers was a little worn compared to his. Maybe they should bring his sofa here. It was important that he had some of his belongings here, too. She stroked the cats that curled around her legs, and headed to the kitchen to give them snacks, thinking about what Dan and Sally had suggested. It was an intriguing suggestion that someone was carrying crossroads magic, essentially boundary magic.

What would this mean for Shadow? Was that a way for her to get home? She shook her head. Unlikely. As they knew from past experience, the power needed for that was huge, and she couldn't feel that much magic so far.

After feeding the cats Avery headed to the attic, spelling on lamps, candles, and the fire as she went. The day was gloomy, and the mist that had lifted earlier was back, blurring the outside world, and making her rooms dark.

She'd already checked the occult section in her shop for books on boundary magic, but hadn't found anything particularly relevant. However, she knew that all the best books were in her private space, anyway. She pulled a few off the shelves and spread them across her wooden worktable, trying to decide where to start, when she realised she hadn't yet phoned Genevieve.

Steeling herself for rebuke, she called her, and Genevieve immediately picked up.

"Hi Genevieve, how are you? It's Avery."

"I'm fine, are you? You don't normally call to chat."

"Damn it. Sprung already," Avery admitted.

Genevieve groaned. "What's happened now?"

She updated her as succinctly as possible and then asked, "Do you know much about crossroads magic?"

Genevieve was silent for moment. "Not really, but there are ways of linking yourself to a crossroads, to carry the power with you. I'll have to do some reading to check exactly how, though."

"No, don't bother, I'll do it. I'm sure you're busy."

"To be honest, I am. Are you sure you don't mind?"

Avery breathed an inward sigh of relief. "No, this call was just to keep you informed. Caspian's offered to help, too."

"Has he now? He's quite the reformed character," she remarked. "Thanks, Avery. Do continue to keep me informed, and if I think of anything, I'll call you."

Happy she'd kept Genevieve up to date and also escaped her ire, Avery turned back to her books, and spent the next half an hour identifying all the ones that had the most relevant articles. Then she turned to her grimoires. She found more crossroads spells in them than she expected, but then again, she'd never looked for such things before. Most talked about the power of boundaries and performing spells on crossroads, and also suggested ways to draw on spirits for their aid. She shuddered. She had no intention of doing that.

As usual, whenever she worked with her original grimoire, she thought of Helena, her ancestor who'd been burned at the stake, and whose ghostly presence inhabited her flat. Naturally, it wasn't long before Helena appeared. She manifested on the opposite side of the table, watching Avery with her cool brown eyes, and she brought the scent of smoke and violets with her. Helena had saved her life when Bethany the vampire had knocked at Avery's window in the middle of the night, trying to tempt her to let her in. As much as Helena unnerved her, and the fact that their past together was complex, Avery liked to see her. She made her feel grounded with her history.

Avery smiled. "Helena, good timing. I'm investigating crossroads magic. Any idea how you link to a crossroads? You know, bring its magic with you?"

Helena was unable to speak, but she did help in other ways, depending on her mood. She frowned, and floated around the table, her long black skirts moving across the floor silently as she arrived next to Avery. She leaned forward over her grimoire and a gentle wind ruffled the pages, finally falling open on a page with a scrawl of writing on it and the images of keys. The spell was written in Middle English, and was difficult to read; no wonder Avery hadn't found it. One word, however, was clear. Hecate, the Goddess of crossroads magic.

Having found the spell, Helena moved away, towards the fireplace. She settled on the small sofa and stared into the flames, a very human activity that was more sorrow-inducing than scary.

Avery called over to her, "Thanks, Helena. By the way, Alex is moving in."

Helena nodded, disinterested, and Avery turned back to the spell. She needed her dictionary if she was to understand this. She settled on a stool and lost herself in the translation.

It was well over an hour later when her phone rang, and she jumped as her silence was disturbed. "Dylan. How did you get on?"

"Pretty well," he said, cautiously. "Do you want to see it?"

"Of course."

"Great. Get the beers in and the witches round, and we'll see you at seven."

After talking to Dylan, Avery decided she should call Shadow, too. It was only fair, and she had proven useful the night they had first surveyed the campgrounds. It was a short conversation. She agreed to join them without hesitation.

Avery had one more call that afternoon from Newton, and his mood was grim. "We prioritised the post-mortem on the young man we found this morning. His death is like the others. His organs are atrophied and old, as if his insides were older than his body."

Avery fell silent for a moment as she took in what he was saying.

"Are you still there?" Newton asked.

"Yes, sorry. I guess that was only to be expected. I think we are making progress, though. Dylan is bringing the footage we've captured around later if you want to see it."

"Of course I bloody do," he said brusquely.

"Did you find any evidence on the body?"

"Nothing. Just like the others. I hope you have something on this, Avery. Otherwise, this will keep happening, and the pressure's on."

"We're moving on this as fast as we can, Newton!"

Now it was his turn to fall silent, before he eventually admitted, "I know. I miss Briar."

Avery's heart sank. "She's still your friend—most of the time."

Newton made a grunting sound. "Is HE coming down again?" He meant Hunter.

"Not for a couple of weeks. It's too far to travel very often, so you don't have to force yourself to be polite."

"Good. And I'm always polite."

Avery threw her head back and laughed loudly, disturbing both the cats and Helena, who still reclined on the sofa. "You know that's bullshit, right?"

"Oh, sod off," he said, impatiently. "I'll see you later."

7

Briar was the first to appear that evening, and she brought crisps and dips to share.

As Avery welcomed her, she couldn't help but notice how pretty Briar looked, and how content. "Have you been chatting to Hunter?" she asked her.

Briar glanced at Avery as she filled a bowl with crisps. "Yes, why?"

"You have a glow."

She wrinkled her nose. "I do not."

"Yes, you do. Don't deny it. I'm pleased for you. Is he treating you well?"

Briar blushed. "Yes. He says the sweetest things."

"Sweet is not the word I was expecting to hear describing Hunter."

She grinned mischievously. "There are times that he's very naughty."

"How naughty?"

"Too naughty to share with you!"

Avery laughed. "Excellent. You deserve some naughtiness. No regrets about Newton?"

Briar met her eyes. "No. It was the right call. Does he ever say anything?"

"He grumps about Hunter, but he knows he has no right to. He'll get over it. We met his new detective friend, Walker, today. He doesn't seem to be sharing much about us at the moment, which is a relief until we know her."

"Good. It will be interesting to see how she deals with the paranormal world."

"Maybe she's involved because she knows a lot of it already. Looks like she'll keep Newton on his toes, anyway."

They were disturbed by the arrival of some of the others, and before long, everyone was present. After a flurry of snack-grabbing and finding drinks, they crowded onto seats in Avery's living room, wedged either on the sofa, the floor, or on chairs pulled in from the dining table.

Dylan quickly loaded the footage on to Avery's TV. It was taken from the camera that he had wedged into the castle wall, and it was, as usual, shot using thermal imaging. The images were startling.

Reuben leaned forward, watching the screen with his forehead creased. "Is that some kind of spectral mist?"

"It looks like it, doesn't it?" Ben said brightly.

Newton almost growled. "You're not supposed to be excited about this crap!"

Ben looked affronted. "It's not every day you see a spectral mist and get it on camera!"

"I think it's cool!" Reuben declared, still staring intently at the screen.

Briar looked confused. "But where is it coming from? And is it really spectral?"

Dylan narrowed his eyes. "Mist does not normally have a red, pulsing glow. And besides, the whole place was misty! Why is it concentrated around the campsite?"

"And," Ben cut in, wagging his finger at the screen, "you can see it rolling up the hill. This started recording as soon as Dylan put it in the wall, and then these two," he pointed at Avery and Alex, "starting to behave all weird. And then look at this!" He broke off as the image of huge, spectral wings filled the screen, and then dissolved into thousands of birds.

"What the actual f—", Newton started to say. He looked around at the others. "Where did those come from?"

"If you slow the footage down," Dylan said, "you can see the place where the wings seem to come from, but it's quick—a split second. And then, in a few minutes' time, another figure emerges from the mist, walking out of the campsite and up the hill, too. We'd gone by then."

"Can you tell who it is?" Newton asked.

"No, sorry," Dylan said regretfully.

Cassie shook her head in disbelief. "No wonder you were so spooked. Where did the wings come from?"

"The Raven King," Alex answered grimly. "Corbin, the owner, is the Ring Master, and that's his costume. The mythical figures on the site are coming to life."

Newton started to look excited. "So he's the cause?"

"Not necessarily. Remember that conversation we overhead the other night?" Alex pointed out.

Avery nodded in agreement. "We think someone is using crossroads magic."

"Why?" Newton asked. "And why feed on young men?"

"Because they're youthful and vibrant, and their energy will be strong," Shadow said confidently. She had sat on a chair to the side, as if she was unsure of how involved she wanted to be with the group, but she had listened and watched intently, her concentration absolute.

"That makes sense, I suppose," Newton admitted. "That also probably explains why there's a gap between kills. But is this all about powering the circus? It seems extreme." He looked unconvinced.

Alex agreed. "And risky. Why kill to get a few extra customers?"

"There has to be some other reason, then," Shadow suggested. "The circus could be an elaborate cover."

"Or a convenient cover," Avery said.

"Where did the deaths start?" Reuben asked. "If we know that, it may help us work out what the aim is."

Newton pulled his notebook out of his pocket. He was dressed in his jeans and a sweatshirt, rather than his suit, but he still exuded authority. He ruffled through a few pages and then said, "The circus started in Inverness, but the first death didn't happen until they reached Edinburgh. They stay in place for three weeks on average before moving on, and tend to sit a short distance outside of cities, but it varies as it moves down the country."

"You'd think it would be set up outside Truro or Falmouth, rather than here," El said.

Reuben shrugged. "Except for the fact that we are paranormal central right now."

"And how many deaths do you think are associated with it?" Cassie asked.

Newton grimaced. "It's hard to be sure, but we think at least half a dozen."

The collective mood shifted as Briar said, "That many? This is worse than we thought."

Reuben continued to muse on the circus's source. "I wonder if there's a crossroads in Scotland that this circus links to? It would make sense, seeing as how that's where the new concept originated."

Alex reached for a handful of crisps as he said, "I doubt we'll ever know that, but I'd like to know how it's done, if it is."

Avery decided that now was a good time to share the spell she'd found. "I was doing some research this afternoon," she explained, "when Helena appeared and showed me a spell in her grimoire."

Cassie shuddered and looked around as if Helena might appear at any moment. "I don't know how you cope with that! I would freak out if a ghost kept manifesting in my home!"

"You're a ghost hunter," Reuben said, incredulous. "Shouldn't you be excited?"

Cassie looked equally incredulous. "Not if one was in my own home!"

Avery laughed. "I've got used to it, and she's very helpful most of the time. And don't worry—it's mainly upstairs where she appears."

Cassie looked slightly relieved as Avery continued. "The spell suggests that the witch links two keys together using a red ribbon or cord, measured from your heart to the wrist of your left hand, and then you carry them around for one full cycle of the moon. You have to handle the keys every day, developing a personal connection to them. Then when the cycle is complete, you bury one key in the centre of the crossroads, cutting the cord between them. You then keep the other key on you, allowing you to access the boundaries of the crossroads."

"Wow, so there is a way!" El exclaimed, her curiosity piqued.

"There's probably more, and I'm sure that spell could be adapted, but it's the only one I've found so far."

Shadow was even more excited. "It allows the user to cross boundaries between worlds? This could be my chance to go home!"

"I don't think it's that straightforward. I think it's more to draw on the power of the boundary," Avery warned her, but it was clear Shadow wasn't listening.

"But again, something to work on," Newton said, relieved.

Dylan changed the footage. "Here's what the camera picked up from the oak tree. The mist looks similar, but you can see a better shot of the wings, and the figure—whoever it is—moving up the hill. And you can see us, retreating from the wall."

"No wonder we got lost," Alex said, watching the screen. "We veered off in the wrong direction partway up the hill."

"Yeah, but," Ben said, pointing, "we were being herded by the mist, just as we thought. And then unfortunately we move out of view and you can't see us anymore, so we can't tell what may or may not have been stalking us. It might be that figure, but—" he shrugged, his meaning clear.

"But we've made progress," Newton said encouragingly. "We know it's the circus that's behind this, and we know there are at least three key figures involved in some way. But I need more. There's nothing I can act on, not legally, anyway."

"Did you find out if there's a Caitlin employed at the circus?" Alex asked.

Newton grimaced. "No, unfortunately. We're re-examining the list again, just to make sure we're not missing anything. I'll let you know. Is anyone going to the first show on Saturday?"

"A few of us were planning to go," Avery said. "I was thinking we should split up again. Some of us could watch the show, others could patrol the grounds, especially since the campsite should be deserted."

"Great idea," Newton agreed. "There are the stalls in the castle walls, too. We'll need to investigate those. Who wants to do what?"

There was a brief argument about who should go where. Most people wanted to investigate the campsite, but Newton stood firm. "Avery and Alex need to be at the campsite. They already know the layout and where Corbin's van is, but someone there to help them would be good."

"Me," Shadow said forcefully.

Briar, as ever, was diplomatic. "I'm happy to watch the show. I want to see if they use any magic in the performance."

Cassie groaned. "I'd love to join, but I'm just too busy right now. Coming here tonight was tricky."

"Same for us," Ben said, speaking for him and Dylan. "Uni work is stacking up."

"That's fine," Newton told them. "Just keep an eye on the cameras in case anything else appears."

Dylan shook his head. "I'm afraid that's not possible. I checked them today and it's too damp out there. Sorry, guys. I've had to retrieve the cameras. There'll be no more footage."

"Then we'll manage without it." Newton turned to El and Reuben. "That leaves you two to check out the stalls within the castle grounds."

"Excellent," Reuben said sarcastically. "I can gorge myself on candyfloss and try to win a teddy bear."

"What about you, Newton?" Briar asked.

"I can't be too obvious about investigating anything, so I'll come and watch the show with you, Briar, if that's okay?" He looked as innocent as Newton could be, which wasn't very.

Briar merely nodded. "That's fine." She looked perplexed. "Has anyone else noticed how unseasonably warm it is? February is usually miserable. Green shoots are appearing on plants that shouldn't even start to grow until late spring."

"I have," El admitted. "The courtyard plants outside my workshop have sprung to life."

Reuben agreed. "Our nursery is blooming, too. I just thought we were having an unseasonable bit of warmth."

"I told you, it's the Green Man," Shadow said. "He's affecting everything."

"But why hasn't it happened in other places?" El asked. "Surely someone would have said something?"

Shadow shrugged. "Maybe no one noticed. Not enough to comment, anyway."

"For all we know they did, but it didn't make the papers or the Internet," Alex suggested.

"We're supernatural central," Reuben pointed out. "And we have a lot more magic in White Haven than most places. I think it's feeding him. Let's hope it doesn't become too obvious. Anyway, where shall we all meet before the show?"

"Castle car park," Alex said immediately. "But what's our plan? Surely we don't want to engage in some kind of magical battle?"

"Reconnaissance, that's all," Newton said. "Observe, fact find, but nothing else! I'm presuming you don't want to out your magical abilities to the watching crowds?"

"No need for sarcasm, Newton," Reuben said. "But if we're attacked, we may have no choice. Anyway, it must be time for another beer. And can we please order some food before I die of starvation?"

8

After a quiet, uneventful Friday, during which Avery tried to forget all about crossroads magic and suspicious deaths, Saturday was busy. White Haven was again inundated with circus performers as they paraded through the town, drumming up business for the afternoon and evening performances.

Acrobats and jugglers in bright costumes handed out flyers during the morning, and there was a palpable air of anticipation in the town. Two performers on stilts were dressed as giants with huge heads on their shoulders, and although it wasn't clear which giants they were supposed to be, everyone was excited, because Cornwall was well-known for its giants. Everyone who came into the shop was talking about them, and it sounded like the first performances would be sold out. However, by lunchtime the street performers had gone. The afternoon show started at two, and the evening show at seven. Avery hoped they'd avoid most of the crowds of screaming children for the night performance, although that wasn't really an issue for her.

"I thought you wanted to see the show?" Sally asked Avery at lunch.

"I do, but it's more important to investigate the campsite again. I can see it another time," she pointed out. "It's here for over another week before it moves on. I didn't think you were going at all!"

Sally shrugged. "I reconsidered, and the kids were driving me mad. And you're right. Nothing will happen at the show in the middle of the afternoon. I managed to swap the tickets Mairi gave us for the afternoon performance, so it's free too!"

"Just stay away from the ravens," Dan warned. "It's like Hitchcock's The Birds out there."

"What?" Avery asked, thinking he'd gone mad.

"Haven't you noticed? There are a lot of ravens around the town." He walked to the shop window and pointed upwards, and Avery craned her neck to see the roofs above.

Dan was right. Ravens were gathering on gutters, chimneys, and electricity poles up and down the street.

"Oh, wow. I didn't notice," Avery confessed.

"Well, if the Green Man is here, it makes sense that the Raven King is, too. The magic is rising, Avery," Dan said ominously.

Sally laughed and checked her watch. "I'm not scared of birds, and I'd better go, if that's okay."

"Sure," Avery said, waving her off. "Have fun, and see you Monday. But let me know if you notice anything odd."

"Are you going?" she asked Dan, after Sally had left.

"Probably. I'll give it a few days in the hope that the rush dies down—I gave Sally my tickets. Although, it's been all over the news. Have you seen it?"

"No, I've been preoccupied with research. Which reminds me, have you found out anything else?"

"Not much at this stage. Nothing significant, anyway. I'll let you know as soon as I do. And Avery, be careful tonight. This thing worries me because of all we don't know. It's so odd!"

Avery held her hands up and jiggled them. "Competent witch here! Don't worry."

Dan looked over her shoulder and out the window, a frown creasing his face. "That guy's back."

"What guy?" Avery said, turning quickly.

The street was crowded with pedestrians, and cars crawled down the road, stuck in Saturday traffic.

He inclined his head. "That man wearing dark clothes, with grey hair. He's in the entryway between the second-hand store and the butchers, and he seems to be watching our shop. That's the second time I've seen him there."

Avery stared, waiting for a gap in the crowd, and then caught a glimpse of him leaning against the wall. She took a sharp intake of breath. "I know him! Well, not know, but I bumped into him a couple of days ago—literally walked directly into him. He was right behind me, and he seemed to be watching that strange woman."

"Really? And now he seems to be watching us—or rather, you."

"Why me?" Avery asked, startled.

"Well there's nothing interesting about me," Dan said. His eyes narrowed again. "Looks like he's leaving."

Avery made a quick decision. "I'm going to follow him."

"Avery! I'm not sure that's wise."

"I don't care. I want to know who he is. Don't worry, I'll be fine."

And with those brief reassurances, she ran out to the street. The man was striding down the pavement, back towards the high street, and Avery hurried after him, wishing she'd thought to grab her jacket. It might be mild for February, but it still wasn't warm.

The man was tall, and she could just see his head above the crowds as she struggled to keep up. She hadn't decided what she wanted to do. Should she try to speak to him, or just try to see where he went? She struggled through the shoppers, edging between them as quickly as she could, but it was hard going, especially as she didn't want to appear too obvious.

He paused at the bottom of the road, looking left and right as if he couldn't make up his mind where to go, and she slowed as she got closer. Then he turned right swiftly, and headed towards the harbour. For a second, she lost him. The main street was much busier, and she hesitated, uncertain, but then she saw him again just as he turned into an alleyway. She quickened her pace, and when she reached the entrance, she paused and peered around the corner, feeling like a spy. What was she thinking?

He was nowhere in sight, so reassured, but annoyed at the same time, she started up the street, and then cursed herself as she saw him sitting on a large black and silver motorbike. The engine was already running and his helmet was in his hand, but before he rode away, he turned back to look directly at her, and raised his hand to his eyebrow in salute, a slow smile spreading across his lips. And then he pulled his helmet on and roared away.

***

El stood with her hands on her hips as she surveyed the circus tent and the sprawling castle grounds. "Wow. This is pretty impressive. No wonder it's had such rave reviews."

"And we haven't even seen the performance yet," Reuben pointed out. His arm was slung across El's shoulders as they paused at the edge of the site.

El was right. It was spectacular. The castle was always eye-catching, especially when lit up from below by the lights that illuminated the castle walls, but there were now strings of coloured lights as well that added to the party atmosphere. Small vans and stalls created a village to stroll through via narrow walkways, all displaying typical carnival fare, albeit with a twist. Everything was Green Man-themed, with the occasional glimpse of the Raven King's image, and there were huge painted ravens on the sides of some stalls. Dominating everything was the Big Top, camouflaged by paintings of leaves and trees with multiple images of the Green Man peeking through. The arch leading into the main area beckoned the crowd, and instead of just two huge imitation standing stones next to the archway, more now lined the path to the tent. The flaps were drawn back, offering a tantalising glimpse inside, but the lighting was low and mysterious, and Avery felt everyone's excitement rise.

The queue to get into the circus was long, but Briar and Newton had arrived early with Avery's free tickets, and Briar texted to confirm they had got seats.

A dark figure emerged from the Big Top, throwing his hands wide in welcome. As he stepped into the light, Avery caught her breath. It was Corbin, dressed as the Raven King. He looked magnificent. The cloak and mask they had glimpsed the other night were only part of his costume. His calves were covered in shiny, slick black Lycra, but the rest of him was clad in feathers, his chest puffed out. His mask incorporated a long black beak, and the only thing visible of his face was the glint of his eyes. He threw his arms open and the cloak lifted like wings. He must have had something in the sleeves, because as he extended his arms, the wings grew longer. It was quite dramatic. He shouted, "Welcome to the Crossroads Circus! Beware all who enter. The boundaries between worlds are thin tonight! Who knows what may come through?"

With that statement, it seemed as if hundreds of ravens were suddenly overhead again, their wings beating noiselessly, but their caws deafening. Several people flinched and ducked, but they were high-quality visual and sound effects, and as the Raven King dropped his wings and re-entered the tent, the illusion vanished.

"Clever," Reuben observed. "Are you sure that's not what you felt the other night?"

Alex just looked at him, deadpan. "No. I know the difference between an illusion and magic."

Reuben winked. "Just checking."

It was already dark, but fortunately the mist had lifted, leaving a damp, cloudy evening that threatened rain. They had parked in the car park like everyone else, and Avery, Alex, and Shadow joined El and Reuben as they strolled to the stalls.

"We'll separate when the show begins," Alex told them. "The campsite should be at its quietest then."

They entered the mini-village together, and Avery's senses were quickly overloaded with smells of food—candyfloss, doughnuts, burgers, hot dogs, and chips—and also the shouts of teenagers, the hum of generators, and garish lights. She fell into step beside Shadow. "I forgot these places were so loud. Do you have anything like this where you're from?"

Shadow was looking around with curiosity, but she nodded. "Always, but without these— what do you call them? Generators?" Avery nodded and Shadow continued. "We don't have electricity. But the themes are the same, just with a lot more magic and fey, of course."

Avery raised her voice to be heard, "You don't have electricity?"

Shadow looked at her, amused. "No. But we have magic that provides lights beyond candles and oil lamps. It's complicated to explain, but I guess it would be something like your witch lights." She lifted her gaze and frowned. "What's Reuben doing?"

Avery looked across to where Reuben was picking up a pellet gun and talking to a stall owner, and she laughed. "We have to watch this. Reuben is going to try and shoot the targets. The sights are always out, so people can't win."

They watched Reuben square up to shoot the little tin targets that were set up at the back of the stall. He called across to El. "What do you want if I win?"

There was a range of cuddly toys hanging up around the stall, as well as key rings, mugs, and t-shirts. In the middle of the display was a large raven soft toy. "The bird, please," she said, pointing it out.

The stall owner, a florid man dressed all in green, laughed. "You'll need to hit a dozen targets for that."

"No problem," Reuben said. He took the first shot, which missed, and he grinned. "Okay. Now I've got it." And then he reeled off the next several shots like a firecracker, and the tin targets fell one after another.

The stall owner looked flustered and confused. "That was impressive."

"I know. Raven, please."

The stall owner handed it over, and Reuben passed it on to El with a flourish. "For you, my lady."

She laughed as they strolled away, tucking it under her arm. "And what am I supposed to do with this?"

"I don't know. I just wanted to win it. You can give it away, I suppose." He looked insufferably pleased with himself.

"Good," she answered. "I'll give it to the next deserving child I see."

They continued to stroll through the stalls, some of the performers still entertaining the crowds, and when they spotted a hot dog stand, they came to a halt while Alex and Reuben queued for food. Shadow and Avery walked on for a short while, Avery curious to see if they could exit through the back of the stalls to the campsite.

"What do you think we're going to find tonight?" Shadow asked her as they stopped in a corner where they could watch the comings and goings of the crowd.

"I don't know, probably not much if I'm honest. I'm wondering if we gave ourselves away the other night, and now they'll hide everything."

"Maybe, but whoever is behind this has been doing it for some time. They might not worry."

"But anyone who recognises magic—as we do—would know what we are and what we do, even though I thought I'd blocked us the other night." Avery was still annoyed with herself, and frustrated. She must have dropped her guard, which allowed them to be chased across the field. But something was niggling her. She was usually so careful, and she was sure she hadn't acted carelessly.

"No point worrying about it now," Shadow told her. "They're here for a while yet. If we don't find anything tonight, we can come back."

"The other night, you felt the Green Man. Can you feel him now?"

A wicked glint entered Shadow's eyes. "Yes, I can. He's stronger than before. There's a real energy here now. You must feel it, too!"

"I can feel something, I'm just not sure what it is." She considered Shadow's excited expression. "Is he good in your world, or a figure of fear?"

"Generally good, but like all Gods and spirits, they have their own agenda. It's hard to know what he wants here."

And that was the trouble, Avery thought, but while they were speaking, she heard a swell of music come from the big tent. The show must be starting.

Within seconds, Alex joined them, taking final bites of his hot dog. "Are we ready, then?" he asked them.

Avery pointed further along where there was a break in the stalls that led to some portable toilet blocks on the edge of the section. "We can get through that gap."

They wound their way through the still considerable crowds, and finally emerged behind some generators. The campsite was ahead. Avery cloaked them all, and Alex threw in a protective shield, as well.

They threaded through the vans, generators, and general camp detritus, trying to sense anything unusual. Unfortunately, the campsite wasn't as quiet as they'd hoped. There were still plenty of people milling about, some seeming to act as security, and others were performers, now dressed in their outrageous costumes and elaborate makeup as they made their way to the discrete doorway at the rear of the tent where they could enter unseen. Avery saw a dozen acrobats all dressed in green again, but made to look like trees.

"Dryads," Shadow whispered, before she disappeared in her bewildering way, leaving Alex and Avery alone.

"We should try to find Corbin's van," Alex said, striding determinedly ahead, barely visible with the spell that protected him. "We know that will be empty."

Before she could follow, Avery sensed the strange woman's presence again and she whirled around, trying to see her.

She stared into the pools of blackness cast by the vans. Nothing moved, but she could sense the woman just ahead, out of sight. She followed almost blindly. It was tantalising, a wisp of magic she couldn't explain. And then Avery reached the edge of the camp, slipped through a gap in the hedge, and the world fell away.

9

Avery was standing alone on a road made of beaten earth, and ahead she saw a crossroads with four huge standing stones, like sentinels, marking the four corners.

Where was she? More importantly, how was she here?

The sounds of the circus had disappeared, and instead the ragged caw of a bird broke the silence. There was no moon that night in White Haven, it had been covered by thick clouds. But here—wherever here was—the sky was clear and the full moon's ghostly light showed a large raven perched on the furthest standing stone, watching her.

Avery's heart beat wildly in her chest, and she glanced around trying to orientate herself. Nothing looked familiar, and all she could see were four roads stretching into the distance. She glanced behind her. The hedge was gone. Avery started to panic, and she took a deep breath. I'm a witch. I've got this. This has to be an illusion. But creeping dread filled her. This didn't feel like an illusion. It felt very real.

She froze, uncertain of what to do. Breathe, and take notes. This could be important, she reminded herself. She looked around again, trying to find landmarks. There was a gentle rolling hill ahead, and trees covered some of the landscape, but other than the standing stones and crossroads, her surroundings were uneventful. It was as if she was in the middle of the moors somewhere. And why was the road of beaten earth? Why wasn't it made of tarmac?

In the middle of the crossroads a swirl of mist appeared, and within seconds a figure stepped from it. It was the woman from the procession. She stared at Avery, grim amusement in her eyes, and fear struck Avery as she'd never experienced it before, not even when facing the vampires. Avery heard drumming, a faint beat at first, and then it grew louder, wilder, and suddenly she wasn't afraid anymore. She was furious.

"Who are you and what do you want?" she yelled. "I know this isn't real!"

"Isn't it?" the woman said softly, her voice almost husky. "Look around, Avery. Do you know your way home from here?"

"How do you know my name?"

"I know many things. "

"So it seems. Would you like to share?"

"All in good time. You're interfering in things you shouldn't."

"Don't bring your business to my doorstep, then."

The woman laughed. "You're feisty."

"Yes I am, and I don't know what you're doing, but I'll stop you."

"Will you?" the woman asked, walking towards Avery. "You won't have time. I have other plans for you."

Instinctively, Avery gathered air around her, and then hurled it at the approaching woman. The woman staggered as her hair streamed behind her, but she recovered quickly and kept advancing as Avery retreated. What the hell did she want?

Avery shouted, "Stop! Don't come any closer."

The woman ignored her. "Or what?"

As she drew closer, Avery whispered a spell that should have stopped the woman from walking, freezing her steps and sinking her into the earth, and for a moment, it did. But then she pulled her feet free, shaking the earth from them, and advanced again. Avery balled pure energy into her palm and threw it, but again the woman deflected it easily, sending it crashing into a standing stone. She kept coming, and Avery saw that she was older than she had first thought, fine lines marking her face and around her eyes.

Avery had no idea what would happen if she reached her, but sensed it couldn't be good. In fact, she had the distinct impression the woman was absorbing the power from her spells.

A single idea filled her mind. Witch-flight. She didn't know where she was, but she knew where she wanted to be. She envisaged the space in the back of her van that was currently parked in the castle's car park, and summoning all of her power, she disappeared, pleased to see the woman's frustrated look before she vanished from sight.

However, for what felt like several long minutes, Avery felt suspended in time and space, and she was briefly aware that the flight was taking far longer than it should. She focused on her van and only her van, until with a thump, she landed sprawling on the plywood floor behind the front seats. She gasped for breath she didn't even know she needed, and then realised she felt nauseous. She stumbled upright and threw the rear door open, half falling onto the tarmac below where she retched, a cold sweat covering her brow. She took a moment to appreciate that everything was as it should be: the car park, the circus, and night sky above, heavy with clouds. She was safe.

Then she had another thought. *Alex.*

Avery dragged herself to her feet, and raced up the path towards the circus and then, bypassing it and the stalls completely, she ran around the back to the campsite, pulling her phone from her pocket as she went, and flicking to Alex's number. And then she hesitated. If he was hidden and she alerted someone to his presence, that could endanger him.

Damn it!

She slowed as she entered the campground, knowing she needed to be stealthy and not having a clue as to who may be a threat, or if the mysterious woman was here again. She edged in and out of the vans, once again draped in the shadow spell, although now fearing it was useless to protect herself from her attacker.

In the camp it seemed as if nothing had changed, although the place seemed emptier. Maybe more of the performers were now in the tent? But, she couldn't see Alex or Shadow.

What if they had also been spelled away into in another place? She tried to calm herself down. For some reason, the woman was targeting her, not the others. Logically, this meant the others must be okay.

The sound of the crowd in the Big Top erupted behind her as a huge cheer went up, and the sound of clapping and stamping of feet resounded through the night. The clapping kept going and Avery paused. It sounded like it was the end of the performance, but it couldn't be, surely. It had only just started.

She stopped and checked the time on her phone, and nearly stumbled with shock. It was just after half-past nine, and the performance was ending. She had lost two hours of time. Two hours? How?

Avery leant against the side of the closest camper van, checking and re-checking the time. This wasn't possible. She had been gone for minutes only. Before she could think or do anything else, Shadow appeared next to her looking furious. "Where the hell have you been, Avery? Alex is panic-stricken." She stopped long enough to let out a piercing whistle, and then she frowned. "You're as white as a corpse. What happened?"

Avery's mouth felt dry. "I don't know. I ended up on a crossroads, somewhere."

Before Shadow could respond, Alex, Reuben, and El emerged out of the darkness, all of them looking worried. Alex ran forward and hugged her. "Thank the Gods! Where have you been? Are you all right?"

Shadow answered for her. "She's been somewhere else. Let's get out of here, now, and ask questions later."

And with that, Avery was hustled back to the van.

***

"Will everyone stop looking at me as if I've gone mad?" Avery said, frustrated. "I'm fine, honestly."

They were all in Alex's flat, and Reuben had just pressed a large glass of mulled red wine into her hand that he'd fetched from the pub below. "I'm sure you are, but let's face it, alcohol always helps."

She couldn't disagree with that, and she took a healthy sip, enjoying the spicy warmth as it flowed down her throat, heating her whole body. She hadn't even known she felt cold, and she shivered. "Thanks, Reuben. That is good."

Briar sat next to Avery, looking at her anxiously and running her hands over her, several inches from her body. "I have never seen you so pale, and your aura has been depleted." She looked up at Reuben. "Grab my bag, please."

Briar had arrived a few minutes after everyone else, having gone home first for her herbal healing kit, and it was this she asked for now. Reuben placed it at her feet, and Briar reached inside, rummaging about, while Avery tried to focus on the room, which was increasingly hazy. She looked at the wine, confused. She hadn't had that much.

"What's the matter?" Alex asked. He sat on the other side of her, watching her every move.

"I feel slightly weak, as if something is missing," Avery told him, trying to explain the weird sensation.

Shadow weighed in now. "Your magic has been weakened, that's why, not just your aura. I can feel it."

El was sitting on the floor, in front of the fire. "What happened, Avery?"

"It doesn't make sense," she said, struggling to articulate her words.

"That doesn't matter. Just tell us as you remember it."

Avery told them about her mysterious journey to the crossroads, her encounter with the strange, still unknown woman, and the loss of time. "I tried several spells on her, but nothing worked. She seemed to be absorbing my magic."

Briar pressed a large, black gemstone into her hand. "Hold this. It's black onyx and very grounding. I'm going to make you a potion." She leapt to her feet, grabbed her small case, and headed to the kitchen.

"Are you still connected to her in some way?" Alex asked.

Avery tentatively explored her magic and sent her awareness further afield. "No, I don't think so, but I don't feel right. I feel disconnected somehow. Like I'm here, but not here." Avery closed her eyes, feeling ridiculous, but as soon as she did, the crossroads appeared in front of her, wreathed in mist, timeless and draped in power. Her eyes flew open again. "The crossroads, I can see it…"

Shadow stepped closer, extending her own strange fey powers. "You *are* connected, Avery. That's why you're not feeling better."

Everyone turned to her in shock. "What?" Alex asked, his eyes haunted with worry. "How?"

"Boundary magic," Shadow said. "She's connected to you. It's faint, but it's there. I think she's feeding off your power."

Avery put her drink down. "Shit. I think you're right. It's the only thing that explains how I feel. How do we stop her?"

"Protective circle, salt, our magic, the works," Alex said, leaping to his feet. "We break it, now."

Shadow shook her head. "You'll need more than that."

Avery started to feel frightened. Some unknown woman with unknown magic had connected to her like a leech. "Why?"

"Because I think she's connected to your spirit body."

"We can spirit-walk," Alex said immediately. "I can do that easily, and find a way to break it."

Shadow nodded, though slightly apprehensive. "Maybe. But if you cut the link in the wrong way—" She broke off, shrugging.

"It could do more damage," Reuben finished for her.

She turned her violet gaze to him. "Possibly. I don't know much about this—please don't think I do—but that woman's magic is more closely aligned to mine than yours. I can sense the difference, and her odd connection."

Alex sat down again, deflated. "So, what do we do?"

Briar answered from the kitchen, where she was furiously crushing herbs. "We enhance Avery's strength; keep her topped up with magic. It's not ideal, because it means the woman will continue to draw from her, but at least Avery will continue to function. I'm making a potion right now that will help."

"It's a waiting game, then," El said.

Briar nodded. "I'm afraid so."

Avery felt her head spin again. This was all so weird. She felt tricked—manipulated. "I feel like an idiot."

Newton was leaning against the wall, his eyes narrowed. "Of course you're not. But this is our chance to learn more about her and what she wants. The questions we have will eventually give us valuable answers. For example, how could she just take you away without your knowledge?"

"I don't know," she answered, looking up at him, baffled. "It was like nothing I have ever experienced before. Her magic is unlike ours—as Shadow says. I'm sure she's not a witch."

"And you had no idea about the time?" Reuben persisted. He was sitting on the rug next to El, a beer in hand.

"None. It felt like minutes only."

"It's because of the crossroads," Shadow explained. "We know it straddles worlds, and time is different in Otherworlds."

Reuben looked impressed. "Wow. So, you were in some sort of time-flux. That's very *Star Trek*."

"Lucky me," Avery said, feeling not very lucky at all.

Alex sighed heavily. "But why you? We're all witches, with varying strengths, why choose you?"

"Maybe it's to do with your elemental Air powers?" El suggested.

"But what can you do with elemental Air that you can't do with other elements?" Newton asked.

Avery shrugged. "Witch-flight, obviously. But everyone here can use elemental Air to some degree."

"But not as well as you," El reminded her.

Avery flopped against the back of the sofa. "I don't know. I'll need to do some reading about crossroads magic, try to work out why she needs me, and for what."

"*We* need to do some reading," El told her, gently. "You're not alone in this. We'll all help, like you got me out of that curse. I guess the big question is whether this is also linked to the Green Man and the Raven King."

"Bollocks!" Newton said forcefully. He pushed away from the wall and started pacing. "Just when I thought we were getting somewhere, we have more questions!"

"Why don't you tell me what you found while I was elsewhere?" Avery suggested to everyone.

"Very little," Shadow said. "Other than the fact that I could sense the Green Man and his Earth magic again. He's getting stronger."

"I found Corbin's van again," Alex added, "and searched it, but there was nothing in there to tell us what's happening, and I couldn't find Rafe or Mairi."

"There was nothing odd happening around the stalls," Reuben told them. "Just people spending money and eating lots of food. I sensed nothing magical or Otherworldly. No wild magic, nothing like we experienced on Samhain."

"What about inside the tent?" Avery asked Newton and Briar.

Briar continued to prepare ingredients in the kitchen. "I did sense magic in the tent, it was subtle, but there. The performance was amazing."

Newton stopped pacing. "It was very clever. The Raven King commanded the whole thing. It felt like the tent had come alive. The walls were covered in fake greenery, and when you were close enough, you could see it rustling, like it was alive. That was down to wind machines, but it was effective. The light tricks were clever. It felt like ravens flew overhead at one point, and all the performances were folklore themed. The stilt walkers were there, playing Cornish giants, the acrobats were dryads, there was even Beowulf fighting Grendel the monster in some crazy aerial acrobatics, and loads more. "

Briar agreed. "It wasn't quite Cirque De Soleil, but it was close. The subtle use of magic definitely gave everything an extra fizz, but no one without magic would ever know it."

Newton rubbed his face, and suddenly looked incredibly tired. "You can't tell me that the deaths and the crossroads magic is just about putting on a good show? That's nuts."

"No," Alex agreed, "there is definitely something else happening. We just have to figure out what."

"And you," Shadow said to Avery, her eyes bright with intrigue, "are in the perfect position to find out more about our mysterious woman. You're linked to her now. The connection goes both ways."

Avery looked up at her, trying to feel positive. "That's true. I just need to work out where that crossroads is. It's the key to everything."

Once the others had left, Avery turned to Alex. "I don't even know if I can sleep. Every time I close my eyes, I see the crossroads. I'm scared that she'll take me back there in my sleep."

Alex pulled her close, kissing the top of her head, and they sat next to each on the sofa, staring into the bright flames of the fire. "I don't think that will happen. Besides, Briar's potion will help you sleep, deep enough hopefully to dull your connection."

She ran her fingers across his face. "I hope you're right. But if not, promise you'll come and find me? That place felt so eerie."

"I'll find you anywhere," he vowed, taking her hand in his and kissing her fingers one by one. "And if she hurts you in any way, I'll kill her. I'll raze the whole circus to the ground if I have to."

10

For the first few hours of the night Avery slept heavily, drugged by the herbs that Briar had put in the potion, but at some point that all changed, and once again she stood on one of the four roads leading to the crossroads, drenched in the shadow of a standing stone.

It was night, and the full moon was still high above her, giving a silvery sheen to the landscape. Ground mist snaked around her ankles, and undulating moors spread around her to the horizon, except for the low roll of hills ahead of her. A second moon closer to the ground confused her for a moment, before she realised it must be reflected in water. The woman was nowhere in sight.

Avery looked around, desperate to see something that may indicate where she was, but the landscape was almost featureless. The standing stones were the only things of significance. The one closest to her was twice her height, and several feet thick. Up close she could see shapes carved into it, and she frowned, frustrated. She didn't recognise them at all, but she tried to memorise them, hoping to find them later. If there was a later.

Tentatively, she placed her hand on the stone. It was cold, but Avery felt it humming with energy, and with her touch the carvings began to glow with a golden light, as if they were illuminated from within. Avery's first instinct was to step back, but she felt that wouldn't help. Whatever was happening, she needed to understand. She pressed her hand on the surface firmly, watching as the signs continued to light up until they almost burned, and suddenly realising that she could be summoning something, she tried to pull her hand away, but couldn't. It started to pull her closer, and Avery had the terrifying thought that it was trying to absorb her, to pull her in and swallow her whole. She screamed as she struggled to break free, sweat pouring from her. The sound of drums once again filled the air, primeval and tribal, and her blood pounded in her ears.

Alex's voice broke through her panic. "Avery! Avery, wake up!"

Her body was shaking violently, and all of a sudden the crossroads had gone, and she felt Alex's hands on her shoulders. Her body felt like lead, and as if her eyes were welded shut, but she forced them open, her breath short. "I'm here. I'm okay!"

"Thank fuck for that!" He pulled her close, his warmth thawing her immobility. "You scared the shit out of me."

He must have spelled the lamp on, because soft, warm light flooded his bedroom, and reality rushed in. Avery pressed herself against him, soaking up his warmth. "How did you know I was in trouble?"

"Because you were screaming the place down," he said, pulling away and staring down at her. "What happened?"

"I was at the crossroads again, in my dream. It was a dream, right? I was still here?"

"You were still here," he said, reassuring her.

She pushed him away and sat up. "What the hell is happening to me?"

"I don't know, but we'll work it out, I promise." He caught her hand, and went to kiss her palm, but frowned. "What's this?"

"What?"

"This mark?"

A strange, silvery shape glowed within her palm, and she groaned. "It's from the standing stone." She explained what had happened and what caused her to scream.

Alex was annoyed. "I can't believe you touched it! What were you thinking?"

"I don't know, it seemed a good idea!"

"Avery, that place is messing with your mind! She's screwing with you! She needs your power for some reason, and now you're truly linked. You can't trust anything you see or think there."

Avery felt tears well up. "Don't shout. I didn't know. I've never had to doubt my instincts before, never!"

He pulled her close again. "I'm sorry. I didn't mean to yell, but I'm terrified I'm going to lose you. You're strong, Avery, but you can't do this alone. Promise me you won't try."

"I promise," she said, feeling exhausted. "I think I need to sleep again, although I'm terrified of what will happen."

"I'll be right here. Just don't touch anything again."

***

The next time Avery woke, it was morning, and grey light seeped into the room. She smelt coffee and bacon, and she stretched out, noticing how heavy her body felt.

She had managed to sleep well for a few hours, with no dreams. She examined her right palm again, hoping the mark would have disappeared, but it was still there, glowing just beneath her skin.

Alex appeared at the door, and he smiled. He had just come out of the shower and he was half naked, his towel wrapped around his hips, showing off his flat, muscled abs and tattoos. "You're awake. Feeling okay?"

She nodded. "I think so. I actually managed some decent sleep."

"I could tell—your breathing was heavy and slow. Hungry?"

"Starving."

"Want breakfast in bed?"

"No, I'll get up. Thank the Gods it's Sunday and the shop is closed."

She padded into the kitchen, wrapped in his heavy robe, and sat at the counter watching him finish making breakfast. He pushed a coffee in front of her. "This will perk you up." He watched her take a few sips. "I've been thinking about what we should do today, and the first thing should be to decipher that." He pointed at her palm.

"You're right. The more we know, the better. I also want to look up crossroads, famous or otherwise, see if I can find some images that will help find out where it really is." She sighed. "I'm wondering if I could use witch-flight to try and get back there, physically, but I'm not sure that's a good idea."

"It's a very bad idea. Don't you dare try that. But researching it sounds fine." He finished preparing bacon and egg sandwiches for them both, and she tucked in. "Briar has already phoned. She's coming around in about half an hour with another potion. It sounds like she woke up early to make one, and apparently El and Reuben are coming, too. She has some jewellery for you."

"Full house, then."

"For a while." He pointed to the table in the corner where a pile of books was already waiting, including his grimoires. "And then we have some reading to do."

***

When the other three witches arrived, Avery was the centre of attention for the next hour, and she didn't like it one bit. "Please, stop fussing! I'm okay."

Briar placed her hands on her hips and stared Avery down, although she was looking up at her. She was petite and shorter than Avery. "No, you're not. You're going to have to put up with fuss until we work out what's going on and sever the connection to this bitch." Briar hardly ever swore, and everyone looked at her, wide-eyed. "What? She *is* one! And she has really pissed me off. I have made half a dozen potions for you, enough to last a couple of days. One with breakfast, one with lunch, and the red ones are to have before bed."

She handed Avery four small turquoise glass vials filled with a thick liquid, and two red ones. Avery pulled the lid off one and sniffed. "What's in them?"

"Many things. The turquoise ones will enhance your energy. The red ones are to help you sleep. I'm working on some more, too. Take one now."

Avery braced herself and downed it in one go. She knew from experience that potions sometimes tasted horrible. She winced. This one was no exception. "Yuck."

"It will work, that's all that matters."

Reuben laughed. "Briar, I had no idea you could be so bossy."

Briar turned to him and frowned. "Don't you start."

Reuben smelt of the sea again, and his hair was still damp. It was obvious that despite the grey, cold weather and freezing water, he had been for an early surf. He held up his hands in mock surrender. "No chance."

El leaned forward, passing Avery a silver necklace with an oval black stone in a simple setting. "This is from my Crossroads Collection. Jet protects you from evil, violence, and psychic attacks, and will hopefully slow down the pull of your magic that woman is using." Avery slipped it over her head, feeling the weight of the stone rest just below her throat; its steady, thrumming energy soothed her.

"Thanks, I feel it already."

El nodded, pleased. "Now, show me your hand. Alex told us you're marked."

Avery held her hand out and the others crowded around.

"It's not a rune," El said confidently. "Unless it's of a type I have never seen before."

"I agree," Reuben said, taking Avery's hand in his rough one and tracing his finger over it. "Is it a sigil of some sort?" He looked at her with piercing blue eyes. "Was this on that standing stone you touched?"

Avery nodded. "Yes. It was covered in them, of different designs, all carved by hand, and I didn't recognise any of them. They started to glow when I put my hand on the stone. It hummed with power, and then started to suck me in… Sorry, it sounds mad, but that's exactly how it felt." She shuddered at the memory.

"What about the other three stones?" Reuben asked. "Did they glow?"

Avery paused for a moment, thinking back to her dream. "No, I don't think so, but I was so focused on the stone I was attached to that I didn't really look."

"That's a good question," Briar said, looking bleak. "It would indicate if they're all connected. And you have no idea where that crossroads is?"

"No. The landscape was completely unrecognisable. Surely a crossroads with four standing stones marking each corner is weird, though?"

Alex frowned, "Maybe, maybe not. Standing stones are littered across the UK, and in Europe. They might not be obviously on crossroads now, but maybe some were in the past. There are hundreds of standing stones and strange cairns in Cornwall, and there's the Castlerigg Stone Circle close to Hunter, but I don't recall any crossroads."

Avery closed her eyes for a few seconds, but already the crossroads was fainter in her mind, harder to recall. "I think this is good news—it's not as close to me now."

"That's the potion and the necklace working," Briar told her. "Was the woman there? I presume not."

"No, fortunately, but I felt her guiding hand on all of it. But," Avery continued, "something I do remember is how old the place felt. I mean, truly ancient."

Alex headed to his coffee machine and started another brew. "What if this isn't just a distance location, but a time one as well?"

"Surely I couldn't have travelled to my van on the car park last night so easily?" Avery reasoned, feeling a chill sweep through her. "I mean, if I had moved through time in any significant way, that would have affected everything."

Alex stared at her for a moment, nodding. "Probably. It was just a thought."

"You know, there is something I forgot to tell you," Avery confessed. "There's a strange American man in town who seems to be watching our mysterious woman, and my shop."

"What!" Alex exclaimed. "Why didn't you say?"

"I forgot, sorry."

"Tell us everything," Reuben instructed.

Avery related her two encounters with the man, and how he'd disappeared on a motorbike.

"Bollocks!" Alex said. "What the hell has he got to do with all this?"

"If it's any reassurance, I didn't feel threatened by him," Avery told them.

"I'll keep an eye out for him, and let Newton know," Reuben said. "You concentrate on feeling better."

Briar picked up her bag, and slung it over her shoulder. "Right, we'll leave you to it. I'm heading back to do some spell research for you. I'll let Eli know about this man tomorrow, just in case he's seen him in town."

El and Reuben made to leave, too. "We'll see what we can find," El said, pulling Avery into a hug. "In the meantime, Avery, stay safe, and don't rush off on your own. This woman will be around for a while. We have time to deal with this. We only have a few pieces of the puzzle so far, but we'll work it out."

For the next few hours, Avery and Alex worked quietly side by side, looking through signs and sigils, before moving on to standing stones and crossroads, but by lunch, Avery was ready to tear her hair out.

"I am utterly stumped," she confessed. "And I'm hungry."

Alex slapped his book shut with a resounding *thud*. "I think we should go and see Shadow."

"You do? Why?"

He looked at her for a second, and Avery could see the worry in his eyes. "I don't want you to freak out, but I've been thinking about that mark and why we can't find out what it is. Last night you were at a boundary, an active boundary. What if the marks aren't from our world?"

Avery looked down at her hand, and then back up at him. "You might be right."

He leapt up, and grabbed his keys. "Come on, I'll drive."

"Can we swing by my flat on the way and feed the cats? I'm afraid they'll think I've abandoned them."

"Ah, the children," he said, laughing. "Of course."

By the time they got to the old farmhouse on the hill, a fine drizzle had set in, and the surrounding fields were a murky grey and green. Alex complained all the way up the bumpy lane, as they jolted along. "I'm sure Gabe makes this road even worse, just to deter visitors."

He pulled into the courtyard surrounded by outbuildings, and they ran to Shadow's place, the converted stable. There was no answer there, so they headed for the main house instead, Avery running with her coat over her head to keep from getting wet.

For a few moments their knocking went unanswered again, and then they heard heavy footfalls. Gabe answered the door, dressed in black fatigues and a black t-shirt, but his feet were bare, and his short dark hair, which was slightly longer than usual, looked damp. He frowned. "Alex and Avery! Didn't expect to see you two. Come on in."

He led them up the hall into the big rustic kitchen at the rear of the house, and Avery noticed that although the place looked as bare as usual, at least it was warm. To her surprise, Shadow was in the kitchen, stirring something in a pot, from which an aromatic smell drifted. A fire was burning in the fireplace, and plates, bowls, and cooking paraphernalia covered most surfaces.

Shadow looked around and smiled. "Hi, guys. I'm cooking. I've found it's a great way to de-stress." She wore an overlarge set of striped pyjamas, which draped her slender frame, and Avery found her mouth dropping open in surprise before she clamped it shut.

Gabe rolled his eyes as he headed to the kettle. "What de-stresses Shadow, distresses me. Look at the mess. Tea, coffee, or beer?"

As one, Avery and Alex said, "Beer, please."

"Good call," Gabe said, heading to the fridge and grabbing four beers. "I've just got back from work, and this is what I find." He popped the caps, handed them out and took a drink. "Grab a seat," he told them gesturing towards the table and taking a seat himself.

"Were you working for Caspian?" Alex asked, as they joined him.

Gabe nodded. "Yeah. He had a big shipment last night, at his Falmouth warehouse, so I was supervising that."

Alex looked puzzled. "I thought you did security?"

"It involves a few things. Turns out that Caspian likes having us Nephilim around."

Intriguing, Avery thought watching him. It made her wonder quite what Caspian's business was sometimes. *Perhaps best she didn't know.* "Are all of you helping him?"

He jerked his head back, indicating Shadow. "She helps sometimes, just enough to earn her keep, and the other guys roster through, although Barak, Nahum, and Niel do most of it."

Shadow snorted. "Enough to earn my keep, indeed! You great-winged idiot. I pull my weight." Avery sniggered. *Great-winged idiot?* She continued, unabashed. "I'm making a hot pot for you! Do you want to try some?"

"Is it safe?" Gabe asked, his eyebrows rising.

"Of course. I'm fey."

"Always with the fey thing," he said, sighing. "Dish it up then, and I'll try not to throw up."

"You know you won't," she retorted, as she grabbed some bowls and started to spoon it out.

Avery and Alex exchanged an amused glance. *What was this weird, domestic set-up?*

"What about you two?" Shadow asked.

"Saves us a pub lunch," Avery found herself saying. "And to be honest, it smells great."

"It's rabbit. I shot them yesterday, using my bow, obviously. I need to keep my skills up."

"Great," Avery said, hating the thought of hunting, but the dish that appeared in front of her looked delicious, and she tucked in regardless.

Shadow sat next to them, placing some slices of fresh bread on a plate in the middle, and then looked at Avery knowingly. "What happened to you last night?"

"You know what happened. I ended up at some weird crossroads."

"I know that. I mean afterwards. In the night. You look terrible," she said bluntly.

"Thanks so much for your honesty. I visited the crossroads again, in my dream, sort of." Avery shook her head, confused. "I don't know if I can call it a dream, because I was there. It was so real!"

Alex interrupted. "She screamed the place down. I had to shake her out of it."

Shadow looked nonplussed. "I told you that you were connected, psychically. I'm not surprised."

Avery put her spoon down. "Well, go you! This isn't that easy for me to accept. It was bloody scary! I almost got sucked into a standing stone, and now I'm marked!" She thrust her palm in front of Shadow.

Shadow blanched. "By Herne's curly horns. That's fey script! How did this happen?"

"Fey script?" Avery looked at her hand. "No wonder we couldn't decipher it."

"I did think it was a possibility," Alex said, "but I honestly hoped I was wrong. It seemed too surreal."

Shadow's nonchalant attitude disappeared and she became very excited. "If you have fey script on your hand, it must mean the boundaries are weakened. This could be my chance!" She narrowed her eyes at them. "I told you there was more than one way!"

"Do you think we can forget about your way home for one second?" Avery asked, annoyed. "I've been marked. What the hell does it mean?"

"You have been claimed."

"I've been sodding *what*?"

"Claimed. By the Goddess of the Crossroads."

The room fell silent as they all stopped eating and looked at Shadow.

Alex found his voice first. "Do you mean Hecate?"

"The three-headed Goddess who sees past, present, and future? Yes."

"The maiden, the mother, and the crone," he said, elaborating.

Shadow looked confused. "If you say so. We have many Gods and Goddesses in our world. She is one of them. We keep out of their business and they keep out of ours, most of the time. Apart from, you know, a few months ago."

Alex was struggling to remain calm. "What do you mean, *claimed*?"

To be fair to Shadow, she looked a bit flustered, too. "Avery has been marked as a sacrifice. That's what that writing says. It's ancient."

Avery closed her eyes, willing herself to be calm. She opened her eyes again, staring into Shadow's violet ones, which were beguiling and cunning all at the same time. "The writing on the standing stones must have all been in fey script."

A calculating look swept across Shadow's face. "Probably. Tell me more."

Avery resumed eating, and in between mouthfuls told Shadow exactly what had happened in her dream.

"We need to find this crossroads," Shadow said, and looked to Gabe for support. "I need to go there!"

"Just slow down a second," Alex said. "Of course we need to go there, but we need to find out more about it! Why is Avery being targeted? There are four other witches that woman could have picked on. *And who the hell is she?*"

But it wasn't Shadow who answered—it was Gabe. "The Gods always like their sacrifices."

"Well, Avery won't be one," Alex said, jabbing his fork forcefully at him and Shadow. "We need to break this, but to do that we need to know what she is to be sacrificed for."

"Not will be, will *try* to be," Avery pointed out, annoyed.

"Well, that's the big question, isn't it?" Shadow said, absently playing with the food in her bowl. "The obvious answer would be to increase Hecate's power. But of course, it could be to strengthen the woman's power. She could be drawing on power from Hecate for a spell. Or it could be that something needs to manifest from the crossroads, and they need Hecate's power for that to happen."

"But surely they're already drawing on that power," Avery said. "That's how the Raven King and the Green Man are becoming real! And what about the deaths? And the strange conversation we heard: 'Its power feeds this place, don't forget that.' Who or what is *it*?"

"I wonder if there's a way for me to travel to the crossroads with you," Shadow mused. "It would allow me to decipher the script on the standing stones."

"That would be useful," Alex conceded. "What if we psychically linked with you, Avery? Like we did with Gabe once. Remember, we were able to see the cave where you were?" he said to Gabe.

Gabe grunted. "I remember that. You were surprisingly strong."

Alex flashed him a surprised grin. "Thanks. We could use the same technique. Then hopefully, wherever it is that you go, Avery, we could go with you."

Avery started to feel the tiniest bit hopeful. "Maybe, but that could be dangerous. You had to drag me back last night. If you're there with me, who brings us back?"

"Our coven. I'll need them, too."

"Where do we do this?" Shadow asked.

"My place," Alex volunteered. "I've been thinking about the other night, when you and Briar felt Earth magic, and you said you could feel something drawing on you. Do you think that's because of the boundary magic, that it knew you were fey?"

Shadow nodded. "I've been thinking on that too, and I think you're right. In the end, though, whatever it was wanted you more, Avery."

"Lucky me."

Alex rose to his feet. "Thanks for the food, Shadow, but we better go. I want to prepare for tonight." He held his hand out for Avery. "Come on. Let's get you home."

She stood, feeling lethargic and heavy. *Damn it.* Whatever was happening was not stopping. It was a strange sensation knowing that something was draining her power. A chill swept through her as she realised she could lose her magic, if not her life. That could not happen. A life without magic was no life at all.

11

Avery and Alex spent a quiet afternoon at Alex's flat, and while Alex prepared for the ritual ahead, Avery continued her research.

Halfway through the afternoon, he declared, "I'm going to need Caspian."

"Why?"

"You'll be in the circle centre with me, linked over the crystal ball, and so will Shadow. We need someone to represent elemental Air, and he's strong."

"Do we have to involve him?" she asked, groaning.

"Yes. You know I wouldn't suggest him if we didn't need to, and he did offer to help. Besides, we need as much power as we can to do this, and he's powerful."

She sighed dramatically. "All right, then."

While Alex made the arrangements, Avery continued to research crossroads and stone circles and found out one fact that was particularly unpleasant. "Do you know that standing stones are supposed to represent witches in some places? They were frozen in place, transformed!"

Alex was in the kitchen grinding herbs in his pestle and mortar. He stopped and looked up at her. "No, but you said you felt you were being sucked in."

"This gets worse. I'm going to be immortalised in stone."

"No, you're not. Go on, tell me more."

She glanced down at the page again. "Standing stones in many places are supposed to represent witches, or other figures frozen in time. One of the most well known is Long Meg and her Daughters. It's a stone circle, not far from where Hunter is from. Apparently, they were turned to stone for dancing on the Sabbath. The circle is supposed to be magical, and many say you can't count the same number of stones twice. To do so will break the spell. Some legends also suggest that witches were buried at crossroads under standing stones, as a way of neutralising their power."

Alex resumed grinding his herbs. "That's good to know. It's a link. You can't identify four standing stones on a crossroads, though?"

"No, annoyingly."

"That's okay. We'll find a way."

"What if this is exactly what that woman wants us to do? We could be walking into a trap!"

"And that's why we have back-up."

***

As the afternoon progressed, Avery felt more and more lethargic, so that by the time everyone else arrived, buzzing with energy and intent, she was drowsy.

Alex had prepared the salt circle in front of the fire again, and the room was filled with candles and was bathed in firelight.

Briar took one look at Avery and ran over to hug her. "You look worse."

"Thanks Briar, I thought Reuben was the one who was going to tell me that."

"You do look terrible," Reuben agreed.

Briar ignored him. "I've been working on spells to break this connection, and I'm struggling."

"We all have," Caspian told her, as he arrived partway through their conversation. "But to break a psychic connection with force is very dangerous." His dark eyes fell on Avery. "That alone could kill you."

"Is there any positive news?" Avery asked, trying to subdue her panic.

"Yes, your link to her is her weakness," Shadow said confidently. She had dressed for battle, wearing black fatigues, and Avery could see the glint of her knives in the sheaths on her thighs.

"Exactly," Reuben said. He pointed at the salt circle on the floor. "Shall we sit?"

Alex nodded. "Yes please. The elemental places are marked by candles and compass points. The usual. Avery, Shadow, let's take our place in the circle, too. Caspian, are you ready?"

He nodded and sat between Briar and El, opposite Reuben, a purple candle in front of each of them. Alex, Shadow, and Avery sat virtually knee-to-knee around one solitary candle in the centre.

"We're going to raise a protective circle before we begin," Alex instructed, "and then we three need to drink this potion. It will help relax us to enter the necessary mind state."

"We're not connected, then?" El asked. "We were last time."

"I'm not going to link to you. You four are our magical protection and support," Alex told them. "It may also take longer than we think, considering Avery thought she'd been gone for minutes and it turned out to be a couple of hours. Are we all clear?"

They nodded, and the four witches in their elemental positions started the ritual to raise protection, while Alex drank some of the potion from the silver goblet and handed it to Shadow and Avery.

Avery could feel the heat and low lighting begin to work on her already weakened state, and the potion quickly exacerbated it. Within seconds she felt the protective circle around her activate, and all noises of the outside world disappeared.

Alex held his hands out. "We need to join hands, and then say the spell after me. This will link us, so that where you go, we follow."

Shadow looked wary. "I have never done magic like this before."

"Trust me, it's safe. Do you want to see this place?"

She nodded.

"Come on, then."

She linked hands with Alex and Avery, and as they repeated the spell after Alex, Avery felt their energies connect; Shadow's sharp, wild energy was distinctly different to Alex's. They all took a moment to adjust, and then Alex guided them again. "Avery, just focus on the crossroads. Don't resist it."

She nodded and closed her eyes. It didn't take long. The crossroads was lurking just beneath her waking mind, a constant presence that she had battled to ignore all day long. But in this state, it rushed in, and so did her fear.

She stood next to the standing stone she had connected to before. A full moon was again overhead, illuminating everything with its silver light. She stepped away from the stone, already feeling its hum of energy, and it took every part of her to resist its pull. The markings on it were already starting to glow with the strange light that looked like molten gold. Once again, no one was here, and the landscape stretched around her, devoid of life.

Avery immediately heard Alex's voice in her head. *You're blocking us, Avery.*

I'm not, I promise.

It's your fear, he replied. I can feel it. Relax, let us in.

Avery took a deep breath and then another, willing herself to calm down. She hated it here, alone. She needed them.

For another few seconds nothing happened, and then suddenly they were there, standing on either side of her.

"Wow," Shadow said, turning slowly. The crossroads enhanced her otherness in ways that were indefinable, but obvious at the same time. "This is amazing. I feel the fey magic rising." She trembled slightly. "It's so odd to feel my home when I haven't in weeks."

Alex squeezed Avery's hand gently. "I knew it would work. I can see why you were freaking out. This place definitely has Otherworldly vibes." He looked at Shadow and his voice was sharp. "Focus on the stone. What does it say?"

Shadow ran her hands gently across the surface, and the writing became more visible. She was silent for a few moments as she read the script. "It's ancient and I don't recognise some phrases, but essentially this stone calls to the energy of the wind. It demands that someone who commands it be made sacrifice so as to give honour to Hecate, Goddess of the Crossroads. Those who are sacrificed will receive her eternal blessing."

Avery felt a cold fear wash over her. "She chose me because I wield elemental Air. Which means—" She broke off, looking at the other three stones, and Alex followed her gaze.

Shadow had already anticipated them, and she reached the next closest one. She didn't need to touch it; the writing was already glowing with golden light. "The language is identical. I presume they were all placed here at the same time, but the script calls to the Fire element instead. They must represent the four elements," she said, confirming their suspicions.

While she made her way to the two remaining stones, Alex asked Avery, "But why only you? Why aren't the other witches being called here?"

"I don't know, but the other stones remain lit from within, unlike this one. I have a bad feeling about this. We need to get out of here."

Alex turned around, taking in their surroundings. "Not yet. Is there something that will help us find this place again, in the real world?"

Avery threw her arms wide. "Look at it! It's virtually featureless! And the moon never changes. It should be waning by now—I've been here three times. It's still full and overhead. I feel as if we're in a bubble."

Shadow re-joined them, and it was clear she'd overheard the conversation. "We ARE in some sort of stasis, like a spell that has frozen this place in time. That's how it feels to me, anyway. The fey magic that surrounds here is," she frowned, as she tried to find the right word. "It's less wild…harnessed, like a horse."

"And why isn't that woman here?" Avery asked. "I keep expecting her to appear at any time!"

"Because she doesn't need to appear," Shadow explained. "Her job is done. She brought you here, and now you're linked to that." She pointed at the stone dedicated to elemental Air. "It's draining your power, even now. I don't know about you, but I can feel its energy growing. And I think I know why the other stones are lit, and it's not good news. And I think you know why, too."

Avery swallowed, fearing she also knew the answer, but she'd been trying to ignore her suspicions. "I think these have already been activated—if that's the right word."

Shadow nodded. "Yes. Their power is already complete, which means?"

"Other witches have already been sacrificed to them," Alex finished for her. He raked his hands through his hair, his eyes wild with worry. "So how do we break the connection before Avery dies?"

Avery felt sick. Three witches with strong elemental magic had already been sacrificed to these stones, and she could be next. "Where did that woman get the other witches from?"

"It might not be where, but *when*," Shadow suggested. "This stasis could have existed for a very long time."

"Which suggests that this woman has also been doing this for a long time," Alex said. "Who the hell is she?"

Before she could answer, Avery staggered as her energy dipped and her vision dimmed, and Alex quickly stepped forward, supporting her before she could fall. "Time to get you out of here."

Alex extended his left hand to Shadow, still holding Avery with his right arm. "Grab my hand and don't resist."

For endless seconds, nothing seemed to happen, and then with a rush, Avery was back in the centre of the circle, and the room dissolved into blackness.

12

Avery heard the murmur of voices all around her, and then slowly a warm, orange light began to seep into the blackness that surrounded her like a shroud.

As the voices grew louder, Avery began to make out words. It sounded like a spell. Why could she hear a spell?

A male voice shouted, "Her eyes are fluttering, she's coming around!"

And then she heard Alex's voice and felt his hand slide into her own. "Avery, can you hear me? Are you all right?"

She tried to speak, but it felt like her mouth was full of dust and grit. With the greatest effort, she opened her eyes and then quickly closed them. The light seemed blinding. "I'm fine," she finally muttered, realising as she said it that she was not fine at all. "Water."

"Here," Briar said, and she felt arms slide under shoulders and lift her so she was sitting up.

"Let me," she heard Reuben say from somewhere behind her, and suddenly she felt a warm, solid mass behind her, and she leaned into it with relief.

Alex said, "Have some water, Avery, just a sip."

A glass was pressed to her lips and she took a few sips of cold water, thinking she'd never tasted anything so delicious in her life. It was only when she finished drinking that she opened her eyes again, squinting against the light for a few moments until her vision adjusted. The fire still burned, candles still illuminated the room, and Alex's worried face swam in front of her.

"Hello, gorgeous. Glad to have you back."

"Glad to be back," she croaked. "What happened?"

"Crossroads bloody magic, that's what," Reuben said from above and behind her. Avery realised a pair of legs were stretched out on either side of her, and she twisted to look up into Reuben's anxious face. She must be leaning against Reuben's chest. "You had us worried then, Ave."

"Sorry. It wasn't exactly what I planned."

Now that she was awake, she could see Alex next to her, and beside him was Caspian. On her right was Briar, and at her feet was El, all of them white-faced with worry. Shadow was watching from beyond the circle.

"By the Goddess," Briar said, "you had me worried. You're very weak."

"I feel as weak as a kitten. What happened?"

Alex explained, "I think that stone drained your magic while at the crossroads, far quicker than it would by just your psychic link. We shouldn't risk you going there again."

"How can I not go?" she asked. "It's there, all the time, in my head! I see it every time I close my eyes!" She could hear her own panic rising, and she tried to subdue it.

"I have made a suggestion," Caspian said, his voice low. "It should help, but not everyone agrees."

Alex shot him a look of annoyance. "I'm just not sure that another magical link will be a good move."

Briar's calm tones interjected. "But it could buy us valuable time—at Caspian's expense."

"I've told you that I'm happy to do it. I'm the only one who can." He looked around at the other witches. "And you know I'm right."

Avery held a hand to her head. "I'm not thinking particularly clearly right now. Can you be more specific?"

Briar took Avery's hand in her small, soft one. "Since Caspian also commands elemental Air, his power will supplement your own, and hopefully feed that standing stone that continues to drain your power, until we can sever the link completely."

Avery looked at Caspian and knew he was completely serious. "I think that's too dangerous, Caspian."

"But it's too dangerous for you not to have support. How long do you think you've been out for, Avery?"

She looked around at the others' faces and noted how tired they looked. "An hour or two?"

"Try five or six."

"What!" She tried to sit upright, but her limbs still felt heavy, and she sagged back against Reuben again. "How is that possible? How long were we at the crossroads?"

"For us, a matter of minutes," Alex said. "But in reality, over an hour."

"We were starting to panic," El told her. She still sat cross-legged at Avery's feet, her blonde hair loose around her shoulders. "You three were motionless. It was freaky. And when you finally came out of your weird psychic trance, you just collapsed. For the last few hours, Briar has been trying a variety of healing spells on you."

"With very limited success," Briar said, grudgingly.

Caspian was impatient. "You haven't got time to wait, Avery, and you have very few options. Do you want to link with me? It will help slow the drain of your power."

Avery glanced at Alex, not sure what to do. Caspian was probably right, but she wasn't certain it would be a good thing, and she wasn't sure Alex would like it, either.

Before she could respond, Briar said, "For the record, I think it's a good idea, Avery. Tell us honestly how you feel."

She met her calm, quiet gaze. "I'm shattered. My limbs feel heavy, and my thoughts are clouded. I can't feel my magic as much, either. It actually feels pretty scary."

"Well, I think you have your answer then," she said softly. Briar looked at Alex. "You know Caspian is right, and I know you want to do this, but Caspian is the only one to truly wield elemental Air like Avery. And his magic is strong. Your powers are different, and we're going to need you to help Avery break this link. That is your strength, Alex."

Alex looked stricken for a moment, and then nodded. "Agreed. Avery?"

She nodded. "Agreed."

Alex turned to Caspian. "Thank you. What do you suggest?"

Caspian could swagger when he wanted to, but he must have realised how difficult this was for Alex, because he said, "You're the expert on this. What do you think?"

Alex thought for a moment, looking at their arrangement within the broken circle of salt. "I don't think what we three have just done is the way to go. That was for a short-term connection only. A type of binding might be more effective."

Caspian nodded thoughtfully. "But it has to link me to the crossroads too, or it's pointless."

"I think whoever links to Avery now will be bound to the crossroads, regardless," Briar said. She held her hands a few inches above Avery, sweeping over her body. "I can feel it. You're sort of vibrating with it. It has changed your energy."

"I agree," Shadow said. "As soon as we connected, it was obvious."

Alex nodded as he started to look excited. "Yes, you're right. We needed to connect mentally and psychically because we needed to visit the crossroads with you, but Caspian doesn't. He just needs to lend his power to yours. The connection you have to that place will automatically feed from Caspian, too."

"I think you're right," Avery agreed. "But Caspian, I think you'll get flashes of the crossroads anyway."

"Good. There are positive aspects to this link. It links us to her, too—whoever she is."

"Exactly," Reuben said from behind her.

Alex rose to his feet. "I'm just going to get my grimoire. I have a binding that should work, but happy to take any suggestions."

"We trust you," Briar said, still gauging Avery's energy levels. "I've brought more potions with me. You have to drink them every two hours. I've upped the dose."

"Whatever, I'll drink anything at this stage. I might have to increase my alcohol consumption, too."

"I've already beat you to that," Reuben said. He shifted slightly, and Avery tried to sit up on her own, but failed. "Stay put," he commanded, his hands resting on her shoulders. "I can cope with a numb ass."

Avery reached up and rested her hands on his for a moment. "Thank you."

Alex returned to the circle, and sat cross-legged with his grimoire on his lap. "You two need to sit in the middle, knee to knee, hands linked," he instructed Avery and Caspian.

Avery reluctantly pulled herself away from Reuben, summoning all of her remaining reserves of energy to sit upright, and sat opposite Caspian.

She watched his expression, wondering if this was really a good idea. He liked her, he'd made that clear, and she hoped this link between them wouldn't make his feelings stronger. But he gave nothing away; he just looked his normal, collected self. He held his hands out and she took them in hers, uncomfortably aware of his strong, sure grip, and the light touch of his knees resting against hers.

Alex pulled a white cord from his pocket. "I'll say the spell, and you repeat it after me. As we continue, I'll wrap this cord around your wrists. The cord will then be kept safe in a cedar wood box until we break the binding." Alex then spoke to El, Reuben, and Briar. "You all can join in, too. Our magic will reinforce the binding and act as a sort of secondary defence."

They murmured their agreement, and moved back into their positions, and then Alex began to chant.

The spell was short and succinct, and they all repeated it over and over again, as Alex wound the cord around Avery and Caspian's linked hands. Avery felt the power of the spell rise quickly, and a tingle ran up her arms and across her body as the binding took hold.

Her link to the standing stone and the crossroads reverberated through her, as if it recognised a second power enter her body. Avery watched Caspian carefully. He shuddered, and Avery guessed he could feel the crossroads magic now, too.

Caspian's magic felt cool in her veins, and she started to sense it beyond her arms, as it travelled across her body, along her trunk, and down her legs. His magic was strong. She'd always known that, but feeling it flow through her now, she realised how much she had underestimated him. He met her eyes as the binding took hold, and she thought she detected a hint of triumph in his face, which he quickly masked. She knew her magic was flowing around him too, as weak as it was right now.

The chanting continued, and with relief Avery felt her magic and energy lift, and her muddled thoughts became clearer. For the first time in hours, she began to feel they could defeat this woman, and that she would not become stone fodder in some time-frozen place.

Alex ended the spell, and the cord that bound her and Caspian's hands burned with a bright white light for a few seconds before extinguishing. She was now bound to Caspian until this thing was over, and he looked a damn sight happier about it than she was.

Alex gently untied the cord. "Feeling better, Avery?"

She smiled at him. "Much better. It happened quicker than I thought. It's very odd to feel someone else's magic in your body." She kept it light as she looked at Caspian. "Thank you. How are you?"

He rolled his shoulders. "Fine so far, but I can feel the pull of the crossroads. Blunted though, probably because I'm not directly linked. Unfortunately, I can't feel that woman. I'd like to pick up her power signature. It might help us work out who she is."

Briar wriggled closer to Avery and extended her hand again, her face impassive as she concentrated furiously for a moment. Then she relaxed and sighed with pleasure. "Excellent. I can feel your magic rising. Great job, everyone."

Reuben scooted around, looked at her, and then nodded wisely. "Yes, I agree, you do look less like shit than you did earlier."

"Thanks Reuben, you always say the nicest things," Avery replied.

"Always here to please, you know that, Ave. So, what now?"

"Now we find out who that woman is and what she wants."

"She must have some other role in the circus," Caspian suggested.

El shrugged. "Maybe her role is to give the circus magic? Odd though, that she should parade around the town with the other performers."

Avery eased away from Caspian and stretched out her cramped limbs, and the others started to move too, breaking up the circle. "The more I think about it, the more I think she has no circus role, not as a performer anyway. She has to be our number one priority. She's the key to everything."

Shadow warned, "That will be hard. She protects herself well, and can obviously defend herself against magic."

"So there are two things going on, really," El surmised. "The creature that is hunting people, and the woman who controls the crossroads—who could be Caitlin, if Newton can find out who she is. And yes, they have to be linked, but essentially there are two problems. We need to keep searching for that crossroads."

"Two teams," Shadow said. "We divide and conquer."

"But," Alex said, looking at Avery. "You can't come to the campgrounds."

"Why not?" she asked, annoyed.

"You know why not. She knows you. A trip to that site could trigger another trip to the stones. We can't risk that."

"No, you can't," Caspian said, unexpectedly agreeing with Alex. "You had just enough energy to fly out of there last time—which, by the way, suggests it's located here in this world somewhere, but is a long way from here. You might not be able to do that again. We need to know where it is and how that woman links to it. We should concentrate on that."

"As in, we," Avery said, gesturing between them.

"Yes. If we find the crossroads, we're halfway to breaking the link. She is anchored to something there."

Briar groaned. "So many questions. It hurts my head."

"That's tiredness," Reuben said, as he rose to his feet and extended his hand, pulling Briar to her feet, too. "We all need sleep. It's nearly three in the morning."

El grabbed her jacket and headed to the door with Reuben next to her. "And it's Monday. So no lie-in either. Do we meet tonight, then?"

Alex put his grimoire away in the large wooden chest he kept a lot of his magic paraphernalia in. "After the show. It has to be then. We want them in the campground, not in the tent, if we're to spy effectively."

"Midnight then," Reuben said. "I'll call you to confirm. You in, Shadow?"

"Of course."

Briar confirmed that she would be there too, and left with Shadow, Reuben, and El, leaving Caspian the only one remaining. He pulled on his coat as he spoke. "I'm going to chat to Estelle. She has a knack for 'finding' spells. There must be something we can adapt to help us find the crossroads. I'll call you later, Avery. Perhaps while the others are searching the campgrounds, we could try this. Midnight would be a good time for us, too. Liminal boundaries are stronger at those times. You should come to my place."

"Are you sure Estelle will want to help?" she asked. Estelle, Caspian's sister, had never liked them, and despite Caspian's acceptance of the White Haven witches, she had never softened her stance. And Avery didn't like Estelle, either. She was abrupt and rude, with a solid superiority complex.

"She has no choice. I'm the head of the family now, and the head of our coven."

Alex shook Caspian's hand. "Thanks, that sounds a good plan. And thanks for tonight."

"Anything to help Avery," Caspian murmured, and with a final glance at her, he left.

Alex shut the door and turned to look at her. "I hate that you're bound to him." His dark eyes burned with a fierce intensity she didn't often see. Behind it she could sense his worry, and maybe some fear.

"I hate it, too," she reassured him, "but I really do feel better. And I love you even more for doing this. You have nothing to fear, you know."

He reached forward and pulled her close, kissing her passionately. When he released her, she was breathless. "I don't want to lose you, to anything or anyone."

"You won't. Now come to bed." She grabbed his hand and pulled him after her.

13

Avery's eyes felt gritty the next morning, and she stumbled into her flat with a heavy head from too few hours of sleep. But at least she *had* slept, which must have been a result of extreme tiredness, Briar's potions, and Caspian's magic.

She felt horribly guilty. She'd hardly been home at all the previous day, and she gave Medea and Circe a big fuss when she arrived. They meowed loudly, and wound around her legs until she'd fed them, and then she headed down to the shop.

Sally and Dan were already in the kitchen, and the smell of coffee filled the space. Avery inhaled greedily. "One for me please," she said as she stepped through the door.

"No problem," Sally called, reaching for cups, and then she turned to look at Avery and frowned. "What have you been up to?"

Avery just groaned. "Too many things. Mainly getting myself into trouble with some crazy circus lady."

"Again?" Dan said, as Sally poured the coffee, sugared it, and then handed Avery her cup. "Tell us everything. No, wait. Let me guess. It must be the mysterious woman."

"Spot on, and our connection just got a lot weirder." She filled them in on everything that had happened over the weekend.

Sally gaped at her. "You're linked to Caspian now?"

"Temporarily! His magic is shoring up mine. It's weird. I didn't think such a thing was possible, not like this anyway. I mean, you connect to another witch's magic when you do spells together, but this is something else entirely."

"Does that mean he's in your head?"

"No! That would NOT be okay. This is a magical link, not psychic. But I'm really annoyed—they've banned me from going to the circus with them tonight."

"Sounds sensible," Dan said, leading the way into the shop, ready to open the doors for the day. "You're clearly very vulnerable right now. Do you want to do your thing?" He gestured around vaguely.

"Do you mean enhance my protection spells? Yes, that's probably a good idea."

Sally and Dan gave her space as she walked around, lighting incense and reinforcing her spells—one for protection, and one that helped her customers find that special something they didn't know they needed. Her rituals calmed her, so that by the time the doors opened, she almost felt her usual self.

Avery joined Sally and Dan at the counter, where they were finishing their coffee. Dan had found Robert Johnson's blues music, and its moody sounds already filled the shop. "Did you go to the circus in the end, Sally?" Avery asked.

She nodded. "I did. It was amazing. The kids loved it. But I did feel the slightest bit of magic, although I doubt anyone else could."

That made Avery pause. "You can sense magic?"

"Only slightly, and only because of you. I think I've been overexposed to it. Anyway, I felt it at the circus, but it didn't detract from the performers. They were still brilliant."

Avery shifted her weight as she leaned against the counter. "What do you think the magic did?"

Sally thought for a moment. "I think it gave the atmosphere a buzz, and the tent walls seemed to rustle as if something was alive in that fake greenery. But, the whole performance was magical, really."

"Interesting. Briar said the same thing."

"What will you do while the others are at the circus?" Dan asked.

"Try to find the crossroads with Caspian and his sister."

"That bitch, Estelle?" Sally looked appalled.

"I don't have much choice. We need to find the crossroads to break my link to it—and the mysterious woman's. Estelle is good at 'finding' spells, apparently."

"What happens if you can't break the link?"

"The standing stone will eventually sap all my power and I'll die."

Dan and Sally fell silent, looking at her wide-eyed and open-mouthed. Dan recovered first. "You'll solve it, Avery. You always do."

Avery's usual positivity was failing her, and she confessed, "Yes, but I'm not normally the one at risk. I'm already not functioning as well as usual. You should have seen me before Caspian helped."

"I did try and find out more about the Green Man and the Raven King," Dan said. "But, to be honest, I've found nothing ground-breaking."

"Tell me what you have found. I need something to cheer me up."

"Well, the Green Man is a nature spirit, and has been around for centuries. Images show him surrounded by green leaves and vines, and he's associated with death, rebirth, and fertility, and particularly with Beltane and May Day celebrations."

Avery nodded. "I remember. Isn't he the consort to the May Queen?"

"Usually. His title is quite recent. It's attributed to a woman called Lady Raglan, back in the 1930s, if I remember the date correctly. Before then he was called Jack in the Green. People mostly associate him with nature, forests, and woods. He's always been depicted in pagan beliefs, but his image is commonly found carved into stone and wood in churches. Depending on where you are in the country, he has been mixed up with Robin Hood, and even Herne the Hunter."

"Really?" Sally asked, surprised. "Why would churches have pagan images carved on them?"

"It's believed that many churches were built on pagan places of worship. And many people who were involved in building churches would have still clung to the old beliefs. He's likely carved into All Souls and Old Haven Church."

"I love how the old beliefs sneak into Christianity. I might have to go and have a look at All Souls," Avery said, thinking it would be good to speak to James anyway.

Dan continued, "He's also been associated with the Green Knight, you know, from the Arthurian Legend, Sir Gawain and the Green Knight. He was interesting! Gawain chopped his head off, and the knight picked it up and challenged him to the same thing the next year."

"You think he's here now because he's linked to the Otherworld, and has been summoned by crossroads magic?" Avery asked.

"I reckon," Dan said. "The circus is all about boundaries and English folklore, and how figures from our ancient past shape our present." He smiled. "I always like to think he's around when I'm walking across the fields and down country lanes, especially in the woods, and particularly at twilight, when the light is fading and the animals are busy. I can almost sense something else there, just beyond my vision."

"That's exactly what I think, too," Sally agreed. "I like to think the old ways lurk behind the everyday."

"You two never cease to surprise me," Avery said, laughing.

"And that's why we like working here," Sally said. "Go on, Dan. What about the Raven King?"

"He's based on Welsh mythology. Have you heard of Brân the Blessed, or *Brân ap Llyr*?"

Avery frowned, thinking that something about the name sounded familiar. "Vaguely."

"He's the legendary Welsh King of Britain. Brân is the God of music, poetry, and prophecy, and *brân* means 'raven' in Welsh. Ravens are associated with prophecy, too, and seen as messengers between the Otherworld and our world." He shrugged. "They have their place in lots of other cultures, and were associated with Apollo in Greek myths. Anyway, here in Britain, the raven is identified with Brân. He's the son of Llyr, which is why you might remember him, Avery."

"Llyr, as in the father of the crazy mermaids we fought in the summer last year?"

"The very same. The God who represents the powers of darkness. But Brân wasn't a dark figure—he was revered and honoured as being wise and brave. Ravens have always been associated with him."

"And hence he's a liminal figure, because ravens carry messages between our world and the Otherworld," Avery said, grasping the connections. "And he was a God of prophecy."

"And as a God, he stepped between worlds anyway," Dan agreed. "Did you know he's the source of the myths of the ravens and the Tower of London?"

Avery shook her head. "No."

"Brân was injured in a fight with the Irish, shot by a poisoned spear. He commanded that his head be chopped off and buried on the White Mount, in London, with him facing France. The White Mount is where the Tower of London now stands. It is believed his head is a talisman, protecting Britain from foreign invasion. And it was a talking head, too! He continued to advise and entertain on his journey to London."

Sally gasped. "That's so cool! I did not know that. And that's why ravens are associated with the Tower?"

He nodded. "Yes. The ravens gather to respect their fallen king, and it is rumoured that should ravens leave the Tower, Britain will fall. Therefore the Tower has a raven master to ensure that the Tower always has ravens."

"So the Raven King is another figure who crosses between worlds," Avery said thoughtfully. "The circus master's costume certainly did it justice the other night. I just wonder how much Corbin has to do with what's going on there. He certainly didn't sound very happy when we overheard him the other night."

Dan finished his coffee and thumped his cup on the counter. "Maybe he's the weak link—someone to work on to help you."

Avery looked at the shelves stacked with books, seeing nothing but the Raven King in her mind. "Maybe he is, Dan." Her hand itched, and she looked at her palm as the mark glowed again.

Sally had followed her gaze, and she frowned. "What's that on your hand?"

Avery looked guilty. "I neglected to mention that. The stone I mentioned marked me. It's fey script."

Sally edged around the counter, grabbed Avery's hand, and pulled her closer to the front window to examine it carefully. "Wow. That's scary."

Dan took her hand too. "That's some dream that can do this."

"I know. The power of the crossroads is real. No wonder they used to bury their dead there. Maybe they thought it helped their souls cross to a better place."

Dan dropped her hand and rubbed his chin thoughtfully. "You know, you talk of the crossroads as an evil place, and Hecate can be a dark mistress, but she isn't always. She's a chthonic Goddess, a Goddess of the Underworld, but she's not inherently evil."

"I know. What are you suggesting?" Avery asked.

"Well, neither are the Raven King and the Green Man. They're liminal figures, after all. Their presence is not evil, even though it probably felt scary the other night when they were in the field with you. But surely the presence of a God and a nature spirit is bound to feel scary. You're in the presence of powerful beings. More importantly, Brân was a power for good. He protected the weak, and if you believe the myths, he protects England right now."

For a moment, Avery was speechless as she processed Dan's words, and a bright spark of hope started to fill her. "You're absolutely right! If anything, they should be on our side!" She started to pace the front of the shop as her head filled with possibilities. "We need to use them, or at least trust in them."

Sally sat on the sofa beneath the window of the shop, watching her pace. "I don't know. They haven't helped so far—those young men have still died. That doesn't sound positive to me."

"But it's like what Shadow says, and what you have said before too, Avery," Dan reminded them. "Gods don't interfere in the affairs of men, and neither do pagan spirits. They are separated from the affairs of mortals—in general—unless you appeal to them. Whoever this woman is, she appealed to Hecate for help, and there was clearly a price to pay. You could appeal for help too, and enlist the Raven King to Team Witch."

Avery stopped pacing and looked at them both. "But what if there is another price to pay?"

Dan folded his arms across his chest. "You're already paying the ultimate price. I don't think you've got much to lose."

***

Avery looked up at All Souls Church and squinted at the stone work. It was a gloomy day, and the sky was filled with heavy clouds. She felt it had been days since she'd seen the sun, but that wasn't unusual in February. What was unusual was the warmth to the air, and the ever increasing number of ravens in the town and up at the castle.

The image of the Green Man with his mischievous, grinning face stared down at her from the archway above the church entrance. It was tucked to the side, but it was unmistakable. Other faces were also there, strange gargoyles with their wild, ugly expressions. She felt they watched her as she set off around the church, trying to spot more carvings. She was so lost in her thoughts that she didn't hear James, the vicar, until he spoke from behind her.

"What are you up to, Avery?"

She looked around, jumping with surprise. "You were quiet! I was looking for the Green Man. He's in quite a few places." She pointed up at him, high up the wall on a buttress.

James laughed. "Oh, yes. He's a cheeky thing, isn't he?"

"Do you mind that he's carved here? He's a pagan symbol, not Christian."

"Of course not. He's an ancient symbol of fertility and rebirth. I quite like it that he connects us to our past. Besides," James said, grinning, "he was probably put there to encourage the pagans to come in. You know, make the Church a place for everyone, and then convert them to the true faith."

He said this with a glint of humour, and Avery laughed. "Of course! That makes perfect sense. What about those, though?" she asked, pointing to the gargoyles that projected from the corners of the building.

"Oh, now they have two purposes. They funnel water from the roof to prevent erosion, and also remind people that the devil exists. That's why they're so grotesque—to encourage people to pray."

Avery was surprised. "They funnel water?"

James pointed. "See, its mouth is open. I believe the word is French originally, it means throat or gullet."

"That's so cool. I'm learning so much today."

"What else are you learning about?"

"The Green Man and the Raven King."

"Is that because of the circus?"

"Sort of," she confessed. She hadn't seen James for a while, and he looked good; happy, and free from worry. He also seemed pleased to see her, which was nice, as they'd had their ups and downs in the past. Fortunately, when she'd last seen him before Christmas, he'd been happy to bless some water for them to help in their fight with the vampires.

James became serious again. "Is something happening again?"

"Yes, but you don't need to be involved."

"I think I owe you a coffee or two, and maybe some biscuits. And if I'm honest, you look a little pale. Come on in." He turned and led the way to the vicarage, clearly not accepting no for an answer, and Avery fell into step beside him.

"I'm sure you're busy, James."

"Never too busy for one of my flock."

"I'm pretty sure I'm not one of those."

"You are to me," he said softly, in a way that had Avery pausing in surprise.

He headed inside and she followed him through the toy-strewn living room, into the kitchen, and watched him as he filled the kettle and prepared cups.

"Where's your wife?" she asked him.

"Volunteering at the children's nursery. She does a few things to help the community." She remained silent, and he looked at her. "Did I surprise you?"

"Yes, actually. You know I'm not a believer in your faith."

"That's okay, Avery. I've decided that I don't need you to believe. And besides, you look after our community, too. I imagine the vampires were pretty scary to deal with?"

"Terrifying. I hope I never have to face them again."

He switched the kettle on, grabbed a packet of shortbread, and then sat at the kitchen table, gesturing her to join him. He offered her a biscuit as he asked, "Were you the ones to tell the police about the bodies in the caves beneath West Haven?"

"Yes. That's where we found Lupescu, the chief vampire."

"And you found those two girls?"

"Me and my coven, yes."

"In the middle of the worst snowstorm that we have seen for years?"

She smiled ruefully. "It was pretty bad, wasn't it? But yes. We tracked it and found its lair, and then waited for it to return. Lupescu killed Grace, the girl who worked at The Wayward Son."

His eyes closed briefly. "I thought it must be so. Poor girl. But you saved two more."

She took a bite of her biscuit, enjoying the sugar hit. "I wish we could have saved even more. The vampire had been hunting for years."

"Were there others?"

"I'm afraid so, but we think we killed them all."

"Only think?"

"We can't be sure, but we're pretty confident."

"And what do the police really think?"

"They know vampires were behind it all."

The kettle boiled and he stood to make their drinks, and then brought them to the table, placing one in front of Avery. "Do they know about you?"

"One of them does."

"And the press?"

"I hope not!" She sipped her drink, watching him over the rim of the cup. "We try to keep a low profile."

He nodded. "And you do. What about that house they found the passages under? The medium's house?"

She tried not to roll her eyes. "That was the root of the problem, actually. But hopefully that will never get out, even though the owners are going to run tours."

"They want to run tours of White Haven, not just their house. That's what Stan was telling me, anyway."

Avery felt a stir of worry deep in the pit of her stomach. "I know. He wants to put my shop on his tour."

"He strikes me as an opportunist."

"Oh, he's definitely one of those."

James looked at her thoughtfully for a moment. "I feel I should tell you that I've heard rumblings of concern from my parishioners."

"Concern about what?"

"Black magic. They think that's what the deaths and all those bones were caused by."

For understandable reasons, angry hordes and Helena flashed into Avery's head, and she had a vision of Helena's final moments as she was burned at the stake. "What did you say to them?"

"I've told them it's ridiculous, of course. Have you had any problems in your shop?"

"None!" Avery's customers were always book and occult lovers in general anyway, and she certainly hadn't detected any animosity.

He nodded, relieved. "Good. The last thing we want is a modern day witch-hunt."

She shook her head, perplexed. "No. I hadn't even considered it."

"Just to reassure you, there were only a few concerned people. Many who live in White Haven appreciate it for what it is, and love its mysticism and magic, but I just wanted to warn you. I hope that man doesn't stir things up. What's his name again?"

"Rupert." She remembered his resentment once he'd learned she was a descendant of Helena, and wondered if he would create trouble for her. There was something about him that none of the witches liked.

"That's it. Are you sure I can't help you with anything? I mean, this current issue with the circus. There was a death the other day, on one of the beaches."

Avery nodded. "Yes, there was, and someone in the circus is responsible, but we're working on it. You can stay out of this one, but thanks for asking anyway." She didn't see any point in sharing her current predicament. There was nothing he could do.

He smiled, but it didn't mask his worry. "Fair enough. Have another biscuit."

14

Alex nearly spat his pint out as Avery repeated what she'd discussed with Dan and Sally.

"Will you please stop talking about dying!"

"It's a possibility, you know that. Facing my own mortality is weird. But I have to trust this will work tonight. I haven't got a death wish! And as much as you don't want me linked to Caspian, I don't want to trust Estelle. But we have to find the crossroads!"

"But do we? I've been thinking on this all day. Is there another way?"

Alex and Avery were sitting in a secluded corner of Penny Lane Bistro, the former home of Helena, waiting for their starters to arrive. Avery had brought him up to date with all the latest developments, theories, and suggestions, before they went their separate ways later that night. She was drinking a hearty red wine, and Alex was drinking a pint of Skullduggery Ale, his latest favourite tipple.

Avery lowered her voice and leaned closer to Alex. "I could not affect that woman in any way with my magic. And I have great magic, as you know. I can only presume that Hecate's magic protects her, and wow, I wish I had that protection. She was virtually immune! If her link to the crossroads is protecting her, we have to sever it. Only then will she be vulnerable. Only then can we stop me from turning into a standing stone, and stop whatever is killing those young men."

Alex scowled. "I hate it when you're so logical."

She smirked. "Like you, I've also been thinking this through all day, and I believe it's our only option. I haven't seen the woman again since the other night. Some of the circus performers have been all through the town this morning, and she wasn't with them—well, not that I saw anyway. Or the American."

Alex sipped his pint thoughtfully. "Dan might be right about Corbin. If we can see he's still doubtful, I'm happy to talk to him. We have to know who the other woman is. I can't believe how many performers there are. It's like looking for a needle in a haystack."

He was right, Avery reflected. The circus was much bigger than she had anticipated, and a very slick affair. "I think he's right about the Raven King and the Green Man too, but how do we recruit them to our side?"

Alex was silent for a moment as their starters were delivered, but as soon as they were alone, he suggested, "What about an invocation?"

"Like summoning a demon or a spirit?"

"They are spirits of a sort, so why not?"

"Wow. I hadn't considered that as an option, but I guess you're right. But, because they're already present at the circus at certain times, wouldn't that mean they are under someone's control?"

Alex groaned with exasperation. "Maybe? We still don't know enough about how this works. But I really don't think you can control them like that. I think they've just been released, you know what I mean, like they have found a way to cross to our world and are tethered to the circus, but are otherwise free to do what they like. Maybe Hecate summoned them." He shrugged and paused to take a few mouthfuls of food and then said, "Rationally, when I think back to that night in the field when we were pursued, it didn't feel threatening, initially. It was disorientating and confusing, but it wasn't until the end when it changed and we felt something else pursuing us. It's a bit jumbled in my mind, but I think that's right."

"I agree, but I think we need to shelve that idea for another time." Avery chinked her glass with Alex's. "Good luck, and be careful."

***

Caspian's manor house was dark except for a few windows on the ground floor through which a subdued yellow light peeked, and subtle garden lights illuminated the drive, shrubs, and specimen trees.

Avery knocked on his front door, feeling nervous for what the night may bring, and her mood wasn't helped when Estelle answered. Her long, dark hair was loose around her shoulders, and her face was pinched with annoyance. She looked disapproving at Avery. "Avery, you'd better come in."

"I better had, unless we want to do this on your lawn."

Estelle just ignored her, leading the way wordlessly into the large reception hall. She turned left down a long corridor and headed to Caspian's study, which Avery knew from her previous visit was at the rear of the house, overlooking a knot garden, which had been there for years but was recently renovated.

Caspian was standing in the middle of the room wearing a black t-shirt and loose black cotton trousers. The room was painted dark moss green, the parts of the wall Avery could see, anyway. The rest was lined with oak bookshelves, and a large desk sat to the side of the room, covered in old leather books. On the opposite wall was a stone fireplace, and a fire blazed within it. The whole place was masculine and expensively furnished.

However, it was the arrangement on the floor that caught Avery's eye. A large map was spread out on a Persian rug, and a salt circle had been drawn around the whole area, leaving plenty of space for people to sit within it.

Caspian was staring at it, and he looked up as they entered, a trace of a smile on his face. "How are you today, Avery?"

"Better, thank you. I've been taking Briar's tonic all day, and with your magic, I feel stronger. How are you?"

"Pretty good, but I can feel the pull of the crossroads, very faintly."

Estelle was dismissive, watching her brother with her arms crossed over her chest. "You're an idiot. It could have affected you, too. It still could."

Caspian didn't even look at her, looking back at the map. "We've been through this. I wasn't about to let Avery die for the sake of father's old grudges. I've moved on, and so should you." He looked up suddenly, flashing her a hard look, before turning to Avery. "I've put this map together from several maps I had. We needed something detailed and big, and this is it. It's the best I could do in the short term. However, I have a feeling we need only concentrate on Scotland."

Avery took her coat off and placed it over the back of a chair, and put her bag next to it, before she joined Caspian. "That makes sense. It seems it's where all this started."

"There was an article on the circus in one of the Sunday papers. Did you see it?"

"No, I don't read them, and besides, I was busy feeling terrible."

"I didn't read it until today. It expands on what Newton told you, and talks about how the circus became so successful."

Avery was intrigued. "Did it give details?"

He shook his head. "Not really. It was a piece about how long the circus has been going, and how they were struggling until Corbin had the brilliant idea to reinvent it after a summer break. He said the history and the wildness of his surroundings inspired him. It mentions Inverness and Loch Ness, but nothing more specific."

Avery stared at the map. "It's a shame we can't narrow it down further. I didn't notice any recognisable landmarks, other than water. It could be the loch or the sea. Inverness is close to both. The only reason I could tell there was water close by was because the moon was reflected in it."

"Excellent. Knowing it's near a body of water will help."

Estelle interrupted. "You don't need to know anymore if you'd both have a little more faith in my spell," she said acerbically. "We can pinpoint the area—if you two can get your part right."

"I think you know better than to doubt my magic, thank you, Estelle," Caspian said dryly.

Avery winced inwardly. There was certainly no sibling affection between them, but maybe that was because she was there, and she knew Estelle didn't like her. That was confirmed when Estelle said, "It's not yours I doubt."

"You should know better than to doubt mine, too," Avery pointed out, resisting the urge to smack Estelle's arrogant face. "But I think it's best we don't look back, don't you?" She was referring to a couple of their previous battles, where she had beaten Estelle, and saved her from attack by the Nephilim when they were still in spirit form.

Estelle chose to ignore her. "We should start to prepare, then. You two sit on the rug, next to the map. I'll get my grimoire."

While Caspian and Avery sat at the base of the map on the soft rug, Estelle collected her grimoire from the table, and sat at right angles to them. "This is a reasonably simple spell," she told them. "We don't need potions or herbs, it's just an incantation. However, we are following your magic, Avery, which means we need a thread of it to follow. And I guess yours too, Caspian, although your connection will be weaker."

Avery frowned. "A thread? How do you mean?"

"The magic you release when you throw energy balls or command air, but rather than releasing it in bulk, we need a tiny part of it."

"It's like when we use witch-flight," Caspian explained. "When I showed you how, we slowed it down. That's what we do now."

Avery nodded. "I know what you mean. What then?"

Estelle huffed, impatient. "You're tethered to a place. That thread will lead us there—in theory. I haven't tried to do anything such as this before. However, I have used a version of this to find lost objects that are closely associated with someone."

Caspian added, "Because my magic is linked to yours, we should have double the magic to find it."

"All you need to do," Estelle said, "is clear your mind, and let the spell do its work. Don't resist it. I'll seal the circle first. You two need to link hands."

Avery shuffled closer to Caspian, until they were both in the same position they had been the previous night, cross-legged and knee to knee, but as Avery reached her hand out, Caspian took her right hand and turned it palm upward. "The mark is still there."

"Unfortunately, yes. It itches sometimes."

Gently, his index finger traced the lines, almost intimately, and Avery was suddenly grateful that Estelle was there, as she subdued a shiver at his touch. She felt the power of his magic again, boosting hers. It was a strange feeling, and one she'd be glad to see the back of. "The mark is unfortunate," he said, softly, "but it will help us tonight."

"Done," Estelle said, satisfied, as Avery felt the circle close. "Now, bring forth your magic."

Caspian cupped his left hand beneath her right one, and Avery cupped his right hand in her left. Within seconds a thin stream of what appeared to be smoke left the centre of Caspian's palm and floated upwards, and it reminded Avery of the cord that linked her to her spirit body. She did the same with her magic, focusing on releasing some into her right palm. Her magic had a similar appearance, but it was golden rather than smoky. It curled in the air as it rose, stopping in her eye line.

Estelle then started the finding spell, her voice low but clear, and Avery's magic started to swirl lazily, drifting across to the map, followed by Caspian's. Avery watched, fascinated as the spool of magical thread uncoiled, still linked to her hand. And then she felt a pull in her stomach, and an image of the crossroads flashed before her eyes. She blinked, suddenly dizzy, and took a deep breath to steady herself.

Caspian murmured, "Don't resist it, Avery. We must follow it."

She nodded, and opened up her mind to the crossroads again, desperately trying to keep anchored in Caspian's study, rather than lose herself at the standing stones. Her magic drifted over the map of Cornwall, and then it was joined by Caspian's, both swirling over White Haven, and then they started to snake their way up the country.

Their threads of magic passed over Bodmin Moor and into Devon, then through Salisbury, across to London, and then northwards, moving back and forth across the country.

"Why is it moving so haphazardly?" Avery asked.

"It's not. It's following the path the circus took," Caspian told her. "See how it's lingering over certain spots where they performed? Places where the boundary magic surged for a brief time."

Avery was impressed with the strength of Estelle's spell. While they watched, Estelle continued to chant, and unbidden the image of the crossroads became stronger in Avery's mind, and she shivered. Caspian's hands gripped hers tighter, sending a pulse of magic her way, and she embraced it hungrily. The farther north they moved, the stronger the image became.

Avery closed her eyes, almost unwillingly, and suddenly she was there, standing at the edge of the crossroads again. She heard Caspian, his voice almost muffled. "I can see it too, Avery, open your eyes."

But Avery's eyelids felt as if they were welded shut, and once again the standing stone glowed, its script pulsing with golden light, and the itch in Avery's palm began to burn.

Then a searing white light flashed into her mind, and Caspian's voice boomed in her head as he commanded, "Avery, open your eyes! NOW!" Magic raced through her, and her eyes flew open. She found Caspian staring at her, panic-stricken, and her hands ached through the fierceness of his grip.

"I'm here. It's okay."

"You almost weren't," he said, his voice rough.

Estelle spoke calmly. "It worked. Look." The threads of their magic whirled lazily above a spot in the far north of Scotland. "Don't move." She jumped to her feet, headed to the top of the map, and then crouched, her face close to the surface. "It's by Inverness, a place called Lochend, which is at the end of Loch Ness." She looked smug. "See, I told you it would work."

"How the hell do we get there?" Avery asked, bewildered. "It's so far!"

Caspian looked at her, a smile playing gently across his lips. "You forget I've seen it now, too."

"But how? I don't understand. We're not psychically linked."

"We didn't need to be. The further north you went, the stronger the pull, the stronger the image. And because my magic is linked to yours, and I *am* an elemental Air witch, I saw it too, clearly. Fortunately, I am not anchored there as you are, and could pull back. However," he smiled triumphantly, "I can take us there."

"I'm not sure that's a good idea," Estelle said. "You may be good at witch-flight, Caspian, but it works best when going to a place you know well."

"To a place I've *seen*," he reminded her, finally dropping Avery's hands. "I saw it well enough to take us there, especially now that I know where it is."

Avery hated to agree with Estelle, but… "I think Estelle's right," she said. "Taking me could be a disaster. I only have to creep towards it on a map and I can't think straight. And that's probably where I flew back from the other night. That's why it seemed to take longer than usual, *and* I was nauseous when I arrived. It was pretty scary."

Estelle's superior expression changed. "Wait a minute. How did she get you there?"

"She called me, sort of, in my head. I passed through a gap in the hedge, and I was just there!"

"No sensation of flight?"

"None! I can't explain it."

Estelle frowned, looking interested for the first time all evening. "Fascinating. How did she manage that?" She clearly didn't expect an answer. Instead, she narrowed her eyes at Caspian. "You don't know what links the woman to that place yet. Whatever it is, it's strong, abnormally strong. To break her link, you have to know what it is. If you go there, you need to be fully informed with a clear plan."

Avery eased away from Caspian. "Let's do some more investigating. If Alex and the others have managed to find Corbin tonight, we may be able to discover more. Or they may even have seen the woman again. She must have something that links her to the boundary magic. They might know what that is. In fact," she said, becoming excited, "we may be able to break her link from here, if we can get close enough. We might not need to go there at all!"

"All right," he said crossly, "you win. For now. But I have a feeling we will have to go there regardless. Hecate's magic makes her too strong—you know that better than anyone."

Avery's phone started to ring, and she headed to her bag and grabbed it. It was Alex, and she answered quickly, asking, "Any luck?"

"Yes, we managed to get Corbin alone, and he's willing to talk, tomorrow morning. No, this morning now, at ten. Neutral ground."

"That's fantastic," she said, breathing a sigh of relief. "Where's neutral ground?"

"Old Haven Church."

"Excellent, that's nice and quiet. Any reason he's decided to help?"

"Haven't you heard?" Alex asked, his voice dropping. "There's been another death tonight. They found the body before midnight on the edge of town."

Avery sank into the closest chair, turning to Caspian to find him watching her. She said, "Are all of you okay?"

Alex laughed dryly, "Sort of, but I'm knackered. I'll head to yours, meet you there?"

"Sure, I'll be leaving soon."

She rang off and looked at Caspian. "There's been another death, outside White Haven. But the good news is Corbin has agreed to help. We're meeting him tomorrow at Old Haven Church."

"Good. I'll come, too."

"No, that's a bad idea," Avery told him. "You haven't been to the circus, and no one—as far as we know—knows you. We should keep it that way. You're our secret weapon."

He laughed. "I've never been called that before."

"You may never be called it again, either," Avery said, teasing him.

"All right," he said, softly. "You're welcome to stay here tonight."

Estelle frowned at Caspian, but Avery shook her head, "No, I'll head home, but thank you, both of you, for tonight. We're one step closer to stopping this. Hopefully I won't end up sacrificed to Hecate after all."

15

A fine drizzle was falling by the time Alex and Avery reached Old Haven Church the next morning, and they ran up the gravel path to the large porch that covered the entrance and sheltered beneath it, waiting for the others to arrive.

After an argument on the phone that morning about who should go and meet Corbin, mainly from Reuben who wanted to meet 'the mad bastard' who had agreed to use crossroads magic, they had finally agreed that for all to show up would be equally mad. The less Corbin knew about them the better, and he had only met Alex the night before. Alex had told Avery how they had waited until the camp had finally fallen silent, and Alex had snuck into his van, using glamour to momentarily silence Corbin while he spoke to him. It seemed Corbin was so shocked about the second death in White Haven that he agreed to help. They had, however, agreed that Shadow should join them. Her knowledge of fey magic might be useful.

Alex leaned against the thick wooden door of the church, looking out at the increasingly heavy rain. "What if he changes his mind?"

"Then we got back to plan B, and try to break whatever links the woman to the crossroads."

"I don't like that option. She seems to have disappeared."

Avery watched the rain spatter off the bare branches and headstones of the dead, and felt the gloomy day lower her spirits. "Well, she can't have gone far. If the second death is caused by whoever is responsible at the circus, and I guess we're waiting to have Newton confirm that, she must be close by, pulling strings."

"At least *you* achieved something last night," he said, watching her. "Even if we never see her again, we know where the crossroads is."

She nodded. "It was a great spell. I was surprised by how accurate it was, and Estelle was a pain, but she helped. But it was also a bit too real, *again*. I don't like how close it is to my reality, and I told you how it affected Caspian, too."

"He'll like that. It makes him feel closer to you."

Alex's voice had an edge to it, and Avery tried not to feel annoyed. If he was linked magically to someone she knew fancied Alex, and didn't particularly hide it, she'd hate it, too. She would be scared she'd lose him. "I don't like it any more than you do, but right now, we couldn't do this without him. In fact, I think I'd be dead. I imagine that woman is feeling pretty damn angry I'm still alive."

"Yes, she is," a deep voice said, making her jump. Avery and Alex raised their hands, and a ball of fire appeared in Alex's palms as Avery summoned what little magic she had available. They hadn't heard Corbin arrive, and he raised his hands as if surrendering. "Sorry. I didn't mean to startle you."

It was the first time that Avery had seen him properly, in daylight, without his costume. He was tall and gaunt, his face long like his limbs, with a thick shock of black hair, greying at the temples, and his eyes were dark, almost black as well. He stared at both of them, taking in their appearance, too.

Alex relaxed his stance, the fire disappearing. "You came. I wasn't sure you would."

Corbin glanced at Alex's hands uneasily as he stepped into the shelter of the porch. "How did you do that?"

"I'm a superhero," Alex answered dryly.

"I mean it. If I'm to trust you, I want to know."

"I need to trust you, too," Alex said. "But I guess you're here. I'm a witch, a good one. And so is Avery, when some bitch isn't messing with her powers."

Corbin swallowed nervously, and despite his height, almost seemed to cower in the corner. "Caitlin is stronger and more dangerous than I realised. I hadn't expected the death toll to be so high."

"Caitlin is the woman who controls the crossroads. The woman with auburn hair?" Alex asked.

Corbin nodded.

"We suspected as much," he said.

Avery subdued a snort. "But you did expect a death toll?"

Corbin glanced at her nervously, and then away, looking out to the graveyard. "Not exactly, but I thought there may be. I guess I willingly misunderstood."

"But you didn't try to stop this sooner!" Avery said, incredulous. "It clearly didn't bother you that much."

Corbin glared at her. "And just who should I ask to stop this madness? Should I have told the police? I would have sounded insane. I had no idea what to do—until now!"

Alex shot her a glance and Avery fell silent, knowing now wasn't the time to antagonise him. Before anyone could say anything else, Shadow appeared at the porch entrance, staring intently at Corbin. "Sorry I'm late to the party."

Alex said, "No, you're just in time. Let's head inside."

Alex unlocked the church door with a spell, and they headed inside, walking to the rear pews to take a seat. Avery shivered. It was colder in here than outside. Corbin folded himself into the narrow pew, looking around nervously. It seemed that even here he was scared.

Alex sat next to Corbin. "We didn't have time to talk last night, not properly. Why don't you tell us how this all started?"

"Last summer, the circus was in trouble. We had returned from Europe with poor sales and little money, despite our performers being excellent. We'd actually cut our tour short because we couldn't afford to keep going. Unfortunately, we looked tired, and weren't competing, and some people were threatening to leave." He smiled briefly. "Fortunately we've been running for years, and most people are loyal. I'm lucky that they wanted to keep trying. We all agreed that we needed to do something new. And then, Rafe and Mairi, my two newest managers, suggested we go to Scotland. They're originally from there, just outside Inverness. They said the place would inspire us, allow us to rebuild and re-think, so that's what we did."

Alex frowned. "Sounds pretty innocuous."

"It was, and they were right. We stayed outside Inverness. It's beautiful there, close to Loch Ness. It gave us time to think. And then Rafe suggested something else." Corbin shuffled in his seat. "Rafe and Mairi as well as being managers are also investors, and have sank a lot of their money into the circus. They had been with us for only a year, but they were hard working and ambitious, and everyone seemed to like them, but I guess now I can say they were always odd. Anyway, they said they knew of a wise woman who could help the circus. They reassured me, joking almost, about how old magic would make us rich. I admit, I was desperate. We were running out of money, and I was intrigued, so I agreed to meet her." He fell silent for a moment, staring at the back of the pew in front of him. "I could tell Caitlin was unusual from the start. She had a strange intensity—eyes that saw too much, if you know what I mean."

"What did she propose?" Shadow asked.

"She said I should embrace the old ways, the myths and the magic of the wild, and the stories would bring their own reward. We talked about the Raven King and the Green Man, King Arthur, Beowulf, giants, pixies, goblins, elves, so many things, and how a circus based on these would be unique and exciting. I loved it!" He became animated, his voice rising as he looked at them. "I could see it all, and I became excited about our future for the first time in a long time. And then she said that she had ways of allowing the magic of the Otherworld to fuel our performance." He shook his head. "I laughed, initially, not realising she was being literal. She said she could ask at the crossroads for the spirits to join us, and asked if I would give my permission. I thought she was mad, but essentially harmless, so I said yes. Caitlin then explained that she would perform the ritual on the night of the next full moon, and I thought that was that."

Avery looked at Alex and Shadow. "That explains the full moon over the crossroads, then."

Corbin looked confused. "You've been there?"

"Unfortunately, yes." Avery looked at his confused face and sensed he was genuinely shocked. "Don't you know what has happened to me?"

"No, I don't think I do."

"I have been marked for sacrifice to Hecate. I should be dead right now—if it wasn't for my friends."

Corbin blanched. "Hecate? How?"

"I've been linked to one of the standing stones there. It's draining me of my magic."

Corbin looked really uncomfortable now. "I've never been. I stayed away from all that. Only Rafe and Mairi went with her."

"Go on," Alex prompted. "What happened next?"

"I focused on developing the new programme, with other key performers. No one else knew about Caitlin's involvement, just the three of us. Nothing more was said about the full moon ritual, and I forgot about it, almost, and when I did think about it, I thought it was probably some crazy something she did in her back garden. Anyway, two weeks or so later, I felt a change in the camp, the stirrings of something happening, something I couldn't quite place."

"Like what?" Shadow asked. "Or are you in denial again?"

Corbin frowned at her. "I worked out, eventually, that what I felt was the presence of a wild spirit, something bigger than all of us. I called Rafe and Mairi into my office, and asked them what was going on, and they laughed, said the ritual had worked, and wasn't that fantastic? At that point, I knew I'd entered into something I couldn't control, but even then I had no idea of the extent of it."

"When did you?" Avery asked.

"Not until weeks later. We were ready to start performing by the end of the summer, and our first performances were for the local crowd. From the start we were a huge success, and that first night I experienced the power of the Raven King for the first time. I felt him, actually *felt* him!" Corbin looked at them, wide-eyed with surprise. "I felt him fill me up, take over me, animate my costume…it was subtle, but it was there. And the Green Man was on the grounds, everywhere, every night. I admit, for a while I loved it."

Shadow watched him, her hands in her pockets as she leaned against the pew. "But not anymore?"

"They exhaust me, and I know it sounds odd, but I sense their frustration. They are as tied to us as we are to them."

"Has anyone else noticed?" Avery asked.

He shook his head. "That's the weird thing—no one else seems to notice that anything's going on. Apart from our success, of course. But the supernatural stuff—nothing."

"Did you know Caitlin would be travelling with you?"

"No. It was only when we were ready to leave Inverness that she announced she was coming, too. I was shocked. She's not part of the circus, and I asked why. She said if I wanted to keep our success that she had to, and Rafe and Mairi were keen, so I agreed, and she's been with us ever since."

"Tell us about the deaths," Alex said.

"They started as soon as we left Inverness, but I didn't associate them with us for weeks. It was only when I noticed that Caitlin was behaving more oddly than usual that I asked what was going on, and Rafe told me, but not at first. I had to ask again and again."

Corbin's voice started to rise with panic, and Alex tried to reassure him, keen to keep the story coming, although it seemed to Avery that Corbin wouldn't stop now. He'd had no one to talk to and no one to help him, and now that they were listening, he needed to tell them everything. "It's okay," Alex said. "How odd did Caitlin become?"

"She became short tempered, angry, distant, odd. Other performers started to complain about her. I knew it had to be bad, she kept to herself most of the time, so if others had noticed—" He broke off, his meaning clear. "Her mood could last for weeks, and then she'd be fine again. I threatened to make her leave at one point when she became so bad. I thought to hell with the success, and that's when Rafe told me I couldn't. Caitlin is tied to the heart of the ritual. She's what Hecate wants most. She carries Empusa."

"Who?" Alex and Avery asked in unison.

"Oh, that's bad news," Shadow said, her hands moving to her daggers and resting on the hilts. "You have an Empusa in your company?"

Corbin looked flustered, "You've heard of her?"

"I've heard of *them*. They are shape-shifting females who consume young men. They're a type of Lamia. They're dangerous, violent, slippery, and tricky to kill."

Avery's thoughts reeled. "Are you saying Caitlin is an Empusa?"

Corbin shook his head. "No, she carries one within her. At the moment they are two separate beings, the Empusa within Caitlin's body. She kills through Caitlin, when she needs to feed." He shuddered as if he couldn't believe what he was saying, and then looked at Shadow. "You sound like you think there's more than one."

"There are, where I come from."

"But Rafe describes her as *the* Empusa, and so does Caitlin, as if there's only one. It is Hecate's wish that she becomes real. That's what she demanded for giving us the Raven King and Green Man—what you call Otherworld magic. But I swear I didn't know this for weeks, and there's *nothing* I can do!"

There was more to this, there had to be. Avery asked, "What does Caitlin get out of this?"

"Youth and immortality. She's getting steadily younger, day by day. More youthful, stronger, fitter."

Shadow rolled her eyes. "Longevity is not all it's cracked up to be."

"Says the woman who is a fey immortal," Alex pointed out.

"Not immortal, just long-lived, so I should know, right? It's fine when you're surrounded by others like you, but sucks when you outlive them."

Corbin barked out a laugh. "Try telling her that. I have learned that they—the Empusa and Caitlin—will become one, but something has to happen first."

Avery met Alex's eyes as understanding dawned, but it was Corbin she addressed. "Me dying at the standing stones as a crossroads sacrifice has to happen. No wonder she's angry. I'm the end point of her ritual."

Shadow added, "And that's why we couldn't find her last night, Alex. She was out, hunting."

Corbin took several deep breaths and he started to shake. "I feel sick. Men are dying because of what I agreed to. I've been a fool."

Shadow pulled one of her daggers out of its leather sheath and balanced it with the tip on the end of her finger, effortlessly. "Has your circus been struggling for a while?"

"Yes, actually, how did you know?"

She didn't answer. "And did you find Rafe and Mairi, or did they come to you, like a miracle?"

His shoulders dropped as he saw where she was leading. "They came to me."

Shadow twirled her dagger round her fingers, spinning it so quickly that they all watched, mesmerised, until she caught it in her palm and threw it at an ornately carved wooden column, one of the many running down the sides of the church. The dagger point landed dead centre on the carving of a Green Man. She smiled, satisfied, and then looked at Corbin. "You've been played. They make lots of money—and so do you—and she gets youth and beauty and power. I think this has less to do with what Hecate wants than what Caitlin wants."

Corbin's expression changed from fear to confusion and then rested on anger. "How do I stop them?"

Shadow grinned. "That's better. We break Caitlin's link to the crossroads. Or just kill her, which would solve everything."

16

"There'll be no more killing!" Alex said, looking at Shadow like she was insane. "This isn't the Wild West."

Shadow walked over to the pillar to retrieve her knife. "I have no idea what the Wild West is, but in my world, that's what we do."

"It's not your world, either! It's ours, and there are consequences to killing."

"There are bigger consequences for her remaining alive and becoming an Empusa," Shadow reasoned. "If she becomes one, she could disappear, change form constantly, and we'd never find her."

Avery was outraged. "And I would be dead! I'd like a solution that doesn't involve my death."

"And so would I, obviously," Alex agreed.

As Avery watched Shadow and Alex arguing about how best to corner Caitlin, she huddled inside her jacket, wishing she'd worn something thicker and warmer, and also wishing she'd had more sleep. She was reluctant to use her warming spell; it seemed an unnecessary use of her power. The rain was heavy, drumming on the roof of the old church, and inside it felt damp and cold. One good thing about the cold was that it kept her awake, but she had a feeling she'd need to sleep that afternoon. All these late nights were catching up with her, and the pull of the standing stone didn't help.

Shadow suggested she was best suited to the job. She stood with her hands on her hips, looking at Alex. "I'm fey, and therefore stronger and faster than you."

"I'm a witch, and therefore better than you at tackling magical enchantments."

Shadow smirked. "That does not wash with me."

Avery held her hand up. "Can I interrupt? Corbin, I have a question. Does Caitlin carry something with her all the time, like a necklace, or a ring, or some kind of object that she has in her pocket? Anything at all that you've noticed seems significant to her?"

Corbin had been leaning back in his pew, looking out of one of the stained glass windows, seemingly miles away, but he turned to her and frowned. His face was grey and lined, and his fear and frustration seemed genuine. Avery hoped they were right to trust him. "She wears an ornate ring on her finger. It looks as if it should interlock with another, if you know what I mean. Anyway, she twirls it constantly. Why?"

"She's not a witch, therefore she doesn't wield magic, and she can't create spells. All of her magic comes from the ritual she performed. So, how can she carry the magic of the crossroads with her? A spell I found suggests there is a way to do it, but it involves two linked objects. That ring could be it. We need to get it off her."

Corbin ran his hand across his face, as if he could wipe his problems away. "I can't believe I've done this. I've been stupid, greedy."

"You wanted to save your circus, it's understandable," Avery said, feeling sorry for him despite her predicament, but not really sure it was that understandable at all.

Shadow wasn't so kind. "Anyone who embarks on a deal that relies on magic—with someone you don't know—is insane. If we can end this, just promise me you won't do this again."

Corbin looked at her, incredulous. "Are you kidding me? Of course I won't."

Shadow pursed her lips. "Avery, do you think removing this ring will stop the magic?"

"It will, in theory, break her link and sever her power. Meaning, she is no longer impervious to our magic. She would no longer carry the Empusa, and it should also break my bond to the stone." She shrugged. "I'm not sure if removing the ring will be enough. We might have to destroy it, somehow."

"I'm not convinced," Shadow said. "I'd still rather kill her."

Alex ignored her. "Corbin, you know Caitlin's routines better than anyone. How do we get to her to get that ring?"

"When she sleeps?" He shrugged. "She watches everything and everyone. I don't know if you can get close to her. Her caravan is next to Rafe and Mairi's, which offers her extra protection, but I don't think she needs it."

Alex considered his suggestion for a moment. "It will be too quiet. If she resists, it could get loud. We'll wake everyone up, people will come running, and Rafe and Mairi will interfere. Is there another time when the camp is otherwise occupied, and the noise will go unnoticed?"

"It would have to be either during the performance or straight after it." Corbin weighed the options. "Probably right at the end. It's chaos. The crowds take a while to leave. Some of them get autographs, then many head to the stalls and games. The team hangs around in the Big Top, just talking through performance issues, tidying up, celebrating, and unwinding. People can hang around in there for a while before they head to the showers. There's no good time, but that's the best."

Alex looked hopeful, finally. "Great. Obviously we'll protect you and anyone else if they get involved, but hopefully that won't be an issue."

"Okay." Corbin paused, looking awkward. "And look, I need to tell you something else."

All three looked at him suspiciously.

"What?" Shadow asked.

"There's been a man hanging around the circus for the last few performances, from about two or three towns ago, wherever we were then. I lose track. I've noticed him because he comes alone."

"Why does that matter?" Alex asked.

"People generally don't come to a circus on their own, repeatedly, and there's something about him I don't like. It's the way he watches us all. He's tall, grey hair, in his forties, wears bike leathers sometimes, other times just jeans and boots. But he's imposing."

Warning bells went off in Avery's head. "I've seen him, too. In the town—twice now. The first time he was watching Caitlin, and the second time, my shop. He's intense looking, but I didn't sense any kind of magic power about him. It has to be the same guy."

"I think he's searching for something," Corbin said. "But don't ask me what."

Alex exchanged a nervous glance with Avery. "Have Rafe and Mairi noticed him? Is he with them?"

"I don't think so. They don't spend as much time in the tent as me, or around the grounds during the performances. They stick to managing the staff."

Avery couldn't believe her ears. She didn't need something else to worry about. "What makes you think he's searching for something?"

"Because he's so relentless. Initially I was worried one of the females had a stalker, but it's not that. I've asked around, just casually, but no one seems to know him."

"Bollocks!" Alex said. "Who the hell is he and what does he want?"

Corbin looked at the floor and then at Alex. "I don't know. I'm starting to feel hemmed in by forces beyond my control."

"This is getting interesting," Shadow said, the only one who looked excited by the news.

Alex looked up at the ceiling as if divine intervention would strike. "I'll update Newton, in case it helps him find out anything about him. Which I doubt."

Avery rose to her feet and started to walk up and down the aisle to warm up. "Great. A mysterious man who could make things worse, and we have no idea how to get that ring from Caitlin. I'm going to pretend that man doesn't exist for now, and think only about her."

Alex sighed. "Can I suggest we get out of this freezing church and regroup later? Then we can think of a plan, which doesn't involve killing someone!" He looked at Shadow pointedly.

"If you have no stomach for it, I'm fine with handling it," she told him.

"I'm not fine with you doing it, either!"

"You aren't my moral protector. This is the way the world works where I come from. Many of us carry weapons—swords, daggers, bows—all the time. This system of *police* you have doesn't exist." She said the word as if it tasted like poison. "We manage things ourselves."

"At some point, you have to learn to live in our world, like it or not." Alex turned back to Corbin, ignoring Shadow's sceptical expression. "How do we keep in touch with you?"

Corbin stood up as he prepared to leave, and fear crept into his eyes again. "You don't. I'll keep in touch with you. I told you, she's uncanny. I feel she sees through me. I'm already worried that if she asks me something, I won't be able to keep my mouth shut."

Alex looked at Avery. "We need a spell, something to help him."

Corbin backed away, alarmed. "No! I've had enough magic!"

As scared as Corbin was, Alex was right, and Avery tried to reassure him. She held her hands up, palms out. "This is only to protect you. A small spell that will seal your lips about this meeting. If she asks you anything, you'll deny it. You'll say you went for a walk."

"In this weather?"

The rain was now falling heavier than ever.

"Say you set out across the fields to the beach, and the rain came in. It's true enough. It wasn't that bad earlier," Avery said. "Did she see you leave?"

"No," he admitted. "She was sleeping heavily. Probably after her feed last night."

"Good. With luck, she's still sleeping. We've only been here for an hour. I have just the spell, unless…" She looked at Alex. "You have one?"

"I do, you should conserve your strength. Corbin?"

His shoulders dropped. "All right, then."

Alex stepped close and began to cast the spell, his fingers weaving shapes in the air. For a second Corbin's eyes glazed, and then he blinked and focussed.

Alex dropped his hands, satisfied, but offered one final word of advice. "Okay. Done. But don't speak of today to anyone. Let her ask if she needs to. Hopefully, she won't. Can you try to call us tonight, just so we can update you?"

"I'll try. If I'm still alive," Corbin said ominously, before heading out the door.

***

"You were right," Avery told Dan when she returned to the shop at lunchtime, Shadow at her side.

"I was? About what?"

"About Corbin. He did want to help us."

"Really? Go me. I am useful, after all." Dan preened slightly, and was rewarded when Shadow smiled at him.

Shadow said, "I think you're very useful. I wanted to know if you thought I could use this crossroads magic to go home?"

His face fell. "Why are you asking me? I don't know about that, but I'd guess that as a boundary, the lines between our worlds are blurring, enough for your fey magic to cross, but not enough for you." He looked at Avery, throwing her a look that appealed for help. "Am I right?"

Avery tried not to show her impatience, but her tiredness meant she showed it anyway. "Yes. I keep telling you, Shadow, the magic that brought you here opened an actual portal—a real portal, not just a blurring of boundaries and a seep of magic! You know this!"

Shadow glared at her. "But an Empusa has crossed. That suggests it is closer to a portal than not!"

"A Medusa?" Dan asked, horrified. "You two kept that quiet!"

"Not a Medusa, dummy," Avery said. "An Empusa, which according to Madame here, is some kind of Lamia, and a man-eating monster. And it hasn't crossed, like through a portal. It is actually the spirit of one, summoned by Hecate. That's different."

Dan glanced around, checking that no one was close enough to hear this strange conversation. "I've heard of Lamias. You're talking Greek myth now. Give me a moment." He ran to the myth section and darted back within seconds, bringing a selection of books. He selected one and flicked through it until he came to a stop, and then looked at them, grinning. "The Empusa is a servant of Hecate, one of several who are worshipped at crossroads. It's reputed to have a leg of copper, and is a shape-shifting female."

Shadow looked triumphant. "Told you she was a shape-shifter. Never seen one with a leg of copper, though. And we have more than one of them in my world. And," she jabbed a finger at Dan, "I'm not from Greek myth. I think you'll find all creatures belong everywhere. Maybe just their names change sometimes."

"Yes ma'am," Dan said, a new note of admiration in his gaze.

"But that must be what Corbin meant, when he said The Empusa," Avery said, excited. "Maybe she's the mother of all Empusas."

"Well, that does not sound good," Dan declared, turning back to the book. "But maybe I can find out more about it."

"Ask me! I know," Shadow said, joining him behind the counter.

Avery left them talking, and headed to the back room to see Sally. She put the kettle on and said, "Break time."

Sally looked up and smiled, left the computer, and joined her at the table. "Thank you. How are you bearing up?"

Avery decided to confess. "I'm not, really. I've been sacrificed to Hecate, and my magic is draining away. Every time I close my eyes, I see that damn crossroads. My hand itches where the stupid mark is, and if it weren't for Caspian, I'd be dead by now. I'm exhausted and pissed off, and it's really hard to stay positive right now. And I feel I owe Caspian. I'm not sure I like that, either. Alex certainly doesn't." Now that she'd declared all, she felt tearful.

Sally grabbed her hand. "I'm sorry, Avery. This sucks, and I'm scared for you, too. I think we're all trying to make light of this, because it makes us feel better. But Alex would do anything for you—anything. That includes tolerating you being magically linked to Caspian."

Suddenly Avery realised the root of her fear. "I worry he'll leave me over this. That me and Caspian will end up in some weird relationship."

Sally frowned and squeezed her hand. "Is that what you want?"

"No! Alex and I were talking about moving in together. He suggested it! That's what I want. I don't want Caspian."

Sally smiled softly. "You idiot. Then that's what will happen. Things are scary now because you can't control what's happening. You were taken against your will, your palm marked with fey script, and you doubt your magic for the first time—ever. But don't. You'll work it out. You always do. Tell me what you found out this morning."

Avery relayed their conversation with Corbin, and then said, "So, we have a rough plan. But we need the help of the Raven King and the Green Man, too."

"But the Raven King comes to Corbin, right? He inhabits him, gives him power, isn't that what you said?"

Avery nodded, her thoughts woolly and confused.

"It sounds like Corbin thinks he's powerless, too," Sally went on, "but he's not. He becomes the Raven King—in short bursts, admittedly—and he desperately wants out of this arrangement. If you ask me, you've got some pretty big guns on your side."

As Sally's words registered, Avery started to feel hopeful, and the fog in her brain started to clear. "By the great Goddess. You're a freaking genius, Sally. You and Dan. What would I do without you?"

Sally winked. "You'd have to work a damn sight harder than you do now, that's for sure. Now, get up those stairs, hit those books, and make it work!"

17

All afternoon Avery worked hard, looking through her grimoires and other books for a way to defeat Caitlin. She eventually fell asleep on her attic sofa, wrapped in a blanket with the cats curled around her, while the fire smouldered and her incense burned. It was the image of the crossroads that woke her.

Once again it was dark and a full moon shone above her, casting its bright white light all around, and throwing shadows on the ground from the standing stones. Three of the stones' scripts glowed with a fiery gold light, except for the one closest to her. It beckoned her, and she felt its insidious pull. She stepped closer and closer, her palm raised, ready to place it on the stone, but the voice in her head was shouting at her to pull away. For a few seconds she couldn't place it, and then realised it was her own voice, from somewhere deep inside, warning her to run.

She dropped her hand, clenched it into a fist, and backed away. She turned, trying to get her bearings, anything that would help pinpoint exactly where she was, but other than the stones and the moors, there was nothing. Surely, she thought, now that they knew it was close to Lochend, it couldn't be hard to find four standing stones in one spot. She took a deep breath, inhaling the smell of something sweet and flowery that merged with the scent of grass and earth.

Drumming started again, a solitary drum that beat slowly, ominously, and the centre of the crossroads became shrouded in mist. She knew what this meant. Caitlin was coming back. She tried to run, but her feet felt as if they were bound to the earth. Caitlin's misty form solidified and she smiled, her eyes filling with a feral glint as she saw Avery. Corbin was right. She looked younger than she had even days before.

She spoke with a low rasp, her Scottish accent hard and accusatory. "I felt you here. It's time. You need to stop resisting. It won't hurt."

She stepped towards Avery.

"No," Avery answered, retreating as her heart thumped and her mouth went dry. "You will not win. I will stop you."

Caitlin threw back her head and laughed, and for a second her features distorted, showing something else beneath the surface of her skin. Something inhuman. "You're too late. And who will rescue you? You're alone."

Avery felt something at her back, something cold and immovable, and she looked around, alarmed to find the standing stone behind her. How had that happened? She had put distance between them.

Once again, everything whirled as she felt her magic drain away.

And then she heard another voice, shouting desperately. Avery, wake up! Something stung her cheek, and she lifted her hand to it, feeling its heat, and then a surge of magic filled her and the last thing she saw was Caitlin's anguished face as she ran at her.

Caspian's pale face was in front of hers, and she felt his hand across her face again, stinging her cheek with a resounding slap.

"Ouch! What the f—"

Caspian looked terrified and appalled all at once. "Sorry, Avery. You wouldn't wake, I shook you, and then I thought slapping you would work."

He sank to the floor as she struggled to sit up, the blanket falling from her shoulders.

"Shit. I was there again. And so was she." She stared at Caspian as the full implications of what had happened hit her. "I could control the pull of the stone for a while, and then she appeared, and I was so disorientated! The stone was right behind me, but I moved away from it, I know I did." She stopped talking, realising she was rambling incoherently, and took several deep breaths. "How are you here? How did you know?"

"Our magic, remember? We're linked, which means I am linked to the crossroads, too. I felt its pull, and I knew you were in trouble. I used witch-flight to get here." He rubbed his face and laughed unexpectedly. "I was in the middle of a meeting and literally ran out of the room. They'll think I'm insane."

Avery's eyes widened with surprise as she noted his smart suit and crisp white shirt. "Oops. Sorry. But thank you, I think you just saved my life—again. I mean, really, thank you. I'm sure this wasn't what you signed up for."

"I knew exactly what I was signing up for, and I'd do it again in a heartbeat." His eyes met hers, holding her gaze for a fraction too long to be comfortable before he stood up, brushing down his trousers and straightening his lapels. She tried to stand too, but her legs felt weak, and he gestured for her to sit again. "Stay there. Do you want some water, tea, whiskey?"

"No, I'm fine. I can get it myself. I just need a minute."

He nodded, his dark eyes unfathomable. "All right, I should probably go. I need to fly back into the bathroom cubicle, like bloody Superman. Let's hope no one else is there."

"Are you sure you have the strength?" she asked him, concerned.

"Yes. The pull was weak for me. Briar has given me tonics too, to bolster my magic. Just promise me you won't go back to sleep again."

"No chance. We're meeting tonight—we have good news about Corbin."

"Great. Seven?"

"Right here. Well, downstairs."

"Later then, Avery," he said softly, before disappearing in a whirl of wind.

Avery's head fell back on the pillow as she contemplated her near miss, and Caspian's undeniable feelings for her. Crap.

***

Alex took a long look at Avery, and then brushed his hand across her cheek. "It still looks red."

"It still hurts. But it saved my life."

"If he touches you again, I'll kill him."

"Alex! Didn't you hear me? He saved my life. *I should be dead!*"

His long, dark hair was pulled back in a half-pony, and his chin and cheeks were grazed with stubble. As usual he wore an old band t-shirt, jeans, and boots. He couldn't be more different from Caspian. His shoulders dropped, and his aggression disappeared as he pulled her close, hugging the breath out of her. "I'm sorry. It should be me saving you, not him." His voice was rough next to her ear.

"You did. You cast the spell that linked our magic." Avery slid her hands around his waist and pulled him closer, savouring his warmth. "If you want to kill anyone, it should be Caitlin."

"True." He released her. "We need to find her tonight. The sooner we end this, the better."

"I don't want to sleep again. Despite Caspian's magic and Briar's tonics, I still succumbed to the magic." They were standing in Avery's kitchen, waiting for everyone else to arrive, and she had just updated Alex on her day. She poured herself a glass of wine, slid a beer towards him, and then leaned against the counter. "Have you had any ideas?"

"Other than isolate her and try to get that ring from her? No."

"I think we'll have to do more than steal it off her."

"We can destroy it. We have spells that will destroy jewellery or melt metal, especially El. It will be easy for her."

"I have a feeling that won't be enough. She told me I was *too late*, when I told her I'd win. Maybe we are?"

He tried to reassure her. "Then why does she still need you dead, sacrificed? It's not over yet."

The door slammed and they were interrupted by Briar shouting, "We're here."

Avery and Alex headed through to the living area to see Briar had arrived with El and Reuben. Reuben was carrying half a dozen pizza boxes, and the smell of spicy tomatoes, cheese, and meats filled the room.

"That smells amazing," Avery said, pointing at the dining table that was already stacked with plates, knives, and forks. "Drop them there, please."

He grinned. "No problem." Then he paused and frowned. "Avery, you look pale. What's happened?"

She shrugged, self-conscious. "I had another episode this afternoon, but I'm okay."

"No, you're not," Alex said gruffly. "You almost died. Again."

Briar left her bowl of salad on the table, and raced to her side. "How?"

"I dozed off on the sofa upstairs, and well, I ended up at the crossroads. If it wasn't for Caspian, I'd be dead right now."

At that point, the door slammed below them and the chatter of voices announced that Shadow, Newton, and Caspian had arrived at the same time. Caspian appeared at the top of the stairs first, and stopped. "Why are you all looking at me like that?"

"Sorry," Briar said. "We've just found out Avery nearly died and you saved her."

"Ah, that." He looked uncomfortable at the attention, and moved into the room to make way for Shadow and Newton behind him. "That *was* the purpose of our magical link."

Newton looked confused. "What's happened?"

Avery sighed, as uncomfortable to be the centre of attention as Caspian. "Grab pizza, everyone, and we'll fill you in."

For the next few minutes there was a flurry of activity as everyone poured drinks, plated up food, and found seats either around the table or on the sofa. By the time she and Caspian had finished telling everyone about the afternoon, the mood was sombre.

"We can't let this carry on anymore," Reuben declared. "We have to act tonight."

"But are we even close to being ready?" El asked. "Don't get me wrong, we have to do something, but Avery has already told us that magic won't work on Caitlin. What are our options?"

Shadow shrugged. "It's simple. I'll kill her."

Newton looked appalled. "You will not!"

Shadow was unimpressed. "Your laws don't apply to me."

"They bloody well do! I can lock a fey up for murder just as I would anyone."

She smirked. "You could try. Gabe had to use an iron cage to keep me in."

An ugly flush of red started to spread up Newton's neck and his face. "You will not kill anyone. You're in our world now, and I do not condone this."

"That's just what I told her," Alex said.

Briar intervened. "No one condones it. Shadow, we're going to try other options." Then she paused as she looked around. "I presume we have other options."

"Perhaps you should hear what we found out from Corbin first," Shadow suggested. "Our options are small."

Newton jabbed a finger at Shadow. "This is not over!"

She shrugged and reached for another slice of pizza. "Someone update him, please."

"Allow me, Madame," Alex said sarcastically. He started to relay their morning meeting with Corbin, and the energy in the room started to lift, until he mentioned the Empusa.

"A what?" Briar asked, frowning.

"It's a shape-shifting female who likes to feed on young men," Shadow told them. "I've been researching them this afternoon with Dan. I originally thought they were a type of Lamia—we have them in our world, too. But it seems they're sisters…sort of."

El looked baffled. "What's a Lamia?"

"Both the Lamia and the Empusa are either daughters of Hecate or her servants, depending what source you read," Shadow explained. "The Lamia is half-snake, half-woman, and again, she likes devouring young men. The Empusa also takes the form of a beautiful young woman, but she has a copper leg and donkey's leg."

Reuben looked horrified. "Sorry for pointing this out, but a woman with a donkey's leg does not sound that beautiful to me."

Shadow tossed her hair seductively, and a shimmer of sensuality passed over her, making her look dazzlingly beautiful. "She will use her magic, just like this. Her powers to seduce are legendary. You wouldn't even notice. And besides, she shape-shifts. She could look like anything! Even El!" She shook away her glamour, leaving the others momentarily silent.

Reuben looked suspiciously at El, and she shook her head. "Idiot." She turned back to Shadow. "But at the moment she's inside Caitlin?"

"Yes. Some accounts say they followed Hecate from the Underworld. They are commonly called demonic vampires, and both are associated with crossroads. But, like all legends, there are lots of stories and little fact. Most commonly, they are thought to be spirits or wraiths, which also sort of fits, because they came from the Underworld."

Newton groaned. "So Caitlin willingly allowed an Empusa into her? Why?"

Alex laughed, incredulous. "Because it's a sure fire way to achieve youth and immortality. We think that's what this is about—Caitlin's wish for youth. This has nothing to do with Hecate wanting her daughter or servant to walk the Earth."

"Hold on," Newton said, holding up his hand. "So this Caitlin is the woman who you keep seeing, Avery?"

She nodded. "It seems so. I guess you can stop searching to find out who she is."

"How old is she?"

"Well, she looks to be in her thirties now, but Corbin said she was an old, wise woman."

"I guess that fits, then. The only Caitlin I could find was Mairi's great-grandmother, and initially I dismissed her as being too old, but now it makes sense."

"Mairi's great-grandmother?" Avery asked, astonished. "I suppose that also explains the feeling that the spell has gone on a long time, and that the crossroads is sort of timeless. Maybe it was something she once started and had to stop?"

"Well, we may know who she is, but that doesn't help us stop her," Newton said, sighing.

Reuben looked troubled. "So if she's already hunting, and getting younger, why does she need Avery as a sacrifice?"

"To complete the transformation," Caspian said. "At the moment, it inhabits her. I believe she wants to become one with it. Once the final standing stone has an elemental Air witch, she will no longer need the boundary magic. Which brings me to the important question. *How* does she access that power?"

"By a ring she wears," Alex told them. "She must have its counterpart at the crossroads. It would work like the spell that Avery found."

"I've told Avery I can take us to the actual place," Caspian said. "We can try to find the ring there. That would save us from needing to take her on."

Alex glared at him. "No way! It could be a disaster. It's in Scotland, anyway. How are you going to get there?"

"Witch-flight."

Reuben choked on his beer. "Is it even possible to go that far—to a place you haven't seen?"

"Yes! And I have seen it. I got a glimpse of it, from Avery. And she's seen it several times. And that's how Avery got back from there the first and only time she went there!"

Alex was really angry now. "And it made her really sick to travel that far! Are you for real? You know the threat that place poses to Avery. That's where it wants her to be! It's dangerous enough with just a psychic link!"

"I am well aware of that," Caspian said evenly. "I saved her from it this afternoon. But she won't survive another night if she sleeps. Neither my magic nor Briar's tonics are working. The standing stone is too strong. Hecate's magic is too strong. Avery could manage one night without sleep, but two or more? Unlikely."

The room fell silent, broken only by Alex's chair scraping back across the floor as he left the table and paced around the room. "This is shit."

"Just wait," Avery said, desperately trying to calm everyone down. "Corbin is on our side."

"At least someone is," El sighed.

Avery continued, "And so are the Green Man and the Raven King. Both Sally and Dan have pointed out valuable things to me recently, and so did Corbin today. Both the God and the nature spirit have been bound against their will. Corbin knows it! He feels it. During every performance, the Raven King inhabits him and they become one. He feels his frustration and annoyance. Which means, the enemy of our enemy is our friend! They will help us stop Caitlin!"

After a brief silence, in which everyone glanced at each other speculatively, Briar said, "It certainly seems logical, but it also sounds as if Corbin has little control of it. For example, how can he help if he's being the Ring Master? We were thinking of going during the performance. Which doesn't leave us a lot of time, by the way," she said, glancing at her watch. "It's after eight now. Corbin only feels the Raven King during the performance—we think. We need to find out if he can channel him at other times…and if he even likes the idea. And how the hell do we enlist the Green Man?"

"And importantly, how do we isolate Caitlin from the rest of the performers?" El pointed out. "Her gypsy caravan might be at the back of the field, but it's still close to the others. We know that there are always performers around, or their security. They could very well be dragged into this."

Shadow added, "And what about Rafe and Mairi? As far as we know, they're regular human people, but what if they're not? We need to know. Although," she shrugged, "I'm sure I could handle it, anyway."

"Wow," Newton said, aghast. "Your ego knows no bounds!"

"I am fey, that says it all," she declared.

Despite her exhaustion, Avery tried to quash a giggle. That saying would end up on a t-shirt someday soon.

"Have you investigated the other circus members?" Reuben asked Newton.

He nodded. "I haven't mentioned it because we didn't find anything of significance for any of them. They are all exactly who they say they are. We looked into the management again—which includes Rafe and Mairi—particularly closely, but again, nothing. They come from Inverness, they've held management jobs all over the place for years, and as Corbin told you, joined his circus a couple of years ago. Nothing untoward has been associated with them. However, that's not to say that Rafe and Mairi haven't got some kind of magical *something.*" He grimaced. "Our investigations don't cover that."

Alex caught Avery's eye. "We have something else to share, too. The man Avery has seen in White Haven, the one outside the shop, has been hanging around the circus, too. Following their tour. Corbin thinks it's suspicious."

"Just great!" Newton said. "I'm doubly worried about him now."

El sighed. "Okay, it seems we're not as ready as we need to be. Which means attacking tonight sounds increasingly stupid. Agreed?"

There was a mumble of grumbling and nods, except from Alex and Caspian, who together said, "What about Avery?"

They looked warily at each other, and then back to the group.

Avery answered, "I agree. It's madness to go tonight. Someone needs to contact Corbin and ask if he can manipulate the Raven King, and prepare him for tomorrow night. And then we need to work on spells, plans, anything to lure Caitlin away. We can try first to disarm her to break her crossroads connection before we have to visit there. But if it fails, I will go with Caspian."

"And what about tonight, Avery?" Alex asked. He had stopped pacing, and instead leaned against the wall, watching her.

She pushed her wine glass aside. "I guess I live on caffeine, find a spell to keep me awake, and then spend all night carrying on the spell searches I started this afternoon. I'm guessing that we'll only get one shot at this before she dives for cover. She's comfortable now. She thinks she holds all the cards—well, other than me frustrating her. Everything else is going to plan. Let's do it right and wait until tomorrow." She looked at Newton. "The death last night? Was that her?"

He nodded and became very official. "It looks like it. Once again, the victim was a young man. There are no obvious causes of death, other than his organs looking withered and older than they should. It's certainly not a normal death. I'm fielding a lot of questions at the station, and have loads of pressure on me to solve this."

"I saw it on the news," El told them, looking grim. "There's a lot of speculation—although of course they didn't mention details. However, they did refer to the caves under West Haven, and the investigation. They are wondering if they're linked."

"Makes sense," Reuben said. "Caves of bones, young men dying, on the back of those gruesome deaths before Christmas. This doesn't make White Haven look good."

"James said he's heard rumblings of concern about black magic from his parishioners," Avery told them. "He said it was only from a few people, but this is a small place. I'm worried it will set off something bigger."

"Like a witch hunt?" Briar asked, eyes-wide.

Reuben groaned. "It's the twenty-first century, Briar. Chill out. If anything, those rumours will make this place more attractive."

"It's not hampering my sales yet," El said.

Briar shuffled uncomfortably. "Nor mine."

"Avery?" Reuben asked.

"No, not mine, either," she admitted. "But it might. Rupert is planning to do ghost tours of White Haven, apparently. That might add a new dimension of interest."

Reuben was still dismissive. "Loads of places do that. And besides, he's an idiot. Let's focus on tomorrow. What can we do to prepare?"

Alex joined them back at the table. "Corbin said he'll call me later. I can update him on our plan, and question him about the Raven King. I'll call you when I know more. He'll be performing now." He looked across to El. "We need spells to destroy jewellery, or magic in jewellery, or anything like that! And say Caitlin turns into the Empusa while we're attacking her. What then? What are its weaknesses?"

At this point, Shadow grinned. "I bet a blade of pure dragonium will do the trick."

"What the hell is that?" Newton asked.

"A very special metal with very special properties, and I happen to know it is the only metal able to slay a Lamia, so it's likely the same will apply here." She stared at Newton, hard. "I presume you have no problem with me slaying the Empusa?"

He squared his shoulders. "Only as last resort."

She raised an eyebrow. "So you're planning on taking an Empusa into custody?"

Newton thumped the table with a clenched fist. "Bollocks! All right, then. Yes!"

"Thank you," she said silkily.

El leaned forward, her eyes alight with curiosity. "You have a sword of pure dragonium? I've never heard of that. Is that something to do with *dragons*?"

"It most certainly is," she replied enigmatically.

"There are dragons in your world?"

"Of course! What a stupid question." Shadow looked incredulous at everyone around the table, as they had all paused mid-bite or mid-drink to look at her, astonished.

El ignored the jibe. "How do you happen to have such a marvellous sword?"

"I made it my business to have one when I discovered how useful they are. It's back at the farmhouse. It gets a bit tricky carrying it around all the time."

"Awesome," El said, clearly excited. "I need to look at that sometime."

Shadow merely shrugged. "Sure, sister."

Wow, Avery thought, *Shadow just kept getting more and more interesting.* She dragged a box of pizza towards her, deciding she needed another slice if she was to keep going all night. "Newton, you know you can't come tomorrow, right?"

He grimaced. "I had a feeling you were going to say that."

"You know the rules. If it's not official police business, you're out."

"And what about you, missy?" he replied. "You're out, too."

Avery bristled. "We'll see about that."

18

"Do you have a death wish?" Alex asked Avery once the others had left.

"Of course not! But equally I am not about to be left out of the fight."

"If Caitlin sees you tomorrow night, you could end up back at the crossroads in seconds. The real place. And you wouldn't be able to fly back, because you're too weak, and you would be alone. And then dead."

The more Alex talked, the crosser he became, and he glared at her.

She glared right back. "But that's where I need to be. She doesn't know that I know we have to break the crossroads link and sever her power."

"But that supposes that our idea is right. We don't know that for sure, not really. And when you're there, you're automatically weaker. And you won't be with Caspian if you get into trouble."

Avery sighed. "What worries me is that Caspian says he can take us, but what if he's wrong? He's weaker because of his connection to me. And you know how witch-flight works. You need to know a place well—he doesn't, despite everything he's saying. If you can't get close to her to take away the ring, then we *have* to get to that place! *I* have to!"

Alex fell silent, watching her speculatively. "You're saying, the very thing she wants to do will be the very thing that ends this. That it will work against her."

"Yes."

He closed his eyes briefly, and then looked into hers. "Bollocks. It's logical, but risky. Hugely risky!"

"Will you help me to keep awake, and find a spell to locate the ring in that crossroads? And while we're at it, a spell to destroy it or deactivate it?"

"Of course I will." He walked across to her, and pulled her close, nuzzling his lips to her neck. "I'll do anything to keep you alive. I'd go with you too, but I'm pretty sure that's not possible."

"I know you would," she mumbled into his chest. "Thank you."

After one final squeeze, he released her. "Right. An energising tea coming up, and then a spell to keep us both awake."

"No! Just me. You should sleep while you can."

"Nope. We're in this together."

He headed to the kitchen and she went upstairs to her attic. The first thing she did was select incense that would keep them alert. She already had some special mixes prepared, including a few she'd bought from Briar. She found the one she wanted and started it burning in the corner. She said a spell to accompany it, and within a few minutes started to feel their benefit.

She threw a log on the fire, and with a word lit the candles placed around her room. Avery then took a few deep breaths to ground herself, releasing them slowly. *Right.* She was ready for this. *Wait for it, Caitlin. You don't know who you're messing with.*

She pulled her old grimoire towards her and found the spell Helena had shown her that detailed the crossroads link using a talisman. She was still studying it when Alex appeared with their drinks.

"Extra strong," he said, placing it on the table.

She took a sip and sighed with pleasure. "Delicious. Thanks. Right, look at this spell. What we need to work out is how to break the connection. I assume it will be simply a case of finding said talisman and digging it up. Agreed?"

"Agreed. But you'll be too weak to fly back with it, and as long as you're still there, the talisman will still work, so you will need to destroy it." He stared at her. "I still don't like this. What if the standing stone's power saps your will when you arrive? You'll never have a chance to even find the ring."

"One problem at a time. How do I destroy it?"

He thought for a second, and then grinned. "I know what we can use."

She narrowed her eyes at him. "You sound excited. Go on."

"El made a knife that could cut through any metal, remember? It was part of those objects we made for Ben and the others."

Avery nearly spilled her tea with shock. "Of course! I'll ring her."

She grabbed her phone and flicked through to El's number, relieved when El answered quickly, asking Avery, "Are you okay?"

"Fine. Do you remember that knife you made for Ben, the one that cut through any metal? That's what we need to destroy the ring."

El laughed. "Strange you should mention that. Guess what I'm working on right now?"

"You're in your workshop making a knife!"

"Too right. You're not the only one pulling an all-nighter. You'll need a holster for it, but Reuben is on that. It's a long and complicated spell, and I'm annoyed with myself for not making another one straight away, so I'd better get on with it."

She rang off and Avery turned to Alex. "I'm getting a knife!"

"Excellent. Now we have to work out what to do about that standing stone."

"Something to block its pull."

He nodded. "And something to protect you against Hecate's influence." At her obvious confusion, he continued, "Hecate can point you in the right direction, or make you lose your way—Goddess of the Crossroads, remember? If she acts against you, and she might if her plans for her Empusa are thwarted, you need to be able to fight that, too."

Avery nodded. "So I need a spell to see through glamour, to find the true way."

"And wear silver. Lots of it."

Silver had many positive properties. It offered protection from negative energies, stimulated psychic awareness, increased perception, amplified certain gemstones, and was particularly identified with the moon. "Well, that's easy enough. I have a lot of silver jewellery. And I've got the necklace El made for me. Maybe I should pair it with another one, with chalcedony." Chalcedony was a gemstone known for its calming and energising properties, its ability to absorb negative energies, and confer protection from abuse and conflict. Combined with silver, these properties would be multiplied.

"Have you got one?"

Avery pointed to her shelves, which held a small selection of gemstones, not anywhere near as many as El, but she did stock the main ones. "Yep, and I have some silver wire I can bind it in."

"Good. You should wear it now. And," Alex added, "I've decided I'm going to do some scrying tonight."

"On who?" she asked, heading over to grab the gemstone.

"Caitlin."

Avery paused, hand on the basket of stones, all cleansed on the day she had bought them. "Is that wise?"

"Why not? No reason to think she would know. I want to double check that what Corbin says is right. If I can watch her for while, and confirm the ring is the talisman, I'll be much happier."

"Okay." Avery searched the basket for the chalcedony, and found the biggest piece she had. It was coloured a waxy greyish-blue, and was about 3 centimetres in diameter, in a rough, misshapen circle. She warmed it in her palm as she returned to the table. "What are you using to scry?"

"I've brought my silver bowl with me. I'll set up in front of the fire, and turn the lamps off there. The darker the better. I'll do it now, if that's okay?"

She smiled. "Of course. I'll start on a spell to keep us awake first."

He headed over to his bag that was on the floor, crouched down, and pulled out the materials he needed. After a few seconds he called over. "You know, I like this. Not under these current circumstances, but in general."

Avery paused, her hand on her grimoire. "What do you mean?"

"Us, working together on spells in your attic. It feels right. When I move in, this could be our new normal."

Avery felt a warm flush of pleasure race through her. "This *will* be our normal. I like it, too. When's it going to happen?"

"As soon as this crap is over."

She beamed at him. "Good. And you can bring your gorgeous sofa. We'll put mine at your place."

Now he smiled at her. "Really? I do love my sofa."

"Really. And you can put up more shelves for your stuff, over there," she said pointing to a patch of wall. "And whatever else you want to bring, we'll find room for. It will be our home, not just mine."

"You're on. Now get on with your spells," he instructed, blowing her a kiss.

She turned away grinning, determined that Caitlin, Hecate, or a demonic, vampire man-eating Empusa would not stop her domestic bliss. She placed both of her grimoires next to each other on the table, and then scribbled a list on a piece of paper of the things she needed to find. She knew all too well how easy it was to lose track when she started hunting through her spells. They sent her down a rabbit hole.

First was the spell to keep them awake, and she found one quickly. It was a simple incantation that needed something personal from both of them. She took a pair of scissors and snipped some of her hair, and then snipped some of Alex's. She placed the locks in a small metal dish with a simple concoction of dried herbs, and then said the incantation as she burnt them. The acrid fumes filled the air, and Avery wrinkled her face in disgust. *Ugh.* The smell alone was enough to keep her awake. But as the ingredients burnt away to a fine powder, she felt a renewed energy flow through her, and combined with everything else they had set up, she thought she'd be awake for days.

"Wow!" Alex called over. "I can really feel that."

"Good. Me, too. I think we'll crash later, but frankly, that's fine."

He turned back to his preparations, and she returned to her books. She realised that her mind was focusing sharper than it had done in days, and ideas fired quickly. She searched for blocking spells, which were stronger than protection spells, more specific. There were spells to deflect ill-will, curses, and hexes. None of them were specific to her needs, but there were some that could be adapted, and she reminded herself that adapting spells was something she was good at. This was a fact she'd almost forgotten in recent days as her magic had been sapped by the stones. She found a spell that talked about cursed objects and decided that would be her best bet. And then the itch in her palm made her open her hand and stare at the mark again.

The fiery mark beneath her skin was more visible in the low lighting. She had fey script on her hand. *How weird was that?* She wondered what type of stone the standing stone was made of, if even knowing that would help. *Probably not.* And there was no way she could find that out now. And how did *fey script even end up there?* There was so much that she still didn't know about magic. It was this that made it so dangerous, and also so attractive. There was always so much to learn. A lifetime of study couldn't encompass it all.

As Avery stared at the mark, it suddenly seemed incredibly important that she know more about it. She glanced over to where Alex sat cross-legged on the rug in front of the fire. His head was bent over the silver scrying bowl, now filled with water. He was unnaturally still, which meant he was already in his trance.

Grabbing her phone, Avery headed downstairs to the living room to call Shadow. It rang for a while before she finally picked up, and when she answered, Shadow was breathless.

"Avery. Are you all right?"

These were the first words anyone ever said to her now, and it wasn't casual. It was always in a worried, panicked, *has something happened* voice.

"I'm fine," she said, mustering her patience, and reminding herself to be grateful for her friend's concern. "Are you? You sound out of breath."

"I've been fighting with Gabe."

Now Avery was alarmed. "*What*? Why?"

"Sparring with swords. He's insisting on using proper ones, which I told him was hazardous for his health, but he won't listen to me. I've almost taken his life, twice. "

Avery heard Gabe shout in the background. "Once, you liar!"

"And why are you sparring?" Avery asked, as she headed to the kitchen to brew more tea.

"Just making sure I've not grown rusty in the last few weeks." She sounded smug. "I haven't."

"So you're sure you'll need to use it?"

"I hope I will. Anything you need, Avery, or was this just a late night chat? I need to get back to teaching Gabe how to fight."

"I wanted to know what the script on my hand says, exactly."

"I've told you. It means you're sacrificed."

Avery bit back her impatience. "But is that what it *says*? Words mean everything in magic, and they have multiple meanings."

Shadow huffed. "Send me a picture so I can check."

Avery took a photo with her phone and pressed *send*, and there was a pause for a moment.

"It's a word. It looks short, but the translation is 'soul-yoked,' which generally in fey understanding means you're connected until death. That's why I said you were sacrificed. And remember that the stone called to elemental Air as a sacrifice to Hecate. It's not a good word, Avery."

"Okay, thanks Shadow. Good luck with Gabe."

She laughed. "It's not me who'll need the luck."

Avery hung up and walked upstairs with a fresh pot of tea, pondering the meaning of *soul-yoked*. While it might feel ominous to Shadow, she wasn't convinced. She was connected to a standing stone that was dedicated to elemental Air, and that stood on a crossroads dedicated to Hecate. Hecate was a powerful Goddess, and like all Gods served their own purposes before anything. But she was a Goddess known for her love of witches. And Avery was a witch. A powerful witch. If anything, Hecate should do *her* bidding, not Caitlin's.

Alex was still bent over the water in front of the fire, so she took a sip of tea, pulled Helena's grimoire closer, and cast a spell to search for spells that invoked Hecate. The pages ruffled and then started to turn of their own accord, falling still at certain points, which allowed Avery to mark them with paper. When the spell had finished, there were at least a dozen spells to investigate, and like many in Helena's book, they were very old and written with tiny script in arcane language. Fortunately, months of studying them had allowed her to become familiar with the language used, so she could quickly work out which ones were worth investing more time in. After a while, she whispered, "Bingo." *There it is. A spell to invoke the Crossroads Goddess.*

She quickly started to make notes, translating it into modern English, and checking her ingredients on the shelf. At this stage she wasn't sure she wanted to summon Hecate, but she needed options, and this was one of them.

The silence of the room was broken by a log cracking and hissing in the grate, and she walked over and topped it up with another, checking on Alex while she was there. She crouched down and saw that his eyes were transfixed on the water. The round, shallow bowl was about 12 centimetres in diameter, and a ripple continuously passed across the water's surface, which in this light looked black. Avery couldn't see a thing in it. Satisfied that Alex seemed fine, his breathing deep and even, she returned to her list and realised she still hadn't found a blocking spell, but would she need one now? Could she subvert the stone's power and use it for herself?

Ultimately, Avery needed a finding spell, something that would help her locate the talisman buried at the crossroads. She glanced at her watch. It was nearly midnight. She'd better get on with it.

***

Avery was just starting to get worried about Alex when he finally stirred from his trance.

He stretched and rolled his shoulders, blinking to clear his vision, before finally turning to face her. "How long was I gone?"

"Nearly three hours."

"Wow. No wonder I feel stiff."

Avery poured him a glass of water and took it to him. "Did you have any luck?"

"I certainly did." He winced. "Unfortunately, it's more complicated than it looks."

All of Avery's enthusiasm started to fall. "Why?"

"There's more tethered to that crossroads than we thought. But it's okay," he reassured her. "Forewarned is forearmed."

She sat next to him on the rug, holding her hands in front of the fire. "I need to be convinced. Go on."

"I started to watch the whole circus, at first. It took me a while to zero in on Caitlin. It was pretty interesting, eavesdropping on their conversations. There seems to be some dissension in the ranks." He looked at her, one eyebrow raised like Spock.

"Not such happy campers, then? Who causes the problems?"

"Rafe and Mairi. It seems they are getting a little bit too bossy and have been for a while, and they're undermining Corbin. I get the impression most people really like him, especially as he's making the circus so successful, so when they undermine him, it doesn't go down too well."

"They don't think Rafe and Mairi help with the success?"

"They know they do, but because their attitude sucks, they overlook it. And of the few I overheard, no one likes Caitlin. They think she's odd and wish she'd leave."

"Do they notice that she's looking younger?"

He shook his head. "Not that I could tell. Maybe they don't see enough of her."

"If we manage to stop Caitlin—no wait," she corrected herself. "When we stop Caitlin, what will Rafe and Mairi do?"

"That's a good question. Fight? Argue? Run? Who knows! But I do know how she's harnessed the Green Man and the Raven King. She has totems of both of them. A bundle of leaves and wood all bound together, which must represent the Green Man, and a bundle of feathers, claws, and skull of a raven."

"Do you think the same totems are buried at the crossroads?"

"I'm not sure. She never spoke about them. I just saw them in her gypsy caravan. She's got them on a small shelf, laid out a little bit like an altar. And I saw a bit more of the Empusa that lurks within her. She is one scary-looking creature."

Avery was shocked. "How did you see it?"

"In the mirror. Caitlin seemed to call it somehow. As she looked at herself, her features changed. I can understand why it's called a demonic vampire. Its face is barely human; high cheekbones, dark eyes that were all pupils, and big, sharp teeth. I could just see it beneath Caitlin's skin, and for a second, it became clear." He shuddered. "Its shape-shifting ability must be good, because no one would be seduced by that. I can't believe there is something in existence that is both demon and vampire. Just our bloody luck."

Avery frowned. "There are layers to this. It may take more than just finding the other half of the ring to break her link. Do you think Rafe and Mairi are bound to it, too?"

"Not that I could tell."

Avery stared into the flames, pondering the complexity of the situation. "You'd think Mairi would be appalled at her wanting to become an Empusa. I don't get that at all. What does she get out of it?"

"I don't know and I don't care," Alex said. "As long as we stop Caitlin, it doesn't matter."

Avery wasn't convinced. She hated unknowns, and wanted to reduce the variables as much as possible. "Did you see Corbin? Was he safe?"

"I did, and he was. It seems the animosity between Corbin and the other three is simmering, and Corbin is keeping his distance anyway. So far they don't seem to know about our meeting." Alex broke off, looking at his watch. "He never phoned me. I guess it's too late now. Maybe he'll call tomorrow."

"He might think it's safer then, especially if the others sleep in late."

Alex changed the subject. "How have you got on?"

"Good. I have a selection of spells to use, including a finding spell, especially for something underground. It might not be as good as something Estelle would have done, but it should work. And I think I have something that might bring Hecate to my side."

"That sounds dangerous."

"This whole thing is dangerous."

He rose to his feet, pulling her with him. "Come and show me, and then seeing as I'm feeling very alert and energetic, I've thought of other ways to pass the night."

"Alex Bonneville!" Avery exclaimed, pretending to be shocked. "What are you suggesting?"

"Sex. And lot's of it. So let's get this other stuff out of the way quickly."

***

Alex came down to the shop with Avery the next morning, both of them bounding downstairs, full of energy.

Dan was unpacking some new stock on the shop floor, and he eyed them suspiciously. "What's going on? You look surprisingly alert. And you, Avery, are never alert at this hour."

"We've got some pretty hard core spells going on to keep us awake," Avery explained. "As well as energising teas, and incense. I feel wired!"

"And we had hours of sex," Alex told him.

Avery slapped his arm. "Alex!"

"We have sex, Avery. Everyone knows it."

Dan groaned. "Yes, I know it, but I don't need to be reminded of what I'm not having." He rose to his feet, picking the empty box up with him, and headed to the front door. "I'll open up. Why have you pulled a Barry Whiter?"

"A what?" Alex asked.

"An all-nighter."

"Ah, of course. Avery can't sleep or she'll end up back at the crossroads, which strangely is where she now wants to be. So, obviously, I kept her company."

"Like the gentleman you are," Dan acknowledged. "Plotting Caitlin's downfall, I hope."

"Of course, along with other things."

"Enough, thank you!" Avery said, glaring at him.

Alex blew her a kiss and continued. "Anyway Dan, you and Sally have to keep an eye on her today, and make sure she renews that spell to keep her awake. Tonight's the night."

Immediately, Dan stopped joking. "Are you ready? Really ready? I don't want my favourite boss to die."

"We're ready," she reassured him. "Or as ready as we possibly can be."

"So when is it all happening?"

"After tonight's performance, we hope," Alex told him. "I'm waiting to hear from Corbin."

"Anything I can do?" Dan asked.

"Just your usual," Avery said. "And if you think of any useful bit of lore or myth that might help, just say so. And keep the coffee coming."

He saluted her. "Yes, boss."

This was going to be a long day.

***

While Dan and Sally were at lunch later that day, Avery relaxed on the stool behind the counter, reading one of the books Dan had brought in on myths and folklore. Her solitude was disturbed when the bell rang over the door and a man walked in.

But not just any man. It was the American, and Avery felt a tight tangle of worry start in the pit of her stomach.

He stood just inside the entrance and looked around the shop, and for a second he didn't see her, allowing her the time to study him properly. He was tall, lean, and somewhere in his forties, Avery guessed. His hair was dark and shot through with grey, and it was swept back at the temples, revealing a clean-shaven square jaw, and he wore scuffed jeans and a motorbike jacket.

As if he felt her gaze on him, he turned and saw her behind the counter. For a moment he paused, and she had the feeling he was assessing her too, and then he walked over.

"I think it's time we had a chat," he announced.

There was something dangerous about this man. Avery couldn't detect magic, but she was pretty sure he was familiar with it.

"You're probably right. You can start by telling me why you've been watching my shop."

"Because I think you're searching for the same thing that I am."

An Empusa? She doubted that.

"I'm sorry," she said, "you're going to have to enlighten me."

His lips tightened into a thin line. "Playing it like this, are we?"

Avery stood up, shoving the book beneath the counter. She kept her voice low, because she knew there were customers browsing the shelves, but this man was infuriating. "Don't you dare come into my shop and accuse me of playing games, you arrogant prick. What do you want?"

"I want the Ring of Callanish."

"I don't even know what that is!" Even as she said it, she had a horrible feeling she knew exactly what it was.

His eyes were as hard as his voice, and leaned over the counter so that they were almost nose-to-nose. "I think you do, and I think it holds your fate. Want to talk now?"

"You're talking gibberish. Who are you?"

"You know that I'm not talking gibberish, Avery. Can't we be civil?"

Avery was itching to hex him. Her magic was weakened, but she could still do that. However, this was not the time, and she was intrigued. "Civility starts with greetings and introductions. We seem to have skipped that part."

He drew back, but Avery didn't move. "I'm a collector, and I work with other collectors, and we want the ring that's at that circus."

"Name?"

"Harlan Beckett."

"And you know my name how?"

"I asked around. You're very well known. Now, the circus. I know you're investigating there. We can't get to it, but I think you can."

"I beg your pardon? You're still talking in riddles, and I need more than that."

"I am a collector, admittedly of unusual things, and sometimes it's a dangerous job. The woman up there who wields the Ring of Callanish is more dangerous than most. She's summoning things that soon she won't be able to control. But you know that. Do you want to talk now?"

Avery studied him. He seemed serious, and there was an urgency to his tone, a desperation he was trying to hide. Maybe they could help each other. It was worth talking to him, at least.

"Why are you coming to me?" she asked him, softening her voice.

He glanced around at her shop, and then looked out of the window before looking at her again. "White Haven has gained quite a reputation lately, more than it's ever had before. The events at Old Haven Church, The Walk of the Spirits, the latest deaths at West Haven and the caves… We make it our business to follow up on things like that. They led us to you, and some of your friends. I may even be able to help you."

Avery saw a customer heading her way with a couple of books to buy, and she made a decision. She needed to talk to him, it would be stupid not to, but she didn't want him in the back of her shop.

"There's a cafe down the street, Sea Spray Cafe. I'll meet you there in 15 minutes."

19

When Avery arrived at the cafe, she saw Harlan seated at a table next to the window, and once she'd ordered her coffee, she sat across from him. He'd taken his jacket off, revealing a long-sleeved cotton t-shirt, the sleeves of which he'd pushed up his forearms. They showed a tattooed script that ran up the inside of each arm, but Avery didn't recognise the language. His arms were corded with muscle, and beneath his shirt Avery could see the swell of muscle across his chest and shoulders. This man knew how to fight; she could see it behind his eyes. But at the moment, their predominant emotion was relief.

"I wasn't sure you'd come," he told her.

"I wasn't sure either, but in the end, you had me sufficiently intrigued. So Harlan, tell me more."

"Caitlin Murray has harnessed the power of the Ring of Callanish. She's using its power to summon crossroads magic, and she's left a trail of deaths across the country."

She nodded. "We know that. I didn't, however, know the ring had a name."

His eyes narrowed. "It's the ring I'm interested in the most. We will pay you a good price for it if you'll help us get it."

"Who's *us*?"

"My colleagues. There are a few of us, and we all search for items that have a rich mythical and magical provenance, and sometimes we sell them on."

"Sometimes?" Avery allowed herself a small smile. "I know a black market organisation when I hear one."

"There's nothing black market about it. It's not illegal," and then he paused as he met her eyes, and added, "most of the time. But, I will admit, it's not a regular market."

Avery waited while the waitress placed her coffee in front of her, and then asked, "What's so special about this ring?"

"It conducts magic particularly well. It's been around for centuries, rumoured to have been forged by a sorcerer to enhance his spells. The years have added potency to its myth and power. It's particularly interesting because it breaks into two parts, and she has chosen to use it most effectively. It had been thought to be lost, and then all of sudden—" He spread his hands wide. "It reappears in the hands of Caitlin and the Crossroads Circus."

"Isn't Callanish a famous ring of stones in Scotland?"

"It is."

"Is that what it's named after?"

His eyes were amused as he looked at her. "We think so."

Avery sipped her coffee and asked, "How do you *know* she has that particular ring? She keeps to herself, and barely leaves the grounds."

"A buyer alerted us to the unusual events that have followed the circus. He suggested the ring was the source—it seems he's been looking for it for a long time. I was assigned to find out if that was true, and if so, who uses it." He sighed. "I've studied that circus for weeks. You're right. She keeps to herself, only venturing out at their arrival in each new place, as if she's searching for something. I spotted the ring upon her finger, but have been unable to get any closer. And I admit, I was curious. What is she using such a powerful ring for? And then I found out that White Haven was on their event list, quite a recent change to their schedule. I imagined the circus wanted to take advantage of this place's reputation, too. I followed them here, and watched her do her usual visit to the town on her arrival, but this time her visit was short." He fixed his pale grey eyes on her and drummed his fingers on the table. "She found you, and I wondered what was so special about you."

"Nothing at all," Avery said smoothly.

He shook his head. "I thought we were being honest? You are a witch. I know how to recognise those who wield magic. It's my job to know it. And you're not the only one here, either. I've brought some products from Charming Balms, and jewellery from The Silver Bough. I've studied them carefully. I've been in your shop when you weren't there, and I've had a drink in The Wayward Son. I know magic when I see it. But, it's *you* who she wants."

That was unnerving. She considered denying everything, but it wouldn't achieve much. "You're right. She wants me because I control elemental Air. It seems she needs me, my power."

"To do what?"

"To complete her ritual."

He looked as if he was going to ask more, but instead he said, "So you believe me?"

Avery sat back in her chair and looked out of the window as she considered what he'd said. The ring would explain the potency of the crossroads magic, and when that mixed with the remnants of their magic that still drifted across the town from the events of the previous summer, it would create even more power.

She looked at Harlan to find him watching her. "I believe you. It makes sense. However, we've come up with a plan to stop her, and you won't like it."

"Why?"

"We're going to destroy it."

"Impossible," he said softly. "It's not just any ring, remember?"

"I'm not just anyone, either. I have a weapon that will destroy any metal."

Harlan's eyebrows shot up. "How did you get that? Oh wait, your friend from The Silver Bough?"

"You have been busy."

"I'm thorough. It's my job." He crossed his arms in front of his chest and leaned back too. "But it won't work. The ring is too strong. Sorcerer-made, remember?"

Avery's confidence faltered. "Is that a fact, or a theory?"

"A theory, but a good one. The legends suggest that the sorcerer used crossroads magic himself, that the ring was specifically designed for it, so it is particularly suited to this situation."

"If you think we can't destroy it, how were you planning on stopping her?"

"Well, that's where it gets tricky."

Avery let out a barely there laugh. "You don't know, do you?"

Harlan straightened his shoulders and an edge entered his voice. "Actually, yes I do. If the two halves of the ring are joined back together, it should break the bond with the crossroads, stripping her of her power. However, the particular details of this ring are lost in time, so this is also a theory."

"Didn't you say you did this for a living?"

"Yes. And I'm very good at it. However, Caitlin has thought this through well and is particularly well protected."

"I agree with you there. However, I'm not sure I agree with your ring theory. First you'd have to get it off her finger, second, putting them together could just make one gigantic spell." She frowned at him. "Does this mean you know where the other half of the ring is and can get it?"

He had the grace to look sheepish. "Actually, no. It's in Scotland. I think we both know that. It's where she's from, but we cannot find the crossroads. I have colleagues up there now searching for it, but they've had no luck."

"Are they looking outside Inverness?"

"Yes, along the shores of Loch Ness, and according to the locals there is one there, somewhere, but it's proving impossible to find."

"She must have managed to hide the crossroads, using the magic it generates. Using Hecate."

"Boundary magic," he said.

"I've been there," she confessed, "but it's sort of stuck in a stasis, or at least that's what it felt like."

Harlan leaned across the table. "How have you been there?"

"She took me there, and it wasn't by choice. I escaped by the skin of my teeth."

"How?"

Avery sighed as she weighed her options. She had only just met this man, and here she was sharing things that most people would have her locked up for. But it was clear that he was no ordinary man.

She lowered her voice and answered him with a question. "It doesn't bother you that I'm a witch?"

"I know magic, and I know other witches. No, it doesn't bother me. It's what I do. Not many places, however, have as much magic around the town as here."

"Probably not," she admitted. "We had a *thing* last year."

"A *thing*? Care to elaborate?"

"Not really."

Harlan laughed, and it made him look far less menacing. "Fair enough. But the Green Man is strong here. Your spring has arrived early. And the

Raven King is here, too. I can feel him. You have a lot of ravens in town at the moment. That hasn't happened anywhere else I've been."

"I think that's probably to do with the *thing* that happened. It should work to our advantage."

"I presume you won't elaborate."

"I'd rather not."

"You haven't told me how you escaped from the crossroads."

"I flew out of there, on my broomstick."

He laughed loudly. "You have a sense of humour! I like it. But, I think you mean witch-flight."

"You are surprisingly well-informed."

"My job, remember?"

"You seem to know a lot about me. What about you? What's an American doing in England? Not enough myths there?"

"There are plenty there, but it's a long story. I tend to move around." He eased back in his chair. "Where does this leave us, Avery? We both want to stop Caitlin, but we have different ideas of how to do it. And at this moment, you have far more ability to succeed than me. But, I would like that ring."

And that was the rub, Avery thought. She wanted to destroy it, they all did; no good could come of it. *But what if they couldn't? What if he was right?* And even if he was, they'd be better at keeping it safe than giving it to him.

"Say you're right, and we can't destroy the ring. What will you do with it?"

"I have a buyer."

"I'm not sure I like that option. What if your buyer decides to do something equally dangerous with it?"

"I doubt he will. He's a collector. It will probably be displayed in a deep, dark personal vault somewhere. And I'll pay, remember?"

"I don't need your money, Harlan."

Anger flashed behind his eyes. "So, what now?"

Avery's mind raced. She needed to speak to the others. They were going to stop this tonight, and they had a plan…of sorts. If she couldn't destroy the ring, they had to try his suggestion. It might even work. But whatever happened, they certainly didn't want him with them. He had his own interests at heart and would only jeopardise theirs.

"Harlan, it's been good to meet you, but I'm not sure we can help you. I don't think any of us will want that ring going somewhere else, and I will try to destroy it before I try anything else."

He stared at her for a moment and sighed, before sliding a business card across the table. "I appreciate your honesty, and I certainly don't want to antagonise you. But I'll be honest, too. I want that ring, and I will try to get it, so if you won't help me, I'll try another way. You have my number if you change your mind."

And with that he stood, grabbed his jacket, and left.

20

"What's happened now?" Dan asked when she arrived back in the shop.

"Is it that obvious?"

"That you look annoyed and distracted? Yes. And Sally said you had a mysterious assignation with a strange man."

"I said no such thing!" Sally exclaimed as she joined them. "You're such an exaggerator. But seriously, who was he, and where did you go?"

Avery groaned. "There's a new player in town—the American!"

Dan whistled. "The guy who was watching the shop?"

"The very same! He's a collector of arcane things, and guess what he's here for?"

"Something circusy?" Dan asked suspiciously.

"Too right." She told them about her meeting.

Sally frowned. "So he thinks Caitlin has a powerful ring?"

"Yep. He's seen it, and is convinced that it's the one he wants. And he clearly knows a lot more about us than we do about him. But, we have Newton, and I have his card and his name, so I'm off to make a phone call."

Avery headed to the back room, and stuck some bread in the toaster while she made the call. Newton picked up quickly. "Are you all right?"

"I'm fine. I'm juiced up on spells to keep me awake. Look, I had a strange meeting today. Have you got time to chat?"

"Sure. How strange?"

"I met the American man who's been watching my shop and the circus. He's called Harlan Beckett, and he works for The Orphic Guild. They collect arcane artefacts for private buyers. He wants Caitlin's ring, which is apparently famous in the paranormal world, but I hadn't heard of it. I wondered if you could find out anything about him?"

"Excellent, no problem. At least we have a name. Did he threaten you?"

Avery thought for a moment as the toaster popped and she buttered her toast. "No, not really. But he made it clear he wanted the ring, and I made it clear he shouldn't have it, so we have opposing agendas."

"Tell me what he looks like."

Avery gave him the best description she could. "We're meeting tonight in the pub, before we go to the circus if you want to join us."

"I've been thinking I should come to the circus with you," he said. She could hear voices in the background, and they went quiet as he seemed to move rooms.

"Are you sure that's a good idea, Newton?"

"No. But I'm coming anyway. Tell Reuben to bring his shotgun and salt shells. See you later."

Despite all their planning, Avery felt increasingly nervous and underprepared. She carried the plate of toast to the table and sat down, brushing aside boxes of books and incense. There were too many variables—Corbin, boundary magic, Hecate, the Green Man, and the Raven King, trying to isolate Caitlin while keeping the circus safe, and Shadow. She hated to have doubts about her, but they barely knew her. She said she wanted to help, but Avery knew she had her own agenda, too. She wanted to use the boundary magic to get home, even though they had told her it wasn't like the portal that had brought her here. She was headstrong and stubborn. And now there was Harlan who knew far too much about them, and Avery had the sinking suspicion that Shadow's agenda was more closely aligned to his than their own. Hadn't she talked only recently about treasure hunting, and how she used to do that in her own world?

The toast tasted like cardboard, but she forced it down anyway into her churning stomach. What was the matter with her? They could deal with this. They had before. Except, she reminded herself, her own life hadn't been at risk before. Not like this. Not soul-yoked to a mystical standing stone that wanted her essence, her power.

She pressed her palms to her eyes and closed her eyes tightly, and immediately the crossroads was there, eerie under a full moon, the mist writhing across the ground. Shit! Her eyes flew open, and she was relieved to find she was still at the shop. *Time to renew her spell and keep herself awake.*

Before she could move, her phone rang, vibrating across the table, and she saw Shadow's name light up the screen. Now what?

"Hey Shadow, everything okay?"

"I'm going to head to the circus on my horse, so I'll meet you there," she announced. "Remind me, what time are you going?"

"We'll arrive just before the show ends. The stalls will be open for another hour or so, so we'll blend in with the crowds post-performance."

They had theorised that with the hustle of people leaving, the stalls still full, and the circus performers busy celebrating in the Big Top, that it was the best time to isolate Caitlin.

"Good. I'll text you, but maybe we should meet in the far corner of the castle, under the walls. It will be well away from the main place."

"Where we put the camera? Sure," Avery agreed. "How will you disguise your sword?"

"Fey glamour. It will be sufficient for a few hours."

A horrible suspicion entered Avery's mind. "Any reason you don't want to meet us at the pub?"

"None. I just thought it was a good way to do extra reconnaissance on the way. In the fields behind the circus is where I feel the Green Man the most."

"Okay, we'll see you there. But don't do anything crazy!"

Shadow laughed impatiently. "Course not. Laters."

Avery hung up and looked at the phone for a long moment, perplexed as to how quickly Shadow had picked up English slang and idioms. Maybe it was a fey thing, and her strange magic. Shadow was smart and quick-witted. Not much escaped her. But more importantly, Avery's paranoia was back. Was she imagining things, or did Shadow sound cagey? If Harlan knew about the witches, he must know about Shadow and Gabe. It sounded like he'd been watching them long enough. *Had he just made Shadow a better offer?* Avery rose to her feet. Well, whatever happened, it was ending tonight, one way or another. Time to renew the energy spell.

***

When Avery joined Dan and Sally back in the shop, she felt freakishly alert again, like she'd had too much caffeine. The spell was effective, but the side effects were unpleasant. Both of them looked at her, worry written all over their faces.

Sally's hands rested on her hips and Avery realised she was about to be lectured. "I think you should delay this again. It's too dangerous."

"It's too dangerous not to!" Avery said softly. She pointed towards the windows and the street beyond. "You've seen what's happening. White Haven is unseasonably warm, and that's because the Green Man is here. Now, don't get me wrong, I love the Green Man, he's a nature spirit and he's doing his thing. But it's not right! It shouldn't be spring now. And there are ravens everywhere, not just at the castle." As if to prove her point, two appeared on the eaves of the shop opposite, cocking their heads to look at her. "They prove the Raven King is here. I can feel the flap of his wings over the town and the castle. They're feeding off our magic, too!"

Dan watched the ravens and then looked at her. "I presumed that was the case. The crossroads magic is mixing with yours."

"Sort of. It's the only explanation. Harlan said this hasn't happened anywhere else—well, not to this extent. And the longer this continues, the stronger it will get." Avery's voice rose with exasperation. "And I can't sleep, or I'll end up at that bloody crossroads. We can't wait."

Sally's shoulders sagged as the reality of the situation hit her, but Dan said, "I looked up that ring, admittedly in the few resources I have on hand, but I found nothing. However, I'm sure you've heard of Callanish and know where it is?"

"I know that it's a ring of stones in Scotland," Avery admitted.

"Callanish is a village in the far north of Scotland, on the Isle of Lewis. It's famous for the standing stones there, which predate Stonehenge by about five hundred years." He showed them the images he'd found on his phone.

"Another group of stones?" Sally exclaimed.

"They're arranged in a circle and a cross, and as usual there are legends associated with them. Nothing about a sorcerer, though. Not that I could find, anyway."

Avery groaned. "Damn it. They're too far north to be where I was, and they look different, but that is interesting. Perhaps the ring was made for that site and Caitlin has made it work for her. After all, a cross within a circle is a sort of crossroads. Thanks Dan, that's good to know. Anyway, I'm going to go and do some restocking, just to keep me busy," and she turned and headed to the back room to collect some stock.

In the end, the afternoon passed all too quickly. As she finished locking up the shop and said goodnight to Dan and Sally, Sally enveloped her in a big hug. "Please don't do anything stupid tonight!"

"Of course not! Have a little faith."

"I have lots of faith," Sally said softly, as she released her from her iron grip. "But I know how you push yourself. Just be careful." Her face was etched in worry.

"I promise I'll be very careful, and you'll see me tomorrow, safe and sound."

Uncharacteristically, Dan hugged her, too. "Yes, please be careful. I'll buy coffee and cakes tomorrow if you make it." He flashed a grin. "Kidding. You will make it. You'd better, I can't put up with Sally alone. Although, there will be more of Sally's delicious cake for me…"

"Dan!" Sally slapped his arm. "You'll be lucky if you get any more of anything from me." She had another long look at Avery. "Okay, I have to go or I'll cry. I'll see you tomorrow."

"Yes, you will," Avery said, resolutely. "And thanks for your help, both of you. You've helped us a lot with your awesome suggestions." She waved them off, locked the door, and headed up to her flat, hoping that wasn't a horrible lie and that she wouldn't die that night. She fed the cats, giving them an extra big fuss, and then headed to the attic to collect all of her prepared gear. While she'd been restocking shelves, she'd used the time to memorise spells, and had written down a few on a piece of paper, just in case her memory failed her.

She dressed all in black—jeans, t-shirt, hoody, and a black leather jacket, and her knee-length, flat-heeled leather boots. She had a small black shoulder pack that she threw a selection of herbs in and another tonic from Briar, and then put some more silver jewellery on. She'd been wearing El's necklace and her own with the chalcedony stone all day. The stones felt warm against her skin, and she'd sensed their protection all day. After taking one last look around the room to ensure she had everything she needed, she headed to The Wayward Son where they were meeting for food and a final debrief, at Reuben's suggestion. He argued that you couldn't work on an empty stomach. *No surprise there*, Avery thought as she headed out the door. The day Reuben stopped being hungry was a day to really worry.

***

"You met him on your own!" Alex said, appalled. His drink was halfway to his lips, but he slammed it down hard and his beer sloshed over the rim and onto the table. "Bollocks!" Briar threw a handful of paper napkins at him, and grabbing some herself, helped to mop up, while Alex continued to complain. "Why didn't you call me?"

Avery had just updated them on her meeting with Harlan. "I tried and couldn't get through. Besides, it's okay, I'm fine," she tried to reassure him but clearly failed. "I met him in the Sea Spray Cafe, surrounded by pensioners and families."

"Why did he come to you and not one of us?"

"Because he knows that it's me Caitlin wants."

The anxiety levels had already been high when they had all met, and now they were even higher. Caspian had joined their coven, and they were waiting on Newton and their food; as usual, they were sitting in the small room overlooking the courtyard at the back of the pub.

"Bloody hell, Ave," Reuben said. "We were only talking about black market stuff a couple of months ago. Do you think he's after things from us? You know, like the magical items we gave Ben?"

She shook her head. "I doubt it. He's after proper collectors' stuff, old arcane objects with history and provenance. But, I could be wrong. What is really worrying me is why Shadow isn't here. It's suspicious timing. I think she's Harlan's back-up."

All the witches exchanged nervous glances, and Caspian cleared his throat. "You're probably right, which means we have to make a plan to contain both of them, too."

El grimaced. "I'm not so sure. I doubt she'd double-cross us that quickly."

Reuben pointed a finger at her. "You were the one who said she had the bit between her teeth on this treasure hunting business. You can't change your mind now."

"I'm not changing my mind," she explained, "I just don't think she'd betray us—certainly not harm us deliberately."

"But if we stood in her way?" Briar asked. "And we don't know Harlan at all. Who knows what he's capable of?"

Before anyone could continue, Newton arrived and sat in the remaining empty chair. "I take it you've updated them," he said to Avery.

"Yup. That's why everyone looks pissed off."

"Give us some hope," Reuben said. "What did you find on him?"

"Very little. He has no criminal record, and no social media profiles. All I know for sure is that he arrived in the UK ten years ago and lives in London.

He pays his bills and his taxes, and owns a motorbike, a Moto Guzzi V7, and a Mercedes SCL300."

"Those are seriously nice toys!" Reuben exclaimed. "He must make good money."

"And the company he works for?" Alex asked. He'd mopped up his spilt beer and had balled the napkins up in a pile.

"It's legit, but very hush-hush. Have you checked the website?"

"I did," Avery admitted. "It says very little. Just a page with the barest of information and an email address. It's all in black and grey with some fancy font."

"What's the name of the company again?" Caspian asked, pulling his phone out, ready to start searching.

Avery checked the business card. "It's called The Orphic Guild. Very mystical."

While Caspian searched, Alex persisted. "It must have an address?"

"Not on the site," Newton told him. "Just an email. I found the address through company records. Again, it's in London. A private residence."

"Is that unusual?" El asked.

Newton shrugged. "It depends on the business, so no, not particularly." He looked around at their disappointed faces. "Sorry. That's all I can give you. Whatever they do, they keep their noses clean."

Before anyone could comment, one of the bar staff came over, bringing their food, and they fell silent for a moment.

As soon as they were alone again, El said, "The dagger's ready, and I think you should carry it, Avery, even though we're hoping you won't need to go to the crossroads. It just means you will have to be close to Caitlin to destroy the ring."

"*If* we can destroy the ring," Avery said, reminding them of Harlan's information.

Newton looked unimpressed. "We still have to try."

Reuben grinned. "Can I start calling you Frodo after this?"

"No. Piss off," Avery said, and threw a chip at him.

He caught it deftly and ate it with a smirk.

"I still think you should keep well away from Caitlin," Alex said.

Avery grimaced. "I'll try, but I'm going, regardless. I have to, I just know it."

El pulled the knife from her bag and slid it across the table. "Here's my labour of love for the last twenty-four hours." It was a steel blade with runes etched down it, and it had a small hilt with a simple design, but as soon as Avery took it from her, she felt its hum of power. El reminded her, "It will pretty much cut through or destroy any metal."

"So we can destroy her ring, either here or at the crossroads."

"Yep, which should break her bond."

"Even though it's the Ring of Callanish?" Reuben asked. "If it's been made by a sorcerer, it may have extra levels of protection."

"It's still metal," El said.

Caspian took the dagger from Avery, examining it with admiration. "Nice job, El. Do you take commissions?"

El's eyes widened with surprise. "Of course. You thinking of anything in particular?"

He ran his finger down the blade. "I have a few ideas. I'll chat to you once all this is over."

"Sure," she said, nodding.

Caspian handed the knife back to Avery. "I feel confident we can get to the crossroads anyway, Avery."

Avery met his gaze. "Unfortunately, I think I'll be there on my own, despite our best intentions."

Alex watched her speculatively and then turned to Caspian. "We think Caitlin will send her there as soon as she can, just like the first time it happened."

"So I'll follow," Caspian reasoned.

Briar grimaced. "And we'll be in a lot of trouble if none of this works, because she'll still have the power of the boundary magic."

"At least I heard from Corbin," Alex said, looking very relieved he'd finally got in touch. "The good news is that he thinks he can call the Raven King even without the circus performance. He sounded nervous, though."

Briar pushed her plate away. "He would be. What if he can't? What if I can't call the Green Man?" Over food, Briar had announced that she thought she had a way to connect to the nature spirit, and use his magic to help them.

"If anyone can, it's you," Avery said. "Earth magic is your thing. You're a green witch, essentially. He should connect with you. And your place, more than anyone else's, has gone mad with spring growth."

As she said it, Avery glanced outside, and noted the climbing plants that clambered up the walls of the courtyard garden were already showing strong green shoots.

Reuben pulled something from his jacket pocket. "This is the holster I found for you. It's a belt that I got from Chi."

"Chihiro from the tattoo place?" Avery asked as she took it from him.

"The very same. She has a thing for knives."

Avery remembered Chi's cool beauty and stunning tattoos. She had an enigmatic edge to her. "That doesn't surprise me. Where does the blade go?"

"In the scabbard at the back. I'll help you fit it when we get there."

Briar picked at her food, deep in thought. "What if Shadow is with Harlan? What can we do?"

Avery placed her fork down. "Harlan needs us, that's a fact. He can't get to Caitlin. And Shadow does not have the magic we have. I think they'll be opportunistic. If he's there, and I think he will be, he'll bide his time and strike when he see his chance."

"The chance Shadow might create for him," Alex said.

Avery shrugged. "Perhaps."

Newton groaned. "I hate all these variables!""

"We'll work with what we've got, we always do," Reuben pointed out. He pushed his plate away and checked his watch. "We should get going. Final thoughts, anyone?"

Alex held his fingers up, counting off one by one. "We have the knife to destroy the ring. Corbin to call the Raven King. Briar to bring the Green Man. We've got spells to draw Caitlin away. Shadow has her sword to slay the Empusa. And Harlan bloody Becket, who could well jeopardise everything. Let's go."

21

As soon as Avery stepped out of her van into the field below the circus, she felt the Green Man's spirit around her.

She turned to the others. "He feels even stronger tonight. Can you feel him?"

Briar nodded. "The Green Man? Absolutely. He's like a gentle tickle on the senses." She crouched and pressed her hands into the earth, closing her eyes briefly. A spark of light lifted from her fingers and hung in the air, almost like glitter, until it drifted away on the night breeze. She stood and smiled softly. "He's curious about us and our magic. Let's hope it means he'll come more easily to me later."

Avery thought she heard a laugh, a deep throaty chuckle, and her head whipped around, searching the darkness. "Did you hear that?"

All of the witches nodded, and Briar reassured her. "It's okay, it's just him."

Briar sounded so relaxed about it, but it felt odd. It was one thing to know that his spirit was strong, it was quite another to hear him.

"Belt time," Reuben said, pulling it from his pocket and dragging Avery back to practicalities. "It's a horizontal sheath that sits on the small of your back."

He passed it to her and Avery strapped the leather belt in place, along the top of her jeans. The sheath felt comfortable, but Reuben stepped forward and adjusted it slightly, and then taking the knife from El, slid it into place. "Reach your hand behind you. Can you feel the hilt?"

Avery felt the cool metal in her fingers. "Easy. This feels good." She pulled the knife out in one smooth movement.

"Just be careful when you slide it back in. It will take practice to do it quickly," he told her. "And watch your fingers."

She grinned at him. "I feel like an assassin."

"That's worrying."

The others had been watching as they gathered their packs, and Alex said, "Please be careful with that. I've seen you chopping vegetables."

"Thanks for the vote of confidence," she told him, but he just laughed.

Reuben rummaged in the back of the van and pulled out the shotgun. "Here you go, Newton, and some shells." He pushed the box into his free hand and Newton quickly loaded both barrels.

The group headed up the hill, cutting directly across the field to where they could see a break in the hedge, and the edge of the car park. The castle was lit up against the night sky, its golden light a beacon in the darkness, and a short distance away was the roof of the Big Top, the huge circus tent that currently looked like a fairy palace. They were halfway there when they heard a rush of wings, and instinctively they all ducked. The wingspan felt huge, and the wind rolled over them before heading back to the circus.

"The Raven King," Caspian murmured. "Do you think Corbin knows we're here?"

"Let's hope so," Alex said, pushing on.

They could hear the crowd in the tent laughing and cheering, but made their way to the series of stalls. There were a lot of people there, their excitement palpable. Avery glanced up and almost faltered. Above them, perched on the castle walls, were hundreds of ravens. *A Conspiracy, that's what they were called collectively, or an Unkindness. Both ominous words*, Avery reflected.

The witches strolled through the scene, taking their time as they kept watch for anything unusual, but the crowds were excited and noisy. Avery looked for Harlan, but she didn't see him. They passed the small, square space where some of the cast were doing ad hoc performances—fire breathers and jugglers, tumblers, acrobats, and the couple on stilts, dressed as giants. The excitement was infectious, and despite the fight ahead, Avery's spirit lifted.

Within ten minutes the applause from the tent exploded, and whoops and cheers mixed with the tinny music from the stalls. *Time to get in position.* They pushed their way through to the far end, and slipped one by one through a gap between stalls and behind generators, until they reached the empty space beyond. If anything, it seemed too dark after leaving the brightness of the circus. Over to the right, the Big Top was still lit up, and beyond that were the fields of the circus folk. Caitlin's van was at the rear of the final one, close to the hedge and a good distance away from the others. *An easy escape to get out and hunt*, Avery mused.

They headed to the far corner of the castle, well away from everything else, and beneath its thick, crumbling walls and sitting on a tumble of stone, they found Shadow.

"I thought you'd changed your mind," Shadow greeted, rising to her feet. Her huge sword was already in her hand, and her daggers were strapped to her thighs. Avery couldn't help but stare at her imposing stature. Shadow was dressed in a sturdy leather jacket and tight fitting trousers, the breast of the jacket layered like armour. Metal arm guards protected her forearms, and her long hair was tied back into a high pony tail; she looked ready to fight. Avery had a sudden flashback to the Wild Hunt and swallowed her fear.

"We agreed not to be too early," Alex said, ignoring her jibe. "If you'd have come with us, you wouldn't have had to wait."

"I wanted to scope the place out again, get a feel for it. Kailen is no ordinary horse, either. He is sensitive to fey magic, just like me."

Avery looked beyond Shadow. "Where is your horse?"

Shadow gestured behind her. "The far side of the field, out of the way, but he'll come if I need him."

There was no moon tonight; it was obscured by cloud cover, and once again a thick mist was rising. It made it impossible for Avery to see anything. If Harlan were out there, they'd never know. She sent her magic out anyway, hoping to feel something, but she couldn't, and she pulled her concentration back to the others.

"Do you feel fey magic?" Caspian asked Shadow.

She looked disappointed. "Not really. A trace, like a whisper on the wind. But I feel the nature spirit, and the Raven King himself. It's incredible to me that they can't!" She jerked her chin up, in the direction of the crowds.

"It's the nature of magic," Briar told her. "You know that. People will rationalise anything that they don't understand. Make excuses for it. And besides, they use lights and sound to enhance the show, so it's easy to explain away."

Caspian agreed. "True, the non-magical are always willing to look away from the truth of things."

"This is a great philosophical discussion, but now's not the time," Reuben said, rolling his shoulders and neck to loosen up. "Me and El will go and scope out the campsite, makes sure it's as quiet as Corbin says, and then we'll cordon it off. Meet us in five."

"I better get prepared, too," Briar said, and she left the group to stand in the field a short distance away.

Avery watched Briar slip her shoes off, wriggle her feet into the grass, and raise her hands to the sky, silently invoking the spirit of the Green Man, but Avery's attention was pulled back to the conversation when she heard Shadow's raised voice.

"What's going on?" Shadow asked, suspicious. "I thought we were luring her out?"

Alex's eyes were bright. "We're going to throw up a magical wall between Caitlin and the rest of the camp, and then we don't have to lure her anywhere."

Shadow started to look worried. "I thought magic wouldn't work on her?"

"The magic separates the camp, it's not attacking her. And besides, we're going to use it on her anyway. With luck and skill, we'll overwhelm her."

"But you said we had more space out here."

"This seemed simpler," Alex argued. "And besides, you get a chance to use your sword quicker."

"Why's that?"

"You keep reminding us you're fey, so here's your chance. Wield your mighty sword and we'll get the ring off her quickly."

Avery pulled the knife from the holster. "And then I'll use this to destroy it."

Shadow's eyes narrowed. "I preferred the first plan."

"Well, you should have been there for the second discussion, then," Alex said.

It was unlike Shadow to look worried, and it immediately raised Avery's suspicions. Harlan must be out there somewhere. She stared into the darkness again, and then stumbled as she felt a shift in the earth beneath her. Looking around at Briar, she saw that below her feet grass was growing, and Briar's feet were sinking into the earth.

Briar continued to raise her arms to the sky, and then stopped, bending swiftly and pulling bare earth into her hands. Avery's mouth fell open as she watched Briar smear the earth across her brow and down her cheeks, and rub her hands with it. And then astonishingly, Briar's eyes filled with a bright, green glow that pulsed softly and then disappeared. Power swelled in the air around her, and Avery stepped back as magic unfurled across the field. The Green Man had arrived.

Briar lowered her hands and looked across at Avery, but it wasn't the Briar that Avery knew. She spoke, her voice rougher, deeper than usual. "I am ready. I shall call the King." She turned to the campsite and raised her arms again.

Avery was aware that the others had grown quiet behind her, waiting expectantly in the deep, rich silence that had suddenly fallen. A thick wall of mist rolled out between them, the campsite and the stalls a short distance away. The thumps of the music and the shrieks of laughter disappeared, and the lights winked out as the mist grew ever thicker.

Reuben's plan was working. It had been his suggestion to use his magic to manipulate the mist, and it was a good one. But despite all their plans, Avery still felt nervous. She reached into her bag and drank one of Briar's tonics, wincing at its bitterness, and then renewed the spell that kept her awake. Despite it, she could feel that she was tired. Very tired. It was like the false high that caffeine gave, and she knew once the spell was gone she'd feel terrible.

Then Avery felt a shift in the air around them again, and the mist stirred in whirlpools. Alex spoke close to her ear. "It feels like a few nights ago, when we walked across the fields."

Avery nodded. "But much stronger."

Briar walked towards the campsite and they followed her into the mist that hung like a curtain. For a few seconds Avery could see nothing, and then it lifted slightly and the Raven King emerged.

Avery's breath caught in her chest. It was Corbin, but it wasn't. Just as Briar had changed, so had he. He was still dressed in his costume of black feathers, and as he lifted his wings, the mist eddied outwards in ripples. But his face carried an Otherness that was inexplicable. His eyes burned with a fierce orange light that pierced the darkness, and his face was transformed into cold, hard planes, his expression grim.

He waited for Briar to reach him, and then turned and led the way to Caitlin.

Caspian spoke from behind Avery. "I'm not sure we're leading this anymore."

"Quickly, we can't lose them," Alex urged as they picked up their pace and ran after them.

As soon as they entered the campsite, the mist receded, forming a thick wall to their right, and Reuben and El walked out of it, the spell complete.

Caitlin's gypsy caravan stood alone, the hedge behind it. Briar flicked her hand out, and the hedge started to grow higher. A writhing, tangled mass of branches reached out to Caitlin's van, thrusting through its walls, and driving Caitlin from its depths, and right behind her were Rafe and Mairi. While Caitlin exuded confidence, Rafe and Mairi looked worried, and almost cowered behind her, although they lifted their heads in defiance as they tried to hide it.

Caitlin stood at the entrance, the yellow lamplight illuminating her from behind and casting her face in shadow, and she laughed. "So, the Raven King and the Green Man seek to break free! You're both fools. And so are all of you!"

"Are we?" Briar asked. "I am already stronger than you could ever be."

In response, Caitlin pulled two objects out of her pockets, and walked down the short flight of steps to the small fire that burned in front of her van, where her expression could be seen clearly, and so could the rings that glinted on her fingers.

Damn it. Which ring was it?

Caitlin laughed, her voice rough. "You can't hurt me! I have the power of the crossroads!"

"Crap!" Alex said. "She's got the totems."

She made as if to drop the totems in the fire, but Reuben was too quick, and he hurled a powerful shot of water at her. Caitlin reacted quickly, deflecting it with a wave of her hand, but Reuben succeeded in dowsing the fire, and she hissed at him, like a snake. And it was then that Avery realised she was starting to change into the Empusa. The air shimmered around her as her shape began to transform, simultaneously closing her hands around the totems and crushing them. Immediately, Briar and the Raven King fell to their knees.

Caitlin grew taller as her face narrowed, and strong, high cheekbones and a long jaw emerged. Her eyes burned with fire, and as her mouth opened, she revealed sharp teeth like a shark. Her clothes fell away, revealing the glint of armour and the strange copper leg the legends talked of. Avery blinked, barely able to believe her eyes.

Shadow didn't hesitate. She raced forward, her sword drawn, covering the ground between them in seconds, and slashed at the Empusa. In retaliation, the Empusa pulled two swords out, their blades flashing with fire, and struck back. Shadow pulled her dagger free too, and a blur of steel whirled between them.

And then several things happened at once.

Alex raced across the ground, running for the totems that she had tossed to the side, while El ran to join Shadow, her sword burning with its blue flame.

Avery couldn't believe she was still there and not at the crossroads, and she turned, ready to help Briar, but Briar's hands were sunk deep into the earth, and the ground shook beneath her as she pulled power from it. She staggered to her feet and changed form too, her body wreathed in foliage as she grew in size. The hedge suddenly exploded into life, and Alex, who was scrabbling at its base for the totems, disappeared in a mass of branches. The clearing was becoming a wood. Saplings were erupting from the earth around them, rapidly maturing into trees, and branches swept through the air, reaching for them with clawing fingers.

Next to Briar, the Raven King dissolved into hundreds of birds as he scattered across the night, and the area around Caitlin's caravan descended into chaos.

Avery tried to move, but couldn't. She felt her magic draining from her, and she wasn't even doing anything. She couldn't fight at all, and she realised with horrible clarity that Caitlin was drawing on her power now.

Mairi and Rafe looked terrified, and ran from Caitlin as if running for cover, but Newton intercepted them, tackling Rafe to the ground. Mairi screamed and tried to intervene, but Reuben ran to help.

Caspian grabbed Avery's arm. "This is impossible. We need to get to the crossroads."

"But Alex—he's trapped!"

"There's no way we're getting to that ring here. Shadow and El between them can't even get close to her. We have to go!"

"But I can't even move. She's anchored me here." Avery was bewildered. "I thought she'd send me to the crossroads."

Caspian's face was pale. "You're magnifying her link. You're probably of more use to her here than there."

Avery swayed on her feet, suddenly dizzy. "Shit. I think you're right. What about you? Are you connected with her because of me?"

"Not yet, but it's only a matter of time. We're going, now!" He stepped behind her, pulling her close. "Work with me. Close your eyes and see the crossroads."

Avery was trembling with weakness, but she did as she was told and closed her eyes tightly.

22

Avery was at the crossroads. And she was alone. She'd left her friends battling the Empusa, Rafe and Mairi, and she had no idea if she'd ever see them again.

Where is Caspian?

The thick mist had vanished and once again the full moon was overhead. The crossroads waited as if with baited breath. Three of the standing stones were lit up, the fiery gold script speaking of the untold magic of the fey and of the witches whose powers the stones had taken. And the fourth standing stone was silent and grey, waiting for her.

Suddenly, a voice yelled at her, as if it was coming from the depths of a well, and once again she felt a sharp sting on her cheek and she cried out in shock. The voice was louder now. "*Avery! Come back to me*!"

She wrenched her eyes open to see Caspian's panic-stricken face inches from her own. As soon as she opened her eyes, he relaxed. "Sorry, Avery. That was a stupid suggestion, but it did help."

"What's happened? Are we here?"

"You tell me. We'd better be."

Avery felt dizzy and sick, but she forced herself to focus and look around.

They were standing dead centre of the crossroads, but now the stones were sentinel, dark and forbidding. The full moon was still overhead, casting the place in sharp relief, and a gentle breeze carried the scent of honey and pollen. The feeling of stasis was still prevalent there. The moon was like a malevolent eye watching them, and Avery had to remind herself that the moon was also her friend, not just Hecate's.

She sighed with relief. "Yes, this is it."

Caspian exhaled heavily. "Good." He fell to his knees, retching.

Avery dropped next to him, her hand on his back. "What's wrong?"

"Alex was right. That was far harder than I expected. Especially bringing two of us. I'll be okay. Just give me a minute."

She looked deep into his weary eyes, and listened to his laboured breathing. "Liar. This has half-killed you."

He glared at her. "I'll be fine."

"I'm sorry. This is my fault. Look what I've done to you."

"Caitlin, not you. And I volunteered."

She rummaged in her pack, and found Briar's last tonic. "Drink this."

"You'll need it."

"Not as much as you do."

"No," he said stubbornly.

"Take it! Right now you're weaker than I am. Be logical."

She thrust it at him, and he reluctantly took it, knocking it back in one go.

Avery stood up, trying to steady the shaking in her limbs. "I have to act now. I can feel it…the stone is pulling me." She looked at her itching palm, and the glow of the mark became stronger. "Bollocks. I have to find the ring."

Caspian nodded. "I feel it, too. Which stone is it?"

Unlike in her dreams, these didn't glow with a magical light. "I'm not sure."

But even as she spoke, the stone to her right started to glow, the carved script igniting with the fiery light.

Caspian gave a hollow laugh. "That one, I presume."

"Well, it can wait," she answered, desperately trying to ignore its pull. She'd got used to it now. "Move away."

Caspian dragged himself across the ground to the edge of the crossroads, well away from the beckoning stone, and Avery said the spell to find the ring, the spell she'd rehearsed all day.

Nothing happened.

"Damn it!" she shouted into the night.

"You're too weak," Caspian told her.

Avery didn't answer him, instead grounding herself and calling the wind to her, wrapping it close like a blanket. She felt it giving her strength, and she said the spell again, uttering it with conviction as she shaped the necessary signs in the air.

Again, her words tumbled across the moors, meaningless and spent.

Avery struggled to focus, her thoughts jumbled, as the script on the stones virtually ignited. She collapsed to the ground, her body shaking uncontrollably as her magic start to ebb.

"Draw on me!" Caspian shouted. "We're linked. Use it!"

"You're not strong enough!"

Avery looked around her at the stones and faint silver lines of the four roads leading away across the moors, and she felt despair and loss. She would die here, away from Alex, away from her friends, and they would die, too. Caitlin and the Empusa would win, and Hecate would once again have her crossroads sacrifice.

The loud screeching of a bird shattered her reverie, and she jerked around, seeing an enormous raven perched on a standing stone. It looked at her, its head cocked, and its dark eyes reflected the silver of the full moon. It screeched again, burning through her foggy thoughts, and she suddenly remembered all she'd planned that day.

Sacrifice be damned.

Avery was soul-yoked to a stone that channelled fey magic from beyond the boundaries of their world. That magic was now hers. She slipped her boots off and wriggled her feet in the loamy earth of the moor, and then stood on her trembling limbs. The moor started to spin around her, but she threw her arms wide and faced the standing stone, allowing it to feel her soul, opening herself up to its power. The tiny pull she'd felt before became a rope of sinewy magic, as old as the Earth itself. She grabbed it with her mind and pulled it back to her, and it was like flipping a switch. Power flooded into her so quickly that she felt as if she'd dissolved into it. Her feet left the earth and she turned slowly, her hair streaming around her.

This is power! This is magic!

Images flashed through her mind—strange faces and stranger places, beings whose lives were different from her own, from another place and time. The moors seemed to move, the earth rustling as if it was waking, and she heard the drums again, far in the distance.

They didn't frighten her anymore. They were the drums of the fey shaman calling to their Gods, and one of them was already here.

She uttered the spell to summon Hecate. It was time to remind her who she was.

Within seconds there was a rumble of thunder, the earth shook, and the sky ignited with forked lightning. A bright white jagged finger crashed down into the crossroads, and the earth sizzled. Avery could smell the ozone, but she didn't flinch.

A figure rose from the ground, mist-wrapped and wraithlike, until she finally revealed herself. A woman towered over her, regal, imposing, and draped in darkness. Stars whirled around her head, and snakes hissed at her feet. She was ageless—maiden, mother, and crone all at the same time.

"You called me, child?" Her voice was as a soft as a feather and as hard as steel, and the weight of worlds lay within it.

Avery was still hovering in the air, fey magic flooding through her. "Yes! I demand an apology! I have been summoned here as sacrifice to you! How dare you keep me here? I am a witch! I carry your power, as all witches do! Release me from this binding."

Hecate regarded her silently for a moment, her eyes narrowed, and Avery knew she was being judged. "I do not keep you here, nor do I ask for sacrifice. Others act in my name, but it is not of my choosing."

"You promised Caitlin the Empusa! She wields it now. She kills with it."

"The Empusa has always been a difficult servant…wilful, spiteful, eager to dabble in the affairs of men. This place," she gestured around her, "was always her place more than mine. It is the Empusa who controls your fate, not me." She stepped closer to Avery, bringing the scent of decay and earth with her, as well as the stench of death. She looked into her eyes. "Break your bonds, I will not interfere. That which you seek is beneath your feet. You have the power to find it."

Hecate vanished in the blink of an eye, as if she had never been there at all, and relief washed through Avery. She'd been terrified that Hecate would stop her, or try to kill her, but she hadn't. She slowed her breathing, and at the same time eased her grip on the standing stone magic, slowly lowering herself to the earth.

Caspian looked up at her. He was still prostrate on the ground, his face whiter than before. "Well, that was something else."

"Did I imagine that?"

"Nope." He gestured to the centre of the crossroads. "Time to get the ring."

Avery looked down. The fey magic still affected her vision. The earth seemed to shimmer and move, as if there was another Earth just out of sight. She smiled. There probably was, she just couldn't normally see it.

She held her hands out, cupping her palms, and said the spell to find the ring. Within seconds, the earth writhed and buckled, and a small box rocketed upwards, as if it had been spat out. It landed in her outstretched hands and she opened it cautiously. There, on a bed of black velvet, was an elaborately designed silver ring with a deep red stone set within it. Next to it was a bundle of feathers, and a bundle of twigs and leaves. *The totems of the Raven King and the Green Man.*

She grinned at Caspian. "Got them. Shall I destroy it?"

"I think you should try, after all this."

She dropped to her knees, pulled the knife from her belt, and then placed the ring on the grass. She brought the knife down on the ring, gently at first, but nothing happened. Then she raised it above her head and brought it down quickly, stabbing the metal. Sparks flew outwards, sending Avery backwards in shock.

"Damn it!" She looked at Caspian. "Harlan was right."

"It seems the sorcerer knew his stuff."

"We're going to have to go back and get that ring off her finger after all. Are you better?" she asked, concerned.

"I can fight, the tonic has helped, but I can't fly."

A horrible thought struck Avery. "What if the time thing works against us? We could have been gone for hours." Her heart almost stopped. "They could all be dead!"

Caspian rolled to his knees and looked around. "Tricky to say. The boundary magic is making everything weird. But, you have got fey magic, temporarily at least. Use it. Think of the place *and* the time you want to return to."

The screech of the raven shattered the night and sent the sound of the drums fleeing, and at that Avery stood, pulled her boots on, and held her hand out to pull Caspian up. "Time to go. I'm strong enough now to take both of us."

He looked up at her for a moment, his expression deadly serious. "You're extraordinary, do you know that? I don't think you've ever looked more beautiful."

Avery felt incredibly self-conscious, and her voice faltered. "I'm not extraordinary or beautiful. It's the fey magic."

"No, it's not. You always are. I wish I had found you sooner, Avery."

Caspian looked suddenly lost, defeated, and with horrible clarity, Avery realised the depth of his feelings for her.

She started to speak, fumbling for her words, "Caspian, I'm sorry, but—"

"I know. You love Alex."

"I really do." She smiled at him, tears threatening to fall. "But thank you. You're quite extraordinary, too. I couldn't have done this without you."

"We're not done yet." He took her outstretched hand, and she pulled him to his feet.

"True. But when we get back and this is all over, because we *are* going to kick Caitlin's butt, I'm going to find you a girlfriend."

He stood behind her, sliding his arms around her waist, and said softly in her ear, "She won't be you."

"But she'll be amazing. Trust me. I'm a witch."

23

The fey magic was strong, and Avery and Caspian arrived back in the madness and chaos of the area around Caitlin's gypsy caravan. Caspian reluctantly released her.

The wood that had appeared out of nowhere was thick and rustling with life, and from somewhere in its dark confines, Avery heard the *clang* of steel on steel, and the *zing* of magic and spells. A figure appeared just at the edge of her peripheral vision, and Avery turned, catching the briefest glimpse of a strange, green-skinned, almost ethereal creature before it stepped back into the trunk of tree, disappearing from sight.

Avery blinked, doubting what she'd seen, but this was not the time to think. It was time to act.

She and Caspian ran towards the noise, and it seemed as if they had arrived only minutes after they left.

Reuben and Newton were fighting with Rafe and Mairi, Newton trading punches with Rafe, while Reuben ensnared Mairi with magic. El and Shadow were fighting furiously with the Empusa. Shadow was moving so quickly that Avery could barely follow her, but El ran forward when she could, making quick jabbing thrusts and flinging fireballs at the Empusa when there was no danger of hitting Shadow. Briar and the Raven King were everywhere all at once. Tree roots and branches were tearing through Caitlin's home, and the fire in front of her van had reignited, fed by chunks of wood that fell onto it. Overhead, ravens screeched, wheeling through the branches above them.

Avery left Caspian to help El fight the Empusa and ran to the hedge, just in time to see Alex break free, leaves exploding outwards as he spelled his way out. She launched herself at him, wrapping him in a hug. "You're okay!"

He plucked twigs and leaves from his hair. "I'm fine, if half-crushed by a crazed hedge. What happened to you? You're sort of glowing."

"Am I?" She looked down at herself properly, and saw that she shimmered, as if she was covered in gold dust. She grinned at him. "Fey magic. I'll tell you later. Take this. I found it at the crossroads. It has the ring and the talismans in it. I can't destroy the ring—Harlan was right. We have to take it off her. Can you break her bonds with the Raven King and Green Man?"

He looked bewildered. "Sure, but—" He looked around. "I think they're doing just fine!"

"But they can't attack her. This is as much as they can do. That's why the ravens are overhead."

He nodded. "That makes sense. What are you doing?"

"Getting the ring, of course. Keep that half safe."

Avery ran to where the Empusa was fighting, and skidded to a halt. El and Caspian arrived next to her, breathless. El was exasperated. "Nothing works! I've tried spell after spell, but nothing gets through! If it weren't for Shadow keeping her pre-occupied, we'd all be dead."

Caspian nodded. "I've tried, too. She's impervious."

For a few seconds they watched them fight, and Avery felt breathless just watching. Although Shadow was quick, the Empusa always seemed to have the edge, but Shadow wasn't backing down. Both had cuts to their arms, and the Empusa had a long wound down her side, but it didn't slow her down as she relentlessly advanced on Shadow. In turn, she rolled, slashed and parried, while they both darted around trees and jumped over tree roots.

"I bet she's not impervious to this," Avery said, raising her hands. "Let's see how she likes being on the *punishing* end of boundary magic."

Avery summoned the wild fey magic that still coursed through her, and although it was not as strong as it had been, she sent a tendril of magic across the ground. It writhed over roots until it reached the Empusa's feet, and it started to wrap around them.

Realising what was happening, the Empusa slashed at the magic, slicing through it with ease, but the distraction meant that Shadow could get closer, and the Empusa couldn't fight both, not successfully. With renewed enthusiasm, Avery whipped magic at the Empusa again, and it snagged around her limbs, tangling her feet and arms in bonds she couldn't get to quick enough. With a snap of her fingers, Avery dragged her to the ground, and Shadow kicked the swords from her hands and stood over her, her blade to the Empusa's throat.

Screams and a skirmish behind them made Avery turn briefly to see Reuben and Newton dragging Rafe and Mairi into the small clearing. Both Newton and Rafe were bleeding, but Rafe had a black eye and appeared unconscious. Mairi, mute with anger, was next to him.

As Avery turned back to Shadow and the Empusa, a *boom* resounded across the newly grown wood as Alex broke the bonds tying the Green Man and Raven King. If the wood was impressive before, it was nothing compared to what was happening there now. The trees soared higher, their trunks growing broader, becoming alive with a mysterious Otherness, and already feeling ancient, even though they had appeared only minutes before.

Alex skidded to Avery's side, the box in his hands.

Through the tangled branches, ravens cawed and dived earthwards, until they coalesced in the shape of the Raven King. He brought his own luminescence with him, illuminating the space around him with a soft white light, and throwing the Empusa's figure into sharp relief. He watched her writhing furiously on the ground, his face impassive.

Avery tightened her fingers and the fey magic tightened too, until the Empusa could barely move, allowing Shadow to stand back, breathless and bleeding, her eyes alive with curiosity.

Corbin had vanished, and in his place stood the Raven King alone. He was taller, his shoulders broader, and he had long black hair, as glossy as a raven's plumage, and shot through with midnight blue. He wore a long black cloak, black clothes, and black boots, his eyes were as dark as night, and his white face was square jawed. A raven perched on his shoulder, rustling his wings and looked around imperiously.

"You desire the ring?" the Raven King asked Shadow, his voice deep and melodious.

Shadow nodded, unusually silent for once.

"Take it."

Shadow leaned forward, stepping on the Empusa's closest hand to keep her immobile, and not knowing which ring to choose, tried to pull them all free, but they were trapped on the larger fingers of the creature, far larger than Caitlin's hands. With a grim smile Shadow raised her sword and brought it down quickly, severing the hand.

The Empusa screamed, and behind her scratchy voice, Avery heard Caitlin's. "Hecate will make you pay for that!"

Avery's voice carried across the rustles and scurries that filled the night. "No, she won't. She told me your deal had nothing to do with her."

Avery felt all heads turn to look at her, but none so swiftly as the Raven King's. His black eyes met hers. "You met her?"

"Briefly."

"You carry fey magic. You finally understand what soul-yoked means."

Avery nodded, feeling the power of his words trembling though her. "I did, finally. Thanks to you."

He looked at Shadow holding the Empusa's hand. "You have the ring?"

Shadow grimaced as she pulled one free. "I do now." She held it up. "Is this it?"

Alex walked over and took it from her, holding it next to the one he held. "That's the one." He looked around at the others and then hesitantly at the Raven King. "Shall I?"

"Wait. Where's Briar?" Avery said. "She should be here."

"She's here," the Raven King said, gesturing around him. "She's everywhere!"

Alex looked at them hesitantly, and then pushed both rings together. They clicked as they joined, and with it came an audible *snap* as the power of the ring released, throwing them to the ground or crushing them against tree trunks. Alex loosed his grip on the ring in shock and it flew into the air, but Shadow and her lightning-fast reflexes recovered quickly, and she leapt forward and grabbed it, squeezing her palm around it tightly.

With a frustrated scream, the Empusa disappeared, leaving Caitlin in her wake, blood pouring from the end of her arm. Within seconds, her youth ebbed away, and she was left an old woman, her face deeply wrinkled, her hair grey, and her frame withered. Her eyes, however, burned with fierce hatred as she glared at Avery, but if she was going to say anything, it stalled on her lips as the Raven King stood over her.

"What should I do with her?" he asked. "I can take her with me."

Newton looked anguished. At his feet, Rafe and Mairi were bound with magic, lips sealed, but their faces were furious. "I have no idea if I can ever prove what they've done. There's no evidence, nothing that I can hold them with! They could do this again, and more could die."

The King cocked his head, birdlike, as he looked at Caitlin. "Was it all to be young again?"

"You will never know the frustration of age, and the loss of power and beauty. When I found the Ring of Callanish, I saw a way to save myself, and I took it!"

He looked at her with distaste, then turned to Reuben, and pointed to Rafe and Mairi. "Let them speak. I would like to know what they wanted."

Reuben eased his spell, watching them dispassionately.

"Tell me," the King prompted. "What should I do with you?"

Neither answered, their fury burning away into fear as seconds ticked by.

"You're right," the King finally said to Newton. "They will never get the justice they deserve, so I will take them all."

Shadow was trembling, too. "You will take them to the Otherworld? Take me with you! Take me home!"

He shook his head. "I shall take these somewhere far worse. They will go to the Underworld to answer for their crimes."

"But you *could* take me home," she said, almost pleading. "It is within your power."

"Child, your destiny lies here, at least for now. I cannot take you." His voice was gentle, but firm.

She jerked her chin up, eyes flashing, and her hand gripped her sword tightly. "What destiny? You lie!"

"Do not challenge me; it is a fight you shall lose. You must trust me. Your path is long and varied. It is for you to discover."

Shadow fell silent, but Avery saw her swallow and blink, as if to chase away the tears.

He turned to the witches, looking at each one in turn, and dropping his head in acknowledgement. "I thank you for releasing me from my bonds. We may meet again, one day, when the worlds turn and boundaries collide. Until then, some of my friends will stay here, in this place of ancient magic." The raven flew from his shoulder to the tree above them, settling on a branch, as the King dragged Caitlin to her feet, looking more like a bundle of rags than a person. He then marched over to Rafe and Mairi. They cowered, but he didn't care. He swirled his cloak around his shoulders, covering all of them, and then with a rustle of feathers and a snap of air he was gone, taking them with him, and leaving Corbin behind, his body spent as he collapsed on the ground.

Avery ran to his side, and felt for his pulse, relieved to find it was there, unexpectedly steady. Corbin's eyelids fluttered and Avery gripped his hands. "Corbin, wake up! You did it!"

He groaned. "Am I dead?"

Reuben laughed. "No mate, you are most definitely alive."

He struggled to sit up, and he looked around, confused. "Where am I?"

"At the campsite—sort of," Avery said gently. "Do you remember anything?"

"Flashes of things, and *him*, I remember him." His eyes came into sharp focus. "Was it real? Did it work?"

"It did. You saved your circus, and us."

"I did? You'll have to tell me how." And then he fell back on the ground and looked up through the branches to the night sky above.

Avery realised she was shaking, and she sat on the rich soil, feeling Alex's hand grip her nape, and then his warmth as he sat next to her, his arm sliding across her shoulders. He murmured, "What the hell just happened?"

"We have had the most extraordinary moment," Reuben said softly, and he patted Newton on the arm, and pulled El into a hug.

Shadow's voice was almost a whisper. "He left me. I am stuck here!" She couldn't help herself as tears poured down her cheeks. "I could taste home, it was so close."

Caspian did the most unexpected thing. He gathered her into his arms and held her as she shook and trembled. His eyes met Avery's and he smiled, his face full of sorrow.

"Where's Briar?" Newton asked, as he pulled himself together. "She must be here somewhere!"

"I'm here," she called as she emerged from the darkness. Her hair cascaded down her back, and she wore a crown of leaves, a certain wildness emanating from her eyes. "The Green Man has gone."

Newton held the tops of her arms as he examined her. "Are you okay? You look…" He struggled for words. "Different."

She cupped his face in her hands. "I'm not sure I'll ever be the same again. And I don't think you will be, either."

"We need a fire," El declared, easing herself out of Reuben's hug. "And I want to sit here while we can, in this amazing wood. Can we?"

"I should think so," Alex answered, "before we have to go back to reality. I'm not even sure what that is anymore."

The fire in front of Caitlin's smashed home was still smouldering, so El reignited it with a word, and they dragged chairs and wood from the remnants and sat around it, the flames throwing shapes onto the wildness of their surroundings.

"What is this place, Briar?" Avery asked. "It can't last, surely?"

Briar laughed. "Oh, I'm afraid it can. This isn't going anywhere!"

"You have got to be kidding!" Reuben said, looking at her as if she'd gone mad. "How do we explain how a bloody great wood grew overnight?"

"We don't." She grinned impishly. "It's nothing to do with us. He called it his gift to us, and White Haven."

"No, no, no!" Newton said, appalled. "This place can't get any weirder! You have to keep the magic here that hides it. It is hidden now, right Reuben?"

Reuben nodded. "Yep, my giant wall of mist is still there. We're hidden for now, but it will be a hell of spell to hide it forever."

Briar's voice was sharp. "It is not meant to be hidden. He said that no one would question it. It would be as if it had been here forever."

There was a universal, "*What?*" expressed by the group.

"It's his magic, not mine," she explained. "I think it was more for you, Shadow, than anyone. To bring you closer to home," she said gently.

Shadow sighed as she stared into the fire. "So be it, then. I will be glad of it. It will be a long life so far from home."

"Have you still got the ring?" Alex asked.

She patted her pocket. "Right here." And then she took a sharp intake of breath. "Harlan! I left him outside by my horse."

"I knew it!" Alex said accusingly. "You double-crossing, fey-blooded—" He spluttered as he tried to find words.

She just looked at him. "I'm here, aren't I? Did I leave you to die at her hands? No. I risked my life for you!"

Avery placed a hand on his arm. "It's true, Alex. Thank you, Shadow. And I'm sorry you're still here, but if I'm honest, I quite like you, and am glad you're staying."

"So am I, sister," El said, winking at her across the fire.

"What are we going to do about Harlan?" Reuben asked. "Shall we go fetch him?"

"I think you should," Newton said, ominously. "I'd like to know more about him. Planning on giving him the ring, Shadow?"

She looked shifty. "Maybe."

"I'd like some assurances, first," Alex said.

Shadow jumped to her feet. "Come on then, Reuben. Let's introduce Harlan to the team."

Newton held his hand out. "Hand it over first."

She glared at him. "Don't trust me?"

"No."

She reluctantly pulled the ring from her pocket and placed it on his palm, before turning her back and marching away.

24

When Reuben finally returned with Harlan, he had a wry smile on his face.

"The Green Man has outdone himself!"

"What do you mean?" Alex asked, suspiciously.

"This wood covers the entire field behind this one, right up to the lane that runs across the back. We had a bit of trouble finding Harlan."

"I wondered what was taking you so long," Newton said. He had the shotgun on the ground next to him, in easy reach in case anything else happened, and he still looked on edge.

Shadow was grinning from ear to ear. "It's amazing. It's like the woods from home! It's tangled and ancient and mysterious and I love it!"

Harlan, however, looked in shock as he stepped into their circle. "This is quite some trick you've pulled off."

"It ain't no trick," Reuben drawled as he pointed to a salvaged bench. "Take a seat." He quickly made introductions as they settled themselves down.

"Hi, Harlan," Avery said, with a mischievous smile. "Fancy meeting you again."

"Yes, fancy that. You're very resourceful."

"I know."

He leaned forward to rub his hands over the fire. "It's cold out there. How have you managed all of this?" He lifted his chin to indicate the trees around them.

"We didn't, the Green Man did," Briar told him.

For a moment Harlan didn't answer as he looked at them all, examining each face as though to memorise them. He stared a little longer at Corbin in his Raven King costume. "I've seen many strange things in my life, but nothing as strange as this."

Newton frowned. "What *did* you see? We've received reassurances that no one would notice—incredible though that sounds. And yet, you have."

"I was at the edge of the field, on Shadow's horse, when I saw the mist thicken until I couldn't see a thing. And then all of a sudden, I was surrounded by an ancient forest. It just appeared—literally in the blink of an eye. It gave me quite a shock, but the horse was completely fine with it."

"That's because he's from the Otherworld," Shadow explained. "He has his own magic, like me. That's why you remember it happening." She shrugged. "At least I think so. Otherwise, the Green Man is wrong and there'll be a lot of questions tomorrow."

"Makes sense," Caspian said, nodding. He narrowed his eyes at Harlan. "Avery and Shadow tell us that you want that ring. We need some assurances first. Who are you, and what will you do with it?"

"And make it good," Newton added. "Or it stays with me."

"I work for The Orphic Guild. We acquire unusual things for buyers for their private collections. Sometimes these objects have magical or mythical histories, sometimes not. And that's it. It's nothing dodgy. You can look it up. We have a website and contact numbers."

Newton leaned forward, his arms on his knees. "I did. It tells me very little."

Harlan's expression was as steely as Newton's. "We like to keep things private, that's why. Our clients pay a lot for our services and discretion."

"Will someone be paying a lot for this?" Newton laid the ring on the palm of his hand.

"Yes. It will be placed somewhere as an object of art, for appreciation only."

Newton snorted. "I doubt that."

Harlan straightened his shoulders. "Have you ever found anything of a criminal nature about us?"

"No. And believe me, I checked. You haven't even had a parking ticket."

Harlan smiled tightly. "Well, there you go then."

Avery watched Harlan carefully. He had recovered his composure, but he still looked wary, glancing nervously over his shoulder from time to time. She couldn't blame him. She was doing the same herself, they all were. There were strange rustlings from behind them, and the feeling that something was watching them, something maybe like the strange, green-skinned creature she had seen so briefly before it vanished into the tree. The feeling of age that came from these trees was unnatural, as if it had not just grown there, but had been pulled from somewhere else.

Perhaps the firelight was playing tricks on her. It cast the branches' shadows into strange, contorted shapes, and the rich smell of loam beneath their feet was heady, making her almost giddy, but maybe that was just tiredness as the events caught up with her.

Newton's voice was sharp, and she focused on the conversation again. "What's your role in this, Shadow?"

"Are you interrogating me?" she asked, her hand on her sword hilt.

"Yes," he said bluntly.

She scowled at him like a child. "I'm stuck here, and I need to make a life, and money. Harlan offered me a finder's fee for my help when Avery refused."

Newton looked between Shadow and Harlan. "And how did you two become acquainted?"

Harlan answered. "I make it my business to know about unusual things and places. This town has been on my radar for a while, and *she* is noticeable."

Shadow smirked. "I am fey."

"I think we know," Alex said, wearily.

Newton ignored her, focusing on Harlan. "Who's your buyer for this?"

"I can't tell you that, but I can tell you that it will be far safer with the buyer than anywhere else."

Newton looked at the other witches. "What do you think?"

"It caused a lot of trouble," Caspian said, taking it from Newton and holding it close to the firelight. "It seems so innocuous now, if it weren't for the power it exudes." He looked at Harlan. "How old is it?"

"It was made sometime in the twelfth century. It's impossible to say exactly when."

"And the sorcerer's name?"

Harlan rubbed his jaw and looked up at the sky before saying, "It escapes me right now."

"Of course it does," Caspian said.

"May I?" El asked. Caspian passed it to her, and she examined it. "It's been made with great skill. The design is intricate and unusual, and the metal feels different."

"Your knife wouldn't work on it," Avery told her.

El's head jerked up. "Really? Damn it. I thought I'd covered everything."

Harlan's tone was even, but impatience was creeping in. "Like I said, it's very special."

Newton persisted. "Are you sure it won't be used again?"

"As sure as I can be." Harlan looked at his watch. "It's late, and I need to go. The ring?" He held his hand out.

Newton nodded, and El placed it on his palm. Harlan immediately put it into a small box he pulled from an inside pocket and tucked it away safely. "Excellent, and now I must leave. Shadow, will you escort me?"

Shadow had spent the last few minutes polishing her sword and cleaning the blood from it, and she slid it into her scabbard, and then picked up one of the Empusa's swords that lay at her feet. She examined its finely wrought blade and unusual hilt. "This is made of bronze. I'll take these if no one has any objections?"

El reached forward and picked the other one up, running her finger down its blade. "Actually, I'd like one. Don't ask me why, but I'd feel happier if they were separated."

Shadow looked as if she might complain, but then she rose to her feet. "You might be right."

Harlan's stared at the one that Shadow held, but he didn't say a word, and Avery wondered if another transaction was about to take place. He stood and made a short bow. "I'm sure we'll meet again sometime. Meanwhile, it's been a pleasure."

Shadow merely smiled enigmatically as she led him away.

Reuben waited a few moments until he was sure they had left. "Is it me, or have we just witnessed the start of an unholy relationship?"

Caspian picked up a stick and poked the fire. "She needs something. She's stuck here, and it might be just what she's looking for."

"I'm just glad it's all over for now," Newton said. "I'll worry about it another time. Are you all right, Corbin?"

Corbin had sat quietly for a long time, staring almost vacantly into the fire. Avery had almost forgotten he was there. He'd edged back from the others, and his cloak of feathers was pulled closely around him. He dragged his gaze from the fire. "It's been a long night. It's been a long few months, actually. A nightmare."

Briar patted his arm. "You have your circus back now, and memories to last a lifetime."

"How do I move on from this? I feel…*different*."

"That's magic for you. And you did become the Raven King," she pointed out. "That's something to treasure, surely?"

"But what about my circus?" His eyes were wild. "Will it be as successful without magic? How do I explain Rafe and Mairi just disappearing? And this forest! We're so close—what if they noticed something?"

"We'll see soon enough," Alex said. "In the meantime, let's enjoy the peace and quiet, and I'd like to know what happened at the crossroads." He nudged Avery with his shoulder. "Fey magic?"

Avery laughed. "Things got very weird."

"I admit, it was bit strange there for a while," Caspian said, leaning back in the old deckchair he'd found. "You tell them what happened, Avery. I was a mere spectator!"

"Not true," she remonstrated. "But I'll start."

Between them they told the others about Hecate and the standing stones, and then Briar talked about her experience with the Green Man, but it wasn't long before Avery's head started to nod.

"You're tired. We need to go home," Alex said.

Reuben jumped to his feet. "Bed sounds good. Let's get rid of my magic wall of mist and we'll see what's happening out there. Give me a moment." He disappeared into the trees and within minutes they heard shouts, laughter, and music. Lights appeared at the edge of the wood as the campsite reappeared. There was a gap where Rafe and Mairi's van had been parked a few meters away from Caitlin's destroyed van, but Corbin's was still there, looking completely untouched.

Corbin walked away from the fire as Alex quickly doused it. "Their van! Where is it?"

"All gone! Maybe you won't have much explaining to do after all," El said.

One of the performers walked towards Corbin, the greasepaint now wiped from his face. "Corbin! There you are. We've been looking for you. It was another good night. Are you coming for a drink?" He looked beyond him. "Who are your friends?"

"Just some locals, they're heading home now," Corbin explained, and he raised his hand to them. "I'll see you soon."

They watched him leave, and it was clear the performer had no concerns about the wood that had suddenly materialised.

"That answers that, then," Reuben noted, and he slung his arms around El's shoulders as he led the way across the castle grounds.

25

The following day, the five White Haven witches met in the early afternoon in front of Hawk House, El's old family home, and they walked to the edge of the hill to look down on the castle and the circus.

Alex let out a short laugh. "Look at the size of that!"

"I don't think I'm ever going to get used to it," El said, as they stared at the newly created wood below them.

Reuben whistled. "That is quite unexpected. It's bigger than I thought."

The wood stretched from the back of the campsite, starting more or less by the hedge, cutting over the corner where Caitlin's van had been, and spread to the entire field beyond it. It finally stopped at the roads that bordered it to the top and the side, and ran to the cliff's edge on the other end. Most of the castle was unaffected, other than the remnants of the wall at the rear corner.

"Unbelievable," Avery said, taking it all in. "If you hadn't had your magic wall of mist up, sealing the area off, it might have spread the other way, too, Reuben."

"Maybe. I did have to work really hard to keep it going once the Green Man did his thing."

They all watched Briar, who stood quietly taking in the scene below her.

"Are you okay?" El asked her.

She nodded and finally looked at them, her eyes haunted. "I'm fine. I think I have a Green Man hangover. I've barely slept, even though I'm exhausted. I had the weirdest dreams."

"Like what?" Avery asked.

"I was still in the wood, and I saw strange things—dryads, satyrs, sprites, and other things I can't explain. Maybe it was like when you kept seeing the crossroads, Avery?"

Avery nodded. "Maybe. Although, I'm glad to say that did not happen for me last night, and I slept like the dead."

"Is the mark still on your hand?" El asked.

"All gone," she said, showing them her unmarked palm. "Which is quite a relief. I thought being soul-yoked might mean forever."

"Come on," Reuben prompted them. "I want to get down there and walk in it."

Fifteen minutes later, after they had navigated the lanes, they pulled up next to a gate in the hedge and walked into the newly formed ancient woodland. As soon as they were beneath its broad branches, a deep, dreamy silence enveloped them, broken only by birdsong.

"It really does feel old," Alex said, as they walked along a barely there path, which was more of an animal track than anything made by humans.

Thick moss covered patches of ground and the occasional fallen branch lay rotting in deep shadow. Shafts of sunlight pierced the canopy, and the farther in they walked, the quieter the wood became.

"This is insane," Reuben murmured, as he pushed back overhanging branches. "You really outdid yourself, Briar."

"It's got nothing to do with me."

"Not true," Avery said. "You allowed him to do this. You helped him break free."

"We all did," she replied. "He was using our White Haven magic. That's why the spring came early. I just gave him a nudge in the right direction."

El swatted another branch away. "Has anyone said anything to you guys about this?"

"No one!" Alex said. "Just like we were promised."

They paused in a small clearing, enjoying the pale rays of the sun, and Avery asked, "Has this place got a name?"

Reuben laughed. "It sure has. I Googled it earlier. It's called Ravens' Wood."

"No way!" Avery said, astonished.

"It's there, on the map, just like it's been here forever."

Avery turned slowly, squinting as she peered into the wood's murky depths. "I thought I saw a dryad last night."

"You probably did," Briar told her. "That fey magic you channelled for a while allowed that to happen. I think there are more of them, too—although I doubt we'll ever see them."

El's eyes were shining, and she was almost bouncing with excitement. "We were part of something astonishing last night. This is where we should have our solstice celebrations from now on. What do you think?"

"I think that's a brilliant idea," Reuben said. "But I have a feeling it's going to be popular with everyone."

A shimmer of movement disturbed them, and they turned swiftly, hands raised, but it was only Shadow doing her usual fey appearance trick. She leaned against the trunk of the closest tree, grinning at them.

"This is officially my favourite place in White Haven. How are you all?"

"Pretty good," Avery admitted. "What about you?"

"I'm aching a little. I haven't had such a good fight in a long time—even against Gabe."

El walked over and hugged her. "Thanks for last night, Shadow. We couldn't have done this without you."

Although Shadow looked uncomfortable at first, she eventually responded, giving El a quick hug in return. "Thank you, sister."

"Things go well with Harlan?" Reuben asked, a wry smile on his face.

Shadow looked impish. "Very well, thank you. He's a very generous man."

"Of course he is," Alex said. "I'm sure you'll have a beautiful friendship."

Shadow pushed away from the tree. "A girl's got to keep herself busy, and that's all I have to say on that."

"Fair enough," Avery said laughing, and then quickly sobered. "I'm sorry you're stuck here, though. I can't imagine how that must feel."

Shadow's eyes darkened to a stormy blue. "I'll survive. At least now I have this place—a taste of home."

"Is it really?" Briar asked. "It feels magical to us, but does it to you, too?"

"It does." She spread her arms wide and turned slowly. "The Green Man will always be strong here, a little oasis of fey magic. Something to feed my soul if there are dark days ahead. I have a feeling there are things hidden here that only I can find." Her eyes lit up again.

She was irrepressible, Avery thought, feeling a flood of affection for her.

"Well, this is great," Reuben declared, "but now I'm starving. Let's head to the pub for a late lunch. Magic is hungry work."

***

Early on the following Saturday, the final night of the circus's stay in White Haven, Avery entered the back room of Happenstance Books. However, she didn't beat Sally, who was already there and putting the coffee machine on.

"Have you moved in and I don't know about it?" Avery asked, watching her work.

Sally laughed. "Not likely. You know me, the kids wake early and I've abandoned them to Sam. He gets the joy of sorting them out on a Saturday. Has Alex moved in yet?"

Avery grinned sheepishly. "His sofa arrives today. Reuben's going to help him load mine into the back of my van, and then take mine to his place and do a swap. But he's already moved his clothes, and toiletries, and books and stuff. They're picking up more boxes today."

Sally hugged her. "That's fantastic. I'm so pleased for you. I like Alex, I always have, but I've told you that before."

"I know. All those months ago, and you were right."

Sally gave her a final squeeze before releasing her. "I always am. Heard anything else from Shadow?"

"She's been suspiciously quiet, probably setting up some new business venture with Harlan."

"The American?" Sally asked, as she finished preparing the coffee.

"Yeah, and I haven't seen him, either."

"Maybe he left as soon as he'd got the ring."

Avery nodded. "He probably did. If it was so precious, his buyer wouldn't want to wait."

Sally leaned against the counter, her expression thoughtful. "And what about Caspian?"

"Nothing all week. I guess he's busy. We asked him if he wanted to come with us tonight, but he says he'll be away on business for a while."

"Good. I think he needs to get away."

Avery mulled over what she was thinking, but in the end said it anyway. "I feel guilty, like I've led him on, and that it's my fault he developed these feelings for me."

"Don't be ridiculous. You've done no such thing. It's very obvious that you love Alex, and that he loves you, and you two moving in together makes that very clear. Caspian's a grown man, Avery, not a kid. He'll move on. This is his way of doing that."

Avery nodded. "I guess so. I feel I've driven him away."

Sally rolled her eyes. "Stop being a drama queen. How's Alex doing?"

"Being calm and rational as usual, and very pleased about moving in. He's up there right now reorganising the kitchen, which is why I'm here. He says my cupboards are as disorderly as my mind. Cheeky sod."

Sally sniggered. "It's part of your charm."

"Oh, don't you start!"

"Start what?" Dan said, catching the end of the conversation as he barrelled through the door.

"Criticising my organisation skills."

"They are legendary for their nonexistence," Dan admitted. "But it's okay, that's why you have us."

Avery folded her arms. "Don't you start, either. I'm not a child!"

"That is not what we're saying. It's what allows you to be such a creative witch," he said as he took his jacket off. "Anything you can do about the cold?"

"No. It's February, suck it up."

Sally poured them all coffees and passed one to each of them. "I miss the Green Man. Do you think he'll come back?"

Avery sipped her drink, enjoying its sweet warmth. "I doubt it, not like that again, anyway. All the green shoots in my garden have got frost damage, and the early spring warmth has gone. Every now and again, I feel he's here, looking over my shoulder."

"What about Briar? How's she doing?" Sally asked.

Both she and Dan knew that Briar had become the Green Man for a few hours over a week ago.

"It's changed her. She sort of carries this Otherness now, and her magic is even stronger. You should see her garden, and her allotment! She showed me a few days ago. The other gardeners think she has magical compost. They're not wrong, but not quite in the way they think! Hunter arrived last night. I think she needs him now more than ever. He's good for her."

"So he's going tonight, too?" Dan asked.

Avery nodded. "We all are. Corbin has given us free tickets. I can't wait."

Sally said, "Caitlin's disappearance doesn't seem to have ruined the show. Everyone still loves it, from what I've heard."

"You're right, and the performers are happier, too, although I don't think they actually remember her anyway. Or Rafe and Mairi."

"I must admit, I have trouble remembering them," Dan said, his forehead wrinkling with concentration. "If you didn't keep telling me, I wouldn't give them a second thought. I can't even picture what they look like."

Avery stared at them both, as she prepared to ask the question she'd been repeating all week. "And you're sure that wood has been there, next to the castle, all along?"

Sally and Dan exchanged a glance, and Sally said, "One hundred percent. You can't magic an entire wood overnight, not ancient woodland!"

"But the Green Man did!" Avery insisted. "You know about him, you can remember that much."

Dan grabbed a biscuit to dunk into his coffee. "Of course. We're not idiots." He winked at Avery. "But I like the fact that you're trying to tell us it just appeared overnight. Another layer of mystery to White Haven. But trust me, it has enough already."

Unbelievable. The Raven King had effectively made three people disappear, and the Green Man had spelled an entire wood into existence. Their magic was insanely powerful. No one had questioned the appearance of the ancient wood. No one. Not the locals, the visitors, the circus folk, or the news. If they weren't there during the spell, it hadn't happened.

She nodded, giving up. "You're right, it has. I'm just messing with you."

"You look better, though," Dan continued. "You've finally caught up on your sleep."

"I have. The crossroads no longer appear in my head every time I close my eyes, and my magic is back to its normal self."

"And your fey magic has gone?" Sally asked.

"Completely, which is probably a good thing. It was very odd," Avery reflected, remembering how she could feel and see things that weren't really there—not in her world, anyway. "I'm enjoying normality. Speaking of which, I'm going to open up and refresh my spells." She left them to walk through her shop, enjoying its peace and security as she mulled over the latest crazy happenings in White Haven.

***

It was dark when Avery arrived at the circus with Alex, and they parked at the normal car park rather than down the lane behind the hedge.

"This is already feeling weird," Avery told him.

Alex laughed. "We can walk across the fields if you prefer."

"The car park is just fine," she said as she exited the car. "I'm hoping we can enjoy the show like ordinary people."

"Got the tickets?"

She patted her bag. "In my purse. I gave the others theirs earlier, so we'll meet them in there."

As they walked up the path to the castle and the entrance of the circus, it was clear that the circus hadn't suffered from losing the magic of the Raven King and The Green Man. There were as many people milling around as on the first night. A few circus performers were entertaining the crowds—a juggler sent balls whirling in a bewildering show of skill as he balanced on a unicycle, a young man was walking on his hands, and a female acrobat dressed as a dryad cart-wheeled and back-flipped at the edge of the crowd.

They made their way under the arched entrance at the beginning of the path, the fake standing stones looking over them like guards. There were still ravens at the castle, and one was perched on top of one of the stones, cawing loudly as they passed by. Avery gave an involuntary jump.

"Bad memories?" Alex asked, pulling her close.

She shook her head. "It was the raven at the crossroads that made me act so quickly. It was like the Raven King himself was watching over me."

Alex kissed her forehead. "He probably was. He's very resourceful."

"Speaking of which." Avery pointed to the entrance of the Big Top, where the tent sides were pulled back, revealing a glimpse of a shadowy interior. To the side, welcoming the crowd, stood Corbin as the Raven King. His costume still looked amazing, and when he saw them, he lifted his caped and feathered arms, shouting, "Welcome to the Crossroads Circus!"

The screeching sound of hundreds of ravens filled the air, and the light show flashed images of dark wings across the tent behind him. They smiled at him as they passed, but didn't speak. There were too many people around, and it would have ruined the illusion, but he looked their way, and for the briefest of moments, Avery thought his eyes turned inky black, before people came between them, obscuring him from view. She strained to look back. Did his eyes change for a moment, or did she imagine it?

As soon as Avery entered the tent, she knew for certain. The Raven King was still there, and it was still his circus. She felt like an excited child again as she made her way to her seat, Alex's warm hand in her own, to watch the old myths come to life.

Please leave a review and make me very happy!

You can join my readers group for free short stories and up to date news about my writing and new releases - **https://tjgreen.nz/landing/**

Or join my Facebook group, TJ's Inner Circle, for teasers, giveaways, and other fun stuff!

https://www.facebook.com/groups/696140834516292/

Titles available by TJ Green:

Rise of the King Series

A Young Adult series about a teen called Tom who's summoned to wake King Arthur. It's a fun adventure about King Arthur in the Otherworld!

Call of the King #1

King Arthur is destined to return, and Tom is destined to wake him.

When sixteen year old Tom's grandfather mysteriously disappears, Tom stops at nothing to find him, even when that means crossing to a mysterious and unknown world.

When he gets there, Tom discovers that everything he thought he knew about himself and his life was wrong. Vivian, the Lady of the Lake, has been watching over him and manipulating his life since his birth. And now she needs his help.

The Silver Tower #2

Merlin disappeared over a thousand years ago. Now they risk everything to find him.

Vivian needs King Arthur's help. Nimue, a powerful witch and priestess who lives on Avalon, has disappeared.

King Arthur, Tom, and his friends set off across the Other to find her, following Nimue's trail to Nimue seems to have a quest of her own, one she's deliberately hiding. Arthur is convinced it's about Merlin, and he's determined to find him.

The Cursed Sword #3

An ancient sword. A dark secret. A new enemy.

Tom loves his new life in the Otherworld. He lives with Arthur in New Camelot, and Arthur is hosting a tournament. Eager to test his sword-fighting skills, Tom's competing.

But while the games are being played, his friends are attacked and everything he loves is threatened. Tom has to find the intruder before anyone else gets hurt.

Tom's sword seems to be the focus of these attacks. Their investigations uncover its dark history and a terrible betrayal that a family has kept secret for generations.

White Haven Witches Series

Witches, secrets, myth and folklore, set on the Cornish coast!

Buried Magic #1

Love witchy fiction? Welcome to White Haven – where secrets are deadly.

Avery, a witch who lives on the Cornish coast, finds her past holds more secrets than she ever imagined in this spellbinding mystery.

For years witches have lived in quirky White Haven, all with an age-old connection to the town's magical roots, but Avery has been reluctant to join a coven, preferring to work alone.

However, when she inherits a rune covered box and an intriguing letter, Avery learns that their history is darker than she realised. And when the handsome Alex Bonneville tells her he's been having ominous premonitions, they know that trouble's coming.

Magic Unbound #2

Avery and the other witches are now being hunted, and they know someone is betraying them.

The question is, who?

One thing is certain.

They have to find their missing grimoires before their attackers do, and they have to strike back.

If you love urban fantasy, filled with magic and a twist of romance, you'll love Magic Unbound.

Magic Unleashed #3

Old magic, new enemies. The danger never stops in White Haven.

Avery and the White Haven witches have finally found their grimoires and defeated the Favershams, but their troubles are only just beginning.

Something escaped from the spirit world when they battled beneath All Souls Church, and now it wants to stay, unleashing violence across Cornwall.

On top of that, the power they released when they reclaimed their magic is attracting powerful creatures from the deep, creatures that need men to survive.

All Hallows' Magic #4

When Samhain arrives, worlds collide.

A Shifter family arrives in White Haven, one of them close to death. Avery offers them sanctuary, only to find their pursuers are close behind, intent on retribution. In an effort to help them, Avery and Alex are dragged into a fight they didn't want but must see through.

As if that weren't enough trouble, strange signs begin to appear at Old Haven Church. Avery realises that an unknown witch has wicked plans for Samhain, and is determined to breach the veils between worlds.

Avery and her friends scramble to discover who the mysterious newcomer is, all while being attacked one by one.

Undying Magic #5

Winter grips White Haven, bringing death in its wake.

It's close to the winter solstice when Newton reports that dead bodies have been found drained of their blood.

Then people start disappearing, and Genevieve calls a coven meeting. What they hear chills their blood.

This has happened before, and it's going to get worse. The witches have to face their toughest challenge yet – vampires.

Crossroads Magic #6

When Myths become real, danger stalks White Haven.

The Crossroads Circus has a reputation for bringing myths to life, but it also seems that where the circus goes, death follows. When the circus sets up on the castle grounds, Newton asks Avery and the witches to investigate.

This proves trickier than they expected when an unexpected encounter finds Avery bound to a power she can't control.

Strange magic is making the myths a little too real.

Crown of Magic #7

Passions run deep at Beltane - too deep.

With the Beltane Festival approaching, the preparations in White Haven are in full swing, but when emotions soar out of control, the witches suspect more than just high spirits.

As part of the celebrations, a local theatre group is rehearsing Tristan and Isolde, but it seems Beltane magic is affecting the cast, and all sorts of old myths are brought to the surface.

The May Queen brings desire, fertility, and the promise of renewal, but love can also be dark and dangerous.

White Haven Hunters

The fun-filled spin-off to the White Haven Witches, with Gabe, Shadow, and the Orphic Guild.

Spirit of the Fallen #1

Kill the ghost, save the host.

Shadow is an over-confident fey stranded in White Haven after the Wild Hunt is defeated on Samhain.

Gabe is a Nephilim, newly arrived from the spirit world along with six of his companions. He has a violent history that haunts him, and a father he wants answers from - if he ever finds him.

When they set up in business together with the Orphic Guild, they're expecting adventure, intrigue and money.

But their first job is more complicated than they expected.

When they break fey magic that seals an old tomb, they find it contains more than they bargained for. Now they're hunting for a rogue spirit, and he always seems one step ahead.

The fight leads them in a direction they never expected.

Gabe could leave his past behind, or he could delve into the darkest secrets of mankind. Shadow has no intention of being left out.

Author's Note

Thank you for reading White Haven Winter, books 4 -6 in my witches' series.

As usual, I have mixed myths and legends into my fictional world, and of course kept my focus on the witches. They are the heart of this series, and I love them all. I try to represent witchcraft honestly and positively, but of course, I have taken some liberties with facts.

I love Halloween and the magical lore that surrounds the night. I thought it would be a great subject for book four. It was fun reading up on druids, yew trees, the Wild Hunt, and ley lines.

Another favourite is vampires, so what better subject for book five! Witch-bottles really exist, and there was a news article about one quite recently. It's also true that mediums and séances were very popular in the 1920's and '30's. Arthur Conan Doyle was a huge fan and an ardent believer in spiritualism. It's also true that vampires are called Strigoi in Romania, and that Bram Stoker took his inspiration from them.

After the crazy evil of the vampires of Undying Magic, I fancied turning to the old myths again, specifically the Raven King and the Green Man. I had an idea for a circus with a twist, and thought this was a great way to bring these myths to White Haven. The Green Man and the Raven King have special places in English mythology, and are familiar and beloved figures. I couldn't wait to have them interact with White Haven magic.

As usual, my characters continue to grow and change and I thought it was only natural that Alex and Avery's relationship should evolve, but of course Caspian did, too. I'm sure there'll be more to come of his story!

I'm very fond of my new character, Shadow, and I think Harlan Beckett could become a new favourite, too. These two, and the Nephilim of course, will get their own spin-off series, and I'm writing that right now!

I hope you enjoyed our new enemy, Caitlin. The Empusa is a real myth as well, and I love crossroads magic, so what a perfect fit!

There will be seventh book, as soon as book 1 of White Haven Hunters is complete. I'll keep you updated on the release information. Join my readers' group by going to **https://tjgreen.nz/**to keep up to date, or follow my **Facebook** page - **https://www.facebook.com/tjgreenauthor/**. I post there reasonably frequently.

Thanks to Fiona Jayde Media for my awesome cover, and thanks to Kyla Stein at Missed Period Editing for ironing out the kinks!

Thanks also to my beta readers and launch team, who give valuable feedback on typos and are happy to review on release. It's lovely to hear from them - you know who you are - and their feedback is always so encouraging. I'm lucky to have them on my team! I love hearing from all my readers, so I welcome you to get in touch.

Thanks of course to my partner, Jason, who does most of the cooking while I'm feverishly writing in the study. Without his unfailing support and encouragement, my life would be so much harder - and I'd starve.

I've dedicated this book to my readers. You are all fantastic. I couldn't do this, and certainly wouldn't enjoy writing so much, without your support!

If you'd like to read a bit more background to the stories, please head to my website - www.tjgreen.nz - where I'll be blogging about the books I've read and the research I've done on the series - in fact there's lots of stuff on there about my other series, Rise of the King, too.

If you'd like to read more of my writing, please join my mailing list by visiting my website - www.tjgreen.nz. You can get a free short story called Jack's Encounter, describing how Jack met Fahey – a longer version of the prologue in Call of the King – by subscribing to my newsletter. You'll also get a FREE copy of Excalibur Rises, a short story prequel.

You will also receive free character sheets on all of my main characters in White Haven Witches - exclusive to my email list!

By staying on my mailing list you'll receive free excerpts of my new books, as well as short stories and news of giveaways. I'll also be sharing information about other books in this genre you might enjoy.

I look forward to you joining my readers' group. www.tjgreen.nz/landing

About the Author

I grew up in England and now live in the Hutt Valley, near Wellington, New Zealand, with my partner Jason, and my cats Sacha and Leia. When I'm not writing, you'll find me with my head in a book, gardening, or doing yoga. And maybe getting some retail therapy!

In a previous life I've been a singer in a band, and have done some acting with a theatre company – both of which were lots of fun. On occasions I make short films with a few friends, which begs the question, where are the book trailers? Thinking on it ...

I'm currently working on more books in the White Haven Witches series, musing on a prequel, and planning for a fourth book in Tom's Arthurian Legacy series.

Please follow me on social media to keep up to date with my news, or join my mailing list - I promise I don't spam! Join my mailing list by visiting www.tjgreen.nz.

You can follow me on social media -

Website: http://www.tjgreen.nz
Facebook: https://www.facebook.com/tjgreenauthor/
Twitter: https://twitter.com/tjay_green
Pinterest:
https://nz.pinterest.com/mount0live/my-books-and-writing/
Goodreads:
https://www.goodreads.com/author/show/15099365.T_J_Green
Instagram: https://www.instagram.com/mountolivepublishing/
BookBub: https://www.bookbub.com/authors/tj-green
Amazon:
https://www.amazon.com/TJ-Green/e/B01D7V8LJK/

Lightning Source UK Ltd.
Milton Keynes UK
UKHW011832130921
390533UK00006B/359/J

9 780995 138650